THE MONK

THE MONK
A Romance

Matthew Gregory Lewis

edited by D.L. Macdonald and Kathleen Scherf

broadview literary texts

National Library of Canada Cataloguing in Publication

Lewis, Matthew Gregory, 1775–1818
The monk : a romance / Matthew Gregory Lewis ; edited by
D.L. Macdonald and Kathleen Scherf.

(Broadview literary texts)
Includes bibliographical references.
ISBN 1-55111-227-2

I. Macdonald, David Lorne, 1955–. II. Scherf, Kathleen, 1960–. III. Title. IV. Series.

PR4887.M7 2003   823'.6   C2003-905394-6

Broadview Press Ltd. is an independent, international publishing house, incorporated in 1985. Broadview believes in shared ownership, both with its employees and with the general public; since the year 2000 Broadview shares have traded publicly on the Toronto Venture Exchange under the symbol BDP.

We welcome comments and suggestions regarding any aspect of our publications – please feel free to contact us at the addresses below or at broadview@broadviewpress.com.

North America
Post Office Box 1243, Peterborough, Ontario, Canada K9J 7H5
3576 California Road, Orchard Park, NY, USA 14127
Tel: (705) 743-8990; Fax: (705) 743-8353;
e-mail: customerservice@broadviewpress.com

UK, Ireland, and continental Europe
Plymbridge Distributors Ltd.
Estover Road
Plymouth PL6 7PY UK Tel: (01752) 202301; Fax: (01752) 202333
e-mail: orders@plymbridge.com

Australia and New Zealand
UNIREPS, University of New South Wales
Sydney, NSW, 2052
Tel: 61 2 9664 0999; Fax: 61 2 9664 5420
email: info.press@unsw.edu.au

www.broadviewpress.com

Series Editor: Professor L.W. Conolly
Advisory editor for this volume: Colleen Franklin
Typesetting and assembly: True to Type Inc., Mississauga, Canada.

PRINTED IN CANADA

Contents

Acknowledgements

We are grateful to the Department of English and the Faculty of Arts, University of New Brunswick, and to the Faculties of Communication and Culture and of Humanities, University of Calgary, for their generous financial support of this project. We are grateful to the librarians at the British Library and the University of Calgary Library, and especially to David C. Devenish, Gill Rayment, and Robert Bell of the Wisbech and Fenland Museum, for their expert and courteous assistance.

We are grateful to the British Library, for permission to reproduce a photograph of a page from the third edition of *The Monk*, by Matthew Gregory Lewis, with the author's holograph revisions; to the Clarendon Press, for permission to quote from *The Writings and Speeches of Edmund Burke*, general editor Paul Langford; to Louis Crompton, for permission to quote from *Byron and Greek Love*, by Louis Crompton; to the Kensington Publishing Corporation, for permission to quote from *The Complete Writings of Thomas Paine*, edited by Philip S. Foner; to the National Library of Jamaica, for permission to publish "France and England in 1793," a poem by M.G. Lewis; to Penguin Books Limited, for permission to quote from *Clarissa*, by Samuel Richardson, edited by Angus Ross, and from the Introduction, by Mario Praz, to *Three Gothic Novels*, edited by Peter Fairclough; and to the University Press of Kentucky, for permission to quote from *The Guardian*, edited by John Calhoun Stephens. We have made every effort to identify and contact copyright holders; we would be grateful for any information concerning any we may have missed.

We are grateful to our research assistants, Jay Gamble, Renée Laaja, Darren Matthies, Chris Olbey, Matte Robinson, and Nikki Sheppy, for collation, proofreading, checking translations and references, photocopying, and a variety of other tedious and exacting tasks, all of which they performed meticulously, promptly, and cheerfully. It was a pleasure to work with them.

For assistance, advice, and encouragement, we are grateful to Julie Abbott, Kevin Binfield, Estelle Dansereau, David Harrison, Matthew Heilman, Sandra Hoenle, Hermina Joldersma, Roberta Jackson, Daniel Maher, Anne McWhir, David Oakleaf, Vivienne Rundle, Florentine Strzelczyk, and Martha Wells.

Engraved by Ridley, from a Picture by Drummond.

M. G. LEWIS Esq.ʳ M.P.

AUTHOR OF THE MONK.

Introduction

The Monk was written in ten weeks by a nineteen-year-old who was at once bored out of his mind and in increasing danger; this combination of circumstances may partly account for its peculiarly frantic quality.[1] In 1794, Matthew Gregory Lewis was an attaché at the British embassy in The Hague, and the French Revolutionary Armée du Nord was approaching inexorably from the South. It is not known what his duties were (it has been suggested, implausibly, that he was a spy [Winter 29]); they do not seem to have taken up much of his time and energy, but they did on one occasion take him to the front lines, where he saw a man and his three-year-old child mutilated by French artillery. Back in The Hague, social life was so tedious that one of Lewis's fellow-guests at an evening party, "quite overcome with its stupidity, yawned so terribly that He fairly dislocated his jaw" (Peck 212). Lewis turned to Gothic fiction as a relief from boredom and an escape from anxiety.

Lewis was born in 1775, the oldest child of Matthew Lewis, a Jamaica planter and the Deputy Secretary at War, and Frances Maria Sewell Lewis. The Lewises went on to have three more children, but in 1781 the family was broken forever when Mrs. Lewis eloped with Samuel Harrison, a music teacher. Mr. Lewis succeeded in obtaining a judicial separation, but he failed to obtain a divorce (these were very rare in the eighteenth century). The Lewises remained married, and Mr. Lewis supported his estranged wife, for the rest of his life. (In time, their son would use the income from his writings to help support her.) She managed to regain her respectability (she became a lady-in-waiting to the Princess of Wales), and Lewis remained devoted to her, but there is reason to believe that he never fully recovered from the trauma of the separation.[2] He never married. He was educated at Winchester School and at Christ Church College, Oxford; during his Oxford years, he travelled to Paris in 1791 and to

---

1 For a fuller account of the composition of the novel, and a detailed interpretation, see D.L. Macdonald, *Monk Lewis* (2000), especially Chapter 5.

2 Odd details in *The Monk* suggest an ongoing feeling of abandonment. Elvira and Gonzalvo, fleeing to Cuba to escape the wrath of his father, leave behind their two-year-old son, who grows up to become Ambrosio, the monk of the title. Similarly, when Marguerite the bandit's wife helps Raymond to escape from her husband and his gang, they leave behind her four-year-old son. And the live entombment of Agnes recalls a morbid fantasy of the guilt-stricken Mrs. Lewis: see Macdonald, *Monk Lewis* 7.

Weimar in 1792-93, to study languages in preparation for the diplomatic career his father intended for him.

The French invasion of Holland brought this career to a premature end, so his father brought him home and bought him a seat in Parliament (it is said to have cost more than £2600). Lewis's Parliamentary duties do not seem to have occupied him any more than his diplomatic ones had, and he gave up his seat in 1802. Meanwhile, he published a great deal of fiction, poetry, and drama of all kinds, from blank-verse tragedy to knockabout farce. *The Monk* is his most important novel; his most important play is *The Castle Spectre*, a Gothic melodrama first produced in 1797 and published in 1798. He abruptly stopped writing in 1812, when his father died and he came into his inheritance, which included two sugar plantations in Jamaica. He travelled to Jamaica twice, in 1815-16 and 1817-18, to inspect and if possible to improve the living and working conditions of his slaves; these voyages inspired his last book, *Journal of a West India Proprietor* (1834). In between, he made a trip to Europe, including a stop in Geneva, where he met Byron and the Shelleys: his conversation may have influenced the writing of *Frankenstein* and certainly did that of *Manfred*. He died of yellow fever on his second return voyage from Jamaica.

Literary Sources

Lewis began trying to write "a Roma[nce] in the style of the Castle of Otranto" as early as March 1792 (Peck 189), but he seems to have made little progress on it until 1794, when, in addition to the stimuli of life in war-torn Holland, he encountered two important literary influences: Ann Radcliffe's *The Mysteries of Udolpho* (1794), which he described as "one of the most interesting Books that ever have been published" (Peck 208), and William Godwin's *Caleb Williams* (1794), which he described as "in a new style, and well written," adding (in the shadow of the Armée du Nord): "Unluckily the Author is half a Democrate" (Peck 213). *The Monk* combined Godwin's narrative drive, and his interest in crime and punishment, with Radcliffe's preoccupation with the supernatural, but Lewis rejected Godwin's radical politics, and he famously refused to provide Radcliffean rational explanations of the supernatural events in his novel.[1] Godwin's radicalism and Radcliffe's rationalism were both aspects of an Enlightenment ideology that Lewis superficially endorsed (as in

---

1 Only two incidents are in Radcliffe's mode: when Ambrosio sees what he takes to be the ghost of the murdered Elvira but which turns out to be her maid in a white dress, and when the groans of the entombed Agnes ʹ

his narrator's, and his heroes', many criticisms of the "superstition" of Catholicism) but on a deeper level found uncongenial. Indeed, *The Monk* is not just anti-Enlightenment; it is also, in a sense, "anticivilization." As Stephen King, who should know, puts it:

> [A]nticivilization emotions don't go away, and they demand periodic exercise[....] The mythic horror movie, like the sick joke [or the Gothic novel], has a dirty job to do. It deliberately appeals to all that is worst in us. It is morbidity unchained, our most base instincts let free, our nastiest fantasies realized[....] I like to see the most aggressive of them [...] as lifting a trapdoor in the civilized forebrain and throwing a basket of raw meat to the hungry alligators swimming around in that subterranean river underneath.
>
> Why bother? Because it keeps them from getting out, man. It keeps them down there and me up here. (177)

"[G]ood liberal [...] critics," as King calls us (189), have a hard time with this sort of thing, and *The Monk* has been called reactionary, racist, and sexist. There is some reason to call it all these things, but we should remember that it's also simply *bad*. dismissive?

Radcliffe and Godwin may have inspired *The Monk*, but Lewis found the idea for his main plot (as he explains in his prefatory "Advertisement") in "The History of Santon Barsisa," a moral fable that Sir Richard Steele (1672-1729) had taken from Tonson's *Turkish Tales* (1708) and published in his short-lived periodical *The Guardian* in 1713 (Appendix A.1). In expanding it to novel length, Lewis gave his readers an intimate sense—some found it too intimate—of what succumbing to temptation is like. Steele's concise and elegant tale scarcely has room to give his hero an inner life, but the story of Ambrosio's damnation is focalized almost exclusively through Ambrosio himself.[1] As John Berryman pointed out in 1952, in what is still

---

are mistaken for those of a ghost. More characteristic of the novel is the episode of the Bleeding Nun, where what appears to be a natural event—the elopement of two lovers—turns out to have an unexpected supernatural component (cf. Miles 53). Just as *The Monk* is, in part, Lewis's response to *The Mysteries of Udolpho*, so Radcliffe's *The Italian* (1797) is, in part, her response to *The Monk*; see Conger, "Sensibility Restored." Interestingly, it contains at least one (supererogatory) example of the unexplained supernatural: a premonitory dream.

1 It is this focalization of the story of a rapist through the rapist himself that gives the novel its quasi-pornographic character (cf. Williams 106-7, Winter 28).

one of the most perceptive accounts of the novel, "It is surprising, after all, how *long* it takes—how *difficult* it is—to be certain of damnation" (13). Each of the steps in Ambrosio's career of crime—from breaking his monastic vows to rape, murder, and black magic—is duly weighed beforehand and duly regretted afterwards, but his regrets never quite prevent him from going on to his next, greater offence.

Ambrosio's progress is facilitated by Matilda, the most fascinating and troubling character in the novel. She not only talks him into most of his crimes, she provides the equipment for many of them: the magic myrtle he uses for his second attempt to rape Antonia, the opiate he uses for his successful third attempt, the dagger he uses to stab her, and finally the book he uses to summon the Devil. Along the way, she goes through a bewildering series of transformations, from a timid (and apparently male) novice, to a virtuous if unconventional woman, an enthusiastic and expert sexual partner, a Sadean super-villain,[1] and finally a glamorous witch. She is so variable, so indefatigable, so resourceful, so suspiciously willing to further Ambrosio's pursuit of another woman, and so well equipped, that many readers have been inclined to accept the Devil's explanation that she is not actually a woman at all, but "a subordinate but crafty spirit" (361)—the Mephistopheles to Ambrosio's Faust (Conger, *Matthew G. Lewis* 29-30). But the Devil is, after all, the father of lies; and a number of passages in the novel, especially those focalized through Matilda, make no sense unless we assume that she really is a woman.[2] There is plenty of reason to believe, both from the biographical record and from the portrayal of women in the novel itself—from the sympathetic, suffering Marguerite, Agnes, Elvira, and Antonia to the grotesque baroness of Lindenberg and the monstrous prioress of St. Clare—that Lewis had profoundly ambivalent feelings about women. Matilda sums up that ambivalence in a single character. The near-impossibility of deciding whether she is a woman or a demon is one expression of that ambivalence (cf. Miles 52-53, Todorov 25).[3]

---

1 *Justine* was on sale when Lewis visited Paris in 1791. There is no evidence that he ever actually read it—but then, his only surviving letter from Paris is to his mother (Peck 184-86).

2 E.g., "Matilda with every succeeding day grew more attached to the friar. Since he had obtained her favours, he was become dearer to her than ever" (212), and "Matilda was next ordered to the torture; but, terrified by the sight of the friar's sufferings, her courage totally deserted her" (350).

3 It is only fair to add that Lewis seems also to have been ambivalent about men. With the notable exception of the villainous Ambrosio, most of the men in the novel have, as Pope would put it, no characters at all (*Moral Essays* 2.2).

In connection with Lewis's conflicted sexual politics, Berryman refers to the "strange, tenuous, but saving" influence of *Clarissa* on *The Monk*. This influence has not received much attention, perhaps because until recently the academy has not been much used to thinking about a monument of the Great Tradition and a Gothic thriller at the same time;[1] but Lewis himself drew attention to a specific, and not at all tenuous, example of it in a footnote to his fourth edition (see Appendix E, entry for 55.28). Lorenzo's prophetic dream, at the beginning of his novel, recalls a prophetic dream of Lovelace's, near the *end* of Richardson's; and the fulfillment of Lorenzo's dream-prophecy in the rape and murder of Antonia, at the end of Lewis's novel, recalls a dream of Clarissa's, near the *beginning* of Richardson's (see Appendix A.2). Lewis's taking on of Richardson shows an ambition, and his complex use of him shows a sophistication, for which he has not always been given credit.

Lewis drew inspiration from more than English literature. During his stay in Weimar, he met Goethe ("the celebrated author of Werter," as he airily told his mother: "so that you must not be [s]urprized if I should shoot myself one of these fine Mornings" [Peck 190]) and other authors, and he read widely in modern German literature. Syndy M. Conger has usefully surveyed the use he made of it in *Matthew G. Lewis, Charles Robert Maturin and the Germans* (1977). Ambrosio's story is, broadly speaking, Faustian; and Conger has noted a number of specific similarities between *The Monk* and Goethe's *Faust: Ein Fragment* (1790), especially between Ambrosio's attempted seduction of Antonia and Faust's seduction of Gretchen (12-42). The characterization both of Ambrosio and of the Wandering Jew draws on Schiller's *Der Geisterseher* ("The Ghost-Seer," 1787-89). Raymond's adventure with the robbers draws on Lorenz Flammenberg's *Der Geisterbanner* ("The Necromancer," 1792). His wild ride with the Bleeding Nun, and the ballad of "Alonzo the Brave and Fair Imogine" draw on Bürger's "Lenore" (1773). "The Water-King" is a free translation of Herder's "Der Wassermann" (1779). The agonizing death of Ambrosio is taken straight from the conclusion to Weber's *Die Teufelsbeschwörung* ("The Exorcism," 1791). Perhaps Lewis's most interesting uses of German pre-texts are of "Die Entführung" ("The Elopement"), from *Volksmärchen der Deutschen* ("Folk Tales of the Germans," 1782-86), by Johann Karl August Musäus (1735-87; Appendix

---

1 See D.L. Macdonald, "'A Dreadful Dreadful Dream': Transvaluation, Realization, and Literalization of *Clarissa* in *The Monk*," forthcoming in *Gothic Studies*.

A.3), and "Der ewige Jude" ("The Eternal Jew," 1784), by Christian Friedrich Daniel Schubart (1739-91; Appendix A.4).[1]

Lewis's Advertisement, and a later letter to Walter Scott (Guthke 219), suggest that he had not read Musäus, but a comparative reading of "Die Entführung" and the story of the Bleeding Nun suggests that he had listened closely to someone who had. In expanding Musäus's tale, however, Lewis increases the element of suspense by focalizing the elopement through the man rather than through the woman, so that for a moment the reader does not understand that Raymond has eloped with the real Bleeding Nun. He deepens the tone, from Musäus's lighthearted humour to a horror only occasionally lightened by humour (Conger, *Matthew G. Lewis* 99). He gives the Nun a history of immoderate passions, thus integrating the story with the main themes of his novel (Conger, *Matthew G. Lewis* 103-4). And he replaces the colourless conjurer who rescues Musäus's hero with the Wandering Jew, drawn from Schubart's poem. This tormented, suicidal character greatly impressed Lewis's readers and inspired a number of imitations, most notably Byron's *Manfred* (1817). The episode of the Bleeding Nun, the first conclusively supernatural incident in the novel, is an outrage both intellectually (an example of the truth of the "superstition" about which Agnes so sensibly complains [142]) and morally (Raymond has done nothing to deserve the Nun's spectral persecution). It foreshadows the increasingly irrational and nightmarish quality of the rest of the book, which abundantly illustrates both what Hamlet has to say about philosophy (1.5.166-67) and what Alice Miller, in *For Your Own Good*, calls "the sad truth that cruelty is often inflicted upon the innocent" (158). Robert Miles draws a link between the intellectual and moral scandals of the book: "What *The Monk* finally contests is the system of justice that relies upon notions of fixed identity, upon standards of truth capable of distinguishing the natural from the unnatural" (54).

The Monk has a number of other literary pre-texts, some identified in the Advertisement and some in the footnotes to the fourth edition. One more is worth comment here. The last stanza of Theodore's poem "Love and Age," a footnote tells us (see Appendix E, entry for 185.18), is "taken from the first Ode of Anacreon"; that is, from one of the poems then attributed to Anacreon (they are now known to be by later, anonymous imitators of Anacreon: see Rosenmeyer, *The Poetics of Imitation*). But the whole poem, as the footnote does not tell us, is an imitation of an anacreontic ode

---

1 Lewis's specific uses of pre-texts are indicated in the footnotes.

that Lewis had translated while a schoolboy at Westminster (Appendix A.5). This is important because some scholars have speculated that Lewis was homosexual (e.g., Miles 44-45);[1] and his translation, like the original poem, is frankly homoerotic. The poem published in the novel, however, has been carefully heterosexualized.

Lewis's age did not have a highly developed idea of intertextuality, and it virtually invented the idea of originality as a literary value; Lewis's own embarrassed term for his use of pre-texts is "plagiarisms" (38). The *Monthly Review* understood his method: "This may be called plagiarism; yet it deserves some praise. The great art of writing consists in selecting what is most stimulant from the works of our predecessors, and in uniting the gathered beauties in a new whole, more interesting than the tributary models" (451). Nevertheless, Lewis was soon accused of plagiarism in the narrow sense, and when, early in the twentieth century, a scholar discovered a German adaptation of *The Monk*, he assumed it was the original from which Lewis had plagiarized (Conger, *Matthew G. Lewis* 2, 8n13). After the publication of Genette's *Palimpsests*, we can see that Lewis's adaptation and combination of such a variety of pre-texts is part of the interest, the sophistication, and even the originality of his novel (but cf. Clery 142-43, 200n30).

Historical Contexts

The Monk was not inspired only by other books. It is a response to some of the most pressing issues of Lewis's time—though it makes the typical Gothic move of displacing them onto a distant time and place, seventeenth-century Spain. Foremost among these issues, as Lewis's contemporaries realized right away and as Ronald Paulson has cogently argued in *Representations of Revolution* (219-22), was the French Revolution. Raised a Protestant, Lewis obviously found the anti-Catholicism of the Revolution congenial.[2] One of his most important literary pre-texts (too tedious to be excerpted here) is *Les Victimes cloîtrées*, an anti-Catholic melodrama by Jacques-Marie Boutet de Monvel, which he had seen in Paris in 1791 and which he would later translate as *Venoni; or, The Novice of St. Mark's* (1808);

---

1 See Macdonald, *Monk Lewis*, Chapter 4, which, among other points, stresses that yes, there *were* homosexuals before 1870; even Foucault says so (Eribon 316).

2 In *Art of Darkness*, Anne Williams links Lewis's anti-Catholicism with his anti-feminism, arguing that his fear of "Mother Church" (117) is only an example of the "horror of the female [that] drives and shapes the narrative" of the male Gothic in general and *The Monk* in particular (114).

and the release of Agnes from her live entombment, like the release of Boutet de Monvel's cloistered victims, is strikingly reminiscent of the release of the seven prisoners from the Bastille. But Lewis, like most English writers in 1794, was alarmed by the excesses to which the Revolution had given rise; and both his main plot and his subplot concern initially justifiable or sympathetic revolts which get out of hand. Lewis actually describes Ambrosio as "having undergone a thorough revolution" because of his affair with Matilda (209), and he initially treats that affair almost as indulgently as he later makes Mother St. Ursula treat the similar offence of Agnes (298).Yet it leads Ambrosio to rape and murder. At the climax of the subplot, the crowd's anger as Mother St. Ursula exposes the crimes of the prioress is understandable, but it leads to a scene of horrific mob violence reminiscent of the September Massacres.

In his poem "France and England in 1793" (Appendix B.1.b), Lewis makes Marie Antoinette, imprisoned in the Temple, into a Gothic heroine, "Almost debarred the coarse support of life" like Agnes (386), and weeping over her children like Agnes over her dead child. His account of the rape and murder of Antonia is clearly based not only on Clarissa's dream but also on the famous account of the (alleged) attempted rape and murder of the French queen in Burke's *Reflections on the Revolution in France* (1790; see Appendix B.1.a)—and Antonia is presumably named after Marie Antoinette. The way that the demonic Matilda presides over this double crime is particularly reminiscent of the way that the enforced return of the French royal family to Paris is, according to Burke, accompanied by "all the unutterable abominations of the furies of hell, in the abused shape of the vilest of women." In one passage, however, Lewis seemed to his contemporaries to endorse some of the most radical ideas of the Revolutionary period: Ambrosio's reflections on discovering that Antonia has been reading the Bible (230-31) are, no doubt unintentionally but very strikingly, reminiscent of *The Age of Reason* (1794-95; see Appendix B.1.c), Thomas Paine's attack on revealed religion. Paine's and Lewis's comments on some of the narrative content, and the diction, of the Bible actually have some cogency, but that did not save an English bookseller named Thomas Williams from being imprisoned for publishing a cheap edition of Paine's book. Lewis, too, would get into trouble.

Towards the end of the long second chapter of *The Monk*, Matilda has revealed her true sex, and Ambrosio has persuaded her to leave the abbey. For a moment, it looks as though his virtue will be saved after all. Then she asks him to pick a flower for her to take as a keepsake to the convent where she proposes to spend the rest of her life. As he does so, he is bitten by what he calls a "serpent." The intervention of this creature is one of the most decisive events in the whole novel—the bite is poisonous; Matilda sucks out the poison; it is, in large part, because of the reflection that she has saved his life at the risk of her own that Ambrosio becomes her lover; and it is in order to save her life and continue their affair that she first resorts to magic—and the scene of a man, a woman, and a serpent in a garden has reminded critics (e.g., Williams 116) of the Garden of Eden. But the creature is not really a serpent at all. It is a centipede, which, as Lewis takes the trouble to tell us in the only footnote to the first edition, "is supposed to be a native of Cuba, and to have been brought into Spain from that island in the vessel of Columbus" (90). It is an early example of the empire biting back to the centre. The colonial margin shadows much of the action of this novel set in one imperial capital, written in a second, and published in a third. Ambrosio's parents fled to Cuba when he was two, leaving him behind to be brought up as a monk. Lorenzo, who has "an estate, though not of value, in Hispaniola" (196), proposes eloping there with Antonia. This reminds us that Lewis's father had an estate of considerable value, and a half-share in another, in Jamaica; when he died in 1812, Lewis inherited them—and several hundred slaves.[1] Slavery is a key concept in his novel, both metaphorically, as part of its attack on Catholicism ("You cannot but be aware, that your parents were unfortunately slaves to the grossest superstition" [134]), and literally, in Matilda's account of her first conjuration: "I saw the dæmon obedient to my orders: I saw him trembling at my frown; and found that, instead of selling my soul to a master, my courage had purchased for myself a slave" (237). The relationship between master and slave—even between such comparatively benign masters as Lewis and his father, and their slaves—is one of absolute domination, sustained by violence and liable to overthrow by violence: the slave revolt in St. Domingue (formerly Lorenzo's Hispaniola, later Haiti and the Dominican Republic) had broken out in 1791 and was marked by atrocities on both sides; the Jamaica that Lewis visited twice at the end of his life was constantly threatened by similar revolts, as he recorded in *Journal of a West India Proprietor* (see Appendix B.2.b).[2] Even if Matilda is telling the truth about her encounter with Lucifer, one might ask how long she will

---

1 See Macdonald, *Monk Lewis*, especially Chapter 8.
2 He also recorded a curious encounter with a centipede, on 5 February 1818: see p. 210 in Judith Terry's edition.

be able to keep the Devil down. In *Subjects of Slavery, Agents of Change: Women and Power in Gothic Novels and Slave Narratives, 1790-1865*, Kari J. Winter draws a distinction between the "unexplained supernatural" of Lewis and the "explained supernatural" of Radcliffe that is extremely suggestive in this colonial context:

> [M]ale Gothic novelists from the 1790s to the 1860s lingered over horrible spectacles of sexual violence, gore, and death, locating evil in the "other"—women, Catholics, Jews [to which list we might add: African slaves], and ultimately the devil. In contrast, female Gothic novelists uncovered the terror of the familiar: the routine brutality and injustice of the patriarchal family, conventional religion, and classist social structures. (21)

Winter's analysis sheds light on Lewis's portrayal both of Matilda and of the Devil—who, when he shows up in his true form, is black (356).

For what it's worth, the *Journal of a West India Proprietor* does show that Lewis was capable of sympathy for the slaves. He also seems to have been aware of subtler dangers for the master than open revolt—especially of the corrupting nature of absolute power. His first play, *The Castle Spectre* (1797; see Appendix B.2.a), contains the anachronistic but striking figure of Hassan, an African who has been so embittered by his enslavement that he has declared war on the entire European race. He prosecutes this war by faithfully serving his master, the villain of the play: "Oh! 'tis a thought which I would not barter for empires, to know that in this world he makes others suffer, and will suffer himself for their tortures in the next!" (389).[1] When the gods wish to punish us, Wilde says, they answer our prayers; when the Devil wishes to damn us, Lewis implies, he obeys our orders.

The search for historical contexts for the novel, as for literary pre-texts, could be carried on indefinitely; one more is important to mention here. We have referred above to the possibility that Lewis was gay; and Louis Crompton has characterized Lewis's age as the most homophobic in English history—which, given English history, is saying something. The apparatus of sexual repression embodied in the novel in the figure of the prioress reflects the apparatus of repression which Lewis could see around him in English society, and of which he may have felt a potential object. The death of the prioress recalls not only the violence of the French and Haitian Revolutions but also the violence to which

---

1 The speeches of Hassan quoted in Appendix B.2.a were cut by the censor from the performance version of the play: see Jeffrey N. Cox, *Seven Gothic Dramas, 1789-1825* (1992) 160, 196.

English homosexuals, with full official complicity, were regularly subjected. The usual penalty for attempted sodomy was exposure in the pillory, an opportunity for mob violence which the mob did not let slip. The most vivid account we have found comes from a publication of 1810, *The Trying and Pilloring of the Vere Street Club* (see Appendix B.3.a). It is not, of course, a source for *The Monk*, but it is uncannily similar to Lewis's disturbing incident, which, read in this light, looks like a revenge fantasy—the turning of the violence of sexual repression onto a figure who herself personifies that repression.[1]

Critical Reception

Lewis may have been encouraged to sign the second edition of his novel by favourable early reviews, such as the one in the radical *Analytical Review* (Appendix C.1), which complained that the sub-plot "weaken[ed] the main interest" but thought that the novel as a whole "display[ed] no common powers." It raised questions (not for the last time) about the role of Matilda, but thought that her relations with Ambrosio were "very finely conceived, and truly picturesque; indeed the whole temptation is so artfully contrived, that a man, it should seem, were he made as other men are, would deserve to be d—ned who could resist even devilish spells, conducted with such address, and assuming such a heavenly form." (It is pleasant to think that the reviewer may have been Mary Wollstonecraft, who was then embarking on the one happy sexual relationship of her life, with William Godwin.) Even the conservative *European Review* (Appendix C.2) conceded Lewis's "genius and talents," and especially admired his interpolated poems, though it disapproved of the novel as "an *oblique attack* upon *venerable establishments*," of a kind that "the presses of the Continent teemed with [...] while the Revolution was preparing in France."

The most thoughtful, most influential, and most negative review of the novel was by Samuel Taylor Coleridge, published in the *Critical Review* (Appendix C.3). Coleridge was not entirely unappreciative: he admired the "truly terrific" subplot, the characterization of Matilda, the interpolated poems, and in general Lewis's "rich, powerful, and fervid" imagination. But he disapproved of Lewis's invocation of the supernatural, of his gratuitous "[s]ituations of torment, and images of naked horror," and especially of his eroticism. He

---

1   Miles similarly argues that "Ambrosio's spectacular punishment takes on the character of a sodomite in the stocks experiencing the rough justice of the crowd" (54).

drew particular attention to the passage about Antonia's Bible, accusing Lewis of "first [...] inflam[ing] the fleshly appetites, and then [...] pour[ing] contempt on the only book which would be adequate to the task of recalming them." Coming from a member of parliament, this was outrageous: "Yes! the author of the Monk signs himself a LEGISLATOR!—We stare and tremble."

The *Monthly Mirror*, which had already published a favourable review, a biographical note, and a portrait of Lewis, now published "An Apology for the Monk" (Appendix C.4), by "A Friend to Genius," which attempted to answer Coleridge point by point. Ambrosio's sensual temptations had to be vividly described to show how "a man of strong understanding, austerity of manners, and great self command" succumbed to them. The "horrors consequent on his vicious conduct," far from being an additional problem, actually "destroy the momentary effect, if any were produced, of the passages which are rather warm in description." As for the Bible passage, everybody knew that some parts of the Bible, such as the Song of Solomon, "must certainly be improper [reading] for young females." The Friend to Genius even accused Coleridge, in his own words, of having responded to *The Monk* as perversely as he had accused Lewis of responding to the Bible: "The most innocent expressions may become the first link in the chain of association, when a man's soul has been poisoned and depraved by the habit of reading lewd and voluptuous tales; and we believe it not absolutely impossible that he might extract pollution from the word of purity, and turn the grace of God into wantonness." This must be the only time that anyone has ever compared *The Monk* to the Bible.

Lewis was grateful for this defence, and wrote to the *Monthly Mirror* to say so; but Coleridge's view prevailed. According to Lewis's first biographer, "the Attorney-general was actually instructed, by one of the societies for the suppression of vice, to move for an injunction to restrain [the] sale [of the novel]" (Baron-Wilson 1: 153-54). It is not clear what action, if any, the authorities actually took. Lewis had already shown some signs of a loss of nerve when he published the second edition under his own name: he deleted the long description of Ambrosio's dying agonies and added a coda:

Haughty Lady, why shrunk you back when yon poor frail-one drew near? Was the air infected by her errors? Was your purity soiled by her passing breath? Ah! Lady, smooth that insulting brow: stifle the reproach just bursting from your scornful lip: wound not a soul, that bleeds already! She has suffered, suffers still. Her air is gay, but her heart is broken; her dress sparkles, but her bosom groans.

Lady, to look with mercy on the conduct of others, is a virtue no less than to look with severity on your own. (See Appendix E, entry for 363.21)

This gave a possibly unexpected indication of Lewis's target audience (though Gothic fiction was considered largely a women's genre), and it suggested, oddly, that Agnes was his central character, but it did draw attention to the one offence—his merciless treatment of Agnes—which was unambiguously Ambrosio's own fault, and it did insist that the novel had a moral.[1] Now, in response to the threat of legal action, Lewis extensively expurgated the fourth edition of the novel (see Appendix E).[2] He cut the discussion of the Bible (230-31) and carefully revised his other references to religion, replacing appeals to "God" with more discreet ones to "heaven," and spelling "Bible" with an upper-case *B* throughout. His expurgations of sexual material were more extensive. He completely cut, or drastically abbreviated, the opening discussion of Ambrosio's chastity (47), the description of Matilda's breast (84-85; see the illustration on 456), Ambrosio's erotic dreams (86, 89), the sex scenes between Ambrosio and Matilda (104, 204-5), the attempted and successful rapes (233, 262, 318-21), and the vision of Antonia in the magic mirror (239-40).[3] As with the references to religion, he paid attention to detail, erasing the word "Lust!" from the forehead of the monster in Lorenzo's prophetic dream (55) and arranging for Elvira to arrive just "in time," rather than "just in time" to interrupt Ambrosio's second attempted rape (263). He was especially careful to delete the sexual use of the verb "enjoy." He also added a number of helpful footnotes and some new poems; one of these, "Giles Jollup the Grave and Brown Sally Green," was a parody of "Alon-

---

1 This particular moral would have been especially important to Lewis, because of the experience of his mother. In more general terms, Conger points out that sympathy for unwed mothers was one of the values of the *Sturm und Drang* authors (like Goethe) on whom Lewis drew (*Matthew G. Lewis* 39).

2 In advertising this edition, Lewis's publisher was careful to point out not only that "the Author had paid particular attention to some passages that have been objected to," but also that "A few remaining copies of the original edition" were still available—at twice the original price (Todd 20).

3 Other passages offensive to modern taste, such as the killing of the prioress and the decomposition of Agnes's baby, went completely untouched.

zo the Brave and Fair Imogine," perhaps the most popular of the poems in the first version of the novel. The *Monthly Mirror*, which had faithfully defended Lewis all along, and which did not fail to welcome his "judicious corrections and *additions*" to the fourth edition, remarked: "we cannot help expressing our astonishment that the author should have subjoined to his justly popular poem of *Alonzo and Imogine* a ridiculous parody, expressly calculated to ruin the interest, and pervert the effect of the original" (5: 157). It is hard not to see in this gesture Lewis's protest against the way he had been forced to ruin the interest and pervert the effect of his book.

Lewis left two comments on the controversy, one private and one public. Just after expurgating the book, he wrote to his father (Appendix C.5), essentially repeating the arguments of the Friend to Genius, but conceding that they were in error: "convinced of my object being unexceptionable, I did not sufficiently examine whether the means by which I attained that object were generally so[....] I thought that the stronger my colours, the more effect would my picture produce; and it never struck me, that the exhibition of vice, in her temporary triumph, might possibly do as much harm as her final exposure and punishment would do good." In 1801, in the Preface to his melodrama *Adelmorn, the Outlaw* (Appendix C.6), he just admitted that his judgement had been wrong, insisted that his intentions had been good, and asked to be left alone. The whole experience had a profoundly inhibiting effect on him as a writer: none of his numerous later works is as shocking as *The Monk*, and none, with the exception of the *Journal of a West India Proprietor*, is as interesting.

The novel was a success in Revolutionary France, where readers did not find it offensive. We have chosen two representative reviews. The *Décade philosophique* (Appendix C.7) praised Lewis's understanding of monasticism and his "profound knowledge of the human heart"; the *Spectateur du Nord* (Appendix C.8) drew attention to the "great and fearful lesson" taught by the book. Both defended Lewis's use of the supernatural; the *Spectateur du Nord* made the standard distinction between the "unexplained supernatural" of Lewis and the "explained supernatural" of Radcliffe. Both are above all aesthetic critiques, concentrating on the novel's powerful effect on the reader; insofar as the English reviews had raised this issue, they had limited themselves largely to worrying about its effects on the reader's morals. Like the *Spectateur du Nord,* the Marquis de Sade discussed the difference between the unexplained and explained supernatural (Appendix C.9); not surprisingly, he preferred Lewis's mode to that of the more refined Radcliffe, but he understood that both were responses to the Revolution. When Radcliffe herself came to reflect on the difference between her Gothic mode, which she called "terror," and Lewis's, which she called "horror" (Appendix C.10),[1] she concentrated not on whether the author explains the supernatural events away at the end of the story, but on how much information s/he gives about them as the characters experience them, and (like the French reviews) on the effect that this management of information has on the reader. By leaving the experience obscure, terror "expands the soul, and awakens the faculties to a high degree of life"; by making it explicit, horror "contracts, freezes, and nearly annihilates them." It is this distinction, rather than that between the explained and the unexplained, which is still current in Gothic fiction, according to Stephen King. In the tale of terror, "We actually *see* nothing outright nasty[....] the imagination alone is stimulated" (21-22). Horror is more explicit, evoking a bodily response. King even accepts, in theory, Radcliffe's valorization of terror, though he confesses to a more Lewis-like practice: "I recognize terror as the finest emotion [...] and so I will try to terrorize the reader. But if I find I cannot terrify him/her, I will try to horrify; and if I find I cannot horrify, I'll go for the gross-out. I'm not proud" (25). Neither was Lewis.

Cultural Responses

In addition to the amount of critical comment it received, another measure of the impact of *The Monk* is the number of imitations and adaptations it spawned. Dramatic adaptations included James Boaden's serious, blank-verse *Aurelio and Miranda* (1798), which was a flop (despite the star power of John Philip Kemble and Sarah Siddons), and Charles Farley's pantomime *Raymond and Agnes; or, The Castle of Lindenbergh* (1797), which was a great success—not to mention Charles Louis Didelot's *Alonzo the Brave and the Fair Imogine; A Grand Ballet* (1801), W.H. Grosette's *Raymond and Agnes! or, The Bleeding Nun of Lindenberg. A Melo Drama* (1825), Henry M. Milner's *Alonzo the Brave and the Fair Imogine; or, The Spectre Bride! A Legendary Romantic Melo-Drama* (1852), Francis Cowley Burnand's *Alonzo the Brave; or, Faust and the Fair Imogene. A Tragical, Comical, Demoniacal, and whatever-you-like-to-call-it Burlesque, Uniting in its Construction the Romantic Pathos of the Well-Known Ballad, "Alonzo and Imogene" with the Thrilling Horrors of Goethe's "Faust"* (1863),

---

1 Williams argues that terror is characteristic of the female and horror of the male Gothic (104-6).

Samuel M. Harrison's *Alonzo ye Brave and ye Fayre Imogene: An Hysterical Drama, in Three Acts* (1876)—and *Le Moine* (1972) a film co-written by Luis Buñuel and Jean-Claude Carrière, and directed by Ado Kyrou. Popular chapbooks—intended for readers who could not afford to buy, or were not literate enough to read, a whole novel—included *Father Innocent, Abbot of the Capuchins; or, The Crimes of Cloisters* (1803), *Almagro & Claude; or, Monastic Murder; Exemplified in the Dreadful Doom of an Unfortunate Nun* (1810), and Sarah Wilkinson's *Castle of Lindenberg; or, The History of Raymond and Agnes; including Raymond's Adventures with the Banditti in the Forest of Rosenwald, and his Being Haunted by the Spectre of the Bleeding Nun. Abridged from the Celebrated Novel of The Monk, Written by the Late G.M.* [sic] *Lewis, Esq. A Spanish Tale* (c. 1820). For a more highbrow prose redaction, the reader may consult Antonin Artaud's *Le Moine* (1966). We have chosen three such adaptations, one from each of the major literary genres, and all based on the subplot, since this seems to have been the more popular part of the novel.

Only two London theatres, Covent Garden and Drury Lane, were licensed to present "legitimate" spoken drama, but a wide variety of dramatic forms not reliant on the spoken word flourished at a large number of other theatrical spaces, and the legitimate theatres also included these in their programs, to vary the evening's entertainment. Pantomimes became an increasingly important part of the programming at the legitimate theatres, in part simply because they were popular, in part because the theatres had become so large—both could accommodate over three thousand people—that they had become, as a disapproving contemporary put it, "theatres for spectators rather than playhouses for hearers" (Cox 8-9). Charles Farley (1771-1859) was one of the most prominent writers, directors, and actors of pantomime in the period; he was especially celebrated for his use of theatrical machinery.[1] His *Raymond and Agnes; or, The Castle of Lindenbergh* (Appendix D.1) was produced at Covent Garden in March 1797, with Farley as Raymond. It is certainly spectacular, taking the actors through thirteen different scenes. Through a combination of pantomime, song, and a couple of well-placed written placards, it manages to dramatize most of the subplot, with a few changes for enhanced theatrical effect. It is Agnes, not her aunt, who meets Raymond in the bandits' cottage, so that, in accordance with a long-standing dramatic tradition, she

---

1 In 1811, Farley directed and starred in Lewis's last original play, the spectacular equestrian melodrama *Timour the Tartar*.

can fall in love with the man who has saved her life. The bandits are brought back at the end of the play, so that Raymond can rescue Agnes (again) from a fate livelier than live entombment. Most importantly, the Bleeding Nun is not Raymond's distant relative but Agnes's murdered mother, and she appears not in order to persecute Raymond but to warn him that Agnes is in danger from the bandits—thus integrating the two parts of the subplot more neatly than Lewis himself had done. Lewis was duly impressed with this maternal ghost, and especially with the "great applause" which greeted her "ascending to heaven [...] in a sort of postchaise made of paste-board" (*Adelmorn* v). He made a virtually identical ghost the title character of *The Castle Spectre*.

The publication of Thomas Percy's *Reliques of Ancient English Poetry* (1765) gave rise to a new interest in the ballad and inspired the writing of a number of imitation ballads, of which perhaps Wordsworth and Coleridge's *Lyrical Ballads* (1798) are the most distinguished. This movement resulted in some interesting interchanges between popular and élite culture. Just as oral folk ballads could be published as broadsides and broadside ballads could enter the oral tradition (Laws 2), so an élite poem like Wordsworth's "We Are Seven" was republished as a popular broadside, and the songs of Burns entered (or re-entered) the oral tradition (Friedman 271-72). Lewis's own "Alonzo the Brave and Fair Imogine" apparently became part of the oral tradition of Nebraska in the 1940s, and of Portugal in the 1980s (Dias Marques, Pound).

Since many of the ballads collected by Percy and others had supernatural themes, and since the new interest in the ballad coincided with the ascendancy of the Gothic, it is not surprising that many of the imitation ballads were Gothic. In 1801, Lewis published *Tales of Wonder*, a collection of sixty Gothic ballads, some reprinted from Percy and other sources and some original. One of the originals is "The Bleeding Nun" (Appendix D.2), an anonymous poem which combines the subplot of Lewis's novel with some motifs from "The Water-King" and "Alonzo the Brave and Fair Imogine."

The mostly anonymous booklets known as chapbooks (apparently because they were sometimes sold by chapmen, or peddlers) had been an important part of popular literary culture since the sixteenth century. They covered every conceivable subject, from religion and morality through household hints, history, and criminal biography, and according to one estimate, hundreds of thousands of them were in circulation at any one time (Weiss 6). Chapbook redactions of popular novels flourished from the early eighteenth century—that is, from the rise of the novel itself—until the 1820s, when they were largely superseded as popular entertainment by the monthly magazine (Weiss 6, 56). Ranging in price from less than a penny to about a shilling (the first edition of *The Monk* cost ten shillings and sixpence), they brought at least some idea of a novel to a much larger readership than it would otherwise have had—though without a corresponding increase in income for the original author. *Almagro and Claude* (Appendix D.3) was published in 1810, fifteen years after Lewis's novel, by Thomas Tegg (1776-1845), who specialized in these ripoffs (Weiss 25-26). It gives an accurate account of the subplot (despite the eye-catching subtitle, Claude, as the redactor renames Agnes, is not actually murdered). Perhaps the most interesting things about it are its tone (the redactor avoids Lewis's humour) and its pacing—or what Genette, in *Narrative Discourse*, calls *duration*: when the redactor is especially interested in an incident—or perhaps when s/he expects her readers to be especially interested—s/he slows down, incorporating many of Lewis's own words into the dialogue and narration. (S/he seems especially drawn to the embedded narratives of Marguerite/Antoinette, the Wandering Jew, and Agnes/Claude.) When s/he is less interested, s/he can summarize remorselessly. This is most evident in his/her treatment of the main plot, to which s/he devotes the last five pages of the chapbook, after dwelling on the subplot for the first thirty-three. Perhaps s/he thought that his/her readers would be distracted by the "splitting [of] the interest" between the two plots, of which Wollstonecraft (?) had complained (Appendix C.1); evidently s/he thought they would be confused by Lewis's cutting back and forth between the two. This radical compression necessitated greater changes to the main plot than to the subplot, notably the omission (except for two vague references to "magic" and "witchcraft") of all the supernatural elements, and so of the Devil's final revelation that Ambrosio/Clement's crimes have included matricide and incest.

We have concentrated on popular cultural responses to *The Monk*, but Lewis's novel also inspired responses from a number of élite cultural figures, not only Artaud, Buñuel, and Carrière but also Breton, Charlotte Brontë, Byron, Coleridge (despite his disapproval), Dacre, Dumas père, Éluard, Flaubert, Gounod, Hoffmann, Hugo, Keats, Maturin, Mérimée, Radcliffe, Sand, Scott, and P.B. Shelley. Those alligators get around.

Matthew Gregory Lewis:
A Brief Chronology

1773 Marriage of Matthew Lewis and Frances Maria Sewell (22 February).
1775 Birth of MGL (9 July).
1776 Birth of Fanny Maria Lewis (5 October).
1778 Birth of Barrington Lewis (29 March).
1780 Birth of Sophia Elizabeth Lewis (10 February).
1781 MGL enters Marylebone Seminary (?). Elopement of Mrs. Lewis and Samuel Harrison (June/July).
1782 Birth of Fanny Lacey (half-sister, 3 July).
1783 Judicial separation of Mr. and Mrs. Lewis (27 February); rejection of Mr. Lewis's petition for a parliamentary divorce (6 May); MGL enters Westminster School (19 June).
1789 Storming of the Bastille (14 July).
1790 MGL enters Christ Church College, Oxford (April).
1791 MGL travels to Paris to learn French (September). Slave revolt and civil war in St. Domingue.
1792 First reference to "a Roma[nce] in the style of the Castle of Otranto" (March); MGL travels to Weimar to learn German (July), meets Goethe and Wieland.
1793 France declares war on Britain and Holland (1 February); MGL returns to Oxford (May), visits Bothwell Castle (December).
1794 MGL receives B.A. from Christ Church, Oxford; arrives at The Hague as attaché to the British Embassy (15 May); finishes *The Monk* (23 September).
1796 Publication of *The Monk* (12 March); of *Village Virtues* (dramatic satire). Election to Parliament.
1797 MGL receives M.A. Publication of *The Minister* (translation of Schiller, *Kabale und Liebe*); production of *The Castle Spectre* (melodrama, Drury Lane, 14 December; published 1798).
1798 Publication of the expurgated fourth edition of *Ambrosio; or, The Monk*. Meeting with Walter Scott.
1799 Publication of *The Love of Gain* (imitation of Juvenal, Satire 13); of *Rolla, the Peruvian Hero* (translation of Kotzebue, *Die Spanier in Peru*); production of *The Twins* (translation of a German/French farce, Drury Lane, 8

April); of *The East Indian* (comedy, Drury Lane, 22 April; published 1800).

1800 Death of Barrington Lewis (13 January).

1801 MGL moves to Barnes. Meeting with Thomas Moore (March). Publication of *Tales of Wonder* (collection of Gothic ballads); of *Alfonso, King of Castile* (tragedy); of *Adelmorn, the Outlaw* (melodrama); production of *Adelmorn* (Drury Lane, 4 May).

1802 Production of *Alfonso* (Covent Garden, 15 January). MGL resigns his seat in Parliament.

1803 Break with his father. Production of *The Captive* (monodrama, Covent Garden, 22 March); of *The Harper's Daughter* (stage version of *The Minister*, Covent Garden, 4 May).

1805 Publication of *The Bravo of Venice* (translation of H. Zschokke, *Aballino der Grosse Bandit*); of *Rugantino* (dramatization of *The Bravo of Venice*); production of *Rugantino* (Covent Garden, 18 October).

1806 Publication of *Adelgitha; or, The Fruits of a Single Error* (tragedy); of *Feudal Tyrants* (translation of Christiane Naubert, *Elisabeth, Erbin von Toggenburg*).

1807 Production of *The Wood Daemon* (melodrama, Drury Lane, 1 April); of *Adelgitha* (Drury Lane, 30 April). Abolition of the slave trade.

1808 Publication of *He Loves and He Rides Away* (ballad); of *Twelve Ballads* (for which MGL composed the music as well as the lyrics); of *Romantic Tales* (four-volume collection of tales and ballads); production of *Venoni; or, The Novice of St. Mark's* (adaptation of Jacques-Marie Boutet de Monvel, *Les Victimes cloîtrées*, Drury Lane, 1 December; published 1809).

1809 Recitation (Drury Lane, 14 February) and publication of *Monody on the Death of Sir John Moore*; production of *Temper; or, The Domestic Tyrant* (adaptation of David-Augustin Brueys and Jean Palaprat, *Le Grondeur*, Drury Lane at Lyceum, 1 May). MGL takes quarters in the Albany (June).

1811 Production and publication of *Timour the Tartar* (melodrama, Covent Garden, 29 April) and *One O'Clock! or, The Knight and the Wood-Daemon* (revision of *The Wood Daemon*, Lyceum, 1 August).

1812 Death of his father (17 May). Production of *Rich and Poor* (musical version of *The East Indian*, Lyceum, 22 July); publication of *Poems*.

1813 Meeting with Byron.
1814 Publication of *Rich and Poor*.
1815 Departure for Jamaica (10 November).
1816 Arrival in Jamaica (1 January); departure from Jamaica (1 April); arrival at Gravesend (5 June); trip to Geneva (August), Florence (October), Rome (December).
1817 Naples (January–March); return via Venice (July–August) and Paris (September); second departure for Jamaica (5 November).
1818 Arrival in Jamaica (24 January); departure on second return voyage (4 May); death at sea (16 May).
1822 Death of his mother.
1833 Emancipation of the West Indian slaves.
1834 Publication of *Journal of a West India Proprietor*.
1839 Publication of *The Life and Correspondence of M.G. Lewis*, by Margaret Baron-Wilson.

A Note on the Text

This edition of *The Monk* is based on the first edition: to be precise, on the British Library's copy (Cup.401.d.35). With the aid of our research assistants, we have collated this with copies of the second (12654.a.14), third (C.28.b.4-6: this is the copy that Lewis marked up to expurgate the novel), fourth (012612.ff.35), and fifth (C.124.aaa.32) editions. We have also examined the manuscript (Townshend MS ix, Wisbech and Fenland Museum, Wisbech, Cambridgeshire) but were unable to collate it with the first edition; such a collation can be found in Anderson's edition (443-53).

No modern scholar has based an edition of the novel on any version later than Lewis's first edition; the critical consensus, which we endorse, is that the later lifetime editions represent successive retreats from, rather than refinements on, the author's original vision. (We have included our collation of all five editions [Appendix E] because these retreats reveal much about eighteenth-century standards of literary propriety, and Lewis's belated attempt to conform to them.) In 1973, Howard Anderson published an edition based on the manuscript in the Wisbech and Fenland Museum. This manuscript, which is slightly incomplete, otherwise has considerable authority: it is a fair copy in Lewis's handwriting,[1] marked up in ways that indicate that the compositors used it for setting type (Anderson xxiv). Anderson's collation identifies about 150 substantive differences between the manuscript and the first edition. Most of them have three things in common: they are minor, they do not look like typographical errors, and they stand uncorrected in all five lifetime editions. Eighteen look like corrections of slips in the manuscript: for example, "*whom* I knew, could only be a burthen to me" (p. 128, line 5 in Anderson's edition of the manuscript) becomes "*who* I knew could only be a burthen to me" (p. 131, line 12-13 in our edition of the first edition); "He had neither Servants *or* Baggage" (167.18-19) becomes "He had neither

---

1 Lewis's handwriting is unusually good for the period, but it is sometimes difficult to tell whether or not a letter is capitalized. We believe that this difficulty misled Anderson (xxvi) into adopting a system of capitalization which is not found in any of Lewis's published works (or any other published works of the period), and which modern readers find distracting. We have followed the capitalization of the first edition.

servants *nor* baggage" (161.11); "and never appeared more devoted to Heaven *as* since He had broken through his engagements" (226.23-25) becomes "and never appeared more devoted to heaven *than* since he had broken through his engagements" (206.22-23); and "The top was also covered, and in it was *practised* a small grated Door" (403.5-6) becomes "The top was also covered, and in it was *fitted* a small grated door" (335.8; italics added in each case). We infer that Lewis used the proofs, which have since been lost, to make a number of corrections and other small changes, and that he remained satisfied with most of these changes.

In twenty-five cases, however, he did not remain satisfied with the changes; in these cases, a change between the manuscript and the first edition is changed back to the manuscript reading in a later edition, sometimes as early as the second, sometimes not until the fourth (in the preparation of which Lewis evidently went over the text much more closely than he had for the second or third, in order to expurgate it). Some of these change-backs look like, and all of them could be, typographical errors in the first edition; once changed back, most of them stay that way for the rest of the lifetime editions. In these cases, we have therefore emended the first edition to match the reading of the manuscript and the later editions. In the following list of our emendations, we give first the page and line numbers indicating where the emendation occurs in our edition; then the reading in the first edition; then a right square bracket; then the page and line numbers of Anderson's edition of the manuscript, and the numbers of the later lifetime editions, where the alternate reading is found; then the alternate reading itself (which is also what will be found in our own text):

97.4   sunk] Ms. 81.11, 4-5 sank
102.27 sunk] Ms. 88.18, 4-5 sank
124.33-34 light lightning] Ms. 119.9, 2-5 like lightning
127.8   sunk] Ms. 122.15, 4-5 sank
147.2   farther] Ms. 147.27, 4-5 further
153.2   sunk] Ms. 156.5, 4-5 sank
156.32 sunk] Ms. 161.15, 4-5 sank
157.28 sunk] Ms. 162.20, 4-5 sank
167.14 drunk] Ms. 175.21, 2, 4-5 drank
170.28 their servants] Ms. 179.31, 3-5 the servants
199.3   drunk] Ms. 216.19, 2, 4-5 drank
220.26 looks] Ms. 246.4, 2-5 locks
221.28 bid] Ms. 247.17 ("bad"), 2-5 bade

222.29　bid] Ms. 248.34 ("bad"), 2-5 bade
227.22　praise] Ms. 255.4, 2-5 prize
232.1　a husband] Ms. 260.31, 2-5 an husband
242.35　himself] Ms. 275.23, 2-5 herself
266.38　great may be] Ms. 307.4, 2-5 great might be
271.1　sunk] Ms. 312.36, 4-5 sank
272.15　at the castle] Ms. 314.21, 2-5 of the castle
276.17　throw on her oil] Ms. 319.17, 2-5 throw on her veil
281.1　I would] Ms. 326.2, 2-5 I should
297.17　tempers, that this] Ms. 352.2 (n.b.: Anderson's edition,
　　　　but not the manuscript itself, includes the redundant
　　　　"that"), 2-5 tempers, this
316.8　with Don] Ms. 376.1 ("with one Don"), 2-5 with
　　　　one, Don
325.12　is fallen] Ms. 389.16, 4-5 has fallen

One other error persists from the manuscript through the first
three editions; Lewis did not catch it until the fourth. Antonia has
not seen her suitor, Lorenzo, for some time, and "with every day his
image grew less feebly impressed upon her bosom" (231.34-35).
This is obviously the opposite of what Lewis means; in the fourth
and fifth editions he changed "feebly" to "forcibly," and we have
made the same change.

In addition to these emendations, we have replaced the eighteenth-century long S, deleted running quotation marks, regularized the length of dashes, and silently corrected a few trivial and
obvious typographical errors (e.g., "h" for "he"). Otherwise, we
have not regularized or modernized Lewis's text in any way (e.g.,
we have not regularized the past tenses of strong verbs, about which
Lewis never did make up his mind).

THE MONK:
A
ROMANCE.

Somnia, terrores magicos, miracula, sagas,
Nocturnos lemures, portentaque.

HORAT.[1]

Dreams, magic terrors, spells of mighty power,
Witches, and ghosts who rove at midnight hour.

IN THREE VOLUMES.
VOL. I.

LONDON:
PRINTED FOR J. BELL, OXFORD-STREET.
M.DCC.XCVI.

---

1 Horace (Quintus Horatius Flaccus, 65-8 B.C.), *Epistles* 2.2.208-9.

PREFACE.
IMITATION OF HORACE,
EP. 20.—B. I.[1]

METHINKS, Oh! vain ill judging book,
I see thee cast a wishful look,
Where reputations won and lost are
In famous row called Paternoster.[2]
Incensed to find your precious olio
Buried in unexplored port-folio,
You scorn the prudent lock and key,
And pant well bound and gilt to see
Your volume in the window set
Of Stockdale, Hookham, or Debrett.[3]
Go then, and pass that dangerous bourne
Whence never book can back return:[4]
And when you find, condemned, despised,
Neglected, blamed, and criticised,
Abuse from all who read you fall,
(If haply you be read at all)
Sorely will you your folly sigh at,
And wish for me, and home, and quiet.

Assuming now a conjuror's office, I
Thus on your future fortune prophesy:—
Soon as your novelty is o'er,
And you are young and new no more,
In some dark dirty corner thrown,
Mouldy with damps, with cobwebs strown,
Your leaves shall be the book-worm's prey;
Or sent to chandler-shop away,
And doomed to suffer public scandal,
Shall line the trunk, or wrap the candle!

But should you meet with approbation,
And some one find an inclination

---

1 Imitated from Horace, *Epistles* 1.20.
2 "Our father" (Latin): a London street, north of St. Paul's Churchyard, where a number of booksellers had their premises.
3 Booksellers.
4 Cf. Shakespeare, *Hamlet* 3.1.79–80.

To ask, by natural transition,
Respecting me and my condition;
That I am one, the enquirer teach,
Nor very poor, nor very rich;
Of passions strong, of hasty nature,
Of graceless form and dwarfish stature;
By few approved, and few approving;
Extreme in hating and in loving;
Abhorring all whom I dislike,
Adoring who my fancy strike;
In forming judgments never long,
And for the most part judging wrong;
In friendship firm, but still believing
Others are treacherous and deceiving,
And thinking in the present æra
That friendship is a pure chimæra:
More passionate no creature living,
Proud, obstinate, and unforgiving,
But yet for those who kindness show,
Ready through fire and smoke to go.

Again, should it be asked your page,
"Pray, what may be the author's age?"
Your faults, no doubt, will make it clear,
I scarce have seen my twentieth year,
Which passed, kind Reader, on my word,
While England's throne held George the Third.

Now then your venturous course pursue:
Go, my delight! dear book, adieu!

HAGUE,
Oct. 28, 1794.   M.G.L.

TABLE OF THE POETRY.

ADVERTISEMENT.

THE first idea of this Romance was suggested by the story of the *Santon Barsisa*, related in The Guardian.[1]—The *Bleeding Nun* is a tradition still credited in many parts of Germany; and I have been told, that the ruins of the castle of *Lauenstein*, which she is supposed to haunt, may yet be seen upon the borders of *Thuringia*.[2]—The *Water-King*, from the third to the twelfth stanza, is the fragment of an original Danish ballad—And *Belerma and Durandarte* is translated from some stanzas to be found in a collection of old Spanish poetry, which contains also the popular song of *Gayferos and Melesindra*, mentioned in Don Quixote.—I have now made a full avowal of all the plagiarisms of which I am aware myself; but I doubt not, many more may be found, of which I am at present totally unconscious.

---

1 Richard Steele, *Guardian* 148 (Monday 31 August 1713): see Appendix A.1.
2 See Appendix A.3.

THE MONK.
CHAP. I.

——Lord Angelo is precise;
Stands at a guard with envy; scarce confesses
That his blood flows, or that his appetite
Is more to bread than stone.

MEASURE FOR MEASURE.[1]

SCARCELY had the abbey-bell tolled for five minutes, and already was the church of the Capuchins[2] thronged with auditors. Do not encourage the idea, that the crowd was assembled either from motives of piety or thirst of information. But very few were influenced by those reasons; and in a city where superstition reigns with such despotic sway as in Madrid, to seek for true devotion would be a fruitless attempt. The audience now assembled in the Capuchin church was collected by various causes, but all of them were foreign to the ostensible motive. The women came to show themselves, the men to see the women: some were attracted by curiosity to hear an orator so celebrated; some came, because they had no better means of employing their time till the play began; some, from being assured that it would be impossible to find places in the church; and one half of Madrid was brought thither by expecting to meet the other half. The only persons truly anxious to hear the preacher, were a few antiquated devotees, and half a dozen rival orators, determined to find fault with and ridicule the discourse. As to the remainder of the audience, the sermon might have been omitted altogether, certainly without their being disappointed, and very probably without their perceiving the omission.

Whatever was the occasion, it is at least certain, that the Capuchin church had never witnessed a more numerous assembly. Every corner was filled, every seat was occupied. The very statues which ornamented the long aisles were pressed into the service. Boys suspended themselves upon the wings of cherubims; St. Francis[3] and St. Mark bore each a spectator on his shoulders; and St.

---

1 Shakespeare, *Measure for Measure* 1.3.50-53.
2 Franciscan friars. Strictly speaking, friars are not monks, and their superior should be referred to as their guardian, not (like Ambrosio) their abbot. Lewis's knowledge of Catholicism is not very accurate.
3 St. Francis of Assisi (1181-1226) founded the Franciscan order in 1208.

Agatha found herself under the necessity of carrying double. The consequence was, that, in spite of all their hurry and expedition, our two newcomers, on entering the church, looked round in vain for places.

However, the old woman continued to move forwards. In vain were exclamations of displeasure vented against her from all sides: in vain was she addressed with—"I assure you, Segnora, there are no places here."—"I beg, Segnora, that you will not crowd me so intolerably!"—"Segnora, you cannot pass this way. Bless me! How can people be so troublesome!"—The old woman was obstinate, and on she went. By dint of perseverance and two brawny arms she made a passage through the crowd, and managed to bustle herself into the very body of the church, at no great distance from the pulpit. Her companion had followed her with timidity and in silence, profiting by the exertions of her conductress.

"Holy Virgin!" exclaimed the old woman in a tone of disappointment, while she threw a glance of enquiry round her; "Holy Virgin! what heat! what a crowd! I wonder what can be the meaning of all this. I believe we must return: there is no such thing as a seat to be had, and nobody seems kind enough to accommodate us with theirs."

This broad hint attracted the notice of two cavaliers, who occupied stools on the right hand, and were leaning their backs against the seventh column from the pulpit. Both were young, and richly habited. Hearing this appeal to their politeness pronounced in a female voice, they interrupted their conversation to look at the speaker. She had thrown up her veil in order to take a clearer look round the cathedral. Her hair was red, and she squinted. The cavaliers turned round, and renewed their conversation.

"By all means," replied the old woman's companion; "by all means, Leonella, let us return home immediately; the heat is excessive, and I am terrified at such a crowd."

These words were pronounced in a tone of unexampled sweetness. The cavaliers again broke off their discourse, but for this time they were not contented with looking up: both started involuntarily from their seats, and turned themselves towards the speaker.

The voice came from a female, the delicacy and elegance of whose figure inspired the youths with the most lively curiosity to view the face to which it belonged. This satisfaction was denied them. Her features were hidden by a thick veil; but struggling through the crowd had deranged it sufficiently to discover a neck which for symmetry and beauty might have vied with the

Medicean Venus.[1] It was of the most dazzling whiteness, and received additional charms from being shaded by the tresses of her long fair hair, which descended in ringlets to her waist. Her figure was rather below than above the middle size: it was light and airy as that of an Hamadryad.[2] Her bosom was carefully veiled. Her dress was white; it was fastened by a blue sash, and just permitted to peep out from under it a little foot of the most delicate proportions. A chaplet of large grains hung upon her arm, and her face was covered with a veil of thick black gauze. Such was the female, to whom the youngest of the cavaliers now offered his seat, while the other thought it necessary to pay the same attention to her companion.

The old lady with many expressions of gratitude, but without much difficulty, accepted the offer, and seated herself: the young one followed her example, but made no other compliment than a simple and graceful reverence. Don Lorenzo (such was the cavalier's name, whose seat she had accepted) placed himself near her; but first he whispered a few words in his friend's ear, who immediately took the hint, and endeavoured to draw off the old woman's attention from her lovely charge.

"You are doubtless lately arrived at Madrid," said Lorenzo to his fair neighbour; "it is impossible that such charms should have long remained unobserved; and had not this been your first public appearance, the envy of the women and adoration of the men would have rendered you already sufficiently remarkable."

He paused, in expectation of an answer. As his speech did not absolutely require one, the lady did not open her lips: After a few moments he resumed his discourse:

"Am I wrong in supposing you to be a stranger to Madrid?"

The lady hesitated; and at last, in so low a voice as to be scarcely intelligible, she made shift to answer,—"No, Segnor."

"Do you intend making a stay of any length?"

"Yes, Segnor."

"I should esteem myself fortunate, were it in my power to contribute to making your abode agreeable. I am well known at Madrid, and my family has some interest at court. If I can be of any service, you cannot honour or oblige me more than by permitting

---

1 The Venus de' Medici was then one of the most highly regarded classical statues. Lewis went to see it in Florence in 1816.

2 A tree-nymph.

me to be of use to you."—"Surely," said he to himself, "she cannot answer that by a monosyllable; now she must say something to me."

Lorenzo was deceived, for the lady answered only by a bow.

By this time he had discovered, that his neighbour was not very conversible; but whether her silence proceeded from pride, discretion, timidity, or idiotism, he was still unable to decide.

After a pause of some minutes—"It is certainly from your being a stranger," said he, "and as yet unacquainted with our customs, that you continue to wear your veil. Permit me to remove it."

At the same time he advanced his hand towards the gauze: the lady raised hers to prevent him.

"I never unveil in public, Segnor."

"And where is the harm, I pray you?" interrupted her companion somewhat sharply. "Do not you see, that the other ladies have all laid their veils aside, to do honour no doubt to the holy place in which we are? I have taken off mine already; and surely, if I expose my features to general observation, you have no cause to put yourself in such a wonderful alarm! Blessed Maria! Here is a fuss and a bustle about a chit's face! Come, come, child! Uncover it! I warrant you that nobody will run away with it from you——"

"Dear aunt, it is not the custom in Murcia——"

"Murcia, indeed! Holy St. Barbara, what does that signify? You are always putting me in mind of that villanous province. If it is the custom in Madrid, that is all that we ought to mind; and therefore I desire you to take off your veil immediately. Obey me this moment, Antonia, for you know that I cannot bear contradiction."[1]

Her niece was silent, but made no further opposition to Don Lorenzo's efforts, who, armed with the aunt's sanction, hastened to remove the gauze. What a seraph's head presented itself to his admiration! Yet it was rather bewitching than beautiful; it was not so lovely from regularity of features, as from sweetness and sensibility of countenance. The several parts of her face considered separately, many of them were far from handsome; but, when examined together, the whole was adorable. Her skin, though fair, was not entirely without freckles; her eyes were not very large, nor their lashes particularly long. But then her lips were of the most rosy freshness; her fair and undulating hair, confined by a simple rib-

---

1   Antonia is named after Marie Antoinette, Queen of France.

band, poured itself below her waist in a profusion of ringlets; her neck was full and beautiful in the extreme; her hand and arm were formed with the most perfect symmetry; her mild blue eyes seemed an heaven of sweetness, and the crystal in which they moved sparkled with all the brilliance of diamonds. She appeared to be scarcely fifteen; an arch smile, playing round her mouth, declared her to be possessed of liveliness, which excess of timidity at present repressed. She looked round her with a bashful glance; and whenever her eyes accidentally met Lorenzo's, she dropped them hastily upon her rosary; her cheek was immediately suffused with blushes, and she began to tell her beads; though her manner evidently showed that she knew not what she was about.

Lorenzo gazed upon her with mingled surprise and admiration; but the aunt thought it necessary to apologize for Antonia's *mauvaise honte*.

"'Tis a young creature," said she, "who is totally ignorant of the world. She has been brought up in an old castle in Murcia, with no other society than her mother's, who, God help her! has no more sense, good soul, than is necessary to carry her soup to her mouth. Yet she is my own sister, both by father and mother."

"And has so little sense?" said Don Christoval with feigned astonishment. "How very extraordinary!"[1]

"Very true, Segnor. Is it not strange? However, such is the fact; and yet only to see the luck of some people! A young nobleman, of the very first quality, took it into his head that Elvira had some pretensions to beauty.—As to pretensions, in truth she had always enough of *them*; but as to beauty!—If I had only taken half the pains to set myself off which she did!—But this is neither here nor there. As I was saying, Segnor, a young nobleman fell in love with her, and married her unknown to his father. Their union remained a secret near three years; but at last it came to the ears of the old marquis, who, as you may well suppose, was not much pleased with the intelligence. Away he posted in all haste to Cordova,[2] determined to seize Elvira, and send her away to some place or other, where she would never be heard of more. Holy St. Paul! How he stormed on finding that she had escaped him, had joined her husband, and that they had embarked together for the Indies! He

---

1 Don Christoval's diversionary courtship of Leonella recalls Mephistopheles' courtship of Marthe in Goethe, *Faust* 54 ("Garden").

2 Córdoba is a city in Andalusia, in south-central Spain.

swore at us all, as if the evil spirit had possessed him; he threw my father into prison—as honest a pains-taking shoe-maker as any in Cordova; and when he went away, he had the cruelty to take from us my sister's little boy, then scarcely two years old, and whom in the abruptness of her flight she had been obliged to leave behind her. I suppose that the poor little wretch met with bitter bad treatment from him, for in a few months after we received intelligence of his death."

"Why, this was a most terrible old fellow, Segnora!"

"Oh! shocking! and a man so totally devoid of taste! Why, would you believe it, Segnor? when I attempted to pacify him, he cursed me for a witch, and wished that, to punish the count, my sister might become as ugly as myself! Ugly indeed! I like him for that."

"Ridiculous!" cried Don Christoval. "Doubtless the count would have thought himself fortunate, had he been permitted to exchange the one sister for the other."

"Oh! Christ! Segnor, you are really too polite. However, I am heartily glad that the condé[1] was of a different way of thinking. A mighty pretty piece of business, to be sure, Elvira has made of it! After broiling and stewing in the Indies for thirteen long years, her husband dies, and she returns to Spain, without an house to hide her head, or money to procure her one! This Antonia was then but an infant, and her only remaining child. She found that her father-in-law had married again, that he was irreconcilable to the condé, and that his second wife had produced him a son, who is reported to be a very fine young man. The old marquis refused to see my sister or her child; but sent her word that, on condition of never hearing any more of her, he would assign her a small pension, and she might live in an old castle which he possessed in Murcia. This had been the favourite habitation of his eldest son; but, since his flight from Spain, the old marquis could not bear the place, but let it fall to ruin and confusion.—My sister accepted the proposal; she retired to Murcia, and has remained there till within the last month."

"And what brings her now to Madrid?" enquired Don Lorenzo, whom admiration of the young Antonia compelled to take a lively interest in the talkative old woman's narration.

"Alas! Segnor, her father-in-law being lately dead, the steward of his Murcian estates has refused to pay her pension any longer.

---

1 Spanish for count or earl.

With the design of supplicating his son to renew it, she is now come to Madrid; but I doubt that she might have saved herself the trouble. You young noblemen have always enough to do with your money, and are not very often disposed to throw it away upon old women. I advised my sister to send Antonia with her petition; but she would not hear of such a thing. She is so obstinate! Well! she will find herself the worse for not following my counsels: the girl has a good pretty face, and possibly might have done much."

"Ah, Segnora!" interrupted Don Christoval, counterfeiting a passionate air; "if a pretty face will do the business, why has not your sister recourse to you?"

"Oh! Jesus! my lord, I swear you quite overpower me with your gallantry! But I promise you that I am too well aware of the danger of such expeditions to trust myself in a young nobleman's power! No, no; I have as yet preserved my reputation without blemish or reproach, and I always knew how to keep the men at a proper distance."

"Of that, Segnora, I have not the least doubt. But permit me to ask you, Have you then any aversion to matrimony?"

"That is an home question. I cannot but confess, that if an amiable cavalier was to present himself———"

Here she intended to throw a tender and significant look upon Don Christoval; but, as she unluckily happened to squint most abominably, the glance fell directly upon his companion. Lorenzo took the compliment to himself, and answered it by a profound bow.

"May I enquire," said he, "the name of the marquis?"

"The marquis de las Cisternas."

"I know him intimately well. He is not at present in Madrid, but is expected here daily. He is one of the best of men; and if the lovely Antonia will permit me to be her advocate with him, I doubt not my being able to make a favourable report of her cause."

Antonia raised her blue eyes, and silently thanked him for the offer by a smile of inexpressible sweetness. Leonella's satisfaction was much more loud and audible. Indeed, as her niece was generally silent in her company, she thought it incumbent upon her to talk enough for both: this she managed without difficulty, for she very seldom found herself deficient in words.

"Oh, Segnor!" she cried; "you will lay our whole family under the most signal obligations! I accept your offer with all possible gratitude, and return you a thousand thanks for the generosity of your proposal. Antonia, why do not you speak, child?

While the cavalier says all sorts of civil things to you, you sit like a statue, and never utter a syllable of thanks, either bad, good, or indifferent!—"

"My dear aunt, I am very sensible that——"

"Fye, niece! How often have I told you, that you never should interrupt a person who is speaking! When did you ever know me do such a thing? Are these your Murcian manners? Mercy on me! I shall never be able to make this girl any thing like a person of good breeding. But pray, Segnor," she continued, addressing herself to Don Christoval, "inform me, why such a crowd is assembled to-day in this cathedral."

"Can you possibly be ignorant, that Ambrosio,[1] abbot of this monastery, pronounces a sermon in this church every Thursday? All Madrid rings with his praises. As yet he has preached but thrice; but all who have heard him are so delighted with his eloquence, that it is as difficult to obtain a place at church, as at the first representation of a new comedy. His fame certainly must have reached your ears?"

"Alas! Segnor, till yesterday I never had the good fortune to see Madrid; and at Cordova we are so little informed of what is passing in the rest of the world, that the name of Ambrosio has never been mentioned in its precincts."

"You will find it in every one's mouth at Madrid. He seems to have fascinated the inhabitants; and, not having attended his sermons myself, I am astonished at the enthusiasm which he has excited. The adoration paid him both by young and old, by man and woman, is unexampled. The grandees load him with presents; their wives refuse to have any other confessor; and he is known through all the city by the name of The Man of Holiness."

"Undoubtedly, Segnor, he is of noble origin?"

"That point still remains undecided. The late superior of the Capuchins found him while yet an infant at the abbey-door. All attempts to discover who had left him there were vain, and the child himself could give no account of his parents. He was educated in the monastery, where he has remained ever since. He early showed a strong inclination for study and retirement; and as soon as he was of a proper age, he pronounced his vows. No one has ever appeared to claim him, or clear up the mystery which conceals his

---

1 Ambrosio is named after St. Ambrose, bishop of Milan (c. 339-97), celebrated as an orator and an advocate of the excellence of virginity.

birth; and the monks, who find their account in the favour which is shewn to their establishment from respect to him, have not hesitated to publish, that he is a present to them from the Virgin. In truth, the singular austerity of his life gives some countenance to the report. He is now thirty years old, every hour of which period has been passed in study, total seclusion from the world, and mortification of the flesh. Till these last three weeks, when he was chosen superior of the society to which he belongs, he had never been on the outside of the abbey-walls. Even now he never quits them except on Thursdays, when he delivers a discourse in this cathedral, which all Madrid assembles to hear. His knowledge is said to be the most profound, his eloquence the most persuasive. In the whole course of his life he has never been known to transgress a single rule of his order; the smallest stain is not to be discovered upon his character; and he is reported to be so strict an observer of chastity, that he knows not in what consists the difference of man and woman. The common people therefore esteem him to be a saint."

"Does that make a saint?" enquired Antonia. "Bless me! then am I one."

"Holy St. Barbara!" exclaimed Leonella, "what a question! Fye, child, fye! these are not fit subjects for young women to handle. You should not seem to remember that there is such a thing as a man in the world, and you ought to imagine every body to be of the same sex with yourself. I should like to see you give people to understand, that you know that a man has no breasts, and no hips, and no.........."

Luckily for Antonia's ignorance, which her aunt's lecture would soon have dispelled, an universal murmur through the church announced the preacher's arrival. Donna Leonella rose from her seat to take a better view of him, and Antonia followed her example.

He was a man of noble port and commanding presence. His stature was lofty, and his features uncommonly handsome. His nose was aquiline, his eyes large, black and sparkling, and his dark brows almost joined together. His complexion was of a deep but clear brown; study and watching had entirely deprived his cheek of colour. Tranquillity reigned upon his smooth unwrinkled forehead; and content, expressed upon every feature, seemed to announce the man equally unacquainted with cares and crimes. He bowed himself with humility to the audience. Still there was a certain severity in his look and manner that inspired universal awe, and few could sustain the glance of his eye, at once fiery and penetrating. Such was Ambrosio, abbot of the Capuchins, and sur-named "The Man of Holiness."

Antonia, while she gazed upon him eagerly, felt a pleasure flut-tering in her bosom which till then had been unknown to her, and for which she in vain endeavoured to account. She waited with impatience till the sermon should begin; and when at length the friar spoke, the sound of his voice seemed to penetrate into her very soul. Though no other of the spectators felt such violent sen-sations as did the young Antonia, yet every one listened with inter-est and emotion. They who were insensible to religion's merits, were still enchanted with Ambrosio's oratory. All found their atten-tion irresistibly attracted while he spoke, and the most profound silence reigned through the crowded aisles. Even Lorenzo could not resist the charm: he forgot that Antonia was seated near him, and listened to the preacher with undivided attention.

In language nervous, clear, and simple, the monk expatiated on the beauties of religion. He explained some abstruse parts of the sacred writings in a style that carried with it universal conviction. His voice, at once distinct and deep, was fraught with all the ter-rors of the tempest, while he inveighed against the vices of human-ity, and described the punishments reserved for them in a future state. Every hearer looked back upon his past offences, and trem-bled: the thunder seemed to roll, whose bolt was destined to crush him, and the abyss of eternal destruction to open before his feet! But when Ambrosio, changing his theme, spoke of the excellence of an unsullied conscience, of the glorious prospect which eterni-ty presented to the soul untainted with reproach, and of the rec-ompense which awaited it in the regions of everlasting glory, his auditors felt their scattered spirits insensibly return. They threw themselves with confidence upon the mercy of their judge; they hung with delight upon the consoling words of the preacher; and while his full voice swelled into melody, they were transported to those happy regions which he painted to their imaginations in colours so brilliant and glowing.

The discourse was of considerable length: yet, when it con-cluded, the audience grieved that it had not lasted longer. Though the monk had ceased to speak, enthusiastic silence still prevailed through the church. At length the charm gradually dis-solving, the general admiration was expressed in audible terms. As Ambrosio descended from the pulpit, his auditors crowded round him, loaded him with blessings, threw themselves at his feet, and kissed the hem of his garment. He passed on slowly, with his hands crossed devoutly upon his bosom, to the door opening into the abbey-chapel, at which his monks waited to receive him. He ascended the steps, and then, turning towards his followers, addressed to them a few words of gratitude and exhortation. While he spoke, his rosary, composed of large grains of amber, fell from his hand, and dropped among the surrounding multitude. It was seized eagerly, and immediately divided amidst the spectators. Whoever became possessor of a bead, preserved it as a sacred relique; and had it been the chaplet of thrice-blessed St. Francis himself, it could not have been disputed with greater vivacity. The abbot, smiling at their eagerness, pronounced his benediction and quitted the church, while humility dwelt upon every feature. Dwelt she also in his heart?

Antonia's eyes followed him with anxiety. As the door closed after him, it seemed to her as she had lost some one essential to her happiness. A tear stole in silence down her cheek.

"He is separated from the world!" said she to herself; "perhaps, I shall never see him more!"

As she wiped away the tear, Lorenzo observed her action.

"Are you satisfied with our orator?" said he; "or do you think that Madrid over-rates his talents?"

Antonia's heart was so filled with admiration for the monk, that she eagerly seized the opportunity of speaking of him: besides, as she now no longer considered Lorenzo as an absolute stranger, she was less embarrassed by her excessive timidity.

"Oh! he far exceeds all my expectations," answered she; "till this moment I had no idea of the powers of eloquence. But when he spoke, his voice inspired me with such interest, such esteem, I might almost say such affection for him, that I am myself astonished at the acuteness of my feelings."

Lorenzo smiled at the strength of her expressions.

"You are young, and just entering into life," said he: "your heart, new to the world, and full of warmth and sensibility, receives its first impressions with eagerness. Artless yourself, you suspect not others of deceit; and viewing the world through the medium of your own truth and innocence, you fancy all who surround you to deserve your confidence and esteem. What pity, that these gay visions must soon be dissipated! What pity, that you must soon discover the baseness of mankind, and guard against your fellow-creatures as against your foes!"

"Alas! Segnor," replied Antonia, "the misfortunes of my parents have already placed before me but too many sad examples of the perfidy of the world! Yet surely in the present instance the warmth of sympathy cannot have deceived me."

"In the present instance, I allow that it has not. Ambrosio's character is perfectly without reproach; and a man who has passed the whole of his life within the walls of a convent, cannot have found the opportunity to be guilty, even were he possessed of the inclination. But now, when, obliged by the duties of his situation, he must enter occasionally into the world, and be thrown into the way of temptation, it is now that it behoves him to show the brilliance of his virtue. The trial is dangerous; he is just at that period of life when the passions are most vigorous, unbridled, and despotic; his established reputation will mark him out to seduction as an illustrious victim; novelty will give additional charms to the allurements of pleasure; and even the talents with which nature has endowed him will contribute to his ruin, by facilitating the means of obtaining his object. Very few would return victorious from a contest so severe."

"Ah! surely Ambrosio will be one of those few."

"Of that I have myself no doubt: by all accounts he is an exception to mankind in general, and envy would seek in vain for a blot upon his character."

"Segnor, you delight me by this assurance! It encourages me to indulge my prepossession in his favour; and you know not with what pain I should have repressed the sentiment! Ah! dearest aunt, entreat my mother to choose him for our confessor."

"I entreat her?" replied Leonella; "I promise you that I shall do no such thing. I do not like this same Ambrosio in the least; he has a look of severity about him that made me tremble from head to foot. Were he my confessor, I should never have the courage to avow one half of my peccadilloes, and then I should be in a rare condition! I never saw such a stern-looking mortal, and hope that I never shall see such another. His description of the devil, God bless us! almost terrified me out of my wits, and when he spoke about sinners he seemed as if he was ready to eat them."

"You are right, Segnora," answered Don Christoval. "Too great severity is said to be Ambrosio's only fault. Exempted himself from human failings, he is not sufficiently indulgent to those of others; and though strictly just and disinterested in his decisions, his government of the monks has already shown some proofs of his inflexibility. But the crowd is nearly dissipated: will you permit us to attend you home?"

"O Christ! Segnor," exclaimed Leonella affecting to blush; "I would not suffer such a thing for the universe! If I came home attended by so gallant a cavalier, my sister is so scrupulous that she would read me an hour's lecture, and I should never hear the last of it. Besides, I rather wish you not to make your proposals just at present.——"

"My proposals? I assure you, Segnora."

"Oh! Segnor, I believe that your assurances of impatience are all very true; but really I must desire a little respite. It would not be quite so delicate in me to accept your hand at first sight."

"Accept my hand? As I hope to live and breathe——"

"Oh! dear Segnor, press me no further if you love me! I shall consider your obedience as a proof of your affection; you shall hear from me to-morrow, and so farewell. But pray, cavaliers, may I not enquire your names?"

"My friend's," replied Lorenzo, "is the Condé d'Ossorio, and mine Lorenzo de Medina."

"'Tis sufficient. Well, Don Lorenzo, I shall acquaint my sister with your obliging offer, and let you know the result with all expedition. Where may I send to you?"

"I am always to be found at the Medina palace."

"You may depend upon hearing from me. Farewell, cavaliers. Segnor Condé, let me entreat you to moderate the excessive ardour of your passion. However, to prove that I am not displeased with you, and prevent your abandoning yourself to despair, receive this mark of my affection, and sometimes bestow a thought upon the absent Leonella."

As she said this, she extended a lean and wrinkled hand; which her supposed admirer kissed with such sorry grace and constraint so evident, that Lorenzo with difficulty repressed his inclination to laugh. Leonella then hastened to quit the church: the lovely Antonia followed her in silence; but when she reached the porch, she turned involuntarily, and cast back her eyes towards Lorenzo. He bowed to her, as bidding her farewell; she returned the compliment, and hastily withdrew.

"So, Lorenzo!" said Don Christoval as soon as they were alone, "you have procured me an agreeable intrigue! To favour your designs upon Antonia, I obligingly make a few civil speeches which mean nothing to the aunt, and at the end of an hour I find myself upon the brink of matrimony! How will you reward me for having suffered so grievously for your sake? What can repay me for having kissed the leathern paw of that confounded old witch? Diavolo! She has left such a scent upon my lips, that I shall smell of garlick for this month to come! As I pass along the Prado,[1] I shall be taken for a walking omelet, or some large onion running to seed!"

"I confess, my poor count," replied Lorenzo, "that your service has been attended with danger; yet am I so far from supposing it to be past all endurance, that I shall probably solicit you to carry on your amours still further."

"From that petition I conclude, that the little Antonia has made some impression upon you."

"I cannot express to you how much I am charmed with her. Since my father's death, my uncle the duke de Medina has signified to me his wishes to see me married; I have till now eluded his hints, and refused to understand them; but what I have seen this evening——"

"Well, what have you seen this evening? Why surely, Don Lorenzo, you cannot be mad enough to think of making a wife out of this grand-daughter of 'as honest a pains-taking shoemaker as any in Cordova'?"

"You forget, that she is also the grand-daughter of the late marquis de las Cisternas; but without disputing about birth and titles, I must assure you, that I never beheld a woman so interesting as Antonia."

"Very possibly; but you cannot mean to marry her?"

"Why not, my dear condé? I shall have wealth enough for both of us, and you know that my uncle thinks liberally upon the subject. From what I have seen of Raymond de las Cisternas, I am certain that he will readily acknowledge Antonia for his niece. Her birth therefore will be no objection to my offering her my hand. I should be a villain, could I think of her on any other terms than marriage; and in truth she seems possessed of every quality requisite to make me happy in a wife—young, lovely, gentle, sensible——"

"Sensible? Why, she said nothing but Yes, and No."

"She did not say much more, I must confess—but then she always said Yes or No in the right place."

"Did she so? Oh! your most obedient! That is using a right lover's argument, and I dare dispute no longer with so profound a casuist. Suppose we adjourn to the comedy?"

"It is out of my power. I only arrived last night at Madrid, and

---

1 A street in Madrid.

have not yet had an opportunity of seeing my sister. You know that her convent is in this street, and I was going thither when the crowd which I saw thronging into this church excited my curiosity to know what was the matter. I shall now pursue my first intention, and probably pass the evening with my sister at the parlour-grate."

"Your sister in a convent, say you? Oh! very true, I had forgotten. And how does Donna Agnes?[1] I am amazed, Don Lorenzo, how you could possibly think of immuring so charming a girl within the walls of a cloister!"

"I think of it, Don Christoval? How can you suspect me of such barbarity? You are conscious that she took the veil by her own desire, and that particular circumstances made her wish for a seclusion from the world. I used every means in my power to induce her to change her resolution; the endeavour was fruitless, and I lost a sister!"

"The luckier fellow you: I think, Lorenzo, you were a considerable gainer by that loss; if I remember right, Donna Agnes had a portion of ten thousand pistoles,[2] half of which reverted to your lordship. By St. Jago![3] I wish that I had fifty sisters in the same predicament: I should consent to losing them every soul without much heartburning."

"How, condé?" said Lorenzo in an angry voice; "do you suppose me base enough to have influenced my sister's retirement? do you suppose that the despicable wish to make myself master of her fortune could——"

"Admirable! Courage, Don Lorenzo! Now the man is all in a blaze. God grant that Antonia may soften that fiery temper, or we shall certainly cut each other's throat before the month is over! However, to prevent such a tragical catastrophe for the present, I shall make a retreat, and leave you master of the field. Farewell, my knight of Mount Ætna! Moderate that inflammable disposition, and remember that, whenever it is necessary to make love to yonder harridan, you may reckon upon my services."

---

1 Agnes is named after St. Agnes (d. 1253), sister of St. Clare and first abbess of the Poor Clares' convent in Florence.

2 Spanish gold coins.

3 St. James the Apostle. He is said to have evangelized Spain, though the early date of his martyrdom (42) makes this unlikely. His relics are preserved at Compostella, in northern Spain, goal of one of the great Catholic pilgrimages.

He said, and darted out of the cathedral.

"How wild-brained!" said Lorenzo. "With so excellent an heart, what pity that he possesses so little solidity of judgment!"

The night was now fast advancing. The lamps were not yet lighted. The faint beams of the rising moon scarcely could pierce through the gothic obscurity of the church. Lorenzo found himself unable to quit the spot. The void left in his bosom by Antonia's absence, and his sister's sacrifice which Don Christoval had just recalled to his imagination, created that melancholy of mind, which accorded but too well with the religious gloom surrounding him. He was still leaning against the seventh column from the pulpit. A soft and cooling air breathed along the solitary aisles; the moon-beams darting into the church through painted windows, tinged the fretted roofs and massy pillars with a thousand various shades of light and colours. Universal silence prevailed around, only interrupted by the occasional closing of doors in the adjoining abbey.

The calm of the hour and solitude of the place contributed to nourish Lorenzo's disposition to melancholy. He threw himself upon a seat which stood near him, and abandoned himself to the delusions of his fancy. He thought of his union with Antonia; he thought of the obstacles which might oppose his wishes; and a thousand changing visions floated before his fancy, sad 'tis true, but not unpleasing. Sleep insensibly stole over him, and the tranquil solemnity of his mind when awake, for a while continued to influence his slumbers.

He still fancied himself to be in the church of the Capuchins; but it was no longer dark and solitary. Multitudes of silver lamps shed splendour from the vaulted roofs; accompanied by the captivating chaunt of distant choristers, the organ's melody swelled through the church; the altar seemed decorated as for some distinguished feast; it was surrounded by a brilliant company; and near it stood Antonia arrayed in bridal white, and blushing with all the charms of virgin modesty.

Half hoping, half fearing, Lorenzo gazed upon the scene before him. Sudden the door leading to the abbey unclosed; and he saw, attended by a long train of monks, the preacher advance to whom he had just listened with so much admiration. He drew near Antonia.

"And where is the bridegroom?" said the imaginary friar.

Antonia seemed to look round the church with anxiety. Involuntarily the youth advanced a few steps from his concealment. She saw him; the blush of pleasure glowed upon her cheek; with a graceful motion of her hand she beckoned to him to advance. He disobeyed not the command; he flew towards her, and threw himself at her feet.

She retreated for a moment; then gazing upon him with unutterable delight, "Yes," she exclaimed, "my bridegroom! my destined bridegroom!"

She said, and hastened to throw herself into his arms; but before he had time to receive her, an unknown rushed between them: his form was gigantic; his complexion was swarthy, his eyes fierce and terrible; his mouth breathed out volumes of fire, and on his forehead was written in legible characters—"Pride! Lust! Inhumanity!"

Antonia shrieked. The monster clasped her in his arms, and, springing with her upon the altar, tortured her with his odious caresses. She endeavoured in vain to escape from his embrace. Lorenzo flew to her succour; but, ere he had time to reach her, a loud burst of thunder was heard. Instantly the cathedral seemed crumbling into pieces; the monks betook themselves to flight, shrieking fearfully; the lamps were extinguished, the altar sunk down, and in its place appeared an abyss vomiting forth clouds of flame. Uttering a loud and terrible cry the monster plunged into the gulph, and in his fall attempted to drag Antonia with him. He strove in vain. Animated by supernatural powers, she disengaged herself from his embrace; but her white robe was left in his possession. Instantly a wing of brilliant splendour spread itself from either of Antonia's arms. She darted upwards, and while ascending cried to Lorenzo, "Friend! we shall meet above!"

At the same moment the roof of the cathedral opened; harmonious voices pealed along the vaults; and the glory into which Antonia was received, was composed of rays of such dazzling brightness, that Lorenzo was unable to sustain the gaze. His sight failed, and he sunk upon the ground.[1]

When he awoke he found himself extended upon the pavement of the church: it was illuminated, and the chaunt of hymns sounded from a distance. For a while Lorenzo could not persuade himself that what he had just witnessed had been a dream, so strong an

---

1 As Lewis pointed out in a footnote to the fourth edition (see Appendix E), Lorenzo's dream is based on Lovelace's dream, in Samuel Richardson, *Clarissa* (1747-48) 1218; letter 417 (22 August): see Appendix A.2.a.

impression had it made upon his fancy. A little recollection convinced him of its fallacy: the lamps had been lighted during his sleep, and the music which he heard was occasioned by the monks, who were celebrating their vespers in the abbey-chapel.

Lorenzo rose, and prepared to bend his steps towards his sister's convent; his mind fully occupied by the singularity of his dream. He already drew near the porch, when his attention was attracted by perceiving a shadow moving upon the opposite wall. He looked curiously round, and soon descried a man wrapped up in his cloak, who seemed carefully examining whether his actions were observed. Very few people are exempt from the influence of curiosity. The unknown seemed anxious to conceal his business in the cathedral; and it was this very circumstance which made Lorenzo wish to discover what he was about.

Our hero was conscious that he had no right to pry into the secrets of this unknown cavalier.

"I will go," said Lorenzo. And Lorenzo stayed where he was.

The shadow thrown by the column effectually concealed him from the stranger, who continued to advance with caution. At length he drew a letter from beneath his cloak, and hastily placed it beneath a colossal statue of St. Francis. Then retiring with precipitation, he concealed himself in a part of the church at a considerable distance from that in which the image stood.

"So!" said Lorenzo to himself; "this is only some foolish love affair. I believe, I may as well be gone, for I can do no good in it."

In truth, till that moment it never came into his head that he could do any good in it; but he thought it necessary to make some little excuse to himself for having indulged his curiosity. He now made a second attempt to retire from the church. For this time he gained the porch without meeting with any impediment; but it was destined that he should pay it another visit that night. As he descended the steps leading into the street, a cavalier rushed against him with such violence, that both were nearly overturned by the concussion. Lorenzo put his hand to his sword.

"How now, Segnor?" said he; "what mean you by this rudeness?"

"Ha! is it you, Medina?" replied the new comer, whom Lorenzo by his voice now recognized for Don Christoval. "You are the luckiest fellow in the universe, not to have left the church before my return. In, in! my dear lad! they will be here immediately!"

"Who will be here?"

"The old hen and all her pretty little chickens. In, I say; and then you shall know the whole history."

Lorenzo followed him into the cathedral, and they concealed themselves behind the statue of St. Francis.

"And now," said our hero, "may I take the liberty of asking what is the meaning of all this haste and rapture?"

"Oh! Lorenzo, we shall see such a glorious sight! The prioress of St. Clare[1] and her whole train of nuns are coming hither. You are to know, that the pious father Ambrosio [the Lord reward him for it!] will upon no account move out of his own precincts. It being absolutely necessary for every fashionable convent to have him for its confessor, the nuns are in consequence obliged to visit him at the abbey; since, when the mountain will not come to Mahomet, Mahomet must needs go to the mountain.[2] Now the prioress of St. Clare, the better to escape the gaze of such impure eyes as belong to yourself and your humble servant, thinks proper to bring her holy flock to confession in the dusk: she is to be admitted into the abbey-chapel by yon private door. The porteress of St. Clare, who is a worthy old soul and a particular friend of mine, has just assured me of their being here in a few moments. There is news for you, you rogue! We shall see some of the prettiest faces in Madrid!"

"In truth, Christoval, we shall do no such thing. The nuns are always veiled."

"No! no! I know better. On entering a place of worship, they ever take off their veils, from respect to the saint to whom 'tis dedicated. But hark, they are coming! Silence! silence! Observe, and be convinced."

"Good!" said Lorenzo to himself; "I may possibly discover to whom the vows are addressed of this mysterious stranger."

Scarcely had Don Christoval ceased to speak, when the domina of St. Clare appeared, followed by a long procession of nuns. Each upon entering the church took off her veil. The prioress crossed her hands upon her bosom, and made a profound reverence as she passed the statue of St. Francis, the patron of this cathedral. The nuns followed her example, and several moved onwards

---

1 St. Clare (c. 1193-1253), a disciple of St. Francis, founded the first Franciscan order of nuns, the Poor Clares. Since the Poor Clares are an enclosed order, this visit to the church, like the procession at the climax of the novel, is another of Lewis's mistakes about Catholicism.

2 The proverb is derived from Francis Bacon, "Of Boldness."

without having satisfied Lorenzo's curiosity. He almost began to despair of seeing the mystery cleared up, when, in paying her respects to St. Francis, one of the nuns happened to drop her rosary. As she stooped to pick it up the light flashed full in her face. At the same moment she dexterously removed the letter from beneath the image, placed it in her bosom, and hastened to resume her rank in the procession.

"Ha!" said Christoval in a low voice, "here we have some little intrigue, no doubt."

"Agnes, by heaven!" cried Lorenzo.

"What, your sister? Diavolo! Then somebody, I suppose, will have to pay for our peeping."

"And shall pay for it without delay," replied the incensed brother.

The pious procession had now entered the abbey; the door was already closed upon it. The unknown immediately quitted his concealment, and hastened to leave the church: ere he could effect his intention, he descried Medina stationed in his passage. The stranger hastily retreated, and drew his hat over his eyes.

"Attempt not to fly me!" exclaimed Lorenzo; "I will know who you are, and what were the contents of that letter."

"Of that letter?" repeated the unknown. "And by what title do you ask the question?"

"By a title of which I am now ashamed; but it becomes not you to question me. Either reply circumstantially to my demands, or answer me with your sword."

"The latter method will be the shortest," rejoined the other, drawing his rapier; "come on, Segnor Bravo! I am ready."

Burning with rage, Lorenzo hastened to the attack: the antagonists had already exchanged several passes, before Christoval, who at that moment had more sense than either of them, could throw himself between their weapons.

"Hold! hold! Medina!" he exclaimed; "remember the consequences of shedding blood on consecrated ground!"

The stranger immediately dropped his sword.

"Medina?" he cried. "Great God, is it possible! Lorenzo, have you quite forgotten Raymond de las Cisternas?"

Lorenzo's astonishment increased with every succeeding moment. Raymond advanced towards him; but with a look of suspicion he drew back his hand, which the other was preparing to take.

"You here, Marquis? What is the meaning of all this? You

engaged in a clandestine correspondence with my sister, whose affections——"

"Have ever been, and still are mine. But this is no fit place for an explanation. Accompany me to my hotel,[1] and you shall know every thing. Who is that with you?"

"One whom I believe you to have seen before," replied Don Christoval, "though probably not at church."

"The condé d'Ossorio?"

"Exactly so, marquis."

"I have no objection to entrusting you with my secret, for I am sure that I may depend upon your silence."

"Then your opinion of me is better than my own, and therefore I must beg leave to decline your confidence. Do you go your own way, and I shall go mine. Marquis, where are you to be found?"

"As usual, at the hotel de las Cisternas; but remember that I am incognito, and that, if you wish to see me, you must ask for Alphonso d'Alvarada."

"Good! good! Farewell, cavaliers!" said Don Christoval, and instantly departed.

"You, marquis," said Lorenzo in the accent of surprise; "you, Alphonso d'Alvarada?"

"Even so, Lorenzo: but unless you have already heard my story from your sister, I have much to relate that will astonish you. Follow me, therefore, to my hotel without delay."

At this moment the porter of the Capuchins entered the cathedral to lock up the doors for the night. The two noblemen instantly withdrew, and hastened with all speed to the palace de las Cisternas.

————

"Well, Antonia," said the aunt, as soon as she had quitted the church, "what think you of our gallants? Don Lorenzo really seems a very obliging good sort of young man: he paid you some attention, and nobody knows what may come of it. But as to Don Christoval, I protest to you, he is the very phœnix of politeness; so gallant! so well-bred! so sensible, and so pathetic! Well! if ever man can prevail upon me to break my vow never to marry, it will be

---

1 A mansion or palace, not a hotel in the modern sense.

that Don Christoval. You see, niece, that every thing turns out exactly as I told you: the very moment that I produced myself in Madrid, I knew that I should be surrounded by admirers. When I took off my veil, did you see, Antonia, what an effect the action had upon the condé? And when I presented him my hand, did you observe the air of passion with which he kissed it? If ever I witnessed real love, I then saw it impressed upon Don Christoval's countenance!"

Now Antonia had observed the air with which Don Christoval had kissed this same hand; but as she drew conclusions from it somewhat different from her aunt's, she was wise enough to hold her tongue. As this is the only instance known of a woman's ever having done so, it was judged worthy to be recorded here.

The old lady continued her discourse to Antonia in the same strain, till they gained the street in which was their lodging. Here a crowd collected before their door permitted them not to approach it; and placing themselves on the opposite side of the street, they endeavoured to make out what had drawn all these people together. After some minutes the crowd formed itself into a circle; and now Antonia perceived in the midst of it a woman of extraordinary height, who whirled herself repeatedly round and round, using all sorts of extravagant gestures. Her dress was composed of shreds of various-coloured silks and linens fantastically arranged, yet not entirely without taste. Her head was covered with a kind of turban ornamented with vine-leaves and wild flowers. She seemed much sun-burnt, and her complexion was of a deep olive: her eyes looked fiery and strange; and in her hand she bore a long black rod, with which she at intervals traced a variety of singular figures upon the ground, round about which she danced in all the eccentric attitudes of folly and delirium. Suddenly she broke off her dance, whirled herself round thrice with rapidity, and after a moment's pause she sung the following ballad:

THE GIPSY's SONG.

COME, cross my hand! My art surpasses
All that did ever mortal know:
Come, maidens, come! My magic glasses
Your future husband's form can show:

For 'tis to me the power is given
Unclosed the book of fate to see;

To read the fixed resolves of heaven,
    And dive into futurity.

I guide the pale moon's silver waggon;
    The winds in magic bonds I hold;
I charm to sleep the crimson dragon,
    Who loves to watch o'er buried gold.

Fenced round with spells, unhurt I venture
    Their sabbath strange where witches keep;
Fearless the sorcerer's circle enter,
    And woundless tread on snakes asleep.

Lo! here are charms of mighty power!
    This makes secure an husband's truth;
And this, composed at midnight hour,
    Will force to love the coldest youth.

If any maid too much has granted,
    Her loss this philtre will repair.
This blooms a cheek where red is wanted,
    And this will make a brown girl fair;

Then silent hear, while I discover
    What I in fortune's mirror view;
And each, when many a year is over,
    Shall own the Gipsy's sayings true.

"Dear aunt!" said Antonia when the stranger had finished, "is she not mad?"

"Mad? Not she, child; she is only wicked. She is a gipsy, a sort of vagabond, whose sole occupation is to run about the country telling lyes, and pilfering from those who come by their money honestly. Out upon such vermin! If I were king of Spain, every one of them should be burnt alive, who was found in my dominions after the next three weeks."

These words were pronounced so audibly, that they reached the gipsy's ears. She immediately pierced through the crowd, and made towards the ladies. She saluted them thrice in the eastern fashion, and then addressed herself to Antonia.

THE GIPSY.

"Lady, gentle lady! know,
I your future fate can show;
Give your hand, and do not fear;
Lady, gentle lady! hear!"

"Dearest aunt!" said Antonia, "indulge me this once! let me have
my fortune told me!"
"Nonsense, child! She will tell you nothing but falsehoods."
"No matter; let me at least hear what she has to say. Do, my dear
aunt, oblige me, I beseech you!"
"Well, well! Antonia, since you are so bent upon the thing—
Here, good woman, you shall see the hands of both of us. There is
money for you, and now let me hear my fortune."
As she said this, she drew off her glove, and presented her hand.
The gipsy looked at it for a moment, and then made this
reply:

THE GIPSY.

"Your fortune? You are now so old,
Good dame, that 'tis already told:
Yet, for your money, in a trice
I will repay you in advice.
Astonished at your childish vanity,
Your friends all tax you with insanity,
And grieve to see you use your art
To catch some youthful lover's heart.
Believe me, dame, when all is done,
Your age will still be fifty-one;
And men will rarely take an hint
Of love from two grey eyes that squint.
Take then my counsels; lay aside
Your paint and patches, lust and pride,
And on the poor those sums bestow,
Which now are spent on useless show.
Think on your Maker, not a suitor;
Think on your past faults, not on future;
And think Time's scythe will quickly mow
The few red hairs, which deck your brow."

The audience rang with laughter during the gipsy's address; and—"fifty-one,—squinting eyes,—red hair,—paint and patches,"—&c. were bandied from mouth to mouth. Leonella was almost choked with passion, and loaded her malicious adviser with the bitterest reproaches. The swarthy prophetess for some time listened to her with a contemptuous smile: at length she made her a short answer, and then turned to Antonia.

THE GIPSY.

"Peace, lady! What I said was true.
And now, my lovely maid, to you;
Give me your hand, and let me see
Your future doom, and heaven's decree."

In imitation of Leonella, Antonia drew off her glove, and presented her white hand to the gipsy, who, having gazed upon it for some time with a mingled expression of pity and astonishment, pronounced her oracle in the following words:

THE GIPSY.

"Jesus! what a palm is there!
Chaste, and gentle, young and fair,
Perfect mind and form possessing,
You would be some good man's blessing:
But, alas! this line discovers
That destruction o'er you hovers;
Lustful man and crafty devil
Will combine to work your evil;
And from earth by sorrows driven,
Soon your soul must speed to heaven.
Yet your sufferings to delay,
Well remember what I say.
When you one more virtuous see
Than belongs to man to be,
One, whose self no crimes assailing,
Pities not his neighbour's failing,
Call the gipsy's words to mind:
Though he seem so good and kind,
Fair exteriors oft will hide
Hearts that swell with lust and pride.

Lovely maid, with tears I leave you.
Let not my prediction grieve you:
Rather, with submission bending,
Calmly wait distress impending,
And expect eternal bliss
In a better world than this."

Having said this, the gipsy again whirled herself round thrice, and then hastened out of the street with frantic gesture. The crowd followed her; and Elvira's door being now unembarrassed, Leonella entered the house, out of humour with the gipsy, with her niece, and with the people; in short, with every body but herself and her charming cavalier. The gipsy's predictions had also considerably affected Antonia; but the impression soon wore off, and in a few hours she had forgotten the adventure, as totally as had it never taken place.

CHAP. II.

Fòrse sé tu gustassi una sòl volta
La millésima parte délle giòje,
Ché gusta un còr amato riamando,
Diresti ripentita sospirando,
Perduto è tutto il tempo
Ché in amar non si spènde.

TASSO.[1]

Hadst thou but tasted once the thousandth part
Of joys, which bless the loved and loving heart,
Your words repentant and your sighs would prove,
Lost is the time which is not past in love.

——

THE monks having attended their abbot to the door of his cell, he dismissed them with an air of conscious superiority, in which humility's semblance combated with the reality of pride.

He was no sooner alone, than he gave free loose to the indul-

1 Torquato Tasso (1544-95), *L'Aminta* 1.1.26-31.

gence of his vanity. When he remembered the enthusiasm which his discourse had excited, his heart swelled with rapture, and his imagination presented him with splendid visions of aggrandizement. He looked round him with exultation; and pride told him loudly, that he was superior to the rest of his fellow-creatures.

"Who," thought he, "who but myself has passed the ordeal of youth, yet sees no single stain upon his conscience? Who else has subdued the violence of strong passions and an impetuous temperament, and submitted even from the dawn of life to voluntary retirement? I seek for such a man in vain. I see no one but myself possessed of such resolution. Religion cannot boast Ambrosio's equal! How powerful an effect did my discourse produce upon its auditors! How they crowded round me! How they loaded me with benedictions, and pronounced me the sole uncorrupted pillar of the church! What then now is left for me to do? Nothing, but to watch as carefully over the conduct of my brethren, as I have hitherto watched over my own. Yet hold! May I not be tempted from those paths, which till now I have pursued without one moment's wandering? Am I not a man, whose nature is frail and prone to error? I must now abandon the solitude of my retreat; the fairest and noblest dames of Madrid continually present themselves at the abbey, and will use no other confessor. I must accustom my eyes to objects of temptation, and expose myself to the seduction of luxury and desire. Should I meet in that world which I am constrained to enter, some lovely female—lovely as you—Madona——!"

As he said this, he fixed his eyes upon a picture of the Virgin, which was suspended opposite to him: this for two years had been the object of his increasing wonder and adoration. He paused, and gazed upon it with delight.

"What beauty in that countenance!" he continued after a silence of some minutes; "how graceful is the turn of that head! what sweetness, yet what majesty in her divine eyes! how softly her cheek reclines upon her hand! Can the rose vie with the blush of that cheek? can the lily rival the whiteness of that hand? Oh! if such a creature existed, and existed but for me! were I permitted to twine round my fingers those golden ringlets, and press with my lips the treasures of that snowy bosom! gracious God, should I then resist the temptation? Should I not barter for a single embrace the reward of my sufferings for thirty years? Should I not abandon——Fool that I am! Whither do I suffer my admiration of this picture to hurry me? Away, impure ideas! Let me remember, that woman is for ever lost to me. Never was mortal formed so perfect as this picture. But even did such exist, the trial might be too mighty for a common virtue; but Ambrosio's is proof against temptation. Temptation, did I say? To me it would be none. What charms me, when ideal and considered as a superior being, would disgust me, become woman and tainted with all the failings of mortality. It is not the woman's beauty that fills me with such enthusiasm: it is the painter's skill that I admire; it is the Divinity that I adore. Are not the passions dead in my bosom? have I not freed myself from the frailty of mankind? Fear not, Ambrosio! Take confidence in the strength of your virtue. Enter boldly into the world, to whose failings you are superior; reflect that you are now exempted from humanity's defects, and defy all the arts of the spirits of darkness. They shall know you for what you are!"

Here his reverie was interrupted by three soft knocks at the door of his cell. With difficulty did the abbot awake from his delirium. The knocking was repeated.

"Who is there?" said Ambrosio at length.

"It is only Rosario," replied a gentle voice.[1]

"Enter! enter, my son!"

The door was immediately opened, and Rosario appeared with a small basket in his hand.

Rosario was a young novice belonging to the monastery, who in three months intended to make his profession. A sort of mystery enveloped this youth, which rendered him at once an object of interest and curiosity. His hatred of society, his profound melancholy, his rigid observation of the duties of his order, and his voluntary seclusion from the world, at his age so unusual, attracted the notice of the whole fraternity. He seemed fearful of being recognised, and no one had ever seen his face. His head was continually muffled up in his cowl; yet such of his features as accident discovered, appeared the most beautiful and noble. Rosario was the only name by which he was known in the monastery. No one knew from whence he came, and when questioned on the subject he preserved a profound silence. A stranger, whose rich habit and magnificent equipage declared him to be of distinguished rank, had engaged the monks to receive a novice, and had deposited the necessary sums. The next day he returned

---

1 Rosario's name is associated with the Rosary, and indirectly with the Virgin Mary, who is sometimes addressed as "Madonna del Rosario," Our Lady of the Rosary.

with Rosario, and from that time no more had been heard of him.

The youth had carefully avoided the company of the monks: he answered their civilities with sweetness, but reserve, and evidently showed that his inclination led him to solitude. To this general rule the superior was the only exception. To him he looked up with a respect approaching idolatry: he sought his company with the most attentive assiduity, and eagerly seized every means to ingratiate himself in his favour. In the abbot's society his heart seemed to be at ease, and an air of gaiety pervaded his whole manners and discourse. Ambrosio on his side did not feel less attracted towards the youth; with him alone did he lay aside his habitual severity. When he spoke to him, he insensibly assumed a tone milder than was usual to him; and no voice sounded so sweet to him as did Rosario's. He repaid the youth's attentions by instructing him in various sciences; the novice received his lessons with docility; Ambrosio was every day more charmed with the vivacity of his genius, the simplicity of his manners, and the rectitude of his heart: in short, he loved him with all the affection of a father. He could not help sometimes indulging a desire secretly to see the face of his pupil; but his rule of self-denial extended even to curiosity, and prevented him from communicating his wishes to the youth.

"Pardon my intrusion, father," said Rosario, while he placed his basket upon the table; "I come to you a suppliant. Hearing that a dear friend is dangerously ill, I entreat your prayers for his recovery. If supplications can prevail upon heaven to spare him, surely yours must be efficacious."

"Whatever depends upon me, my son, you know that you may command. What is your friend's name?"

"Vincentio della Ronda."

"'Tis sufficient. I will not forget him in my prayers, and may our thrice-blessed St. Francis deign to listen to my intercession!—What have you in your basket, Rosario?"

"A few of those flowers, reverend father, which I have observed to be most acceptable to you. Will you permit my arranging them in your chamber?"

"Your attentions charm me, my son."

While Rosario dispersed the contents of his basket in small vases, placed for that purpose in various parts of the room, the abbot thus continued the conversation:

"I saw you not in the church this evening, Rosario."

"Yet I was present, father. I am too grateful for your protection to lose an opportunity of witnessing your triumph."

"Alas! Rosario, I have but little cause to triumph: the saint spoke by my mouth; to him belongs all the merit. It seems then you were contented with my discourse?"

"Contented, say you? Oh! you surpassed yourself! Never did I hear such eloquence—save once!"

Here the novice heaved an involuntary sigh.

"When was that once?" demanded the abbot.

"When you preached upon the sudden indisposition of our late superior."

"I remember it: that is more than two years ago. And were you present? I knew you not at that time, Rosario."

"'Tis true, father; and would to God I had expired ere I beheld that day! What sufferings, what sorrows should I have escaped!"

"Sufferings at your age, Rosario?"

"Aye, father; sufferings, which if known to you, would equally raise your anger and compassion! Sufferings, which form at once the torment and pleasure of my existence! Yet in this retreat my bosom would feel tranquil, were it not for the tortures of apprehension. Oh God! oh God! how cruel is a life of fear!—Father! I have given up all; I have abandoned the world and its delights for ever: nothing now remains, nothing now has charms for me, but your friendship, but your affection. If I lose that, father! oh! if I lose that, tremble at the effects of my despair!"

"You apprehend the loss of my friendship? How has my conduct justified this fear? Know me better, Rosario, and think me worthy of your confidence. What are your sufferings? Reveal them to me, and believe, that if 'tis in my power to relieve them——"

"Ah! 'tis in no one's power but yours. Yet I must not let you know them. You would hate me for my avowal! you would drive me from your presence with scorn and ignominy."

"My son, I conjure you! I entreat you——"

"For pity's sake, enquire no further! I must not—I dare not— Hark! the bell rings for vespers! Father, your benediction, and I leave you."

As he said this, he threw himself upon his knees, and received the blessing which he demanded. Then pressing the abbot's hand to his lips, he started from the ground, and hastily quitted the apartment. Soon after Ambrosio descended to vespers (which were celebrated in a small chapel belonging to the abbey), filled with surprise at the singularity of the youth's behaviour.

Vespers being over, the monks retired to their respective cells. The abbot alone remained in the chapel to receive the nuns of St. Clare. He had not been long seated in the confessional chair, before the prioress made her appearance. Each of the nuns was heard in her turn, while the others waited with the domina in the adjoining vestry. Ambrosio listened to the confessions with attention, made many exhortations, enjoined penance proportioned to each offence, and for some time every thing went on as usual: till at last one of the nuns, conspicuous from the nobleness of her air and elegance of her figure, carelessly permitted a letter to fall from her bosom. She was retiring, unconscious of her loss. Ambrosio supposed it to have been written by some one of her relations, and picked it up, intending to restore it to her.

"Stay, daughter," said he; "you have let fall——"

At this moment, the paper being already open, his eye involuntarily read the first words. He started back with surprise. The nun had turned round on hearing his voice: she perceived her letter in his hand, and, uttering a shriek of terror, flew hastily to regain it.

"Hold!" said the friar in a tone of severity; "daughter, I must read this letter."

"Then I am lost!" she exclaimed, clasping her hands together wildly.

All colour instantly faded from her face; she trembled with agitation, and was obliged to fold her arms round a pillar of the chapel to save herself from sinking upon the floor. In the mean while the abbot read the following lines:

"All is ready for your escape, my dearest Agnes! At twelve tomorrow night I shall expect to find you at the garden-door: I have obtained the key, and a few hours will suffice to place you in a secure asylum. Let no mistaken scruples induce you to reject the certain means of preserving yourself and the innocent creature whom you nourish in your bosom. Remember that you had promised to be mine, long ere you engaged yourself to the church; that your situation will soon be evident to the prying eyes of your companions; and that flight is the only means of avoiding the effects of their malevolent resentment. Farewell, my Agnes! my dear and destined wife! Fail not to be at the garden-door at twelve!"

As soon as he had finished, Ambrosio bent an eye stern and angry upon the imprudent nun.

"This letter must to the prioress," said he, and passed her.

His words sounded like thunder to her ears: she awoke from her torpidity only to be sensible of the dangers of her situation. She followed him hastily, and detained him by his garment.

"Stay! oh! stay!" she cried in the accents of despair, while she threw herself at the friar's feet, and bathed them with her tears. "Father, compassionate my youth! Look with indulgence on a woman's weakness, and deign to conceal my frailty! The remainder of my life shall be employed in expiating this single fault, and your lenity will bring back a soul to heaven!"

"Amazing confidence! What! shall St. Clare's convent become the retreat of prostitutes? Shall I suffer the church of Christ to cherish in its bosom debauchery and shame? Unworthy wretch! such lenity would make me your accomplice. Mercy would here be criminal. You have abandoned yourself to a seducer's lust; you have defiled the sacred habit by your impurity; and still dare you think yourself deserving my compassion? Hence, nor detain me longer. Where is the lady prioress?" he added, raising his voice.

"Hold! father, hold! Hear me but for one moment! Tax me not with impurity, nor think that I have erred from the warmth of temperament. Long before I took the veil, Raymond was master of my heart: he inspired me with the purest, the most irreproachable passion, and was on the point of becoming my lawful husband. An horrible adventure, and the treachery of a relation, separated us from each other. I believed him for ever lost to me, and threw myself into a convent from motives of despair. Accident again united us; I could not refuse myself the melancholy pleasure of mingling my tears with his. We met nightly in the gardens of St. Clare, and in an unguarded moment I violated my vows of chastity. I shall soon become a mother. Reverend Ambrosio, take compassion on me; take compassion on the innocent being whose existence is attached to mine. If you discover my imprudence to the domina, both of us are lost. The punishment which the laws of St. Clare assign to unfortunates like myself, is most severe and cruel. Worthy, worthy father! let not your own untainted conscience render you unfeeling towards those less able to withstand temptation! Let not mercy be the only virtue of which your heart is unsusceptible! Pity me, most reverend! Restore my letter, nor doom me to inevitable destruction!"

"Your boldness confounds me. Shall *I* conceal your crime—*I* whom you have deceived by your feigned confession?—No, daughter, no. I will render you a more essential service. I will rescue you from perdition, in spite of yourself. Penance and mortification shall expiate your offence, and severity force you back to the paths of holiness. What, ho! Mother St. Agatha!"[1]

"Father! by all that is sacred, by all that is most dear to you, I supplicate, I entreat——"

"Release me. I will not hear you. Where is the domina? Mother St. Agatha, where are you?"

The door of the vestry opened, and the prioress entered the chapel, followed by her nuns.

"Cruel, cruel!" exclaimed Agnes, relinquishing her hold.

Wild and desperate, she threw herself upon the ground, beating her bosom, and rending her veil in all the delirium of despair. The nuns gazed with astonishment upon the scene before them. The friar now presented the fatal paper to the prioress, informed her of the manner in which he had found it, and added, that it was her business to decide what penance the delinquent merited.

While she perused the letter, the domina's countenance grew inflamed with passion. What! such a crime committed in her convent, and made known to Ambrosio, to the idol of Madrid, to the man whom she was most anxious to impress with the opinion of the strictness and regularity of her house! Words were inadequate to express her fury. She was silent, and darted upon the prostrate nun looks of menace and malignity.

"Away with her to the convent!" said she at length to some of her attendants.

Two of the oldest nuns now approaching Agnes, raised her forcibly from the ground, and prepared to conduct her from the chapel.

"What!" she exclaimed suddenly, shaking off their hold with distracted gestures, "is all hope then lost? Already do you drag me to punishment? Where are you, Raymond? Oh! save me! save me!" Then casting upon the abbot a frantic look, "Hear me!" she continued, "man of an hard heart! Hear me, proud, stern, and cruel! You could have saved me; you could have restored me to happiness and virtue, but would not; you are the destroyer of my soul; you are my murderer, and on you fall the curse of my death and my unborn infant's! Insolent in your yet-unshaken virtue, you disdained the prayers of a penitent; but God will shew mercy, though

---

1 The prioress is named after St. Agatha, a third-century Sicilian martyr. According to legend, she refused the advances of the Roman governor and was tortured by having her breasts cut off. She died in prison.

you shew none. And where is the merit of your boasted virtue? What temptations have you vanquished? Coward! you have fled from it, not opposed seduction. But the day of trial will arrive. Oh! then when you yield to impetuous passions; when you feel that man is weak, and born to err; when, shuddering, you look back upon your crimes, and solicit, with terror, the mercy of your God, oh! in that fearful moment think upon me! think upon your cruelty! think upon Agnes, and despair of pardon."

As she uttered these last words, her strength was exhausted, and she sunk inanimate upon the bosom of a nun who stood near her. She was immediately conveyed from the chapel, and her companions followed her.

Ambrosio had not listened to her reproaches without emotion. A secret pang at his heart made him feel that he had treated this unfortunate with too great severity. He therefore detained the prioress, and ventured to pronounce some words in favour of the delinquent.

"The violence of her despair," said he, "proves that at least vice is not become familiar to her. Perhaps, by treating her with somewhat less rigour than is generally practised, and mitigating in some degree the accustomed penance——"

"Mitigate it, father?" interrupted the lady prioress: "Not I, believe me. The laws of our order are strict and severe; they have fallen into disuse of late; but the crime of Agnes shews me the necessity of their revival.[1] I go to signify my intention to the convent, and Agnes shall be the first to feel the rigour of those laws, which shall be obeyed to the very letter. Father, farewell!"

Thus saying, she hastened out of the chapel.

"I have done my duty," said Ambrosio to himself.

Still did he not feel perfectly satisfied by this reflection. To dissipate the unpleasant ideas which this scene had excited in him, upon quitting the chapel he descended into the abbey-garden. In all Madrid there was no spot more beautiful, or better regulated. It was laid out with the most exquisite taste; the choicest flowers adorned it in the height of luxuriance, and, though artfully arranged, seemed only planted by the hand of Nature. Fountains, springing from basons of white marble, cooled the air with perpetual showers; and the walls were entirely covered by jessamine, vines, and honey-suckles. The hour now

---

1 Cf. Shakespeare, *Measure for Measure* 1.3.19-31.

added to the beauty of the scene. The full moon, ranging through a blue and cloudless sky, shed upon the trees a trembling lustre, and the waters of the fountains sparkled in the silver beam; a gentle breeze breathed the fragrance of orange-blossoms along the alleys, and the nightingale poured forth her melodious murmur from the shelter of an artificial wilderness. Thither the abbot bent his steps.

In the bosom of this little grove stood a rustic grotto, formed in imitation of an hermitage. The walls were constructed of roots of trees, and the interstices filled up with moss and ivy. Seats of turf were placed on either side, and a natural cascade fell from the rock above. Buried in himself, the monk approached the spot. The universal calm had communicated itself to his bosom, and a voluptuous tranquillity spread languor through his soul.

He reached the hermitage, and was entering to repose himself, when he stopped on perceiving it to be already occupied. Extended upon one of the banks lay a man in a melancholy posture. His head was supported upon his arm, and he seemed lost in meditation. The monk drew nearer, and recognised Rosario: he watched him in silence, and entered not the hermitage. After some minutes the youth raised his eyes, and fixed them mournfully upon the opposite wall.

"Yes," said he, with a deep and plaintive sigh, "I feel all the happiness of thy situation, all the misery of my own. Happy were I, could I think like thee! Could I look like thee with disgust upon mankind, could bury myself for ever in some impenetrable solitude, and forget that the world holds beings deserving to be loved! O God! what a blessing would misanthropy be to me!"

"That is a singular thought, Rosario," said the abbot, entering the grotto.

"You here, reverend father?" cried the novice.

At the same time starting from his place in confusion, he drew his cowl hastily over his face. Ambrosio seated himself upon the bank, and obliged the youth to place himself by him.

"You must not indulge this disposition to melancholy," said he: "What can possibly have made you view in so desirable a light, misanthropy, of all sentiments the most hateful?"

"The perusal of these verses, father, which till now had escaped my observation. The brightness of the moon-beams permitted my reading them; and, oh! how I envy the feelings of the writer!"

As he said this, he pointed to a marble tablet fixed against the opposite wall: on it were engraved the following lines:

INSCRIPTION IN AN HERMITAGE.

Whoe'er thou art these lines now reading,
Think not, though from the world receding,
I joy my lonely days to lead in
        This desert drear,
That with remorse a conscience bleeding
        Hath led me here.

No thought of guilt my bosom sours:
Free-willed I fled from courtly bowers;
For well I saw in halls and towers,
        That Lust and Pride,
The Arch-fiend's dearest darkest powers,
        In state preside.

I saw mankind with vice incrusted;
I saw that Honour's sword was rusted;
That few for aught but folly lusted;
That he was still deceiv'd, who trusted
        In love or friend;
And hither came, with men disgusted,
        My life to end.

In this lone cave, in garments lowly,
Alike a foe to noisy folly
And brow-bent gloomy melancholy,
        I wear away
My life, and in my office holy
        Consume the day.

Content and comfort bless me more in
This grot, than e'er I felt before in
A palace; and with thoughts still soaring
        To God on high,
Each night and morn with voice imploring
        This wish I sigh:

"Let me, O Lord! from life retire,
Unknown each guilty worldly fire,
Remorseful throb, or loose desire;
        And when I die,

Let me in this belief expire,
                    To God I fly!"

Stranger, if, full of youth and riot,
As yet no grief has marred thy quiet,
Thou haply throw'st a scornful eye at
                    The Hermit's prayer:
But if thou hast a cause to sigh at
                    Thy fault, or care;

If thou hast known false love's vexation,
Or hast been exil'd from thy nation,
Or guilt affrights thy contemplation,
                    And makes thee pine;
Oh! how must thou lament *thy* station,
                    And envy mine!

"Were it possible," said the friar, "for man to be so totally
wrapped up in himself as to live in absolute seclusion from human
nature, and could yet feel the contented tranquillity which these
lines express, I allow that the situation would be more desirable,
than to live in a world so pregnant with every vice and every folly.
But this never can be the case. This inscription was merely placed
here for the ornament of the grotto, and the sentiments and the
hermit are equally imaginary. Man was born for society. However
little he may be attached to the world, he never can wholly forget
it, or bear to be wholly forgotten by it. Disgusted at the guilt or
absurdity of mankind, the misanthrope flies from it; he resolves to
become an hermit, and buries himself in the cavern of some
gloomy rock. While hate inflames his bosom, possibly he may feel
contented with his situation: but when his passions begin to cool;
when Time has mellowed his sorrows, and healed those wounds
which he bore with him to his solitude, think you that Content
becomes his companion? Ah! no, Rosario. No longer sustained by
the violence of his passions, he feels all the monotony of his way
of living, and his heart becomes the prey of ennui and weariness.
He looks round, and finds himself alone in the universe: the love
of society revives in his bosom, and he pants to return to that world
which he has abandoned. Nature loses all her charms in his eyes:
no one is near him to point out her beauties, or share in his admiration of her excellence and variety. Propped upon the fragment of
some rock, he gazes upon the tumbling water-fall with a vacant

eye; he views, without emotion, the glory of the setting sun. Slowly he returns to his cell at evening, for no one there is anxious for his arrival; he has no comfort in his solitary, unsavoury meal: he throws himself upon his couch of moss despondent and dissatisfied, and wakes only to pass a day as joyless, as monotonous as the former."

"You amaze me, father! Suppose that circumstances condemned you to solitude; would not the duties of religion, and the consciousness of a life well spent, communicate to your heart that calm which——"

"I should deceive myself, did I fancy that they could. I am convinced of the contrary, and that all my fortitude would not prevent me from yielding to melancholy and disgust. After consuming the day in study, if you knew my pleasure at meeting my brethren in the evening! After passing many a long hour in solitude, if I could express to you the joy which I feel at once more beholding a fellow-creature! 'Tis in this particular that I place the principal merit of a monastic institution. It secludes man from the temptations of vice; it procures that leisure necessary for the proper service of the Supreme; it spares him the mortification of witnessing the crimes of the worldly, and yet permits him to enjoy the blessings of society. And do you, Rosario, do you envy an hermit's life? Can you be thus blind to the happiness of your situation? Reflect upon it for a moment. This abbey is become your asylum: your regularity, your gentleness, your talents have rendered you the object of universal esteem: you are secluded from the world which you profess to hate; yet you remain in possession of the benefits of society, and that a society composed of the most estimable of mankind."

"Father! father! 'tis that which causes my torment. Happy had it been for me, had my life been passed among the vicious and abandoned; had I never heard pronounced the name of virtue. 'Tis my unbounded adoration of religion; 'tis my soul's exquisite sensibility of the beauty of fair and good, that loads me with shame—that hurries me to perdition. Oh! that I had never seen these abbey-walls!"

"How, Rosario? When we last conversed, you spoke in a different tone. Is my friendship then become of such little consequence? Had you never seen these abbey-walls, you never had seen me. Can that really be your wish?"

"Had never seen you?" repeated the novice, starting from the bank, and grasping the friar's hand with a frantic air—"You! you! Would to God that lightning had blasted them before you ever met my eyes! Would to God that I were never to see you more, and could forget that I had ever seen you!"

With these words he flew hastily from the grotto. Ambrosio remained in his former attitude, reflecting on the youth's unaccountable behaviour. He was inclined to suspect the derangement of his senses: yet the general tenor of his conduct, the connexion of his ideas, and calmness of his demeanour till the moment of his quitting the grotto, seemed to discountenance this conjecture. After a few minutes Rosario returned. He again seated himself upon the bank: he reclined his cheek upon one hand, and with the other wiped away the tears which trickled from his eyes at intervals.

The monk looked upon him with compassion, and forbore to interrupt his meditations. Both observed for some time a profound silence. The nightingale had now taken her station upon an orange-tree fronting the hermitage, and poured forth a strain the most melancholy and melodious. Rosario raised his head, and listened to her with attention.

"It was thus," said he, with a deep-drawn sigh, "it was thus that, during the last month of her unhappy life, my sister used to sit listening to the nightingale. Poor Matilda! she sleeps in the grave, and her broken heart throbs no more with passion."[1]

"You had a sister?"

"You say right, that I *had*. Alas! I have one no longer. She sunk beneath the weight of her sorrows in the very spring of life."

"What were those sorrows?"

"They will not excite *your* pity. *You* know not the power of those irresistible, those fatal sentiments to which her heart was a prey. Father, she loved unfortunately. A passion for one endowed with every virtue, for a man—oh! rather let me say for a divinity—proved the bane of her existence. His noble form, his spotless character, his various talents, his wisdom solid, wonderful, and glorious, might have warmed the bosom of the most insensible. My sister saw him, and dared to love, though she never dared to hope."

---

1 Cf. Shakespeare, *Twelfth Night* 2.4.106-20. "Matilda" is a distinguished name in Gothic fiction; there is a Matilda in the first Gothic novel, *The Castle of Otranto* (1764), by Horace Walpole, and another in Radcliffe's first novel, *The Castles of Athlin and Dunbayne* (1789). P.B. Shelley later included a Matilda in his first novel, *Zastrozzi* (1810), and Dacre combined the names "Rosario" and "Matilda," publishing poetry as "Rosa Matilda."

"If her love was so well bestowed, what forbad her to hope the obtaining of its object?"

"Father, before he knew her, Julian had already plighted his vows to a bride most fair, most heavenly! Yet still my sister loved, and for the husband's sake she doted upon the wife. One morning she found means to escape from our father's house: arrayed in humble weeds she offered herself as a domestic to the consort of her beloved, and was accepted. She was now continually in his presence: she strove to ingratiate herself into his favour: she succeeded. Her attentions attracted Julian's notice: the virtuous are ever grateful, and he distinguished Matilda above the rest of her companions."

"And did not your parents seek for her? Did they submit tamely to their loss, nor attempt to recover their wandering daughter?"

"Ere they could find her, she discovered herself. Her love grew too violent for concealment; yet she wished not for Julian's person, she ambitioned but a share of his heart. In an unguarded moment she confessed her affection. What was the return? Doting upon his wife, and believing that a look of pity bestowed upon another was a theft from what he owed to her, he drove Matilda from his presence: he forbad her ever again appearing before him. His severity broke her heart: she returned to her father's, and in a few months after was carried to her grave."

"Unhappy girl! Surely her fate was too severe, and Julian was too cruel."

"Do you think so, father?" cried the novice with vivacity: "Do you think that he was cruel?"

"Doubtless I do, and pity her most sincerely."

"You pity her? you pity her? Oh! father! father! then pity me——"

The friar started; when, after a moment's pause, Rosario added with a faltering voice, "for my sufferings are still greater. My sister had a friend, a real friend, who pitied the acuteness of her feelings, nor reproached her with her inability to repress them. I——! I have no friend! The whole wide world cannot furnish an heart that is willing to participate in the sorrows of mine."

As he uttered these words, he sobbed audibly. The friar was affected. He took Rosario's hand, and pressed it with tenderness.

"You have no friend, say you? What then am I? Why will you not confide in me, and what can you fear? My severity? Have I ever used it with you? The dignity of my habit? Rosario, I lay aside the monk, and bid you consider me as no other than your friend, your father. Well may I assume that title, for never did parent watch over a child more fondly than I have watched over you. From the moment in which I first beheld you, I perceived sensations in my bosom till then unknown to me; I found a delight in your society which no one's else could afford; and when I witnessed the extent of your genius and information, I rejoiced as does a father in the perfections of his son. Then lay aside your fears; speak to me with openness: speak to me, Rosario, and say that you will confide in me. If my aid or my pity can alleviate your distress——"

"Yours can; yours only can. Ah! father, how willingly would I unveil to you my heart! how willingly would I declare the secret which bows me down with its weight! But oh! I fear, I fear——"

"What, my son?"

"That you should abhor me for my weakness; that the reward of my confidence should be the loss of your esteem."

"How shall I reassure you? Reflect upon the whole of my past conduct, upon the paternal tenderness which I have ever shown you. Abhor you, Rosario? It is no longer in my power. To give up your society would be to deprive myself of the greatest pleasure of my life. Then reveal to me what afflicts you, and believe me while I solemnly swear——"

"Hold!" interrupted the novice. "Swear, that whatever be my secret, you will not oblige me to quit the monastery till my noviciate shall expire."

"I promise it faithfully; and as I keep my vows to you, may Christ keep his to mankind! Now then explain this mystery, and rely upon my indulgence."

"I obey you. Know then—Oh! how I tremble to name the word! Listen to me with pity, revered Ambrosio! Call up every latent spark of human weakness that may teach you compassion for mine! Father!" continued he, throwing himself at the friar's feet, and pressing his hand to his lips with eagerness, while agitation for a moment choked his voice; "father!" continued he in faltering accents, "I am a woman!"[1]

The abbot started at this unexpected avowal. Prostrate on the ground lay the feigned Rosario, as if waiting in silence the decision of his judge. Astonishment on the one part, apprehension on the

---

1 This recalls the climactic revelation of Biondetta, in *Le Diable amoureux* (1772), by Jacques Cazotte (1719-92): "Je suis le diable" (123). Lewis claimed, however, not to have read Cazotte until after writing *The Monk*.

other, for some minutes chained them in the same attitudes, as they had been touched by the rod of some magician. At length recovering from his confusion, the monk quitted the grotto, and sped with precipitation towards the abbey. His action did not escape the suppliant. She sprang from the ground; she hastened to follow him, overtook him, threw herself in his passage, and embraced his knees. Ambrosio strove in vain to disengage himself from her grasp.

"Do not fly me!" she cried. "Leave me not abandoned to the impulse of despair! Listen, while I excuse my imprudence; while I acknowledge my sister's story to be my own! I am Matilda; you are her beloved."

If Ambrosio's surprise was great at her first avowal, upon hearing her second it exceeded all bounds. Amazed, embarrassed, and irresolute, he found himself incapable of pronouncing a syllable, and remained in silence gazing upon Matilda. This gave her opportunity to continue her explanation as follows:

"Think not, Ambrosio, that I come to rob your bride of your affections. No, believe me: Religion alone deserves you; and far is it from Matilda's wish to draw you from the paths of virtue. What I feel for you is love, not licentiousness. I sigh to be possessor of your heart, not lust for the enjoyment of your person. Deign to listen to my vindication:[1] a few moments will convince you that this holy retreat is not polluted by my presence, and that you may grant me your compassion without trespassing against your vows."—She seated herself. Ambrosio, scarcely conscious of what he did, followed her example, and she proceeded in her discourse:——

"I spring from a distinguished family; my father was chief of the noble house of Villanegas: he died while I was still an infant, and left me sole heiress of his immense possessions. Young and wealthy, I was sought in marriage by the noblest youths of Madrid; but no one succeeded in gaining my affections. I had been brought up under the care of an uncle possessed of the most solid judgment and extensive erudition: he took pleasure in communicating to me some portion of his knowledge. Under his instructions my understanding acquired more strength and justness than generally falls to the lot of my sex: the ability of my preceptor being aided by natural curiosity, I not only made a considerable progress in sciences

---

1 There is some evidence (Macdonald 103-4) that Lewis had read, and disapproved of, *A Vindication of the Rights of Woman* (1792), by Mary Wollstonecraft (1959-97).

universally studied, but in others revealed but to few, and lying under censure from the blindness of superstition. But while my guardian laboured to enlarge the sphere of my knowledge, he carefully inculcated every moral precept: he relieved me from the shackles of vulgar prejudice: he pointed out the beauty of religion: he taught me to look with adoration upon the pure and virtuous; and, wo is me! I have obeyed him but too well.

"With such dispositions, judge whether I could observe with any other sentiment than disgust, the vice, dissipation, and ignorance which disgrace our Spanish youth. I rejected every offer with disdain: my heart remained without a master, till chance conducted me to the cathedral of the Capuchins. Oh! surely on that day my guardian angel slumbered, neglectful of his charge! Then was it that I first beheld you: you supplied the superior's place, absent from illness.—You cannot but remember the lively enthusiasm which your discourse created. Oh! how I drank your words! how your eloquence seemed to steal me from myself! I scarcely dared to breathe, fearing to lose a syllable; and while you spoke, methought a radiant glory beamed round your head, and your countenance shone with the majesty of a god. I retired from the church, glowing with admiration. From that moment you became the idol of my heart; the never-changing object of my meditations. I enquired respecting you. The reports which were made me of your mode of life, of your knowledge, piety, and self-denial, riveted the chains imposed on me by your eloquence. I was conscious that there was no longer a void in my heart; that I had found the man whom I had sought till then in vain. In expectation of hearing you again, every day I visited your cathedral: you remained secluded within the abbey walls, and I always withdrew, wretched and disappointed. The night was more propitious to me, for then you stood before me in my dreams; you vowed to me eternal friendship; you led me through the paths of virtue, and assisted me to support the vexations of life. The morning dispelled these pleasing visions: I awoke, and found myself separated from you by barriers which appeared insurmountable. Time seemed only to increase the strength of my passion: I grew melancholy and despondent; I fled from society, and my health declined daily. At length, no longer able to exist in this state of torture, I resolved to assume the disguise in which you see me. My artifice was fortunate; I was received into the monastery, and succeeded in gaining your esteem.

"Now, then, I should have felt completely happy, had not my

quiet been disturbed by the fear of detection. The pleasure which I received from your society was embittered by the idea, that perhaps I should soon be deprived of it: and my heart throbbed so rapturously at obtaining the marks of your friendship, as to convince me that I never should survive its loss. I resolved, therefore, not to leave the discovery of my sex to chance—to confess the whole to you, and throw myself entirely on your mercy and indulgence. Ah! Ambrosio, can I have been deceived? Can you be less generous than I thought you? I will not suspect it. You will not drive a wretch to despair; I shall still be permitted to see you, to converse with you, to adore you! Your virtues shall be my example through life; and, when we expire, our bodies shall rest in the same grave."

She ceased.—While she spoke, a thousand opposing sentiments combated in Ambrosio's bosom. Surprise at the singularity of this adventure; confusion at her abrupt declaration; resentment at her boldness in entering the monastery; and consciousness of the austerity with which it behoved him to reply; such were the sentiments of which he was aware: but there were others also which did not obtain his notice. He perceived not that his vanity was flattered by the praises bestowed upon his eloquence and virtue; that he felt a secret pleasure in reflecting that a young and seemingly lovely woman had for his sake abandoned the world, and sacrificed every other passion to that which he had inspired: still less did he perceive, that his heart throbbed with desire, while his hand was pressed gently by Matilda's ivory fingers.

By degrees he recovered from his confusion: his ideas became less bewildered: he was immediately sensible of the extreme impropriety, should Matilda be permitted to remain in the abbey after this avowal of her sex. He assumed an air of severity, and drew away his hand.

"How, lady!" said he, "can you really hope for my permission to remain amongst us? Even were I to grant your request, what good could you derive from it? Think you, that I ever can reply to an affection, which——"

"No, father, no! I expect not to inspire you with a love like mine: I only wish for the liberty to be near you; to pass some hours of the day in your society; to obtain your compassion, your friendship, and esteem. Surely my request is not unreasonable."

"But reflect, lady! reflect only for a moment on the impropriety of my harbouring a woman in the abbey, and that too a woman who confesses that she loves me. It must not be. The risk of your being discovered is too great; and I will not expose myself to so dangerous a temptation."

"Temptation, say you? Forget that I am a woman, and it no longer exists: consider me only as a friend; as an unfortunate, whose happiness, whose life, depends upon your protection. Fear not, lest I should ever call to your remembrance, that love the most impetuous, the most unbounded, has induced me to disguise my sex; or that, instigated by desires, offensive to *your* vows and my own honour, I should endeavour to seduce you from the path of rectitude. No, Ambrosio! learn to know me better: I love you for your virtues: lose them, and with them you lose my affections. I look upon you as a saint: prove to me that you are no more than man, and I quit you with disgust. Is it then from me that you fear temptation? from me, in whom the world's dazzling pleasures created no other sentiment than contempt? from me, whose attachment is grounded on your exemption from human frailty? Oh! dismiss such injurious apprehensions! think nobler of me; think nobler of yourself. I am incapable of seducing you to error; and surely your virtue is established on a basis too firm to be shaken by unwarranted desires. Ambrosio! dearest Ambrosio! drive me not from your presence; remember your promise, and authorise my stay."

"Impossible, Matilda! *your* interest commands me to refuse your prayer, since I tremble for you, not for myself. After vanquishing the impetuous ebullitions of youth; after passing thirty years in mortification and penance, I might safely permit your stay, nor fear your inspiring me with warmer sentiments than pity: but to yourself, remaining in the abbey can produce none but fatal consequences. You will misconstrue my every word and action; you will seize every circumstance with avidity which encourages you to hope the return of your affection; insensibly, your passions will gain a superiority over your reason; and, far from being repressed by my presence, every moment which we pass together will only serve to irritate and excite them. Believe me, unhappy woman! you possess my sincere compassion. I am convinced that you have hitherto acted upon the purest motives; but though you are blind to the imprudence of your conduct, in me it would be culpable not to open your eyes. I feel that duty obliges my treating you with harshness; I must reject your prayer, and remove every shadow of hope which may aid to nourish sentiments so pernicious to your repose. Matilda, you must from hence to-morrow."

"To-morrow, Ambrosio? to-morrow? Oh! surely you cannot

mean it! you cannot resolve on driving me to despair! you cannot have the cruelty——"

"You have heard my decision, and it must be obeyed: the laws of our order forbid your stay: it would be perjury to conceal that a woman is within these walls, and my vows will oblige me to declare your story to the community. You must from hence. I pity you, but can do no more."

He pronounced these words in a faint and trembling voice; then, rising from his seat, he would have hastened towards the monastery. Uttering a loud shriek, Matilda followed, and detained him.

"Stay yet one moment, Ambrosio! hear me yet speak one word!"

"I dare not listen. Release me: you know my resolution."

"But one word! but one last word, and I have done!"

"Leave me. Your entreaties are in vain: you must from hence to-morrow."

"Go then, barbarian! But this resource is still left me."

As she said this, she suddenly drew a poniard. She rent open her garment, and placed the weapon's point against her bosom.

"Father, I will never quit these walls alive."

"Hold! hold, Matilda! what would you do?"

"You are determined, so am I: the moment that you leave me, I plunge this steel in my heart."

"Holy St. Francis! Matilda, have you your senses? Do you know the consequences of your action? that suicide is the greatest of crimes? that you destroy your soul? that you lose your claim to salvation? that you prepare for yourself everlasting torments?"

"I care not, I care not," she replied passionately: "either your hand guides me to paradise, or my own dooms me to perdition. Speak to me, Ambrosio! Tell me that you will conceal my story; that I shall remain your friend and your companion, or this poniard drinks my blood."

As she uttered these last words, she lifted her arm, and made a motion as if to stab herself. The friar's eyes followed with dread the course of the dagger. She had torn open her habit, and her bosom was half exposed. The weapon's point rested upon her left breast: and, oh! that was such a breast! The moon-beams darting full upon it enabled the monk to observe its dazzling whiteness: his eye dwelt with insatiable avidity upon the beauteous orb: a sensation till then unknown filled his heart with a mixture of anxiety and delight; a raging fire shot through every limb; the blood boiled in his veins, and a thousand wild wishes bewildered his imagination.

"Hold!" he cried, in an hurried, faltering voice; "I can resist no longer! Stay then, enchantress! stay for my destruction!"

He said; and, rushing from the place, hastened towards the monastery: he regained his cell, and threw himself upon his couch, distracted, irresolute and confused.

He found it impossible for some time to arrange his ideas. The scene in which he had been engaged, had excited such a variety of sentiments in his bosom, that he was incapable of deciding which was predominant. He was irresolute what conduct he ought to hold with the disturber of his repose; he was conscious that prudence, religion, and propriety, necessitated his obliging her to quit the abbey: but, on the other hand, such powerful reasons authorised her stay, that he was but too much inclined to consent to her remaining. He could not avoid being flattered by Matilda's declaration, and at reflecting that he had unconsciously vanquished an heart which had resisted the attacks of Spain's noblest cavaliers. The manner in which he had gained her affections was also the most satisfactory to his vanity: he remembered the many happy hours which he had passed in Rosario's society; and dreaded that void in his heart which parting with him would occasion. Besides all this, he considered, that as Matilda was wealthy, her favour might be of essential benefit to the abbey.

"And what do I risk," said he to himself, "by authorizing her stay? May I not safely credit her assertions? Will it not be easy for me to forget her sex, and still consider her as my friend and my disciple? Surely her love is as pure as she describes: had it been the offspring of mere licentiousness, would she so long have concealed it in her own bosom? Would she not have employed some means to procure its gratification? She has done quite the contrary: she strove to keep me in ignorance of her sex; and nothing but the fear of detection, and my instances, would have compelled her to reveal the secret: she has observed the duties of religion not less strictly than myself: she has made no attempt to rouse my slumbering passions, nor has she ever conversed with me till this night on the subject of love. Had she been desirous to gain my affections, not my esteem, she would not have concealed from me her charms so carefully: at this very moment I have never seen her face; yet certainly that face must be lovely, and her person beautiful, to judge by her—by what I have seen."

As this last idea passed through his imagination, a blush spread itself over his cheek. Alarmed at the sentiments which he was indulging, he betook himself to prayer: he started from his couch, knelt before the beautiful Madona, and entreated her assistance in stifling such culpable emotions: he then returned to his bed, and resigned himself to slumber.

He awoke heated and unrefreshed. During his sleep, his inflamed imagination had presented him with none but the most voluptuous objects. Matilda stood before him in his dreams, and his eyes again dwelt upon her naked breast; she repeated her protestations of eternal love, threw her arms round his neck, and loaded him with kisses: he returned them; he clasped her passionately to his bosom, and—the vision was dissolved. Sometimes his dreams presented the image of his favourite Madona, and he fancied that he was kneeling before her: as he offered up his vows to her, the eyes of the figure seemed to beam on him with inexpressible sweetness; he pressed his lips to hers, and found them warm: the animated form started from the canvas, embraced him affectionately, and his senses were unable to support delight so exquisite. Such were the scenes on which his thoughts were employed while sleeping: his unsatisfied desires placed before him the most lustful and provoking images, and he rioted in joys till then unknown to him.

He started from his couch, filled with confusion at the remembrance of his dreams: scarcely was he less ashamed when he reflected on his reasons of the former night, which induced him to authorise Matilda's stay. The cloud was now dissipated which had obscured his judgment; he shuddered when he beheld his arguments blazoned in their proper colours, and found that he had been a slave to flattery, to avarice, and self-love. If in one hour's conversation Matilda had produced a change so remarkable in his sentiments, what had he not to dread from her remaining in the abbey? Become sensible of his danger, awakened from his dream of confidence, he resolved to insist on her departing without delay: he began to feel that he was not proof against temptation; and that, however Matilda might restrain herself within the bounds of modesty, he was unable to contend with those passions from which he falsely thought himself exempted.

"Agnes! Agnes!" he exclaimed, while reflecting on his embarrassments, "I already feel thy curse!"

He quitted his cell, determined upon dismissing the feigned Rosario. He appeared at matins; but his thoughts were absent, and he paid them but little attention: his heart and brain were both of them filled with worldly objects, and he prayed without devotion. The service over, he descended into the garden; he bent his steps towards the same spot where on the preceding night he had made this embarrassing discovery: he doubted not that Matilda would seek him there. He was not deceived: she soon entered the hermitage, and approached the monk with a timid air. After a few minutes, during which both were silent, she appeared as if on the point of speaking; but the abbot, who during this time had been summoning up all his resolution, hastily interrupted her. Though still unconscious how extensive was its influence, he dreaded the melodious seduction of her voice.

"Seat yourself by my side, Matilda," said he, assuming a look of firmness, though carefully avoiding the least mixture of severity; "listen to me patiently, and believe that, in what I shall say, I am not more influenced by my own interest than by yours; believe that I feel for you the warmest friendship, the truest compassion; and that you cannot feel more grieved than I do, when I declare to you that we must never meet again."

"Ambrosio!" she cried, in a voice at once expressive both of surprise and of sorrow.

"Be calm, my friend! my Rosario! still let me call you by that name so dear to me: our separation is unavoidable; I blush to own how sensibly it affects me.—But yet it must be so; I feel myself incapable of treating you with indifference; and that very conviction obliges me to insist upon your departure. Matilda, you must stay here no longer."

"Oh! where shall I now seek for probity? Disgusted with a perfidious world, in what happy region does Truth conceal herself? Father, I hoped that she resided here; I thought that your bosom had been her favourite shrine. And you too prove false? Oh God! and you too can betray me?"

"Matilda?"

"Yes, father, yes; 'tis with justice that I reproach you. Oh! where are your promises? My noviciate is not expired, and yet will you compel me to quit the monastery? Can you have the heart to drive me from you? and have I not received your solemn oath to the contrary?"

"I will not compel you to quit the monastery; you have received my solemn oath to the contrary: but yet, when I throw myself upon your generosity; when I declare to you the embarrassments in which your presence involves me, will you not release me from that oath? Reflect upon the danger of a discovery; upon the opprobrium in which such an event would plunge me: reflect, that my honour and reputation are at stake; and that my peace of mind depends on your compliance. As yet, my heart is free; I shall separate from you with regret, but not with despair. Stay here, and a few weeks will sacrifice my happiness on the altar of your charms; you are but too interesting, too amiable! I should love you, I should doat on you! my bosom would become the prey of desires, which honour and my profession forbid me to gratify. If I resisted them, the impetuosity of my wishes unsatisfied would drive me to madness: if I yielded to the temptation, I should sacrifice to one moment of guilty pleasure, my reputation in this world, my salvation in the next. To you, then, I fly for defence against myself. Preserve me from losing the reward of thirty years of sufferings! preserve me from becoming the victim of remorse! *Your* heart has already felt the anguish of hopeless love: oh! then, if you really value me, spare mine that anguish! give me back my promise; fly from these walls. Go, and you bear with you my warmest prayers for your happiness, my friendship, my esteem, and admiration: stay, and you become to me the source of danger, of sufferings, of despair. Answer me, Matilda, what is your resolve?" She was silent.—"Will you not speak, Matilda? Will you not name your choice?"

"Cruel! cruel!" she exclaimed, wringing her hands in agony; "you know too well that you offer me no choice: you know too well that I can have no will but yours!"

"I was not then deceived. Matilda's generosity equals my expectations."

"Yes; I will prove the truth of my affection by submitting to a decree which cuts me to the very heart. Take back your promise. I will quit the monastery this very day. I have a relation, abbess of a convent in Estramadura: to her will I bend my steps, and shut myself from the world for ever. Yet tell me, father, shall I bear your good wishes with me to my solitude? Will you sometimes abstract your attention from heavenly objects to bestow a thought upon me?"

"Ah! Matilda, I fear that I shall think on you but too often for my repose!"

"Then I have nothing more to wish for, save that we may meet in heaven. Farewell, my friend! my Ambrosio! And yet, methinks, I would fain bear with me some token of your regard."

"What shall I give you?"

"Something—any thing—one of those flowers will be sufficient." [Here she pointed to a bush of roses, planted at the door of the grotto.] "I will hide it in my bosom, and, when I am dead, the nuns shall find it withered upon my heart."

The friar was unable to reply: with slow steps, and a soul heavy with affliction, he quitted the hermitage. He approached the bush, and stooped to pluck one of the roses. Suddenly he uttered a piercing cry, started back hastily, and let the flower, which he already held, fall from his hand. Matilda heard the shriek, and flew anxiously towards him.

"What is the matter?" she cried. "Answer me, for God's sake! What has happened?"

"I have received my death," he replied in a faint voice: "concealed among the roses—a serpent——"

Here the pain of his wound became so exquisite, that nature was unable to bear it: his senses abandoned him, and he sunk inanimate into Matilda's arms.

Her distress was beyond the power of description. She rent her hair, beat her bosom, and, not daring to quit Ambrosio, endeavoured by loud cries to summon the monks to her assistance. She at length succeeded. Alarmed by her shrieks, several of the brothers hastened to the spot, and the superior was conveyed back to the abbey. He was immediately put to bed, and the monk, who officiated as surgeon to the fraternity, prepared to examine the wound. By this time Ambrosio's hand had swelled to an extraordinary size: the remedies which had been administered to him, 'tis true, restored him to life, but not to his senses: he raved in all the horrors of delirium, foamed at the mouth, and four of the strongest monks were scarcely able to hold him in his bed.

Father Pablos (such was the surgeon's name) hastened to examine the wounded hand. The monks surrounded the bed, anxiously waiting for the decision: among these the feigned Rosario appeared not the most insensible to the friar's calamity: he gazed upon the sufferer with inexpressible anguish; and his groans, which every moment escaped from his bosom, sufficiently betrayed the violence of his affliction.

Father Pablos probed the wound. As he drew out his lancet, its point was tinged with a greenish hue. He shook his head mournfully, and quitted the bed-side.

"'Tis as I feared," said he; "there is no hope."

"No hope!" exclaimed the monks with one voice; "say you, no hope?"

"From the sudden effects, I suspected that the abbot was stung by a cientipedoro:[1] the venom which you see upon my lancet confirms my idea. He cannot live three days."

"And can no possible remedy be found?" enquired Rosario.

"Without extracting the poison, he cannot recover; and how to extract it is to me still a secret. All that I can do is to apply such herbs to the wound as will relieve the anguish: the patient will be restored to his senses; but the venom will corrupt the whole mass of his blood, and in three days he will exist no longer."

Excessive was the universal grief at hearing this decision. Pablos, as he had promised, dressed the wound, and then retired, followed by his companions. Rosario alone remained in the cell, the abbot, at his urgent entreaty, having been committed to his care. Ambrosio's strength worn out by the violence of his exertions, he had by this time fallen into a profound sleep. So totally was he overcome by weariness, that he scarcely gave any signs of life. He was still in this situation, when the monks returned to enquire whether any change had taken place. Pablos loosened the bandage which concealed the wound, more from a principle of curiosity, than from indulging the hope of discovering any favourable symptoms. What was his astonishment at finding that the inflammation had totally subsided! He probed the hand; his lancet came out pure and unsullied; no traces of the venom were perceptible; and had not the orifice still been visible, Pablos might have doubted that there had ever been a wound.

He communicated this intelligence to his brethren: their delight was only equalled by their surprise. From the latter sentiment, however, they were soon released, by explaining the circumstance according to their own ideas. They were perfectly convinced that their superior was a saint, and thought that nothing could be more natural than for St. Francis to have operated a miracle in his favour. This opinion was adopted unanimously. They declared it so loudly, and vociferated "A miracle! a miracle!" with such fervour, that they soon interrupted Ambrosio's slumbers.

The monks immediately crowded round his bed, and expressed their satisfaction at his wonderful recovery. He was perfectly in his senses, and free from every complaint, except feeling weak and languid. Pablos gave him a strengthening medicine, and advised his

---

1   The cientipedoro is supposed to be a native of Cuba, and to have been brought into Spain from that island in the vessel of Columbus. [Lewis's note.]

keeping his bed for the two succeeding days: he then retired, having desired his patient not to exhaust himself by conversation, but rather to endeavour at taking some repose. The other monks followed his example, and the abbot and Rosario were left without observers.

For some minutes Ambrosio regarded his attendant with a look of mingled pleasure and apprehension. She was seated upon the side of the bed, her head bending down, and, as usual, enveloped in the cowl of her habit.

"And you are still here, Matilda?" said the friar at length; "are you not satisfied with having so nearly effected my destruction, that nothing but a miracle could have saved me from the grave? Ah! surely heaven sent that serpent to punish——"

Matilda interrupted him by putting her hand before his lips with an air of gaiety.

"Hush! father, hush! you must not talk."

"He who imposed that order, knew not how interesting are the subjects on which I wish to speak."

"But I know it, and yet issue the same positive command. I am appointed your nurse, and you must not disobey my orders."

"You are in spirits, Matilda!"

"Well may I be so; I have just received a pleasure unexampled through my whole life."

"What was that pleasure?"

"What I must conceal from all, but most from you."

"But most from me? Nay then, I entreat you, Matilda——"

"Hush! father, hush! you must not talk. But as you do not seem inclined to sleep, shall I endeavour to amuse you with my harp?"

"How! I knew not that you understood music."

"Oh! I am a sorry performer! Yet as silence is prescribed you for eight-and-forty hours, I may possibly entertain you, when wearied of your own reflections. I go to fetch my harp."

She soon returned with it.

"Now, father, what shall I sing? Will you hear the ballad which treats of the gallant Durandarte, who died in the famous battle of Roncevalles?"[1]

"What you please, Matilda."

---

1 Roncesvalles is the pass through the Pyrenees where the rearguard of Charlemagne's army, under the command of Roland, was defeated by the Saracens c. 778.

"Oh! call me not Matilda! Call me Rosario, call me your friend. Those are the names which I love to hear from you lips. Now listen."

She then tuned her harp, and afterwards preluded for some moments with such exquisite taste as to prove her a perfect mistress of the instrument. The air which she played was soft and plaintive. Ambrosio, while he listened, felt his uneasiness subside, and a pleasing melancholy spread itself into his bosom. Suddenly Matilda changed the strain: with an hand bold and rapid, she struck a few loud martial chords, and then chanted the following ballad to an air at once simple and melodious:

DURANDARTE AND BELERMA.[1]

SAD and fearful is the story
Of the Roncevalles fight;
On those fatal plains of glory
Perished many a gallant knight.

There fell Durandarte: never
Verse a nobler chieftain named:
He, before his lips for ever
Clos'd in silence, thus exclaimed:

"Oh! Belerma! Oh! my dear one,
For my pain and pleasure born,
Seven long years I serv'd thee, fair one,
Seven long years my fee was scorn.

"And when now thy heart, replying
To my wishes, burns like mine,
Cruel fate, my bliss denying,
Bids me every hope resign.

"Ah! though young I fall, believe me,
Death would never claim a sigh;
'Tis to lose thee, 'tis to leave thee,
Makes me think it hard to die!

---

1   Cf. Miguel de Cervantes (1547-1615), *Don Quixote* (1604-14) 2.23.

"Oh! my cousin Montesinos,
By that friendship firm and dear,
Which from youth has lived between us,
Now my last petition hear:

"When my soul, these limbs forsaking,
Eager seeks a purer air,
From my breast the cold heart taking,
Give it to Belerma's care.

"Say, I of my lands possessor
Named her with my dying breath:
Say, my lips I op'd to bless her,
Ere they clos'd for aye in death:

"Twice a week, too, how sincerely
I ador'd her, cousin, say:
Twice a week, for one who dearly
Lov'd her, cousin, bid her pray.

"Montesinos, now the hour
Mark'd by fate is near at hand:
Lo! my arm has lost its power!
Lo! I drop my trusty brand.

"Eyes, which forth beheld me going,
Homewards ne'er shall see me hie:
Cousin, stop those tears o'erflowing,
Let me on thy bosom die.

"Thy kind hand my eye-lids closing,
Yet one favour I implore:
Pray thou for my soul's reposing,
When my heart shall throb no more.

"So shall Jesus, still attending,
Gracious to a Christian's vow,
Pleas'd accept my ghost ascending,
And a seat in heaven allow."

Thus spoke gallant Durandarte;
Soon his brave heart broke in twain.

Greatly joy'd the Moorish party,
That the gallant knight was slain.

Bitter weeping, Montesinos
Took from him his helm and glaive;[1]
Bitter weeping, Montesinos
Dug his gallant cousin's grave.

To perform his promise made, he
Cut the heart from out the breast,
That Belerma, wretched lady!
Might receive the last bequest.

Sad was Montesinos' heart, he
Felt distress his bosom rend.
"Oh! my cousin Durandarte,
Woe is me to view thy end!

"Sweet in manners, fair in favour,
Mild in temper, fierce in fight,
Warrior nobler, gentler, braver,
Never shall behold the light.

"Cousin, lo! my tears bedew thee;
How shall I thy loss survive?
Durandarte, he who slew thee,
Wherefore left he me alive?"

While she sung, Ambrosio listened with delight: never had he
heard a voice more harmonious; and he wondered how such
heavenly sounds could be produced by any but angels. But though
he indulged the sense of hearing, a single look convinced him,
that he must not trust to that of sight. The songstress sat at a little
distance from his bed. The attitude in which she bent over her
harp was easy and graceful: her cowl had fallen backwarder than
usual: two coral lips were visible, ripe, fresh, and melting, and a
chin, in whose dimples seemed to lurk a thousand Cupids. Her
habit's long sleeve would have swept along the chords of the
instrument: to prevent this inconvenience she had drawn it above

---

1   Sword.

her elbow; and by this means an arm was discovered, formed in the most perfect symmetry, the delicacy of whose skin might have contended with snow in whiteness. Ambrosio dared to look on her but once: that glance sufficed to convince him, how dangerous was the presence of this seducing object. He closed his eyes, but strove in vain to banish her from his thoughts. There she still moved before him, adorned with all those charms which his heated imagination could supply. Every beauty which he had seen appeared embellished; and those still concealed fancy represented to him in glowing colours. Still, however, his vows, and the necessity of keeping to them, were present to his memory. He struggled with desire, and shuddered when he beheld how deep was the precipice before him.

Matilda ceased to sing. Dreading the influence of her charms, Ambrosio remained with his eyes closed, and offered up his prayers to St. Francis to assist him in this dangerous trial! Matilda believed that he was sleeping: she rose from her seat, approached the bed softly, and for some minutes gazed upon him attentively.

"He sleeps!" said she at length in a low voice, but whose accents the abbot distinguished perfectly: "now then I may gaze upon him without offence; I may mix my breath with his; I may doat upon his features, and he cannot suspect me of impurity and deceit. He fears my seducing him to the violation of his vows. Oh! the unjust! Were it my wish to excite desire, should I conceal my features from him so carefully?—those features, of which I daily hear him——"

She stopped, and was lost in her reflections.

"It was but yesterday," she continued; "but a few short hours have passed since I was dear to him; he esteemed me, and my heart was satisfied: now, oh! now, how cruelly is my situation changed! He looks on me with suspicion; he bids me leave him, leave him for ever. Oh! you, my saint, my idol! You! holding the next place to God in my breast, yet two days, and my heart will be unveiled to you. Could you know my feelings, when I beheld your agony! Could you know how much your sufferings have endeared you to me! But the time will come, when you will be convinced that my passion is pure and disinterested. Then you will pity me, and feel the whole weight of these sorrows."

As she said this, her voice was choaked by weeping. While she bent over Ambrosio, a tear fell upon his cheek.

"Ah! I have disturbed him," cried Matilda, and retreated hastily.

Her alarm was ungrounded. None sleep so profoundly as those who are determined not to wake. The friar was in this predicament: he still seemed buried in a repose, which every succeeding minute rendered him less capable of enjoying. The burning tear had communicated its warmth to his heart.

"What affection! what purity!" said he internally. "Ah! since my bosom is thus sensible of pity, what would it be if agitated by love?"

Matilda again quitted her seat, and retired to some distance from the bed. Ambrosio ventured to open his eyes, and to cast them upon her fearfully. Her face was turned from him. She rested her head in a melancholy posture upon her harp, and gazed on the picture which hung opposite to the bed.

"Happy, happy image!" Thus did she address the beautiful Madona; "'tis to you that he offers his prayers; 'tis on you that he gazes with admiration. I thought you would have lightened my sorrows; you have only served to increase their weight; you have made me feel, that, had I known him ere his vows were pronounced, Ambrosio and happiness might have been mine. With what pleasure he views this picture! With what fervour he addresses his prayers to the insensible image! Ah! may not his sentiments be inspired by some kind and secret genius, friend to my affection? May it not be man's natural instinct which informs him—? Be silent! idle hopes! let me not encourage an idea, which takes from the brilliance of Ambrosio's virtue. 'Tis religion, not beauty, which attracts his admiration; 'tis not to the woman, but the divinity that he kneels. Would he but address to me the least tender expression which he pours forth to this Madona! Would he but say, that were he not already affianced to the church, he would not have despised Matilda! Oh! let me nourish that fond idea. Perhaps he may yet acknowledge that he feels for me more than pity, and that affection like mine might well have deserved a return. Perhaps he may own thus much when I lie on my death-bed. He then need not fear to infringe his vows, and the confession of his regard will soften the pangs of dying. Would I were sure of this! Oh! how earnestly should I sigh for the moment of dissolution!"

Of this discourse the abbot lost not a syllable; and the tone in which she pronounced these last words pierced to his heart. Involuntarily he raised himself from his pillow.

"Matilda!" he said in a troubled voice; "Oh! my Matilda!"

She started at the sound, and turned towards him hastily. The suddenness of her movement made her cowl fall back from her head; her features became visible to the monk's enquiring eye. What was his amazement at beholding the exact resemblance of his admired Madona![1] The same exquisite proportion of features, the same profusion of golden hair, the same rosy lips, heavenly eyes, and majesty of countenance adorned Matilda! Uttering an exclamation of surprise, Ambrosio sank back upon his pillow, and doubted whether the object before him was mortal or divine.

Matilda seemed penetrated with confusion. She remained motionless in her place, and supported herself upon her instrument. Her eyes were bent upon the earth, and her fair cheeks overspread with blushes. On recovering herself, her first action was to conceal her features. She then, in an unsteady and troubled voice, ventured to address these words to the friar:

"Accident has made you master of a secret, which I never would have revealed but on the bed of death: yes, Ambrosio, in Matilda de Villanegas you see the original of your beloved Madona. Soon after I conceived my unfortunate passion, I formed the project of conveying to you my picture. Crowds of admirers had persuaded me that I possessed some beauty, and I was anxious to know what effect it would produce upon you. I caused my portrait to be drawn by Martin Galuppi, a celebrated Venetian at that time resident in Madrid. The resemblance was striking: I sent it to the Capuchin-abbey as if for sale; and the Jew from whom you bought it was one of my emissaries. You purchased it. Judge of my rapture, when informed that you had gazed upon it with delight, or rather with adoration; that you had suspended it in your cell, and that you addressed your supplications to no other saint! Will this discovery make me still more regarded as an object of suspicion? Rather should it convince you how pure is my affection, and engage you to suffer me in your society and esteem. I heard you daily extol the praises of my portrait. I was an eye witness of the transports which its beauty excited in you: yet I forbore to use against your virtue those arms with which yourself had furnished me. I concealed those features from your sight, which you loved unconsciously. I strove not to excite desire by displaying my charms, or to make myself mistress of your heart through the medium of your senses. To attract your notice by studiously attending to religious duties, to endear myself to you by convincing you that my mind was virtuous and my attachment sincere, such was my only aim. I suc-

---

1   In Schiller's *Der Geisterseher* ("The Ghost-Seer," 1787-89), the Prince falls in love with a woman who resembles a portrait of the Madonna (68-69; Letter 5).

ceeded; I became your companion and your friend. I concealed my sex from your knowledge; and had you not pressed me to reveal my secret, had I not been tormented by the fear of a discovery, never had you known me for any other than Rosario. And still are you resolved to drive me from you? The few hours of life which yet remain for me, may I not pass them in your presence? Oh! speak, Ambrosio, and tell me that I may stay."

This speech gave the abbot an opportunity of recollecting himself. He was conscious that, in the present disposition of his mind, avoiding her society was his only refuge from the power of this enchanting woman.

"Your declaration has so much astonished me," said he, "that I am at present incapable of answering you. Do not insist upon a reply, Matilda; leave me to myself, I have need to be alone."

"I obey you; but, before I go, promise not to insist upon my quitting the abbey immediately."

"Matilda, reflect upon your situation; reflect upon the consequences of your stay: our separation is indispensable, and we must part."

"But not to-day, father! Oh! in pity, not to-day!"

"You press me too hard; but I cannot resist that tone of supplication. Since you insist upon it, I yield to your prayer; I consent to your remaining here a sufficient time to prepare, in some measure, the brethren for your departure: stay yet two days; but on the third"—(He sighed involuntarily)—"remember, that on the third we must part for ever!"

She caught his hand eagerly, and pressed it to her lips.

"On the third!" she exclaimed with an air of wild solemnity: "You are right, father, you are right! On the third we must part for ever!"

There was a dreadful expression in her eye as she uttered these words, which penetrated the friar's soul with horror. Again she kissed his hand, and then fled with rapidity from the chamber.

Anxious to authorise the presence of his dangerous guest, yet conscious that her stay was infringing the laws of his order, Ambrosio's bosom became the theatre of a thousand contending passions. At length his attachment to the feigned Rosario, aided by the natural warmth of his temperament, seemed likely to obtain the victory: the success was assured, when that presumption which formed the ground-work of his character came to Matilda's assistance. The monk reflected, that to vanquish temptation was an infinitely greater merit than to avoid it; he thought that he ought rather to rejoice in the opportunity given him of proving the firmness of his virtue. St. Anthony[1] had withstood all seductions to lust, then why should not he? Besides, St. Anthony was tempted by the devil, who put every art into practice to excite his passions; whereas Ambrosio's danger proceeded from a mere mortal woman, fearful and modest, whose apprehensions of his yielding were not less violent than his own.

"Yes," said he, "the unfortunate shall stay; I have nothing to fear from her presence: even should my own prove too weak to resist the temptation, I am secured from danger by the innocence of Matilda."

Ambrosio was yet to learn, that to an heart unacquainted with her, vice is ever most dangerous when lurking behind the mask of virtue.

He found himself so perfectly recovered, that, when father Pablos visited him again at night, he entreated permission to quit his chamber on the day following. His request was granted. Matilda appeared no more that evening, except in company with the monks when they came in a body to enquire after the abbot's health. She seemed fearful of conversing with him in private, and stayed but a few minutes in his room. The friar slept well; but the dreams of the former night were repeated, and his sensations of voluptuousness were yet more keen and exquisite; the same lust-exciting visions floated before his eyes; Matilda, in all the pomp of beauty, warm, tender and luxurious, clasped him to her bosom, and lavished upon him the most ardent caresses. He returned them as eagerly; and already was on the point of satisfying his desires, when the faithless form disappeared, and left him to all the horrors of shame and disappointment.

The morning dawned. Fatigued, harassed, and exhausted by his provoking dreams, he was not disposed to quit his bed: he excused himself from appearing at matins: it was the first morning in his life that he had ever missed them. He rose late: during the whole of the day he had no opportunity of speaking to Matilda without witnesses; his cell was thronged by the monks, anxious to express their concern at his illness; and he was still occupied in receiving their compliments on his recovery, when the bell summoned them to the refectory.

---

1 St. Anthony (251–356), traditionally the father of monasticism, is famous for withstanding all the devil's efforts to lead him into temptation.

After dinner the monks separated, and dispersed themselves in various parts of the garden, where the shade of trees, or retirement of some grotto, presented the most agreeable means of enjoying the siesta. The abbot bent his steps towards the hermitage; a glance of his eye invited Matilda to accompany him: she obeyed, and followed him thither in silence: they entered the grotto, and seated themselves: both seemed unwilling to begin the conversation, and to labour under the influence of mutual embarrassment. At length the abbot spoke: he conversed only on indifferent topics, and Matilda answered him in the same tone; she seemed anxious to make him forget that the person who sat by him was any other than Rosario. Neither of them dared, or indeed wished, to make an allusion to the subject which was most at the hearts of both.

Matilda's efforts to appear gay were evidently forced; her spirits were oppressed by the weight of anxiety; and when she spoke, her voice was low and feeble: she seemed desirous of finishing a conversation which embarrassed her; and, complaining that she was unwell, she requested Ambrosio's permission to return to the abbey. He accompanied her to the door of her cell; and, when arrived there, he stopped her to declare his consent to her continuing the partner of his solitude, so long as should be agreeable to herself.

She discovered no marks of pleasure at receiving this intelligence, though on the preceding day she had been so anxious to obtain the permission.

"Alas, father," she said, waving her head mournfully, "your kindness comes too late; my doom is fixed; we must separate for ever: yet believe that I am grateful for your generosity; for your compassion of an unfortunate who is but too little deserving of it."

She put her handkerchief to her eyes; her cowl was only half drawn over her face. Ambrosio observed that she was pale, and her eyes sunk and heavy.

"Good God!" he cried, "you are very ill, Matilda; I shall send father Pablos to you instantly."

"No, do not; I am ill, 'tis true, but he cannot cure my malady. Farewell, father! Remember me in your prayers to-morrow, while I shall remember you in heaven."

She entered her cell, and closed the door.

The abbot dispatched to her the physician without losing a moment, and waited his report impatiently; but father Pablos soon returned, and declared that his errand had been fruitless. Rosario refused to admit him, and had positively rejected his offers of assistance. The uneasiness which this account gave Ambrosio was not trifling; yet he determined that Matilda should have her own way for that night; but that, if her situation did not mend by the morning, he would insist upon her taking the advice of father Pablos.

He did not find himself inclined to sleep; he opened his casement, and gazed upon the moon-beams as they played upon the small stream whose waters bathed the walls of the monastery. The coolness of the night breeze, and tranquillity of the hour, inspired the friar's mind with sadness; he thought upon Matilda's beauty and affection; upon the pleasures which he might have shared with her, had he not been restrained by monastic fetters. He reflected that, unsustained by hope, her love for him could not long exist; that doubtless she would succeed in extinguishing her passion, and seek for happiness in the arms of one more fortunate. He shuddered at the void which her absence would leave in his bosom; he looked with disgust on the monotony of a convent, and breathed a sigh towards that world from which he was for ever separated. Such were the reflections which a loud knocking at his door interrupted. The bell of the church had already struck two. The abbot hastened to enquire the cause of this disturbance. He opened the door of his cell, and a lay-brother entered, whose looks declared his hurry and confusion.

"Hasten, reverend father!" said he, "hasten to the young Rosario: he earnestly requests to see you; he lies at the point of death."

"Gracious God! where is father Pablos? Why is he not with him? Oh! I fear, I fear——"

"Father Pablos has seen him, but his art can do nothing. He says that he suspects the youth to be poisoned."

"Poisoned? Oh! the unfortunate! It is then as I suspected! But let me not lose a moment; perhaps it may yet be time to save her."

He said, and flew towards the cell of the novice. Several monks were already in the chamber; father Pablos was one of them, and held a medicine in his hand, which he was endeavouring to persuade Rosario to swallow. The others were employed in admiring the patient's divine countenance, which they now saw for the first time. She looked lovelier than ever; she was no longer pale or languid; a bright glow had spread itself over her cheeks; her eyes sparkled with a serene delight, and her countenance was expressive of confidence and resignation.

"Oh! torment me no more!" was she saying to Pablos, when the terrified abbot rushed hastily into the cell; "my disease is far beyond the reach of your skill, and I wish not to be cured of it." Then perceiving Ambrosio—"Ah, 'tis he!" she cried; "I see him once again before we part for ever! Leave me, my brethren; much have I to tell this holy man in private."

The monks retired immediately, and Matilda and the abbot remained together.

"What have you done, imprudent woman?" exclaimed the latter, as soon as they were left alone: "tell me; are my suspicions just? Am I indeed to lose you? Has your own hand been the instrument of your destruction?"

She smiled, and grasped his hand.

"In what have I been imprudent, father? I have sacrificed a pebble, and saved a diamond. My death preserves a life valuable to the world, and more dear to me than my own.—Yes, father, I am poisoned; but know, that the poison once circulated in your veins."

"Matilda!"

"What I tell you I resolved never to discover to you but on the bed of death; that moment is now arrived. You cannot have forgotten the day already, when your life was endangered by the bite of a cientipedoro. The physician gave you over, declaring himself ignorant how to extract the venom. I knew but of one means, and hesitated not a moment to employ it. I was left alone with you; you slept; I loosened the bandage from your hand; I kissed the wound, and drew out the poison with my lips. The effect has been more sudden than I expected. I feel death at my heart; yet an hour, and I shall be in a better world."

"Almighty God!" exclaimed the abbot, and sank almost lifeless upon the bed.

After a few minutes he again raised himself up suddenly, and gazed upon Matilda with all the wildness of despair.

"And you have sacrificed yourself for me! You die, and die to preserve Ambrosio! And is there indeed no remedy, Matilda? And is there indeed no hope? Speak to me, oh! speak to me! Tell me that you have still the means of life!"

"Be comforted, my only friend! Yes, I have still the means of life in my power; but it is a means which I dare not employ; it is dangerous; it is dreadful! Life would be purchased at too dear a rate,—unless it were permitted me to live for you."

"Then live for me, Matilda; for me and gratitude!"—(He caught her hand, and pressed it rapturously to his lips.)—"Remember our late conversations; I now consent to every thing. Remember in what lively colours you described the union of souls; be it ours to realize those ideas. Let us forget the distinctions of sex, despise the world's prejudices, and only consider each other as brother and friend. Live then, Matilda, oh! live for me!"

"Ambrosio, it must not be. When I thought thus, I deceived both you and myself: either I must die at present, or expire by the lingering torments of unsatisfied desire. Oh! since we last conversed together, a dreadful veil has been rent from before my eyes. I love you no longer with the devotion which is paid to a saint; I prize you no more for the virtues of your soul; I lust for the enjoyment of your person. The woman reigns in my bosom, and I am become a prey to the wildest of passions. Away with friendship! 'tis a cold unfeeling word: my bosom burns with love, with unutterable love, and love must be its return. Tremble then, Ambrosio, tremble to succeed in your prayers. If I live, your truth, your reputation, your reward of a life past in sufferings, all that you value, is irretrievably lost. I shall no longer be able to combat my passions, shall seize every opportunity to excite your desires, and labour to effect your dishonour and my own. No, no, Ambrosio, I must not live; I am convinced with every moment that I have but one alternative; I feel with every heart throb, that I must enjoy you or die."

"Amazement! Matilda! Can it be you who speak to me?"

He made a movement as if to quit his seat. She uttered a loud shriek, and, raising herself half out of the bed, threw her arms round the friar to detain him.

"Oh! do not leave me! Listen to my errors with compassion: in a few hours I shall be no more: yet a little, and I am free from this disgraceful passion."

"Wretched woman, what can I say to you? I cannot—I must not—But live, Matilda! oh, live!"

"You do not reflect on what you ask. What? live to plunge myself in infamy? to become the agent of hell? to work the destruction both of you and of myself? Feel this heart, father."

She took his hand. Confused, embarrassed, and fascinated, he withdrew it not, and felt her heart throb under it.

"Feel this heart, father! It is yet the seat of honour, truth, and chastity: if it beats to-morrow, it must fall a prey to the blackest crimes. Oh, let me then die to-day! Let me die while I yet deserve the tears of the virtuous. Thus will I expire!"—(She reclined her head upon his shoulder; her golden hair poured itself over his chest.)—"Folded in your arms, I shall sink to sleep; your hand shall close my eyes for ever, and your lips receive my dying breath. And will you not sometimes think of me? Will you not sometimes shed a tear upon my tomb? Oh, yes, yes, yes! that kiss is my assurance."

The hour was night. All was silence around. The faint beams of a solitary lamp darted upon Matilda's figure, and shed through the chamber a dim, mysterious light. No prying eye or curious ear was near the lovers: nothing was heard but Matilda's melodious accents. Ambrosio was in the full vigour of manhood; he saw before him a young and beautiful woman, the preserver of his life, the adorer of his person; and whom affection for him had reduced to the brink of the grave. He sat upon her bed; his hand rested upon her bosom; her head reclined voluptuously upon his breast. Who then can wonder if he yielded to the temptation? Drunk with desire, he pressed his lips to those which sought them; his kisses vied with Matilda's in warmth and passion: he clasped her rapturously in his arms; he forgot his vows, his sanctity, and his fame; he remembered nothing but the pleasure and opportunity.

"Ambrosio! Oh, my Ambrosio!" sighed Matilda.

"Thine, ever thine," murmured the friar, and sunk upon her bosom.

CHAP. III.

——————These are the villains
Whom all the travellers do fear so much.
——————————Some of them are gentlemen,
Such as the fury of ungovern'd youth
Thrust from the company of awful men.

TWO GENTLEMEN OF VERONA.[1]

THE marquis and Lorenzo proceeded to the hotel in silence. The former employed himself in calling every circumstance to his mind, which related might give Lorenzo's the most favourable idea of his connexion with Agnes. The latter, justly alarmed for the honour of his family, felt embarrassed by the presence of the marquis: the adventure which he had just witnessed forbad his treating him as a friend; and Antonia's interests being entrusted to his mediation, he saw the impolicy of treating him as a foe. He concluded from

---

1 Adapted from Shakespeare, *Two Gentlemen of Verona* 4.1.5-6, 44-46.

these reflections, that profound silence would be the wisest plan, and waited with impatience for Don Raymond's explanation.

They arrived at the hotel de las Cisternas. The marquis immediately conducted him to his apartment, and began to express his satisfaction at finding him at Madrid. Lorenzo interrupted him.

"Excuse me, my lord," said he with a distant air, "if I reply somewhat coldly to your expressions of regard. A sister's honour is involved in this affair: till that is established, and the purport of your correspondence with Agnes cleared up, I cannot consider you as my friend. I am anxious to hear the meaning of your conduct; and hope that you will not delay the promised explanation."

"First give me your word, that you will listen with patience and indulgence."

"I love my sister too well to judge her harshly; and, till this moment, I possessed no friend so dear to me as yourself. I will also confess, that your having it in your power to oblige me in a business which I have much at heart, makes me very anxious to find you still deserving my esteem."

"Lorenzo, you transport me! No greater pleasure can be given me, than an opportunity of serving the brother of Agnes."

"Convince me that I can accept your favours without dishonour, and there is no man in the world to whom I am more willing to be obliged."

"Probably you have already heard your sister mention the name of Alphonso d'Alvarada?"

"Never. Though I feel for Agnes an affection truly fraternal, circumstances have prevented us from being much together. While yet a child, she was consigned to the care of her aunt, who had married a German nobleman. At his castle she remained till two years since, when she returned to Spain, determined upon secluding herself from the world."

"Good God! Lorenzo, you knew of her intention, and yet strove not to make her change it?"

"Marquis, you wrong me: the intelligence which I received at Naples shocked me extremely, and I hastened my return to Madrid for the express purpose of preventing the sacrifice. The moment that I arrived, I flew to the convent of St. Clare, in which Agnes had chosen to perform her noviciate. I requested to see my sister. Conceive my surprise, when she sent me a refusal: she declared positively that, apprehending my influence over her mind, she would not trust herself in my society, till the day before that on which she was to receive the veil. I supplicated the nuns; I insisted upon seeing Agnes; and hesitated not to avow my suspicions, that her being kept from me was against her own inclinations. To free herself from the imputation of violence, the prioress brought me a few lines, written in my sister's well-known hand, repeating the message already delivered. All future attempts to obtain a moment's conversation with her were as fruitless as the first. She was inflexible, and I was not permitted to see her till the day preceding that on which she entered the cloister, never to quit it more. This interview took place in the presence of our principal relations. It was for the first time since her childhood that I saw her, and the scene was most affecting: she threw herself upon my bosom, kissed me, and wept bitterly. By every possible argument, by tears, by prayers, by kneeling, I strove to make her abandon her intention. I represented to her all the hardships of a religious life; I painted to her imagination all the pleasures which she was going to quit; and besought her to disclose to me what occasioned her disgust to the world. At this last question she turned pale, and her tears flowed yet faster. She entreated me not to press her on that subject; that it sufficed me to know that her resolution was taken, and that a convent was the only place where she could now hope for tranquillity. She persevered in her design, and made her profession. I visited her frequently at the grate; and every moment that I passed with her made me feel more affliction at her loss. I was shortly after obliged to quit Madrid; I returned but yesterday evening, and, since then, have not had time to call at St. Clare's convent."

"Then, till I mentioned it, you never heard the name of Alphonso d'Alvarada?"

"Pardon me: my aunt wrote me word, that an adventurer so called had found means to get introduced into the castle of Lindenberg; that he had insinuated himself into my sister's good graces; and that she had even consented to elope with him. However, before the plan could be executed, the cavalier discovered, that the estates which he believed Agnes to possess in Hispaniola,[1] in reality belonged to me. This intelligence made him change his intention; he disappeared on the day that the elopement was to have taken place; and Agnes, in despair at his perfidy and meanness, had resolved upon seclusion in a convent. She added, that as this adventurer had given himself out

---

1   At the time of writing, the Caribbean island was the scene of a slaves' revolt that later led to its being divided into Haiti and the Dominican Republic.

to be a friend of mine, she wished to know whether I had any knowledge of him. I replied in the negative. I had then very little idea, that Alphonso d'Alvarada and the marquis de las Cisternas were one and the same person: the description given me of the first, by no means tallied with what I knew of the latter."

"In this I easily recognize Donna Rodolpha's perfidious character. Every word of this account is stamped with marks of her malice, of her falsehood, of her talents for misrepresenting those whom she wishes to injure. Forgive me, Medina, for speaking so freely of your relation. The mischief which she has done me authorises my resentment; and when you have heard my story, you will be convinced that my expressions have not been too severe."

He then began his narrative in the following manner:—

HISTORY OF DON RAYMOND, MARQUIS DE LAS CISTERNAS.

LONG experience, my dear Lorenzo, has convinced me how generous is your nature: I waited not for your declaration of ignorance respecting your sister's adventures, to suppose that they had been purposely concealed from you. Had they reached your knowledge, from what misfortunes should both Agnes and myself have escaped! Fate had ordained it otherwise. You were on your travels when I first became acquainted with your sister; and as our enemies took care to conceal from her your direction, it was impossible for her to implore by letter your protection and advice.

On leaving Salamanca, at which university, as I have since heard, you remained a year after I quitted it, I immediately set out upon my travels. My father supplied me liberally with money; but he insisted upon my concealing my rank, and presenting myself as no more than a private gentleman. This command was issued by the counsels of his friend the duke of Villa Hermosa, a nobleman for whose abilities and knowledge of the world I have ever entertained the most profound veneration.

"Believe me," said he, "my dear Raymond, you will hereafter feel the benefits of this temporary degradation. 'Tis true, that as the condé de las Cisternas you would have been received with open arms, and your youthful vanity might have felt gratified by the attentions showered upon you from all sides. At present, much will depend upon yourself; you have excellent recommendations, but it must be your own business to make them of use to you: you must lay yourself out to please; you must labour to gain the approbation

of those to whom you are presented: they who would have courted the friendship of the condé de las Cisternas will have no interest in finding out the merits, or bearing patiently with the faults,
of Alphonso d'Alvarada: consequently, when you find yourself really liked, you may safely ascribe it to your good qualities, not your
rank; and the distinction shewn you will be infinitely more flattering. Besides, your exalted birth would not permit your mixing
with the lower classes of society, which will now be in your power,
and from which, in my opinion, you will derive considerable benefit. Do not confine yourself to the illustrious of those countries
through which you pass. Examine the manners and customs of the
multitude: enter into the cottages; and, by observing how the vas-
sals of foreigners are treated, learn to diminish the burthens, and
augment the comforts, of your own. According to my ideas of
those advantages which a youth destined to the possession of
power and wealth may reap from travel, he should not consider as
the least essential, the opportunity of mixing with the classes below
him, and becoming an eye-witness of the sufferings of the people."

Forgive me, Lorenzo, if I seem tedious in my narration: the close
connexion which now exists between us, makes me anxious that
you should know every particular respecting me; and in my fear of
omitting the least circumstance which may induce you to think
favourably of your sister and myself, I may possibly relate many
which you may think uninteresting.

I followed the duke's advice; I was soon convinced of its wisdom.
I quitted Spain, calling myself by the assumed title of Don Alphonso d'Alvarada, and attended by a single domestic of approved fidelity. Paris was my first station. For some time I was enchanted with
it, as indeed must be every man who is young, rich, and fond of
pleasure. Yet, among all its gaieties, I felt that something was want-
ing to my heart: I grew sick of dissipation: I discovered that the people among whom I lived, and whose exterior was so polished and
seducing, were at bottom frivolous, unfeeling, and insincere. I
turned from the inhabitants of Paris with disgust, and quitted that
theatre of luxury without heaving one sigh of regret.

I now bent my course towards Germany, intending to visit most
of the principal courts. Prior to this expedition, I meant to make
some little stay at Strasbourg. On quitting my chaise[1] at Luneville,

---

1   "A carriage for travelling, having a closed body and seated for one to
    three persons, the driver sitting on one of the horses" (*OED*).

to take some refreshment, I observed a splendid equipage, attended by four domestics in rich liveries, waiting at the door of the Silver Lion. Soon after, as I looked out of the window, I saw a lady of noble presence, followed by two female attendants, step into the carriage, which drove off immediately.

I enquired of the host who the lady was that had just departed.

"A German baroness, monsieur, of great rank and fortune; she has been upon a visit to the duchess of Longueville, as her servants informed me. She is going to Strasbourg, where she will find her husband, and then both return to their castle in Germany."

I resumed my journey, intending to reach Strasbourg that night. My hopes, however, were frustrated by the breaking down of my chaise: the accident happened in the middle of a thick forest, and I was not a little embarrassed as to the means of proceeding. It was the depth of winter; the night was already closing round us; and Strasbourg, which was the nearest town, was still distant from us several leagues. It seemed to me that my only alternative to passing the night in the forest, was to take my servant's horse and ride on to Strasbourg; an undertaking at that season very far from agreeable. However, seeing no other resource, I was obliged to make up my mind to it: accordingly, I communicated my design to the postillion, telling him that I would send people to assist him as soon as I reached Strasbourg. I had not much confidence in his honesty; but Stephano being well armed, and the driver, to all appearance, considerably advanced in years, I believed I ran no risk of losing my baggage.

Luckily, as I then thought, an opportunity presented itself of passing the night more agreeably than I expected. On mentioning my design of proceeding by myself to Strasbourg, the postillion shook his head in disapprobation.

"It is a long way," said he; "you will find it a difficult matter to arrive there without a guide: besides, monsieur seems unaccustomed to the season's severity; and 'tis possible that, unable to sustain the excessive cold——"

"What use is there to present me with all these objections?" said I, impatiently interrupting him: "I have no other resource; I run still greater risk of perishing with cold by passing the night in the forest."

"Passing the night in the forest?" he replied. "Oh, by St. Denis! we are not in quite so bad a plight as that comes to yet. If I am not mistaken, we are scarcely five minutes walk from the cottage of my old friend Baptiste: he is a wood-cutter, and a very honest fellow. I doubt not but he will shelter you for the night with pleasure. In the mean time, I can take the saddle-horse, ride to Strasbourg, and be back with proper people to mend your carriage by break of day."

"And, in the name of God," said I, "how could you leave me so long in suspense? Why did you not tell me of this cottage sooner? What excessive stupidity!"

"I thought, that perhaps monsieur would not deign to accept——"

"Absurd! Come, come; say no more, but conduct us without delay to the woodman's cottage."

He obeyed, and we moved onwards: the horses contrived, with some difficulty, to drag the shattered vehicle after us. My servant was become almost speechless, and I began to feel the effects of the cold myself before we reached the wished-for cottage. It was a small but neat building: as we drew near it, I rejoiced at observing through the window the blaze of a comfortable fire. Our conductor knocked at the door: it was some time before any one answered; the people within seemed in doubt whether we should be admitted.

"Come, come, friend Baptiste!" cried the driver with impatience, "what are you about? Are you asleep? Or will you refuse a night's lodging to a gentleman, whose chaise has just broken down in the forest?"

"Ah! is it you, honest Claude?" replied a man's voice from within: "wait a moment, and the door shall be opened."

Soon after the bolts were drawn back; the door was unclosed, and a man presented himself to us with a lamp in his hand: he gave the guide an hearty reception, and then addressed himself to me:

"Walk in, monsieur; walk in, and welcome. Excuse me for not admitting you at first; but there are so many rogues about this place that, saving your presence, I suspected you to be one."

Thus saying, he ushered me into the room where I had observed the fire. I was immediately placed in an easy chair, which stood close to the hearth. A female, whom I supposed to be the wife of my host, rose from her seat upon my entrance, and received me with a slight and distant reverence. She made no answer to my compliment, but, immediately re-seating herself, continued the work on which she had been employed. Her husband's manners were as friendly as hers were harsh and repulsive.

"I wish I could lodge you more conveniently, monsieur," said he, "but we cannot boast of much spare room in this hovel. However, a chamber for yourself and another for your servant, I think, we can make shift to supply. You must content yourself with sorry fare; but to what we have, believe me, you are heartily welcome."— Then, turning to his wife—"Why, how you sit there, Marguerite, with as much tranquillity as if you had nothing better to do! Stir about, dame! stir about! Get some supper; look out some sheets. Here, here! throw some logs upon the fire, for the gentleman seems perished with cold."

The wife threw her work hastily upon the table, and proceeded to execute his commands with every mark of unwillingness. Her countenance had displeased me on the first moment of my examining it: yet, upon the whole, her features were handsome unquestionably; but her skin was sallow, and her person thin and meagre: a louring gloom overspread her countenance, and it bore such visible marks of rancour and ill-will, as could not escape being noticed by the most inattentive observer: her every look and action expressed discontent and impatience; and the answers which she gave Baptiste, when he reproached her good-humouredly for her dissatisfied air, were tart, short, and cutting. In fine, I conceived at first sight equal disgust for her, and prepossession in favour of her husband, whose appearance was calculated to inspire esteem and confidence. His countenance was open, sincere, and friendly; his manners had all the peasant's honesty, unaccompanied by his rudeness: his cheeks were broad, full, and ruddy; and in the solidity of his person he seemed to offer an ample apology for the leanness of his wife's. From the wrinkles on his brow, I judged him to be turned of sixty; but he bore his years well, and seemed still hearty and strong. The wife could not be more than thirty, but in spirits and vivacity she was infinitely older than the husband.

However, in spite of her unwillingness, Marguerite began to prepare the supper, while the woodman conversed gaily on different subjects. The postillion, who had been furnished with a bottle of spirits, was now ready to set out for Strasbourg, and enquired whether I had any further commands.

"For Strasbourg?" interrupted Baptiste; "you are not going thither to-night?"

"I beg your pardon: if I do not fetch workmen to mend the chaise, how is monsieur to proceed to-morrow?"

"That is true, as you say, I had forgotten the chaise. Well, but Claude, you may at least eat your supper here? That can make you lose very little time; and monsieur looks too kind-hearted to send you out with an empty stomach on such a bitter cold night as this is."

To this I readily assented, telling the postillion that my reaching Strasbourg the next day an hour or two later would be perfectly immaterial. He thanked me, and then leaving the cottage with Stephano, put up his horses in the woodman's stable. Baptiste followed them to the door, and looked out with anxiety.

"'Tis a sharp, biting wind," said he: "I wonder what detains my boys so long! Monsieur, I shall shew you two of the finest lads that ever stepped in shoe of leather: the eldest is three-and-twenty, the second a year younger: their equals for sense, courage, and activity, are not to be found within fifty miles of Strasbourg. Would they were back again! I begin to feel uneasy about them."

Marguerite was at this time employed in laying the cloth.

"And are you equally anxious for the return of your sons?" said I to her.

"Not I," she replied peevishly; "they are no children of mine."

"Come, come, Marguerite!" said the husband, "do not be out of humour with the gentleman for asking a simple question: had you not looked so cross, he would never have thought you old enough to have a son of three-and-twenty; but you see how many years ill-temper adds to you!—Excuse my wife's rudeness, monsieur; a little thing puts her out; and she is somewhat displeased at your not thinking her to be under thirty.—That is the truth, is it not, Marguerite? You know, monsieur, that age is always a ticklish subject with a woman. Come, come, Marguerite! clear up a little. If you have not sons as old, you will some twenty years hence; and I hope that we shall live to see them just such lads as Jacques and Robert."

Marguerite clasped her hands together passionately.

"God forbid!" said she, "God forbid! If I thought it, I would strangle them with my own hands."

She quitted the room hastily, and went up stairs.

I could not help expressing to the woodman how much I pitied him for being chained for life to a partner of such ill-humour.

"Ah, Lord! monsieur, every one has his share of grievances, and Marguerite has fallen to mine. Besides, after all, she is only cross, and not malicious: the worst is, that her affection for two children by a former husband, makes her play the step-mother with my two sons; she cannot bear the sight of them; and, by her good will, they would never set a foot within my door. But on this point I always stand firm, and never will consent to abandon the poor lads to the world's mercy, as she has often solicited me to do. In every thing else I let her have her own way; and truly she manages a family rarely, that I must say for her."

We were conversing in this manner, when our discourse was interrupted by a loud halloo, which rang through the forest.

"My sons, I hope!" exclaimed the woodman, and ran to open the door.

The halloo was repeated. We now distinguished the trampling of horses; and, soon after, a carriage attended by several cavaliers stopped at the cottage door. One of the horsemen enquired how far they were still from Strasbourg. As he addressed himself to me, I answered in the number of miles which Claude had told me; upon which a volley of curses was vented against the drivers for having lost their way. The persons in the coach were now informed of the distance of Strasbourg; and also that the horses were so fatigued as to be incapable of proceeding further. A lady, who appeared to be the principal, expressed much chagrin at this intelligence; but as there was no remedy, one of the attendants asked the woodman whether he could furnish them with lodging for the night.

He seemed much embarrassed, and replied in the negative; adding, that a Spanish gentleman and his servant were already in possession of the only spare apartments in his house. On hearing this, the gallantry of my nation would not permit me to retain those accommodations of which a female was in want. I instantly signified to the woodman, that I transferred my right to the lady: he made some objections, but I over-ruled them, and, hastening to the carriage, opened the door, and assisted the lady to descend. I immediately recognized her for the same person whom I had seen at the inn at Luneville. I took an opportunity of asking one of her attendants what was her name?

"The baroness Lindenberg," was the answer.

I could not but remark how different a reception our host had given these new-comers and myself. His reluctance to admit them was visibly expressed on his countenance; and he prevailed on himself with difficulty to tell the lady that she was welcome. I conducted her into the house, and placed her in the arm-chair which I had just quitted. She thanked me very graciously, and made a thousand apologies for putting me to an inconvenience. Suddenly the woodman's countenance cleared up.

"At last I have arranged it!" said he, interrupting her excuses. "I can lodge you and your suite, madam, and you will not be under the necessity of making this gentleman suffer for his politeness. We have two spare chambers, one for the lady, the other, monsieur, for you: my wife shall give up hers to the two waiting-women: as for the men servants, they must content themselves with passing the night in a large barn, which stands at a few yards distance from the house; there they shall have a blazing fire, and as good a supper as we can make shift to give them."

After several expressions of gratitude on the lady's part, and opposition on mine to Marguerite's giving up her bed, this arrangement was agreed to. As the room was small, the baroness immediately dismissed her male domestics. Baptiste was on the point of conducting them to the barn which he had mentioned, when two young men appeared at the door of the cottage.

"Hell and furies!" exclaimed the first, starting back, "Robert, the house is filled with strangers!"

"Ha! there are my sons!" cried our host. "Why, Jacques! Robert! whither are you running, boys? There is room enough still for you."

Upon this assurance the youths returned. The father presented them to the baroness and myself; after which he withdrew with our domestics, while, at the request of the two waiting-women, Marguerite conducted them to the room designed for their mistress.

The two new-comers were tall, stout, well-made young men, hard-featured, and very much sun-burnt. They paid their compliments to us in few words, and acknowledged Claude, who now entered the room, as an old acquaintance. They then threw aside their cloaks in which they were wrapped up, took off a leathern belt to which a large cutlass was suspended, and each drawing a brace of pistols from his girdle laid them upon a shelf.

"You travel well armed," said I.

"True, monsieur," replied Robert.—"We left Strasbourg late this evening, and 'tis necessary to take precautions at passing through this forest after dark; it does not bear a good repute, I promise you."

"How?" said the baroness, "are there robbers hereabout?"

"So it is said, madame: for my own part, I have travelled through the wood at all hours, and never met with one of them."

Here Marguerite returned. Her step-sons drew her to the other end of the room, and whispered her for some minutes. By the looks which they cast towards us at intervals, I conjectured them to be enquiring our business in the cottage.

In the mean while, the baroness expressed her apprehensions that her husband would be suffering much anxiety upon her account. She had intended to send on one of her servants to inform the baron of her delay; but the account which the young men gave of the forest rendered this plan impracticable. Claude relieved her from her embarrassment: he informed her, that he was under the necessity of reaching Strasbourg that night; and that, would she trust him with a letter, she might depend upon its being safely delivered.

"And how comes it," said I, "that you are under no apprehension of meeting these robbers?"

"Alas! monsieur, a poor man with a large family must not lose certain profit because 'tis attended with a little danger; and perhaps my lord the baron may give me a trifle for my pains: besides, I have nothing to lose except my life, and that will not be worth the robbers taking."

I thought his arguments bad, and advised his waiting till the morning; but, as the baroness did not second me, I was obliged to give up the point. The baroness Lindenberg, as I found afterwards, had long been accustomed to sacrifice the interests of others to her own, and her wish to send Claude to Strasbourg blinded her to the danger of the undertaking. Accordingly, it was resolved that he should set out without delay. The baroness wrote her letter to her husband; and I sent a few lines to my banker, apprising him that I should not be at Strasbourg till the next day. Claude took our letters, and left the cottage.

The lady declared herself much fatigued by her journey: besides having come from some distance, the drivers had contrived to lose their way in the forest. She now addressed herself to Marguerite, desiring to be shewn to her chamber, and permitted to take half an hour's repose. One of the waiting-women was immediately summoned; she appeared with a light, and the baroness followed her up stairs. The cloth was spreading in the chamber where I was, and Marguerite soon gave me to understand that I was in her way. Her hints were too broad to be easily mistaken; I therefore desired one of the young men to conduct me to the chamber where I was to sleep, and where I could remain till supper was ready.

"Which chamber is it, mother?" said Robert.

"The one with green hangings," she replied. "I have just been at the trouble of getting it ready, and have put fresh sheets upon the bed: if the gentleman chooses to lollop and lounge upon it, he may make it again himself, for me."

"You are out of humour, mother; but that is no novelty. Have the goodness to follow me, monsieur."

He opened the door, and advanced towards a narrow stair-case.

"You have got no light," said Marguerite; "is it your own neck or the gentleman's that you have a mind to break?"

She crossed by me, and put a candle into Robert's hand; having received which, he began to ascend the stair-case. Jacques was employed in laying the cloth, and his back was turned towards me. Marguerite seized the moment when we were unobserved: she caught my hand, and pressed it strongly.

"Look at the sheets!" said she as she passed me, and immediately resumed her former occupation.

Startled by the abruptness of her action, I remained as if petrified. Robert's voice desiring me to follow him recalled me to myself. I ascended the stair-case. My conductor ushered me into a chamber where an excellent wood fire was blazing upon the hearth. He placed the light upon the table, enquired whether I had any further commands, and, on my replying in the negative, left me to myself. You may be certain, that the moment when I found myself alone, was that on which I complied with Marguerite's injunction. I took the candle hastily, approached the bed, and turned down the coverture. What was my astonishment, my horror, at finding the sheets crimsoned with blood!

At that moment a thousand confused ideas passed before my imagination. The robbers who infested the wood, Marguerite's exclamation respecting her children, the arms and appearance of the two young men, and the various anecdotes which I had heard related respecting the secret correspondence which frequently exists between banditti and postillions; all these circumstances flashed upon my mind, and inspired me with doubt and apprehension. I ruminated on the most probable means of ascertaining the truth of my conjectures. Suddenly I was aware of some one below pacing hastily backwards and forwards. Every thing now appeared to me an object of suspicion. With precaution I drew near the window, which, as the room had been long shut up, was left open in spite of the cold. I ventured to look out. The beams of the moon permitted me to distinguish a man, whom I had no difficulty to recognize for my host. I watched his movements. He walked swiftly, then stopped and seemed to listen: he stamped upon the ground, and beat his stomach with his arms, as if to guard himself from the inclemency of the season: at the least noise, if a voice was heard in the lower part of the house, if a bat flitted past him, or the wind rattled amidst the leafless boughs, he started, and looked round with anxiety.

"Plague take him!" said he at length with extreme impatience; "what can he be about?"

He spoke in a low voice; but as he was just below my window, I had no difficulty to distinguish his words.

I now heard the steps of one approaching. Baptiste went towards the sound; he joined a man, whom his low stature and the horn suspended from his neck declared to be no other than my faithful Claude, whom I had supposed to be already on his way to Strasbourg. Expecting their discourse to throw some light upon my situation, I hastened to put myself in a condition to hear it with safety. For this purpose I extinguished the candle, which stood upon a table near the bed: the flame of the fire was not strong enough to betray me, and I immediately resumed my place at the window.

The objects of my curiosity had stationed themselves directly under it. I suppose that, during my momentary absence, the woodman had been blaming Claude for tardiness, since when I returned to the window the latter was endeavouring to excuse his fault.

"However," added he, "my diligence at present shall make up for my past delay."

"On that condition," answered Baptiste, "I shall readily forgive you: but in truth, as you share equally with us in our prizes, your own interest will make you use all possible diligence. 'Twould be a shame to let such a noble booty escape us. You say that this Spaniard is rich?"

"His servant boasted at the inn, that the effects in his chaise were worth above two thousand pistoles."

Oh! how I cursed Stephano's imprudent vanity.

"And I have been told," continued the postillion, "that this baroness carries about her a casket of jewels of immense value."

"May be so, but I had rather she had stayed away. The Spaniard was a secure prey; the boys and myself could easily have mastered him and his servant, and then the two thousand pistoles would have been shared between us four. Now we must let in the band for a share, and perhaps the whole covey may escape us. Should our friends have betaken themselves to their different posts before you reach the cavern, all will be lost. The lady's attendants are too numerous for us to overpower them. Unless our associates arrive in time, we must needs let these travellers set out to-morrow without damage or hurt."

"'Tis plaguy unlucky that my comrades who drove the coach should be those unacquainted with our confederacy! But never fear, friend Baptiste: an hour will bring me to the cavern; it is now but ten o'clock, and by twelve you may expect the arrival of the band. By the bye, take care of your wife: you know how strong is her repugnance to our mode of life, and she may find means to give information to the lady's servants of our design."

"Oh! I am secure of her silence; she is too much afraid of me, and fond of her children, to dare to betray my secret. Besides, Jacques and Robert keep a strict eye over her, and she is not permitted to set a foot out of the cottage. The servants are safely lodged in the barn. I shall endeavour to keep all quiet till the arrival of our friends. Were I assured of your finding them, the strangers should be dispatched this instant; but as it is possible for you to miss the banditti, I am fearful of being summoned by their domestics to produce them in the morning."

"And suppose either of the travellers should discover your design?"

"Then we must poniard those in our power, and take our chance about mastering the rest. However, to avoid running such a risk, hasten to the cavern; the banditti never leave it before eleven, and if you use diligence you may reach it in time to stop them."

"Tell Robert that I have taken his horse; my own has broken his bridle, and escaped into the wood. What is the watch-word?"

"The reward of courage."

"'Tis sufficient. I hasten to the cavern."

"And I to rejoin my guests, lest my absence should create suspicion. Farewell, and be diligent."

These worthy associates now separated; the one bent his course towards the stable, while the other returned to the house.

You may judge what must have been my feelings during this conversation, of which I lost not a single syllable. I dared not trust myself to my reflections, nor did any means present itself to escape the dangers which threatened me. Resistance I knew to be vain; I was unarmed, and a single man against three. However, I resolved at least to sell my life as dearly as I could. Dreading lest Baptiste should perceive my absence, and suspect me to have overheard the message with which Claude was dispatched, I hastily re-lighted my candle and quitted the chamber. On descending, I found the table spread for six persons. The baroness sat by the fire-side; Marguerite was employed in dressing a sallad, and her step-sons were whispering together at the further end of the room. Baptiste, having the round of the garden to make ere he could reach the cottage door, was not yet arrived. I seated myself quietly opposite to the baroness.

A glance upon Marguerite told her that her hint had not been thrown away upon me. How different did she now appear to me! What before seemed gloom and sullenness, I now found to be disgust at her associates and compassion for my danger. I looked up to her as to my only resource; yet knowing her to be watched by her husband with a suspicious eye, I could place but little reliance on the exertions of her good will.

In spite of all my endeavours to conceal it, my agitation was but too visibly expressed upon my countenance. I was pale, and both my words and actions were disordered and embarrassed. The young men observed this, and enquired the cause. I attributed it to excess of fatigue, and the violent effect produced on me by the severity of the season. Whether they believed me or not, I will not pretend to say; they at least ceased to embarrass me with their questions. I strove to divert my attention from the perils which surrounded me, by conversing on different subjects with the baroness. I talked of Germany, declaring my intention of visiting it immediately: God knows, that I little thought at that moment of ever seeing it! She replied to me with great ease and politeness, professed that the pleasure of making my acquaintance amply compensated for the delay in her journey, and gave me a pressing invitation to make some stay at the castle of Lindenberg. As she spoke thus, the youths exchanged a malicious smile, which declared that she would be fortunate if she ever reached that castle herself. This action did not escape me; but I concealed the emotion which it excited in my breast. I continued to converse with the lady; but my discourse was so frequently incoherent that, as she has since informed me, she began to doubt whether I was in my right senses. The fact was, that while my conversation turned upon one subject, my thoughts were entirely occupied by another. I meditated upon the means of quitting the cottage, finding my way to the barn, and giving the domestics information of our host's designs. I was soon convinced how impracticable was the attempt. Jacques and Robert watched my every movement with an attentive eye, and I was obliged to abandon the idea. All my hopes now rested upon Claude's not finding the banditti. In that case, according to what I had overheard, we should be permitted to depart unhurt.

I shuddered involuntarily as Baptiste entered the room. He made many apologies for his long absence, but "he had been detained by affairs impossible to be delayed." He then entreated permission for his family to sup at the same table with us, without which, respect would not authorize his taking such a liberty. Oh! how in my heart I cursed the hypocrite! how I loathed his presence, who was on the point of depriving me of an existence, at that time infinitely dear! I had every reason to be satisfied with life; I had youth, wealth, rank, and education, and the fairest prospects presented themselves before me. I saw those prospects on the point of closing in the most horrible manner: yet was I obliged to dissimulate, and to receive with a semblance of gratitude the false civilities of him who held the dagger to my bosom.

The permission which our host demanded was easily obtained. We seated ourselves at the table. The baroness and myself occupied one side; the sons were opposite to us, with their backs to the door. Baptiste took his seat by the baroness, at the upper end; and the place next to him was left for his wife. She soon entered the room, and placed before us a plain but comfortable peasant's repast. Our host thought it necessary to apologize for the poorness of the supper: "he had not been apprized of our coming; he could only offer us such fare as had been intended for his own family."

"But," added he, "should any accident detain my noble guests longer than they at present intend, I hope to give them a better treatment."

The villain! I well knew the accident to which he alluded. I shuddered at the treatment which he taught us to expect.

My companion in danger seemed entirely to have got rid of her chagrin at being delayed. She laughed, and conversed with the family with infinite gaiety. I strove, but in vain, to follow her example. My spirits were evidently forced, and the constraint which I put upon myself escaped not Baptiste's observation.

"Come, come, monsieur, cheer up!" said he; "you seem not quite recovered from your fatigue. To raise your spirits, what say you to a glass of excellent old wine which was left me by my father? God rest his soul, he is in a better world! I seldom produce this wine; but as I am not honoured with such guests every day, this is an occasion which deserves a bottle."

He then gave his wife a key, and instructed her where to find the wine of which he spoke. She seemed by no means pleased with the commission; she took the key with an embarrassed air, and hesitated to quit the table.

"Did you hear me?" said Baptiste in an angry tone.

Marguerite darted upon him a look of mingled anger and fear, and left the chamber. His eyes followed her suspiciously till she had closed the door.

She soon returned with a bottle sealed with yellow wax. She placed it upon the table, and gave the key back to her husband. I suspected that this liquor was not presented to us without design, and I watched Marguerite's movements with inquietude. She was employed in rinsing some small horn goblets. As she placed them before Baptiste, she saw that my eye was fixed upon her; and at the moment when she thought herself unobserved by the banditti, she motioned to me with her head not to taste the liquor. She then resumed her place.

In the mean while our host had drawn the cork, and, filling two of the goblets, offered them to the lady and myself. She at first made some objections, but the instances of Baptiste were so urgent, that she was obliged to comply. Fearing to excite suspicion, I hesitated not to take the goblet presented to me. By its smell and colour, I guessed it to be champagne; but some grains of powder floating upon the top convinced me that it was not unadulterated. However, I dared not to express my repugnance to drinking it; I lifted it to my lips, and seemed to be swallowing it: suddenly starting from my chair, I made the best of my way towards a vase of water at some distance, in which Marguerite had been rinsing the goblets. I pretended to spit out the wine with disgust, and took an opportunity, unperceived, of emptying the liquor into the vase.

The banditti seemed alarmed at my action. Jacques half rose from his chair, put his hand into his bosom, and I discovered the haft of a dagger. I returned to my seat with tranquillity, and affected not to have observed their confusion.

"You have not suited my taste, honest friend," said I, addressing myself to Baptiste: "I never can drink champagne without its producing a violent illness. I swallowed a few mouthfuls ere I was aware of its quality, and fear that I shall suffer for my imprudence."

Baptiste and Jacques exchanged looks of distrust.

"Perhaps," said Robert, "the smell may be disagreeable to you?"

He quitted his chair, and removed the goblet. I observed, that he examined whether it was nearly empty.

"He must have drank sufficient," said he to his brother in a low voice, while he re-seated himself.

Marguerite looked apprehensive that I had tasted the liquor. A glance from my eye re-assured her.

I waited with anxiety for the effects which the beverage would produce upon the lady. I doubted not but the grains which I had observed were poisonous, and lamented that it had been impossible for me to warn her of the danger. But a few minutes had elapsed, before I perceived her eyes grow heavy; her head sank upon her shoulder, and she fell into a deep sleep. I affected not to attend to this circumstance, and continued my conversation with Baptiste, with all the outward gaiety in my power to assume. But he no longer answered me without constraint. He eyed me with distrust and astonishment, and I saw that the banditti were frequently whispering among themselves. My situation became every moment more painful: I sustained the character of confidence with a worse grace than ever. Equally afraid of the arrival of their accomplices, and of their suspecting my knowledge of their designs, I knew not how to dissipate the distrust which the banditti evidently entertained for me. In this new dilemma the friendly Marguerite again assisted me. She passed behind the chairs of her step-sons, stopped for a moment opposite to me, closed her eyes, and reclined her head upon her shoulder. This hint immediately dispelled my incertitude. It told me, that I ought to imitate the baroness, and pretend that the liquor had taken its full effect upon me. I did so, and in a few minutes seemed perfectly overcome with slumber.

"So!" cried Baptiste, as I fell back in my chair, "at last he sleeps! I began to think that he had scented our design, and that we should have been forced to dispatch him at all events."

"And why not dispatch him at all events?" enquired the ferocious Jacques: "why leave him the possibility of betraying our secret? Marguerite, give me one of my pistols: a single touch of the trigger will finish him at once."

"And supposing," rejoined the father, "supposing that our friends should not arrive to-night, a pretty figure we should make when the servants .enquire for him in the morning! No, no, Jacques; we must wait for our associates. If they join us, we are strong enough to dispatch the domestics as well as their masters, and the booty is our own. If Claude does not find the troop, we must take patience, and suffer the prey to slip through our fingers. Ah! boys, boys, had you arrived but five minutes sooner, the Spaniard would have been done for, and two thousand pistoles our own. But you are always out of the way when you are most wanted. You are the most unlucky rogues——"

"Well, well, father!" answered Jacques; "had you been of my mind, all would have been over by this time. You, Robert, Claude, and myself—why the strangers were but double the number, and I warrant you we might have mastered them. However, Claude is gone; 'tis too late to think of it now. We must wait patiently for the arrival of the gang; and if the travellers escape us to-night, we must take care to way-lay them to-morrow."

"True! true!" said Baptiste; "Marguerite, have you given the sleeping-draught to the waiting-women?"

She replied in the affirmative.

"All then is safe. Come, come, boys; whatever falls out, we have no reason to complain of this adventure. We run no danger, may gain much, and can lose nothing."

At this moment I heard a trampling of horses. Oh! how dreadful was the sound to my ears! A cold sweat flowed down my forehead, and I felt all the terrors of impending death. I was by no means re-assured by hearing the compassionate Marguerite exclaim, in the accents of despair,

"Almighty God! they are lost."

Luckily the woodman and his sons were too much occupied by the arrival of their associates to attend to me, or the violence of my agitation would have convinced them that my sleep was feigned.

"Open! open!" exclaimed several voices on the outside of the cottage.

"Yes! yes!" cried Baptiste joyfully; "they are our friends, sure enough. Now then our booty is certain. Away! lads, away! Lead them to the barn; you know what is to be done there."

Robert hastened to open the door of the cottage.

"But first," said Jacques, taking up his arms, "first let me dispatch these sleepers."

"No, no, no!" replied his father: "Go you to the barn, where your presence is wanted. Leave me to take care of these and the women above."

Jacques obeyed, and followed his brother. They seemed to converse with the new-comers for a few minutes; after which I heard the robbers dismount, and, as I conjectured, bend their course towards the barn.

"So! that is wisely done!" muttered Baptiste; "they have quitted their horses, that they may fall upon the strangers by surprise. Good! good! and now to business."

I heard him approach a small cupboard which was fixed up in a distant part of the room, and unlock it. At this moment I felt myself shaken gently.

"Now! now!" whispered Marguerite.

I opened my eyes. Baptiste stood with his back towards me. No one else was in the room save Marguerite and the sleeping lady. The villain had taken a dagger from the cupboard, and seemed examining whether it was sufficiently sharp. I had neglected to furnish myself with arms; but I perceived this to be my only chance of escaping, and resolved not to lose the opportunity. I sprang from my seat, darted suddenly upon Baptiste, and, clasping my hands round his throat, pressed it so forcibly as to prevent his uttering a single cry. You may remember, that I was remarkable at Salamanca for the power of my arm. It now rendered me an essential service. Surprised, terrified, and breathless, the villain was by no means an equal antagonist. I threw him upon the ground; I grasped him still tighter; and while I fixed him without motion upon the floor, Marguerite, wresting the dagger from his hand, plunged it repeatedly in his heart till he expired.

No sooner was this horrible but necessary act perpetrated, than Marguerite called on me to follow her.

"Flight is our only refuge," said she, "quick! quick! away!"

I hesitated not to obey her; but unwilling to leave the baroness a victim to the vengeance of the robbers, I raised her in my arms still sleeping, and hastened after Marguerite. The horses of the banditti were fastened near the door. My conductress sprang upon one of them. I followed her example, placed the baroness before me, and spurred on my horse. Our only hope was to reach Strasbourg, which was much nearer than the perfidious Claude had assured me. Marguerite was well acquainted with the road, and galloped on before me. We were obliged to pass by the barn, where the robbers were slaughtering our domestics. The door was open: we distinguished the shrieks of the dying, and imprecations of the murderers. What I felt at that moment language is unable to describe.

Jacques heard the trampling of our horses, as we rushed by the barn. He flew to the door with a burning torch in his hand, and easily recognised the fugitives.

"Betrayed! betrayed!" he shouted to his companions.

Instantly they left their bloody work, and hastened to regain their horses. We heard no more. I buried my spurs in the sides of my courser, and Marguerite goaded on hers with the poniard which had already rendered us such good service. We flew like lightning, and gained the open plains. Already was Strasbourg's steeple in sight, when we heard the robbers pursuing us. Marguerite looked back, and distinguished our followers descending a small hill at no great distance. It was in vain that we urged on our horses: the noise approached nearer with every moment.

"We are lost!" she exclaimed; "the villains gain upon us!"

"On! on!" replied I; "I hear the trampling of horses coming from the town."

We redoubled our exertions, and were soon aware of a numerous band of cavaliers, who came towards us at full speed. They were on the point of passing us.

"Stay! stay!" shrieked Marguerite; "save us! for God's sake, save us!"

The foremost, who seemed to act as guide, immediately reined in his steed.

"'Tis she! 'tis she!" exclaimed he, springing upon the ground: "Stop, my lord, stop! they are safe! 'tis my mother!"

At the same moment Marguerite threw herself from her horse, clasped him in her arms, and covered him with kisses. The other cavaliers stopped at the exclamation.

"The baroness Lindenberg!" cried another of the strangers eagerly: "Where is she? Is she not with you?"

He stopped on beholding her lying senseless in my arms. Hastily he caught her from me. The profound sleep in which she was plunged, made him at first tremble for her life; but the beating of her heart soon re-assured him.

"God be thanked!" said he, "she has escaped unhurt."

I interrupted his joy by pointing out the brigands, who continued to approach. No sooner had I mentioned them, than the greatest part of the company, which appeared to be chiefly composed of soldiers, hastened forward to meet them. The villains staid not to receive their attack. Perceiving their danger, they turned the heads of their horses, and fled into the wood, whither they were followed by our preservers. In the mean while the stranger, whom I guessed to be the baron Lindenberg, after thanking me for my care of his lady, proposed our returning with all speed to the town. The baroness, on whom the effects of the opiate had not ceased to operate, was placed before him; Marguerite and her son remounted their horses; the baron's domestics followed, and we soon arrived at the inn, where he had taken his apartments.

This was at the Austrian Eagle, where my banker, whom before my quitting Paris I had apprised of my intention to visit Strasbourg, had prepared lodgings for me. I rejoiced at this circumstance. It gave me an opportunity of cultivating the baron's acquaintance, which I foresaw would be of use to me in Germany. Immediately upon our arrival, the lady was conveyed to bed. A physician was sent for, who prescribed a medicine likely to counteract the effects of the sleepy potion; and after it had been poured down her throat, she was committed to the care of the hostess. The baron then addressed himself to me, and entreated me to recount the particulars of this adventure. I complied with his request instantaneously; for, in pain respecting Stephano's fate, whom I had been compelled to abandon to the cruelty of the banditti, I found it impossible for me to repose till I had some news of him. I received but too soon the intelligence that my trusty servant had perished. The soldiers who had pursued the brigands, returned while I was employed in relating my adventure to the baron. By their account, I found that the robbers had been overtaken. Guilt and true courage are incompatible: they had thrown themselves at the feet of their pursuers, had surrendered themselves without striking a blow, had discovered their secret retreat, made known their signals by which the rest of the gang might be seized, and, in short, had betrayed every mark of cowardice and baseness. By this means the whole of the band, consisting of near sixty persons, had been made prisoners, bound, and conducted to Strasbourg. Some of the soldiers hastened to the cottage, one of the banditti serving them as guide. Their first visit was to the fatal barn, where they were fortunate enough to find two of the baron's servants still alive, though desperately wounded. The rest had expired beneath the swords of the robbers, and of these my unhappy Stephano was one.

Alarmed at our escape, the robbers, in their haste to overtake us, had neglected to visit the cottage; in consequence, the soldiers found the two waiting-women unhurt, and buried in the same death-like slumber which had overpowered their mistress. There was nobody else found in the cottage, except a child not above four years old, which the soldiers brought away with them. We were busying ourselves with conjectures respecting the birth of this little unfortunate, when Marguerite rushed into the room with the baby in her arms. She fell at the feet of the officer who was making us this report, and blessed him a thousand times for the preservation of her child.[1]

When the first burst of maternal tenderness was over, I besought her to declare by what means she had been united to a man whose principles seemed so totally discordant with her own. She bent her eyes downwards, and wiped a few tears from her cheek.

"Gentlemen," said she, after a silence of some minutes, "I would request a favour of you. You have a right to know on whom you confer an obligation; I will not, therefore, stifle a confession which

1   Cf. the episodes of the robbers in Tobias Smollett, *The Adventures of Ferdinand Count Fathom* (1753), chapters 20-21, and Lorenz Flammenberg, *Der Geisterbanner* ("The Necromancer," 1792) 145-54.

covers me with shame; but permit me to comprise it in as few words as possible.

"I was born in Strasbourg, of respectable parents; their names I must at present conceal. My father still lives, and deserves not to be involved in my infamy. If you grant my request, you shall be informed of my family name. A villain made himself master of my affections, and to follow him I quitted my father's house. Yet, though my passions overpowered my virtue, I sank not into that degeneracy of vice but too commonly the lot of women who make the first false step. I loved my seducer, dearly loved him! I was true to his bed: this baby, and the youth who warned you, my lord baron, of your lady's danger, are the pledges of our affection. Even at this moment I lament his loss, though 'tis to him that I owe all the miseries of my existence.

"He was of noble birth, but he had squandered away his paternal inheritance. His relations considered him as a disgrace to their name, and utterly discarded him. His excesses drew upon him the indignation of the police. He was obliged to fly from Strasbourg; and saw no other resource from beggary than an union with the banditti who infested the neighbouring forest, and whose troop was chiefly composed of young men of family in the same predicament with himself. I was determined not to forsake him. I followed him to the cavern of the brigands, and shared with him the misery inseparable from a life of pillage. But though I was aware that our existence was supported by plunder, I knew not all the horrible circumstances attached to my lover's profession: these he concealed from me with the utmost care. He was conscious that my sentiments were not sufficiently depraved to look without horror upon assassination. He supposed, and with justice, that I should fly with detestation from the embraces of a murderer. Eight years of possession had not abated his love for me; and he cautiously removed from my knowledge every circumstance which might lead me to suspect the crimes in which he but too often participated. He succeeded perfectly. It was not till after my seducer's death that I discovered his hands to have been stained with the blood of innocence.

"One fatal night he was brought back to the cavern, covered with wounds: he received them in attacking an English traveller, whom his companions immediately sacrificed to their resentment. He had only time to entreat my pardon for all the sorrows which he had caused me: he pressed my hand to his lips, and expired. My grief was inexpressible. As soon as its violence abated, I resolved to return to Strasbourg, to throw myself, with my two children, at my father's feet, and implore his forgiveness, though I little hoped to obtain it. What was my consternation when informed, that no one entrusted with the secret of their retreat was ever permitted to quit the troop of the banditti; that I must give up all hopes of ever rejoining society, and consent instantly to accept one of their band for my husband! My prayers and remonstrances were vain. They cast lots to decide to whose possession I should fall. I became the property of the infamous Baptiste. A robber, who had once been a monk, pronounced over us a burlesque rather than a religious ceremony: I and my children were delivered into the hands of my new husband, and he conveyed us immediately to his home.

"He assured me that he had long entertained for me the most ardent regard; but that friendship for my deceased lover had obliged him to stifle his desires. He endeavoured to reconcile me to my fate, and for some time treated me with respect and gentleness. At length, finding that my aversion rather increased than diminished, he obtained those favours by violence which I persisted to refuse him. No resource remained for me but to bear my sorrows with patience; I was conscious that I deserved them but too well. Flight was forbidden. My children were in the power of Baptiste; and he had sworn, that if I attempted to escape, their lives should pay for it. I had had too many opportunities of witnessing the barbarity of his nature, to doubt his fulfilling his oath to the very letter. Sad experience had convinced me of the horrors of my situation. My first lover had carefully concealed them from me; Baptiste rather rejoiced in opening my eyes to the cruelties of his profession, and strove to familiarise me with blood and slaughter.

"My nature was licentious and warm, but not cruel: my conduct had been imprudent, but my heart was not unprincipled. Judge, then, what I must have felt at being a continual witness of crimes the most horrible and revolting! Judge how I must have grieved at being united to a man, who received the unsuspecting guest with an air of openness and hospitality, at the very moment that he meditated his destruction! Chagrin and discontent preyed upon my constitution; the few charms bestowed on me by nature withered away, and the dejection of my countenance denoted the sufferings of my heart. I was tempted a thousand times to put an end to my existence; but the remembrance of my children held my hand. I trembled to leave my dear boys in my tyrant's power, and trembled yet more for their virtue than their lives. The second was still too young to benefit by my instructions; but in the heart of my eldest

I laboured unceasingly to plant those principles which might enable him to avoid the crimes of his parents. He listened to me with docility, or rather with eagerness. Even at his early age, he shewed that he was not calculated for the society of villains; and the only comfort which I enjoyed among my sorrows, was to witness the dawning virtues of my Theodore.

"Such was my situation when the perfidy of Don Alphonso's postillion conducted him to the cottage. His youth, air, and manners interested me most forcibly in his behalf. The absence of my husband's sons gave me an opportunity which I had long wished to find, and I resolved to risque every thing to preserve the stranger. The vigilance of Baptiste prevented me from warning Don Alphonso of his danger. I knew that my betraying the secret would be immediately punished with death; and however embittered was my life by calamities, I wanted courage to sacrifice it for the sake of preserving that of another person. My only hope rested upon procuring succour from Strasbourg. At this I resolved to try; and should an opportunity offer of warning Don Alphonso of his danger unobserved, I was determined to seize it with avidity. By Baptiste's orders I went up stairs to make the stranger's bed: I spread upon it sheets in which a traveller had been murdered but a few nights before, and which still were stained with blood. I hoped that these marks would not escape the vigilance of our guest, and that he would collect from them the designs of my perfidious husband. Neither was this the only step which I took to preserve the stranger. Theodore was confined to his bed by illness. I stole into his room unobserved by my tyrant, communicated to him my project, and he entered into it with eagerness. He rose in spite of his malady, and dressed himself with all speed. I fastened one of the sheets round his arms, and lowered him from the window. He flew to the stable, took Claude's horse, and hastened to Strasbourg. Had he been accosted by the banditti, he was to have declared himself sent upon a message by Baptiste, but fortunately he reached the town without meeting any obstacle. Immediately upon his arrival at Strasbourg, he entreated assistance from the magistrate: his story passed from mouth to mouth, and at length came to the knowledge of my lord the baron. Anxious for the safety of his lady, who he knew would be upon the road that evening, it struck him that she might have fallen into the power of the robbers. He accompanied Theodore, who guided the soldiers towards the cottage, and arrived just in time to save us from falling once more into the hands of our enemies."

Here I interrupted Marguerite to enquire why the sleepy potion had been presented to me. She said, that Baptiste supposed me to have arms about me, and wished to incapacitate me from making resistance: it was a precaution which he always took, since, as the travellers had no hopes of escaping, despair would have incited them to sell their lives dearly.

The baron then desired Marguerite to inform him what were her present plans. I joined him in declaring my readiness to shew my gratitude to her for the preservation of my life.

"Disgusted with a world," she replied, "in which I have met with nothing but misfortunes, my only wish is to retire into a convent. But first I must provide for my children. I find that my mother is no more—probably driven to an untimely grave by my desertion. My father is still living. He is not an hard man. Perhaps, gentlemen, in spite of my ingratitude and imprudence, your intercessions may induce him to forgive me, and to take charge of his unfortunate grandsons. If you obtain this boon for me, you will repay my services a thousand-fold."

Both the baron and myself assured Marguerite, that we would spare no pains to obtain her pardon: and that, even should her father be inflexible, she need be under no apprehensions respecting the fate of her children. I engaged myself to provide for Theodore, and the baron promised to take the youngest under his protection. The grateful mother thanked us with tears for what she called generosity, but which in fact was no more than a proper sense of our obligations to her. She then left the room to put her little boy to bed, whom fatigue and sleep had completely overpowered.

The baroness, on recovering, and being informed from what dangers I had rescued her, set no bounds to the expressions of her gratitude. She was joined so warmly by her husband in pressing me to accompany them to their castle in Bavaria, that I found it impossible to resist their entreaties. During a week which we passed at Strasbourg, the interests of Marguerite were not forgotten. In our application to her father we succeeded as amply as we could wish. The good old man had lost his wife. He had no children but this unfortunate daughter, of whom he had received no news for almost fourteen years. He was surrounded by distant relations, who waited with impatience for his decease, in order to get possession of his money. When therefore Marguerite appeared again so unexpectedly, he considered her as a gift from Heaven. He received her and her children with open arms, and insisted upon their establishing themselves in his house without delay. The disappointed cousins were obliged to give place. The old man would not hear of his daughter's retiring into a convent. He said, that she was too necessary to his happiness, and she was easily persuaded to relinquish her designs. But no persuasions could induce Theodore to give up the plan which I had at first marked out for him. He had attached himself to me most sincerely during my stay at Strasbourg; and when I was on the point of leaving it, he besought me with tears to take him into my service. He set forth all his little talents in the most favourable colours, and tried to convince me that I should find him of infinite use to me upon the road. I was unwilling to charge myself with a lad scarcely turned of thirteen, who I knew could only be a burthen to me: however, I could not resist the entreaties of this affectionate youth, who in fact possessed a thousand estimable qualities. With some difficulty he persuaded his relations to let him follow me; and that permission once obtained, he was dubbed with the title of my page. Having passed a week at Strasbourg, Theodore and myself set out for Bavaria, in company with the baron and his lady. These latter, as well as myself, had forced Marguerite to accept several presents of value, both for herself and her youngest son. On leaving her, I promised his mother faithfully, that I would restore Theodore to her within the year.

I have related this adventure at length, Lorenzo, that you might understand the means by which "the adventurer Alphonso d'Alvarada got introduced into the castle of Lindenberg." Judge from this specimen, how much faith should be given to your aunt's assertions.

END OF THE FIRST VOLUME.

obligations
hospitality
judgements

THE MONK.
[VOLUME II]
CHAP. IV.

Avaunt! and quit my sight! Let the earth hide thee!
Thy bones are marrowless; thy blood is cold;
Thou hast no speculation in those eyes
Which thou dost glare with! Hence, horrible shadow!
Unreal mockery, hence!

MACBETH.[1]

CONTINUATION OF
THE HISTORY OF DON RAYMOND.

MY journey was uncommonly agreeable: I found the baron a man of some sense, but little knowledge of the world. He had passed a great part of his life without stirring beyond the precincts of his own domains, and consequently his manners were far from being the most polished; but he was hearty, good-humoured, and friendly. His attention to me was all that I could wish, and I had every reason to be satisfied with his behaviour. His ruling passion was hunting, which he had brought himself to consider as a serious occupation; and, when talking over some remarkable chace, he treated the subject with as much gravity as it had been a battle on which the fate of two kingdoms was depending. I happened to be a tolerable sportsman: soon after my arrival at Lindenberg, I gave some proofs of my dexterity. The baron immediately marked me down for a man of genius, and vowed to me an eternal friendship.

That friendship was become to me by no means indifferent. At the castle of Lindenberg, I beheld for the first time your sister, the lovely Agnes. For me, whose heart was unoccupied, and who grieved at the void, to see her and to love her were the same. I found in Agnes all that was requisite to secure my affection. She was then scarcely sixteen; her person light and elegant was already formed; she possessed several talents in perfection, particularly those of music and drawing: her character was gay, open, and good-humoured; and the graceful simplicity of her dress and manners formed an advantageous contrast to the art and studied coquetry of the Parisian dames, whom I had just quitted. From the moment

---

1 Shakespeare, *Macbeth* 3.4.93-96, 106-7.

that I beheld her, I felt the most lively interest in her fate. I made many enquiries respecting her of the baroness.

"She is my niece," replied that lady; "you are still ignorant, Don Alphonso, that I am your country-woman. I am sister to the duke of Medina Celi. Agnes is the daughter of my second brother, Don Gaston: she has been destined to the convent from her cradle, and will soon make her profession at Madrid."

[Here Lorenzo interrupted the marquis by an exclamation of surprise.

"Intended for the convent from her cradle!" said he: "By heaven, this is the first word that I ever heard of such a design."

"I believe it, my dear Lorenzo," answered Don Raymond; "but you must listen to me with patience. You will not be less surprised, when I relate some particulars of your family still unknown to you, and which I have learnt from the mouth of Agnes herself."

He then resumed his narrative as follows:]

You cannot but be aware, that your parents were unfortunately slaves to the grossest superstition: when this foible was called into play, their every other sentiment, their every other passion, yielded to its irresistible strength. While she was big with Agnes, your mother was seized by a dangerous illness, and given over by her physicians. In this situation Donna Inesilla vowed, that if she recovered from her malady, the child then living in her bosom, if a girl, should be dedicated to St. Clare; if a boy, to St. Benedict. Her prayers were heard; she got rid of her complaint; Agnes entered the world alive, and was immediately destined to the service of St. Clare.

Don Gaston readily chimed in with his lady's wishes: but knowing the sentiments of the duke, his brother, respecting a monastic life, it was determined that your sister's destination should be carefully concealed from him. The better to guard the secret, it was resolved that Agnes should accompany her aunt, Donna Rodolpha, into Germany, whither that lady was on the point of following her new-married husband, baron Lindenberg. On her arrival at that estate, the young Agnes was put into a convent, situated but a few miles from the castle. The nuns, to whom her education was confided, performed their charge with exactitude: they made her a perfect mistress of many accomplishments, and strove to infuse into her mind a taste for the retirement and tranquil pleasures of a convent. But a secret instinct made the young recluse sensible that she was not born for solitude: in all the freedom of youth and gaiety, she scrupled not to treat as ridiculous many ceremonies which the nuns regarded with awe; and she was never more happy than when her lively imagination inspired her with some scheme to plague the stiff lady abbess, or the ugly ill-tempered old porteress. She looked with disgust upon the prospect before her: however, no alternative was offered to her, and she submitted to the decree of her parents, though not without secret repining.

That repugnance she had not art enough to conceal long: Don Gaston was informed of it. Alarmed, Lorenzo, lest your affection for her should oppose itself to his projects, and lest you should positively object to your sister's misery, he resolved to keep the whole affair from *your* knowledge as well as the duke's, till the sacrifice should be consummated. The season of her taking the veil was fixed for the time when you should be upon your travels: in the mean while no hint was dropped of Donna Inesilla's fatal vow. Your sister was never permitted to know your direction. All your letters were read before she received them, and those parts effaced which were likely to nourish her inclination for the world: her answers were dictated either by her aunt, or by dame Cunegonda, her governess. These particulars I learnt partly from Agnes, partly from the baroness herself.

I immediately determined upon rescuing this lovely girl from a fate so contrary to her inclinations, and ill-suited to her merit. I endeavoured to ingratiate myself into her favour: I boasted of my friendship and intimacy with you. She listened to me with avidity; she seemed to devour my words while I spoke in your praise, and her eyes thanked me for my affection to her brother. My constant and unremitted attention at length gained me her heart, and with difficulty I obliged her to confess that she loved me. When, however, I proposed her quitting the castle of Lindenberg, she rejected the idea in positive terms.

"Be generous, Alphonso," she said; "you possess my heart, but use not the gift ignobly. Employ not your ascendancy over me in persuading me to take a step at which I should hereafter have to blush. I am young and deserted: my brother, my only friend, is separated from me, and my other relations act with me as my enemies. Take pity on my unprotected situation. Instead of seducing me to an action which would cover me with shame, strive rather to gain the affections of those who govern me. The baron esteems you. My aunt, to others ever harsh, proud, and contemptuous, remembers that you rescued her from the hands of murderers, and wears with you alone the appearance of kindness and benignity. Try then your influence over my guardians. If they consent to our union, my hand is yours. From your account of my brother, I cannot doubt your obtaining his approbation: and when they find the impossibility of executing their design, I trust that my parents will excuse my disobedience, and expiate by some other sacrifice my mother's fatal vow."

From the first moment that I beheld Agnes, I had endeavoured to conciliate the favour of her relations. Authorised by the confession of her regard, I redoubled my exertions. My principal battery was directed against the baroness: it was easy to discover, that her word was law in the castle: her husband paid her the most absolute submission, and considered her as a superior being. She was about forty: in her youth she had been a beauty; but her charms had been upon that large scale which can but ill sustain the shock of years: however, she still possessed some remains of them. Her understanding was strong and excellent when not obscured by prejudice, which unluckily was but seldom the case. Her passions were violent: she spared no pains to gratify them, and pursued with unremitting vengeance those who opposed themselves to her wishes. The warmest of friends, the most inveterate of enemies, such was the baroness Lindenberg.

I laboured incessantly to please her: unluckily I succeeded but too well. She seemed gratified by my attention, and treated me with a distinction accorded by her to no one else. One of my daily occupations was reading to her for several hours: those hours I should much rather have passed with Agnes; but as I was conscious that complaisance for her aunt would advance our union, I submitted with a good grace to the penance imposed upon me. Donna Rodolpha's library was principally composed of old Spanish romances: these were her favourite studies, and once a day one of these unmerciful volumes was put regularly into my hands. I read the wearisome adventures of "*Perceforest,*" "*Tirante the White,*" "*Palmerin of England,*" and "*the Knight of the Sun,*"[1] till the book was on the point of falling from my hands through ennui. However, the increasing pleasure which the baroness seemed to take in my society, encouraged me to persevere; and latterly she shewed for me a

---

1 These are chivalric romances: *Perceforest* is French, composed between 1314 and 1340. The other three are Spanish: *Tirante the White* (1460-90), is by Johanot Martorell and Martí Johán de Galba; *Palmerin of England* (1547), by Francisco de Moraes (d. 1572); they are mentioned in Cervantes, *Don Quixote* 1.1 and 1.6, as items in the library that drives Don Quixote crazy.

partiality so marked, that Agnes advised me to seize the first opportunity of declaring our mutual passion to her aunt.

One evening I was alone with Donna Rodolpha, in her own apartment. As our readings generally treated of love, Agnes was never permitted to assist at them. I was just congratulating myself on having finished "*the Loves of Tristan and the Queen Iseult*——"[1]

"Ah! the unfortunates!" cried the baroness: "How say you, Segnor? Do you think it possible for man to feel an attachment so disinterested and sincere?"

"I cannot doubt it," replied I; "my own heart furnishes me with the certainty. Ah! Donna Rodolpha, might I but hope for your approbation of my love! might I but confess the name of my mistress, without incurring your resentment!"

She interrupted me.

"Suppose I were to spare you that confession? Suppose I were to acknowledge that the object of your desires is not unknown to me? Suppose I were to say, that she returns your affection, and laments not less sincerely than yourself the unhappy vows which separate her from you?"

"Ah! Donna Rodolpha!" I exclaimed, throwing myself upon my knees before her, and pressing her hand to my lips, "you have discovered my secret! What is your decision? Must I despair, or may I reckon upon your favour?"

She withdrew not the hand which I held; but she turned from me, and covered her face with the other.

"How can I refuse it you?" she replied: "Ah! Don Alphonso, I have long perceived to whom your attentions were directed, but till now I perceived not the impression which they made upon my heart. At length, I can no longer hide my weakness either from myself or from you. I yield to the violence of my passion, and own that I adore you! For three long months I stifled my desires; but growing stronger by resistance, I submit to their impetuosity. Pride, fear, and honour, respect for myself, and my engagements to the baron, all are vanquished. I sacrifice them to my love for you, and it still seems to me that I pay too mean a price for your possession."

She paused for an answer.—Judge, my Lorenzo, what must have been my confusion at this discovery. I at once saw all the magnitude of this obstacle, which I had myself raised to my happiness.

---

1 Presumably *Tristán*, another chivalric romance; the baroness may find it especially touching because the love of Tristan and Iseult is adulterous.

The baroness had placed those attentions to her own account, which I had merely paid her for the sake of Agnes: and the strength of her expressions, the looks which accompanied them, and my knowledge of her revengeful disposition, made me tremble for myself and my beloved. I was silent for some minutes. I knew not how to reply to her declaration: I could only resolve to clear up the mistake without delay, and for the present to conceal from her knowledge the name of my mistress. No sooner had she avowed her passion, than the transports which before were evident in my features gave place to consternation and constraint. I dropped her hand, and rose from my knees. The change in my countenance did not escape her observation.

"What means this silence?" said she in a trembling voice: "Where is that joy which you led me to expect?"

"Forgive me, Segnora," I answered, "if what necessity forces from me should seem harsh and ungrateful. To encourage you in an error, which, however it may flatter myself, must prove to you the source of disappointment, would make me appear criminal in every eye. Honour obliges me to inform you, that you have mistaken for the solicitude of love what was only the attention of friendship. The latter sentiment is that which I wished to excite in your bosom: to entertain a warmer, respect for you forbids me, and gratitude for the baron's generous treatment. Perhaps these reasons would not be sufficient to shield me from your attractions, were it not that my affections are already bestowed upon another. You have charms, Segnora, which might captivate the most insensible; no heart unoccupied could resist them. Happy is it for me, that mine is no longer in my possession, or I should have to reproach myself for ever with having violated the laws of hospitality. Recollect yourself, noble lady! recollect what is owed by you to honour, by me to the baron, and replace by esteem and friendship those sentiments which I never can return."

The baroness turned pale at this unexpected and positive declaration: she doubted whether she slept or woke. At length recovering from her surprise, consternation gave place to rage, and the blood rushed back into her cheeks with violence.

"Villain!" she cried; "Monster of deceit! Thus is the avowal of my love received? Is it thus that.... but, no, no! it cannot, it shall not be! Alphonso, behold me at your feet! Be witness of my despair! Look with pity on a woman who loves you with sincere affection! She who possesses your heart, how has she merited such a treasure? What sacrifice has she made to you? What raises her above Rodolpha?"

I endeavoured to lift her from her knees.

"For God's sake, Segnora, restrain these transports; they disgrace yourself and me. Your exclamations may be heard, and your secret divulged to your attendants. I see that my presence only irritates you: permit me to retire."

I prepared to quit the apartment: the baroness caught me suddenly by the arm.

"And who is this happy rival?" said she in a menacing tone; "I will know her name, and *when* I know it.....! She is some one in my power; you entreated my favour, my protection! Let me but find her, let me but know who dares to rob me of your heart, and she shall suffer every torment which jealousy and disappointment can inflict. Who is she? Answer me this moment. Hope not to conceal her from my vengeance! Spies shall be set over you; every step, every look shall be watched; your eyes will discover my rival; I shall know her; and when she is found, tremble, Alphonso, for her and for yourself."

As she uttered these last words, her fury mounted to such a pitch as to stop her powers of respiration. She panted, groaned, and at length fainted away. As she was falling I caught her in my arms, and placed her upon a sopha. Then hastening to the door, I summoned her women to her assistance; I committed her to their care, and seized the opportunity of escaping.

Agitated and confused beyond expression, I bent my steps towards the garden. The benignity with which the baroness had listened to me at first, raised my hopes to the highest pitch: I imagined her to have perceived my attachment for her niece, and to approve of it. Extreme was my disappointment at understanding the true purport of her discourse. I knew not what course to take: the superstition of the parents of Agnes, aided by her aunt's unfortunate passion, seemed to oppose such obstacles to our union as were almost insurmountable.

As I passed by a low parlour, whose windows looked into the garden, through the door which stood half open I observed Agnes seated at a table. She was occupied in drawing, and several unfinished sketches were scattered round her. I entered, still undetermined whether I should acquaint her with the declaration of the baroness.

"Oh! is it only you?" said she, raising her head: "You are no stranger, and I shall continue my occupation without ceremony. Take a chair, and seat yourself by me."

I obeyed, and placed myself near the table. Unconscious what I was doing, and totally occupied by the scene which had just passed, I took up some of the drawings, and cast my eyes over them. One of the subjects struck me from its singularity. It represented the great hall of the castle of Lindenberg. A door conducting to a narrow stair-case stood half open. In the foreground appeared a group of figures, placed in the most grotesque attitudes; terror was expressed upon every countenance. Here was one upon his knees, with his eyes cast up to heaven, and praying most devoutly; there, another was creeping away upon all fours. Some hid their faces in their cloaks, or the laps of their companions; some had concealed themselves beneath a table, on which the remnants of a feast were visible; while others, with gaping mouths and eyes wide-stretched, pointed to a figure supposed to have created this disturbance. It represented a female of more than human stature, clothed in the habit of some religious order. Her face was veiled; on her arm hung a chaplet of beads; her dress was in several places stained with the blood which trickled from a wound upon her bosom. In one hand she held a lamp, in the other a large knife, and she seemed advancing towards the iron gates of the hall.

"What does this mean, Agnes?" said I: "Is this some invention of your own?"

She cast her eyes upon the drawing.

"Oh! no," she replied; "'tis the invention of much wiser heads than mine. But can you possibly have lived at Lindenberg for three whole months without hearing of the bleeding nun?"[1]

"You are the first who ever mentioned the name to me. Pray, who may the lady be?"

"That is more than I can pretend to tell you. All my knowledge of her history comes from an old tradition in this family, which has been handed down from father to son, and is firmly credited throughout the baron's domains. Nay, the baron believes it himself; and as for my aunt, who has a natural turn for the marvellous, she would sooner doubt the veracity of the Bible than of the bleeding nun. Shall I tell you this history?"

I answered, that she would oblige me much by relating it: she resumed her drawing, and then proceeded as follows in a tone of burlesqued gravity:

"It is surprising that in all the chronicles of past times this

---

1 Cf. Johann August Musäus, "Die Entführung" ("The Elopement") from *Die Volksmärchen der Deutschen* (1782-86): see Appendix A.3.

remarkable personage is never once mentioned. Fain would I recount to you her life; but unluckily till after her death she was never known to have existed. Then first did she think it necessary to make some noise in the world, and with that intention she made bold to seize upon the castle of Lindenberg. Having a good taste, she took up her abode in the best room of the house; and once established there, she began to amuse herself by knocking about the tables and chairs in the middle of the night. Perhaps she was a bad sleeper, but this I have never been able to ascertain. According to the tradition, this entertainment commenced about a century ago. It was accompanied with shrieking, howling, groaning, swearing, and many other agreeable noises of the same kind. But though one particular room was more especially honoured with her visits, she did not entirely confine herself to it. She occasionally ventured into the old galleries, paced up and down the spacious halls; or, sometimes stopping at the doors of the chambers, she wept and wailed there to the universal terror of the inhabitants. In these nocturnal excursions she was seen by different people, who all describe her appearance as you behold it here traced by the hand of her unworthy historian."

The singularity of this account insensibly engaged my attention.

"Did she never speak to those who met her?" said I.

"Not she. The specimens indeed which she gave nightly of her talents for conversation, were by no means inviting. Sometimes the castle rung with oaths and execrations: a moment after she repeated her paternoster:[1] now she howled out the most horrible blasphemies, and then chaunted De profundis[2] as orderly as if still in the choir. In short, she seemed a mighty capricious being: but whether she prayed or cursed, whether she was impious or devout, she always contrived to terrify her auditors out of their senses. The castle became scarcely habitable; and its lord was so frightened by these midnight revels, that one fine morning he was found dead in his bed. This success seemed to please the nun mightily, for now she made more noise than ever. But the next baron proved too cunning for her. He made his appearance with a celebrated exorciser in his hand, who feared not to shut himself up for a night in the haunted chamber. There it seems that he had a hard battle with the ghost before she would promise to be quiet. She was obstinate,

---

1 "Our Father" (Latin): the Lord's Prayer (Matthew 6.9-13).
2 "Out of the depths" (Latin): the first words of Psalm 130.

but he was more so; and at length she consented to let the inhabitants of the castle take a good night's rest. For some time after no news was heard of her. But at the end of five years the exorciser died, and then the nun ventured to peep abroad again. However, she was now grown much more tractable and well-behaved. She walked about in silence, and never made her appearance above once in five years. This custom, if you will believe the baron, she still continues. He is fully persuaded, that on the fifth of May of every fifth year, as soon as the clock strikes one, the door of the haunted chamber opens. [Observe, that this room has been shut up for near a century.] Then out walks the ghostly nun with her lamp and dagger: she descends the stair-case of the eastern tower, and crosses the great hall. On that night the porter always leaves the gates of the castle open, out of respect to the apparition: not that this is thought by any means necessary, since she could easily whip through the key-hole if she chose it; but merely out of politeness, and to prevent her from making her exit in a way so derogatory to the dignity of her ghostship."

"And whither does she go on quitting the castle?"

"To heaven, I hope; but if she does, the place certainly is not to her taste, for she always returns after an hour's absence. The lady then retires to her chamber, and is quiet for another five years."

"And you believe this, Agnes?"

"How can you ask such a question? No, no, Alphonso! I have too much reason to lament superstition's influence to be its victim myself. However, I must not avow my incredulity to the baroness: she entertains not a doubt of the truth of this history. As to dame Cunegonda, my governess, she protests that fifteen years ago she saw the spectre with her own eyes. She related to me one evening, how she and several other domestics had been terrified while at supper by the appearance of the bleeding nun, as the ghost is called in the castle: 'tis from her account that I drew this sketch, and you may be certain that Cunegonda was not omitted. There she is! I shall never forget what a passion she was in, and how ugly she looked while she scolded me for having made her picture so like herself!"

Here she pointed to a burlesque figure of an old woman in an attitude of terror.

In spite of the melancholy which oppressed me, I could not help smiling at the playful imagination of Agnes: she had perfectly preserved dame Cunegonda's resemblance, but had so much exaggerated every fault, and rendered every feature so irresistibly laughable, that I could easily conceive the duenna's anger.

"The figure is admirable, my dear Agnes! I knew not that you possessed such talents for the ridiculous."

"Stay a moment," she replied; "I will shew you a figure still more ridiculous than dame Cunegonda's. If it pleases you, you may dispose of it as seems best to yourself."

She rose, and went to a cabinet at some little distance: unlocking a drawer, she took out a small case, which she opened, and presented to me.

"Do you know the resemblance?" said she, smiling.

It was her own.

Transported at the gift, I pressed the portrait to my lips with passion: I threw myself at her feet, and declared my gratitude in the warmest and most affectionate terms. She listened to me with complaisance, and assured me that she shared my sentiments; when suddenly she uttered a loud shriek, disengaged the hand which I held, and flew from the room by a door which opened to the garden. Amazed at this abrupt departure, I rose hastily from my knees. I beheld with confusion the baroness standing near me, glowing with jealousy, and almost choaked with rage. On recovering from her swoon, she had tortured her imagination to discover her concealed rival. No one appeared to deserve her suspicions more than Agnes. She immediately hastened to find her niece, tax her with encouraging my addresses, and assure herself whether her conjectures were well-grounded. Unfortunately she had already seen enough to need no other confirmation. She arrived at the door of the room, at the precise moment when Agnes gave me her portrait. She heard me profess an everlasting attachment to her rival, and saw me kneeling at her feet. She advanced to separate us; we were too much occupied by each other to perceive her approach, and were not aware of it till Agnes beheld her standing by my side.

Rage on the part of Donna Rodolpha, embarrassment on mine, for some time kept us both silent. The lady recovered herself first.

"My suspicions then were just," said she; "the coquetry of my niece has triumphed, and 'tis to her that I am sacrificed. In one respect, however, I am fortunate; I shall not be the only one who laments a disappointed passion. You, too, shall know what it is to love without hope! I daily expect orders for restoring Agnes to her parents. Immediately upon her arrival in Spain, she will take the veil, and place an insuperable barrier to your union. You may spare your supplications." She continued, perceiving me on the point of speaking: "My resolution is fixed and immoveable. Your mistress shall remain a close prisoner in her chamber, till she exchanges this castle for the cloister. Solitude will perhaps recall her to a sense of her duty: but to prevent your opposing that wished event, I must inform you, Don Alphonso, that your presence here is no longer agreeable either to the baron or myself. It was not to talk nonsense to my niece, that your relations sent you to Germany: your business was to travel, and I should be sorry to impede any longer so excellent a design. Farewell, Segnor; remember, that to-morrow morning we meet for the last time."

Having said this, she darted upon me a look of pride, contempt, and malice, and quitted the apartment. I also retired to mine, and consumed the night in planning the means of rescuing Agnes from the power of her tyrannical aunt.

After the positive declaration of its mistress, it was impossible for me to make a longer stay at the castle of Lindenberg. Accordingly, I the next day announced my immediate departure. The baron declared that it gave him sincere pain; and he expressed himself in my favour so warmly, that I endeavoured to win him over to my interest. Scarcely had I mentioned the name of Agnes when he stopped me short, and said, that it was totally out of his power to interfere in the business. I saw that it was in vain to argue; the baroness governed her husband with despotic sway, and I easily perceived that she had prejudiced him against the match. Agnes did not appear. I entreated permission to take leave of her, but my prayer was rejected. I was obliged to depart without seeing her.

At quitting him, the baron shook my hand affectionately, and assured me that, as soon as his niece was gone, I might consider his house as my own.

"Farewell, Don Alphonso!" said the baroness, and stretched out her hand to me.

I took it, and offered to carry it to my lips. She prevented me. Her husband was at the other end of the room, and out of hearing.

"Take care of yourself," she continued; "my love is become hatred, and my wounded pride shall not be unatoned. Go where you will, my vengeance shall follow you!"

She accompanied these words with a look sufficient to make me tremble. I answered not, but hastened to quit the castle.

As my chaise drove out of the court, I looked up to the windows of your sister's chamber: nobody was to be seen there. I threw myself back despondent in my carriage. I was attended by no other servants than a Frenchman, whom I had hired at Strasbourg in Stephano's room, and my little page, whom I before mentioned to you. The fidelity, intelligence, and good temper of Theodore had already made him dear to me; but he now prepared to lay an obligation on me, which made me look upon him as a guardian genius. Scarcely had we proceeded half a mile from the castle, when he rode up to the chaise door.

"Take courage, Segnor!" said he in Spanish, which he had already learnt to speak with fluency and correctness: "While you were with the baron, I watched the moment when dame Cunegonda was below stairs, and mounted into the chamber over that of donna Agnes. I sang, as loud as I could, a little German air, well known to her, hoping that she would recollect my voice. I was not disappointed, for I soon heard her window open. I hastened to let down a string with which I had provided myself. Upon hearing the casement closed again, I drew up the string and, fastened to it, I found this scrap of paper."

He then presented me with a small note, addressed to me. I opened it with impatience. It contained the following words, written in pencil:

"Conceal yourself for the next fortnight in some neighbouring village. My aunt will believe you to have quitted Lindenberg, and I shall be restored to liberty. I will be in the west pavilion at twelve on the night of the thirtieth. Fail not to be there, and we shall have an opportunity of concerting our future plans. Adieu.

"AGNES."

At perusing these lines my transports exceeded all bounds; neither did I set any to the expressions of gratitude which I heaped upon Theodore. In fact, his address and attention merited my warmest praise. You will readily believe that I had not entrusted him with my passion for Agnes; but the arch youth had too much discernment not to discover my secret, and too much discretion not to conceal his knowledge of it. He observed in silence what was going on, nor strove to make himself an agent in the business till my interests required his interference. I equally admired his judgment, his penetration, his address, and his fidelity. This was not the first occasion in which I had found him of infinite use, and I was every day more convinced of his quickness and capacity. During my short stay at Strasbourg, he had applied himself diligently to learning the rudiments of Spanish. He continued to study it, and with so much success, that he spoke it with the same facility as his native language. He passed the greatest part of his time in reading.

He had acquired much information for his age; and united the advantages of a lively countenance and prepossessing figure to an excellent understanding and the very best of hearts. He is now fif-teen. He is still in my service; and, when you see him, I am sure that he will please you. But excuse this digression; I return to the subject which I quitted.

I obeyed the instructions of Agnes. I proceeded to Munich: there I left my chaise under the care of Lucas, my French servant, and then returned on horseback to a small village about four miles distant from the castle of Lindenberg. Upon arriving there, a story was related to the host at whose inn I alighted, which prevented his wondering at my making so long a stay in his house. The old man, fortunately, was credulous and incurious: he believed all I said, and sought to know no more than what I thought proper to tell him. Nobody was with me but Theodore: both were disguised; and as we kept ourselves close, we were not suspected to be other than what we seemed. In this manner the fortnight passed away. During that time I had the pleasing conviction that Agnes was once more at liberty. She passed through the village with dame Cunegonda: she seemed in good health and spirits, and talked to her compan-ion without any appearance of constraint.

"Who are those ladies?" said I to my host as the carriage passed.

"Baron Lindenberg's niece, with her governess," he replied: "she goes regularly every Friday to the convent of St. Catharine, in which she was brought up, and which is situated about a mile from hence."

You may be certain that I waited with impatience for the ensu-ing Friday. I again beheld my lovely mistress. She cast her eyes upon me as she passed the inn door. A blush which overspread her cheek, told me that, in spite of my disguise, I had been recognised. I bowed profoundly. She returned the compliment by a slight incli-nation of the head, as if made to one inferior, and looked another way till the carriage was out of sight.

The long-expected, long wished-for night arrived. It was calm, and the moon was at the full. As soon as the clock struck eleven I hastened to my appointment, determined not to be too late. Theodore had provided a ladder; I ascended the garden wall with-out difficulty. The page followed me, and drew the ladder after us. I posted myself in the west pavilion, and waited impatiently for the approach of Agnes. Every breeze that whispered, every leaf that fell, I believed to be her foot-step, and hastened to meet her. Thus was I obliged to pass a full hour, every minute of which appeared to me an age. The castle bell at length tolled twelve, and scarcely could I believe the night to be no further advanced. Another quarter of an hour elapsed, and I heard the light foot of my mistress approaching the pavilion with precaution. I flew to receive her, and conducted her to a seat. I threw myself at her feet, and was expressing my joy at seeing her, when she thus interrupted me:

"We have no time to lose, Alphonso: the moments are precious; for, though no more a prisoner, Cunegonda watches my every step. An express is arrived from my father; I must depart immediately for Madrid, and 'tis with difficulty that I have obtained a week's delay. The superstition of my parents, supported by the representations of my cruel aunt, leaves me no hope of softening them to compassion. In this dilemma, I have resolved to commit myself to your honour. God grant that you may never give me cause to repent my resolution! Flight is my only resource from the horrors of a convent; and my imprudence must be excused by the urgency of the danger. Now listen to the plan by which I hope to effect my escape.

"We are now at the thirtieth of April. On the fifth day from this the visionary nun is expected to appear. In my last visit to the convent I provided myself with a dress proper for the character. A friend whom I have left there, and to whom I made no scruple to confide my secret, readily consented to supply me with a religious habit. Provide a carriage, and be with it at a little distance from the great gate of the castle. As soon as the clock strikes 'one,' I shall quit my chamber, dressed in the same apparel as the ghost is supposed to wear. Whoever meets me will be too much terrified to oppose my escape: I shall easily reach the door, and throw myself under your protection. Thus far success is certain: but, oh! Alphonso, should you deceive me! Should you despise my imprudence, and reward it with ingratitude, the world will not hold a being more wretched than myself! I feel all the dangers to which I shall be exposed. I feel that I am giving you a right to treat me with levity: but I rely upon your love, upon your honour! The step which I am on the point of taking will incense my relations against me. Should you desert me; should you betray the trust reposed in you, I shall have no friend to punish your insult, or support my cause. On yourself alone rests all my hope; and if your own heart does not plead in my behalf, I am undone for ever!"

The tone in which she pronounced these words was so touching that, in spite of my joy at receiving her promise to follow me, I could not help being affected. I also repined in secret at not having taken the precaution to provide a carriage at the village; in which case, I might have carried off Agnes that very night. Such an attempt was now impracticable; neither carriage nor horses were to be procured nearer than Munich, which was distant from Lindenberg two good days journey. I was therefore obliged to chime in with her plan, which, in truth, seemed well arranged. Her disguise would secure her from being stopped in quitting the castle, and would enable her to step into the carriage at the very gate, without difficulty or losing time.

Agnes reclined her head mournfully upon my shoulder, and, by the light of the moon, I saw tears flowing down her cheek. I strove to dissipate her melancholy, and encouraged her to look forward to the prospect of happiness. I protested in the most solemn terms that her virtue and innocence would be safe in my keeping; and that, till the church had made her my lawful wife, her honour should be held by me as sacred as a sister's. I told her, that my first care should be to find you out, Lorenzo, and reconcile you to our union; and I was continuing to speak in the same strain, when a noise without alarmed me. Suddenly the door of the pavilion was thrown open, and Cunegonda stood before us. She had heard Agnes steal out of her chamber, followed her into the garden, and perceived her entering the pavilion. Favoured by the trees which shaded it, and unperceived by Theodore, who waited at a little distance, she had approached in silence, and overheard our whole conversation.

"Admirable!" cried Cunegonda, in a voice shrill with passion, while Agnes uttered a loud shriek. "By St. Barbara, young lady, you have an excellent invention! You must personate the bleeding nun, truly? What impiety! What incredulity! Marry, I have a good mind to let you pursue your plan. When the real ghost met you, I warrant you would be in a pretty condition! Don Alphonso, you ought to be ashamed of yourself for seducing a young, ignorant creature to leave her family and friends. However, for this time, at least, I shall mar your wicked designs. The noble lady shall be informed of the whole affair, and Agnes must defer playing the spectre till a better opportunity. Farewell, Segnor.—Donna Agnes, let me have the honour of conducting your ghostship back to your apartment."

She approached the sopha on which her trembling pupil was seated, took her by the hand, and prepared to lead her from the pavilion.

I detained her, and strove by entreaties, soothing, promises, and flattery to win her to my party; but, finding all that I could say of no avail, I abandoned the vain attempt.

"Your obstinacy must be its own punishment," said I; "but one resource remains to save Agnes and myself, and I shall not hesitate to employ it."

Terrified at this menace, she again endeavoured to quit the pavilion; but I seized her by the wrist, and detained her forcibly. At the same moment Theodore, who had followed her into the room, closed the door, and prevented her escape. I took the veil of Agnes; I threw it round the duenna's head, who uttered such piercing shrieks that, in spite of our distance from the castle, I dreaded their being heard. At length I succeeded in gagging her so completely, that she could not produce a single sound. Theodore and myself, with some difficulty, next contrived to bind her hands and feet with our handkerchiefs; and I advised Agnes to regain her chamber with all diligence. I promised that no harm should happen to Cunegonda; bade her remember that, on the fifth of May, I should be in waiting at the great gate of the castle, and took of her an affectionate farewell. Trembling and uneasy, she had scarce power enough to signify her consent to my plans, and fled back to her apartment in disorder and confusion.

In the mean while Theodore assisted me in carrying off my antiquated prize. She was hoisted over the wall, placed before me upon my horse, like a portmanteau, and I galloped away with her from the castle of Lindenberg. The unlucky duenna never had made a more disagreeable journey in her life. She was jolted and shaken till she was become little more than an animated mummy; not to mention her fright, when we waded through a small river, through which it was necessary to pass in order to regain the village. Before we reached the inn, I had already determined how to dispose of the troublesome Cunegonda. We entered the street in which the inn stood; and while the page knocked, I waited at a little distance. The landlord opened the door with a lamp in his hand.

"Give me the light," said Theodore, "my master is coming."

He snatched the lamp hastily, and purposely let it fall upon the ground. The landlord returned to the kitchen to re-light the lamp, leaving the door open. I profited by the obscurity, sprang from my horse with Cunegonda in my arms, darted up stairs, reached my chamber unperceived, and, unlocking the door of a spacious closet, stowed her within it, and then turned the key. The landlord and Theodore soon after appeared with lights: the former expressed himself surprised at my returning so late, but asked no impertinent questions. He soon quitted the room, and left me to exult in the success of my undertaking.

I immediately paid a visit to my prisoner. I strove to persuade her submitting with patience to her temporary confinement. My attempt was unsuccessful. Unable to speak or move, she expressed her fury by her looks; and, except at meals, I never dared to unbind her, or release her from the gag. At such times I stood over her with a drawn sword, and protested that, if she uttered a single cry, I would plunge it in her bosom. As soon as she had done eating, the gag was replaced. I was conscious that this proceeding was cruel, and could only be justified by the urgency of circumstances. As to Theodore, he had no scruples upon the subject. Cunegonda's captivity entertained him beyond measure. During his abode in the castle, a continual warfare had been carried on between him and the duenna; and, now that he found his enemy so absolutely in his power, he triumphed without mercy: he seemed to think of nothing but how to find out new means of plaguing her. Sometimes he affected to pity her misfortune, then laughed at, abused, and mimicked her: he played her a thousand tricks, each more provoking than the other; and amused himself by telling her, that her elopement must have occasioned much surprise at the baron's. This was in fact the case. No one, except Agnes, could imagine what was become of dame Cunegonda. Every hole and corner was searched for her: the ponds were dragged, and the woods underwent a thorough examination. Still no dame Cunegonda made her appearance. Agnes kept the secret, and I kept the duenna: the baroness, therefore, remained in total ignorance respecting the old woman's fate, but suspected her to have perished by suicide. Thus passed away five days, during which I had prepared every thing necessary for my enterprise. On quitting Agnes, I had made it my first business to dispatch a peasant with a letter to Lucas, at Munich, ordering him to take care that a coach and four should arrive about ten o'clock on the fifth of May at the village of Rosenwald. He obeyed my instructions punctually; the equipage arrived at the time appointed. As the period of her lady's elopement drew nearer, Cunegonda's rage increased. I verily believe, that spite and passion would have killed her, had I not luckily discovered her prepossession in favour of cherry-brandy. With this favourite liquor she was plentifully supplied, and, Theodore always remaining to guard her, the gag was occasionally removed. The liquor seemed to have a wonderful effect in softening the acrimony of her nature; and her confinement not admitting of any other amusement, she got drunk regularly once a-day, just by way of passing the time.

The fifth of May arrived, a period by me never to be forgotten! Before the clock struck twelve, I betook myself to the scene of action. Theodore followed me on horseback. I concealed the carriage in a spacious cavern of the hill on whose brow the castle was situated. This cavern was of considerable depth, and, among the peasants, was known by the name of Lindenberg Hole. The night was calm and beautiful: the moon-beams fell upon the antient towers of the castle, and shed upon their summits a silver light. All was still around me: nothing was to be heard except the night-breeze sighing among the leaves, the distant barking of village dogs, or the owl who had established herself in a nook of the deserted eastern turret. I heard her melancholy shriek, and looked upwards: she sat upon the ridge of a window, which I recognized to be that of the haunted room. This brought to my remembrance the story of the bleeding nun, and I sighed while I reflected on the influence of superstition, and weakness of human reason. Suddenly I heard a faint chorus steal upon the silence of the night.

"What can occasion that noise, Theodore?"

"A stranger of distinction," replied he, "passed through the village to-day in his way to the castle: he is reported to be the father of Donna Agnes. Doubtless the baron has given an entertainment to celebrate his arrival."

The castle bell announced the hour of midnight. This was the usual signal for the family to retire to bed. Soon after I perceived lights in the castle, moving backwards and forwards in different directions. I conjectured the company to be separating. I could hear the heavy doors grate as they opened with difficulty; and as they closed again, the rotten casements rattled in their frames. The chamber of Agnes was on the other side of the castle. I trembled lest she should have failed in obtaining the key of the haunted room. Through this it was necessary for her to pass, in order to reach the narrow stair-case by which the ghost was supposed to descend into the great hall. Agitated by this apprehension, I kept my eyes constantly fixed upon the window, where I hoped to perceive the friendly glare of a lamp borne by Agnes. I now heard the massy gates unbarred. By the candle in his hand, I distinguished old Conrad, the porter. He set the portal doors wide open, and retired. The lights in the castle gradually disappeared, and at length the whole building was wrapt in darkness.

While I sat upon a broken ridge of the hill, the stillness of the scene inspired me with melancholy ideas not altogether unpleasing. The castle, which stood full in my sight, formed an object equally awful and picturesque. Its ponderous walls, tinged by the moon with solemn brightness; its old and partly ruined towers, lifting themselves into the clouds, and seeming to frown on the plains around them; its lofty battlements, overgrown with ivy; and folding gates, expanding in honour of the visionary inhabitant, made me sensible of a sad and reverential horror. Yet did not these sensations occupy me so fully as to prevent me from witnessing with impatience the slow progress of time. I approached the castle, and ventured to walk round it. A few rays of light still glimmered in the chamber of Agnes. I observed them with joy. I was still gazing upon them, when I perceived a figure draw near the window, and the curtain was carefully closed to conceal the lamp which burned there. Convinced by this observation that Agnes had not abandoned our plan, I returned with a light heart to my former station.

The half-hour struck! The three-quarters struck! My bosom beat high with hope and expectation. At length, the wished-for sound was heard. The bell tolled "one," and the mansion echoed with the noise loud and solemn. I looked up to the casement of the haunted chamber. Scarcely had five minutes elapsed when the expected light appeared. I was now close to the tower. The window was not so far from the ground, but that I fancied I perceived a female figure with a lamp in her hand moving slowly along the apartment. The light soon faded away, and all was again dark and gloomy.

Occasional gleams of brightness darted from the stair-case windows as the lovely ghost passed by them. I traced the light through the hall: it reached the portal, and at length I beheld Agnes pass through the folding gates. She was habited exactly as she had described the spectre. A chaplet of beads hung upon her arm; her head was enveloped in a long white veil; her nun's dress was stained with blood; and she had taken care to provide herself with a lamp and dagger. She advanced towards the spot where I stood. I flew to meet her, and clasped her in my arms.

"Agnes!" said I, while I pressed her to my bosom,

> "Agnes! Agnes! thou art mine!
> Agnes! Agnes! I am thine!
> In my veins while blood shall roll,
> Thou art mine!
> I am thine!
> Thine my body! thine my soul!"

Terrified and breathless, she was unable to speak. She dropp« her lamp and dagger, and sank upon my bosom in silence. I raisea her in my arms, and conveyed her to the carriage. Theodore remained behind in order to release dame Cunegonda. I also charged him with a letter to the baroness, explaining the whole affair, and entreating her good offices in reconciling Don Gaston to my union with his daughter. I discovered to her my real name. I proved to her that my birth and expectations justified my pretending to her niece; and assured her, though it was out of my power to return her love, that I would strive unceasingly to obtain her esteem and friendship.

I stepped into the carriage, where Agnes was already seated. Theodore closed the door, and the postillions drove away. At first I was delighted with the rapidity of our progress; but as soon as we were in no danger of pursuit, I called to the drivers, and bade them moderate their pace. They strove in vain to obey me; the horses refused to answer the rein, and continued to rush on with astonishing swiftness. The postillions redoubled their efforts to stop them; but, by kicking and plunging, the beasts soon released themselves from this restraint. Uttering a loud shriek, the drivers were hurled upon the ground. Immediately thick clouds obscured the sky: the winds howled around us, the lightning flashed, and the thunder roared tremendously. Never did I behold so frightful a tempest! Terrified by the jar of contending elements, the horses seemed every moment to increase their speed. Nothing could interrupt their career; they dragged the carriage through hedges and ditches, dashed down the most dangerous precipices, and seemed to vie in swiftness with the rapidity of the winds.

All this while my companion lay motionless in my arms. Truly alarmed by the magnitude of the danger, I was in vain attempting to recall her to her senses, when a loud crash announced that a stop was put to our progress in the most disagreeable manner. The carriage was shattered to pieces. In falling, I struck my temple against a flint. The pain of the wound, the violence of the shock, and apprehension for the safety of Agnes, combined to overpower me so completely, that my senses forsook me, and I lay without animation on the ground.

I probably remained for some time in this situation, since, when I opened my eyes, it was broad day-light. Several peasants were standing round me, and seemed disputing whether my recovery was possible. I spoke German tolerably well. As soon as I could utter an articulate sound, I enquired after Agnes. What was my surprise and distress, when assured by the peasants that nobody had been seen answering the description which I gave of her! They told me, that in going to their daily labour they had been alarmed by observing the fragments of my carriage, and by hearing the groans of an horse, the only one of the four which remained alive: the other three lay dead by my side. Nobody was near me when they came up, and much time had been lost before they succeeded in recovering me. Uneasy beyond expression respecting the fate of my companion, I besought the peasants to disperse themselves in search of her. I described her dress, and promised immense rewards to whoever brought me any intelligence. As for myself, it was impossible for me to join in the pursuit: I had broken two of my ribs in the fall; my arm being dislocated hung useless by my side; and my left leg was shattered so terribly, that I never expected to recover its use.

The peasants complied with my request; all left me except four, who made a litter of boughs, and prepared to convey me to the neighbouring town. I enquired its name: it proved to be Ratisbon, and I could scarcely persuade myself that I had travelled to such a distance in a single night. I told the countrymen, that at one o'clock that morning I had passed through the village of Rosen-wald. They shook their heads wistfully, and made signs to each other that I must certainly be delirious. I was conveyed to a decent inn, and immediately put to bed. A physician was sent for, who set my arm with success: he then examined my other hurts, and told me that I need be under no apprehension of the consequences of any of them, but ordered me to keep myself quiet, and be prepared for a tedious and painful cure. I answered him, that if he hoped to keep me quiet, he must first endeavour to procure me some news of a lady who had quitted Rosenwald in my company the night before, and had been with me at the moment when the coach broke down. He smiled, and only replied by advising me to make myself easy, for that all proper care should be taken of me. As he quitted me, the hostess met him at the door of the room.

"The gentleman is not quite in his right senses," I heard him say to her in a low voice; "'tis the natural consequence of his fall, but that will soon be over."

One after another the peasants returned to the inn, and informed me that no traces had been discovered of my unfortunate mistress. Uneasiness now became despair. I entreated them to renew their search in the most urgent terms, doubling the promises which I had already made them. My wild and frantic manner confirmed the by-standers in the idea of my being delirious. No signs of the lady having appeared, they believed her to be a creature fabricated by my over-heated brain, and paid no attention to my entreaties. However, the hostess assured me, that a fresh enquiry should be made; but I found afterwards that her promise was only given to quiet me. No further steps were taken in the business.

Though my baggage was left at Munich under the care of my French servant, having prepared myself for a long journey, my purse was amply furnished: besides, my equipage proved me to be of distinction, and in consequence all possible attention was paid me at the inn. The day passed away: still no news arrived of Agnes. The anxiety of fear now gave place to despondency. I ceased to rave about her, and was plunged in the depth of melancholy reflections. Perceiving me to be silent and tranquil, my attendants believed my delirium to have abated, and that my malady had taken a favourable turn. According to the physician's order, I swallowed a composing medicine; and as soon as the night shut in, my attendants withdrew, and left me to repose.

That repose I wooed in vain. The agitation of my bosom chased away sleep. Restless in my mind, in spite of the fatigue of my body, I continued to toss about from side to side, till the clock in a neighbouring steeple struck "one." As I listened to the mournful hollow sound, and heard it die away in the wind, I felt a sudden chillness spread itself over my body. I shuddered without knowing wherefore; cold dews poured down my forehead, and my hair stood bristling with alarm. Suddenly I heard slow and heavy steps ascending the stair-case. By an involuntary movement I started up in my bed, and drew back the curtain. A single rush-light, which glimmered upon the hearth, shed a faint gleam through the apartment, which was hung with tapestry. The door was thrown open with violence. A figure entered, and drew near my bed with solemn measured steps. With trembling apprehension I examined this midnight visitor. God Almighty! it was the bleeding nun! It was my lost companion! Her face was still veiled, but she no longer held her lamp and dagger. She lifted up her veil slowly. What a sight presented itself to my startled eyes! I beheld before me an animated corse. Her countenance was long and haggard; her cheeks and lips were bloodless; the paleness of death was spread over her features; and her eye-balls, fixed stedfastly upon me, were lustreless and hollow.

I gazed upon the spectre with horror too great to be described. My blood was frozen in my veins. I would have called for aid, but the sound expired ere it could pass my lips. My nerves were bound up in impotence, and I remained in the same attitude inanimate as a statue.

The visionary nun looked upon me for some minutes in silence: there was something petrifying in her regard. At length, in a low sepulchral voice, she pronounced the following words:

> "Raymond! Raymond! Thou art mine!
> Raymond! Raymond! I am thine!
> In thy veins while blood shall roll,
> I am thine!
> Thou art mine!
> Mine thy body! Mine thy soul!"——

Breathless with fear, I listened while she repeated my own expressions. The apparition seated herself opposite to me at the foot of the bed, and was silent. Her eyes were fixed earnestly upon mine: they seemed endowed with the property of the rattlesnake's, for I strove in vain to look off her. My eyes were fascinated, and I had not the power of withdrawing them from the spectre's.

In this attitude she remained for a whole long hour without speaking or moving; nor was I able to do either. At length the clock struck two. The apparition rose from her seat, and approached the side of the bed. She grasped with her icy fingers my hand, which hung lifeless upon the coverture, and, pressing her cold lips to mine, again repeated,

> "Raymond! Raymond! Thou art mine!
> Raymond! Raymond! I am thine!" &c.—

She then dropped my hand, quitted the chamber with slow steps, and the door closed after her. Till that moment the faculties of my body had been all suspended; those of my mind had alone been waking. The charm now ceased to operate; the blood which had been frozen in my veins rushed back to my heart with violence; I uttered a deep groan, and sank lifeless upon my pillow.

The adjoining room was only separated from mine by a thin partition; it was occupied by the host and his wife: the former was roused by my groan, and immediately hastened to my chamber; the hostess soon followed him. With some difficulty they succeeded in restoring me to my senses, and immediately sent for the physician, who arrived in all diligence. He declared my fever to be very much increased, and that, if I continued to suffer such violent agitation, he would not take upon him to ensure my life. Some medicines which he gave me, in some degree tranquillized my spirits. I fell into a sort of slumber towards day-break, but fearful dreams prevented me from deriving any benefit from my repose. Agnes and the bleeding nun presented themselves by turns to my fancy, and combined to harass and torment me. I awoke fatigued and unrefreshed. My fever seemed rather augmented than diminished; the agitation of my mind impeded my fractured bones from knitting: I had frequent fainting fits, and during the whole day the physician judged it expedient not to quit me for two hours together.

The singularity of my adventure made me determine to conceal it from every one, since I could not expect that a circumstance so strange should gain credit. I was very uneasy about Agnes. I knew not what she would think at not finding me at the rendezvous, and dreaded her entertaining suspicions of my fidelity. However, I depended upon Theodore's discretion, and trusted that my letter to the baroness would convince her of the rectitude of my intentions. These considerations somewhat lightened my inquietude upon her account; but the impression left upon my mind by my nocturnal visitor, grew stronger with every succeeding moment. The night drew near; I dreaded its arrival; yet I strove to persuade myself that the ghost would appear no more, and at all events I desired that a servant might sit up in my chamber.

The fatigue of my body, from not having slept on the former night, co-operating with the strong opiates administered to me in profusion, at length procured me that repose of which I was so much in need. I sank into a profound and tranquil slumber, and had already slept for some hours, when the neighbouring clock roused me by striking "one." Its sound brought with it to my memory all the horrors of the night before. The same cold shivering seized me. I started up in my bed, and perceived the servant fast asleep in an arm-chair near me. I called him by his name: he made no answer. I shook him forcibly by the arm, and strove in vain to wake him: he was perfectly insensible to my efforts. I now heard the heavy steps ascending the stair-case; the door was thrown open, and again the bleeding nun stood before me. Once more my limbs were chained in second infancy: once more I heard those fatal words repeated,

> "Raymond! Raymond! Thou art mine!
> Raymond! Raymond! I am thine!" &c.—

The scene which had shocked me so sensibly on the former night, was again presented. The spectre again pressed her lips to mine, again touched me with her rotting fingers, and, as on her first appearance, quitted the chamber as soon as the clock told "two."

Every night was this repeated. Far from growing accustomed to the ghost, every succeeding visit inspired me with greater horror. Her idea pursued me continually, and I became the prey of habitual melancholy. The constant agitation of my mind naturally retarded the re-establishment of my health. Several months elapsed before I was able to quit my bed; and when, at length, I was moved to a sopha, I was so faint, spiritless, and emaciated, that I could not cross the room without assistance. The looks of my attendants sufficiently denoted the little hope which they entertained of my recovery. The profound sadness which oppressed me without remission, made the physician consider me to be an hypochondriac. The cause of my distress I carefully concealed in my own bosom, for I knew that no one could give me relief. The ghost was not even visible to any eye but mine. I had frequently caused attendants to sit up in my room; but the moment that the clock struck "one," irresistible slumber seized them, nor left them till the departure of the ghost.

You may be surprised that during this time I made no enquiries after your sister. Theodore, who with difficulty had discovered my abode, had quieted my apprehensions for her safety; at the same time he convinced me, that all attempts to release her from captivity must be fruitless, till I should be in a condition to return to Spain. The particulars of her adventure, which I shall now relate to you, were partly communicated to me by Theodore, and partly by Agnes herself.

On the fatal night when her elopement was to have taken place, accident had not permitted her to quit her chamber at the appointed time. At length she ventured into the haunted room, descended the stair-case leading into the hall, found the gates open as she expected, and left the castle unobserved. What was her surprise at not finding me ready to receive her! She examined the cavern, ranged through every alley of the neighbouring wood, and passed two full hours in this fruitless enquiry. She could discover no traces either of me or of the carriage. Alarmed and disappointed, her only resource was to return to the castle before the baroness missed her; but here she found herself in a fresh embarrassment. The bell had already tolled "two," the ghostly hour was past, and the careful porter had locked the folding gates. After much irresolution, she ventured to knock softly. Luckily for her, Conrad was still awake: he heard the noise, and rose, murmuring at being called up a second time. No sooner had he opened one of the doors, and beheld the supposed apparition waiting there for admittance, than he uttered a loud cry, and sunk upon his knees. Agnes profited by his terror: she glided by him, flew to her own apartment, and, having thrown off her spectre's trappings, retired to bed, endeavouring in vain to account for my disappearing.

In the mean while, Theodore having seen my carriage drive off with the false Agnes, returned joyfully to the village. The next morning he released Cunegonda from her confinement, and accompanied her to the castle. There he found the baron, his lady, and Don Gaston, disputing together upon the porter's relation. All of them agreed in believing the existence of spectres; but the latter contended, that for a ghost to knock for admittance was a proceeding till then unwitnessed, and totally incompatible with the immaterial nature of a spirit. They were still discussing the subject, when the page appeared with Cunegonda, and cleared up the mystery. On hearing his deposition, it was agreed unanimously, that the Agnes whom Theodore had seen step into my carriage must have been the bleeding nun, and that the ghost who had terrified Conrad was no other than Don Gaston's daughter.

The first surprise which this discovery occasioned being over, the baroness resolved to make it of use in persuading her niece to take the veil. Fearing lest so advantageous an establishment for his daughter should induce Don Gaston to renounce his resolution, she suppressed my letter, and continued to represent me as a needy unknown adventurer. A childish vanity had led me to conceal my real name even from my mistress; I wished to be loved for myself, not for being the son and heir of the marquis de las Cisternas. The consequence was, that my rank was known to no one in the castle except the baroness, and she took good care to confine the knowledge to her own breast. Don Gaston having approved his sister's design, Agnes was summoned to appear before them. She was taxed with having meditated an elopement, obliged to make a full confession, and was amazed at the gentleness with which it was received: but what was her affliction, when informed that the failure of her project must be attributed to me! Cunegonda, tutored by the baroness, told her, that when I released her I had desired her to inform her lady that our connexion was at an end, that the whole affair was occasioned by a false report, and that it by no means suited my circumstances to marry a woman without fortune or expectations.

To this account my sudden disappearing gave but too great an air of probability. Theodore, who could have contradicted the story, by Donna Rodolpha's order was kept out of her sight. What proved a still greater confirmation of my being an impostor, was the arrival of a letter from yourself, declaring that you had no sort of acquaintance with Alphonso d'Alvarada. These seeming proofs of my perfidy, aided by the artful insinuations of her aunt, by Cunegonda's flattery, and her father's threats and anger, entirely conquered your sister's repugnance to a convent. Incensed at my behaviour, and disgusted with the world in general, she consented to receive the veil. She passed another month at the castle of Lindenberg, during which my non-appearance confirmed her in her resolution, and then accompanied Don Gaston into Spain. Theodore was now set at liberty. He hastened to Munich, where I had promised to let him hear from me; but finding from Lucas that I never arrived there, he pursued his search with indefatigable perseverance, and at length succeeded in rejoining me at Ratisbon.

So much was I altered, that scarcely could he recollect my features: the distress visible upon his, sufficiently testified how lively was the interest which he felt for me. The society of this amiable boy, whom I had always considered rather as a companion than a servant, was now my only comfort. His conversation was gay, yet sensible, and his observations shrewd and entertaining. He had picked up much more knowledge than is usual at his age; but what rendered him most agreeable to me, was his having a delightful voice, and some skill in music. He had also acquired some taste in poetry, and even ventured sometimes to write verses himself. He occasionally composed little ballads in Spanish. His compositions were but indifferent, I must confess, yet they were pleasing to me from their novelty; and hearing him sing them to his guitar was the only amusement which I was capable of receiving. Theodore perceived well enough that something preyed upon my mind; but as I concealed the cause of my grief even from him, respect would not permit him to pry into my secrets.

One evening I was lying upon my sopha, plunged in reflections very far from agreeable: Theodore amused himself by observing from the window a battle between two postillions, who were quarrelling in the inn-yard.

"Ha! ha!" cried he, suddenly, "yonder is the Great Mogul."[1]

---

1   The Muslim Emperor of India.

"Who?" said I.

"Only a man who made me a strange speech at Munich."

"What was the purport of it?"

"Now you put me in mind of it, Segnor, it was a kind of message to you, but truly it was not worth delivering. I believe the fellow to be mad, for my part. When I came to Munich in search of you, I found him living at 'the King of the Romans,' and the host gave me an odd account of him. By his accent he is supposed to be a foreigner, but of what country nobody can tell. He seemed to have no acquaintance in the town, spoke very seldom, and never was seen to smile. He had neither servants nor baggage; but his purse seemed well furnished, and he did much good in the town. Some supposed him to be an Arabian astrologer, others to be a travelling mountebank, and many declared that he was Doctor Faustus,[1] whom the devil had sent back to Germany. The landlord, however, told me, that he had the best reasons to believe him to be the Great Mogul incognito."

"But the strange speech, Theodore——"

"True, I had almost forgotten the speech: indeed, for that matter, it would not have been a great loss if I had forgotten it altogether. You are to know, Segnor, that while I was enquiring about you of the landlord, this stranger passed by. He stopped, and looked at me earnestly—'Youth,' said he, in a solemn voice, 'he whom you seek, has found that which he would fain lose. My hand alone can dry up the blood. Bid your master wish for me when the clock strikes "one."'"

"How?" cried I, starting from my sopha. [The words which Theodore had repeated, seemed to imply the stranger's knowledge of my secret.] "Fly to him, my boy! Entreat him to grant me one moment's conversation."

Theodore was surprised at the vivacity of my manner: however, he asked no questions, but hastened to obey me. I waited his return impatiently. But a short space of time had elapsed, when he again appeared, and ushered the expected guest into my chamber. He was a man of majestic presence; his countenance was strongly

---

1   There was a sixteenth-century magician (possibly two) named Faust. The legends that accumulated around him after his death in 1540 were collected in Johann Spiess's *Faustbuch* (1587). Lewis may have known the story from *Dr. Faustus* (1604, 1616) by Christopher Marlowe or *Faust, ein Fragment* (1790) by Goethe. Lewis had met Goethe in Weimar in 1792.

marked, and his eyes were large, black, and sparkling: yet there was a something in his look, which, the moment that I saw him, inspired me with a secret awe, not to say horror. He was dressed plainly, his hair was unpowdered, and a band of black velvet which encircled his forehead, spread over his features an additional gloom. His countenance wore the marks of profound melancholy, his step was slow, and his manner grave, stately, and solemn.[1]

He saluted me with politeness; and having replied to the usual compliments of introduction, he motioned to Theodore to quit the chamber. The page instantly withdrew.

"I know your business," said he, without giving me time to speak. "I have the power of releasing you from your nightly visitor; but this cannot be done before Sunday. On the hour when the sabbath morning breaks, spirits of darkness have least influence over mortals. After Saturday the nun shall visit you no more."

"May I not enquire," said I, "by what means you are in possession of a secret, which I have carefully concealed from the knowledge of every one?"

"How can I be ignorant of your distresses, when their cause at this moment stands beside you?"

I started. The stranger continued.

"Though to you only visible for one hour in the twenty-four, neither day nor night does she ever quit you; nor will she ever quit you till you have granted her request."

"And what is that request?"

"That she must herself explain: it lies not in my knowledge. Wait with patience for the night of Saturday: all shall be then cleared up."

I dared not press him further. He soon after changed the conversation, and talked of various matters. He named people who had ceased to exist for many centuries, and yet with whom he appeared to have been personally acquainted. I could not mention a country, however distant, which he had not visited, nor could I sufficiently admire the extent and variety of his information. I remarked to him, that having travelled, seen and known so much, must have given him infinite pleasure. He shook his head mournfully.

"No one," he replied, "is adequate to comprehending the misery of my lot! Fate obliges me to be constantly in movement; I am

---

1 Cf. the description of the Armenian in Schiller, *The Ghost-Seer* 8.

not permitted to pass more than a fortnight in the same place. I have no friend in the world, and, from the restlessness of my destiny, I never can acquire one. Fain would I lay down my miserable life, for I envy those who enjoy the quiet of the grave: but death eludes me, and flies from my embrace. In vain do I throw myself in the way of danger. I plunge into the ocean; the waves throw me back with abhorrence upon the shore: I rush into fire; the flames recoil at my approach: I oppose myself to the fury of banditti; their swords become blunted, and break against my breast. The hungry tiger shudders at my approach, and the alligator flies from a monster more horrible than itself.[1] God has set his seal upon me, and all his creatures respect this fatal mark."

He put his hand to the velvet, which was bound round his forehead. There was in his eyes an expression of fury, despair, and malevolence, that struck horror to my very soul. An involuntary convulsion made me shudder. The stranger perceived it.

"Such is the curse imposed on me," he continued: "I am doomed to inspire all who look on me with terror and detestation. You already feel the influence of the charm, and with every succeeding moment will feel it more. I will not add to your sufferings by my presence. Farewell till Saturday. As soon as the clock strikes twelve, expect me at your chamber-door."

Having said this he departed, leaving me in astonishment at the mysterious turn of his manner and conversation. His assurances that I should soon be relieved from the apparition's visits, produced a good effect upon my constitution. Theodore, whom I rather treated as an adopted child than a domestic, was surprised at his return to observe the amendment in my looks. He congratulated me on this symptom of returning health, and declared himself delighted at my having received so much benefit from my conference with the Great Mogul. Upon enquiry I found that the stranger had already passed eight days in Ratisbon. According to his own account, therefore, he was only to remain there six days longer. Saturday was still at the distance of three. Oh! with what impatience did I expect its arrival! In the interim, the bleeding nun continued her nocturnal visits; but hoping soon to be released from them altogether, the effects which they produced on me became less violent than before.

The wished-for night arrived. To avoid creating suspicion I

---

1 See Appendix A.4.

retired to bed at my usual hour. But as soon as my attendants had left me, I dressed myself again, and prepared for the stranger's reception. He entered my room upon the turn of midnight. A small chest was in his hand, which he placed near the stove. He saluted me without speaking; I returned the compliment, observing an equal silence. He then opened his chest. The first thing which he produced was a small wooden crucifix: he sunk upon his knees, gazed upon it mournfully, and cast his eyes towards heaven. He seemed to be praying devoutly. At length he bowed his head respectfully, kissed the crucifix thrice, and quitted his kneeling posture. He next drew from the chest a covered goblet: with the liquor which it contained, and which appeared to be blood, he sprinkled the floor; and then dipping in it one end of the crucifix, he described a circle in the middle of the room. Round about this he placed various reliques, sculls, thigh-bones, &c. I observed, that he disposed them all in the forms of crosses. Lastly, he took out a large bible, and beckoned me to follow him into the circle. I obeyed.

"Be cautious not to utter a syllable!" whispered the stranger: "step not out of the circle, and as you love yourself, dare not to look upon my face!"

Holding the crucifix in one hand, the bible in the other, he seemed to read with profound attention. The clock struck one! As usual I heard the spectre's steps upon the stair-case: but I was not seized with the accustomed shivering. I waited her approach with confidence. She entered the room, drew near the circle, and stopped. The stranger muttered some words, to me unintelligible. Then raising his head from the book, and extending the crucifix towards the ghost, he pronounced, in a voice distinct and solemn,

"Beatrice! Beatrice! Beatrice!"

"What wouldst thou?" replied the apparition in a hollow faltering tone.

"What disturbs thy sleep? Why dost thou afflict and torture this youth? How can rest be restored to thy unquiet spirit?"

"I dare not tell! I must not tell! Fain would I repose in my grave, but stern commands force me to prolong my punishment!"

"Knowest thou this blood? Knowest thou in whose veins it flowed? Beatrice! Beatrice! In his name, I charge thee to answer me."

"I dare not disobey my taskers."

"Darest thou disobey me?"

He spoke in a commanding tone, and drew the sable band from his forehead. In spite of his injunctions to the contrary, curiosity would not suffer me to keep my eyes off his face: I raised them, and beheld a burning cross impressed upon his brow. For the horror with which this object inspired me I cannot account, but I never felt its equal. My senses left me for some moments: a mysterious dread overcame my courage; and had not the exorciser caught my hand, I should have fallen out of the circle.

When I recovered myself, I perceived that the burning cross had produced an effect no less violent upon the spectre. Her countenance expressed reverence and horror, and her visionary limbs were shaken by fear.

"Yes!" she said at length, "I tremble at that mark! I respect it! I obey you! Know then, that my bones lie still unburied: they rot in the obscurity of Lindenberg Hole. None but this youth has the right of consigning them to the grave. His own lips have made over to me his body and his soul: never will I give back his promise, never shall he know a night devoid of terror, unless he engages to collect my mouldering bones, and deposit them in the family vault of his Andalusian castle. Then let thirty masses be said for the repose of my spirit, and I trouble this world no more. Now let me depart. Those flames are scorching!"

He let the hand drop slowly which held the crucifix, and which till then he had pointed towards her. The apparition bowed her head, and her form melted into air. The exorciser led me out of the circle. He replaced the bible, &c. in the chest, and then addressed himself to me, who stood near him speechless from astonishment.

"Don Raymond, you have heard the conditions on which repose is promised you. Be it your business to fulfil them to the letter. For me, nothing more remains than to clear up the darkness still spread over the spectre's history, and inform you, that when living Beatrice bore the name of las Cisternas. She was the great aunt of your grandfather. In quality of your relation, her ashes demand respect from you, though the enormity of her crimes must excite your abhorrence. The nature of those crimes no one is more capable of explaining to you than myself. I was personally acquainted with the holy man who proscribed her nocturnal riots in the castle of Lindenberg, and I hold this narrative from his own lips.

"Beatrice de las Cisternas took the veil at an early age, not by her own choice, but at the express command of her parents. She was then too young to regret the pleasures of which her profession deprived her: but no sooner did her warm and voluptuous character begin to be developed, than she abandoned herself freely to the impulse of her passions, and seized the first opportunity to procure their gratification. This opportunity was at length presented, after many obstacles which only added new force to her desires. She contrived to elope from the convent, and fled to Germany with the baron Lindenberg. She lived at his castle several months as his avowed concubine. All Bavaria was scandalized by her impudent and abandoned conduct. Her feasts vied in luxury with Cleopatra's, and Lindenberg became the theatre of the most unbridled debauchery. Not satisfied with displaying the incontinence of a prostitute, she professed herself an atheist: she took every opportunity to scoff at her monastic vows, and loaded with ridicule the most sacred ceremonies of religion.

"Possessed of a character so depraved, she did not long confine her affections to one object. Soon after her arrival at the castle, the baron's younger brother attracted her notice by his strong-marked features, gigantic stature, and herculean limbs. She was not of an humour to keep her inclinations long unknown: but she found in Otto von Lindenberg her equal in depravity. He returned her passion just sufficiently to increase it; and when he had worked it up to the desired pitch, he fixed the price of his love at his brother's murder. The wretch consented to this horrible agreement. A night was pitched upon for perpetrating the deed. Otto, who resided on a small estate a few miles distant from the castle, promised that, at one in the morning, he would be waiting for her at Lindenberg-hole; that he would bring with him a party of chosen friends, by whose aid he doubted not being able to make himself master of the castle; and that his next step should be the uniting her hand to his. It was this last promise which over-ruled every scruple of Beatrice, since, in spite of his affection for her, the baron had declared positively, that he never would make her his wife.

"The fatal night arrived. The baron slept in the arms of his perfidious mistress, when the castle bell struck 'one.' Immediately Beatrice drew a dagger from underneath her pillow, and plunged it in her paramour's heart. The baron uttered a single dreadful groan, and expired. The murderess quitted her bed hastily, took a lamp in one hand, in the other the bloody dagger, and bent her course towards the cavern. The porter dared not to refuse opening the gates to one more dreaded in the castle than its master. Beatrice reached Lindenberg-hole unopposed, where, according to promise, she found Otto waiting for her. He received, and listened to her narrative with transport: but ere she had time to ask why he came unaccompanied, he convinced her that he wished for no witnesses to their interview. Anxious to conceal his share in the murder, and to free himself from a woman whose violent and atrocious character made him tremble with reason for his own safety, he had resolved on the destruction of his wretched agent. Rushing upon her suddenly, he wrested the dagger from her hand. He plunged it, still reeking with his brother's blood, in her bosom, and put an end to her existence by repeated blows.

"Otto now succeeded to the barony of Lindenberg. The murder was attributed solely to the fugitive nun, and no one suspected him to have persuaded her to the action. But though his crime was unpunished by man, God's justice permitted him not to enjoy in peace his blood-stained honours. Her bones lying still unburied in the cave, the restless soul of Beatrice continued to inhabit the castle. Dressed in her religious habit, in memory of her vows broken to heaven, furnished with the dagger which had drank the blood of her paramour, and holding the lamp which had guided her flying steps, every night did she stand before the bed of Otto. The most dreadful confusion reigned through the castle. The vaulted chambers resounded with shrieks and groans; and the spectre, as she ranged along the antique galleries, uttered an incoherent mixture of prayers and blasphemies. Otto was unable to withstand the shock which he felt at this fearful vision: its horrors increased with every succeeding appearance. His alarm at length became so insupportable, that his heart burst, and one morning he was found in his bed totally deprived of warmth and animation. His death did not put an end to the nocturnal riots. The bones of Beatrice continued to lie unburied, and her ghost continued to haunt the castle.

"The domains of Lindenberg now fell to a distant relation. But terrified by the accounts given him of the bleeding nun [so was the spectre called by the multitude] the new baron called to his assistance a celebrated exorciser. This holy man succeeded in obliging her to temporary repose: but though she discovered to him her history, he was not permitted to reveal it to others, or cause her skeleton to be removed to hallowed ground. That office was reserved for you; and till your coming her ghost was doomed to wander about the castle, and lament the crime which she had there committed. However, the exorciser obliged her to silence during his life-time. So long as he existed, the haunted chamber was shut up, and the spectre was invisible. At his death, which happened in five years after, she again appeared, but only once on every fifth year, on the same day and at the same hour when she plunged her knife in the heart of her sleeping lover: she then visited the cavern which held her mouldering skeleton, returned to the castle as soon as the clock struck two, and was seen no more till the next five years had elapsed.

"She was doomed to suffer during the space of a century. That period is past. Nothing now remains but to consign to the grave the ashes of Beatrice. I have been the means of releasing you from your visionary tormentor; and amidst all the sorrows which oppress me, to think that I have been of use to you, is some consolation. Youth, farewell! May the ghost of your relation enjoy that rest in the tomb, which the Almighty's vengeance has denied to me for ever!"

Here the stranger prepared to quit the apartment.

"Stay yet one moment!" said I; "you have satisfied my curiosity with regard to the spectre, but you leave me a prey to yet greater respecting yourself. Deign to inform me to whom I am under such real obligations. You mention circumstances long past, and persons long dead: you were personally acquainted with the exorciser, who, by your own account, has been deceased near a century. How am I to account for this? What means that burning cross upon your forehead, and why did the sight of it strike such horror to my soul?"

On these points he for some time refused to satisfy me. At length, overcome by my entreaties, he consented to clear up the whole, on condition that I would defer his explanation till the next day. With this request I was obliged to comply, and he left me. In the morning my first care was to enquire after the mysterious stranger. Conceive my disappointment, when informed that he had already quitted Ratisbon. I dispatched messengers in pursuit of him, but in vain. No traces of the fugitive were discovered. Since that moment I never have heard any more of him, and 'tis most probable that I never shall.

[Lorenzo here interrupted his friend's narrative:

"How!" said he, "you have never discovered who he was, or even formed a guess?"

"Pardon me," replied the marquis: "when I related this adventure to my uncle, the cardinal-duke, he told me, that he had no doubt of this singular man's being the celebrated character known universally by the name of *the wandering Jew*.[1] His not being per-

---

1 The story of the Wandering Jew, who insulted Christ on his way to Calvary and was consequently condemned to wander the earth until the Second Coming, has been traced to John 21.20-22. It is first elaborated in *Flores Historiarum* (1228), by Roger of Wendover. Lewis probably knew

mitted to pass more than fourteen days on the same spot, the burning cross impressed upon his forehead, the effect which it produced upon the beholders, and many other circumstances, gave this supposition the colour of truth. The cardinal is fully persuaded of it; and for my own part I am inclined to adopt the only solution which offers itself to this riddle. I return to the narrative from which I have digressed."]

From this period I recovered my health so rapidly as to astonish my physicians. The bleeding nun appeared no more, and I was soon able to set out for Lindenberg. The baron received me with open arms. I confided to him the sequel of my adventure; and he was not a little pleased to find that his mansion would be no longer troubled with the phantom's quinquennial visits. I was sorry to perceive, that absence had not weakened Donna Rodolpha's imprudent passion. In a private conversation which I had with her during my short stay at the castle, she renewed her attempts to persuade me to return her affection. Regarding her as the primary cause of all my sufferings, I entertained for her no other sentiment than disgust. The skeleton of Beatrice was found in the place which she had mentioned. This being all that I sought at Lindenberg, I hastened to quit the baron's domains, equally anxious to perform the obsequies of the murdered nun, and escape the importunity of a woman whom I detested. I departed, followed by Donna Rodolpha's menaces, that my contempt should not be long unpunished.

I now bent my course towards Spain with all diligence. Lucas with my baggage had joined me during my abode at Lindenberg. I arrived in my native country without any accident, and immediately proceeded to my father's castle in Andalusia. The remains of Beatrice were deposited in the family vault, all due ceremonies performed, and the number of masses said which she had required. Nothing now hindered me from employing all my endeavours to discover the retreat of Agnes. The baroness had assured me, that her niece had already taken the veil: this intelligence I suspected to have been forged by jealousy, and hoped to find my mistress still at liberty to accept my hand. I enquired after her family; I found that before her daughter could reach Madrid, Donna Inesilla was no more: you, my dear Lorenzo, were said to be abroad, but where I

it from Christian Friedrich Daniel Schubart, "Der ewige Jude" (1784; Appendix A.4), from which he borrows some details. See also Appendix E, note to 169.6.

could not discover: your father was in a distant province, on a visit to the duke de Medina; and as to Agnes, no one could or would inform me what was become of her. Theodore, according to promise, had returned to Strasbourg, where he found his grandfather dead, and Marguerite in possession of his fortune. All her persuasions to remain with her were fruitless: he quitted her a second time, and followed me to Madrid. He exerted himself to the utmost in forwarding my search: but our united endeavours were unattended by success. The retreat which concealed Agnes remained an impenetrable mystery, and I began to abandon all hopes of recovering her.

About eight months ago I was returning to my hotel in a melancholy humour, having passed the evening at the play-house. The night was dark, and I was unaccompanied. Plunged in reflections which were far from being agreeable, I perceived not that three men had followed me from the theatre, till, on turning into an unfrequented street, they all attacked me at the same time with the utmost fury. I sprang back a few paces, drew my sword, and threw my cloak over my left arm. The obscurity of the night was in my favour. For the most part the blows of the assassins, being aimed at random, failed to touch me. I at length was fortunate enough to lay one of my adversaries at my feet: but before this I had already received so many wounds, and was so warmly pressed, that my destruction would have been inevitable, had not the clashing of swords called a cavalier to my assistance. He ran towards me with his sword drawn: several domestics followed him with torches. His arrival made the combat equal: yet would not the bravoes abandon their design, till the servants were on the point of joining us. They then fled away, and we lost them in the obscurity.[1]

The stranger now addressed himself to me with politeness, and enquired whether I was wounded. Faint with the loss of blood, I could scarcely thank him for his seasonable aid, and entreat him to let some of his servants convey me to the hotel de las Cisternas. I no sooner mentioned the name than he professed himself an acquaintance of my father's, and declared that he would not permit my being transported to such a distance, before my wounds had been examined. He added, that his house was hard by, and begged me to accompany him thither. His manner was so earnest, that I

---

1 Cf. the attempted assassination of Civitella in Schiller, *The Ghost-Seer* 55-56 (Letter 2).

could not reject his offer; and, leaning upon his arm, a few minutes brought me to the porch of a magnificent hotel.

On entering the house, an old grey-headed domestic came to welcome my conductor: he enquired when the duke, his master, meant to quit the country, and was answered, that he would remain there yet some months. My deliverer then desired the family surgeon to be summoned without delay: his orders were obeyed. I was seated upon a sopha in a noble apartment; and my wounds being examined, they were declared to be very slight. The surgeon, however, advised me not to expose myself to the night air; and the stranger pressed me so earnestly to take a bed in his house, that I consented to remain where I was for the present.

Being now left alone with my deliverer, I took the opportunity of thanking him in more express terms than I had done hitherto; but he begged me to be silent upon the subject.

"I esteem myself happy," said he, "in having had it in my power to render you this little service; and I shall think myself eternally obliged to my daughter for detaining me so late at the convent of St. Clare. The high esteem in which I have ever held the marquis de las Cisternas, though accident has not permitted our being so intimate as I could wish, makes me rejoice in the opportunity of making his son's acquaintance. I am certain that my brother, in whose house you now are, will lament his not being at Madrid to receive you himself: but, in the duke's absence, I am master of the family, and may assure you, in his name, that every thing in the hotel de Medina is perfectly at your disposal."

Conceive my surprise, Lorenzo, at discovering, in the person of my preserver, Don Gaston de Medina. It was only to be equalled by my secret satisfaction at the assurance, that Agnes inhabited the convent of St. Clare. This latter sensation was not a little weakened, when, in answer to my seemingly indifferent questions, he told me that his daughter had really taken the veil. I suffered not my grief at this circumstance to take root in my mind: I flattered myself with the idea, that my uncle's credit at the court of Rome would remove this obstacle, and that, without difficulty, I should obtain for my mistress a dispensation from her vows. Buoyed up with this hope, I calmed the uneasiness of my bosom; and I redoubled my endeavours to appear grateful for the attention, and pleased with the society, of Don Gaston.

A domestic now entered the room, and informed me that the bravo whom I had wounded, discovered some signs of life. I desired that he might be carried to my father's hotel, and said that, as soon as he recovered his voice, I would examine him respecting his reasons for attempting my life. I was answered that he was already able to speak, though with difficulty. Don Gaston's curiosity made him press me to interrogate the assassin in his presence; but this curiosity I was by no means inclined to gratify. One reason was, that, doubting from whence the blow came, I was unwilling to place before Don Gaston's eyes the guilt of a sister. Another was, that I feared to be recognized for Alphonso d'Alvarada, and precautions taken in consequence to keep me from the sight of Agnes. To avow my passion for his daughter, and endeavour to make him enter into my schemes, what I knew of Don Gaston's character convinced me would be an imprudent step; and considering it to be essential that he should know me for no other than the condé de las Cisternas, I was determined not to let him hear the bravo's confession. I insinuated to him, that as I suspected a lady to be concerned in the business, whose name might accidentally escape from the assassin, it was necessary for me to examine the man in private. Don Gaston's delicacy would not permit his urging the point any longer, and, in consequence, the bravo was conveyed to my hotel.

The next morning I took leave of my host, who was to return to the duke on the same day. My wounds had been so trifling, that, except being obliged to wear my arm in a sling for a short time, I felt no inconvenience from the night's adventure. The surgeon who examined the bravo's wound declared it to be mortal: he had just time to confess, that he had been instigated to murder me by the revengeful Donna Rodolpha, and expired in a few minutes after.

All my thoughts were now bent upon getting to the speech of my lovely nun. Theodore set himself to work, and, for this time, with better success. He attacked the gardener of St. Clare so forcibly with bribes and promises, that the old man was entirely gained over to my interests; and it was settled that I should be introduced into the convent in the character of his assistant. The plan was put into execution without delay. Disguised in a common habit, and a black patch covering one of my eyes, I was presented to the lady prioress, who condescended to approve of the gardener's choice. I immediately entered upon my employment. Botany having been a favourite study with me, I was by no means at a loss in my new station. For some days I continued to work in the convent-garden without meeting the object of my disguise. On the fourth morning I was more successful. I heard the voice of Agnes, and was speeding towards the sound, when the sight of the domina stopped me. I drew back with caution, and concealed myself behind a thick clump of trees.

The prioress advanced, and seated herself with Agnes on a bench at no great distance. I heard her, in an angry tone, blame her companion's continual melancholy. She told her, that to weep the loss of any lover, in her situation, was a crime; but that to weep the loss of a faithless one was folly and absurdity in the extreme. Agnes replied in so low a voice that I could not distinguish her words, but I perceived that she used terms of gentleness and submission. The conversation was interrupted by the arrival of a young pensioner, who informed the domina that she was waited for in the parlour. The old lady rose, kissed the cheek of Agnes, and retired. The new-comer remained. Agnes spoke much to her in praise of somebody whom I could not make out; but her auditor seemed highly delighted, and interested by the conversation. The nun shewed her several letters: the other perused them with evident pleasure, obtained permission to copy them, and withdrew for that purpose to my great satisfaction.

No sooner was she out of sight, than I quitted my conceal-ment. Fearing to alarm my lovely mistress, I drew near her gently, intending to discover myself by degrees. But who for a moment can deceive the eyes of love? She raised her head at my approach, and recognised me, in spite of my disguise, at a single glance. She rose hastily from her seat with an exclamation of surprise, and attempted to retire; but I followed her, detained her, and entreat-ed to be heard. Persuaded of my falsehood, she refused to listen to me, and ordered me positively to quit the garden. It was now my turn to refuse. I protested that, however dangerous might be the consequences, I would not leave her till she had heard my justifi-cation. I assured her, that she had been deceived by the artifices of her relations: that I could convince her, beyond the power of doubt, that my passion had been pure and disinterested; and I asked her what should induce me to seek her in the convent, were I influenced by the selfish motives which my enemies had ascribed to me.

My prayers, my arguments, and vows not to quit her till she had promised to listen to me, united to her fears lest the nuns should see me with her, to her natural curiosity, and to the affection which she still felt for me, in spite of my supposed desertion, at length prevailed. She told me, that to grant my request at that moment was impossible; but she engaged to be in the same spot at eleven that night, and to converse with me for the last time. Having obtained this promise, I released her hand, and she fled back with rapidity towards the convent.

I communicated my success to my ally, the old gardener: he pointed out an hiding place, where I might shelter myself till night without fear of a discovery. Thither I betook myself at the hour when I ought to have retired with my supposed master, and waited impatiently for the appointed time. The chillness of the night was in my favour, since it kept the other nuns confined to their cells. Agnes alone was insensible of the inclemency of the air, and, before eleven, joined me at the spot which had witnessed our former interview. Secure from interruption, I related to her the true cause of my disappearing on the fatal fifth of May. She was evidently much affected by my narrative. When it was concluded, she confessed the injustice of her suspicions, and blamed herself for having taken the veil through despair at my ingratitude.

"But now it is too late to repine!" she added; "the die is thrown:[1] I have pronounced my vows, and dedicated myself to the service of heaven. I am sensible how ill I am calculated for a convent. My disgust at a monastic life increases daily: ennui and discontent are my constant companions; and I will not conceal from you, that the passion which I formerly felt for one so near being my husband, is not yet extinguished in my bosom: but we must part! Insuperable barriers divide us from each other, and on this side the grave we must never meet again!"

I now exerted myself to prove, that our union was not so impossible as she seemed to think it. I vaunted to her the cardinal-duke of Lerma's influence at the court of Rome. I assured her, that I should easily obtain a dispensation from her vows; and I doubted not but Don Gaston would coincide with my views, when informed of my real name and long attachment. Agnes replied, that since I encouraged such an hope, I could know but little of her father. Liberal and kind in every other respect, superstition formed the only stain upon his character. Upon this head he was inflexible: he sacrificed his dearest interests to his scruples, and would consider it an insult to suppose him capable of authorising his daughter to break her vows to heaven.

"But suppose," said I, interrupting her—"suppose that he should disapprove of our union: let him remain ignorant of my

---

1 Agnes compares herself to Julius Caesar crossing the Rubicon: Suetonius, *Divus Julius* 32.

proceedings till I have rescued you from the prison in which you are now confined. Once my wife, you are free from his authority. I need from him no pecuniary assistance; and when he sees his resentment to be unavailing, he will doubtless restore you to his favour. But, let the worst happen; should Don Gaston be irreconcileable, my relations will vie with each other in making you forget his loss; and you will find in my father a substitute for the parent of whom I shall deprive you."

"Don Raymond," replied Agnes, in a firm and resolute voice, "I love my father: he has treated me harshly in this one instance; but I have received from him, in every other, so many proofs of love, that his affection is become necessary to my existence. Were I to quit the convent, he never would forgive me; nor can I think that, on his death-bed, he would leave me his curse, without shuddering at the very idea. Besides, I am conscious myself, that my vows are binding. Wilfully did I contract my engagement with heaven: I cannot break it without a crime. Then banish from your mind the idea of our being ever united. I am devoted to religion; and however I may grieve at our separation, I would oppose obstacles myself, to what I feel would render me guilty."

I strove to over-rule these ill-grounded scruples. We were still disputing upon the subject, when the convent-bell summoned the nuns to matins. Agnes was obliged to attend them; but she left me not till I had compelled her to promise, that on the following night she would be at the same place at the same hour. These meetings continued for several weeks uninterrupted: and 'tis now, Lorenzo, that I must implore your indulgence. Reflect upon our situation, our youth, our long attachment. Weigh all the circumstances which attended our assignations, and you will confess the temptation to have been irresistible: you will even pardon me when I acknowledge that, in an unguarded moment, the honour of Agnes was sacrificed to my passion.

[Lorenzo's eyes sparkled with fury; a deep crimson spread itself over his face: he started from his seat, and attempted to draw his sword. The marquis was aware of his movement, and caught his hand: he pressed it affectionately:

"My friend! my brother! hear me to the conclusion! Till then restrain your passion; and be at least convinced, that if what I have related is criminal, the blame must fall upon me, and not upon your sister."

Lorenzo suffered himself to be prevailed upon by Don Raymond's entreaties: he resumed his place, and listened to the rest of the narrative with a gloomy and impatient countenance. The marquis thus continued:]

Scarcely was the first burst of passion past, when Agnes, recovering herself, started from my arms with horror. She called me infamous seducer, loaded me with the bitterest reproaches, and beat her bosom in all the wildness of delirium. Ashamed of my imprudence, I with difficulty found words to excuse myself. I endeavoured to console her: I threw myself at her feet, and entreated her forgiveness. She forced her hand from me, which I had taken and would have pressed to my lips.

"Touch me not!" she cried, with a violence which terrified me. "Monster of perfidy and ingratitude, how have I been deceived in you! I looked upon you as my friend, my protector: I trusted myself in your hands with confidence, and, relying upon your honour, thought that mine ran no risk: and 'tis by you, whom I adored, that I am covered with infamy! 'Tis by you that I have been seduced into breaking my vows to God, that I am reduced to a level with the basest of my sex! Shame upon you, villain, you shall never see me more!"

She started from the bank on which she was seated. I endeavoured to detain her; but she disengaged herself from me with violence, and took refuge in the convent.

I retired, filled with confusion and inquietude. The next morning I failed not, as usual, to appear in the garden; but Agnes was no where to be seen. At night I waited for her at the place where we generally met. I found no better success. Several days and nights passed away in the same manner. At length I saw my offended mistress cross the walk, on whose borders I was working: she was accompanied by the same young pensioner, on whose arm she seemed, from weakness, obliged to support herself. She looked upon me for a moment, but instantly turned her head away. I waited her return; but she passed on to the convent without paying any attention to me, or the penitent looks with which I implored her forgiveness.

As soon as the nuns were retired, the old gardener joined me with a sorrowful air.

"Segnor," said he, "it grieves me to say, that I can be no longer of use to you; the lady whom you used to meet has just assured me, that if I admitted you again into the garden, she would discover the whole business to the lady prioress. She bade me tell you also, that your presence was an insult, and that, if you still possess the least respect for her, you will never attempt to see her more. Excuse me then for informing you, that I can favour your disguise no longer. Should the prioress be acquainted with my conduct, she might not be contented with dismissing me her service: out of revenge, she might accuse me of having profaned the convent, and cause me to be thrown into the prisons of the Inquisition."[1]

Fruitless were my attempts to conquer his resolution. He denied me all future entrance into the garden; and Agnes persevered in neither letting me see or hear from her. In about a fortnight after, a violent illness which had seized my father obliged me to set out for Andalusia. I hastened thither, and, as I imagined, found the marquis at the point of death. Though, on its first appearance, his complaint was declared mortal, he lingered out several months; during which, my attendance upon him in his malady, and the occupation of settling his affairs after his decease, permitted not my quitting Andalusia. Within these four days I returned to Madrid, and, on arriving at my hotel, I there found this letter waiting for me.

[Here the marquis unlocked a drawer of a cabinet; he took out a folded paper, which he presented to his auditor. Lorenzo opened it, and recognised his sister's hand. The contents were as follows:

"INTO what an abyss of misery have you plunged me! Raymond, you force me to become as criminal as yourself. I had resolved never to see you more; if possible, to forget you; if not, only to remember you with hate. A being, for whom I already feel a mother's tenderness, solicits me to pardon my seducer, and apply to his love for the means of preservation. Raymond, your child lives in my bosom. I tremble at the vengeance of the prioress. I tremble much for myself, yet more for the innocent creature whose existence depends upon mine. Both of us are lost, should my situation be discovered. Advise me, then, what steps to take, but seek not to see me. The gardener, who undertakes to deliver this, is dismissed, and we have nothing to hope from that quarter. The man engaged in his place is of incorruptible fidelity. The best means of conveying to me your answer, is by concealing it under the great statue of St. Francis, which stands in the Capuchin cathedral; thither I go every Thursday to confession, and shall easily have an

---

1 A papal judicial institution dedicated to combating heresy, witchcraft, and other offences. The Spanish inquisition was founded in 1478; it was finally abolished in 1834. It is a common topic in British anti-Catholic writing; the partly positive role it plays in *The Monk* is unusual.

opportunity of securing your letter. I hear that you are now absent from Madrid. Need I entreat you to write the very moment of your return? I will not think it. Ah! Raymond! mine is a cruel situation! Deceived by my nearest relations, compelled to embrace a profession the duties of which I am ill calculated to perform, conscious of the sanctity of those duties, and seduced into violating them by one whom I least suspected of perfidy, I am now obliged, by circumstances, to choose between death and perjury. Woman's timidity, and maternal affection, permit me not to balance in the choice. I feel all the guilt into which I plunge myself when I yield to the plan which you before proposed to me. My poor father's death, which has taken place since we met, has removed one obstacle. He sleeps in his grave, and I no longer dread his anger. But from the anger of God, oh! Raymond! who shall shield me? Who can protect me against my conscience, against myself? I dare not dwell upon these thoughts; they will drive me mad. I have taken my resolution. Procure a dispensation from my vows. I am ready to fly with you. Write to me, my husband! Tell me that absence has not abated your love! Tell me that you will rescue from death your unborn child, and its unhappy mother. I live in all the agonies of terror. Every eye which is fixed upon me, seems to read my secret and my shame. And you are the cause of those agonies! Oh! when my heart first loved you, how little did it suspect you of making it feel such pangs!

"AGNES."

Having perused the letter, Lorenzo restored it in silence. The marquis replaced it in the cabinet, and then proceeded:]

Excessive was my joy at reading this intelligence, so earnestly desired, so little expected. My plan was soon arranged. When Don Gaston discovered to me his daughter's retreat, I entertained no doubt of her readiness to quit the convent: I had, therefore, entrusted the cardinal-duke of Lerma with the whole affair, who immediately busied himself in obtaining the necessary bull.[1] Fortunately, I had afterwards neglected to stop his proceedings. Not long since I received a letter from him, stating that he expected daily to receive the order from the court of Rome. Upon this I would willingly have relied; but the cardinal wrote me word, that I must find some means of conveying Agnes out of the convent, unknown to

---

1 "A papal or episcopal edict" (*OED*).

the prioress. He doubted not but this latter would be much incensed by losing a person of such high rank from her society, and consider the renunciation of Agnes as an insult to her house. He represented her as a woman of a violent and revengeful character, capable of proceeding to the greatest extremities. It was therefore to be feared lest, by confining Agnes in the convent, she should frustrate my hopes, and render the pope's mandate unavailing. Influenced by this consideration, I resolved to carry off my mistress, and conceal her till the arrival of the expected bull in the cardinal-duke's estate. He approved of my design, and professed himself ready to give a shelter to the fugitive. I next caused the new gardener of St. Clare to be seized privately, and confined in my hotel. By this means I became master of the key to the garden-door, and I had now nothing more to do than prepare Agnes for the elopement. This was done by the letter which you saw me deliver this evening. I told her in it, that I should be ready to receive her at twelve to-morrow night; that I had secured the key of the garden, and that she might depend upon a speedy release.

You have now, Lorenzo, heard the whole of my long narrative. I have nothing to say in my excuse, save that my intentions towards your sister have been ever the most honourable: that it has always been, and still is, my design to make her my wife; and that I trust, when you consider these circumstances, our youth, and our attachment, you will not only forgive our momentary lapse from virtue, but will aid me in repairing my faults to Agnes, and securing a lawful title to her person and her heart.

CHAP. V.

O you! whom Vanity's light bark conveys
On Fame's mad voyage by the wind of Praise,
With what a shifting gale your course you ply,
For ever sunk too low, or borne too high!
Who pants for glory finds but short repose:
A breath revives him, and a breath o'erthrows.

POPE.[1]

---

1   Alexander Pope, "The First Epistle of the Second Book of Horace Imitated, To Augustus" (1736) 296-301.

HERE the marquis concluded his adventures. Lorenzo, before he could determine on his reply, passed some moments in reflection. At length he broke silence.

"Raymond," said he, taking his hand, "strict honour would oblige me to wash off in your blood the stain thrown upon my family; but the circumstances of your case forbid me to consider you as an enemy. The temptation was too great to be resisted. 'Tis the superstition of my relations which has occasioned these misfortunes, and they are more the offenders than yourself and Agnes. What has passed between you cannot be recalled, but may yet be repaired by uniting you to my sister. You have ever been, you still continue to be, my dearest, and indeed my only friend. I feel for Agnes the truest affection, and there is no one on whom I would bestow her more willingly than on yourself. Pursue, then, your design. I will accompany you to-morrow night, and conduct her myself to the house of the cardinal. My presence will be a sanction for her conduct, and prevent her incurring blame by her flight from the convent."

The marquis thanked him in terms by no means deficient in gratitude. Lorenzo then informed him, that he had nothing more to apprehend from Donna Rodolpha's enmity. Five months had already elapsed since, in an excess of passion, she broke a blood-vessel, and expired in the course of a few hours. He then proceeded to mention the interests of Antonia. The marquis was much surprised at hearing of this new relation. His father had carried his hatred of Elvira to the grave, and had never given the least hint that he knew what was become of his eldest son's widow. Don Raymond assured his friend, that he was not mistaken in supposing him ready to acknowledge his sister-in-law, and her amiable daughter. The preparations for the elopement would not permit his visiting them the next day; but, in the mean while, he desired Lorenzo to assure them of his friendship, and to supply Elvira, upon his account, with any sums which she might want. This the youth promised to do, as soon as her abode should be known to him. He then took leave of his future brother, and returned to the palace de Medina.

The day was already on the point of breaking when the marquis retired to his chamber. Conscious that his narrative would take up some hours, and wishing to secure himself from interruption, on returning to the hotel he ordered his attendants not to sit up for him; consequently, he was somewhat surprised, on entering his anti-room, to find Theodore established there. The page sat near a table with a pen in his hand, and was so totally occupied by his employment, that he perceived not his lord's approach. The marquis stopped to observe him. Theodore wrote a few lines, then paused, and scratched out a part of the writing; then wrote again, smiled, and seemed highly pleased with what he had been about. At last he threw down his pen, sprang from his chair, and clapped his hands together joyfully.

"There it is!" cried he aloud: "now they are charming!"

His transports were interrupted by a laugh from the marquis, who suspected the nature of his employment.

"What is so charming, Theodore?"

The youth started, and looked round: he blushed, ran to the table, seized the paper on which he had been writing, and concealed it in confusion.

"Oh! my lord, I knew not that you were so near me. Can I be of use to you? Lucas is already gone to bed."

"I shall follow his example when I have given my opinion of your verses."

"My verses, my lord?"

"Nay, I am sure that you have been writing some, for nothing else could have kept you awake till this time of the morning. Where are they, Theodore? I shall like to see your composition."

Theodore's cheeks glowed with still deeper crimson: he longed to shew his poetry, but first chose to be pressed for it.

"Indeed, my lord, they are not worthy your attention."

"Not these verses, which you just now declared to be so charming? Come, come, let me see whether our opinions are the same. I promise that you shall find in me an indulgent critic."

The boy produced his paper with seeming reluctance; but the satisfaction which sparkled in his dark expressive eyes betrayed the vanity of his little bosom. The marquis smiled while he observed the emotions of an heart as yet but little skilled in veiling its sentiments. He seated himself upon a sopha. Theodore, while hope and fear contended on his anxious countenance, waited with inquietude for his master's decision, while the marquis read the following lines:

LOVE AND AGE.[1]

THE night was dark; the wind blew cold;
Anacreon, grown morose and old,
Sat by his fire, and fed the cheerful flame:
  Sudden the cottage-door expands,
  And, lo! before him Cupid stands,
Casts round a friendly glance, and greets him by his name.

"What! is it thou?" the startled sire
In sullen tone exclaimed, while ire
With crimson flushed his pale and wrinkled cheek:
  "Wouldst thou again with amorous rage
  Inflame my bosom? Steeled by age,
Vain boy, to pierce my breast thine arrows are too weak.

"What seek you in this desert drear?
No smiles or sports inhabit here;
Ne'er did these vallies witness dalliance sweet:
  Eternal winter binds the plains;
  Age in my house despotic reigns;
My garden boasts no flower, my bosom boasts no heat.

"Begone, and seek the blooming bower,
Where some ripe virgin courts thy power,
Or bid provoking dreams flit round her bed;
  On Damon's amorous breast repose;
  Wanton on Chloe's lip of rose,
Or make her blushing cheek a pillow for thy head.

"Be such thy haunts! These regions cold
Avoid! Nor think grown wise and old
This hoary head again thy yoke shall bear:
  Remembering that my fairest years
  By thee were marked with sighs and tears,
I think thy friendship false, and shun the guileful snare.

---

1 This is an imitation of one of the odes attributed in Lewis's time to
  Anacreon (c. 570-485 B.C.) but now known to have been composed by
  anonymous imitators of Anacreon in the Hellenistic and Byzantine peri-
  ods. See Appendix A.5 for Lewis's translation of the poem imitated here.

"I have not yet forgot the pains
I felt, while bound in Julia's chains:
The ardent flames with which my bosom burned;
The nights I passed deprived of rest;
The jealous pangs which racked my breast;
My disappointed hopes, and passion unreturned.

"Then fly, and curse mine eyes no more!
Fly from my peaceful cottage-door!
No day, no hour, no moment shalt thou stay.
I know thy falsehood, scorn thy arts,
Distrust thy smiles, and fear thy darts:
Traitor, begone, and seek some other to betray!"—

"Does age, old man, your wits confound?"
Replied the offended god, and frowned:
[His frown was sweet as is the virgin's smile!]
"Do you to me these words address?
To me, who do not love you less,
Though you my friendship scorn, and pleasures past revile!

"If one proud fair you chanced to find,
An hundred other nymphs were kind,
Whose smiles might well for Julia's frowns atone:
But such is man! his partial hand
Unnumbered favours writes on sand,
But stamps one little fault on solid lasting stone.

"Ingrate! Who led thee to the wave,
At noon where Lesbia loved to lave?
Who named the bower alone where Daphne lay?
And who, when Celia shrieked for aid,
Bade you with kisses hush the maid?
What other was't than Love, oh! false Anacreon, say!

"Then you could call me—'Gentle boy!
My only bliss! my source of joy!'
Then you could prize me dearer than your soul!
Could kiss, and dance me on your knees;
And swear, not wine itself would please,
Had not the lip of Love first touched the flowing bowl!

"Must those sweet days return no more?
Must I for aye your loss deplore,
Banished your heart, and from your favour driven?
Ah! no; my fears that smile denies;
That heaving breast, those sparkling eyes
Declare me ever dear, and all my faults forgiven.

"Again beloved, esteemed, caressed,
Cupid shall in thine arms be pressed,
Sport on thy knees, or on thy bosom sleep:
My torch thine age-struck heart shall warm;
My hand pale winter's rage disarm,
And Youth and Spring shall here once more their revels
        keep."—

A feather now of golden hue
He smiling from his pinion drew;
This to the poet's hand the boy commits;
And straight before Anacreon's eyes
The fairest dreams of fancy rise,
And round his favoured head wild inspiration flits.

His bosom glows with amorous fire;
Eager he grasps the magic lyre;
Swift o'er the tuneful chords his fingers move:
The feather plucked from Cupid's wing
Sweeps the too-long neglected string,
While soft Anacreon sings the power and praise of love.

Soon as that name was heard, the woods
Shook off their snows; the melting floods
Broke their cold chains, and winter fled away.
Once more the earth was decked with flowers;
Mild zephyrs breathed through blooming bowers;
High towered the glorious sun, and poured the blaze of day.

Attracted by the harmonious sound,
Sylvans and fauns the cot surround,
And curious crowd the minstrel to behold:
The wood-nymphs haste the spell to prove;
Eager they run; they list, they love,
And, while they hear the strain, forget the man is old.

Cupid, to nothing constant long,
　　Perched on the harp attends the song,
Or stifles with a kiss the dulcet notes:
　　Now on the poet's breast reposes,
　　Now twines his hoary locks with roses,
Or borne on wings of gold in wanton circle floats.

Then thus Anacreon—"I no more
　　At other shrines my vows will pour,
Since Cupid deigns my numbers to inspire:
　　From Phœbus or the blue-eyed maid[1]
　　Now shall my verse request no aid,
For Love alone shall be the patron of my lyre.

"In lofty strain, of earlier days,
　　I spread the king's or hero's praise,
And struck the martial chords with epic fire:
　　But farewell, hero! farewell, king!
　　Your deeds my lips no more shall sing,
For Love alone shall be the subject of my lyre."

The marquis returned the paper with a smile of encouragement.

"Your little poem pleases me much," said he: "however, you must not count my opinion for any thing. I am no judge of verses, and for my own part never composed more than six lines in my life: those six produced so unlucky an effect, that I am fully resolved never to compose another. But I wander from my subject. I was going to say that you cannot employ your time worse than in making verses. An author, whether good or bad, or between both, is an animal whom every body is privileged to attack: for though all are not able to write books, all conceive themselves able to judge them. A bad composition carries with it its own punishment—contempt and ridicule. A good one excites envy, and entails upon its author a thousand mortifications: he finds himself assailed by partial and ill-humoured criticism: one man finds fault with the plan, another with the style, a third with the precept which it strives to inculcate; and they who cannot succeed in finding fault

---

1　Phœbus is Apollo, god of the sun and of poetry; the blue-eyed maid is
　　Athena (in Latin, Minerva), goddess of wisdom.

with the book, employ themselves in stigmatizing its author. They maliciously rake out from obscurity every little circumstance which may throw ridicule upon his private character or conduct, and aim at wounding the man since they cannot hurt the writer. In short, to enter the lists of literature is wilfully to expose yourself to the arrows of neglect, ridicule, envy, and disappointment. Whether you write well or ill, be assured that you will not escape from blame. Indeed this circumstance contains a young author's chief consolation: he remembers that Lope de Vega and Calderona[1] had unjust and envious critics, and he modestly conceives himself to be exactly in their predicament. But I am conscious that all these sage observations are thrown away upon you. Authorship is a mania, to conquer which no reasons are sufficiently strong; and you might as easily persuade me not to love, as I persuade you not to write. However, if you cannot help being occasionally seized with a poetical paroxysm, take at least the precaution of communicating your verses to none but those whose partiality for you secures their approbation."

"Then, my lord, you do not think these lines tolerable?" said Theodore, with an humble and dejected air.

"You mistake my meaning. As I said before, they have pleased me much: but my regard for you makes me partial, and others might judge them less favourably. I must still remark, that even my prejudice in your favour does not blind me so much as to prevent my observing several faults. For instance, you make a terrible confusion of metaphors; you are too apt to make the strength of your lines consist more in the words than sense; some of the verses only seem introduced in order to rhyme with others; and most of the best ideas are borrowed from other poets, though possibly you are unconscious of the theft yourself. These faults may occasionally be excused in a work of length; but a short poem must be correct and perfect."

"All this is true, segnor; but you should consider that I only write for pleasure."

"Your defects are the less excusable. Their incorrectness may be forgiven, who work for money, who are obliged to complete a given task in a given time, and are paid according to the bulk, not value of their productions. But in those whom no necessity forces

---

1   Lope de Vega (1562-1635) and Pedro Calderón de la Barca (1600-81),
    dramatists of Spain's Golden Age.

to turn author, who merely write for fame, and have full leisure to polish their compositions, faults are unpardonable, and merit the sharpest arrows of criticism."

The marquis rose from the sopha; the page looked discouraged and melancholy; and this did not escape his master's observation.

"However," added he, smiling, "I think that these lines do you no discredit. Your versification is tolerably easy, and your ear seems to be just. The perusal of your little poem upon the whole gave me much pleasure; and if it is not asking too great a favour, I shall be highly obliged to you for a copy."

The youth's countenance immediately cleared up. He perceived not the smile, half approving, half ironical, which accompanied the request, and he promised the copy with great readiness. The marquis withdrew to his chamber, much amused by the instantaneous effect produced upon Theodore's vanity by the conclusion of his criticism. He threw himself upon his couch, sleep soon stole over him, and his dreams presented him with the most flattering pictures of happiness with Agnes.

On reaching the hotel de Medina, Lorenzo's first care was to enquire for letters. He found several waiting for him; but that which he sought was not amongst them. Leonella had found it impossible to write that evening. However, her impatience to secure Don Christoval's heart, on which she flattered herself with having made no slight impression, permitted her not to pass another day without informing him where she was to be found. On her return from the Capuchin-church, she had related to her sister, with exultation, how attentive an handsome cavalier had been to her; as also how his companion had undertaken to plead Antonia's cause with the marquis de las Cisternas. Elvira received this intelligence with sensations very different from those with which it was communicated. She blamed her sister's imprudence in confiding her history to an absolute stranger, and expressed her fears lest this inconsiderate step should prejudice the marquis against her. The greatest of her apprehensions she concealed in her own breast. She had observed, with inquietude, that at the mention of Lorenzo a deep blush spread itself over her daughter's cheek. The timid Antonia dared not to pronounce his name. Without knowing wherefore, she felt embarrassed when he was made the subject of discourse, and endeavoured to change the conversation to Ambrosio. Elvira perceived the emotions of this young bosom: in consequence, she insisted upon Leonella's breaking her promise to the cavaliers. A sigh, which on hearing this order escaped from Antonia, confirmed the wary mother in her resolution.

Through this resolution Leonella was determined to break: she conceived it to be inspired by envy, and that her sister dreaded her being elevated above her. Without imparting her design to any one, she took an opportunity of dispatching the following note to Lorenzo: it was delivered to him as soon as he woke:

"Doubtless, Segnor Don Lorenzo, you have frequently accused me of ingratitude and forgetfulness: but on the word of a virgin it was out of my power to perform my promise yesterday. I know not in what words to inform you, how strange a reception my sister gave your kind wish to visit her. She is an odd woman, with many good points about her; but her jealousy of me frequently makes her conceive notions quite unaccountable. On hearing that your friend had paid some little attention to me, she immediately took the alarm: she blamed my conduct, and has absolutely forbidden me to let you know our abode. My strong sense of gratitude for your kind offers of service, and——shall I confess it? my desire to behold once more the too amiable Don Christoval, will not permit my obeying her injunctions. I have therefore stolen a moment to inform you, that we lodge in the strada di San Jago, four doors from the palace d'Albornos, and nearly opposite to the barber's Miguel Coello. Enquire for Donna Elvira Dalfa, since, in compliance with her father-in-law's order, my sister continues to be called by her maiden name. At eight this evening you will be sure of finding us: but let not a word drop, which may raise a suspicion of my having written this letter. Should you see the Condé d'Ossorio, tell him——I blush while I declare it——tell him that his presence will be but too acceptable to the sympathetic

"LEONELLA."

The latter sentences were written in red ink, to express the blushes of her cheek while she committed an outrage upon her virgin modesty.

Lorenzo had no sooner perused this note, than he set out in search of Don Christoval. Not being able to find him in the course of the day, he proceeded to Donna Elvira's alone, to Leonella's infinite disappointment. The domestic by whom he sent up his name having already declared his lady to be at home, she had no excuse for refusing his visit: yet she consented to receive it with much reluctance. That reluctance was increased by the changes which his approach produced in Antonia's countenance; nor was it by any means abated, when the youth himself appeared. The symmetry of his person, animation of his features, and natural elegance of his manners and address, convinced Elvira that such a guest must be dangerous for her daughter. She resolved to treat him with distant politeness, to decline his services with gratitude for the tender of them, and to make him feel, without offence, that his future visits would be far from acceptable.

On his entrance he found Elvira, who was indisposed, reclining upon a sopha; Antonia sat by her embroidery frame; and Leonella, in a pastoral dress, held "*Montemayor's Diana*."[1] In spite of her being the mother of Antonia, Lorenzo could not help expecting to find in Elvira Leonella's true sister, and the daughter of "as honest a pains-taking shoemaker as any in Cordova." A single glance was sufficient to undeceive him. He beheld a woman whose features, though impaired by time and sorrow, still bore the marks of distinguished beauty: a serious dignity reigned upon her countenance, but was tempered by a grace and sweetness which rendered her truly enchanting. Lorenzo fancied that she must have resembled her daughter in her youth, and readily excused the imprudence of the late Condé de las Cisternas. She desired him to be seated, and immediately resumed her place upon the sopha.

Antonia received him with a simple reverence, and continued her work: her cheeks were suffused with crimson, and she strove to conceal her emotion by leaning over her embroidery frame. Her aunt also chose to play off her airs of modesty: she affected to blush and tremble, and waited with her eyes cast down to receive, as she expected, the compliments of Don Christoval. Finding, after some time, that no sign of his approach was given, she ventured to look round the room, and perceived with vexation that Medina was unaccompanied. Impatience would not permit her waiting for an explanation: interrupting Lorenzo, who was delivering Raymond's message, she desired to know what was become of his friend.

He, who thought it necessary to maintain himself in her good graces, strove to console her under her disappointment by committing a little violence upon truth.

"Ah! segnora," he replied in a melancholy voice, "how grieved will he be at losing this opportunity of paying you his respects! A

---

1   *Diana Enamorada*, a Spanish pastoral, by Jorge de Montemayor (c. 1521-61), mentioned in Cervantes, *Don Quixote* 1.6.

relation's illness has obliged him to quit Madrid in haste: but on his return he will doubtless seize the first moment with transport to throw himself at your feet!"

As he said this, his eyes met those of Elvira: she punished his falsehood sufficiently by darting at him a look expressive of displeasure and reproach. Neither did the deceit answer his intention. Vexed and disappointed, Leonella rose from her seat, and retired in dudgeon to her own apartment.

Lorenzo hastened to repair the fault which had injured him in Elvira's opinion. He related his conversation with the marquis respecting her: he assured her that Raymond was prepared to acknowledge her for his brother's widow; and that, till it was in his power to pay his compliments to her in person, Lorenzo was commissioned to supply his place. This intelligence relieved Elvira from an heavy weight of uneasiness: she had now found a protector for the fatherless Antonia, for whose future fortunes she had suffered the greatest apprehensions. She was not sparing of her thanks to him, who had interfered so generously in her behalf; but still she gave him no invitation to repeat his visit. However, when upon rising to depart he requested permission to enquire after her health occasionally, the polite earnestness of his manner, gratitude for his services, and respect for his friend the marquis, would not admit of a refusal. She consented reluctantly to receive him: he promised not to abuse her goodness, and quitted the house.

Antonia was now left alone with her mother: a temporary silence ensued. Both wished to speak upon the same subject, but neither knew how to introduce it. The one felt a bashfulness which sealed up her lips, and for which she could not account; the other feared to find her apprehensions true, or to inspire her daughter with notions to which she might be still a stranger. At length Elvira began the conversation.

"That is a charming young man, Antonia; I am much pleased with him. Was he long near you yesterday in the cathedral?"

"He quitted me not for a moment while I staid in the church: he gave me his seat, and was very obliging and attentive."

"Indeed? Why then have you never mentioned his name to me? Your aunt launched out in praise of his friend, and you vaunted Ambrosio's eloquence: but neither said a word of Don Lorenzo's person and accomplishments. Had not Leonella spoken of his readiness to undertake our cause, I should not have known him to be in existence."

She paused. Antonia coloured, but was silent.

"Perhaps you judge him less favourably than I do. In my opinion his figure is pleasing, his conversation sensible, and manners engaging. Still he may have struck you differently: you may think him disagreeable, and——"

"Disagreeable? Oh! dear mother, how should I possibly think him so? I should be very ungrateful were I not sensible of his kindness yesterday, and very blind if his merits had escaped me. His figure is so graceful, so noble! His manners so gentle, yet so manly! I never yet saw so many accomplishments united in one person, and I doubt whether Madrid can produce his equal."

"Why then were you so silent in praise of this phœnix of Madrid? Why was it concealed from me, that his society had afforded you pleasure?"

"In truth, I know not: you ask me a question which I cannot resolve myself. I was on the point of mentioning him a thousand times; his name was constantly on my lips; but when I would have pronounced it, I wanted courage to execute my design. However, if I did not speak of him, it was not that I thought of him the less."

"That I believe. But shall I tell you why you wanted courage? It was because, accustomed to confide to me your most secret thoughts, you knew not how to conceal, yet feared to acknowledge, that your heart nourished a sentiment which you were conscious I should disapprove. Come hither to me, my child."

Antonia quitted her embroidery frame, threw herself upon her knees by the sopha, and hid her face in her mother's lap.

"Fear not, my sweet girl! Consider me equally as your friend and parent, and apprehend no reproof from me. I have read the emotions of your bosom; you are yet ill skilled in concealing them, and they could not escape my attentive eye. This Lorenzo is dangerous to your repose; he has already made an impression upon your heart. 'Tis true that I perceive easily that your affection is returned: but what can be the consequences of this attachment? You are poor and friendless, my Antonia; Lorenzo is the heir of the duke of Medina Celi. Even should himself mean honourably, his uncle never will consent to your union; nor, without that uncle's consent, will I. By sad experience I know what sorrow she must endure, who marries into a family unwilling to receive her. Then struggle with your affection: whatever pains it may cost you, strive to conquer it. Your heart is tender and susceptible: it has already received a strong impression; but when once convinced that you should not encourage such sentiments, I trust that you have sufficient fortitude to drive them from your bosom."

Antonia kissed her hand, and promised implicit obedience. Elvira then continued——

"To prevent your passion from growing stronger, it will be needful to prohibit Lorenzo's visits. The service which he has rendered me permits not my forbidding them positively; but unless I judge too favourably of his character, he will discontinue them without taking offence, if I confess to him my reasons, and throw myself entirely on his generosity. The next time that I see him, I will honestly avow to him the embarrassment which his presence occasions. How say you, my child? Is not this measure necessary?"

Antonia subscribed to every thing without hesitation, though not without regret. Her mother kissed her affectionately, and retired to bed. Antonia followed her example, and vowed so frequently never more to think of Lorenzo, that till sleep closed her eyes she thought of nothing else.

While this was passing at Elvira's, Lorenzo hastened to rejoin the marquis. Every thing was ready for the second elopement of Agnes; and at twelve the two friends with a coach and four were at the garden-wall of the convent. Don Raymond drew out his key, and unlocked the door. They entered, and waited for some time in expectation of being joined by Agnes. At length the marquis grew impatient: beginning to fear that his second attempt would succeed no better than the first, he proposed to reconnoitre the convent. The friends advanced towards it. Every thing was still and dark. The prioress was anxious to keep the story a secret, fearing lest the crime of one of its members should bring disgrace upon the whole community, or that the interposition of powerful relations should deprive her vengeance of its intended victim. She took care therefore to give the lover of Agnes no cause to suppose that his design was discovered, and his mistress on the point of suffering the punishment of her fault. The same reason made her reject the idea of arresting the unknown seducer in the garden: such a proceeding would have created much disturbance, and the disgrace of her convent would have been noised about Madrid. She contented herself with confining Agnes closely: as to the lover, she left him at liberty to pursue his designs. What she had expected was the result. The marquis and Lorenzo waited in vain till the break of day; they then retired without noise, alarmed at the failure of their plan, and ignorant of the cause of its ill success.

The next morning Lorenzo went to the convent, and requested to see his sister. The prioress appeared at the grate with a melancholy countenance. She informed him that for several days Agnes had appeared much agitated; that she had been pressed by the nuns in vain to reveal the cause, and apply to their tenderness for advice and consolation; that she had obstinately persisted in concealing the cause of her distress; but that on Thursday evening it had produced so violent an effect upon her constitution, that she had fallen ill, and was actually confined to her bed. Lorenzo did not credit a syllable of this account: he insisted upon seeing his sister; if she was unable to come to the grate, he desired to be admitted to her cell. The prioress crossed herself! she was shocked at the very idea of a man's profane eye pervading the interior of her holy mansion, and professed herself astonished that Lorenzo could think of such a thing. She told him that his request could not be granted; but that, if he returned the next day, she hoped that her beloved daughter would then be sufficiently recovered to join him at the parlour grate. With this answer Lorenzo was obliged to retire, unsatisfied, and trembling for his sister's safety.

He returned the next morning at an early hour. "Agnes was worse; the physician had pronounced her to be in imminent danger; she was ordered to remain quiet, and it was utterly impossible for her to receive her brother's visit." Lorenzo stormed at this answer, but there was no resource. He raved, he entreated, he threatened; no means were left untried to obtain a sight of Agnes. His endeavours were as fruitless as those of the day before, and he returned in despair to the marquis. On his side, the latter had spared no pains to discover what had occasioned his plot to fail. Don Christoval, to whom the affair was now entrusted, endeavoured to worm out the secret from the old porteress of St. Clare, with whom he had formed an acquaintance; but she was too much upon her guard, and he gained from her no intelligence. The marquis was almost distracted, and Lorenzo felt scarcely less inquietude. Both were convinced that the purposed elopement must have been discovered: they doubted not but the malady of Agnes was a pretence, but they knew not by what means to rescue her from the hands of the prioress.

Regularly every day did Lorenzo visit the convent: as regularly was he informed that his sister rather grew worse than better. Certain that her indisposition was feigned, these accounts did not alarm him: but his ignorance of her fate, and of the motives which induced the prioress to keep her from him, excited the most serious uneasiness. He was still uncertain what steps he ought to take, when the marquis received a letter from the cardinal-duke of Lerma. It inclosed the pope's expected bull, ordering that Agnes should be released from her vows, and restored to her relations. This essential paper decided at once the proceedings of her friends; they resolved that Lorenzo should carry it to the domina without delay, and demand that his sister should be instantly given up to him. Against this mandate illness could not be pleaded: it gave her brother the power of removing her instantly to the palace de Medina, and he determined to use that power on the following day.

His mind relieved from inquietude respecting his sister, and his spirits raised by the hope of soon restoring her to freedom, he now had time to give a few moments to love and to Antonia. At the same hour as on his former visit, he repaired to Donna Elvira's. She had given orders for his admission. As soon as he was announced, her daughter retired with Leonella; and when he entered the chamber, he found the lady of the house alone. She received him with less distance than before, and desired him to place himself near her upon the sopha. She then, without losing time, opened her business, as had been agreed between herself and Antonia.

"You must not think me ungrateful, Don Lorenzo, or forgetful how essential are the services which you have rendered me with the marquis. I feel the weight of my obligations: nothing under the sun should induce my taking the step to which I am now compelled, but the interest of my child, of my beloved Antonia. My health is declining; God only knows how soon I may be summoned before his throne. My daughter will be left without parents, and, should she lose the protection of the Cisternas family, without friends. She is young and artless, uninstructed in the world's perfidy, and with charms sufficient to render her an object of seduction. Judge then how I must tremble at the prospect before her! Judge, how anxious I must be to keep her from their society, who may excite the yet dormant passions of her bosom. You are amiable, Don Lorenzo; Antonia has a susceptible, a loving heart, and is grateful for the favours conferred upon us by your interference with the marquis. Your presence makes me tremble: I fear lest it should inspire her with sentiments which may embitter the remainder of her life, or encourage her to cherish hopes in her situation unjustifiable and futile. Pardon me, when I avow my terrors, and let my frankness plead in my excuse. I cannot forbid you my house, for gratitude restrains me; I can only throw myself upon your generosity, and entreat you to spare the feelings of an anxious, of a doting mother. Believe me, when I assure you, that I lament the necessity of rejecting your acquaintance; but there is no remedy, and Antonia's interest obliges me to beg you to forbear your visits. By complying with my request, you will increase the esteem which I already feel for you, and of which every thing convinces me that you are truly deserving."

"Your frankness charms me," replied Lorenzo: "You shall find, that in your favourable opinion of me you were not deceived; yet I hope that the reasons now in my power to allege, will persuade you to withdraw a request which I cannot obey without infinite reluctance. I love your daughter, love her most sincerely; I wish for no greater happiness than to inspire her with the same sentiments, and receive her hand at the altar as her husband. 'Tis true I am not rich myself, my father's death has left me but little in my own possession; but my expectations justify my pretending to the Condé de las Cisternas' daughter."

He was proceeding, but Elvira interrupted him——

"Ah! Don Lorenzo, you forget in that pompous title the meanness of my origin. You forget that I have now passed fourteen years in Spain, disavowed by my husband's family, and existing upon a stipend barely sufficient for the support and education of my daughter. Nay, I have even been neglected by most of my own relations, who out of envy affect to doubt the reality of my marriage. My allowance being discontinued at my father-in-law's death, I was reduced to the very brink of want. In this situation I was found by my sister, who, amongst all her foibles, possesses a warm, generous, and affectionate heart. She aided me with the little fortune which my father left her, persuaded me to visit Madrid, and has supported my child and myself since our quitting Murcia. Then, consider not Antonia as descended from the Condé de las Cisternas; consider her as a poor and unprotected orphan, as the grandchild of the tradesman Torribio Dalfa, as the needy pensioner of that tradesman's daughter. Reflect upon the difference between such a situation and that of the nephew and heir of the potent duke of Medina. I believe your intentions to be honourable; but as there are no hopes that your uncle will approve of the union, I foresee that the consequences of your attachment must be fatal to my child's repose."

"Pardon me, Segnora; you are misinformed if you suppose the duke of Medina to resemble the generality of men. His sentiments are liberal and disinterested; he loves me well, and I have no reason to dread his forbidding the marriage, when he perceives that my happiness depends upon Antonia. But supposing him to refuse his sanction, what have I still to fear? My parents are no more; my little fortune is in my own possession; it will be sufficient to support Antonia, and I shall exchange for her hand Medina's dukedom without one sigh of regret."

"You are young and eager; it is natural for you to entertain such ideas. But experience has taught me to my cost, that curses accompany an unequal alliance. I married the Condé de las Cisternas in opposition to the will of his relations; many an heart-pang has punished me for the imprudent step. Wherever we bent our course, a father's execration pursued Gonzalvo. Poverty overtook us, and no friend was near to relieve our wants. Still our mutual affection existed, but, alas! not without interruption. Accustomed to wealth and ease, ill could my husband support the transition to distress and indigence. He looked back with repining to the comforts which he once enjoyed. He regretted the situation which for my sake he had quitted; and, in moments when despair possessed his mind, has reproached me with having made him the companion of want and wretchedness. He has called me his bane! the source of his sorrows, the cause of his destruction! Ah! God! he little knew how much keener were my own heart's reproaches! He was ignorant that I suffered trebly, for myself, for my children, and for him! 'Tis true that his anger seldom lasted long: his sincere affection for me soon revived in his heart, and then his repentance for the tears which he had made me shed, tortured me even more than his reproaches. He would throw himself on the ground, implore my forgiveness in the most frantic terms, and load himself with curses for being the murderer of my repose. Taught by experience, that an union contracted against the inclinations of families on either side must be unfortunate, I will save my daughter from those miseries which I have suffered. Without your uncle's consent, while I live, she never shall be yours. Undoubtedly he will disapprove of the union; his power is immense, and Antonia shall not be exposed to his anger and persecution."

"His persecution? How easily may that be avoided! Let the worst happen, it is but quitting Spain. My wealth may easily be realised. The Indian islands will offer us a secure retreat. I have an estate, though not of value, in Hispaniola: thither will we fly, and I shall consider it to be my native country, if it gives me Antonia's undisturbed possession."

"Ah! youth, this is a fond, romantic vision. Gonzalvo thought the same. He fancied that he could leave Spain without regret; but the moment of parting undeceived him. You know not yet what it is to quit your native land: to quit it, never to behold it more! You know not what it is to exchange the scenes where you have passed your infancy, for unknown realms and barbarous climates!—to be forgotten, utterly, eternally forgotten by the companions of your youth!—to see your dearest friends, the fondest objects of your affection, perishing with diseases incidental to Indian atmospheres, and find yourself unable to procure for them necessary assistance! I have felt all this! My husband and two sweet babes found their graves in Cuba: nothing would have saved my young Antonia, but my sudden return to Spain. Ah! Don Lorenzo, could you conceive what I suffered during my absence! Could you know how sorely I regretted all that I left behind, and how dear to me was the very name of Spain! I envied the winds which blew towards it: and when the Spanish sailor chaunted some well-known air as he passed my window, tears filled my eyes, while I thought upon my native land. Gonzalvo too——my husband——"

Elvira paused. Her voice faltered, and she concealed her face with her handkerchief. After a short silence she rose from the sopha, and proceeded——

"Excuse my quitting you for a few moments: the remembrance of what I have suffered has much agitated me, and I need to be alone. Till I return, peruse these lines. After my husband's death I found them among his papers. Had I known sooner that he entertained such sentiments, grief would have killed me. He wrote these verses on his voyage to Cuba, when his mind was clouded by sorrow, and he forgot that he had a wife and children. What we are losing ever seems to us the most precious. Gonzalvo was quitting Spain for ever, and therefore was Spain dearer to his eyes than all else which the world contained. Read them, Don Lorenzo, they will give you some idea of the feelings of a banished man."

Elvira put a paper into Lorenzo's hand, and retired from the chamber. The youth examined the contents, and found them to be as follows:

THE EXILE.

FAREWELL, oh native Spain! farewell for ever!
    These banished eyes shall view thy coasts no more:
A mournful presage tells my heart, that never
    Gonzalvo's steps again shall press thy shore.

Hushed are the winds; while soft the vessel sailing
    With gentle motion plows the unruffled main,

I feel my bosom's boasted courage failing,
     And curse the waves which bear me far from Spain.

I see it yet! Beneath yon blue clear heaven
     Still do the spires, so well-beloved, appear.
From yonder craggy point the gale of even
     Still wafts my native accents to mine ear.

Propped on some moss-crowned rock, and gaily singing,
     There in the sun his nets the fisher dries;
Oft have I heard the plaintive ballad, bringing
     Scenes of past joys before my sorrowing eyes.

Ah! happy swain! he waits the accustomed hour,
     When twilight-gloom obscures the closing sky;
Then gladly seeks his loved paternal bower,
     And shares the feast his native fields supply.

Friendship and Love, his cottage guests, receive him
     With honest welcome and with smile sincere:
No threatening woes of present joys bereave him;
     No sigh his bosom owns, his cheek no tear.

Ah! happy swain! such bliss to me denying,
     Fortune thy lot with envy bids me view;
Me, who, from home and Spain an exile flying,
     Bid all I value, all I love, adieu.

No more mine ear shall list the well-known ditty
     Sung by some mountain-girl, who tends her goats,
Some village-swain imploring amorous pity,
     Or shepherd chanting wild his rustic notes.

No more my arms a parent's fond embraces,
     No more my heart domestic calm must know;
Far from these joys, with sighs which memory traces,
     To sultry skies and distant climes I go.

Where Indian suns engender new diseases,
     Where snakes and tigers breed, I bend my way
To brave the feverish thirst no art appeases,
     The yellow plague, and madding blaze of day.

But not to feel slow pangs consume my liver,
      To die by piece-meal in the bloom of age,
My boiling blood drank by insatiate fever,
      And brain delirious with the day-star's rage,

Can make me know such grief, as thus to sever,
      With many a bitter sigh, dear land! from thee;
To feel this heart must dote on thee for ever,
      And feel that all thy joys are torn from me!

Ah me! how oft will fancy's spells, in slumber,
      Recall my native country to my mind!
How oft regret will bid me sadly number
      Each lost delight, and dear friend left behind!

Wild Murcia's vales and loved romantic bowers,
      The river on whose banks a child I played,
My castle's antient halls, its frowning towers,
      Each much-regretted wood, and well-known glade;

Dreams of the land where all my wishes centre,
      Thy scenes, which I am doomed no more to know,
Full oft shall memory trace, my soul's tormentor,
      And turn each pleasure past to present woe.

But, lo! the sun beneath the waves retires;
      Night speeds apace her empire to restore;
Clouds from my sight obscure the village-spires,
      Now seen but faintly, and now seen no more.

Oh! breathe not, winds! Still be the water's motion!
      Sleep, sleep, my bark, in silence on the main!
So, when to-morrow's light shall gild the ocean,
      Once more mine eyes shall see the coast of Spain.

Vain is the wish! My last petition scorning,
      Fresh blows the gale, and high the billows swell:
Far shall we be before the break of morning:
      Oh! then, for ever, native Spain, farewell!

Lorenzo had scarcely time to read these lines, when Elvira
returned to him: the giving a free course to her tears had

relieved her, and her spirits had regained their usual compo-
sure.

"I have nothing more to say, my lord," said she; "you have heard
my apprehensions, and my reasons for begging you not to repeat
your visits. I have thrown myself in full confidence upon your honour. I am certain that you will not prove my opinion of you to have
been too favourable."

"But one question more, Segnora, and I leave you. Should the
duke of Medina approve my love, would my addresses be unacceptable to yourself and the fair Antonia?"

"I will be open with you, Don Lorenzo: there being little probability of such an union taking place, I fear that it is desired but too
ardently by my daughter. You have made an impression upon her
young heart which gives me the most serious alarm: to prevent that
impression from growing stronger, I am obliged to decline your
acquaintance. For me, you may be sure that I should rejoice at
establishing my child so advantageously. Conscious that my constitution, impaired by grief and illness, forbids me to expect a long
continuance in this world, I tremble at the thought of leaving her
under the protection of a perfect stranger. The marquis de las Cisternas is totally unknown to me. He will marry: his lady may look
upon Antonia with an eye of displeasure, and deprive her of her
only friend. Should the duke, your uncle, give his consent, you
need not doubt obtaining mine and my daughter's; but, without
his, hope not for ours. At all events, whatever steps you may take,
whatever may be the duke's decision, till you know it, let me beg
your forbearing to strengthen, by your presence, Antonia's prepossession. If the sanction of your relations authorises your addressing
her as your wife, my doors fly open to you. If that sanction is
refused, be satisfied to possess my esteem and gratitude, but
remember that we must meet no more."

Lorenzo promised reluctantly to conform to this decree: but he
added, that he hoped soon to obtain that consent, which would
give him a claim to the renewal of their acquaintance. He then
explained to her why the marquis had not called in person; and
made no scruple of confiding to her his sister's history. He concluded by saying, "that he hoped to set Agnes at liberty the next
day; and that, as soon as Don Raymond's fears were quieted upon
this subject, he would lose no time in assuring Donna Elvira of his
friendship and protection."

The lady shook her head.

"I tremble for your sister," said she; "I have heard many traits of the domina of St. Clare's character from a friend who was educated in the same convent with her: she reported her to be haughty, inflexible, superstitious, and revengeful. I have since heard, that she is infatuated with the idea of rendering her convent the most regular in Madrid, and never forgave those whose imprudence threw upon it the slightest stain. Though naturally violent and severe, when her interests require it, she well knows how to assume an appearance of benignity. She leaves no means untried to persuade young women of rank to become members of her community: she is implacable when once incensed, and has too much intrepidity to shrink at taking the most rigorous measures for punishing the offender. Doubtless, she will consider your sister's quitting the convent as a disgrace thrown upon it: she will use every artifice to avoid obeying the mandate of his holiness; and I shudder to think that Donna Agnes is in the hands of this dangerous woman."

Lorenzo now rose to take leave. Elvira gave him her hand at parting, which he kissed respectfully; and, telling her that he soon hoped for the permission to salute that of Antonia, he returned to his hotel. The lady was perfectly satisfied with the conversation which had passed between them: she looked forward with satisfaction to the prospect of his becoming her son-in-law; but prudence bade her conceal from her daughter's knowledge the flattering hopes which herself now ventured to entertain.

Scarcely was it day, and already Lorenzo was at the convent of St. Clare, furnished with the necessary mandate. The nuns were at matins. He waited impatiently for the conclusion of the service; and at length the prioress appeared at the parlour-grate. Agnes was demanded. The old lady replied with a melancholy air, that the dear child's situation grew hourly more dangerous: that the physicians despaired of her life; but that they had declared the only chance for her recovery to consist in keeping her quiet, and not to permit those to approach her whose presence was likely to agitate her. Not a word of all this was believed by Lorenzo, any more than he credited the expressions of grief and affection for Agnes with which this account was interlarded. To end the business, he put the pope's bull into the hands of the domina, and insisted that, ill or in health, his sister should be delivered to him without delay.

The prioress received the paper with an air of humility; but no sooner had her eye glanced over the contents than her resentment baffled all the efforts of hypocrisy. A deep crimson spread itself over her face, and she darted upon Lorenzo looks of rage and menace.

"This order is positive," said she, in a voice of anger, which she in vain strove to disguise: "willingly would I obey it, but, unfortunately, it is out of my power."

Lorenzo interrupted her by an exclamation of surprise.

"I repeat it, Segnor, to obey this order is totally out of my power. From tenderness to a brother's feelings, I would have communicated the sad event to you by degrees, and have prepared you to hear it with fortitude. My measures are broken through: this order commands me to deliver up to you the sister Agnes without delay; I am, therefore, obliged to inform you, without circumlocution, that on Friday last she expired."

Lorenzo started back with horror, and turned pale. A moment's recollection convinced him that this assertion must be false, and it restored him to himself.

"You deceive me!" said he, passionately: "but five minutes past you assured me that, though ill, she was still alive. Produce her this instant! See her I must and will; and every attempt to keep her from me will be unavailing."

"You forget yourself, Segnor: you owe respect to my age as well as my profession. Your sister is no more. If I at first concealed her death, it was from dreading lest an event so unexpected should produce on you too violent an effect. In truth, I am but ill repaid for my attention. And what interest, I pray you, should I have in detaining her? To know her wish of quitting our society is a sufficient reason for me to wish her absence, and think her a disgrace to the sisterhood of St. Clare: but she has forfeited my affection in a manner yet more culpable. Her crimes were great; and when you know the cause of her death, you will doubtless rejoice, Don Lorenzo, that such a wretch is no longer in existence. She was taken ill on Thursday last on returning from confession in the Capuchin chapel: her malady seemed attended with strange circumstances; but she persisted in concealing its cause. Thanks to the Virgin, we were too ignorant to suspect it! Judge then what must have been our consternation, our horror, when she was delivered the next day of a still-born child, whom she immediately followed to the grave. How, Segnor? Is it possible that your countenance expresses no surprise, no indignation? Is it possible that your sister's infamy was known to you, and that still she possessed your affection? In that case, you have no need of my compassion. I can say nothing more, except repeat my inability of obeying the orders of his holiness. Agnes is no more; and, to convince you that what I say is true, I swear by our blessed Saviour, that three days have passed since she was buried."

Here she kissed a small crucifix which hung at her girdle: she then rose from her chair, and quitted the parlour. As she withdrew she cast upon Lorenzo a scornful smile.

"Farewell, Segnor," said she; "I know no remedy for this accident. I fear that even a second bull from the pope will not procure your sister's resurrection."

Lorenzo also retired, penetrated with affliction: but Don Raymond's, at the news of this event, amounted to madness: he would not be convinced that Agnes was really dead; and continued to insist that the walls of St. Clare still confined her. No arguments could make him abandon his hopes of regaining her. Every day some fresh scheme was invented for procuring intelligence of her, and all of them were attended with the same success.

On his part, Medina gave up the idea of ever seeing his sister more; yet he believed that she had been taken off by unfair means. Under this persuasion, he encouraged Don Raymond's researches, determined, should he discover the least warrant for his suspicions, to take a severe vengeance upon the unfeeling prioress. The loss of his sister affected him sincerely: nor was it the least cause of his distress, that propriety obliged him for some time to defer mentioning Antonia to the duke. In the mean while, his emissaries constantly surrounded Elvira's door. He had intelligence of all the movements of his mistress. As she never failed every Thursday to attend the sermon in the Capuchin cathedral, he was secure of seeing her once a week; though, in compliance with his promise, he carefully shunned her observation. Thus two long months passed away. Still no information was procured of Agnes. All but the marquis credited her death: and now Lorenzo determined to disclose his sentiments to his uncle: he had already dropped some hints of his intention to marry: they had been as favourably received as he could expect; and he harboured no doubt of the success of his application.

CHAP. VI.

> While in each other's arms entranced they lay,
> They blessed the night, and cursed the coming day.
>
> LEE.[1]

---

1 Adapted from Nathaniel Lee (1653?-92), *Sophonisba; or, Hannibal's Overthrow* 1.1.240-41.

rst of transport was passed: Ambrosio's lust was satisfied. : fled, and Shame usurped her seat in his bosom. Confused rified at his weakness, he drew himself from Matilda's arms: rjury presented itself before him: he reflected on the scene which had just been acted, and trembled at the consequences of a discovery: he looked forward with horror: his heart was despondent, and became the abode of satiety and disgust: he avoided the eyes of his partner in frailty. A melancholy silence prevailed, during which both seemed busied with disagreeable reflections.

Matilda was the first to break it. She took his hand gently, and pressed it to her burning lips.

"Ambrosio!" she murmured, in a soft and trembling voice.

The abbot started at the sound: he turned his eyes upon Matilda's; they were filled with tears; her cheeks were covered with blushes, and her supplicating looks seemed to solicit his compassion.

"Dangerous woman!" said he; "into what an abyss of misery have you plunged me! Should your sex be discovered, my honour, nay, my life, must pay for the pleasure of a few moments. Fool that I was, to trust myself to your seductions! What can now be done? How can my offence be expiated? What atonement can purchase the pardon of my crime? Wretched Matilda, you have destroyed my quiet for ever!"

"To me these reproaches, Ambrosio? to me, who have sacrificed for you the world's pleasures, the luxury of wealth, the delicacy of sex, my friends, my fortune, and my fame? What have you lost which I preserved? Have *I* not shared in *your* guilt? Have *you* not shared in *my* pleasure? Guilt, did I say? In what consists ours, unless in the opinion of an ill-judging world? Let that world be ignorant of them, and our joys become divine and blameless! Unnatural were your vows of celibacy; man was not created for such a state: and were love a crime, God never would have made it so sweet, so irresistible! Then banish those clouds from your brow, my Ambrosio. Indulge in those pleasures freely, without which life is a worthless gift. Cease to reproach me with having taught you what is bliss, and feel equal transports with the woman who adores you!"

As she spoke, her eyes were filled with a delicious languor: her bosom panted: she twined her arms voluptuously round him, drew him towards her, and glued her lips to his. Ambrosio again raged with desire: the die was thrown:[1] his vows were already broken: he

---

1 Another allusion to Suetonius, *Divus Julius* 32; cf. 174n.

had already committed the crime, and why should he refrain from enjoying its reward? He clasped her to his breast with redoubled ardour. No longer repressed by the sense of shame, he gave a loose to his intemperate appetites; while the fair wanton put every invention of lust in practice, every refinement in the art of pleasure, which might heighten the bliss of her possession, and render her lover's transports still more exquisite. Ambrosio rioted in delights till then unknown to him. Swift fled the night, and the morning blushed to behold him still clasped in the embraces of Matilda.

Intoxicated with pleasure, the monk rose from the syren's luxurious couch: he no longer reflected with shame upon his incontinence, or dreaded the vengeance of offended heaven: his only fear was lest death should rob him of enjoyments, for which his long fast had only given a keener edge to his appetite. Matilda was still under the influence of poison; and the voluptuous monk trembled less for his preserver's life than his concubine's. Deprived of her, he would not easily find another mistress with whom he could indulge his passions so fully, and so safely; he therefore pressed her with earnestness to use the means of preservation which she had declared to be in her possession.

"Yes!" replied Matilda; "since you have made me feel that life is valuable, I will rescue mine at any rate. No dangers shall appal me: I will look upon the consequences of my action boldly, nor shudder at the horrors which they present: I will think my sacrifice scarcely worthy to purchase your possession; and remember, that a moment passed in your arms in this world, o'erpays an age of punishment in the next. But before I take this step, Ambrosio, give me your solemn oath never to enquire by what means I shall preserve myself."

He did so, in a manner the most binding.

"I thank you, my beloved. This precaution is necessary; for, though you know it not, you are under the command of vulgar prejudices. The business on which I must be employed this night might startle you, from its singularity, and lower me in your opinion. Tell me, are you possessed of the key of the low door on the western side of the garden?"

"The door which opens into the burying-ground common to us and the sisterhood of St. Clare? I have not the key, but can easily procure it."

"You have only this to do. Admit me into the burying-ground at midnight. Watch while I descend into the vaults of St. Clare, lest some prying eye should observe my actions. Leave me there alone for an hour, and that life is safe which I dedicate to your pleasures. To prevent creating suspicion, do not visit me during the day. Remember the key, and that I expect you before twelve. Hark! I hear steps approaching! Leave me; I will pretend to sleep."

The friar obeyed, and left the cell. As he opened the door, father Pablos made his appearance.

"I come," said the latter, "to enquire after the health of my young patient."

"Hush!" replied Ambrosio, laying his finger upon his lip; "speak softly; I am just come from him: he has fallen into a profound slumber, which doubtless will be of service to him. Do not disturb him at present, for he wishes to repose."

Father Pablos obeyed, and, hearing the bell ring, accompanied the abbot to matins. Ambrosio felt embarrassed as he entered the chapel. Guilt was new to him, and he fancied that every eye could read the transactions of the night upon his countenance. He strove to pray: his bosom no longer glowed with devotion: his thoughts insensibly wandered to Matilda's secret charms. But what he wanted in purity of heart, he supplied by exterior sanctity. The better to cloak his transgression, he redoubled his pretensions to the semblance of virtue, and never appeared more devoted to heaven than since he had broken through his engagements. Thus did he unconsciously add hypocrisy to perjury and incontinence: he had fallen into the latter errors from yielding to seduction almost irresistible: but he was now guilty of a voluntary fault, by endeavouring to conceal those into which another had betrayed him.

The matins concluded, Ambrosio retired to his cell. The pleasures which he had just tasted for the first time were still impressed upon his mind: his brain was bewildered, and presented a confused chaos of remorse, voluptuousness, inquietude, and fear: he looked back with regret to that peace of soul, that security of virtue, which till then had been his portion: he had indulged in excesses whose very idea, but four-and-twenty hours before, he had recoiled at with horror: he shuddered at reflecting that a trifling indiscretion on his part, or on Matilda's, would overturn that fabric of reputation which it had cost him thirty years to erect, and render him the abhorrence of that people of whom he was then the idol. Conscience painted to him in glaring colours his perjury and weakness; apprehension magnified to him the horrors of punishment, and he already fancied himself in the prisons of the Inquisition. To these tormenting ideas succeeded Matilda's beauty, and those delicious

lessons, which once learnt can never be forgotten. A single gla[nce]
thrown upon these reconciled him with himself: he considered the
pleasures of the former night to have been purchased at an easy
price by the sacrifice of innocence and honour. Their very remembrance filled his soul with ecstacy: he cursed his foolish vanity,
which had induced him to waste in obscurity the bloom of life,
ignorant of the blessings of love and woman: he determined, at all
events, to continue his commerce with Matilda, and called every
argument to his aid which might confirm his resolution: he asked
himself, provided his irregularity was unknown, in what would his
fault consist, and what consequences he had to apprehend? By
adhering strictly to every rule of his order save chastity, he doubted not to retain the esteem of men, and even the protection of
heaven: he trusted easily to be forgiven so slight and natural a deviation from his vows; but he forgot that, having pronounced those
vows, incontinence, in laymen the most venial of errors, became in
his person the most heinous of crimes.

Once decided upon his future conduct, his mind became more
easy: he threw himself upon his bed, and strove by sleeping to
recruit his strength, exhausted by his nocturnal excesses. He awoke
refreshed, and eager for a repetition of his pleasures. Obedient to
Matilda's order, he visited not her cell during the day. Father Pablos mentioned in the refectory, that Rosario had at length been
prevailed upon to follow his prescription; but that the medicine
had not produced the slightest effect, and that he believed no mortal skill could rescue him from the grave. With this opinion the
abbot agreed, and affected to lament the untimely fate of a youth
whose talents had appeared so promising.

The night arrived. Ambrosio had taken care to procure from the
porter the key of the low door opening into the cemetery. Furnished with this, when all was silent in the monastery, he quitted
his cell, and hastened to Matilda's. She had left her bed, and was
dressed before his arrival.

"I have been expecting you with impatience," said she; "my life
depends upon these moments. Have you the key?"

"I have."

"Away then to the garden. We have no time to lose. Follow
me!"

She took a small covered basket from the table. Bearing this in
one hand, and the lamp, which was flaming upon the hearth, in the
other, she hastened from the cell. Ambrosio followed her. Both
maintained a profound silence. She moved on with quick but cau-

tious steps, passed through the cloisters, and reached the western side of the garden: her eyes flashed with a fire and wildness which impressed the monk at once with awe and horror. A determined desperate courage reigned upon her brow: she gave the lamp to Ambrosio; then taking from him the key, she unlocked the low door, and entered the cemetery. It was a vast and spacious square, planted with yew-trees; half of it belonged to the abbey, the other half was the property of the sisterhood of St. Clare, and was protected by a roof of stone: the division was marked by an iron railing, the wicket of which was generally left unlocked.

Thither Matilda bent her course: she opened the wicket, and sought for the door leading to the subterraneous vaults where reposed the mouldering bodies of the votaries of St. Clare. The night was perfectly dark; neither moon nor stars were visible. Luckily there was not a breath of wind, and the friar bore his lamp in full security: by the assistance of its beams, the door of the sepulchre was soon discovered. It was sunk within the hollow of a wall, and almost concealed by thick festoons of ivy hanging over it. Three steps of rough-hewn stone conducted to it, and Matilda was on the point of descending them, when she suddenly started back.

"There are people in the vaults!" she whispered to the monk; "conceal yourself till they are passed."

She took refuge behind a lofty and magnificent tomb, erected in honour of the convent's foundress. Ambrosio followed her example, carefully hiding his lamp, lest its beams should betray them. But a few moments had elapsed when the door was pushed open leading to the subterraneous caverns. Rays of light proceeded up the stair-case: they enabled the concealed spectators to observe two females dressed in religious habits, who seemed engaged in earnest conversation. The abbot had no difficulty to recognize the prioress of St. Clare in the first, and one of the elder nuns in her companion.

"Every thing is prepared," said the prioress: "her fate shall be decided to-morrow; all her tears and sighs will be unavailing. No! In five-and-twenty years that I have been superior of this convent, never did I witness a transaction more infamous!"

"You must expect much opposition to your will," the other replied in a milder voice: "Agnes has many friends in the convent, and in particular the mother St. Ursula will espouse her cause most warmly. In truth, she merits to have friends; and I wish I could prevail upon you to consider her youth, and her peculiar situation. She seems sensible of her fault; the excess of her grief proves her penitence, and I am convinced that her tears flow more from contrition than fear of punishment. Reverend mother, would you be persuaded to mitigate the severity of your sentence; would you but deign to overlook this first transgression; I offer myself as the pledge of her future conduct."

"Overlook it, say you? Mother Camilla, you amaze me! What? after disgracing me in the presence of Madrid's idol, of the very man on whom I most wished to impress an idea of the strictness of my discipline? How despicable must I have appeared to the reverend abbot! No, mother, no! I never can forgive the insult. I cannot better convince Ambrosio that I abhor such crimes, than by punishing that of Agnes with all the rigour of which our severe laws admit. Cease then your supplications, they will all be unavailing. My resolution is taken. To-morrow Agnes shall be made a terrible example of my justice and resentment."

The mother Camilla seemed not to give up the point, but by this time the nuns were out of hearing. The prioress unlocked the door which communicated with St. Clare's chapel, and having entered with her companion, closed it again after them.

Matilda now asked, who was this Agnes with whom the prioress was thus incensed, and what connexion she could have with Ambrosio. He related her adventure; and he added, that since that time his ideas having undergone a thorough revolution, he now felt much compassion for the unfortunate nun.

"I design," said he, "to request an audience of the domina to-morrow, and use every means of obtaining a mitigation of her sentence."

"Beware of what you do," interrupted Matilda; "your sudden change of sentiment may naturally create surprise, and may give birth to suspicions which it is most our interest to avoid. Rather redouble your outward austerity, and thunder out menaces against the errors of others, the better to conceal your own. Abandon the nun to her fate. Your interfering might be dangerous, and her imprudence merits to be punished: she is unworthy to enjoy love's pleasures, who has not wit enough to conceal them. But in discussing this trifling subject, I waste moments which are precious. The night flies apace, and much must be done before morning. The nuns are retired, all is safe. Give me the lamp, Ambrosio, I must descend alone into these caverns: wait here, and if any one approaches warn me by your voice; but as you value your existence, presume not to follow me, your life would fall a victim to your imprudent curiosity."

Thus saying, she advanced towards the sepulchre, still holding her lamp in one hand, and her little basket in the other. She touched the door, it turned slowly upon its grating hinges, and a narrow winding stair-case of black marble presented itself to her eyes. She descended it; Ambrosio remained above, watching the faint beams of the lamp, as they still receded down the stairs. They disappeared, and he found himself in total darkness.

Left to himself, he could not reflect without surprise on the sudden change in Matilda's character and sentiments. But a few days had passed, since she appeared the mildest and softest of her sex, devoted to his will, and looking up to him as to a superior being. Now she assumed a sort of courage and manliness in her manners and discourse, but ill calculated to please him. She spoke no longer to insinuate, but command: he found himself unable to cope with her in argument, and was unwillingly obliged to confess the superiority of her judgment. Every moment convinced him of the astonishing powers of her mind; but what she gained in the opinion of the man, she lost with interest in the affection of the lover. He regretted Rosario, the fond, the gentle, and submissive; he grieved that Matilda preferred the virtues of his sex to those of her own; and when he thought of her expressions respecting the devoted nun, he could not help blaming them as cruel and unfeminine. Pity is a sentiment so natural, so appropriate to the female character, that it is scarcely a merit for a woman to possess it, but to be without it is a grievous crime. Ambrosio could not easily forgive his mistress for being deficient in this amiable quality. However, though he blamed her insensibility, he felt the truth of her observations; and though he pitied sincerely the unfortunate Agnes, he resolved to drop the idea of interposing in her behalf.

Near an hour had elapsed since Matilda descended into the caverns; still she returned not. Ambrosio's curiosity was excited. He drew near the stair-case—he listened—all was silent, except that at intervals he caught the sound of Matilda's voice, as it wound along the subterraneous passages, and was re-echoed by the sepulchre's vaulted roofs. She was at too great a distance for him to distinguish her words, and ere they reached him, they were deadened into a low murmur. He longed to penetrate into this mystery. He resolved to disobey her injunctions, and follow her into the cavern. He advanced to the stair-case; he had already descended some steps, when his courage failed him. He remembered Matilda's menaces if he infringed her orders, and his bosom was filled with a secret unaccountable awe. He returned up the stairs, resumed his former station, and waited impatiently for the conclusion of this adventure.

Suddenly he was sensible of a violent shock. An earthquake rocked the ground, the columns which supported the roof under which he stood, were so strongly shaken, that every moment menaced him with its fall, and at the same moment he heard a loud and tremendous burst of thunder; it ceased, and his eyes being fixed upon the stair-case, he saw a bright column of light flash along the caverns beneath. It was seen but for an instant. No sooner did it disappear, than all was once more quiet and obscure. Profound darkness again surrounded him, and the silence of night was only broken by the whirring bat as she flitted slowly by him.

With every instant Ambrosio's amazement increased. Another hour elapsed, after which the same light again appeared, and was lost again as suddenly. It was accompanied by a strain of sweet but solemn music, which, as it stole through the vaults below, inspired the monk with mingled delight and terror. It had not long been hushed, when he heard Matilda's steps upon the stair-case. She ascended from the cavern; the most lively joy animated her beautiful features.

"Did you see any thing?" she asked.

"Twice I saw a column of light flash up the stair-case."

"Nothing else?"

"Nothing."

"The morning is on the point of breaking, let us retire to the abbey, lest day-light should betray us."

With a light step she hastened from the burying-ground. She regained her cell, and the curious abbot still accompanied her. She closed the door, and disembarrassed herself of her lamp and basket.

"I have succeeded!" she cried, throwing herself upon his bosom; "succeeded beyond my fondest hopes! I shall live, Ambrosio, shall live for you! the step, which I shuddered at taking, proves to me a source of joys inexpressible! Oh! that I dared communicate those joys to you! Oh! that I were permitted to share with you my power, and raise you as high above the level of your sex, as one bold deed has exalted me above mine!"

"And what prevents you, Matilda?" interrupted the friar, "Why is your business in the cavern made a secret? Do you think me undeserving of your confidence? Matilda, I must doubt the truth of your affection, while you have joys in which I am forbidden to share."

"You reproach me with injustice; I grieve sincerely that I am obliged to conceal from you my happiness: but I am not to blame; the fault lies not in me, but in yourself, my Ambrosio. You are still too much the monk, your mind is enslaved by the prejudices of education; and superstition might make you shudder at the idea of that which experience has taught me to prize and value. At present you are unfit to be trusted with a secret of such importance; but the strength of your judgment, and the curiosity which I rejoice to see sparkling in your eyes, makes me hope that you will one day deserve my confidence. Till that period arrives, restrain your impatience. Remember that you have given me your solemn oath, never to enquire into this night's adventures. I insist upon your keeping this oath; for, though," she added smiling, while she sealed his lips with a wanton kiss, "though I forgive your breaking your vows to heaven, I expect you to keep your vows to me."

The friar returned the embrace, which had set his blood on fire. The luxurious and unbounded excesses of the former night were renewed, and they separated not till the bell rang for matins.

The same pleasures were frequently repeated. The monks rejoiced in the feigned Rosario's unexpected recovery, and none of them suspected his real sex. The abbot possessed his mistress in tranquillity, and, perceiving his frailty unsuspected, abandoned himself to his passions in full security. Shame and remorse no longer tormented him. Frequent repetitions made him familiar with sin, and his bosom became proof against the stings of conscience. In these sentiments he was encouraged by Matilda; but she soon was aware that she had satiated her lover by the unbounded freedom of her caresses. Her charms becoming accustomed to him, they ceased to excite the same desires which at first they had inspired. The delirium of passion being past, he had leisure to observe every trifling defect; where none were to be found, satiety made him fancy them. The monk was glutted with the fullness of pleasure. A week had scarcely elapsed, before he was wearied of his paramour: his warm constitution still made him seek in her arms the gratification of his lust. But when the moment of passion was over, he quitted her with disgust, and his humour, naturally inconstant, made him sigh impatiently for variety.

Possession, which cloys man, only increases the affection of women. Matilda with every succeeding day grew more attached to the friar. Since he had obtained her favours, he was become dearer to her than ever, and she felt grateful to him for the pleasures in which they had equally been sharers. Unfortunately as her passion grew ardent, Ambrosio's grew cold; the very marks of her fondness excited his disgust, and its excess served to extinguish the flame which already burned but feebly in his bosom. Matilda could not but remark that her society seemed to him daily less agreeable; he was inattentive while she spoke; her musical talents, which she possessed in perfection, had lost the power of amusing him; or if he deigned to praise them, his compliments were evidently forced and cold. He no longer gazed upon her with affection, or applauded her sentiments with a lover's partiality. This Matilda well perceived, and redoubled her efforts to revive those sentiments which he once had felt. She could not but fail, since he considered as importunities, the pains which she took to please him, and was disgusted by the very means which she used to recall the wanderer. Still, however, their illicit commerce continued; but it was clear that he was led to her arms, not by love, but the cravings of brutal appetite. His constitution made a woman necessary to him, and Matilda was the only one with whom he could indulge his passions safely. In spite of her beauty, he gazed upon every other female with more desire; but fearing that his hypocrisy should be made public, he confined his inclinations to his own breast.

It was by no means his nature to be timid: but his education had impressed his mind with fear so strongly, that apprehension was now become part of his character. Had his youth been passed in the world, he would have shown himself possessed of many brilliant and manly qualities. He was naturally enterprizing, firm, and fearless: he had a warrior's heart, and he might have shone with splendour at the head of an army. There was no want of generosity in his nature: the wretched never failed to find in him a compassionate auditor: his abilities were quick and shining, and his judgment vast, solid, and decisive. With such qualifications he would have been an ornament to his country: that he possessed them he had given proofs in his earliest infancy, and his parents had beheld his dawning virtues with the fondest delight and admiration. Unfortunately, while yet a child, he was deprived of those parents. He fell into the power of a relation, whose only wish about him was never to hear of him more: for that purpose he gave him in charge to his friend, the former superior of the Capuchins. The abbot, a very monk, used all his endeavours to persuade the boy that happiness existed not without the walls of a convent. He succeeded fully. To deserve admittance into the order of St. Francis was Ambrosio's highest ambition. His instructors carefully repressed those virtues, whose grandeur and disinterestedness were ill suited to the cloister. Instead of universal benevolence, he adopted a selfish partiality for his own particular establishment: he was taught to consider compassion for the errors of others as a crime of the blackest dye: the noble frankness of his temper was exchanged for servile humility; and in order to break his natural spirit, the monks terrified his young mind, by placing before him all the horrors with which superstition could furnish them: they painted to him the torments of the damned in colours the most dark, terrible and fantastic, and threatened him at the slightest fault with eternal perdition.[1] No wonder that his imagination constantly dwelling upon these fearful objects should have rendered his character timid and apprehensive. Add to this, that his long absence from the great world, and total unacquaintance with the common dangers of life, made him form of them an idea far more dismal than the reality. While the monks were busied in rooting out his virtues, and narrowing his sentiments, they allowed every vice which had fallen to his share to arrive at full perfection. He was suffered to be proud, vain, ambitious, and disdainful: he was jealous of his equals, and despised all merit but his own: he was implacable when offended, and cruel in his revenge. Still in spite of the pains taken to pervert them, his natural good qualities would occasionally break through the gloom cast over them so carefully. At such times the contest for superiority between his real and acquired character was striking and unaccountable to those unacquainted with his original disposition. He pronounced the most severe sentences upon offenders, which the moment after compassion induced him to mitigate: he undertook the most daring enterprizes, which the fear of their consequences soon obliged him to abandon: his inborn genius darted a brilliant light upon subjects the most obscure; and almost instantaneously his superstition replunged them in darkness more profound than that from which they had just been rescued. His brother monks, regarding him as a superior being, remarked not this contradiction in their idol's conduct. They were persuaded that what he did must be right, and supposed him to have good reasons for changing his resolutions. The fact was, that the different sentiments with which education and nature had inspired him, were combating in his bosom: it remained for his passions, which as yet no opportunity had called into play, to decide the victory. Unfortunately his passions were the very worst judges to whom he could possibly have applied. His monastic seclusion had till now been in

---

1 Cf. the education of the Prince in Schiller, *The Ghost-Seer* 46.

his favour, since it gave him no room for discovering his bad qualities. The superiority of his talents raised him too far above his companions to permit his being jealous of them: his exemplary piety, persuasive eloquence, and pleasing manners had secured him universal esteem, and consequently he had no injuries to revenge: his ambition was justified by his acknowledged merit, and his pride considered as no more than proper confidence. He never saw, much less conversed with the other sex: he was ignorant of the pleasures in woman's power to bestow; and if he read in the course of his studies

"That men were fond, he smiled, and wondered how."[1]

For a time spare diet, frequent watching, and severe penance cooled and repressed the natural warmth of his constitution: but no sooner did opportunity present itself, no sooner did he catch a glimpse of joys to which he was still a stranger, than religion's barriers were too feeble to resist the overwhelming torrent of his desires. All impediments yielded before the force of his temperament, warm, sanguine, and voluptuous in the excess. As yet his other passions lay dormant; but they only needed to be once awakened, to display themselves with violence as great and irresistible.

He continued to be the admiration of Madrid. The enthusiasm created by his eloquence seemed rather to increase than diminish. Every Thursday, which was the only day when he appeared in public, the Capuchin cathedral was crowded with auditors, and his discourse was always received with the same approbation. He was named confessor to all the chief families in Madrid; and no one was counted fashionable who was injoined penance by any other than Ambrosio. In his resolution of never stirring out of his convent he still persisted. This circumstance created a still greater opinion of his sanctity and self-denial. Above all, the women sang forth his praises loudly, less influenced by devotion than by his noble countenance, majestic air, and well-turned graceful figure. The abbey-door was thronged with carriages from morning to night; and the noblest and fairest dames of Madrid confessed to the abbot their secret peccadilloes. The eyes of the luxurious friar devoured their charms. Had his penitents consulted those interpreters, he would have needed no other means of expressing his desires. For

---

1 Adapted from Shakespeare, *Measure for Measure* 2.2.187.

his misfortune, they were so strongly persuaded of his continence, that the possibility of his harbouring indecent thoughts never once entered their imaginations. The climate's heat, 'tis well known, operates with no small influence upon the constitutions of the Spanish ladies: but the most abandoned would have thought it an easier task to inspire with passion the marble statue of St. Francis than the cold and rigid heart of the immaculate Ambrosio.

On his part, the friar was little acquainted with the depravity of the world: he suspected not that but few of his penitents would have rejected his addresses. Yet had he been better instructed on this head, the danger attending such an attempt would have sealed up his lips in silence. He knew that it would be difficult for a woman to keep a secret so strange and so important as his frailty; and he even trembled, lest Matilda should betray him. Anxious to preserve a reputation which was infinitely dear to him, he saw all the risque of committing it to the power of some vain giddy female; and as the beauties of Madrid affected only his senses without touching his heart, he forgot them as soon as they were out of his sight. The danger of discovery, the fear of being repulsed, the loss of reputation; all these considerations counselled him to stifle his desires; and though he now felt for it the most perfect indifference, he was necessitated to confine himself to Matilda's person.

One morning, the confluence of penitents was greater than usual. He was detained in the confessional chair till a late hour. At length the crowd was dispatched, and he prepared to quit the chapel, when two females entered, and drew near him with humility. They threw up their veils, and the youngest entreated him to listen to her for a few moments. The melody of her voice, of that voice to which no man ever listened without interest, immediately caught Ambrosio's attention. He stopped. The petitioner seemed bowed down with affliction: her cheeks were pale, her eyes dimmed with tears, and her hair fell in disorder over her face and bosom. Still her countenance was so sweet, so innocent, so heavenly, as might have charmed an heart less susceptible than that which panted in the abbot's breast. With more than usual softness of manner he desired her to proceed, and heard her speak as follows, with an emotion which increased every moment.

"Reverend father, you see an unfortunate threatened with the loss of her dearest, of almost her only friend! My mother, my excellent mother lies upon the bed of sickness. A sudden and dreadful malady seized her last night, and so rapid has been its progress that the physicians despair of her life. Human aid fails me; nothing remains for me but to implore the mercy of heaven. Father, all Madrid rings with the report of your piety and virtue. Deign to remember my mother in your prayers: perhaps they may prevail on the Almighty to spare her; and should that be the case, I engage myself every Thursday in the next three months to illuminate the shrine of St. Francis in his honour."

"So!" thought the monk; "here we have a second Vincentio della Ronda. Rosario's adventure began thus;" and he wished secretly that this might have the same conclusion.

He acceded to the request. The petitioner returned him thanks with every mark of gratitude, and then continued:

"I have yet another favour to ask. We are strangers in Madrid: my mother needs a confessor, and knows not to whom she should apply. We understand that you never quit the abbey, and, alas! my poor mother is unable to come hither! If you would have the goodness, reverend father, to name a proper person, whose wise and pious consolations may soften the agonies of my parent's death-bed, you will confer an everlasting favour upon hearts not ungrateful."

With this petition also the monk complied. Indeed, what petition would he have refused, if urged in such enchanting accents? The suppliant was so interesting! Her voice was so sweet, so harmonious! Her very tears became her, and her affliction seemed to add new lustre to her charms. He promised to send to her a confessor that same evening, and begged her to leave her address. The companion presented him with a card on which it was written, and then withdrew with the fair petitioner, who pronounced before her departure a thousand benedictions on the abbot's goodness. His eyes followed her out of the chapel. It was not till she was out of sight that he examined the card, on which he read the following words:

"Donna Elvira Dalfa, strada di San Iago, four doors from the palace d'Albornos."

The suppliant was no other than Antonia, and Leonella was her companion. The latter had not consented without difficulty to accompany her niece to the abbey: Ambrosio had inspired her with such awe, that she trembled at the very sight of him. Her fears had conquered even her natural loquacity, and while in his presence she uttered not a single syllable.

The monk retired to his cell, whither he was pursued by Antonia's image. He felt a thousand new emotions springing in his bosom, and he trembled to examine into the cause which gave them birth. They were totally different from those inspired by Matilda, when she first declared her sex and her affection. He felt not the provocation of lust; no voluptuous desires rioted in his bosom; nor did a burning imagination picture to him the charms which modesty had veiled from his eyes. On the contrary, what he now felt was a mingled sentiment of tenderness, admiration, and respect. A soft and delicious melancholy infused itself into his soul, and he would not have exchanged it for the most lively transports of joy. Society now disgusted him: he delighted in solitude, which permitted his indulging the visions of fancy: his thoughts were all gentle, sad, and soothing; and the whole wide world presented him with no other object than Antonia.

"Happy man!" he exclaimed in his romantic enthusiasm, "happy man, who is destined to possess the heart of that lovely girl! what delicacy in her features! what elegance in her form! how enchanting was the timid innocence of her eyes! and how different from the wanton expression, the wild luxurious fire, which sparkles in Matilda's! Oh! sweeter must one kiss be, snatched from the rosy lips of the first, than all the full and lustful favours bestowed so freely by the second. Matilda gluts me with enjoyment even to loathing, forces me to her arms, apes the harlot, and glories in her prostitution. Disgusting! Did she know the inexpressible charm of modesty, how irresistibly it enthrals the heart of man, how firmly it chains him to the throne of beauty, she never would have thrown it off. What would be too dear a price for this lovely girl's affections? What would I refuse to sacrifice, could I be released from my vows, and permitted to declare my love in the sight of earth and heaven? While I strove to inspire her with tenderness, with friendship and esteem, how tranquil and undisturbed would the hours roll away! Gracious God! to see her blue downcast eyes beam upon mine with timid fondness! to sit for days, for years, listening to that gentle voice! to acquire the right of obliging her, and hear the artless expressions of her gratitude! to watch the emotions of her spotless heart! to encourage each dawning virtue! to share in her joy when happy, to kiss away her tears when distressed, and to see her fly to my arms for comfort and support! Yes; if there is perfect bliss on earth, 'tis his lot alone who becomes that angel's husband."

While his fancy coined these ideas, he paced his cell with a disordered air. His eyes were fixed upon vacancy: his head reclined upon his shoulder: a tear rolled down his cheek, while he reflected that the vision of happiness for him could never be realized.

"She is lost to me;" he continued, "by marriage she cannot be mine: and to seduce such innocence, to use the confidence reposed in me to work her ruin—Oh! it would be a crime, blacker than yet the world ever witnessed! Fear not, lovely girl! your virtue runs no risque from me. Not for Indies would I make that gentle bosom know the tortures of remorse."

Again he paced his chamber hastily. Then stopping, his eye fell upon the picture of his once-admired Madona. He tore it with indignation from the wall: he threw it on the ground, and spurned it from him with his foot.

"The prostitute!"

Unfortunate Matilda! her paramour forgot, that for his sake alone she had forfeited her claim to virtue; and his only reason for despising her was, that she had loved him much too well.

He threw himself into a chair, which stood near the table. He saw the card with Elvira's address. He took it up, and it brought to his recollection his promise respecting a confessor. He passed a few minutes in doubt: but Antonia's empire over him was already too much decided to permit his making a long resistance to the idea which struck him. He resolved to be the confessor himself. He could leave the abbey unobserved without difficulty: by wrapping up his head in his cowl he hoped to pass through the streets without being recognised: by taking these precautions, and by recommending secrecy to Elvira's family, he doubted not to keep Madrid in ignorance that he had broken his vow never to see the outside of the abbey-walls. Matilda was the only person whose vigilance he dreaded: but by informing her at the refectory, that during the whole of that day business would confine him to his cell, he thought himself secure from her wakeful jealousy. Accordingly, at the hours when the Spaniards are generally taking their siesta, he ventured to quit the abbey by a private door, the key of which was in his possession. The cowl of his habit was thrown over his face: from the heat of the weather the streets were almost totally deserted: the monk met with few people, found the strada di San Iago, and arrived without accident at Donna Elvira's door. He rang, was admitted, and immediately ushered into an upper apartment.

It was here that he ran the greatest risque of a discovery. Had Leonella been at home, she would have recognized him directly. Her communicative disposition would never have permitted her to rest, till all Madrid was informed that Ambrosio had ventured out of the abbey, and visited her sister. Fortune here stood the monk's friend. On Leonella's return home, she found a letter instructing her, that a cousin was just dead, who had left what little he possessed between herself and Elvira. To secure this bequest she was obliged to set out for Cordova without losing a moment. Amidst all her foibles, her heart was truly warm and affectionate, and she was unwilling to quit her sister in so dangerous a state. But Elvira insisted upon her taking the journey, conscious that in her daughter's forlorn situation, no increase of fortune, however trifling, ought to be neglected. Accordingly Leonella left Madrid, sincerely grieved at her sister's illness, and giving some few sighs to the memory of the amiable but inconstant Don Christoval. She was fully persuaded, that at first she had made a terrible breach in his heart; but hearing nothing more of him, she supposed that he had quitted the pursuit, disgusted by the lowness of her origin, and knowing upon other terms than marriage he had nothing to hope from such a dragon of virtue as she professed herself; or else, that being naturally capricious and changeable, the remembrance of her charms had been effaced from the Condé's heart by those of some newer beauty. Whatever was the cause of her losing him, she lamented it sorely. She strove in vain, as she assured every body who was kind enough to listen to her, to tear his image from her too susceptible heart. She affected the airs of a love-sick virgin, and carried them all to the most ridiculous excess. She heaved lamentable sighs, walked with her arms folded, uttered long soliloquies, and her discourse generally turned upon some forsaken maid, who expired of a broken heart! Her fiery locks were always ornamented with a garland of willow. Every evening she was seen straying upon the banks of a rivulet by moonlight; and she declared herself a violent admirer of murmuring streams and nightingales——

> "Of lonely haunts, and twilight groves,
> Places which pale passion loves!"[1]

Such was the state of Leonella's mind when obliged to quit Madrid. Elvira was out of patience at all these follies, and endeavoured at persuading her to act like a reasonable woman. Her advice was thrown away: Leonella assured her at parting, that nothing could make her forget the perfidious Don Christoval. In this point she was fortunately mistaken. An honest youth of Cordova, jour-

---

1 Adapted from William Strode (1602-45), "Melancholy" 12-13.

neyman to an apothecary, found that her fortune would be sufficient to set him up in a genteel shop of his own. In consequence
of this reflection he avowed himself her admirer. Leonella was not
inflexible; the ardour of his sighs melted her heart, and she soon
consented to make him the happiest of mankind. She wrote to
inform her sister of her marriage; but, for reasons which will be
explained hereafter, Elvira never answered her letter.

Ambrosio was conducted into the anti-chamber to that where
Elvira was reposing. The female domestic who had admitted him,
left him alone, while she announced his arrival to her mistress.
Antonia, who had been by her mother's bed-side, immediately
came to him.

"Pardon me, father," said she, advancing towards him; when recognizing his features, she stopped suddenly, and uttered a cry of joy.
"Is it possible?" she continued, "do not my eyes deceive me? Has
the worthy Ambrosio broken through his resolution, that he may
soften the agonies of the best of women? What pleasure will this
visit give my mother! Let me not delay for a moment the comfort
which your piety and wisdom will afford her."

Thus saying, she opened the chamber-door, presented to her
mother her distinguished visitor, and, having placed an arm-chair
by the side of the bed, withdrew into another apartment.

Elvira was highly gratified by this visit: her expectations had
been raised high by general report, but she found them far exceeded. Ambrosio, endowed by nature with powers of pleasing, exerted
them to the utmost, while conversing with Antonia's mother. With
persuasive eloquence he calmed every fear, and dissipated every
scruple. He bade her reflect on the infinite mercy of her judge,
despoiled death of his darts and terrors, and taught her to view
without shrinking the abyss of eternity, on whose brink she then
stood. Elvira was absorbed in attention and delight; while she listened to his exhortations, confidence and comfort stole insensibly
into her mind. She unbosomed to him without hesitation her cares
and apprehensions. The latter respecting a future life he had already
quieted, and he now removed the former, which she felt for the
concerns of this. She trembled for Antonia; she had none to whose
care she could recommend her, save to the marquis de las Cisternas, and her sister Leonella. The protection of the one was very
uncertain; and as to the other, though fond of her niece, Leonella
was so thoughtless and vain, as to make her an improper person to
have the sole direction of a girl so young and ignorant of the
world. The friar no sooner learned the cause of her alarms, than he

begged her to make herself easy upon that head. He doubted not being able to secure for Antonia a safe refuge in the house of one of his penitents, the marchioness of Villa-Franca: this was a lady of acknowledged virtue, remarkable for strict principles and extensive charity. Should accident deprive her of this resource, he engaged to procure Antonia a reception in some respectable convent, that is to say, in quality of boarder; for Elvira had declared herself no friend to a monastic life, and the monk was either candid or complaisant enough to allow that her disapprobation was not unfounded.

These proofs of the interest which he felt for her, completely won Elvira's heart. In thanking him, she exhausted every expression which gratitude could furnish, and protested, that now she should resign herself with tranquillity to the grave. Ambrosio rose to take leave; he promised to return the next day at the same hour, but requested that his visits might be kept secret.

"I am unwilling," said he, "that my breaking through a rule imposed by necessity, should be generally known. Had I not resolved never to quit my convent, except upon circumstances as urgent as that which has conducted me to your door, I should be frequently summoned upon insignificant occasions; that time would be engrossed by the curious, the unoccupied, and the fanciful, which I now pass at the bed-side of the sick, in comforting the expiring penitent, and clearing the passage to eternity from thorns."

Elvira commended equally his prudence and compassion, promising to conceal carefully the honour of his visits. The monk then gave her his benediction, and retired from the chamber.

In the anti-room he found Antonia; he could not refuse himself the pleasure of passing a few moments in her society. He bade her take comfort, for that her mother seemed composed and tranquil, and he hoped that she might yet do well. He enquired who attended her, and engaged to send the physician of his convent to see her, one of the most skilful in Madrid. He then launched out in Elvira's commendation, praised her purity and fortitude of mind, and declared that she had inspired him with the highest esteem and reverence. Antonia's innocent heart swelled with gratitude, joy danced in her eyes, where a tear still sparkled. The hopes which he gave her of her mother's recovery, the lively interest which he seemed to feel for her, and the flattering way in which she was mentioned by him, added to the report of his judgment and virtue, and to the impression made upon her by his eloquence, confirmed the favourable opinion with which his first appearance had inspired Antonia. She replied with diffidence, but without restraint: she feared not to relate to him all her little sorrows, all her little fears and anxieties; and she thanked him for his goodness with all the genuine warmth which favours kindle in a young and innocent heart. Such alone knows how to estimate benefits at their full value. They who are conscious of mankind's perfidy and selfishness, ever receive an obligation with apprehension and distrust; they suspect that some secret motive must lurk behind it; they express their thanks with restraint and caution, and fear to praise a kind action to its full extent, aware that some future day a return may be required. Not so Antonia—she thought the world was composed only of those who resembled her, and that vice existed was to her still a secret. The monk had been of service to her; he said that he wished her well; she was grateful for his kindness, and thought that no terms were strong enough to be the vehicle of her thanks. With what delight did Ambrosio listen to the declaration of her artless gratitude! The natural grace of her manners, the unequalled sweetness of her voice, her modest vivacity, her unstudied elegance, her expressive countenance and intelligent eyes united to inspire him with pleasure and admiration; while the solidity and correctness of her remarks received additional beauty from the unaffected simplicity of the language in which they were conveyed.

Ambrosio was at length obliged to tear himself from this conversation, which possessed for him but too many charms. He repeated to Antonia his wishes, that his visits should not be made known, which desire she promised to observe. He then quitted the house, while his enchantress hastened to her mother, ignorant of the mischief which her beauty had caused. She was eager to know Elvira's opinion of the man whom she had praised in such enthusiastic terms, and was delighted to find it equally favourable, if not even more so, than her own.

"Even before he spoke," said Elvira, "I was prejudiced in his favour; the fervour of his exhortations, dignity of his manner, and closeness of his reasoning, were very far from inducing me to alter my opinion. His fine and full-toned voice struck me particularly; but surely, Antonia, I have heard it before. It seemed perfectly familiar to my ear; either I must have known the abbot in former times, or his voice bears a wonderful resemblance to that of some other, to whom I have often listened. There were certain tones which touched my very heart, and made me feel sensations so singular, that I strive in vain to account for them."

"My dearest mother, it produced the same effect upon me; yet certainly neither of us ever heard his voice till we came to Madrid. I suspect that what we attribute to his voice, really proceeds from his pleasant manners, which forbid our considering him as a stranger. I know not why, but I feel more at my ease while conversing with him, than I usually do with people who are unknown to me. I feared not to repeat to him all my childish thoughts; and somehow I felt confident that he would hear my folly with indulgence. Oh! I was not deceived in him; he listened to me with such an air of kindness and attention; he answered me with such gentleness, such condescension: he did not call me an infant, and treat me with contempt, as our cross old confessor at the Castle used to do. I verily believe, that if I had lived in Murcia a thousand years, I never should have liked that fat old father Dominic!"

"I confess, that father Dominic had not the most pleasing manners in the world; but he was honest, friendly, and well-meaning."

"Ah! my dear mother, those qualities are so common——"

"God grant, my child, that experience may not teach you to think them rare and precious: I have found them but too much so. But tell me, Antonia, why is it impossible for me to have seen the abbot before?"

"Because since the moment when he entered the abbey, he has never been on the outside of its walls. He told me just now, that from his ignorance of the streets, he had some difficulty to find the strada di San Iago, though so near the abbey."

"All this is possible, and still I may have seen him *before* he entered the abbey: in order to come out, it was rather necessary that he should first go in."

"Holy virgin! as you say, that is very true.—Oh! But might he not have been born in the abbey?"

Elvira smiled.

"Why, not very easily."

"Stay, stay! Now I recollect how it was. He was put into the abbey quite a child; the common people say, that he fell from heaven, and was sent as a present to the Capuchins by the Virgin."

"That was very kind of her. And so he fell from heaven, Antonia? He must have had a terrible tumble."

"Many do not credit this; and I fancy, my dear mother, that I must number you among the unbelievers. Indeed, as our landlady told my aunt, the general idea is, that his parents, being poor, and unable to maintain him, left him just born at the abbey-door; the late superior, from pure charity, had him educated in the convent, and he proved to be a model of virtue, and piety, and learning, and

I know not what else besides. In consequence, he was first received as a brother of the order, and not long ago was chosen abbot. However, whether this account or the other is the true one—at least all agree, that when the monks took him under their care, he could not speak; therefore you could not have heard his voice before he entered the monastery, because at that time he had no voice at all."

"Upon my word, Antonia, you argue very closely; your conclusions are infallible. I did not suspect you of being so able a logician."

"Ah! you are mocking me; but so much the better. It delights me to see you in spirits; besides you seem tranquil and easy, and I hope that you will have no more convulsions. Oh! I was sure the abbot's visit would do you good."

"It has indeed done me good, my child. He has quieted my mind upon some points which agitated me, and I already feel the effects of his attention. My eyes grow heavy, and I think I can sleep a little. Draw the curtains, my Antonia: but if I should not wake before midnight, do not sit up with me, I charge you."

Antonia promised to obey her; and having received her blessing, drew the curtains of the bed. She then seated herself in silence at her embroidery frame, and beguiled the hours with building castles in the air. Her spirits were enlivened by the evident change for the better in Elvira, and her fancy presented her with visions bright and pleasing. In these dreams Ambrosio made no despicable figure. She thought of him with joy and gratitude; but for every idea which fell to the friar's share, at least two were unconsciously bestowed upon Lorenzo. Thus passed the time, till the bell in the neighbouring steeple of the Capuchin cathedral announced the hour of midnight. Antonia remembered her mother's injunctions, and obeyed them, though with reluctance. She undrew the curtains with caution. Elvira was enjoying a profound and quiet slumber; her cheek glowed with health's returning colours: a smile declared that her dreams were pleasant, and as Antonia bent over her, she fancied that she heard her name pronounced. She kissed her mother's forehead softly, and retired to her chamber; there she knelt before a statue of St. Rosolia,[1] her patroness; she recommended herself to the protection of heaven, and, as had been her custom from infancy, concluded her devotions by chaunting the following stanzas:

---

1 Possibly St. Rosalia of Sicily (d. 1160?), patron of Palermo.

MIDNIGHT HYMN.

Now all is hush'd; the solemn chime
No longer swells the nightly gale:
Thy awful presence, hour sublime,
With spotless heart once more I hail.

'Tis now the moment still and dread,
When sorcerers use their baleful power;
When graves give up their buried dead
To profit by the sanctioned hour.

From guilt and guilty thoughts secure,
To duty and devotion true,
With bosom light and conscience pure,
Repose, thy gentle aid I woo.

Good angels! take my thanks, that still
The snares of vice I view with scorn;
Thanks, that to-night as free from ill
I sleep, as when I woke at morn.

Yet may not my unconscious breast
Harbour some guilt to me unknown?
Some wish impure, which unreprest
You blush to see, and I to own?

If such there be, in gentle dream
Instruct my feet to shun the snare;
Bid truth upon my errors beam,
And deign to make me still your care.

Chase from my peaceful bed away,
The witching spell, a foe to rest,
The nightly goblin, wanton fay,
The ghost in pain, and fiend unblest.

Let not the tempter in mine ear
Pour lessons of unhallowed joy;[1]

---

1   Cf. Milton, *Paradise Lost* 4.799-803.

Let not the night-mare, wandering near
My couch, the calm of sleep destroy.

Let not some horrid dream affright
With strange fantastic forms mine eyes;
But rather bid some vision bright
Display the bliss of yonder skies.

Shew me the crystal domes of heaven,
The worlds of light where angels lie;
Shew me the lot to mortals given,
Who guiltless live, who guiltless die.

Then shew me how a seat to gain
Amidst those blissful realms of air;
Teach me to shun each guilty stain,
And guide me to the good and fair.

So ev'ry morn and night my voice
To heaven the grateful strain shall raise;
In you as guardian powers rejoice,
Good angels! and exalt your praise.

So will I strive, with zealous fire,
Each vice to shun, each fault correct:
Will love the lessons you inspire,
And prize the virtues you protect.

Then when at length, by high command,
My body seeks the grave's repose,
When death draws nigh with friendly hand,
My failing pilgrim eyes to close:

Pleas'd that my soul has 'scap'd the wreck,
Sighless will I my life resign,
And yield to God my spirit back,
As pure as when it first was mine.

Having finished her usual devotions, Antonia retired to bed.
Sleep soon stole over her senses; and for several hours she
enjoyed that calm repose which innocence alone can know, and

for which many a monarch with pleasure would exchange his crown.[1]

CHAP. VII.

————Ah! how dark
These long-extended realms and rueful wastes;
Where nought but silence reigns, and night, dark night,
Dark as was chaos ere the infant sun
Was rolled together, or had tried its beams
Athwart the gloom profound! The sickly taper,
By glimmering through thy low-browed misty vaults
Furred round with mouldy damps and ropy slime,
Lets fall a supernumerary horror,
And only serves to make thy night more irksome!

BLAIR.[2]

RETURNED undiscovered to the abbey, Ambrosio's mind was filled with the most pleasing images. He was wilfully blind to the danger of exposing himself to Antonia's charms: he only remembered the pleasure which her society had afforded him, and rejoiced in the prospect of that pleasure being repeated. He failed not to profit by Elvira's indisposition to obtain a sight of her daughter every day. At first he bounded his wishes to inspire Antonia with friendship: but no sooner was he convinced that she felt that sentiment in its fullest extent, than his aim became more decided, and his attentions assumed a warmer colour. The innocent familiarity with which she treated him, encouraged his desires. Grown used to her modesty, it no longer commanded the same respect and awe: he still admired it, but it only made him more anxious to deprive her of that quality which formed her principal charm. Warmth of passion, and natural penetration, of which latter, unfortunately both for himself and Antonia, he possessed an ample share, supplied a knowledge of the arts of seduction. He easily distinguished the emotions which were favourable to his designs, and seized every means with avidity of infusing corruption into Antonia's bosom. This he found no easy matter. Extreme simplicity pre-

---

1 Cf. Shakespeare, *2 Henry IV* 3.1.4-31.
2 Robert Blair (1699-1746), *The Grave* (1743) 11-20.

vented her from perceiving the aim to which the monk's insinuations tended; but the excellent morals which she owed to Elvira's care, the solidity and correctness of her understanding, and a strong sense of what was right, implanted in her heart by nature, made her feel that his precepts must be faulty. By a few simple words she frequently overthrew the whole bulk of his sophistical arguments, and made him conscious how weak they were when opposed to virtue and truth. On such occasions he took refuge in his eloquence; he overpowered her with a torrent of philosophical paradoxes, to which, not understanding them, it was impossible for her to reply; and thus, though he did not convince her that his reasoning was just, he at least prevented her from discovering it to be false.[1] He perceived that her respect for his judgment augmented daily, and doubted not with time to bring her to the point desired.

He was not unconscious that his attempts were highly criminal. He saw clearly the baseness of seducing the innocent girl; but his passion was too violent to permit his abandoning his design. He resolved to pursue it, let the consequences be what they might. He depended upon finding Antonia in some unguarded moment; and seeing no other man admitted into her society, nor hearing any mentioned either by her or by Elvira, he imagined that her young heart was still unoccupied. While he waited for the opportunity of satisfying his unwarrantable lust, every day increased his coldness for Matilda. Not a little was this occasioned by the consciousness of his faults to her. To hide them from her, he was not sufficiently master of himself; yet he dreaded lest, in a transport of jealous rage, she should betray the secret, on which his character and even his life depended. Matilda could not but remark his indifference: he was conscious that she remarked it, and, fearing her reproaches, shunned her studiously. Yet, when he could not avoid her, her mildness might have convinced him that he had nothing to dread from her resentment. She had resumed the character of the gentle interesting Rosario: she taxed him not with ingratitude; but her eyes filled with involuntary tears, and the soft melancholy of her countenance and voice uttered complaints far more touching than words could have conveyed. Ambrosio was not unmoved by her sorrow; but, unable to remove its cause, he forbore to show that it affected him. As her conduct convinced him that he needed not

---

1 Cf. Faust's sophistical conversation with Gretchen in Goethe, *Faust* 59-61 ("Marthe's Garden").

fear her vengeance, he continued to neglect her, and avoided her company with care. Matilda saw that she in vain attempted to regain his affections, yet she stifled the impulse of resentment, and continued to treat her inconstant lover with her former fondness and affection.

By degrees Elvira's constitution recovered itself. She was no longer troubled with convulsions, and Antonia ceased to tremble for her mother. Ambrosio beheld this re-establishment with displeasure. He saw that Elvira's knowledge of the world would not be the dupe of his sanctified demeanour, and that she would easily perceive his views upon her daughter. He resolved therefore, before she quitted her chamber, to try the extent of his influence over the innocent Antonia.

One evening, when he had found Elvira almost perfectly restored to health, he quitted her earlier than was his usual custom. Not finding Antonia in the antichamber, he ventured to follow her to her own. It was only separated from her mother's by a closet, in which Flora, the waiting-woman, generally slept. Antonia sat upon a sopha with her back towards the door, and read attentively. She heard not his approach, till he had seated himself by her. She started, and welcomed him with a look of pleasure: then rising, she would have conducted him to the sitting-room; but Ambrosio, taking her hand, obliged her by gentle violence to resume her place. She complied without difficulty: she knew not that there was more impropriety in conversing with him in one room than another. She thought herself equally secure of his principles and her own; and having replaced herself upon the sopha, she began to prattle to him with her usual ease and vivacity.

He examined the book which she had been reading, and had now placed upon the table. It was the Bible.

"How!" said the friar to himself, "Antonia reads the Bible, and is still so ignorant?"

But, upon a further inspection, he found that Elvira had made exactly the same remark. That prudent mother, while she admired the beauties of the sacred writings, was convinced that, unrestricted, no reading more improper could be permitted a young woman. Many of the narratives can only tend to excite ideas the worst calculated for a female breast: every thing is called plainly and roundly by its name; and the annals of a brothel would scarcely furnish a greater choice of indecent expressions. Yet this is the book which young women are recommended to study, which is put into the hands of children, able to comprehend little more than those passages of which they had better remain ignorant, and which but too frequently inculcates the first rudiments of vice, and gives the first alarm to the still sleeping passions. Of this was Elvira so fully convinced, that she would have preferred putting into her daughter's hands "*Amadis de Gaul,*" or "*The Valiant Champion, Tirante the White;*" and would sooner have authorised her studying the lewd exploits of *Don Galaor,* or the lascivious jokes of the *Damsel Plazer di mi vida.*[1] She had in consequence made two resolutions respecting the Bible. The first was, that Antonia should not read it till she was of an age to feel its beauties, and profit by its morality. The second, that it should be copied out with her own hand, and all improper passages either altered or omitted. She had adhered to this determination, and such was the Bible which Antonia was reading: it had been lately delivered to her, and she perused it with an avidity, with a delight that was inexpressible. Ambrosio perceived his mistake, and replaced the book upon the table.

Antonia spoke of her mother's health with all the enthusiastic joy of a youthful heart.

"I admire your filial affection," said the abbot; "it proves the excellence and sensibility of your character; it promises a treasure to him whom Heaven has destined to possess your affections. The breast so capable of fondness for a parent, what will it feel for a lover? Nay, perhaps, what feels it for one even now? Tell me, my lovely daughter, have you known what it is to love? Answer me with sincerity: forget my habit, and consider me only as a friend."

"What it is to love?" said she, repeating his question. "Oh! yes, undoubtedly; I have loved many, many people."

"That is not what I mean. The love of which I speak can be felt only for one. Have you never seen the man whom you wished to be your husband?"

"Oh! no, indeed!"

This was an untruth, but she was unconscious of its falsehood: she knew not the nature of her sentiments for Lorenzo; and never having seen him since his first visit to Elvira, with every day his image grew less forcibly impressed upon her bosom: besides, she

---

1 *Amadis de Gaul* is a chivalric romance of Spanish or Portuguese origin, preserved as recorded by Garci Rodríguez de Montalvo in 1508 (and another item in Don Quixote's library). Don Galaor is Amadis's brother. Plazer di mi vida ("Joy of my life") is a character in *Tirante the White,* a realistic and sometimes obscene work; her witticisms are mentioned in *Don Quixote* 1.6.

thought of an husband with all a virgin's terror, and negatived the friar's demand without a moment's hesitation.

"And do you not long to see that man, Antonia? Do you feel no void in your heart, which you fain would have filled up? Do you heave no sighs for the absence of some one dear to you, but who that some one is you know not? Perceive you not that what formerly could please, has charms for you no longer? that a thousand new wishes, new ideas, new sensations, have sprung in your bosom, only to be felt, never to be described? Or, while you fill every other heart with passion, is it possible that your own remains insensible and cold? It cannot be! That melting eye, that blushing cheek, that enchanting voluptuous melancholy which at times overspreads your features—all these marks belie your words: you love, Antonia, and in vain would hide it from me."

"Father, you amaze me! What is this love of which you speak? I neither know its nature, nor, if I felt it, why I should conceal the sentiment."

"Have you seen no man, Antonia, whom, though never seen before, you seemed long to have sought? whose form, though a stranger's, was familiar to your eyes? the sound of whose voice soothed you, pleased you, penetrated to your very soul? in whose presence you rejoiced, for whose absence you lamented? with whom your heart seemed to expand, and in whose bosom, with confidence unbounded, you reposed the cares of your own? Have you not felt all this, Antonia?"

"Certainly I have: the first time that I saw you, I felt it."

Ambrosio started. Scarcely dared he credit his hearing.

"Me, Antonia?" he cried, his eyes sparkling with delight and impatience, while he seized her hand, and pressed it rapturously to his lips. "Me, Antonia? You felt these sentiments for me?"

"Even with more strength than you have described. The very moment that I beheld you, I felt so pleased, so interested! I waited so eagerly to catch the sound of your voice; and, when I heard it, it seemed so sweet! it spoke to me a language till then so unknown! Methought it told me a thousand things which I wished to hear! It seemed as if I had long known you; as if I had a right to your friendship, your advice, and your protection. I wept when you departed, and longed for the time which should restore you to my sight."

"Antonia! my charming Antonia!" exclaimed the monk, and caught her to his bosom: "Can I believe my senses? Repeat it to me, my sweet girl! Tell me again that you love me, that you love me truly and tenderly!"

"Indeed, I do: let my mother be excepted, and the world holds no one more dear to me."

At this frank avowal Ambrosio no longer possessed himself: wild with desire, he clasped the blushing trembler in his arms. He fastened his lips greedily upon hers, sucked in her pure delicious breath, violated with his bold hand the treasures of her bosom, and wound around him her soft and yielding limbs. Startled, alarmed, and confused at his action, surprise at first deprived her of the power of resistance. At length recovering herself, she strove to escape from his embrace.

"Father!—Ambrosio!" she cried, "release me, for God's sake!"

But the licentious monk heeded not her prayers: he persisted in his design, and proceeded to take still greater liberties. Antonia prayed, wept, and struggled: terrified to the extreme, though at what she knew not, she exerted all her strength to repulse the friar, and was on the point of shrieking for assistance, when the chamber-door was suddenly thrown open. Ambrosio had just sufficient presence of mind to be sensible of his danger. Reluctantly he quitted his prey, and started hastily from the couch. Antonia uttered an exclamation of joy, flew towards the door, and found herself clasped in the arms of her mother.

Alarmed at some of the abbot's speeches, which Antonia had innocently repeated, Elvira resolved to ascertain the truth of her suspicions. She had known enough of mankind, not to be imposed upon by the monk's reputed virtue. She reflected on several circumstances, which, though trifling, on being put together seemed to authorize her fears. His frequent visits, which, as far as she could see, were confined to her family; his evident emotion, whenever she spoke of Antonia; his being in the full prime and heat of manhood; and above all, his pernicious philosophy communicated to her by Antonia, and which accorded but ill with his conversation in her presence; all these circumstances inspired her with doubts respecting the purity of Ambrosio's friendship. In consequence she resolved, when he should next be alone with Antonia, to endeavour at surprising him. Her plan had succeeded. 'Tis true, that when she entered the room, he had already abandoned his prey; but the disorder of her daughter's dress, and the shame and confusion stamped upon the friar's countenance, sufficed to prove that her suspicions were but too well founded. However, she was too prudent to make those suspicions known. She judged, that to unmask the impostor would be no easy matter, the public being so much prejudiced in his favour: and having but few friends, she thought it dangerous to make herself so powerful an enemy. She affected therefore not to remark his agitation, seated herself tranquilly upon the sopha, assigned some trifling reason for having quitted her room unexpectedly, and conversed on various subjects with seeming confidence and ease.

Re-assured by her behaviour, the monk began to recover himself. He strove to answer Elvira without appearing embarrassed: but he was still too great a novice in dissimulation, and he felt that he must look confused and awkward. He soon broke off the conversation, and rose to depart. What was his vexation when, on taking leave, Elvira told him, in polite terms, that being now perfectly re-established, she thought it an injustice to deprive others of his company who might be more in need of it! She assured him of her eternal gratitude, for the benefit which during her illness she had derived from his society and exhortations: and she lamented that her domestic affairs, as well as the multitude of business which his situation must of necessity impose upon him, would in future deprive her of the pleasure of his visits. Though delivered in the mildest language, this hint was too plain to be mistaken. Still he was preparing to put in a remonstrance, when an expressive look from Elvira stopped him short. He dared not press her to receive him, for her manner convinced him that he was discovered: he submitted without reply, took an hasty leave, and retired to the abbey, his heart filled with rage and shame, with bitterness and disappointment.

Antonia's mind felt relieved by his departure; yet she could not help lamenting that she was never to see him more. Elvira also felt a secret sorrow: she had received too much pleasure from thinking him her friend, not to regret the necessity of changing her opinion; but her mind was too much accustomed to the fallacy of worldly friendships to permit her present disappointment to weigh upon it long. She now endeavoured to make her daughter aware of the risk which she had run: but she was obliged to treat the subject with caution, lest, in removing the bandage of ignorance, the veil of innocence should be rent away. She therefore contented herself with warning Antonia to be upon her guard, and ordering her, should the abbot persist in his visits, never to receive them but in company. With this injunction Antonia promised to comply.

Ambrosio hastened to his cell. He closed the door after him, and threw himself upon the bed in despair. The impulse of desire, the stings of disappointment, the shame of detection, and the fear of being publicly unmasked, rendered his bosom a scene of the most horrible confusion. He knew not what course to pursue. Debarred the presence of Antonia, he had no hopes of satisfying that passion which was now become a part of his existence. He reflected that his secret was in a woman's power: he trembled with apprehension when he beheld the precipice before him, and with rage when he thought that, had it not been for Elvira, he should now have possessed the object of his desires. With the direst imprecations he vowed vengeance against her: he swore that, cost what it would, he still would possess Antonia. Starting from the bed, he paced the chamber with disordered steps, howled with impotent fury, dashed himself violently against the walls, and indulged all the transports of rage and madness.

He was still under the influence of this storm of passions, when he heard a gentle knock at the door of his cell. Conscious that his voice must have been heard, he dared not refuse admittance to the importuner. He strove to compose himself, and to hide his agitation. Having in some degree succeeded, he drew back the bolt: the door opened, and Matilda appeared.

At this precise moment there was no one with whose presence he could better have dispensed. He had not sufficient command over himself to conceal his vexation. He started back, and frowned.

"I am busy," said he in a stern and hasty tone; "leave me."

Matilda heeded him not: she again fastened the door, and then advanced towards him with an air gentle and supplicating.

"Forgive me, Ambrosio," said she; "for your own sake I must not obey you. Fear no complaints from me; I come not to reproach you with your ingratitude. I pardon you from my heart; and since your love can no longer be mine, I request the next best gift, your confidence and friendship. We cannot force our inclinations: the little beauty which you once saw in me has perished with its novelty; and if it can no longer excite desire, mine is the fault, not yours. But why persist in shunning me? why such anxiety to fly my presence? You have sorrows, but will not permit me to share them; you have disappointments, but will not accept my comfort; you have wishes, but forbid my aiding your pursuits. 'Tis of this which I complain, not of your indifference to my person. I have given up the claims of the mistress, but nothing shall prevail on me to give up those of the friend."

"Generous Matilda!" he replied, taking her hand, "how far do you rise superior to the foibles of your sex! Yes, I accept your offer. I have need of an adviser, and a confident: in you I find every needful quality united. But to aid my pursuits—— Ah! Matilda, it lies not in your power!"

"It lies in no one's power but mine. Ambrosio, your secret is none to me: your every step, your every action has been observed by my attentive eye. You love."

"Matilda!"

"Why conceal it from me? Fear not the little jealousy which taints the generality of women: my soul disdains so despicable a passion. You love, Ambrosio; Antonia Dalfa is the object of your flame. I know every circumstance respecting your passion. Every conversation has been repeated to me. I have been informed of your attempt to enjoy Antonia's person, your disappointment, and dismission from Elvira's house. You now despair of possessing your mistress; but I come to revive your hopes, and point out the road to success."

"To success? Oh! impossible."

"To those who dare, nothing is impossible. Rely upon me, and you may yet be happy. The time is come, Ambrosio, when regard for your comfort and tranquillity compels me to reveal a part of my history, with which you are still unacquainted. Listen, and do not interrupt me. Should my confession disgust you, remember that in making it my sole aim is to satisfy your wishes, and restore that peace to your heart which at present has abandoned it. I formerly mentioned, that my guardian was a man of uncommon knowledge. He took pains to instil that knowledge into my infant mind. Among the various sciences which curiosity had induced him to explore, he neglected not that which by most is esteemed impious, and by many chimerical: I speak of those arts which relate to the world of spirits. His deep researches into causes and effects, his unwearied application to the study of natural philosophy, his profound and unlimited knowledge of the properties and virtues of every gem which enriches the deep, of every herb which the earth produces, at length procured him the distinction which he had sought so long, so earnestly. His curiosity was fully slaked, his ambition amply gratified. He gave laws to the elements: he could reverse the order of nature: his eye read the mandates of futurity, and the infernal spirits were submissive to his commands. Why shrink you from me? I understand that enquiring look. Your suspicions are right, though your terrors are unfounded. My guardian concealed not from me his most precious acquisition. Yet, had I never seen *you*, I should never have exerted my power. Like you, I shuddered at the thoughts of magic. Like you, I had formed a terrible idea of the consequences of raising a dæmon. To preserve that life which your love had taught me to prize, I had recourse to means which

I trembled at employing. You remember that night which I passed in St. Clare's sepulchre? Then was it that, surrounded by mouldering bodies, I dared to perform those mystic rites, which summoned to my aid a fallen angel. Judge what must have been my joy at discovering that my terrors were imaginary. I saw the dæmon obedient to my orders: I saw him trembling at my frown; and found that, instead of selling my soul to a master, my courage had purchased for myself a slave."

"Rash Matilda! What have you done? You have doomed yourself to endless perdition; you have bartered for momentary power eternal happiness! If on witchcraft depends the fruition of my desires, I renounce your aid most absolutely. The consequences are too horrible. I dote upon Antonia, but am not so blinded by lust, as to sacrifice for her enjoyment my existence both in this world and in the next."

"Ridiculous prejudices! Oh! blush, Ambrosio, blush at being subjected to their dominion. Where is the risque of accepting my offers? What should induce my persuading you to this step, except the wish of restoring you to happiness and quiet? If there is danger, it must fall upon me. It is I who invoke the ministry of the spirits: mine therefore will be the crime, and yours the profit; but danger there is none. The enemy of mankind is my slave, not my sovereign. Is there no difference between giving and receiving laws, between serving and commanding? Awake from your idle dreams, Ambrosio! throw from you these terrors so ill suited to a soul like yours; leave them for common men, and dare to be happy! Accompany me this night to St. Clare's sepulchre; there witness my incantations, and Antonia is your own."

"To obtain her by such means, I neither can nor will. Cease then to persuade me, for I dare not employ hell's agency."

"You *dare* not? How have you deceived me! That mind which I esteemed so great and valiant, proves to be feeble, puerile, and grovelling, a slave to vulgar errors, and weaker than a woman's."

"What? Though conscious of the danger, wilfully shall I expose myself to the seducer's arts? Shall I renounce for ever my title to salvation? Shall my eyes seek a sight which I know will blast them? No, no, Matilda, I will not ally myself with God's enemy."

"Are you then God's friend at present? Have you not broken your engagements with him, renounced his service, and abandoned yourself to the impulse of your passions? Are you not planning the destruction of innocence, the ruin of a creature whom he formed in the mould of angels? If not of dæmons, whose aid would you invoke to forward this laudable design? Will the seraphims protect it, conduct Antonia to your arms, and sanction with their ministry your illicit pleasures? Absurd! But I am not deceived, Ambrosio! It is not virtue which makes you reject my offer; you *would* accept it, but you *dare* not. 'Tis not the crime which holds your hand, but the punishment; 'tis not respect for God which restrains you, but the terror of his vengeance! Fain would you offend him in secret, but you tremble to profess yourself his foe. Now shame on the coward soul, which wants the courage either to be a firm friend, or an open enemy!"

"To look upon guilt with horror, Matilda, is in itself a merit: in this respect I glory to confess myself a coward. Though my passions have made me deviate from her laws, I still feel in my heart an innate love of virtue. But it ill becomes you to tax me with my perjury; you who first seduced me to violate my vows; you who first roused my sleeping vices, made me feel the weight of religion's chains, and bade me be convinced that guilt had pleasures. Yet though my principles have yielded to the force of temperament, I still have sufficient grace to shudder at sorcery, and avoid a crime so monstrous, so unpardonable!"

"Unpardonable, say you? Where then is your constant boast of the Almighty's infinite mercy? Has he of late set bounds to it? Receives he no longer a sinner with joy? You injure him, Ambrosio; you will always have time to repent, and he have goodness to forgive. Afford him a glorious opportunity to exert that goodness: the greater your crime, the greater his merit in pardoning.[1] Away then with these childish scruples; be persuaded to your good, and follow me to the sepulchre."

"Oh! cease, Matilda! That scoffing tone, that bold and impious language is horrible in every mouth, but most so in a woman's. Let us drop a conversation, which excites no other sentiments than horror and disgust. I will not follow you to the sepulchre, or accept the services of your infernal agents. Antonia shall be mine, but mine by human means."

"Then yours she will never be! You are banished her presence; her mother has opened her eyes to your designs, and she is now upon her guard against them. Nay, more, she loves another; a youth of distinguished merit possesses her heart; and unless you interfere, a few days will make her his bride. This intelligence was brought

---

1   Cf. Romans 6.1-2.

me by my invisible servants, to whom I had recourse on first perceiving your indifference. They watched your every action, related
to me all that passed at Elvira's, and inspired me with the idea of
favouring your designs. Their reports have been my only comfort.
Though you shunned my presence, all your proceedings were
known to me; nay, I was constantly with you in some degree,
thanks to this most precious gift!"

With these words she drew from beneath her habit a mirror of
polished steel, the borders of which were marked with various
strange and unknown characters.[1]

"Amidst all my sorrows, amidst all my regrets for your coldness,
I was sustained from despair by the virtues of this talisman. On pronouncing certain words, the person appears in it on whom the
observer's thoughts are bent: thus, though *I* was exiled from *your*
sight, you, Ambrosio, were ever present to mine."

The friar's curiosity was strongly excited.

"What you relate is incredible! Matilda, are you not amusing
yourself with my credulity?"

"Be your own eyes the judge."

She put the mirror into his hand. Curiosity induced him to take
it, and love, to wish that Antonia might appear. Matilda pronounced the magic words. Immediately a thick smoke rose from
the characters traced upon the borders, and spread itself over the
surface. It dispersed again gradually; a confused mixture of colours
and images presented themselves to the friar's eyes, which at length
arranging themselves in their proper places, he beheld in miniature
Antonia's lovely form.

The scene was a small closet belonging to her apartment. She
was undressing to bathe herself. The long tresses of her hair were
already bound up. The amorous monk had full opportunity to
observe the voluptuous contours and admirable symmetry of her
person. She threw off her last garment, and, advancing to the bath
prepared for her, put her foot into the water. It struck cold, and she
drew it back again. Though unconscious of being observed, an in-
bred sense of modesty induced her to veil her charms; and she
stood hesitating upon the brink, in the attitude of the Venus de
Medicis. At this moment a tame linnet flew towards her, nestled its
head between her breasts, and nibbled them in wanton play. The

---

1 Cf. the magic mirrors in Schiller, *The Ghost-Seer* 9 and Goethe, *Faust* 40
("Witch's Kitchen").

smiling Antonia strove in vain to shake off the bird, and at length raised her hands to drive it from its delightful harbour. Ambrosio could bear no more. His desires were worked up to phrensy.

"I yield!" he cried, dashing the mirror upon the ground: "Matilda, I follow you! Do with me what you will!"

She waited not to hear his consent repeated. It was already midnight. She flew to her cell, and soon returned with her little basket and the key of the cemetery, which had remained in her possession since her first visit to the vaults. She gave the monk no time for reflection.

"Come!" she said, and took his hand; "follow me, and witness the effects of your resolve."

This said, she drew him hastily along. They passed into the burying-ground unobserved, opened the door of the sepulchre, and found themselves at the head of the subterraneous stair-case. As yet the beams of the full moon had guided their steps, but that resource now failed them. Matilda had neglected to provide herself with a lamp. Still holding Ambrosio's hand she descended the marble steps; but the profound obscurity with which they were overspread, obliged them to walk slow and cautiously.

"You tremble!" said Matilda to her companion; "fear not, the destined spot is near."

They reached the foot of the stair-case, and continued to proceed, feeling their way along the walls. On turning a corner, suddenly they descried faint gleams of light, which seemed burning at a distance. Thither they bent their steps. The rays proceeded from a small sepulchral lamp which flamed unceasingly before the statue of St. Clare. It tinged with dim and cheerless beams the massy columns which supported the roof, but was too feeble to dissipate the thick gloom in which the vaults above were buried.

Matilda took the lamp.

"Wait for me!" said she to the friar; "in a few moments I am here again."

With these words she hastened into one of the passages which branched in various directions from this spot, and formed a sort of labyrinth. Ambrosio was now left alone. Darkness the most profound surrounded him, and encouraged the doubts which began to revive in his bosom. He had been hurried away by the delirium of the moment. The shame of betraying his terrors, while in Matilda's presence, had induced him to repress them; but, now that he was abandoned to himself, they resumed their former ascendancy. He trembled at the scene which he was soon to witness. He knew not how far the delusions of magic might operate upon his mind: they possibly might force him to some deed, whose commission would make the breach between himself and Heaven irreparable. In this fearful dilemma, he would have implored God's assistance, but was conscious that he had forfeited all claim to such protection. Gladly would he have returned to the abbey; but as he had passed through innumerable caverns and winding passages, the attempt of regaining the stairs was hopeless. His fate was determined; no possibility of escape presented itself. He therefore combated his apprehensions, and called every argument to his succour, which might enable him to support the trying scene with fortitude. He reflected, that Antonia would be the reward of his daring. He inflamed his imagination by enumerating her charms. He persuaded himself, that [as Matilda had observed] he always should have time sufficient for repentance; and that, as he employed *her* assistance, not that of dæmons, the crime of sorcery could not be laid to his charge. He had read much respecting witchcraft; he understood that, unless a formal act was signed renouncing his claim to salvation, Satan would have no power over him. He was fully determined not to execute any such act, whatever threats might be used, or advantages held out to him.

Such were his meditations while waiting for Matilda. They were interrupted by a low murmur, which seemed at no great distance from him. He was startled—he listened. Some minutes passed in silence, after which the murmur was repeated. It appeared to be the groaning of one in pain. In any other situation, this circumstance would only have excited his attention and curiosity. In the present, his predominant sensation was that of terror. His imagination totally engrossed by the ideas of sorcery and spirits, he fancied that some unquiet ghost was wandering near him; or else that Matilda had fallen a victim to her presumption, and was perishing under the cruel fangs of the dæmons. The noise seemed not to approach, but continued to be heard at intervals. Sometimes it became more audible—doubtless, as the sufferings of the person who uttered the groans became more acute and insupportable. Ambrosio now and then thought that he could distinguish accents, and once in particular he was almost convinced that he heard a faint voice exclaim,

"God! Oh! God! No hope! No succour!"

Yet deeper groans followed these words: they died away gradually, and universal silence again prevailed.

"What can this mean?" thought the bewildered monk.

: that moment an idea which flashed into his mind, almost _fied him with horror. He started, and shuddered at himself.

"Should it be possible!" He groaned involuntarily; "should it but be possible; Oh! what a monster am I!"

He wished to resolve his doubts, and to repair his fault, if it were not too late already. But these generous and compassionate sentiments were soon put to flight by the return of Matilda. He forgot the groaning sufferer, and remembered nothing but the danger and embarrassment of his own situation. The light of the returning lamp gilded the walls, and in a few moments after Matilda stood beside him. She had quitted her religious habit: she was now clothed in a long sable robe, on which was traced in gold embroidery a variety of unknown characters: it was fastened by a girdle of precious stones, in which was fixed a poniard. Her neck and arms were uncovered; in her hand she bore a golden wand; her hair was loose, and flowed wildly upon her shoulders; her eyes sparkled with terrific expression; and her whole demeanour was calculated to inspire the beholder with awe and admiration.

"Follow me!" she said to the monk in a low and solemn voice; "all is ready!"

His limbs trembled while he obeyed her. She led him through various narrow passages; and on every side, as they passed along, the beams of the lamp displayed none but the most revolting objects; sculls, bones, graves, and images whose eyes seemed to glare on them with horror and surprise. At length they reached a spacious cavern, whose lofty roof the eye sought in vain to discover. A profound obscurity hovered through the void; damp vapours struck cold to the friar's heart, and he listened sadly to the blast while it howled along the lonely vaults. Here Matilda stopped. She turned to Ambrosio. His cheeks and lips were pale with apprehension. By a glance of mingled scorn and anger she reproved his pusillanimity, but she spoke not. She placed the lamp upon the ground near the basket. She motioned that Ambrosio should be silent, and began the mysterious rites. She drew a circle round him, another round herself; and then, taking a small phial from the basket, poured a few drops upon the ground before her. She bent over the place, muttered some indistinct sentences, and immediately a pale sulphurous flame arose from the ground. It increased by degrees, and at length spread its waves over the whole surface, the circles alone excepted in which stood Matilda and the monk. It then ascended the huge columns of unhewn stone, glided along the roof, and formed the cavern into an immense chamber totally covered with blue trembling fire. It emitted no heat: on the contrary, the extreme chillness of the place seemed to augment with every moment.[1] Matilda continued her incantations; at intervals she took various articles from the basket, the nature and name of most of which were unknown to the friar: but among the few which he distinguished, he particularly observed three human fingers, and an agnus dei[2] which she broke in pieces. She threw them all into the flames which burned before her, and they were instantly consumed.

The monk beheld her with anxious curiosity. Suddenly she uttered a loud and piercing shriek. She appeared to be seized with an access of delirium; she tore her hair, beat her bosom, used the most frantic gestures, and, drawing the poniard from her girdle, plunged it into her left arm. The blood gushed out plentifully; and, as she stood on the brink of the circle, she took care that it should fall on the outside. The flames retired from the spot on which the blood was pouring. A volume of dark clouds rose slowly from the ensanguined earth, and ascended gradually till it reached the vault of the cavern. At the same time a clap of thunder was heard, the echo pealed fearfully along the subterraneous passages, and the ground shook beneath the feet of the enchantress.

It was now that Ambrosio repented of his rashness. The solemn singularity of the charm had prepared him for something strange and horrible. He waited with fear for the spirit's appearance, whose coming was announced by thunder and earthquakes. He looked wildly around him, expecting that some dreadful apparition would meet his eyes, the sight of which would drive him mad. A cold shivering seized his body, and he sunk upon one knee, unable to support himself.

"He comes!" exclaimed Matilda in a joyful accent.

Ambrosio started, and expected the dæmon with terror. What was his surprise when, the thunder ceasing to roll, a full strain of melodious music sounded in the air! At the same time the cloud disappeared, and he beheld a figure more beautiful than fancy's pencil ever drew. It was a youth seemingly scarce eighteen, the perfection of whose form and face was unrivalled. He was

---

1 Cf. Milton, *Paradise Lost* 1.62-63.
2 "Lamb of God" (Latin); that is, Christ. As a common noun, it means either "A figure of a lamb bearing a cross or flag" or "A cake of wax stamped with such a figure and blessed by the Pope" (*OED*); here, it is presumably the latter.

perfectly naked: a bright star sparkled upon his forehead, two crimson wings extended themselves from his shoulders, and his silken locks were confined by a band of many-coloured fires, which played round his head, formed themselves into a variety of figures, and shone with a brilliance far surpassing that of precious stones.

Circlets of diamonds were fastened round his arms and ankles, and in his right hand he bore a silver branch imitating myrtle.[1] His form shone with dazzling glory: he was surrounded by clouds of rose-coloured light, and, at the moment that he appeared, a refreshing air breathed perfumes through the cavern. Enchanted at a vision so contrary to his expectations, Ambrosio gazed upon the spirit with delight and wonder: yet, however beautiful the figure, he could not but remark a wildness in the dæmon's eyes, and a mysterious melancholy impressed upon his features, betraying the fallen angel, and inspiring the spectators with secret awe.

The music ceased. Matilda addressed herself to the spirit: she spoke in a language unintelligible to the monk, and was answered in the same. She seemed to insist upon something which the dæmon was unwilling to grant. He frequently darted upon Ambrosio angry glances, and at such times the friar's heart sank within him. Matilda appeared to grow incensed; she spoke in a loud and commanding tone, and her gestures declared that she was threatening him with her vengeance. Her menaces had the desired effect. The spirit sank upon his knee, and with a submissive air presented to her the branch of myrtle. No sooner had she received it, than the music was again heard; a thick cloud spread itself over the apparition; the blue flames disappeared, and total obscurity reigned through the cave. The abbot moved not from his place: his faculties were all bound up in pleasure, anxiety, and surprise. At length the darkness dispersing, he perceived Matilda standing near him in her religious habit, with the myrtle in her hand. No traces remained of the incantation, and the vaults were only illuminated by the faint rays of the sepulchral lamp.

"I have succeeded," said Matilda, "though with more difficulty than I expected. Lucifer, whom I summoned to my assistance, was at first unwilling to obey my commands: to enforce his compliance, I was constrained to have recourse to my strongest charms. They have produced the desired effect, but I have engaged never

---

1 The myrtle is associated with Venus.

more to invoke his agency in your favour. Beware then how you employ an opportunity which never will return. My magic arts will now be of no use to you: in future you can only hope for supernatural aid, by invoking the dæmons yourself, and accepting the conditions of their service. This you will never do. You want strength of mind to force them to obedience; and unless you pay their established price, they will not be your voluntary servants. In this one instance they consent to obey you; I offer you the means of enjoying your mistress, and be careful not to lose the opportunity. Receive this constellated myrtle: while you bear this in your hand, every door will fly open to you. It will procure you access to-morrow night to Antonia's chamber: then breathe upon it thrice, pronounce her name, and place it upon her pillow. A death-like slumber will immediately seize upon her, and deprive her of the power of resisting your attempts. Sleep will hold her till break of morning. In this state you may satisfy your desires without danger of being discovered; since, when daylight shall dispel the effects of the enchantment, Antonia will perceive her dishonour, but be ignorant of the ravisher. Be happy then, my Ambrosio, and let this service convince you that my friendship is disinterested and pure. The night must be near expiring: let us return to the abbey, lest our absence should create surprise."

The abbot received the talisman with silent gratitude. His ideas were too much bewildered by the adventures of the night, to permit his expressing his thanks audibly, or indeed as yet to feel the whole value of her present. Matilda took up her lamp and basket, and guided her companion from the mysterious cavern. She restored the lamp to its former place, and continued her route in darkness till she reached the foot of the stair-case. The first beams of the rising sun darting down it facilitated the ascent. Matilda and the abbot hastened out of the sepulchre, closed the door after them, and soon regained the abbey's western cloister. No one met them, and they retired unobserved to their respective cells.

The confusion of Ambrosio's mind now began to appease. He rejoiced in the fortunate issue of his adventure, and, reflecting upon the virtues of the myrtle, looked upon Antonia as already in his power. Imagination retraced to him those secret charms betrayed to him by the enchanted mirror, and he waited with impatience for the approach of midnight.

END OF THE SECOND VOLUME.

THE MONK.
[VOLUME III]
CHAP. VIII.

The crickets sing, and man's o'erlaboured sense
Repairs itself by rest: our Tarquin thus
Did softly press the rushes, ere he wakened
The chastity he wounded—Cytherea,
How bravely thou becom'st thy bed! Fresh lily!
And whiter than the sheets!

CYMBELINE.[1]

ALL the researches of the marquis de las Cisternas proved vain.
Agnes was lost to him for ever. Despair produced so violent an
effect upon his constitution, that the consequence was a long and
severe illness. This prevented him from visiting Elvira, as he had
intended; and she being ignorant of the cause of his neglect, it gave
her no trifling uneasiness. His sister's death had prevented Lorenzo
from communicating to his uncle his designs respecting Antonia.
The injunctions of her mother forbade his presenting himself to
her without the duke's consent; and as she heard no more of him
or his proposals, Elvira conjectured that he had either met with a
better match, or had been commanded to give up all thoughts of
her daughter. Every day made her more uneasy respecting Antonia's fate; yet, while she retained the abbot's protection, she bore
with fortitude the disappointment of her hopes with regard to
Lorenzo and the marquis. That resource now failed her. She was
convinced that Ambrosio had meditated her daughter's ruin; and
when she reflected that her death would leave Antonia friendless
and unprotected in a world so base, so perfidious and depraved, her
heart swelled with the bitterness of apprehension. At such times
she would sit for hours gazing upon the lovely girl, and seeming to
listen to her innocent prattle, while in reality her thoughts dwelt
upon the sorrows into which a moment would suffice to plunge
her. Then she would clasp her in her arms suddenly, lean her head
upon her daughter's bosom, and bedew it with her tears.

---

1   Shakespeare, *Cymbeline* 2.2.11-16. In 510 B.C., Sextus Tarquinius, son of
    the last of the Roman kings, raped Lucretia, wife of Collatinus. She com-
    mitted suicide, and the ensuing outrage led to the overthrow of the
    monarchy and the establishment of the Republic: see Shakespeare, *The
    Rape of Lucrece*. Cytherea is Venus.

An event was in preparation, which, had she known it, would have relieved her from her inquietude. Lorenzo now waited only for a favourable opportunity to inform the duke of his intended marriage: however, a circumstance which occurred at this period obliged him to delay his explanation for a few days longer.

Don Raymond's malady seemed to gain ground. Lorenzo was constantly at his bed-side, and treated him with a tenderness truly fraternal. Both the cause and effects of the disorder were highly afflicting to the brother of Agnes; yet Theodore's grief was scarcely less sincere. That amiable boy quitted not his master for a moment, and put every means in practice to console and alleviate his sufferings. The marquis had conceived so rooted an affection for his deceased mistress, that it was evident to all that he never could survive her loss. Nothing could have prevented him from sinking under his grief, but the persuasion of her being still alive, and in need of his assistance. Though convinced of its falsehood, his attendants encouraged him in a belief which formed his only comfort. He was assured daily, that fresh perquisitions were making respecting the fate of Agnes; stories were invented recounting the various attempts made to get admittance into the convent; and circumstances were related, which, though they did not promise her absolute recovery, at least were sufficient to keep his hopes alive. The marquis constantly fell into the most terrible access of passion, when informed of the failure of these supposed attempts. Still he would not credit that the succeeding ones would have the same fate, but flattered himself that the next would prove more fortunate.

Theodore was the only one who exerted himself to realize his master's chimeras. He was eternally busied in planning schemes for entering the convent, or at least of obtaining from the nuns some intelligence of Agnes. To execute these schemes was the only inducement which could prevail on him to quit Don Raymond. He became a very Proteus, changing his shape every day;[1] but all his metamorphoses were to very little purpose. He regularly returned to the palace de las Cisternas without any intelligence to confirm his master's hopes. One day he took it into his head to disguise himself as a beggar; he put a patch over his left eye, took his guitar in hand, and posted himself at the gate of the convent.

---

1 Proteus was a minor sea-god, capable of changing his shape: see Homer, *Odyssey* 4. `

"If Agnes is really confined in the convent," thought he, "and hears my voice, she will recollect it, and possibly may find means to let me know that she is here."

With this idea he mingled with a crowd of beggars who assembled daily at the gate of St. Clare to receive soup, which the nuns were accustomed to distribute at twelve o'clock. All were provided with jugs or bowls to carry it away; but as Theodore had no utensil of this kind, he begged leave to eat his portion at the convent door. This was granted without difficulty. His sweet voice, and, in spite of his patched eye, his engaging countenance, won the heart of the good old porteress, who, aided by a lay-sister, was busied in serving to each his mess. Theodore was bid to stay till the others should depart, and promised that his request should then be granted. The youth desired no better, since it was not to eat soup that he presented himself at the convent. He thanked the porteress for her permission, retired from the door, and, seating himself upon a large stone, amused himself in tuning his guitar while the beggars were served.

As soon as the crowd was gone, Theodore was beckoned to the gate, and desired to come in. He obeyed with infinite readiness, but affected great respect at passing the hallowed threshold, and to be much daunted by the presence of the reverend ladies. His feigned timidity flattered the vanity of the nuns, who endeavoured to re-assure him. The porteress took him into her own little parlour: in the mean while, the lay-sister went to the kitchen, and soon returned with a double portion of soup of better quality than what was given to the beggars. His hostess added some fruits and confections from her own private store, and both encouraged the youth to dine heartily. To all these attentions he replied with much seeming gratitude, and abundance of blessings upon his benefactresses. While he ate, the nuns admired the delicacy of his features, the beauty of his hair, and the sweetness and grace which accompanied all his actions. They lamented to each other in whispers, that so charming a youth should be exposed to the seductions of the world, and agreed that he would be a worthy pillar of the catholic church. They concluded their conference by resolving, that heaven would be rendered a real service, if they entreated the prioress to intercede with Ambrosio for the beggar's admission into the order of capuchins.

This being determined, the porteress, who was a person of great influence in the convent, posted away in all haste to the domina's cell. Here she made so flaming a narrative of Theodore's merits, that the old lady grew curious to see him. Accordingly the porteress was commissioned to convey him to the parlour-grate. In the interim, the supposed beggar was sifting the lay-sister with respect to the fate of Agnes: her evidence only corroborated the domina's assertions. She said, that Agnes had been taken ill on returning from confession, had never quitted her bed from that moment, and that she had herself been present at the funeral. She even attested having seen her dead body, and assisted with her own hands in adjusting it upon the bier. This account discouraged Theodore; yet, as he had pushed the adventure so far, he resolved to witness its conclusion.

The porteress now returned, and ordered him to follow her. He obeyed, and was conducted into the parlour, where the lady prioress was already posted at the grate. The nuns surrounded her, who all flocked with eagerness to a scene which promised some diversion. Theodore saluted them with profound respect, and his presence had the power to smooth for a moment even the stern brow of the superior. She asked several questions respecting his parents, his religion, and what had reduced him to a state of beggary. To these demands his answers were perfectly satisfactory and perfectly false. He was then asked his opinion of a monastic life. He replied in terms of high estimation and respect for it. Upon this the prioress told him, that his obtaining an entrance into a religious order was not impossible; that her recommendation would not permit his poverty to be an obstacle; and that, if she found him deserving it, he might depend in future upon her protection. Theodore assured her, that to merit her favour would be his highest ambition; and having ordered him to return next day, when she would talk with him further, the domina quitted the parlour.

The nuns, whom respect for the superior had till then kept silent, now crowded all together to the grate, and assailed the youth with a multitude of questions. He had already examined each with attention. Alas! Agnes was not amongst them. The nuns heaped question upon question so thickly, that it was scarcely possible for him to reply. One asked where he was born, since his accent declared him to be a foreigner: another wanted to know why he wore a patch upon his left eye: sister Helena enquired whether he had not a sister like him, because she should like such a companion: and sister Rachael was fully persuaded that the brother would be the pleasanter companion of the two. Theodore amused himself with relating to the credulous nuns, for truths, all the strange stories which his imagination could invent. He related to them his supposed adventures, and penetrated every auditor with astonishment, while he talked of giants, savages, shipwrecks, and islands inhabited

> "By anthropophagi, and men whose heads
> Do grow beneath their shoulders,"[1]

with many other circumstances to the full as remarkable. He said that he was born in Terra Incognita, was educated at an Hottentot university, and had passed two years among the Americans of Silesia.

"For what regards the loss of my eye," said he, "it was a just punishment upon me for disrespect to the Virgin, when I made my second pilgrimage to Loretto.[2] I stood near the altar in the miraculous chapel: the monks were proceeding to array the statue in her best apparel. The pilgrims were ordered to close their eyes during this ceremony; but though by nature extremely religious, curiosity was too powerful. At the moment..... I shall penetrate you with horror, reverend ladies, when I reveal my crime!.... At the moment that the monks were changing her shift, I ventured to open my left eye, and gave a little peep towards the statue. That look was my last! The glory which surrounded the Virgin was too great to be supported. I hastily shut my sacrilegious eye, and never have been able to unclose it since!"

At the relation of this miracle the nuns all crossed themselves, and promised to intercede with the blessed Virgin for the recovery of his sight. They expressed their wonder at the extent of his travels, and at the strange adventures which he had met with at so early an age. They now remarked his guitar, and enquired whether he was an adept in music. He replied with modesty, that it was not for him to decide upon his talents, but requested permission to appeal to them as judges. This was granted without difficulty.

"But at least," said the old porteress, "take care not to sing any thing profane."

"You may depend upon my discretion," replied Theodore; "you shall hear how dangerous it is for young women to abandon themselves to their passions, illustrated by the adventure of a damsel, who fell suddenly in love with an unknown knight."

---

1 Adapted from Shakespeare, *Othello* 1.3.144-45.
2 A town in Italy, site of the Holy House of the Virgin, a common goal of pilgrimages.

"But is the adventure true?" enquired the porteress.

"Every word of it. It happened in Denmark; and the heroine was thought so beautiful, that she was known by no other name but that of 'the lovely maid.'"

"In Denmark, say you?" mumbled an old nun: "Are not the people all blacks in Denmark?"

"By no means, reverend lady; they are of a delicate pea-green, with flame-coloured hair and whiskers."

"Mother of God! Pea-green?" exclaimed sister Helena: "Oh! 'tis impossible!"

"Impossible!" said the porteress, with a look of contempt and exultation: "Not at all: when I was a young woman, I remember seeing several of them myself."

Theodore now put his instrument in proper order. He had read the story of a king of England, whose prison was discovered by a minstrel;[1] and he hoped that the same scheme would enable him to discover Agnes, should she be in the convent. He chose a ballad, which she had taught him herself in the castle of Lindenberg: she might possibly catch the sound, and he hoped to hear her replying to some of the stanzas. His guitar was now in tune, and he prepared to strike it.

"But, before I begin," said he, "it is necessary to inform you, ladies, that this same Denmark is terribly infested by sorcerers, witches, and evil spirits. Every element possesses its appropriate dæmons. The woods are haunted by a malignant power, called 'The Erl, or Oak-King:' he it is who blights the trees, spoils the harvest, and commands the imps and goblins. He appears in the form of an old man of majestic figure, with a golden crown, and long white beard. His principal amusement is to entice young children from their parents; and as soon as he gets them into his cave, he tears them into a thousand pieces. The rivers are governed by another fiend, called 'The Water-King:' his province is to agitate the deep, occasion shipwrecks, and drag the drowning sailors beneath the waves. He wears the appearance of a warrior, and employs himself in luring young virgins into his snare: what he does with them, when he catches them in the water, reverend ladies, I leave for you to imagine. 'The Fire-King' seems to be a man all formed of flames: he raises the meteors and wandering

---

1 In 1194, Richard I was held for ransom by Henry VI of Austria on his way back from the crusades. According to legend, his minstrel, Blondel, discovered where he was imprisoned by singing a song he knew Richard would recognize.

lights, which beguile travellers into ponds and marshes, and he directs the lightning where it may do most mischief. The last of these elementary dæmons is called 'The Cloud-King:' his figure is that of a beautiful youth, and he is distinguished by two large sable wings: though his outside is so enchanting, he is not a bit better disposed than the others. He is continually employed in raising storms, tearing up forests by the roots, and blowing castles and convents about the ears of their inhabitants. The first has a daughter, who is queen of the elves and fairies: the second has a mother, who is a powerful enchantress. Neither of these ladies are worth more than the gentlemen. I do not remember to have heard any family assigned to the two other dæmons, but at present I have no business with any of them except the fiend of the waters.[1] He is the hero of my ballad; but I thought it necessary, before I began, to give you some account of his proceedings."

Theodore then played a short symphony; after which, stretching his voice to its utmost extent, to facilitate its reaching the ear of Agnes, he sung the following stanzas:

THE WATER-KING,
A DANISH BALLAD.[2]

WITH gentle murmur flowed the tide,
While by the fragrant flowery side
The lovely maid, with carols gay,
To Mary's church pursued her way.

The water-fiend's malignant eye
Along the banks beheld her hie;
Straight to his mother-witch he sped,
And thus in suppliant accents said:

"Oh! mother! mother! now advise,
How I may yonder maid surprise:
Oh! mother! mother! now explain,
How I may yonder maid obtain."

---

1 Lewis included five poems about these elemental spirits in his anthology *Tales of Wonder* (1801): his own versions of Goethe's "Der Erlkönig" and Herder's "Der Wassermann" and "Erlkönigs Tochter" (see Appendix E, entry for 255.34), his original poem "The Cloud-King," and "The Fire-King," by Walter Scott.
2 Based on "Der Wassermann," from *Volkslieder*, by Johann Gottfried Herder.

The witch, she gave him armour white;
She formed him like a gallant knight;
Of water clear next made her hand
A steed, whose housings were of sand.

The water-king then swift he went;
To Mary's church his steps he bent:
He bound his courser to the door,
And paced the church-yard three times four.

His courser to the door bound he,
And paced the church-yard four times three:
Then hastened up the aisle, where all
The people flocked, both great and small.

The priest said, as the knight drew near,
"And wherefore comes the white chief here?"
The lovely maid, she smiled aside;
"Oh! would I were the white chief's bride!"

He stepped o'er benches one and two;
"Oh! lovely maid, I die for you!"
He stepped o'er benches two and three;
"Oh! lovely maiden, go with me!"

Then sweet she smiled, the lovely maid;
And while she gave her hand, she said,
"Betide me joy, betide me woe,
O'er hill, o'er dale, with thee I go."

The priest their hands together joins:
They dance, while clear the moon-beam shines;
And little thinks the maiden bright,
Her partner is the water-spright.

Oh! had some spirit deigned to sing,
"Your partner is the water-king!"
The maid had fear and hate confessed,
And cursed the hand which then she pressed.

But nothing giving cause to think
How near she strayed to danger's brink,

Still on she went, and hand in hand
The lovers reached the yellow sand.

"Ascend this steed with me, my dear!
We needs must cross the streamlet here:
Ride boldly in; it is not deep;
The winds are hushed, the billows sleep."

Thus spoke the water-king. The maid
Her traitor bride-groom's wish obeyed:
And soon she saw the courser lave
Delighted in his parent wave.

"Stop! stop! my love! The waters blue
E'en now my shrinking foot bedew."
"Oh! lay aside your fears, sweet heart!
We now have reached the deepest part."

"Stop! stop! my love! For now I see
The waters rise above my knee."
"Oh! lay aside your fears, sweet heart!
We now have reached the deepest part."

"Stop! stop! for God's sake, stop! For, oh!
The waters o'er my bosom flow!"—
Scarce was the word pronounced, when knight
And courser vanished from her sight.

She shrieks, but shrieks in vain; for high
The wild winds rising dull the cry;
The fiend exults; the billows dash,
And o'er their hapless victim wash.

Three times, while struggling with the stream,
The lovely maid was heard to scream;
But when the tempest's rage was o'er,
The lovely maid was seen no more.

Warned by this tale, ye damsels fair,
To whom you give your love beware!
Believe not every handsome knight,
And dance not with the water-spright!

The youth ceased to sing. The nuns were delighted with the sweetness of his voice, and masterly manner of touching the instrument; but however acceptable this applause would have been at any other time, at present it was insipid to Theodore. His artifice had not succeeded. He paused in vain between the stanzas; no voice replied to his, and he abandoned the hope of equalling Blondel.

The convent-bell now warned the nuns that it was time to assemble in the refectory. They were obliged to quit the grate: they thanked the youth for the entertainment which his music had afforded them, and charged him to return the next day. This he promised. The nuns, to give him the greater inclination to keep his word, told him that he might always depend upon the convent for his meals, and each of them made him some little present. One gave him a box of sweetmeats; another, an agnus dei; some brought reliques of saints, waxen images, and consecrated crosses; and others presented him with pieces of those works in which the religious excel, such as embroidery, artificial flowers, lace, and needle-work. All these he was advised to sell, in order to put himself into better case; and he was assured that it would be easy to dispose of them, since the Spaniards hold the performances of the nuns in high estimation. Having received these gifts with seeming respect and gratitude, he remarked, that, having no basket, he knew not how to convey them away. Several of the nuns were hastening in search of one, when they were stopped by the return of an elderly woman, whom Theodore had not till then observed. Her mild countenance and respectable air prejudiced him immediately in her favour.

"Hah!" said the porteress, "here comes the mother St. Ursula with a basket."

The nun approached the grate, and presented the basket to Theodore: it was of willow, lined with blue satin, and upon the four sides were painted scenes from the legend of St. Genevieve.

"Here is my gift," said she, as she gave it into his hand: "Good youth, despise it not. Though its value seems insignificant, it has many hidden virtues."

She accompanied these words with an expressive look. It was not lost upon Theodore. In receiving the present, he drew as near the grate as possible.

"Agnes!" she whispered in a voice scarcely intelligible.

Theodore, however, caught the sound. He concluded that some mystery was concealed in the basket, and his heart beat with impatience and joy. At this moment the domina returned. Her air was gloomy and frowning, and she looked if possible more stern than ever.

"Mother St. Ursula, I would speak with you in private."

The nun changed colour, and was evidently disconcerted.

"With me?" she replied in a faltering voice.

The domina motioned that she must follow her, and retired. The mother St. Ursula obeyed her. Soon after, the refectory bell ringing a second time, the nuns quitted the grate, and Theodore was left at liberty to carry off his prize. Delighted that at length he had obtained some intelligence for the marquis, he flew rather than ran till he reached the hotel de las Cisternas. In a few minutes he stood by his master's bed with the basket in his hand. Lorenzo was in the chamber, endeavouring to reconcile his friend to a misfortune which he felt himself but too severely. Theodore related his adventure, and the hopes which had been created by the mother St. Ursula's gift. The marquis started from his pillow. That fire which since the death of Agnes had been extinguished, now revived in his bosom, and his eyes sparkled with the eagerness of expectation. The emotions which Lorenzo's countenance betrayed were scarcely weaker, and he waited with inexpressible impatience for the solution of this mystery. Raymond caught the basket from the hands of his page: he emptied the contents upon the bed, and examined them with minute attention. He hoped that a letter would be found at the bottom. Nothing of the kind appeared. The search was resumed, and still with no better success. At length Don Raymond observed, that one corner of the blue satin lining was unripped: he tore it open hastily, and drew forth a small scrap of paper, neither folded nor sealed. It was addressed to the marquis de las Cisternas, and the contents were as follow:

"Having recognised your page, I venture to send these few lines. Procure an order from the cardinal-duke for seizing my person, and that of the domina; but let it not be executed till Friday at midnight. It is the festival of St. Clare: there will be a procession of nuns by torch-light, and I shall be among them. Beware, not to let your intention be known. Should a syllable be dropped to excite the domina's suspicions, you will never hear of me more. Be cautious, if you prize the memory of Agnes, and wish to punish her assassins. I have that to tell, will freeze your blood with horror.

ST. URSULA."

No sooner had the marquis read the note, than he fell back upon his pillow deprived of sense or motion. The hope failed him which till now had supported his existence; and these lines convinced him but too positively that Agnes was indeed no more. Lorenzo felt this circumstance less forcibly, since it had always been his idea that his sister had perished by unfair means. When he found by the mother St. Ursula's letter how true were his suspicions, the confirmation excited no other sentiment in his bosom than a wish to punish the murderers as they deserved. It was no easy task to recall the marquis to himself. As soon as he recovered his speech, he broke out into execrations against the assassins of his beloved, and vowed to take upon them a signal vengeance. He continued to rave and torment himself with impotent passion, till his constitution, enfeebled by grief and illness, could support itself no longer, and relapsed into insensibility. His melancholy situation sincerely affected Lorenzo, who would willingly have remained in the apartment of his friend; but other cares now demanded his presence. It was necessary to procure the order for seizing the prioress of St. Clare. For this purpose, having committed Raymond to the care of the best physicians in Madrid, he quitted the hotel de las Cisternas, and bent his course towards the palace of the cardinal-duke.

His disappointment was excessive, when he found that affairs of state had obliged the cardinal to set out for a distant province. It wanted but five days to Friday: yet, by travelling day and night, he hoped to return in time for the pilgrimage of St. Clare. In this he succeeded. He found the cardinal-duke, and represented to him the supposed culpability of the prioress, as also the violent effects which it had produced upon Don Raymond. He could have used no argument so forcible as this last. Of all his nephews the marquis was the only one to whom the cardinal-duke was sincerely attached: he perfectly doted upon him, and the prioress could have committed no greater crime in his eyes, than to have endangered the life of the marquis. Consequently, he granted the order of arrest without difficulty. He also gave Lorenzo a letter to a principal officer of the Inquisition, desiring him to see his mandate executed. Furnished with these papers, Medina hastened back to Madrid, which he reached on the Friday a few hours before dark. He found the marquis somewhat easier, but so weak and exhausted, that without great exertion he could neither speak nor move. Having passed an hour by his bed-side, Lorenzo left him to communicate his design to his uncle, as also to give Don Ramirez de Mello the cardinal's letter. The first was petrified with horror, when he learned the fate of his unhappy niece. He encouraged Lorenzo to punish her assassins, and engaged to accompany him at night to St. Clare's convent. Don Ramirez promised his firmest support, and selected a band of trusty archers to prevent opposition on the part of the populace.

But while Lorenzo was anxious to unmask one religious hypocrite, he was unconscious of the sorrows prepared for him by another. Aided by Matilda's infernal agents, Ambrosio had resolved upon the innocent Antonia's ruin. The moment destined to be so fatal to her arrived. She had taken leave of her mother for the night. As she kissed her, she felt an unusual despondency infuse itself into her bosom. She left her, and returned to her instantly, threw herself into her maternal arms, and bathed her cheek with tears. She felt uneasy at quitting her, and a secret presentiment assured her that never must they meet again. Elvira observed, and tried to laugh her out of this childish prejudice. She chid her mildly for encouraging such ungrounded sadness, and warned her how dangerous it was to encourage such ideas.

To all her remonstrances she received no other answer than—
"Mother! Dear mother! Oh! would to God it were morning!"

Elvira, whose inquietude respecting her daughter was a great obstacle to her perfect re-establishment, was still labouring under the effects of her late severe illness. She was this evening more than usually indisposed, and retired to bed before her accustomed hour. Antonia withdrew from her mother's chamber with regret, and, till the door closed, kept her eyes fixed upon her with melancholy expression. She retired to her own apartment: her heart was filled with bitterness. It seemed to her that all her prospects were blasted, and the world contained nothing for which it was worth existing. She sank into a chair, reclined her head upon her arm, and gazed upon the floor with a vacant stare, while the most gloomy images floated before her fancy. She was still in this state of insensibility, when she was disturbed by hearing a strain of soft music breathed beneath her window. She rose, drew near the casement, and opened it to hear it more distinctly. Having thrown her veil over her face, she ventured to look out. By the light of the moon she perceived several men below with guitars and lutes in their hands; and at a little distance from them stood another wrapped in his cloak, whose stature and appearance bore a strong resemblance to Lorenzo's. She was not deceived in this conjecture. It was indeed Lorenzo himself, who, bound by his word not to present himself to Antonia without his uncle's consent, endeavoured, by occasional serenades, to convince his mistress that his attachment still existed. His stratagem had not the desired effect. Antonia was far from supposing that this nightly music was intended as a compliment to her. She was too modest to think herself worthy such attentions; and concluding them to be addressed to some neighbouring lady, she grieved to find that they were offered by Lorenzo.

The air which was played, was plaintive and melodious. It accorded with the state of Antonia's mind, and she listened with pleasure. After a symphony of some length, it was succeeded by the sound of voices, and Antonia distinguished the following words:

SERENADE.

CHORUS.

OH! breathe in gentle strain, my lyre!
'Tis here that beauty loves to rest:
Describe the pangs of fond desire,
Which rend a faithful lover's breast.

SONG.

In every heart to find a slave,
In every soul to fix his reign,
In bonds to lead the wise and brave,
And make the captives kiss his chain;
Such is the power of Love, and oh!
I grieve so well Love's power to know.

In sighs to pass the live-long day,
To taste a short and broken sleep,
For one dear object far away,
All others scorned, to watch and weep;
Such are the pains of Love, and oh!
I grieve so well Love's pains to know.

To read consent in virgin eyes,
To press the lip ne'er prest till then,
To hear the sigh of transport rise,
And kiss, and kiss, and kiss again;
Such are thy pleasures, Love! But oh!
When shall my heart thy pleasures know?

CHORUS.

Now hush, my lyre! My voice, be still!
Sleep, gentle maid! May fond desire
With amorous thoughts thy visions fill,
Though still my voice, and hushed my lyre!

The music ceased: the performers dispersed, and silence prevailed through the street. Antonia quitted the window with regret. She, as usual, recommended herself to the protection of St. Rosolia, said her accustomed prayers, and retired to bed. Sleep was not long absent, and his presence relieved her from her terrors and inquietude.

It was almost two o'clock before the lustful monk ventured to bend his steps towards Antonia's dwelling. It has been already mentioned, that the abbey was at no great distance from the strada di San Iago. He reached the house unobserved. Here he stopped, and hesitated for a moment. He reflected on the enormity of the crime, the consequences of a discovery, and the probability, after what had passed, of Elvira's suspecting him to be her daughter's ravisher. On the other hand it was suggested, that she could do no more than suspect; that no proofs of his guilt could be produced; that it would seem impossible for the rape to have been committed without Antonia's knowing when, where, or by whom; and finally, he believed that his fame was too firmly established to be shaken by the unsupported accusations of two unknown women. This latter argument was perfectly false. He knew not how uncertain is the air of popular applause, and that a moment suffices to make him to-day the detestation of the world, who yesterday was its idol. The result of the monk's deliberations was, that he should proceed in his enterprise. He ascended the steps leading to the house. No sooner did he touch the door with the silver myrtle, than it flew open, and presented him with a free passage. He entered, and the door closed after him of its own accord.

Guided by the moon-beams, he proceeded up the stair-case with slow and cautious steps. He looked round him every moment with apprehension and anxiety. He saw a spy in every shadow, and heard a voice in every murmur of the night-breeze. Consciousness of the guilty business on which he was employed appalled his heart, and rendered it more timid than a woman's. Yet still he proceeded. He reached the door of Antonia's chamber. He stopped, and listened. All was hushed within. The total silence persuaded him that his intended victim was retired to rest, and he ventured to lift up the latch. The door was fastened, and resisted his efforts. But no sooner was it touched by the talisman, than the bolt flew back. The ravisher stepped on, and found himself in the chamber, where slept the innocent girl, unconscious how dangerous a visitor was drawing near her couch. The door closed after him, and the bolt shot again into its fastening.

Ambrosio advanced with precaution. He took care that not a board should creak under his foot, and held in his breath as he approached the bed. His first attention was to perform the magic ceremony, as Matilda had charged him: he breathed thrice upon the silver myrtle, pronounced over it Antonia's name, and laid it upon her pillow. The effects which it had already produced permitted not his doubting its success in prolonging the slumbers of his devoted mistress. No sooner was the inchantment performed, than he considered her to be absolutely in his power, and his eyes flashed with lust and impatience. He now ventured to cast a glance upon the sleeping beauty. A single lamp, burning before the statue of St. Rosolia, shed a faint light through the room, and permitted him to examine all the charms of the lovely object before him. The heat of the weather had obliged her to throw off part of the bed-clothes. Those which still covered her Ambrosio's insolent hand hastened to remove. She lay with her cheek reclining upon one ivory arm: the other rested on the side of the bed with graceful indolence. A few tresses of her hair had escaped from beneath the muslin which confined the rest, and fell carelessly over her bosom, as it heaved with slow and regular suspiration. The warm air had spread her cheek with higher colour than usual. A smile inexpressibly sweet played round her ripe and coral lips, from which every now and then escaped a gentle sigh, or an half-pronounced sentence. An air of enchanting innocence and candour pervaded her whole form; and there was a sort of modesty in her very nakedness, which added fresh stings to the desires of the lustful monk.

He remained for some moments devouring those charms with his eyes, which soon were to be subjected to his ill-regulated passions. Her mouth half-opened seemed to solicit a kiss: he bent over her: he joined his lips to hers, and drew in the fragrance of her breath with rapture. This momentary pleasure increased his longing for still greater. His desires were raised to that frantic height by which brutes are agitated. He resolved not to delay for one instant longer the accomplishment of his wishes, and hastily proceeded to tear off those garments which impeded the gratification of his lust.

"Gracious God!" exclaimed a voice behind him: "Am I not deceived? Is not this an illusion?"

Terror, confusion, and disappointment accompanied these words, as they struck Ambrosio's hearing. He started, and turned towards it. Elvira stood at the door of the chamber, and regarded the monk with looks of surprise and detestation.

A frightful dream had represented to her Antonia on the verge of a precipice. She saw her trembling on the brink: every moment seemed to threaten her fall, and she heard her exclaim with shrieks, "Save me, mother! save me!—Yet a moment, and it will be too late." Elvira woke in terror. The vision had made too strong an impression upon her mind, to permit her resting till assured of her daughter's safety. She hastily started from her bed, threw on a loose night-gown, and, passing through the closet in which slept the waiting-woman, reached Antonia's chamber just in time to rescue her from the grasp of the ravisher.

His shame and her amazement seemed to have petrified into statues both Elvira and the monk. They remained gazing upon each other in silence. The lady was the first to recover herself.

"It is no dream," she cried: "it is really Ambrosio, who stands before me. It is the man whom Madrid esteems a saint, that I find at this late hour near the couch of my unhappy child. Monster of hypocrisy! I already suspected your designs, but forbore your accusation in pity to human frailty. Silence would now be criminal. The whole city shall be informed of your incontinence. I will unmask you, villain, and convince the church what a viper she cherishes in her bosom."

Pale and confused, the baffled culprit stood trembling before her. He would fain have extenuated his offence, but could find no apology for his conduct. He could produce nothing but broken sentences, and excuses which contradicted each other. Elvira was too justly incensed to grant the pardon which he requested. She protested that she would raise the neighbourhood, and make him an example to all future hypocrites. Then hastening to the bed, she called to Antonia to wake; and finding that her voice had no effect, she took her arm, and raised her forcibly from the pillow. The charm operated too powerfully. Antonia remained insensible; and, on being released by her mother, sank back upon the pillow.

"This slumber cannot be natural," cried the amazed Elvira, whose indignation increased with every moment: "some mystery is concealed in it. But tremble, hypocrite! All your villany shall soon be unravelled. Help! help!" she exclaimed aloud: "Within there! Flora! Flora!"

"Hear me for one moment, lady!" cried the monk, restored to himself by the urgency of the danger: "by all that is sacred and holy, I swear that your daughter's honour is still unviolated. Forgive my transgression! Spare me the shame of a discovery, and permit me to regain the abbey undisturbed. Grant me this request in mercy! I promise not only that Antonia shall be secure from me in future, but that the rest of my life shall prove——"

Elvira interrupted him abruptly.

"Antonia secure from you? *I* will secure her. You shall betray no longer the confidence of parents. Your iniquity shall be unveiled to the public eye. All Madrid shall shudder at your perfidy, your hypocrisy, and incontinence. What ho! there! Flora! Flora! I say."

While she spoke thus, the remembrance of Agnes struck upon his mind. Thus had she sued to him for mercy, and thus had he refused her prayer! It was now his turn to suffer, and he could not but acknowledge that his punishment was just. In the mean while Elvira continued to call Flora to her assistance; but her voice was so choaked with passion, that the servant, who was buried in profound slumber, was insensible to all her cries: Elvira dared not go towards the closet in which Flora slept, lest the monk should take that opportunity to escape. Such indeed was his intention: he trusted that, could he reach the abbey unobserved by any other than Elvira, her single testimony would not suffice to ruin a reputation so well established as his was in Madrid. With this idea he gathered up such garments as he had already thrown off, and hastened towards the door. Elvira was aware of his design: she followed him, and, ere he could draw back the bolt, seized him by the arm, and detained him.

"Attempt not to fly!" said she: "you quit not this room without witnesses of your guilt."

Ambrosio struggled in vain to disengage himself. Elvira quitted not her hold, but redoubled her cries for succour. The friar's danger grew more urgent. He expected every moment to hear people assembling at her voice; and, worked up to madness by the approach of ruin, he adopted a resolution equally desperate and savage. Turning round suddenly, with one hand he grasped Elvira's throat so as to prevent her continuing her clamour, and with the other, dashing her violently upon the ground, he dragged her towards the bed. Confused by this unexpected attack, she scarcely had power to strive at forcing herself from his grasp: while the monk, snatching the pillow from beneath her daughter's head, covering with it Elvira's face, and pressing his knee upon her stomach with all his strength, endeavoured to put an end to her existence. He succeeded but too well. Her natural strength increased by the excess of anguish, long did the sufferer struggle to disengage herself, but in vain. The monk continued to kneel upon her breast, witnessed without mercy the convulsive trembling of her limbs beneath him, and sustained with inhuman firmness the spectacle of her agonies, when soul and body were on the point of separating. Those agonies at length were over. She ceased to struggle for life. The monk took off the pillow, and gazed upon her. Her face was covered with a frightful blackness: her limbs moved no more: the blood was chilled in her veins: her heart had forgotten to beat; and her hands were stiff and frozen. Ambrosio beheld before him that once noble and majestic form, now become a corse, cold, senseless, and disgusting.

This horrible act was no sooner perpetrated, than the friar beheld the enormity of his crime. A cold dew flowed over his limbs: his eyes closed: he staggered to a chair, and sank into it almost as lifeless as the unfortunate who lay extended at his feet. From this state he was roused by the necessity of flight, and the danger of being found in Antonia's apartment. He had no desire to profit by the execution of his crime. Antonia now appeared to him an object of disgust. A dead-ly cold had usurped the place of that warmth which glowed in his bosom. No ideas offered themselves to his mind but those of death and guilt, of present shame and future punishment. Agitated by remorse and fear, he prepared for flight: yet his terrors did not so completely master his recollection, as to prevent his taking the pre-cautions necessary for his safety. He replaced the pillow upon the bed, gathered up his garments, and, with the fatal talisman in his hand, bent his unsteady steps towards the door. Bewildered by fear, he fancied that his flight was opposed by legions of phantoms. Wherever he turned, the disfigured corse seemed to lie in his passage, and it was long before he succeeded in reaching the door. The enchanted myr-tle produced its former effect. The door opened, and he hastened down the stair-case. He entered the abbey unobserved; and having shut himself into his cell, he abandoned his soul to the tortures of unavailing remorse, and terrors of impending detection.

CHAP. IX.

Tell us, ye dead, will none of you in pity
To those you left behind disclose the secret?
O! that some courteous ghost would blab it out,
What 'tis you are, and we must shortly be.
I've heard, that souls departed have sometimes
Fore-warned men of their deaths: 'twas kindly done,
To knock, and give the alarum.

BLAIR.[1]

AMBROSIO shuddered at himself when he reflected on his rapid advances in iniquity. The enormous crime which he had just com-mitted, filled him with real horror. The murdered Elvira was contin-ually before his eyes, and his guilt was already punished by the ago-nies of his conscience. Time, however, considerably weakened these

---

1 Robert Blair, *The Grave* 431-37.

impressions: one day passed away; another followed it, and still not the least suspicion was thrown upon him. Impunity reconciled him to his guilt. He began to resume his spirits; and as his fears of detection died away, he paid less attention to the reproaches of remorse. Matilda exerted herself to quiet his alarms. At the first intelligence of Elvira's death, she seemed greatly affected, and joined the monk in deploring the unhappy catastrophe of his adventure: but when she found his agitation to be somewhat calmed, and himself better disposed to listen to her arguments, she proceeded to mention his offence in milder terms, and convince him that he was not so highly culpable as he appeared to consider himself. She represented, that he had only availed himself of the rights which nature allows to every one, those of self-preservation: that either Elvira or himself must have perished; and that her inflexibility and resolution to ruin him had deservedly marked her out for the victim. She next stated, that as he had before rendered himself suspected to Elvira, it was a fortunate event for him that her lips were closed by death; since, without this last adventure, her suspicions, if made public, might have produced very disagreeable consequences. He had therefore freed himself from an enemy, to whom the errors of his conduct were sufficiently known to make her dangerous, and who was the greatest obstacle to his designs upon Antonia. Those designs she encouraged him not to abandon. She assured him that, no longer protected by her mother's watchful eye, the daughter would fall an easy conquest; and by praising and enumerating Antonia's charms, she strove to rekindle the desires of the monk. In this endeavour she succeeded but too well.

As if the crimes into which his passion had seduced him, had only increased its violence, he longed more eagerly than ever to enjoy Antonia. The same success in concealing his present guilt, he trusted, would attend his future. He was deaf to the murmurs of conscience, and resolved to satisfy his desires at any price. He waited only for an opportunity of repeating his former enterprise; but to procure that opportunity by the same means was now impracticable. In the first transports of despair he had dashed the enchanted myrtle into a thousand pieces. Matilda told him plainly, that he must expect no further assistance from the infernal powers, unless he was willing to subscribe to their established conditions. This Ambrosio was determined not to do. He persuaded himself that, however great might be his iniquity, so long as he preserved his claim to salvation, he need not despair of pardon. He therefore resolutely refused to enter into any bond or compact with the fiends; and Matilda, finding him obstinate upon this point, forbore to press him further. She exerted her invention to discover some means of putting Antonia into the abbot's power: nor was it long before that means presented itself.

While her ruin was thus meditating, the unhappy girl herself suffered severely from the loss of her mother. Every morning on waking, it was her first care to hasten to Elvira's chamber. On that which followed Ambrosio's fatal visit, she woke later than was her usual custom: of this she was convinced by the abbey chimes. She started from her bed, threw on a few loose garments hastily, and was speeding to enquire how her mother had passed the night, when her foot struck against something which lay in her passage. She looked down. What was her horror at recognizing Elvira's livid corse! She uttered a loud shriek, and threw herself upon the floor. She clasped the inanimate form to her bosom, felt that it was dead-cold, and, with a movement of disgust, of which she was not the mistress, let it fall again from her arms. The cry had alarmed Flora, who hastened to her assistance. The sight which she beheld penetrated her with horror; but her alarm was more audible than Antonia's. She made the house ring with her lamentations, while her mistress, almost suffocated with grief, could only mark her distress by sobs and groans. Flora's shrieks soon reached the ears of the hostess, whose terror and surprise were excessive on learning the cause of this disturbance. A physician was immediately sent for; but, on the first moment of beholding the corse, he declared that Elvira's recovery was beyond the power of art. He proceeded therefore to give his assistance to Antonia, who by this time was truly in need of it. She was conveyed to bed, while the landlady busied herself in giving orders for Elvira's burial. Dame Jacintha was a plain good kind of woman, charitable, generous, and devout; but her intellects were weak, and she was a miserable slave to fear and superstition. She shuddered at the idea of passing the night in the same house with a dead body. She was persuaded that Elvira's ghost would appear to her, and no less certain that such a visit would kill her with fright. From this persuasion, she resolved to pass the night at a neighbour's, and insisted that the funeral should take place the next day. St. Clare's cemetery being the nearest, it was determined that Elvira should be buried there. Dame Jacintha engaged to defray every expence attending the burial. She knew not in what circumstances Antonia was left; but, from the sparing manner in which the family had lived, she concluded them to be indifferent: consequently she entertained very little hope of ever being recompensed. But this consideration prevented her not from taking care that the interment was performed with decency, and from shewing the unfortunate Antonia all possible respect.

Nobody dies of mere grief; of this Antonia was an instance. Aided by her youth and healthy constitution, she shook off the malady which her mother's death had occasioned; but it was not so easy to remove the disease of her mind. Her eyes were constantly filled with tears; every trifle affected her, and she evidently nourished in her bosom a profound and rooted melancholy. The slightest mention of Elvira, the most trivial circumstance recalling that beloved parent to her memory, was sufficient to throw her into serious agitation. How much would her grief have been increased, had she known the agonies which terminated her mother's existence! But of this no one entertained the least suspicion. Elvira was subject to strong convulsions: it was supposed that, aware of their approach, she had dragged herself to her daughter's chamber in hopes of assistance; that a sudden access of her fits had seized her, too violent to be resisted by her already enfeebled state of health; and that she had expired ere she had time to reach the medicine which generally relieved her, and which stood upon a shelf in Antonia's room. This idea was firmly credited by the few people who interested themselves about Elvira. Her death was esteemed a natural event, and soon forgotten by all, save by her, who had but too much reason to deplore her loss.

In truth Antonia's situation was sufficiently embarrassing and unpleasant. She was alone, in the midst of a dissipated and expensive city; she was ill provided with money, and worse with friends. Her aunt Leonella was still at Cordova, and she knew not her direction. Of the marquis de las Cisternas she heard no news. As to Lorenzo, she had long given up the idea of possessing any interest in his bosom. She knew not to whom she could address herself in her present dilemma. She wished to consult Ambrosio, but she remembered her mother's injunctions to shun him as much as possible; and the last · conversation which Elvira had held with her upon the subject, had given her sufficient lights respecting his designs, to put her upon her guard against him in future. Still all her mother's warnings could not make her change her good opinion of the friar. She continued to feel that his friendship and society were requisite to her happiness: she looked upon his failings with a partial eye, and could not persuade herself that he really had intended her ruin. However, Elvira had positively commanded her to drop his acquaintance, and she had too much respect for her orders to disobey them.

At length she resolved to address herself for advice and protection to the marquis de las Cisternas, as being her nearest relation. She wrote to him, briefly stating her desolate situation; she besought him to compassionate his brother's child, to continue to her Elvira's pension, and to authorise her retiring to his old castle in Murcia, which till now had been her retreat. Having sealed her letter, she gave it to the trusty Flora, who immediately set out to execute her commission. But Antonia was born under an unlucky star. Had she made her application to the marquis but one day sooner, received as his niece, and placed at the head of his family, she would have escaped all the misfortunes with which she was now threatened. Raymond had always intended to execute this plan: but first, his hopes of making the proposal to Elvira through the lips of Agnes, and afterwards his disappointment at losing his intended bride, as well as the severe illness which for some time had confined him to his bed, made him defer from day to day the giving an asylum in his house to his brother's widow. He had commissioned Lorenzo to supply her liberally with money. But Elvira, unwilling to receive obligations from that nobleman, had assured him that she needed no immediate pecuniary assistance. Consequently the marquis did not imagine that a trifling delay on his part would create any embarrassment; and the distress and agitation of his mind might well excuse his negligence.

Had he been informed that Elvira's death had left her daughter friendless and unprotected, he would doubtless have taken such measures as would have ensured her from every danger. But Antonia was not destined to be so fortunate. The day on which she sent her letter to the palace de las Cisternas, was that following Lorenzo's departure from Madrid. The marquis was in the first paroxysms of despair at the conviction that Agnes was indeed no more: he was delirious; and, his life being in danger, no one was suffered to approach him. Flora was informed that he was incapable of attending to letters, and that probably a few hours would decide his fate. With this unsatisfactory answer she was obliged to return to her mistress, who now found herself plunged into greater difficulties than ever.

Flora and Dame Jacintha exerted themselves to console her. The latter begged her to make herself easy, for that as long as she chose to stay with her she would treat her like her own child. Antonia, finding that the good woman had taken a real affection for her, was somewhat comforted by thinking that she had at least one friend in the world. A letter was now brought to her, directed to Elvira. She recognized Leonella's writing, and, opening it with joy, found a detailed account of her aunt's adventures at Cordova. She informed her sister that she had recovered her legacy, had lost her heart, and had received in exchange that of the most amiable of apothecaries, past, present, and to come. She added, that she should be at Madrid on the Tuesday night, and meant to have the pleasure of presenting her caro sposo[1] in form. Though her nuptials were far from pleasing Antonia, Leonella's speedy return gave her niece much delight. She rejoiced in thinking that she should once more be under a relation's care. She could not but judge it to be highly improper for a young woman to be living among absolute strangers, with no one to regulate her conduct, or protect her from the insults to which in her defenceless situation she was exposed. She therefore looked forward with impatience to the Tuesday night.

It arrived. Antonia listened anxiously to the carriages as they rolled along the street. None of them stopped, and it grew late without Leonella's appearing. Still Antonia resolved to sit up till her aunt's arrival; and, in spite of all her remonstrances, Dame Jacintha and Flora insisted upon doing the same. The hours passed on slow and tediously. Lorenzo's departure from Madrid had put a stop to the nightly serenades: she hoped in vain to hear the usual sound of guitars beneath her window. She took up her own, and struck a few chords; but music that evening had lost its charms for her, and she soon replaced the instrument in its case. She seated herself at her embroidery frame, but nothing went right: the silks were missing, the thread snapped every moment, and the needles were so expert at falling that they seemed to be animated. At length a flake of wax fell from the taper which stood near her upon a favourite wreath of violets: this completely discomposed her; she threw down her needle, and quitted the frame. It was decreed that for that night nothing should have the power of amusing her. She was the prey of ennui, and employed herself in making fruitless wishes for the arrival of her aunt.

As she walked with a listless air up and down the chamber, the door caught her eye conducting to that which had been her mother's. She remembered that Elvira's little library was arranged there, and thought that she might possibly find in it some book to amuse her till Leonella should arrive. Accordingly she took her taper from the table, passed through the little closet, and entered the adjoining apartment. As she looked around her, the sight of this room brought to her recollection a thousand painful ideas. It was the first time of her entering it since her mother's death. The total silence prevailing through the chamber, the bed despoiled of its furniture, the cheerless hearth where stood an extinguished lamp, and a few dying plants in the window, which since Elvira's loss had been neglected, inspired Antonia with a melancholy awe. The gloom of night gave strength to this sen-

---

1   "Dear husband" (Italian).

sation. She placed her light upon the table, and sank into a large chair, in which she had seen her mother seated a thousand and a thousand times. She was never to see her seated there again! Tears unbidden streamed down her cheek, and she abandoned herself to the sadness which grew deeper with every moment.

Ashamed of her weakness, she at length rose from her seat; she proceeded to seek for what had brought her to this melancholy scene. The small collection of books was arranged upon several shelves in order. Antonia examined them without finding any thing likely to interest her, till she put her hand upon a volume of old Spanish ballads. She read a few stanzas of one of them. They excited her curiosity. She took down the book, and seated herself to peruse it with ease. She trimmed the taper, which now drew towards its end, and then read the following ballad:

ALONZO THE BRAVE AND FAIR IMOGINE.[1]

A WARRIOR so bold, and a virgin so bright
    Conversed, as they sat on the green;
They gazed on each other with tender delight;
Alonzo the Brave was the name of the knight,
    The maid's was the Fair Imogine.

"And, oh!" said the youth, "since to-morrow I go
    To fight in a far distant land,
Your tears for my absence soon leaving to flow,
Some other will court you, and you will bestow
    On a wealthier suitor your hand."

"Oh! hush these suspicions," Fair Imogine said,
    "Offensive to love and to me!
For, if you be living, or if you be dead,
I swear by the Virgin, that none in your stead
    Shall husband of Imogine be.

"If e'er I, by lust or by wealth led aside,
    Forget my Alonzo the Brave,
God grant, that to punish my falsehood and pride
Your ghost at the marriage may sit by my side,
May tax me with perjury, claim me as bride,
    And bear me away to the grave!"

---

1   Based loosely on Gottfried August Bürger, "Lenore" (1773).

To Palestine hastened the hero so bold;
        His love, she lamented him sore:
But scarce had a twelvemonth elapsed, when behold,
A Baron all covered with jewels and gold
        Arrived at Fair Imogine's door.

His treasure, his presents, his spacious domain
        Soon made her untrue to her vows:
He dazzled her eyes; he bewildered her brain;
He caught her affections so light and so vain,
        And carried her home as his spouse.

And now had the marriage been blest by the priest;
        The revelry now was begun:
The tables they groaned with the weight of the feast;
Nor yet had the laughter and merriment ceased,
        When the bell of the castle told—"one!"

Then first with amazement Fair Imogine found
        That a stranger was placed by her side:
His air was terrific; he uttered no sound;
He spoke not, he moved not, he looked not around,
        But earnestly gazed on the bride.

His vizor was closed, and gigantic his height;
        His armour was sable to view:
All pleasure and laughter were hushed at his sight;
The dogs as they eyed him drew back in affright;
        The lights in the chamber burned blue![1]

His presence all bosoms appeared to dismay;
        The guests sat in silence and fear.
At length spoke the bride, while she trembled; "I pray,
Sir Knight, that your helmet aside you would lay,
        And deign to partake of our chear."

The lady is silent: the stranger complies.
        His vizor he slowly unclosed:
Oh! God! what a sight met Fair Imogine's eyes!

---

1   A sign of the presence of a ghost.

What words can express her dismay and surprise,
   When a skeleton's head was exposed!

All present then uttered a terrified shout;
   All turned with disgust from the scene.
The worms they crept in, and the worms they crept out,
And sported his eyes and his temples about,
   While the spectre addressed Imogine.

"Behold me, thou false one! behold me!" he cried;
   "Remember Alonzo the Brave!
God grants, that to punish thy falsehood and pride
My ghost at thy marriage should sit by thy side,
Should tax thee with perjury, claim thee as bride,
   And bear thee away to the grave!"

Thus saying, his arms round the lady he wound,
   While loudly she shrieked in dismay;
Then sank with his prey through the wide-yawning ground:
Nor ever again was Fair Imogine found,
   Or the spectre who bore her away.

Not long lived the Baron; and none since that time
   To inhabit the castle presume;
For chronicles tell that, by order sublime,
There Imogine suffers the pain of her crime,
   And mourns her deplorable doom.

At midnight four times in each year does her spright,
   When mortals in slumber are bound,
Arrayed in her bridal apparel of white,
Appear in the hall with the Skeleton-Knight,
   And shriek as he whirls her around.

While they drink out of skulls newly torn from the grave,
   Dancing round them the spectres are seen:
Their liquor is blood, and this horrible stave
They howl:—"To the health of Alonzo the Brave,
   And his consort, the False Imogine!"

   The perusal of this story was ill calculated to dispel Antonia's
melancholy. She had naturally a strong inclination to the marvellous;

and her nurse, who believed firmly in apparitions, had related to her, when an infant, so many horrible adventures of this kind, that all Elvira's attempts had failed to eradicate their impressions from her daughter's mind. Antonia still nourished a superstitious prejudice in her bosom: she was often susceptible of terrors, which, when she discovered their natural and insignificant cause, made her blush at her own weakness.[1] With such a turn of mind, the adventure which she had just been reading sufficed to give her apprehensions the alarm. The hour and the scene combined to authorise them. It was the dead of night; she was alone, and in the chamber once occupied by her deceased mother. The weather was comfortless and stormy; the wind howled around the house, the doors rattled in their frames, and the heavy rain pattered against the windows. No other sound was heard. The taper, now burnt down to the socket, sometimes flaring upwards, shot a gleam of light through the room, then sinking again seemed upon the point of expiring. Antonia's heart throbbed with agitation; her eyes wandered fearfully over the objects around her, as the trembling flame illuminated them at intervals. She attempted to rise from her seat, but her limbs trembled so violently that she was unable to proceed. She then called Flora, who was in a room at no great distance; but agitation choked her voice, and her cries died away in hollow murmurs.

She passed some minutes in this situation, after which her terrors began to diminish. She strove to recover herself, and acquire strength enough to quit the room. Suddenly she fancied that she heard a low sigh drawn near her. This idea brought back her former weakness. She had already raised herself from her seat, and was on the point of taking the lamp from the table. The imaginary noise stopped her; she drew back her hand, and supported herself upon the back of a chair. She listened anxiously, but nothing more was heard.

"Gracious God!" she said to herself, "what could be that sound? Was I deceived, or did I really hear it?"

Her reflections were interrupted by a voice at the door scarcely audible; it seemed as if somebody was whispering. Antonia's alarm increased; yet the bolt she knew to be fastened, and this idea in some degree re-assured her. Presently the latch was lifted up softly, and the door moved with caution backwards and forwards. Excess of terror now supplied Antonia with that strength, of which she had till then been deprived. She started from her place, and made towards the clos-

---

1 In this, Antonia resembles Emily, the heroine of Radcliffe's *The Mysteries of Udolpho* (1794).

et door, whence she might soon have reached the chamber where she expected to find Flora and Dame Jacintha. Scarcely had she reached the middle of the room, when the latch was lifted up a second time. An involuntary movement obliged her to turn her head. Slowly and gradually the door turned upon its hinges, and standing upon the threshold she beheld a tall thin figure, wrapped in a white shroud which covered it from head to foot.

This vision arrested her feet; she remained as if petrified in the middle of the apartment. The stranger with measured and solemn steps drew near the table. The dying taper darted a blue and melancholy flame as the figure advanced towards it. Over the table was fixed a small clock; the hand of it was upon the stroke of three. The figure stopped opposite to the clock: it raised its right arm, and pointed to the hour, at the same time looking earnestly upon Antonia, who waited for the conclusion of this scene, motionless and silent.

The figure remained in this posture for some moments. The clock struck. When the sound had ceased, the stranger advanced yet a few steps nearer Antonia.

"Yet three days," said a voice faint, hollow, and sepulchral; "yet three days, and we meet again!"

Antonia shuddered at the words.

"We meet again?" she pronounced at length with difficulty: "Where shall we meet? Whom shall I meet?"

The figure pointed to the ground with one hand, and with the other raised the linen which covered its face.

"Almighty God! My mother?"

Antonia shrieked, and fell lifeless upon the floor.[1]

Dame Jacintha, who was at work in a neighbouring chamber, was alarmed by the cry: Flora was just gone down stairs to fetch fresh oil for the lamp by which they had been sitting. Jacintha therefore hastened alone to Antonia's assistance, and great was her amazement to find her extended upon the floor. She raised her in her arms, conveyed her to her apartment, and placed her upon the bed, still senseless. She then proceeded to bathe her temples, chafe her hands, and use all possible means of bringing her to herself. With some difficulty she succeeded. Antonia opened her eyes, and looked round her wildly.

"Where is she?" she cried in a trembling voice: "Is she gone? Am I safe? Speak to me! Comfort me! Oh! speak to me, for God's sake!"

---

1   Cf. the apparition in Flammenberg, *The Necromancer* 29-30.

"Safe from whom, my child?" replied the astonished Jacintha: "What alarms you? Of whom are you afraid?"

"In three days! She told me that we should meet in three days! I heard her say it! I saw her, Jacintha, I saw her but this moment!"

She threw herself upon Jacintha's bosom.

"You saw her?—Saw whom?"

"My mother's ghost!"

"Christ Jesus!" cried Jacintha; and, starting from the bed, let fall Antonia upon the pillow, and fled in consternation out of the room.

As she hastened down stairs, she met Flora ascending them.

"Go to your mistress, Flora," said she; "here are rare doings! Oh! I am the most unfortunate woman alive! My house is filled with ghosts and dead bodies, and the Lord knows what besides; yet I am sure nobody likes such company less than I do. But go your way to Donna Antonia, Flora, and let me go mine."

Thus saying, she continued her course to the street-door, which she opened; and, without allowing herself time to throw on her veil, she made the best of her way to the Capuchin-abbey. In the mean while, Flora hastened to her lady's chamber, equally surprised and alarmed at Jacintha's consternation. She found Antonia lying upon the bed, insensible. She used the same means for her recovery that Jacintha had already employed; but finding that her mistress only recovered from one fit to fall into another, she sent in all haste for a physician. While expecting his arrival, she undressed Antonia, and conveyed her to bed.

Heedless of the storm, terrified almost out of her senses, Jacintha ran through the streets, and stopped not till she reached the gate of the abbey. She rang loudly at the bell; and as soon as the porter appeared, she desired permission to speak to the superior. Ambrosio was then conferring with Matilda upon the means of procuring access to Antonia. The cause of Elvira's death remaining unknown, he was convinced that crimes were not so swiftly followed by punishment as his instructors the monks had taught him, and as till then he had himself believed. This persuasion made him resolve upon Antonia's ruin, for the enjoyment of whose person dangers and difficulties only seemed to have increased his passion. The monk had already made one attempt to gain admission to her presence; but Flora had refused him in such a manner as to convince him that all future endeavours must be vain. Elvira had confided her suspicions to that trusty servant: she had desired her never to leave Ambrosio alone with her daughter, and, if possible, to prevent their meeting altogether. Flora promised to obey her, and had executed her orders to the very letter. Ambrosio's visit had been rejected that morning, though Antonia was ignorant of it. He saw that to obtain a sight of his mistress by open means was out of the question; and both himself and Matilda had consumed the night in endeavouring to invent some plan, whose event might be more successful. Such was their employment when a lay-brother entered the abbot's cell, and informed him that a woman calling herself Jacintha Zuniga requested audience for a few minutes.

Ambrosio was by no means disposed to grant the petition of his visitor. He refused it positively, and bade the lay-brother tell the stranger to return the next day. Matilda interrupted him——

"See this woman," said she in a low voice; "I have my reasons."

The abbot obeyed her, and signified that he would go to the parlour immediately. With this answer the lay-brother withdrew. As soon as they were alone, Ambrosio enquired why Matilda wished him to see this Jacintha.

"She is Antonia's hostess," replied Matilda; "she may possibly be of use to you; but let us examine her, and learn what brings her hither."

They proceeded together to the parlour, where Jacintha was already waiting for the abbot. She had conceived a great opinion of his piety and virtue; and, supposing him to have much influence over the devil, thought that it must be an easy matter for him to lay Elvira's ghost in the red sea. Filled with this persuasion, she had hastened to the abbey. As soon as she saw the monk enter the parlour, she dropped upon her knees, and began her story as follows:

"Oh! reverend father! such an accident! such an adventure! I know not what course to take; and unless you can help me, I shall certainly go distracted. Well, to be sure, never was woman so unfortunate as myself! All in my power to keep clear of such abomination have I done, and yet that all is too little. What signifies my telling my beads four times a day, and observing every fast prescribed by the calendar? What signifies my having made three pilgrimages to St. James of Compostella, and purchased as many pardons from the pope as would buy off Cain's punishment?[1] Nothing prospers with me! All goes wrong, and God only knows whether any thing will ever go right again! Why now, be your holiness the judge—My lodger dies in convulsions; out of pure kindness I bury her at my own expence; [not that she is any relation of mine, or that I shall be benefited a single pistole by her death: I got nothing by it, and therefore you know, reverend father, that her living or dying was just the same to me. But that is nothing to the purpose; to return to what I was saying], I took care

---

1 Cain was the first murderer: see Genesis 4.1-16.

of her funeral, had every thing performed decently and properly, and put myself to expence enough, God knows! And how do you think the lady repays me for my kindness? Why truly by refusing to sleep quietly in her comfortable deal coffin, as a peaceable well disposed spirit ought to do, and coming to plague me, who never wish to set eyes on her again. Forsooth it well becomes her to go racketing about my house at midnight, popping into her daughter's room through the key-hole, and frightening the poor child out of her wits! Though she be a ghost, she might be more civil than to bolt into a person's house who likes her company so little. But as for me, reverend father, the plain state of the case is this: if she walks into my house, I must walk out of it, for I cannot abide such visitors—not I. Thus you see, your sanctity, that without your assistance I am ruined and undone for ever. I shall be obliged to quit my house: nobody will take it, when 'tis known that she haunts it, and then I shall find myself in a fine situation. Miserable woman that I am! what shall I do? what will become of me?"

Here she wept bitterly, wrung her hands, and begged to know the abbot's opinion of her case.

"In truth, good woman," replied he, "it will be difficult for me to relieve you, without knowing what is the matter with you. You have forgotten to tell me what has happened, and what it is you want."

"Let me die," cried Jacintha, "but your sanctity is in the right. This then is the fact stated briefly—A lodger of mine is lately dead; a very good sort of woman, that I must needs say for her; as far as my knowledge of her went, though that was not a great way. She kept me too much at a distance; for indeed she was given to be upon the high ropes; and whenever I ventured to speak to her, she had a look with her which always made me feel a little queerish: God forgive me for saying so! However, though she was more stately than needful, and affected to look down upon me (though, if I am well informed, I come of as good parents as she could do for her ears, for her father was a shoe-maker at Cordova, and mine was an hatter at Madrid— aye, and a very creditable hatter too, let me tell you), yet for all her pride she was a quiet well-behaved body, and I never wish to have a better lodger. This makes me wonder the more at her not sleeping quietly in her grave; but there is no trusting to people in this world. For my part, I never saw her do amiss, except on the Friday before her death. To be sure, I was then much scandalized by seeing her eat the wing of a chicken. 'How, Madona Flora!' quoth I (Flora, may it please your reverence, is the name of the waiting maid)—'how, Madona Flora!' quoth I, 'does your mistress eat flesh upon Fridays?

Well! well! see the event, and then remember that Dame Jacintha warned you of it!'These were my very words; but, alas! I might as well have held my tongue. Nobody minded me; and Flora, who is somewhat pert and snappish (more is the pity, say I), told me, that there was no more harm in eating a chicken than the egg from which it came: nay she even declared, that if her lady added a slice of bacon, she would not be an inch nearer damnation. God protect us! a poor ignorant sinful soul! I protest to your holiness, I trembled to hear her utter such blasphemies, and expected every moment to see the ground open and swallow her up, chicken and all; for you must know, worshipful father, that while she talked thus, she held the plate in her hand on which lay the identical roast fowl: and a fine bird it was, that I must say for it—done to a turn, for I superintended the cooking of it myself. It was a little gallician of my own raising, may it please your holiness, and the flesh was as white as an egg-shell, as indeed Donna Elvira told me herself. 'Dame Jacintha,' said she very good-humouredly, though to say the truth she was always very polite to me——"

Here Ambrosio's patience failed him. Eager to know Jacintha's business in which Antonia seemed to be concerned, he was almost distracted while listening to the rambling of this prosing old woman. He interrupted her, and protested that if she did not immediately tell her story and have done with it, he should quit the parlour, and leave her to get out of her difficulties by herself. This threat had the desired effect. Jacintha related her business in as few words as she could manage: but her account was still so prolix, that Ambrosio had need of his patience to bear him to the conclusion.

"And so, your reverence," said she, after relating Elvira's death and burial, with all their circumstances—"and so, your reverence, upon hearing the shriek, I put away my work, and away posted I to Donna Antonia's chamber. Finding nobody there, I passed on to the next: but I must own I was a little timorous at going in; for this was the very room where Donna Elvira used to sleep. However in I went, and sure enough there lay the young lady at full length upon the floor, as cold as a stone, and as white as a sheet. I was surprised at this, as your holiness may well suppose: but, oh me! how I shook when I saw a great tall figure at my elbow, whose head touched the cieling! The face was Donna Elvira's, I must confess; but out of its mouth came clouds of fire; its arms were loaded with heavy chains, which it rattled piteously; and every hair on its head was a serpent as big as my arm. At this I was frightened enough, and began to say my ave-maria:[1] but the

---

1 "Hail, Mary" (Latin): a Catholic prayer to the Virgin Mary.

ghost interrupting me uttered three loud groans, and roared out in a terrible voice, 'Oh! that chicken's wing! my poor soul suffers for it.' As soon as she had said this, the ground opened, the spectre sank down; I heard a clap of thunder, and the room was filled with a smell of brimstone. When I recovered from my fright, and had brought Donna Antonia to herself, who told me that she had cried out upon seeing her mother's ghost (and well might she cry, poor soul! had I been in her place, I should have cried ten times louder), it directly came into my head, that if any one had power to quiet this spectre, it must be your reverence. So hither I came in all diligence, to beg that you will sprinkle my house with holy water, and lay the apparition in the Red Sea."

Ambrosio stared at this strange story, which he could not credit.

"Did Donna Antonia also see the ghost?" said he.

"As plain as I see you, reverend father."

Ambrosio paused for a moment. Here was an opportunity offered him of gaining access to Antonia, but he hesitated to employ it. The reputation which he enjoyed in Madrid was still dear to him; and since he had lost the reality of virtue, it appeared as if its semblance was become more valuable. He was conscious that publicly to break through the rule never to quit the abbey-precincts would derogate much from his supposed austerity. In visiting Elvira, he had always taken care to keep his features concealed from the domestics. Except by the lady, her daughter, and the faithful Flora, he was known in the family by no other name than that of father Jerome. Should he comply with Jacintha's request, and accompany her to her house, he knew that the violation of his rule could not be kept a secret. However, his eagerness to see Antonia obtained the victory. He even hoped that the singularity of this adventure would justify him in the eyes of Madrid. But whatever might be the consequences, he resolved to profit by the opportunity which chance had presented to him. An expressive look from Matilda confirmed him in this resolution.

"Good woman," said he to Jacintha, "what you tell me is so extraordinary that I can scarcely credit your assertions. However, I will comply with your request. To-morrow, after matins, you may expect me at your house: I will then examine into what I can do for you; and if it is in my power, will free you from this unwelcome visitor. Now then go home, and peace be with you!"

"Home!" exclaimed Jacintha; "I go home? Not I, by my troth!—except under your protection, I set no foot of mine within the threshold. God help me! the ghost may meet me upon the stairs, and whisk me away with her to the devil! Oh! that I had accepted young Melchior Basco's offer! then I should have had somebody to protect me; but now I am a lone woman, and meet with nothing but crosses and misfortunes. Thank Heaven it is not yet too late to repent. There is Simon Gonzalez will have me any day of the week; and if I live till day-break, I will marry him out of hand: an husband I will have, that is determined; for, now this ghost is once in my house, I shall be frightened out of my wits to sleep alone. But, for God's sake, reverend father! come with me now. I shall have no rest till the house is puri- fied, or the poor young lady either. The dear girl! she is in a piteous taking: I left her in strong convulsions, and I doubt she will not easi- ly recover her fright."

The friar started, and interrupted her hastily.

"In convulsions, say you? Antonia in convulsions? Lead on, good woman, I follow you this moment."

Jacintha insisted upon his stopping to furnish himself with the ves- sel of holy water. With this request he complied. Thinking herself safe under his protection should a legion of ghosts attack her, the old woman returned the monk a profusion of thanks, and they departed together for the strada di San Iago.

So strong an impression had the spectre made upon Antonia, that for the first two or three hours the physician declared her life to be in danger. The fits at length becoming less frequent, induced him to alter his opinion. He said that to keep her quiet was all that was necessary; and he ordered a medicine to be prepared, which would tranquillize her nerves, and procure her that repose which at present she much wanted. The sight of Ambrosio, who now appeared with Jacintha at her bed-side, contributed essentially to compose her ruffled spirits. Elvira had not sufficiently explained herself upon the nature of his designs, to make a girl so ignorant of the world as her daughter aware how dangerous was his acquaintance. At this moment, when penetrat- ed with horror at the scene which had just passed, and dreading to contemplate the ghost's prediction, her mind had need of all the suc- cours of friendship and religion. Antonia regarded the abbot with an eye doubly partial. That strong prepossession in his favour still existed, which she had felt for him at first sight: she fancied, yet knew not wherefore, that his presence was a safeguard to her from every danger, insult, or misfortune. She thanked him gratefully for his visit, and relat- ed to him the adventure which had alarmed her so seriously.

The abbot strove to re-assure her and convince her that the whole had been a deception of her over-heated fancy. The solitude in which she had passed the evening, the gloom of night, the book which she had been reading, and the room in which she sat, were all calculated to place before her such a vision. He treated the idea of ghosts with ridicule, and produced strong arguments to prove the fallacy of such a system. His conversation tranquillized and comforted her, but did not convince her. She could not believe that the spectre had been a mere creature of her imagination: every circumstance was impressed upon her mind too forcibly to permit her flattering herself with such an idea. She persisted in asserting that she had really seen her mother's ghost, had heard the period of her dissolution announced, and declared that she never should quit her bed alive. Ambrosio advised her against encouraging these sentiments, and then quitted her chamber, having promised to repeat his visit on the morrow. Antonia received this assurance with every mark of joy: but the monk easily perceived that he was not equally acceptable to her attendant. Flora obeyed Elvira's injunctions with the most scrupulous observance. She examined with an anxious eye every circumstance likely in the least to prejudice her young mistress, to whom she had been attached for many years. She was a native of Cuba, had followed Elvira to Spain, and loved the young Antonia with a mother's affection. Flora quitted not the room for a moment while the abbot remained there: she watched his every word, his every look, his every action. He saw that her suspicious eye was always fixed upon him; and, conscious that his designs would not bear inspection so minute, he felt frequently confused and disconcerted. He was aware that she doubted the purity of his intentions; that she would never leave him alone with Antonia; and, his mistress defended by the presence of this vigilant observer, he despaired of finding the means to gratify his passion.

As he quitted the house, Jacintha met him, and begged that some masses might be sung for the repose of Elvira's soul, which she doubted not was suffering in purgatory.

He promised not to forget her request; but he perfectly gained the old woman's heart, by engaging to watch during the whole of the approaching night in the haunted chamber. Jacintha could find no terms sufficiently strong to express her gratitude, and the monk departed loaded with her benedictions.

It was broad day when he returned to the abbey. His first care was to communicate what had passed to his confidante. He felt too sincere a passion for Antonia, to have heard unmoved the prediction of her speedy death, and he shuddered at the idea of losing an object so dear to him. Upon this head Matilda re-assured him. She confirmed the arguments which himself had already used: she declared Antonia to have been deceived by the wandering of her brain, by the spleen which oppressed her at the moment, and by the natural turn of her mind to superstition and the marvellous. As to Jacintha's account, the absurdity refuted itself. The abbot hesitated not to believe that she had fabricated the whole story, either confused by terror, or hoping to make him comply more readily with her request. Having over-ruled the monk's apprehensions, Matilda continued thus:

"The prediction and the ghost are equally false: but it must be your care, Ambrosio, to verify the first. Antonia within three days must indeed be dead to the world: but she must live for you. Her present illness, and this fancy which she has taken into her head, will colour a plan which I have long meditated, but which was impracticable without your procuring access to Antonia. She shall be yours, not for a single night, but for ever. All the vigilance of her duenna shall not avail her. You shall riot unrestrained in the charms of your mistress. This very day must the scheme be put in execution, for you have no time to lose. The nephew of the duke of Medina Celi prepares to demand Antonia for his bride: in a few days she will be removed to the palace of her relation, the marquis de las Cisternas, and there she will be secure from your attempts. Thus during your absence have I been informed by my spies, who are ever employed in bringing me intelligence for your service. Now then listen to me. There is a juice extracted from certain herbs known but to few, which brings on the person who drinks it the exact image of death. Let this be administered to Antonia: you may easily find means to pour a few drops into her medicine. The effect will be throwing her into strong convulsions for an hour: after which her blood will gradually cease to flow, and heart to beat: a mortal paleness will spread itself over her features, and she will appear a corse to every eye. She has no friends about her: you may charge yourself unsuspected with the superintendence of her funeral, and cause her to be buried in the vaults of St. Clare. Their solitude and easy access render these caverns favourable to your designs. Give Antonia the soporific draught this evening: eight-and-forty hours after she has drank it, life will revive in her bosom. She will then be absolutely in your power: she will find all resistance unavailing, and necessity will compel her to receive you in her arms."[1]

"Antonia will be in my power!" exclaimed the monk; "Matilda, you transport me! At length then happiness will be mine, and that happiness will be Matilda's gift, will be the gift of friendship! I shall clasp Antonia in my arms, far from every prying eye, from every tor-

---

1 Cf. Shakespeare, *Romeo and Juliet* 4.1.93–112. Lewis may also be thinking of Lovelace's use of an opiate in Richardson's *Clarissa*.

menting intruder! I shall sigh out my soul upon her bosom; shall teach her young heart the first rudiments of pleasure, and revel uncontrouled in the endless variety of her charms! And shall this delight indeed be mine? Shall I give the reins to my desires, and gratify every wild tumultuous wish? Oh! Matilda, how can I express to you my gratitude?"

"By profiting by my counsels. Ambrosio, I live but to serve you; your interest and happiness are equally mine. Be your person Antonia's, but to your friendship and your heart I still assert my claim. Contributing to yours, forms now my only pleasure. Should my exertions procure the gratification of your wishes, I shall consider my trouble to be amply repaid. But let us lose no time. The liquor of which I spoke, is only to be found in St. Clare's laboratory. Hasten then to the prioress, request of her admission to the laboratory, and it will not be denied. There is a closet at the lower end of the great room, filled with liquids of different colours and qualities; the bottle in question stands by itself, upon the third shelf on the left. It contains a greenish liquor: fill a small phial with it when you are unobserved, and Antonia is your own."

The monk hesitated not to adopt this infamous plan. His desires, but too violent before, had acquired fresh vigour from the sight of Antonia. As he sat by her bed-side, accident had discovered to him some of those charms which till then had been concealed from him: he found them even more perfect than his ardent imagination had pictured them. Sometimes her white and polished arm was displayed in arranging the pillow: sometimes a sudden movement discovered part of her swelling bosom: but wherever the new-found charm presented itself, there rested the friar's gloating eyes. Scarcely could he master himself sufficiently to conceal his desires from Antonia and her vigilant duenna. Inflamed by the remembrance of these beauties, he entered into Matilda's scheme without hesitation.

No sooner were matins over, than he bent his course towards the convent of St. Clare; his arrival threw the whole sisterhood into the utmost amazement. The prioress was sensible of the honour done her convent by his paying it his first visit, and strove to express her gratitude by every possible attention. He was paraded through the garden, shewn all the reliques of saints and martyrs, and treated with as much respect and distinction as had he been the Pope himself. On his part, Ambrosio received the domina's civilities very graciously, and strove to remove her surprise at his having broken through his resolution. He stated that among his penitents, illness prevented many from quitting their houses. These were exactly the people who most needed his advice and the comforts of religion. Many representations had been made to him upon this account, and, though highly repugnant to his own wishes, he had found it absolutely necessary, for the service of Heaven, to change his determination, and quit his beloved retirement. The prioress applauded his zeal in his profession, and his charity towards mankind. She declared that Madrid was happy in possessing a man so perfect and irreproachable. In such discourse the friar at length reached the laboratory: he found the closet; the bottle stood in the place which Matilda had described, and the monk seized an opportunity to fill his phial unobserved with the soporific liquor. Then, having partaken of a collation in the refectory, he retired from the convent, pleased with the success of his visit, and leaving the nuns delighted by the honour conferred upon them.

He waited till evening before he took the road to Antonia's dwelling. Jacintha welcomed him with transport, and besought him not to forget his promise to pass the night in the haunted chamber. That promise he now repeated. He found Antonia tolerably well, but still harping upon the ghost's prediction. Flora moved not from her lady's bed, and, by symptoms yet stronger than on the former night, testified her dislike to the abbot's presence. Still Ambrosio affected not to observe them. The physician arrived while he was conversing with Antonia. It was dark already; lights were called for, and Flora was compelled to descend for them herself. However, as she left a third person in the room, and expected to be absent but a few minutes, she believed that she risqued nothing in quitting her post. No sooner had she left the room, than Ambrosio moved towards the table, on which stood Antonia's medicine. It was placed in a recess of the window. The physician, seated in an arm chair, and employed in questioning his patient, paid no attention to the proceedings of the monk. Ambrosio seized the opportunity; he drew out the fatal phial, and let a few drops fall into the medicine: he then hastily left the table, and returned to the seat which he had quitted. When Flora made her appearance with lights, every thing seemed to be exactly as she had left it.

The physician declared that Antonia might quit her chamber the next day with perfect safety. He recommended her following the same prescription which on the night before had procured her a refreshing sleep. Flora replied, that the draught stood ready upon the table: he advised the patient to take it without delay, and then retired. Flora poured the medicine into a cup, and presented it to her mistress. At that moment Ambrosio's courage failed him. Might not Matilda have deceived him? Might not jealousy have persuaded her to destroy her rival, and substitute poison in the room of an opiate?

This idea appeared so reasonable, that he was on the point of preventing her from swallowing the medicine. His resolution was adopted too late. The cup was already emptied, and Antonia restored it into Flora's hands. No remedy was now to be found; Ambrosio could only expect the moment impatiently destined to decide upon Antonia's life or death, upon his own happiness or despair.

Dreading to create suspicion by his stay, or betray himself by his mind's agitation, he took leave of his victim, and withdrew from the room. Antonia parted from him with less cordiality than on the former night. Flora had represented to her mistress, that to admit his visits was to disobey her mother's orders. She described to her his emotion on entering the room, and the fire which sparkled in his eyes while he gazed upon her. This had escaped Antonia's observation, but not her attendant's, who, explaining the monk's designs, and their probable consequences, in terms much clearer than Elvira's, though not quite so delicate, had succeeded in alarming her young lady, and persuading her to treat him more distantly than she had done hitherto. The idea of obeying her mother's will at once determined Antonia. Though she grieved at losing his society, she conquered herself sufficiently to receive the monk with some degree of reserve and coldness. She thanked him with respect and gratitude for his former visits, but did not invite his repeating them in future. It now was not the friar's interest to solicit admission to her presence, and he took leave of her as if not designing to return. Fully persuaded that the acquaintance which she dreaded was now at an end, Flora was so much worked upon by his easy compliance, that she began to doubt the justice of her suspicions. As she lighted him down stairs, she thanked him for having endeavoured to root out from Antonia's mind her superstitious terrors of the spectre's prediction: she added, that as he seemed interested in Donna Antonia's welfare, should any change take place in her situation, she would be careful to let him know it. The monk, in replying, took pains to raise his voice, hoping that Jacintha would hear it. In this he succeeded. As he reached the foot of the stairs with his conductress, the landlady failed not to make her appearance.

"Why surely you are not going away, reverend father?" cried she: "Did you not promise to pass the night in the haunted chamber? Christ Jesus! I shall be left alone with the ghost, and a fine pickle I shall be in by morning! Do all I could, say all I could, that obstinate old brute, Simon Gonzalez, refused to marry me to-day; and before to-morrow comes, I suppose I shall be torn to pieces by the ghosts and goblins, and devils, and what not! For God's sake, your holiness, do not leave me in such a woful condition! On my bended knees I beseech you to keep your promise: watch this night in the haunted chamber; lay the apparition in the red sea, and Jacintha remembers you in her prayers to the last day of her existence!"

This request Ambrosio expected and desired; yet he affected to raise objections, and to seem unwilling to keep his word. He told Jacintha that the ghost existed no where but in her own brain, and that her insisting upon his staying all night in the house was ridiculous and useless. Jacintha was obstinate; she was not to be convinced, and pressed him so urgently not to leave her a prey to the devil, that at length he granted her request. All this show of resistance imposed not upon Flora, who was naturally of a suspicious temper. She suspected the monk to be acting a part very contrary to his own inclinations, and that he wished for no better than to remain where he was. She even went so far as to believe that Jacintha was in his interest; and the poor old woman was immediately set down as no better than a procuress. While she applauded herself for having penetrated into this plot against her lady's honour, she resolved in secret to render it fruitless.

"So then," said she to the abbot with a look half satirical and half indignant—"so then you mean to stay here to-night? Do so, in God's name! Nobody will prevent you. Sit up to watch for the ghost's arrival: I shall sit up too, and the Lord grant that I may see nothing worse than a ghost! I quit not Donna Antonia's bed-side during this blessed night. Let me see any one dare to enter the room, and be he mortal or immortal, be he ghost, devil, or man, I warrant his repenting that ever he crossed the threshold!"

This hint was sufficiently strong, and Ambrosio understood its meaning. But instead of shewing that he perceived her suspicions, he replied mildly, that he approved the duenna's precautions, and advised her to persevere in her intention. This she assured him faithfully that he might depend upon her doing. Jacintha then conducted him into the chamber where the ghost had appeared, and Flora returned to her lady's.

Jacintha opened the door of the haunted room with a trembling hand; she ventured to peep in, but the wealth of India would not have tempted her to cross the threshold. She gave the taper to the monk, wished him well through the adventure, and hastened to be gone. Ambrosio entered. He bolted the door, placed the light upon the table, and seated himself in the chair which on the former night had sustained Antonia. In spite of Matilda's assurances, that the spectre was a mere creation of fancy, his mind was impressed with a certain mysterious horror. He in vain endeavoured to shake it off. The silence of the night, the story of the apparition, the chamber wainscotted with dark oak pannels, the recollection which it brought with it of the murdered Elvira, and his incertitude respecting the nature of the drops given by him to Antonia, made him feel uneasy at his present situation. But he thought much less of the spectre than of the poison. Should he have destroyed the only object which rendered life dear to him; should the ghost's prediction prove true; should Antonia in three days be no more, and he the wretched cause of her death......The supposition was too horrible to dwell upon. He drove away these dreadful images, and as often they presented themselves again before him. Matilda had assured him that the effects of the opiate would be speedy. He listened with fear, yet with eagerness, expecting to hear some disturbance in the adjoining chamber. All was still silent. He concluded that the drops had not begun to operate. Great was the stake for which he now played: a moment would suffice to decide upon his misery or happiness. Matilda had taught him the means of ascertaining, that life was not extinct for ever: upon this assay depended all his hopes. With every instant his impatience redoubled; his terrors grew more lively, his anxiety more awake. Unable to bear this state of incertitude, he endeavoured to divert it by substituting the thoughts of others to his own. The books, as was before mentioned, were ranged upon shelves near the table: this stood exactly opposite to the bed, which was placed in an alcove near the closet-door. Ambrosio took down a volume, and seated himself by the table: but his attention wandered from the pages before him. Antonia's image, and that of the murdered Elvira, persisted to force themselves before his imagination. Still he continued to read, though his eyes ran over the characters without his mind being conscious of their import.

Such was his occupation when he fancied that he heard a footstep. He turned his head, but nobody was to be seen. He resumed his book; but in a few minutes after, the same sound was repeated, and followed by a rustling noise close behind him. He now started from his seat, and looking round him, perceived the closet-door standing half unclosed. On his first entering the room, he had tried to open it, but found it bolted on the inside.

"How is this?" said he to himself; "How comes this door unfastened?"

He advanced towards it, he pushed it open, and looked into the closet: no one was there. While he stood irresolute, he thought that he distinguished a groaning in the adjacent chamber: it was Antonia's, and he supposed that the drops began to take effect. But upon listening more attentively, he found the noise to be caused by Jacintha, who had fallen asleep by the lady's bed-side, and was snoaring most lusti-ly. Ambrosio drew back, and returned to the other room, musing upon the sudden opening of the closet-door, for which he strove in vain to account.

He paced the chamber up and down in silence. At length he stopped, and the bed attracted his attention. The curtain of the recess was but half drawn. He sighed involuntarily.

"That bed," said he in a low voice, "that bed was Elvira's! There has she passed many a quiet night, for she was good and innocent. How sound must have been her sleep! and yet now she sleeps sounder! Does she indeed sleep? Oh! God grant that she may! What if she rose from her grave at this sad and silent hour? What if she broke the bonds of the tomb, and glided angrily before my blasted eyes? Oh! I never could support the sight! Again to see her form distorted by dying agonies, her blood-swollen veins, her livid countenance, her eyes bursting from their sockets with pain!—to hear her speak of future punishment, menace me with Heaven's vengeance, tax me with the crimes I have committed, with those I am going to com-mit..... Great God! what is that?"

As he uttered these words, his eyes, which were fixed upon the bed, saw the curtain shaken gently backwards and forwards. The apparition was recalled to his mind, and he almost fancied that he beheld Elvira's visionary form reclining upon the bed. A few moments consideration sufficed to re-assure him.

"It was only the wind," said he, recovering himself.

Again he paced the chamber; but an involuntary movement of awe and inquietude constantly led his eye towards the alcove. He drew near it with irresolution. He paused before he ascended the few steps which led to it. He put out his hand thrice to remove the cur-tain, and as often drew it back.

"Absurd terrors!" He cried at length, ashamed of his own weak-ness——

Hastily he mounted the steps, when a figure dressed in white start-ed from the alcove, and gliding by him, made with precipitation towards the closet. Madness and despair now supplied the monk with that courage, of which he had till then been destitute. He flew down the steps, pursued the apparition, and attempted to grasp it.

"Ghost, or devil, I hold you!" he exclaimed, and seized the spec-tre by the arm.

"Oh! Christ Jesus!" cried a shrill voice; "Holy father, how you gripe me! I protest that I meant no harm!"

This address, as well as the arm which he held, convinced the abbot that the supposed ghost was substantial flesh and blood. He drew the intruder towards the table, and holding up the light, discovered the features of...... Madona Flora!

Incensed at having been betrayed by this trifling cause into fears so ridiculous, he asked her sternly, what business had brought her to that chamber. Flora, ashamed at being found out, and terrified at the severity of Ambrosio's looks, fell upon her knees, and promised to make a full confession.

"I protest, reverend father," said she, "that I am quite grieved at having disturbed you; nothing was further from my intention. I meant to get out of the room as quietly as I got in; and had you been ignorant that I watched you, you know it would have been the same thing as if I had not watched you at all. To be sure I did very wrong in being a spy upon you—that I cannot deny. But, Lord! your reverence, how can a poor weak woman resist curiosity? Mine was so strong to know what you were doing, that I could not but try to get a little peep without any body knowing any thing about it. So with that I left old Dame Jacintha sitting by my lady's bed, and I ventured to steal into the closet. Being unwilling to interrupt you, I contented myself at first with putting my eye to the key-hole; but as I could see nothing by this means, I undrew the bolt, and while your back was turned to the alcove, I whipt me in softly and silently. Here I lay snug behind the curtain, till your reverence found me out, and seized me ere I had time to regain the closet-door. This is the whole truth, I assure you, holy father, and I beg your pardon a thousand times for my impertinence."

During this speech the abbot had time to recollect himself: he was satisfied with reading the penitent spy a lecture upon the dangers of curiosity, and the meanness of the action in which she had been just discovered. Flora declared herself fully persuaded that she had done wrong; she promised never to be guilty of the same fault again, and was retiring very humble and contrite to Antonia's chamber, when the closet-door was suddenly thrown open, and in rushed Jacintha pale and out of breath.

"Oh! Father! Father!" she cried in a voice almost choked with terror, "What shall I do! What shall I do! Here is a fine piece of work! Nothing but misfortunes! Nothing but dead people, and dying people! Oh! I shall go distracted! I shall go distracted!"

"Speak! Speak!" cried Flora and the monk at the same time; "what has happened? what is the matter?"

"Oh! I shall have another corse in my house! Some witch has certainly cast a spell upon it, upon me, and upon all about me! Poor Donna Antonia! there she lies in just such convulsions as killed her mother! The ghost told her true! I am sure the ghost told her true!"

Flora ran, or rather flew to her lady's chamber: Ambrosio followed her, his bosom trembling with hope and apprehension. They found Antonia as Jacintha had described, torn by racking convulsions, from which they in vain endeavoured to relieve her. The monk dispatched Jacintha to the abbey in all haste, and commissioned her to bring father Pablos back with her without losing a moment.

"I will go for him," replied Jacintha, "and tell him to come hither; but as to bringing him myself, I shall do no such thing. I am sure that the house is bewitched, and burn me if ever I set foot in it again."

With this resolution she set out for the monastery, and delivered to father Pablos the abbot's orders. She then betook herself to the house of old Simon Gonzalez, whom she resolved never to quit till she had made him her husband, and his dwelling her own.

Father Pablos had no sooner beheld Antonia, than he pronounced her incurable. The convulsions continued for an hour; during that time her agonies were much milder than those which her groans created in the abbot's heart. Her every pang seemed a dagger in his bosom, and he cursed himself a thousand times for having adopted so barbarous a project. The hour being expired, by degrees the fits became less frequent, and Antonia less agitated. She felt that her dissolution was approaching, and that nothing could save her.

"Worthy Ambrosio," she said in a feeble voice, while she pressed his hand to her lips; "I am now at liberty to express how grateful is my heart for your attention and kindness. I am upon the bed of death; yet an hour, and I shall be no more. I may therefore acknowledge without restraint, that to relinquish your society was very painful to me: but such was the will of a parent, and I dared not disobey. I die without repugnance: there are few who will lament my leaving them—there are few whom I lament to leave. Among those few, I lament for none more than for yourself; but we shall meet again, Ambrosio! we shall one day meet in heaven: there shall our friendship be renewed, and my mother shall view it with pleasure!"

She paused. The abbot shuddered when she mentioned Elvira. Antonia imputed his emotion to pity and concern for her.

"You are grieved for me, father," she continued; "Ah! sigh not for my loss. I have no crimes to repent, at least none of which I am conscious; and I restore my soul without fear to him from whom I received it. I have but few requests to make; yet let me hope that what few I have shall be granted. Let a solemn mass be said for my soul's repose, and another for that of my beloved mother; not that I doubt her resting in her grave. I am now convinced that my reason wandered, and the falsehood of the ghost's prediction is sufficient to prove my error. But every one has some failing: my mother may have had her's, though I knew them not: I therefore wish a mass to be celebrated for her repose, and the expence may be defrayed by the little wealth of which I am possessed. Whatever may then remain, I bequeath to my aunt Leonella. When I am dead, let the marquis de las Cisternas know that his brother's unhappy family can no longer importune him. But disappointment makes me unjust: they tell me that he is ill, and perhaps, had it been in his power, he wished to have protected me. Tell him, then, father, only that I am dead, and that if he had any faults to me, I forgave him from my heart. This done, I have nothing more to ask for than your prayers. Promise to remember my requests, and I shall resign my life without a pang or sorrow."

Ambrosio engaged to comply with her desires, and proceeded to give her absolution. Every moment announced the approach of Antonia's fate. Her sight failed, her heart beat sluggishly, her fingers stiffened and grew cold, and at two in the morning she expired without a groan. As soon as the breath had forsaken her body, father Pablos retired, sincerely affected at the melancholy scene. On her part, Flora gave way to the most unbridled sorrow. Far different concerns employed Ambrosio; he sought for the pulse whose throbbing, so Matilda had assured him, would prove Antonia's death but temporal. He found it—he pressed it—it palpitated beneath his hand, and his heart was filled with ecstacy. However, he carefully concealed his satisfaction at the success of his plan. He assumed a melancholy air, and, addressing himself to Flora, warned her against abandoning herself to fruitless sorrow. Her tears were too sincere to permit her listening to his counsels, and she continued to weep unceasingly. The friar withdrew, first promising to give orders himself about the funeral, which, out of consideration for Jacintha as he pretended, should take place with all expedition. Plunged in grief for the loss of her beloved mistress, Flora scarcely attended to what he said. Ambrosio hastened to command the burial. He obtained permission from the prioress, that the corse should be deposited in St. Clare's sepulchre: and on the Friday morning, every proper and needful ceremony being performed, Antonia's body was committed to the tomb.

On the same day Leonella arrived at Madrid, intending to present her young husband to Elvira. Various circumstances had obliged her to defer her journey from Tuesday to Friday; and she had no opportunity of making this alteration in her plans known to her sister. As her heart was truly affectionate, and as she had ever entertained a sincere regard for Elvira and her daughter, her surprise at hearing of their sudden and melancholy fate was fully equalled by her sorrow and disappointment. Ambrosio sent to inform her of Antonia's bequest: at her solicitation, he promised, as soon as Elvira's trifling debts were discharged, to transmit to her the remainder. This being settled, no other business detained Leonella in Madrid, and she returned to Cordova with all diligence.

CHAP. X.

> Oh! could I worship aught beneath the skies,
> That earth hath seen, or fancy could devise,
> Thine altar, sacred Liberty, should stand,
> Built by no mercenary vulgar hand,
> With fragrant turf, and flowers as wild and fair,
> As ever dressed a bank, or scented summer air.
>
> COWPER.[1]

HIS whole attention bent upon bringing to justice the assassins of his sister, Lorenzo little thought how severely his interest was suffering in another quarter. As was before mentioned, he returned not to Madrid till the evening of that day on which Antonia was buried. Signifying to the Grand Inquisitor the order of the cardinal-duke (a ceremony not to be neglected when a member of the church was to be arrested publicly), communicating his design to his uncle and Don Ramirez, and assembling a troop of attendants sufficient to prevent opposition, furnished him with full occupation during the few hours preceding midnight. Consequently he had no opportunity to enquire about his mistress, and was perfectly ignorant both of her death and her mother's.

The marquis was by no means out of danger: his delirium was gone, but had left him so much exhausted, that the physicians declined pronouncing upon the consequences likely to ensue. As for Raymond himself, he wished for nothing more earnestly than to join Agnes in the grave. Existence was hateful to him: he saw nothing in the world deserving his attention; and he hoped to hear that Agnes was revenged and himself given over in the same moment.

Followed by Raymond's ardent prayers for success, Lorenzo was at the gates of St. Clare a full hour before the time appointed by the

---

1 William Cowper (1731-1800), *Charity* (1782) 254-59.

other St. Ursula. He was accompanied by his uncle, by Don Ramirez de Mello, and a party of chosen archers. Though in considerable numbers, their appearance created no surprise: a great crowd was already assembled before the convent-doors, in order to witness the procession. It was naturally supposed, that Lorenzo and his attendants were conducted thither by the same design. The duke of Medina being recognised, the people drew back, and made way for his party to advance. Lorenzo placed himself opposite to the great gate, through which the pilgrims were to pass. Convinced that the prioress could not escape him, he waited patiently for her appearance, which she was expected to make exactly at midnight.

The nuns were employed in religious duties established in honour of St. Clare, and to which no prophane was ever admitted. The chapel-windows were illuminated. As they stood on the outside, the auditors heard the full swell of the organ, accompanied by a chorus of female voices, rise upon the stillness of the night. This died away, and was succeeded by a single strain of harmony: it was the voice of her who was destined to sustain in the procession the character of St. Clare. For this office the most beautiful virgin of Madrid was always selected, and she upon whom the choice fell, esteemed it as the highest of honours. While listening to the music, whose melody distance only seemed to render sweeter, the audience was wrapped up in profound attention. Universal silence prevailed through the crowd, and every heart was filled with reverence for religion—every heart but Lorenzo's. Conscious that among those who chaunted the praises of their God so sweetly there were some who cloaked with devotion the foulest sins, their hymns inspired him with detestation at their hypocrisy. He had long observed with disapprobation and contempt the superstition which governed Madrid's inhabitants. His good sense had pointed out to him the artifices of the monks, and the gross absurdity of their miracles, wonders, and supposititious reliques. He blushed to see his countrymen the dupes of deceptions so ridiculous, and only wished for an opportunity to free them from their monkish fetters. That opportunity, so long desired in vain, was at length presented to him. He resolved not to let it slip, but to set before the people, in glaring colours, how enormous were the abuses but too frequently practised in monasteries, and how unjustly public esteem was bestowed indiscriminately upon all who wore a religious habit. He longed for the moment destined to unmask the hypocrites, and convince his countrymen, that a sanctified exterior does not always hide a virtuous heart.

The service lasted till midnight was announced by the convent-bell. That sound being heard, the music ceased: the voices died away softly, and soon after the lights disappeared from the chapel-windows. Lorenzo's heart beat high, when he found the execution of his plan to be at hand. From the natural superstition of the people he had prepared himself for some resistance: but he trusted that the Mother St. Ursula would bring good reasons to justify his proceeding. He had force with him to repel the first impulse of the populace, till his arguments should be heard: his only fear was, lest the domina, suspecting his design, should have spirited away the nun on whose deposition every thing depended. Unless the Mother St. Ursula should be present, he could only accuse the prioress upon suspicion; and this reflection gave him some little apprehension for the success of his enterprise. The tranquillity which seemed to reign through the convent, in some degree re-assured him: still he expected the moment eagerly, when the presence of his ally should deprive him of the power of doubting.

The abbey of Capuchins was only separated from the convent by the garden and cemetery. The monks had been invited to assist at the pilgrimage. They now arrived, marching two by two with lighted torches in their hands, and chaunting hymns in honour of St. Clare. Father Pablos was at their head, the abbot having excused himself from attending. The people made way for the holy train, and the friars placed themselves in ranks on either side of the great gates. A few minutes sufficed to arrange the order of the procession. This being settled, the convent doors were thrown open, and again the female chorus sounded in full melody. First appeared a band of choristers. As soon as they had passed, the monks fell in two by two, and followed with steps slow and measured: next came the novices: they bore no tapers, as did the professed, but moved on with eyes bent downwards, and seemed to be occupied by telling their beads. To them succeeded a young and lovely girl, who represented St. Lucia: she held a golden bason, in which were two eyes: her own were covered by a velvet bandage, and she was conducted by another nun habited as an angel.[1] She was followed by St. Catherine,[2] a palm-branch in one hand, a flaming sword in the other: she was robed in white, and her brow was ornamented with a sparkling diadem. After her appeared St.

---

1 One of the torments that St. Lucy (d. 304?) suffered during her martyrdom was the putting-out of her eyes.

2 St. Catherine of Alexandria (martyred c. 310) was condemned to be killed on a spiked wheel; when it broke, she was beheaded.

Genevieve, surrounded by a number of imps, who putting themselves into grotesque attitudes, drawing her by the robe, and sporting round her with antic gestures, endeavoured to distract her attention from the book, on which her eyes were constantly fixed.[1] These merry devils greatly entertained the spectators, who testified their pleasure by repeated bursts of laughter. The prioress had been careful to select a nun whose disposition was naturally solemn and saturnine. She had every reason to be satisfied with her choice: the drolleries of the imps were entirely thrown away, and St. Genevieve moved on without discomposing a muscle.

Each of these saints was separated from the other by a band of choristers, exalting her praise in their hymns, but declaring her to be very much inferior to St. Clare, the convent's avowed patroness. These having passed, a long train of nuns appeared, bearing like the choristers each a burning taper. Next came the reliques of St. Clare, inclosed in vases equally precious for their materials and workmanship: but they attracted not Lorenzo's attention. The nun who bore the heart occupied him entirely. According to Theodore's description, he doubted not her being the Mother St. Ursula. She seemed to look round with anxiety. As he stood foremost in the rank by which the procession passed, her eye caught Lorenzo's. A flush of joy overspread her till then pallid cheek. She turned to her companion eagerly.

"We are safe," he heard her whisper, "'tis her brother."

His heart being now at ease, Lorenzo gazed with tranquillity upon the remainder of the show. Now appeared its most brilliant ornament: it was a machine fashioned like a throne, rich with jewels, and dazzling with light. It rolled onwards upon concealed wheels, and was guided by several lovely children dressed as seraphs. The summit was covered with silver clouds, upon which reclined the most beautiful form that eyes ever witnessed. It was a damsel representing St. Clare: her dress was of inestimable price, and round her head a wreath of diamonds formed an artificial glory: but all these ornaments yielded to the lustre of her charms. As she advanced, a murmur of delight ran through the crowd. Even Lorenzo confessed secretly, that he never beheld more perfect beauty; and had not his heart been Antonia's, it must have fallen a sacrifice to this enchanting girl. As it was, he considered her only as a fine statue: she obtained from him no tribute save cold admiration; and when she had passed him, he thought of her no more.

---

1 St. Genevieve (c. 422-c. 500) is sometimes portrayed with a devil putting out the candle by which she is reading.

"Who is she?" asked a by-stander in Lorenzo's hearing.

"One whose beauty you must often have heard celebrated. Her name is Virginia de Villa-Franca: she is a pensioner of St. Clare's convent, a relation of the prioress, and has been selected with justice as the ornament of the procession."

The throne moved onwards. It was followed by the prioress herself: she marched at the head of the remaining nuns with a devout and sanctified air, and closed the procession. She moved on slowly: her eyes were raised to heaven: her countenance, calm and tranquil, seemed abstracted from all sublunary things, and no feature betrayed her secret pride at displaying the pomp and opulence of her convent. She passed along, accompanied by the prayers and benedictions of the populace: but how great was the general confusion and surprise when Don Ramirez, starting forward, challenged her as his prisoner!

For a moment amazement held the domina silent and immoveable: but no sooner did she recover herself, than she exclaimed against sacrilege and impiety, and called upon the people to rescue a daughter of the church. They were eagerly preparing to obey her; when Don Ramirez, protected by the archers from their rage, commanded them to forbear, and threatened them with the severest vengeance of the Inquisition. At that dreaded word every arm fell, every sword shrunk back into its scabbard. The prioress herself turned pale, and trembled. The general silence convinced her that she had nothing to hope but from innocence, and she besought Don Ramirez in a faultering voice, to inform her of what crime she was accused.

"That you shall know in time," replied he; "but first I must secure the Mother St. Ursula."

"The Mother St. Ursula?" repeated the domina faintly.

At this moment casting her eyes round, she saw Lorenzo and the duke, who had followed Don Ramirez.

"Ah! great God!" she cried, clasping her hands together with a frantic air, "I am betrayed."

"Betrayed?" replied St. Ursula, who now arrived conducted by some of the archers, and followed by the nun her companion in the procession: "not betrayed, but discovered. In me recognise your accuser: you know not how well I am instructed in your guilt:—Segnor," she continued, turning to Don Ramirez, "I commit myself to your custody. I charge the prioress of St. Clare with murder, and stake my life for the justice of my accusation."

A general cry of surprise was uttered by the whole audience, and an explanation was loudly demanded. The trembling nuns, terrified at the noise and universal confusion, had dispersed, and fled different ways. Some regained the convent: others sought refuge in the dwellings of their relations; and many, only sensible of their present danger, and anxious to escape from the tumult, ran through the streets, and wandered they knew not whither. The lovely Virginia was one of the first to fly. And in order that she might be better seen and heard, the people desired that St. Ursula should harangue them from the vacant throne. The nun complied: she ascended the glittering machine, and then addressed the surrounding multitude as follows:

"However strange and unseemly may appear my conduct, when considered to be adopted by a female and a nun, necessity will justify it most fully. A secret, an horrible secret weighs heavy upon my soul: no rest can be mine till I have revealed it to the world, and satisfied that innocent blood which calls from the grave for vengeance. Much have I dared, to gain this opportunity of lightening my conscience. Had I failed in my attempt to reveal the crime, had the domina but suspected that the mystery was none to me, my ruin was inevitable. Angels who watch unceasingly over those who deserve their favour, have enabled me to escape detection. I am now at liberty to relate a tale, whose circumstances will freeze every honest soul with horror. Mine is the task to rend the veil from hypocrisy, and shew misguided parents to what dangers the woman is exposed, who falls under the sway of a monastic tyrant.

"Among the votaries of St. Clare, none was more lovely, none more gentle, than Agnes de Medina. I knew her well: she entrusted to me every secret of her heart: I was her friend and confidante, and I loved her with sincere affection. Nor was I singular in my attachment. Her piety unfeigned, her willingness to oblige, and her angelic disposition, rendered her the darling of all that was estimable in the convent. The prioress herself, proud, scrupulous and forbidding, could not refuse Agnes that tribute of approbation which she bestowed upon no one else. Every one has some fault. Alas! Agnes had her weakness: she violated the laws of our order, and incurred the inveterate hate of the unforgiving domina. St. Clare's rules are severe: but grown antiquated and neglected, many of late years have either been forgotten, or changed by universal consent into milder punishments. The penance adjudged to the crime of Agnes was most cruel, most inhuman. The law had been long exploded. Alas! it still existed, and the revengeful prioress now determined to revive it. This law decreed, that the offender should be plunged into a private dungeon, expressly constituted to hide from the world for ever the victim of cruelty and tyrannic superstition. In this dreadful abode she was to lead a perpetual solitude, deprived of all society, and believed to be dead by those, whom affection might have prompted to attempt her rescue. Thus was she to languish out the remainder of her days, with no other food than bread and water, and no other comfort than the free indulgence of her tears."

The indignation created by this account was so violent, as for some moments to interrupt St. Ursula's narrative. When the disturbance ceased, and silence again prevailed through the assembly, she continued her discourse, while at every word the domina's countenance betrayed her increasing terrors.

"A council of the twelve elder nuns was called: I was of the number. The prioress in exaggerated colours described the offence of Agnes, and scrupled not to propose the revival of this almost forgotten law. To the shame of our sex be it spoken, that either so absolute was the domina's will in the convent, or so much had disappointment, solitude, and self-denial hardened their hearts and soured their tempers, this barbarous proposal was assented to by nine voices out of the twelve. I was not one of the nine. Frequent opportunities had convinced me of the virtues of Agnes, and I loved and pitied her most sincerely. The mothers Bertha and Cornelia joined my party: we made the strongest opposition possible, and the superior found herself compelled to change her intention. In spite of the majority in her favour, she feared to break with us openly. She knew that, supported by the Medina family, our forces would be too strong for her to cope with: and she also knew that, after being once imprisoned, and supposed dead, should Agnes be discovered, her ruin would be inevitable; she therefore gave up her design, though with much reluctance. She demanded some days to reflect upon a mode of punishment, which might be agreeable to the whole community; and she promised, that as soon as her resolution was fixed, the same council should be again summoned. Two days passed away: on the evening of the third it was announced, that on the next day Agnes should be examined; and that according to her behaviour on that occasion her punishment should be either strengthened or mitigated.

"On the night preceding this examination, I stole to the cell of Agnes at an hour when I supposed the other nuns to be buried in sleep. I comforted her to the best of my power: I bade her take courage, told her to rely upon the support of her friends, and taught her certain signs, by which I might instruct her to answer the domina's questions by an assent or negative. Conscious that her enemy would strive to confuse, embarrass, and daunt her, I feared her being ensnared into some confession prejudicial to her interests. Being anxious to keep my visit secret, I stayed with Agnes but a short time. I bade her not to let her spirits be cast down. I mingled my tears with those which streamed down her cheek, embraced her fondly, and was on the point of retiring, when I heard the sound of steps approaching the cell. I started back. A curtain which veiled a large crucifix offered me a retreat, and I hastened to place myself behind it. The door opened. The prioress entered, followed by four other nuns. They advanced towards the bed of Agnes. The superior reproached her with her errors in the bitterest terms. She told her, that she was a disgrace to the convent, that she was resolved to deliver the world and herself from such a monster, and commanded her to drink the contents of a goblet now presented to her by one of the nuns. Aware of the fatal properties of the liquor, and trembling to find herself upon the brink of eternity, the unhappy girl strove to excite the domina's pity by the most affecting prayers. She sued for life in terms which might have melted the heart of a fiend. She promised to submit patiently to any punishment, to shame, imprisonment, and torture, might she but be permitted to live! Oh! might she but live another month, or week, or day! Her merciless enemy listened to her complaints unmoved: she told her, that at first she meant to have spared her life, and that if she had altered her intention, she had to thank the opposition of her friends. She continued to insist upon her swallowing the poison: she bade her recommend herself to the Almighty's mercy, not to hers; and assured her that in an hour she would be numbered with the dead. Perceiving that it was vain to implore this unfeeling woman, she attempted to spring from her bed, and call for assistance: she hoped, if she could not escape the fate announced to her, at least to have witnesses of the violence committed. The prioress guessed her design: she seized her forcibly by the arm, and pushed her back upon her pillow; at the same time drawing a dagger, and placing it at the breast of the unfortunate Agnes, she protested that if she uttered a single cry, or hesitated a single moment to drink the poison, she would pierce her heart that instant. Already half-dead with fear, she could make no further resistance. The nun approached with the fatal goblet; the domina obliged her to take it, and swallow the contents. She drank, and the horrid deed was accomplished. The nuns then seated themselves round the bed; they answered her groans with reproaches; they interrupted with sarcasms the prayers in which she recommended her parting soul to mercy: they threatened her with heaven's vengeance and eternal perdition: they bade her despair of pardon, and strowed with yet sharper thorns death's painful pillow. Such were the sufferings of this young unfortunate, till released by fate from the malice of her tormentors. She expired in horror of the past, in fears for the future; and her agonies were such as must have amply gratified the hate and vengeance of her enemies. As soon as her victim ceased to breathe, the domina retired, and was followed by her accomplices.

"It was now that I ventured from my concealment. I dared not to assist my unhappy friend, aware that, without preserving her, I should only have brought on myself the same destruction. Shocked and terrified beyond expression at this horrid scene, scarcely had I sufficient strength to regain my cell. As I reached the door of that of Agnes, I ventured to look towards the bed on which lay her lifeless body, once so lovely and so sweet! I breathed a prayer for her departed spirit, and vowed to revenge her death by the shame and punishment of her assassins. With danger and difficulty I have kept my oath. I unwarily dropped some words at the funeral of Agnes, while thrown off my guard by excessive grief, which alarmed the guilty conscience of the prioress. My every action was observed; my every step was traced. I was constantly surrounded by the superior's spies. It was long before I could find the means of conveying to the unhappy girl's relations an intimation of my secret. It was given out, that Agnes had expired suddenly: this account was credited not only by her friends in Madrid, but even by those within the convent. The poison had left no marks upon her body: no one suspected the true cause of her death, and it remained unknown to all, save the assassins and myself.

"I have no more to say; for what I have already said, I will answer with my life. I repeat, that the prioress is a murderess; that she has driven from the world, perhaps from heaven, an unfortunate, whose offence was light and venial; that she has abused the power intrusted to her hands, and has been a tyrant, a barbarian, and an hypocrite. I also accuse the four nuns, Violante, Camilla, Alix, and Mariana, as being her accomplices, and equally criminal."

Here St. Ursula ended her narrative. It created horror and surprise throughout; but when she related the inhuman murder of Agnes, the indignation of the mob was so audibly testified, that it was scarcely possible to hear the conclusion. This confusion increased with every moment. At length a multitude of voices exclaimed, that the prioress should be given up to their fury. To this Don Ramirez positively refused to consent. Even Lorenzo bade the people remember, that she had undergone no trial, and advised them to leave her punishment to the Inquisition. All representations were fruitless; the disturbance grew still more violent, and the populace more exasperated. In vain did Ramirez attempt to convey his prisoner out of the throng. Wherever he turned, a band of rioters barred his passage, and demanded her being delivered over to them more loudly than before. Ramirez ordered his attendants to cut their way through the multitude. Oppressed by numbers, it was impossible for them to draw their swords. He threatened the mob with the vengeance of the Inquisition: but, in this moment of popular phrensy, even this dreadful name had lost its effect. Though regret for his sister made him look upon the prioress with abhorrence, Lorenzo could not help pitying a woman in a situation so terrible: but in spite of all his exertions and those of the duke, of Don Ramirez and the archers, the people continued to press onwards. They forced a passage through the guards who protected their destined victim, dragged her from her shelter, and proceeded to take upon her a most summary and cruel vengeance. Wild with terror, and scarcely knowing what she said, the wretched woman shrieked for a moment's mercy: she protested that she was innocent of the death of Agnes, and could clear herself from the suspicion beyond the power of doubt. The rioters heeded nothing but the gratification of their barbarous vengeance. They refused to listen to her: they shewed her every sort of insult, loaded her with mud and filth, and called her by the most opprobrious appellations. They tore her one from another, and each new tormentor was more savage than the former. They stifled with howls and execrations her shrill cries for mercy, and dragged her through the streets, spurning her, trampling her, and treating her with every species of cruelty which hate or vindictive fury could invent. At length a flint, aimed by some well-directing hand, struck her full upon the temple. She sank upon the ground bathed in blood, and in a few minutes terminated her miserable existence. Yet though she no longer felt their insults, the rioters still exercised their impotent rage upon her lifeless body. They beat it, trod upon it, and ill-used it, till it became no more than a mass of flesh, unsightly, shapeless, and disgusting.[1]

Unable to prevent this shocking event, Lorenzo and his friends had beheld it with the utmost horror: but they were roused from their compelled inactivity, on hearing that the mob was attacking the convent of St. Clare. The incensed populace, confounding the innocent with the guilty, had resolved to sacrifice all the nuns of that order to their rage, and not to leave one stone of the building upon another. Alarmed at this intelligence, they hastened to the convent, resolved to defend it if possible, or at least to rescue the inhabitants from the fury

1   Cf. contemporary accounts of mob violence against homosexuals; e.g., Appendix B.3.a.

of the rioters. Most of the nuns had fled, but a few still remained in their habitation. Their situation was truly dangerous. However, as they had taken the precaution of fastening the inner gates, with this assistance Lorenzo hoped to repel the mob, till Don Ramirez should return to him with a more sufficient force.

Having been conducted by the former disturbance to the distance of some streets from the convent, he did not immediately reach it. When he arrived, the throng surrounding it was so excessive, as to prevent his approaching the gates. In the interim, the populace besieged the building with persevering rage: they battered the walls, threw lighted torches in at the windows, and swore that by break of day not a nun of St. Clare's order should be left alive. Lorenzo had just succeeded in piercing his way through the crowd, when one of the gates was forced open. The rioters poured into the interior part of the building, where they exercised their vengeance upon every thing which found itself in their passage. They broke the furniture into pieces, tore down the pictures, destroyed the reliques, and in their hatred of her servant forgot all respect to the saint. Some employed themselves in searching out the nuns, others in pulling down parts of the convent, and others again in setting fire to the pictures and valuable furniture which it contained. These latter produced the most decisive desolation. Indeed the consequences of their action were more sudden than themselves had expected or wished. The flames rising from the burning piles caught part of the building, which being old and dry, the conflagration spread with rapidity from room to room. The walls were soon shaken by the devouring element. The columns gave way, the roofs came tumbling down upon the rioters, and crushed many of them beneath their weight. Nothing was to be heard but shrieks and groans. The convent was wrapped in flames, and the whole presented a scene of devastation and horror.

Lorenzo was shocked at having been the cause, however innocent, of this frightful disturbance: he endeavoured to repair his fault by protecting the helpless inhabitants of the convent. He entered it with the mob, and exerted himself to repress the prevailing fury, till the sudden and alarming progress of the flames compelled him to provide for his own safety. The people now hurried out as eagerly as they had before thronged in; but their numbers clogging up the door-way, and the fire gaining upon them rapidly, many of them perished ere they had time to effect their escape. Lorenzo's good fortune directed him to a small door in a farther aisle of the chapel. The bolt was already undrawn: he opened the door, and found himself at the foot of St. Clare's sepulchre.

Here he stopped to breathe. The duke and some of his attendants had followed him, and thus were in security for the present. They now consulted what steps they should take to escape from this scene of disturbance; but their deliberations were considerably interrupted by the sight of volumes of fire rising from amidst the convent's massy walls, by the noise of some heavy arch tumbling down in ruins, or by the mingled shrieks of the nuns and rioters, either suffocating in the press, perishing in the flames, or crushed beneath the weight of the falling mansion.

Lorenzo enquired, whither the wicket led? He was answered, to the garden of the Capuchins; and it was resolved to explore an outlet upon that side. Accordingly the duke raised the latch, and passed into the adjoining cemetery. The attendants followed without ceremony. Lorenzo, being the last, was also on the point of quitting the colonnade, when he saw the door of the sepulchre opened softly. Some one looked out, but on perceiving strangers uttered a loud shriek, started back again, and flew down the marble stairs.

"What can this mean?" cried Lorenzo: "Here is some mystery concealed. Follow me without delay!"

Thus saying, he hastened into the sepulchre, and pursued the person who continued to fly before him. The duke knew not the cause of this exclamation, but, supposing that he had good reasons for it, followed him without hesitation. The others did the same, and the whole party soon arrived at the foot of the stairs. The upper door having been left open, the neighbouring flames darted from above a sufficient light to enable Lorenzo's catching a glance of the fugitive running through the long passages and distant vaults; but when a sudden turn deprived him of this assistance, total darkness succeeded, and he could only trace the object of his enquiry by the faint echo of retiring feet. The pursuers were now compelled to proceed with caution: as well as they could judge, the fugitive also seemed to slacken pace, for they heard the steps follow each other at longer intervals. They at length were bewildered by the labyrinth of passages, and dispersed in various directions. Carried away by his eagerness to clear up this mystery, and to penetrate into which he was impelled by a movement secret and unaccountable, Lorenzo heeded not this circumstance till he found himself in total solitude. The noise of foot-steps had ceased, all was silent around, and no clue offered itself to guide him to the flying person. He stopped to reflect on the means most likely to aid his pursuit. He was persuaded that no common cause would have induced the fugitive to seek that dreary place at an hour so unusual: the cry which he had heard, seemed uttered in a voice of terror; and he was convinced that some mystery was attached to this event. After some minutes passed in hesitation, he continued to proceed, feeling his way along the walls of the passage. He had already passed some time in this slow progress, when he descried a spark of light glimmering at a distance. Guided by this observation, and having drawn his sword, he bent his steps towards the place whence the beam seemed to be emitted.

It proceeded from the lamp which flamed before St. Clare's statue. Before it stood several females; their white garments streaming in the blast as it howled along the vaulted dungeons. Curious to know what had brought them together in this melancholy spot, Lorenzo drew near with precaution. The strangers seemed earnestly engaged in conversation. They heard not Lorenzo's steps, and he approached unobserved, till he could hear their voices distinctly.

"I protest," continued she who was speaking when he arrived, and to whom the rest were listening with great attention; "I protest, that I saw them with my own eyes. I flew down the steps, they pursued me, and I escaped falling into their hands with difficulty. Had it not been for the lamp, I should never have found you."

"And what could bring them hither?" said another in a trembling voice; "do you think that they were looking for us?"

"God grant that my fears may be false," rejoined the first; "but I doubt they are murderers! If they discover us, we are lost! As for me, my fate is certain. My affinity to the prioress will be a sufficient crime to condemn me; and though till now these vaults have afforded me a retreat......"

Here looking up, her eye fell upon Lorenzo, who had continued to approach slowly.

"The murderers!" she cried.

She started away from the statue's pedestal on which she had been seated, and attempted to escape by flight. Her companions at the same moment uttered a terrified scream, while Lorenzo arrested the fugitive by the arm. Frightened and desperate, she sank upon her knees before him.

"Spare me!" she exclaimed; "for Christ's sake, spare me! I am innocent, indeed, I am!"

While she spoke, her voice was almost choaked with fear. The beams of the lamp darting full upon her face, which was unveiled, Lorenzo recognized the beautiful Virginia de Villa-Franca. He hastened to raise her from the ground, and besought her to take courage. He promised to protect her from the rioters, assured her that her retreat was still a secret, and that she might depend upon his readiness efend her to the last drop of his blood. During this conversation, the nuns had thrown themselves into various attitudes: one knelt, and addressed herself to Heaven; another hid her face in the lap of her neighbour; some listened motionless with fear to the discourse of the supposed assassin; while others embraced the statue of St. Clare, and implored her protection with frantic cries. On perceiving their mistake, they crowded round Lorenzo, and heaped benedictions on him by dozens. He found that on hearing the threats of the mob, and terrified by the cruelties which from the convent towers they had seen inflicted on the superior, many of the pensioners and nuns had taken refuge in the sepulchre. Among the former was to be reckoned the lovely Virginia, nearly related to the prioress. She had more reason than the rest to dread the rioters, and now besought Lorenzo earnestly not to abandon her to their rage. Her companions, most of whom were women of noble family, made the same request, which he readily granted: he promised not to quit them till he had seen each of them safe in the arms of her relations. But he advised their deferring to quit the sepulchre for some time longer, when the popular fury should be somewhat calmed, and the arrival of military force have dispersed the multitude.

"Would to God," cried Virginia, "that I were already safe in my mother's embraces! How say you, Segnor? will it be long ere we may leave this place? Every moment that I pass here, I pass in torture!"

"I hope, not long," said he; "but till you can proceed with security, this sepulchre will prove an impenetrable asylum. Here you run no risque of a discovery, and I would advise your remaining quiet for the next two or three hours."

"Two or three hours?" exclaimed sister Helena: "If I stay another hour in these vaults, I shall expire with fear! Not the wealth of worlds should bribe me to undergo again what I have suffered since my coming hither. Blessed Virgin! To be in this melancholy place in the middle of night, surrounded by the mouldering bodies of my deceased companions, and expecting every moment to be torn in pieces by their ghosts who wander about me, and complain, and groan, and wail in accents that make my blood run cold.... Christ Jesus! It is enough to drive me to madness!"

"Excuse me," replied Lorenzo, "if I am surprised, that while menaced by real woes you are capable of yielding to imaginary dangers. These terrors are puerile and groundless: combat them, holy sister; I have promised to guard you from the rioters, but against the attacks of superstition you must depend for protection upon yourself. The idea of ghosts is ridiculous in the extreme; and if you continue to be swayed by ideal terrors......"

"Ideal?" exclaimed the nuns with one voice: "Why we heard it ourselves, Segnor! Every one of us heard it! It was frequently repeated, and it sounded every time more melancholy and deep. You will never persuade me that we could all have been deceived. Not we, indeed; no, no; had the noise been merely created by fancy...."

"Hark! hark!" interrupted Virginia, in a voice of terror; "God preserve us! There it is again!"

The nuns clasped their hands together, and sank upon their knees. Lorenzo looked round him eagerly, and was on the point of yielding to the fears which already had possessed the women. Universal silence prevailed. He examined the vault, but nothing was to be seen. He now prepared to address the nuns, and ridicule their childish apprehensions, when his attention was arrested by a deep and long-drawn groan.

"What was that?" he cried, and started.——

"There, Segnor!" said Helena: "Now you must be convinced! You have heard the noise yourself! Now judge whether our terrors are imaginary. Since we have been here, that groaning has been repeated almost every five minutes. Doubtless it proceeds from some soul in pain who wishes to be prayed out of purgatory: but none of us dare ask it the question. As for me, were I to see an apparition, the fright, I am very certain, would kill me out of hand."

As she said this, a second groan was heard yet more distinctly. The nuns crossed themselves, and hastened to repeat their prayers against evil spirits. Lorenzo listened attentively. He even thought that he could distinguish sounds as of one speaking in complaint, but distance rendered them inarticulate. The noise seemed to come from the midst of the small vault in which he and the nuns then were, and which a multitude of passages branching out in various directions formed into a sort of star. Lorenzo's curiosity, which was ever awake, made him anxious to solve this mystery. He desired that silence might be kept. The nuns obeyed him. All was hushed till the general stillness was again disturbed by the groaning, which was repeated several times successively. He perceived it to be most audible, when upon following the sound he was conducted close to the shrine of St. Clare.

"The noise comes from hence," said he: "Whose is this statue?"

Helena, to whom he addressed the question, paused for a moment. Suddenly she clapped her hands together.

"Aye!" cried she, "it must be so. I have discovered the meaning of these groans."

The nuns crowded round her, and besought her eagerly to explain herself. She gravely replied, that for time immemorial the statue had been famous for performing miracles. From this she inferred, that the saint was concerned at the conflagration of a convent which she protected, and expressed her grief by audible lamentations. Not having equal faith in the miraculous saint, Lorenzo did not think this solution of the mystery quite so satisfactory, as the nuns, who subscribed to it without hesitation. In one point 'tis true that he agreed with Helena. He suspected that the groans proceeded from the statue: the more he listened the more was he confirmed in this idea. He drew nearer to the image, designing to inspect it more closely: but perceiving his intention, the nuns besought him for God's sake to desist, since, if he touched the statue, his death was inevitable.

"And in what consists the danger?" said he.

"Mother of God! In what?" replied Helena, ever eager to relate a miraculous adventure: "If you had only heard the hundredth part of those marvellous stories about this statue, which the domina used to recount! She assured us often and often, that if we only dared to lay a finger upon it, we might expect the most fatal consequences. Among other things she told us, that a robber having entered these vaults by night, he observed yonder ruby, whose value is inestimable. Do you see it, Segnor? It sparkles upon the third finger of the hand in which she holds a crown of thorns. This jewel naturally excited the villain's cupidity. He resolved to make himself master of it. For this purpose he ascended the pedestal; he supported himself by grasping the saint's right arm, and extended his own towards the ring. What was his surprise, when he saw the statue's hand raised in a posture of menace, and heard her lips pronounce his eternal perdition! Penetrated with awe and consternation, he desisted from his attempt, and prepared to quit the sepulchre. In this he also failed. Flight was denied him. He found it impossible to disengage the hand which rested upon the right arm of the statue. In vain did he struggle: he remained fixed to the image, till the insupportable and fiery anguish which darted itself through his veins, compelled his shrieking for assistance. The sepulchre was now filled with spectators. The villain confessed his sacrilege, and was only released by the separation of his hand from his body. It has remained ever since fastened to the image. The robber turned hermit, and led ever after an exemplary life. But yet the saint's decree was performed; and tradition says, that he continues to haunt this sepulchre, and implore St. Clare's pardon with groans and lamentations. Now I think of it, those which we have just heard, may very possibly have been uttered by the ghost of this sinner: but of this I will not be positive. All that I can say is, that since that time no one has ever dared to touch the statue. Then do not be fool-hardy, good Segnor! For the love of heaven, give up your design, nor expose yourself unnecessarily to certain destruction."

Not being convinced that his destruction would be so certain as Helena seemed to think it, Lorenzo persisted in his resolution. The nuns besought him to desist, in piteous terms, and even pointed out the robber's hand, which was in effect still visible upon the arm of the statue. This proof, as they imagined, must convince him. It was very far from doing so; and they were greatly scandalized when he declared his suspicion that the dried and shrivelled fingers had been placed there by order of the prioress. In spite of their prayers and threats he approached the statue. He sprang over the iron rails which defended it, and the saint underwent a thorough examination. The image at first appeared to be of stone, but proved on further inspection to be formed of no more solid materials than coloured wood. He shook it, and attempted to move it: but it appeared to be of a piece with the base which it stood upon. He examined it over and over: still no clue guided him to the solution of this mystery, for which the nuns were become equally solicitous, when they saw that he touched the statue with impunity. He paused, and listened: the groans were repeated at intervals, and he was convinced of being in the spot nearest to them. He mused upon this singular event, and ran over the statue with enquiring eyes. Suddenly they rested upon the shrivelled hand. It struck him, that so particular an injunction was not given without cause, not to touch the arm of the image. He again ascended the pedestal: he examined the object of his attention, and discovered a small knob of iron concealed between the saint's shoulder and what was supposed to have been the hand of the robber. This observation delighted him. He applied his fingers to the knob, and pressed it down forcibly. Immediately a rumbling noise was heard within the statue, as if a chain tightly stretched was flying back. Startled at the sound, the timid nuns started away, prepared to hasten from the vault at the first appearance of danger. All remaining quiet and still, they again gathered round Lorenzo, and beheld his proceedings with anxious curiosity.

Finding that nothing followed this discovery, he descended. As he took his hand from the saint, she trembled beneath his touch. This created new terrors in the spectators, who believed the statue to be animated. Lorenzo's ideas upon the subject were widely different. He easily comprehended, that the noise which he had heard was occasioned by his having loosened a chain which attached the image to its pedestal. He once more attempted to move it, and succeeded without much exertion. He placed it upon the ground, and then perceived the pedestal to be hollow, and covered at the opening with an heavy iron grate.

This excited such general curiosity, that the sisters forgot both their real and imaginary dangers. Lorenzo proceeded to raise the grate, in which the nuns assisted him to the utmost of their strength. The attempt was accomplished with little difficulty. A deep abyss now presented itself before them, whose thick obscurity the eye strove in vain to pierce. The rays of the lamp were too feeble to be of much assistance. Nothing was discernible, save a flight of rough unshapen steps, which sank into the yawning gulph, and were soon lost in darkness. The groans were heard no more: but all believed them to have ascended from this cavern. As he bent over it, Lorenzo fancied that he distinguished something bright twinkling through the gloom. He gazed attentively upon the spot where it showed itself, and was convinced, that he saw a small spark of light, now visible, now disappearing. He communicated this circumstance to the nuns: they also perceived the spark: but when he declared his intention to descend into the cave, they united to oppose his resolution. All their remonstrances could not prevail on him to alter it. None of them had courage enough to accompany him; neither could he think of depriving them of the lamp. Alone therefore, and in darkness, he prepared to pursue his design, while the nuns were contented to offer up prayers for his success and safety.

The steps were so narrow and uneven, that to descend them was like walking down the side of a precipice. The obscurity by which he was surrounded, rendered his footing insecure. He was obliged to proceed with great caution, lest he should miss the steps, and fall into the gulph below him. This he was several times on the point of doing. However, he arrived sooner upon solid ground than he had expected. He now found, that the thick darkness and impenetrable mists which reigned through the cavern, had deceived him into the belief of its being much more profound than it proved upon inspection. He reached the foot of the stairs unhurt: he now stopped, and looked round for the spark, which had before caught his attention. He sought it in vain: all was dark and gloomy. He listened for the groans; but his ear caught no sound except the distant murmur of the nuns above, as in low voices they repeated their ave-marias. He stood irresolute to which side he should address his steps. At all events he determined to proceed: he did so, but slowly, fearful lest, instead of approaching, he should be retiring from the object of his search. The groans seemed to announce one in pain, or at least in sorrow, and he hoped to have the power of relieving the mourner's calamities. A plaintive tone, sounding at no great distance, at length reached his hearing: he bent his course joyfully towards it. It became more audible as he advanced; and he soon beheld again the spark of light, which a low projecting wall had hitherto concealed from him.

It proceeded from a small lamp which was placed upon an heap of stones, and whose faint and melancholy rays served rather to point out than dispel the horrors of a narrow gloomy dungeon, formed in one side of the cavern: it also shewed several other recesses of similar construction, but whose depth was buried in obscurity. Coldly played the light upon the damp walls, whose dew-stained surface gave back a feeble reflection. A thick and pestilential fog clouded the height of the vaulted dungeon. As Lorenzo advanced, he felt a piercing chill-ness spread itself through his veins. The frequent groans still engaged him to move forwards. He turned towards them, and by the lamp's glimmering beams beheld, in a corner of this loathsome abode, a creature stretched upon a bed of straw, so wretched, so emaciated, so pale, that he doubted to think her woman. She was half naked: her long dishevelled hair fell in disorder over her face, and almost entire-ly concealed it. One wasted arm hung listlessly upon a tattered rug, which covered her convulsed and shivering limbs: the other was wrapped round a small bundle, and held it closely to her bosom. A large rosary lay near her: opposite to her was a crucifix, on which she bent her sunk eyes fixedly, and by her side stood a basket and a small earthen pitcher.

Lorenzo stopped: he was petrified with horror. He gazed upon the miserable object with disgust and pity. He trembled at the spectacle: he grew sick at heart: his strength failed him, and his limbs were unable to support his weight. He was obliged to lean against the low wall which was near him, unable to go forward or to address the suf-ferer. She cast her eyes towards the stair-case: the wall concealed Lorenzo, and she observed him not.

"No one comes!" she at length murmured.

As she spoke, her voice was hollow, and rattled in her throat: she sighed bitterly.

"No one comes!" she repeated: "no! they have forgotten me! they will come no more!"

She paused for a moment; then continued mournfully:

"Two days! two long, long days, and yet no food! and yet no hope, no comfort! Foolish woman! how can I wish to lengthen a life so wretched!—Yet such a death! O God! to perish by such a death! to linger out such ages in torture! Till now, I knew not what it was to hunger!—Hark!—No! no one comes: they will come no more."

She was silent. She shivered, and drew the rug over her naked shoulders:

"I am very cold: I am still unused to the damps of this dungeon: 'tis strange: but no matter. Colder shall I soon be, and yet not feel it. I shall be cold, cold as thou art."

She looked at the bundle, which lay upon her breast. She bent over it, and kissed it: then drew back hastily, and shuddered with disgust:

"It was once so sweet! It would have been so lovely, so like him! I have lost it for ever. How a few days have changed it! I should not know it again myself. Yet it is dear to me. God! how dear!—I will forget what it is! I will only remember what it was, and love it as well, as when it was so sweet! so lovely! so like him!—I thought that I had wept away all my tears, but here is one still lingering."

She wiped her eyes with a tress of her hair. She put out her hand for the pitcher, and reached it with difficulty. She cast into it a look of hopeless enquiry. She sighed, and replaced it upon the ground.

"Quite a void!—Not a drop!—Not one drop left to cool my scorched-up burning palate!—Now would I give treasures for a draught of water!—And they are God's servants who make me suffer thus!—They think themselves holy, while they torture me like fiends!—They are cruel and unfeeling; and 'tis they who bid me repent; and 'tis they who threaten me with eternal perdition! Saviour, Saviour! you think not so!"

She again fixed her eyes upon the crucifix, took her rosary, and, while she told her beads, the quick motion of her lips declared her to be praying with fervency.

While he listened to her melancholy accents, Lorenzo's sensibility became yet more violently affected. The first sight of such misery had given a sensible shock to his feelings: but that being past, he now advanced towards the captive. She heard his steps, and, uttering a cry of joy, dropped the rosary.

"Hark! hark! hark!" she cried, "some one comes!"

She strove to raise herself, but her strength was unequal to the attempt; she fell back, and, as she sank again upon the bed of straw, Lorenzo heard the rattling of heavy chains. He still approached, while the prisoner thus continued:

"Is it you, Camilla? You are come then at last? Oh! it was time! I thought that you had forsaken me; that I was doomed to perish of hunger. Give me to drink, Camilla, for pity's sake; I am faint with long fasting, and grown so weak that I cannot raise myself from the ground. Good Camilla, give me to drink, lest I expire before you."

Fearing that surprise in her enfeebled state might be fatal, Lorenzo was at a loss how to address her.

"It is not Camilla," said he at length, speaking in a slow and gentle voice.

"Who is it then?" replied the sufferer; "Alix, perhaps, or Violante. My eyes are grown so dim and feeble, that I cannot distinguish your features; but whichever it is, if your breast is sensible of the least compassion, if you are not more cruel than wolves and tigers, take pity on my sufferings. You know that I am dying for want of sustenance. This is the third day since these lips have received nourishment. Do you bring me food? Or come you only to announce my death, and learn how long I have yet to exist in agony?"

"You mistake my business," replied Lorenzo; "I am no emissary of the cruel prioress. I pity your sorrows, and come hither to relieve them."

"To relieve them?" repeated the captive; "said you, to relieve them?"

At the same time starting from the ground, and supporting herself upon her hands, she gazed upon the stranger earnestly.

"Great God!—Is it no illusion?—A man? Speak! Who are you? What brings you hither? Come you to save me, to restore me to liberty, to life and light? Oh! speak, speak quickly, lest I encourage an hope whose disappointment will destroy me."

"Be calm!" replied Lorenzo, in a voice soothing and compassionate; "the domina of whose cruelty you complain, has already paid the forfeit of her offences: you have nothing more to fear from her. A few minutes will restore you to liberty and the embraces of your friends, from whom you have been secluded. You may rely upon my protection. Give me your hand, and be not fearful. Let me conduct you where you may receive those attentions which your feeble state requires."

"Oh! yes! yes! yes!" cried the prisoner with an exulting shriek; "there is a God then, and a just one! Joy! Joy! I shall once more breathe the fresh air, and view the light of the glorious sunbeams! I will go with you! Stranger, I will go with you! Oh! Heaven will bless you for pitying an unfortunate! But this too must go with me," she added, pointing to the small bundle, which she still clasped to her bosom; "I cannot part with this. I will bear it away: it shall convince the world how dreadful are the abodes so falsely termed religious. Good stranger! lend me your hand to rise; I am faint with want, and sorrow, and sickness, and my strength has quite forsaken me! So, that is well!"

As Lorenzo stooped to raise her, the beams of the lamp struck full upon his face.

"Almighty God!" she exclaimed: "Is it possible?—That look! those features!—Oh! yes, it is, it is....."

She extended her arms to throw them round him, but her enfeebled frame was unable to sustain the emotions which agitated her bosom. She fainted, and again sank upon the bed of straw.

Lorenzo was surprised at her last exclamation. He thought that he had before heard such accents as her hollow voice had just formed, but where, he could not remember. He saw, that in her dangerous situation immediate physical aid was absolutely necessary, and he hastened to convey her from the dungeon. He was at first prevented from doing so by a strong chain fastened round the prisoner's body, and fixing her to the neighbouring wall. However, his natural strength being aided by anxiety to relieve the unfortunate, he soon forced out the staple, to which one end of the chain was attached: then taking the captive in his arms, he bent his course towards the stair-case. The rays of the lamp above, as well as the murmur of female voices, guided his steps. He gained the stairs, and in a few minutes after arrived at the iron-grate.

The nuns during his absence had been terribly tormented by curiosity and apprehension. They were equally surprised and delighted on seeing him suddenly emerge from the cave. Every heart was filled with compassion for the miserable creature, whom he bore in his arms. While the nuns, and Virginia in particular, employed themselves in striving to recall her to her senses, Lorenzo related in few words the manner of his finding her. He then observed to them, that by this time the tumult must have been quelled, and that he could now conduct them to their friends without danger. All were eager to quit the sepulchre. Still, to prevent all possibility of ill-usage, they besought Lorenzo to venture out first alone, and examine whether the coast was clear. With this request he complied. Helena offered to conduct him to the stair-case, and they were on the point of departing, when a strong light flashed from several passages upon the adjacent walls. At the same time steps were heard of people approaching hastily, and whose number seemed to be considerable. The nuns were greatly alarmed at this circumstance; they supposed their retreat to be discovered, and the rioters to be advancing in pursuit of them. Hastily quitting the prisoner, who remained insensible, they crowded round Lorenzo, and claimed his promise to protect them. Virginia alone forgot her own danger by striving to relieve the sorrows of another. She supported the sufferer's head upon her knees, bathing her temples with rose-water, chafing her cold hands, and sprinkling her face with tears which were drawn from her by compassion. The strangers approaching nearer, Lorenzo was enabled to dispel the fears of the suppliants. His name pronounced by a number of voices, among which he distinguished the duke's, pealed along the vaults, and convinced him that he was the object of their search. He communicated this intelligence to the nuns, who received it with rapture. A few moments after confirmed his idea. Don Ramirez as well as the duke appeared, followed by attendants with torches. They had been seeking him through the vaults, in order to let him know that the mob was dispersed, and the riot entirely over. Lorenzo recounted briefly his adventure in the cavern, and explained how much the unknown was in want of medical assistance. He besought the duke to take charge of her, as well as of the nuns and pensioners.

"As for me," said he, "other cares demand my attention. While you with one half of the archers convey these ladies to their respective homes, I wish the other half to be left with me. I will examine the cavern below, and pervade the most secret recesses of the sepulchre. I cannot rest till convinced that yonder wretched victim was the only one confined by superstition in these vaults."

The duke applauded his intention. Don Ramirez offered to assist him in his enquiry, and his proposal was accepted with gratitude. The nuns, having made their acknowledgments to Lorenzo, committed themselves to the care of his uncle, and were conducted from the sepulchre. Virginia requested that the unknown might be given to her in charge, and promised to let Lorenzo know, whenever she was sufficiently recovered to accept his visits. In truth, she made this promise more from consideration for herself, than for either Lorenzo or the captive. She had witnessed his politeness, gentleness, and intrepidity with sensible emotion. She wished earnestly to preserve his acquaintance; and in addition to the sentiments of pity which the prisoner excited, she hoped that her attention to this unfortunate would raise her a degree in the esteem of Lorenzo. She had no occasion to trouble herself upon this head. The kindness already displayed by her, and the tender concern which she had shewn for the sufferer, had gained her an exalted place in his good graces. While occupied in alleviating the captive's sorrows, the nature of her employment adorned her with new charms, and rendered her beauty a thousand times more interesting. Lorenzo viewed her with admiration and delight: he considered her as a ministering angel descended to the aid of afflicted innocence; nor could his heart have resisted her attractions, had it not been steeled by the remembrance of Antonia.

The duke now conveyed the nuns in safety to the dwellings of their respective friends. The rescued prisoner was still insensible, and gave no signs of life, except by occasional groans. She was borne upon a sort of litter. Virginia, who was constantly by the side of it, was apprehensive that, exhausted by long abstinence, and shaken by the sudden change from bonds and darkness to liberty and light, her frame would never get the better of the shock. Lorenzo and Don Ramirez still remained in the sepulchre. After deliberating upon their proceedings, it was resolved that, to prevent losing time, the archers should be divided into two bodies: that with one, Don Ramirez should examine the cavern, while Lorenzo, with the other, might penetrate into the further vaults. This being arranged, and his followers being provided with torches, Don Ramirez advanced to the cavern. He had already descended some steps, when he heard people approaching hastily from the interior part of the sepulchre. This surprised him, and he quitted the cave precipitately.

"Do you hear foot-steps?" said Lorenzo. "Let us bend our course towards them. 'Tis from this side that they seem to proceed."

At that moment a loud and piercing shriek induced him to quicken his steps.

"Help! help, for God's sake!" cried a voice, whose melodious tone penetrated Lorenzo's heart with terror.

He flew towards the cry with the rapidity of lightning, and was followed by Don Ramirez with equal swiftness.

CHAP. XI.

Great Heaven! How frail thy creature man is made!
How by himself insensibly betrayed!
In our own strength unhappily secure,
Too little cautious of the adverse power,
On pleasure's flowery brink we idly stray,
Masters as yet of our returning way:
Till the strong gusts of raging passion rise,
Till the dire tempest mingles earth and skies,
And, swift into the boundless ocean borne,
Our foolish confidence too late we mourn:
Round our devoted heads the billows beat,
And from our troubled view the lessening lands retreat.

PRIOR.[1]

---

1   Matthew Prior (1664-1721), *Solomon* 2.525-28, 531-32, 539-44.

ALL this while Ambrosio was unconscious of the dreadful scenes which were passing so near. The execution of his designs upon Antonia employed his every thought. Hitherto he was satisfied with the success of his plans. Antonia had drunk the opiate, was buried in the vaults of St. Clare, and absolutely in his disposal. Matilda, who was well acquainted with the nature and effects of the soporific medicine, had computed that it would not cease to operate till one in the morning. For that hour he waited with impatience. The festival of St. Clare presented him with a favourable opportunity of consummating his crime. He was certain that the friars and nuns would be engaged in the procession, and that he had no cause to dread an interruption: from appearing himself at the head of his monks, he had desired to be excused. He doubted not, that being beyond the reach of help, cut off from all the world, and totally in his power, Antonia would comply with his desires. The affection which she had ever expressed for him, warranted this persuasion: but he resolved, that should she prove obstinate, no consideration whatever should prevent him from enjoying her. Secure from a discovery, he shuddered not at the idea of employing force; or, if he felt any repugnance, it arose not from a principle of shame or compassion, but from his feeling for Antonia the most sincere and ardent affection, and wishing to owe her favours to no one but herself.

The monks quitted the abbey at midnight. Matilda was among the choristers, and led the chaunt. Ambrosio was left by himself, and at liberty to pursue his own inclinations. Convinced that no one remained behind to watch his motions, or disturb his pleasures, he now hastened to the western aisles. His heart beating with hope not unmingled with anxiety, he crossed the garden, unlocked the door which admitted him into the cemetery, and in a few minutes he stood before the vaults. Here he paused: he looked round him with suspicion, conscious that his business was unfit for any other eye. As he stood in hesitation, he heard the melancholy shriek of the screech-owl: the wind rattled loudly against the windows of the adjacent convent, and, as the current swept by him, bore with it the faint notes of the chaunt of choristers. He opened the door cautiously, as if fearing to be overheard; he entered, and closed it again after him. Guided by his lamp, he threaded the long passages, in whose windings Matilda had instructed him, and reached the private vault which contained his sleeping mistress.

Its entrance was by no means easy to discover; but this was no obstacle to Ambrosio, who at the time of Antonia's funeral had observed it too carefully to be deceived. He found the door, which was unfastened, pushed it open, and descended into the dungeon. He approached the humble tomb in which Antonia reposed. He had provided himself with an iron crow and a pick-axe: but this precaution was unnecessary. The grate was slightly fastened on the outside: he raised it, and, placing the lamp upon its ridge, bent silently over the tomb. By the side of three putrid half-corrupted bodies lay the sleeping beauty. A lively red, the forerunner of returning animation, had already spread itself over her cheeks; and as wrapped in her shroud she reclined upon her funeral bier, she seemed to smile at the images of death around her. While he gazed upon their rotting bones and disgusting figures, who perhaps were once as sweet and lovely, Ambrosio thought upon Elvira, by him reduced to the same state. As the memory of that horrid act glanced upon his mind, it was clouded with a gloomy horror; yet it served but to strengthen his resolution to destroy Antonia's honour.

"For your sake, fatal beauty!" murmured the monk, while gazing on his devoted prey, "for your sake have I committed this murder, and sold myself to eternal tortures. Now you are in my power: the produce of my guilt will at least be mine. Hope not that your prayers breathed in tones of unequalled melody, your bright eyes filled with tears, and your hands lifted in supplication, as when seeking in penitence the Virgin's pardon: hope not, that your moving innocence, your beauteous grief, or all your suppliant arts, shall ransom you from my embraces. Before the break of day, mine you must, and mine you shall be!"

He lifted her, still motionless, from the tomb: he seated himself upon a bank of stone, and, supporting her in his arms, watched impatiently for the symptoms of returning animation. Scarcely could he command his passions sufficiently, to restrain himself from enjoying her while yet insensible. His natural lust was increased in ardour by the difficulties which had opposed his satisfying it; as also by his long abstinence from woman, since, from the moment of resigning her claim to his love, Matilda had exiled him from her arms for ever.

"I am no prostitute, Ambrosio," had she told him, when, in the fullness of his lust, he demanded her favours with more than usual earnestness; "I am now no more than your friend, and will not be your mistress. Cease then to solicit my complying with desires which insult me. While your heart was mine, I gloried in your embraces. Those happy times are past; my person is become indifferent to you, and 'tis necessity, not love, which makes you seek my enjoyment. I cannot yield to a request so humiliating to my pride."

Suddenly deprived of pleasures, the use of which had made them an absolute want, the monk felt this restraint severely. Naturally addicted to the gratification of the senses, in the full vigour of manhood and heat of blood, he had suffered his temperament to acquire such ascendancy, that his lust was become madness. Of his fondness for Antonia, none but the grosser particles remained; he longed for the possession of her person; and even the gloom of the vault, the surrounding silence, and the resistance which he expected from her, seemed to give a fresh edge to his fierce and unbridled desires.

Gradually he felt the bosom which rested against his glow with returning warmth. Her heart throbbed again, her blood flowed swifter, and her lips moved. At length she opened her eyes; but, still oppressed and bewildered by the effects of the strong opiate, she closed them again immediately. Ambrosio watched her narrowly, nor permitted a movement to escape him. Perceiving that she was fully restored to existence, he caught her in rapture to his bosom, and closely pressed his lips to hers. The suddenness of his action sufficed to dissipate the fumes which obscured Antonia's reason. She hastily raised herself, and cast a wild look round her. The strange images which presented themselves on every side contributed to confuse her. She put her hand to her head, as if to settle her disordered imagination. At length she took it away, and threw her eyes through the dungeon a second time. They fixed on the abbot's face.

"Where am I?" she said abruptly. "How came I here?— Where is my mother? Methought I saw her! Oh! a dream, a dreadful dreadful dream told me...... But where am I? Let me go! I cannot stay here!"

She attempted to rise, but the monk prevented her.

"Be calm, lovely Antonia!" he replied; "no danger is near you: confide in my protection. Why do you gaze on me so earnestly? Do you not know me? Not know your friend, Ambrosio?"

"Ambrosio? my friend?—Oh! yes, yes; I remember...... But why am I here? Who has brought me? Why are you with me?—Oh! Flora bade me beware.....!—Here are nothing but graves, and tombs, and skeletons! This place frightens me! Good Ambrosio, take me away from it, for it recalls my fearful dream!—Methought I was dead, and laid in my grave!—Good Ambrosio, take me from hence!—Will you not? Oh! will you not?—Do not look on me thus!—Your flaming eyes terrify me!—Spare me, father! Oh! spare me for God's sake!"

"Why these terrors, Antonia?" rejoined the abbot, folding her in his arms, and covering her bosom with kisses which she in vain struggled to avoid. "What fear you from me, from one who adores you? What matters it where you are? This sepulchre seems to me Love's bower. This gloom is the friendly night of Mystery, which he spreads over our delights! Such do I think it, and such must my Antonia. Yes, my sweet girl! yes! Your veins shall glow with the fire which circles in mine, and my transports shall be doubled by your sharing them!"

While he spoke thus, he repeated his embraces, and permitted himself the most indecent liberties. Even Antonia's ignorance was not proof against the freedom of his behaviour. She was sensible of her danger, forced herself from his arms, and her shroud being her only garment, she wrapped it closely round her.

"Unhand me, father!" she cried, her honest indignation tempered by alarm at her unprotected position: "Why have you brought me to this place? Its appearance freezes me with horror! Convey me from hence, if you have the least sense of pity and humanity! Let me return to the house, which I have quitted I know not how; but stay here one moment longer, I neither will nor ought."

Though the monk was somewhat startled by the resolute tone in which this speech was delivered, it produced upon him no other effect than surprise. He caught her hand, forced her upon his knee, and, gazing upon her with gloting eyes, he thus replied to her:

"Compose yourself, Antonia. Resistance is unavailing, and I need disavow my passion for you no longer. You are imagined dead; society is for ever lost to you. I possess you here alone; you are absolutely in my power, and I burn with desires which I must either gratify or die: but I would owe my happiness to yourself. My lovely girl! my adorable Antonia! let me instruct you in joys to which you are still a stranger, and teach you to feel those pleasures in my arms, which I must soon enjoy in yours. Nay, this struggling is childish," he continued, seeing her repel his caresses, and endeavour to escape from his grasp; "no aid is near; neither heaven nor earth shall save you from my embraces. Yet why reject pleasures so sweet, so rapturous? No one observes us; our loves will be a secret to all the world. Love and opportunity invite your giving loose to your passions. Yield to them, my Antonia! yield to them, my lovely girl! Throw your arms thus fondly round me; join your lips thus closely to mine! Amidst all her gifts, has Nature denied her most precious, the sensibility of pleasure? Oh! impossible! Every feature, look, and motion declares you formed to bless, and to be blessed yourself! Turn not on me those supplicating eyes: consult your own charms; they will tell you that I am proof against entreaty. Can I relinquish these limbs so white, so soft, so delicate! these swelling breasts, round, full, and elastic! these lips fraught with such inexhaustible sweetness? Can I relinquish these treasures, and leave them to another's enjoyment? No, Antonia; never, never! I swear it by this kiss! and this! and this!"

With every moment the friar's passion became more ardent, and Antonia's terror more intense. She struggled to disengage herself from his arms. Her exertions were unsuccessful; and, finding that Ambrosio's conduct became still freer, she shrieked for assistance with all her strength. The aspect of the vault, the pale glimmering of the lamp, the surrounding obscurity, the sight of the tomb, and the objects of mortality which met her eyes on either side, were ill calculated to inspire her with those emotions by which the friar was agitated. Even his caresses terrified her from their fury, and created no other sentiment than fear. On the contrary, her alarm, her evident disgust, and incessant opposition, seemed only to inflame the monk's desires, and supply his brutality with additional strength. Antonia's shrieks were unheard; yet she continued them, nor abandoned her endeavours to escape, till exhausted and out of breath she sank from his arms upon her knees, and once more had recourse to prayers and supplications. This attempt had no better success than the former. On the contrary, taking advantage of her situation, the ravisher threw himself by her side. He clasped her to his bosom almost lifeless with terror, and faint with struggling. He stifled her cries with kisses, treated her with the rudeness of an unprincipled barbarian, proceeded from freedom to freedom, and, in the violence of his lustful delirium, wounded and bruised her tender limbs. Heedless of her tears, cries and entreaties, he gradually made himself master of her person, and desisted not from his prey, till he had accomplished his crime and the dishonour of Antonia.

Scarcely had he succeeded in his design, than he shuddered at himself, and the means by which it was effected. The very excess of his former eagerness to possess Antonia now contributed to inspire him with disgust; and a secret impulse made him feel how base and unmanly was the crime which he had just committed. He started hastily from her arms. She, who so lately had been the object of his adoration, now raised no other sentiment in his heart than aversion and rage. He turned away from her; or, if his eyes rested upon her figure involuntarily, it was only to dart upon her looks of hate. The unfortunate had fainted ere the completion of her disgrace: she only recovered life to be sensible of her misfortune. She remained stretched upon the earth in silent despair; the tears chased each other slowly down her cheeks, and her bosom heaved with frequent sobs. Oppressed with grief, she continued for some time in this state of torpidity. At length she rose with difficulty, and, dragging her feeble steps towards the door, prepared to quit the dungeon.

The sound of her foot-steps roused the monk from his sullen apathy. Starting from the tomb against which he reclined, while his eyes wandered over the images of corruption contained in it, he pursued the victim of his brutality, and soon overtook her. He seized her by the arm, and violently forced her back into the dungeon.

"Whither go you?" he cried in a stern voice; "return this instant!" Antonia trembled at the fury of his countenance.

"What would you more?" she said with timidity: "Is not my ruin completed? Am I not undone, undone for ever? Is not your cruelty contented, or have I yet more to suffer? Let me depart: let me return to my home, and weep unrestrained my shame and my affliction!"

"Return to your home?" repeated the monk, with bitter and contemptuous mockery; then suddenly his eyes flaming with passion, "What? That you may denounce me to the world? that you may proclaim me a hypocrite, a ravisher, a betrayer, a monster of cruelty, lust, and ingratitude? No, no, no! I know well the whole weight of my offences; well, that your complaints would be too just, and my crimes too notorious! You shall not from hence to tell Madrid that I am a villain; that my conscience is loaded with sins, which make me despair of Heaven's pardon. Wretched girl, you must stay here with me! Here amidst these lonely tombs, these images of death, these rotting, loathsome, corrupted bodies! here shall you stay, and witness my sufferings; witness what it is to be in the horrors of despondency, and breathe the last groan in blasphemy and curses!—And whom am I to thank for this? What seduced me into crimes, whose bare remembrance makes me shudder? Fatal witch! was it not thy beauty? Have you not plunged my soul into infamy? Have you not made me a perjured hypocrite, a ravisher, an assassin? Nay, at this moment, does not that angel look bid me despair of God's forgiveness? Oh! when I stand before his judgment-throne, that look will suffice to damn me! You will tell my judge, that you were happy, till *I* saw you; that you were innocent, till *I* polluted you! You will come with those tearful eyes, those cheeks pale and ghastly, those hands lifted in supplication, as when you sought from me that mercy which I gave not! Then will my perdition be certain! Then will come your mother's ghost, and hurl me down into the dwellings of fiends, and flames, and furies, and everlasting torments! And 'tis you who will accuse me! 'tis you who will cause my eternal anguish!—you, wretched girl! you! you!"

As he thundered out these words, he violently grasped Antonia's arm, and spurned the earth with delirious fury.

Supposing his brain to be turned, Antonia sank in terror upon her knees; she lifted up her hands, and her voice almost died away ere she could give it utterance.

"Spare me! spare me!" she murmured with difficulty.

"Silence!" cried the friar madly, and dashed her upon the ground——

He quitted her, and paced the dungeon with a wild and disordered air. His eyes rolled fearfully; Antonia trembled whenever she met their gaze. He seemed to meditate on something horrible, and she gave up all hopes of escaping from the sepulchre with life. Yet in harbouring this idea she did him injustice. Amidst the horror and disgust to which his soul was a prey, pity for his victim still held a place in it. The storm of passion once over, he would have given worlds, had he possessed them, to have restored to her that innocence of which his unbridled lust had deprived her. Of the desires which had urged him to the crime, no trace was left in his bosom. The wealth of India would not have tempted him to a second enjoyment of her person. His nature seemed to revolt at the very idea, and fain would he have wiped from his memory the scene which had just passed. As his gloomy rage abated, in proportion did his compassion augment for Antonia. He stopped, and would have spoken to her words of comfort; but he knew not from whence to draw them, and remained gazing upon her with mournful wildness. Her situation seemed so hopeless, so woe-begone, as to baffle mortal power to relieve her. What could he do for her? Her peace of mind was lost, her honour irreparably ruined. She was cut off for ever from society, nor dared he give her back to it. He was conscious that, were she to appear in the world again, his guilt would be revealed, and his punishment inevitable. To one so laden with crimes, death came armed with double terrors. Yet, should he restore Antonia to light, and stand the chance of her betraying him, how miserable a prospect would present itself before her! She could never hope to be creditably established; she would be marked with infamy, and condemned to sorrow and solitude for the remainder of her existence. What was the alternative? A resolution far more terrible for Antonia, but which at least would insure the abbot's safety. He determined to leave the world persuaded of her death, and to retain her a captive in this gloomy prison. There he proposed to visit her every night, to bring her food, to profess his penitence, and mingle his tears with hers. The monk felt that this resolution was unjust and cruel; but it was his only means to prevent Antonia from publishing his guilt and her own infamy. Should he release her, he could not depend upon her silence. His offence was too flagrant to permit his hoping for her forgiveness. Besides, her re-appearing would excite universal curiosity, and the violence of her affliction would prevent her from concealing its cause. He determined, therefore, that Antonia should remain a prisoner in the dungeon.

He approached her with confusion painted on his countenance. He raised her from the ground—her hand trembled as he took it, and he dropped it again as if he had touched a serpent. Nature seemed to recoil at the touch. He felt himself at once repulsed from and attracted towards her, yet could account for neither sentiment. There was something in her look which penetrated him with horror; and though his understanding was still ignorant of it, conscience pointed out to him the whole extent of his crime. In hurried accents, yet the gentlest he could find, while his eye was averted, and his voice scarcely audible, he strove to console her under a misfortune which now could not be avoided. He declared himself sincerely penitent, and that he would gladly shed a drop of his blood for every tear which his barbarity had forced from her. Wretched and hopeless, Antonia listened to him in silent grief; but when he announced her confinement in the sepulchre, that dreadful doom, to which even death seemed preferable, roused her from her insensibility at once. To linger out a life of misery in a narrow loathsome cell, known to exist by no human being save her ravisher, surrounded by mouldering corses, breathing the pestilential air of corruption, never more to behold the light, or drink the pure gale of heaven—the idea was more terrible than she could support. It conquered even her abhorrence of the friar. Again she sank upon her knees; she besought his compassion in terms the most pathetic and urgent: she promised, would he but restore her to liberty, to conceal her injuries from the world; to assign any reasons for her re-appearance, which he might judge proper; and in order to prevent the least suspicion from falling upon him, she offered to quit Madrid immediately. Her entreaties were so urgent as to make a considerable impression upon the monk. He reflected, that as her person no longer excited his desires, he had no interest in keeping her concealed as he had at first intended; that he was adding a fresh injury to those which she had already suffered; and that if she adhered to her promises, whether she was confined or at liberty, his life and reputation were equally secure. On the other hand, he trembled lest in her affliction Antonia should unintentionally break her engagement, or that her excessive simplicity and ignorance of deceit should permit some one more artful to surprise her secret. However well-founded were these apprehensions, compassion, and a sincere wish to repair his fault as much as possible, solicited his complying with the prayers of his suppliant. The difficulty of colouring Antonia's unexpected return to life, after her supposed death and public interment, was the only point which kept him irresolute. He was still pondering on the means of removing this obstacle, when he heard the sound of feet approaching with precipitation. The door of the vault was thrown open, and Matilda rushed in, evidently much confused and terrified.

On seeing a stranger enter, Antonia uttered a cry of joy; but her hopes of receiving succour from him were soon dissipated. The supposed novice, without expressing the least surprise at finding a woman alone with the monk, in so strange a place, and at so late an hour, addressed him thus without losing a moment:

"What is to be done, Ambrosio? We are lost, unless some speedy means is found of dispelling the rioters. Ambrosio, the convent of St. Clare is on fire; the prioress has fallen a victim to the fury of the mob. Already is the abbey menaced with a similar fate. Alarmed at the threats of the people, the monks seek for you every where. They imagine that your authority alone will suffice to calm this disturbance. No one knows what is become of you, and your absence creates universal astonishment and despair. I profited by the confusion, and fled hither to warn you of the danger."

"This will soon be remedied," answered the abbot; "I will hasten back to my cell: a trivial reason will account for my having been missed."

"Impossible!" rejoined Matilda: "The sepulchre is filled with archers. Lorenzo de Medina, with several officers of the Inquisition, searches through the vaults, and pervades every passage. You will be intercepted in your flight; your reasons for being at this late hour in the sepulchre will be examined; Antonia will be found, and then you are undone for ever!"

"Lorenzo de Medina? Officers of the Inquisition? What brings them here? Seek they for me? Am I then suspected? Oh! speak, Matilda! answer me in pity!"

"As yet they do not think of you; but I fear that they will ere long. Your only chance of escaping their notice rests upon the difficulty of exploring this vault. The door is artfully hidden; haply it may not be observed, and we may remain concealed till the search is over."

"But Antonia..... Should the inquisitors draw near, and her cries be heard..."

"Thus I remove that danger!" interrupted Matilda.

At the same time drawing a poniard, she rushed upon her devoted prey.

"Hold! hold!" cried Ambrosio, seizing her hand, and wresting from it the already lifted weapon. "What would you do, cruel woman? The unfortunate has already suffered but too much, thanks to your pernicious counsels! Would to God that I had never followed them! Would to God that I had never seen your face!"

Matilda darted upon him a look of scorn.

"Absurd!" she exclaimed with an air of passion and majesty, which impressed the monk with awe. "After robbing her of all that made it dear, can you fear to deprive her of a life so miserable? But 'tis well! Let her live to convince you of your folly. I abandon you to your evil destiny! I disclaim your alliance! Who trembles to commit so insignificant a crime, deserves not my protection. Hark! hark! Ambrosio; hear you not the archers? They come, and your destruction is inevitable!"

At this moment the abbot heard the sound of distant voices. He flew to close the door, on whose concealment his safety depended, and which Matilda had neglected to fasten. Ere he could reach it, he saw Antonia glide suddenly by him, rush through the door, and fly towards the noise with the swiftness of an arrow. She had listened attentively to Matilda: she heard Lorenzo's name mentioned, and resolved to risque every thing to throw herself under his protection. The door was open. The sounds convinced her that the archers could be at no great distance. She mustered up her little remaining strength, rushed by the monk ere he perceived her design, and bent her course rapidly towards the voices. As soon as he recovered from his first surprise, the abbot failed not to pursue her. In vain did Antonia redouble her speed, and stretch every nerve to the utmost. Her enemy gained upon her every moment: she heard his steps close after her, and felt the heat of his breath glow upon her neck. He overtook her; he twisted his hand in the ringlets of her streaming hair, and attempted to drag her back with him to the dungeon. Antonia resisted with all her strength. She folded her arms round a pillar which supported the roof, and shrieked loudly for assistance. In vain did the monk strive to threaten her to silence.

"Help!" she continued to exclaim; "help! help! for God's sake!"

Quickened by her cries, the sound of foot-steps was heard approaching. The abbot expected every moment to see the inquisitors arrive. Antonia still resisted, and he now enforced her silence by means the most horrible and inhuman. He still grasped Matilda's dagger: without allowing himself a moment's reflection, he raised it, and plunged it twice in the bosom of Antonia! She shrieked, and sank upon the ground. The monk endeavoured to bear her away with him, but she still embraced the pillar firmly. At that instant the light of approaching torches flashed upon the walls. Dreading a discovery, Ambrosio was compelled to abandon his victim, and hastily fled back to the vault, where he had left Matilda.

He fled not unobserved. Don Ramirez happening to arrive the first, perceived a female bleeding upon the ground, and a man flying from the spot, whose confusion betrayed him for the murderer. He instantly pursued the fugitive, with some part of the archers, while the others remained with Lorenzo to protect the wounded stranger. They raised her, and supported her in their arms. She had fainted from excess of pain, but soon gave signs of returning life. She opened her eyes; and on lifting up her head, the quantity of fair hair fell back, which till then had obscured her features.

"God Almighty! it is Antonia!"

Such was Lorenzo's exclamation, while he snatched her from the attendant's arms, and clasped her in his own.

Though aimed by an uncertain hand, the poniard had answered but too well the purpose of its employer. The wounds were mortal, and Antonia was conscious that she never could recover. Yet the few moments which remained for her, were moments of happiness. The concern expressed upon Lorenzo's countenance, the frantic fondness of his complaints, and his earnest enquiries respecting her wounds, convinced her beyond a doubt that his affections were her own. She would not be removed from the vaults, fearing lest motion should only hasten her death; and she was unwilling to lose those moments which she passed in receiving proofs of Lorenzo's love, and assuring him of her own. She told him, that had she still been undefiled she might have lamented the loss of life; but that, deprived of honour and branded with shame, death was to her a blessing: she could not have been his wife; and that hope being denied her, she resigned herself to the grave without one sigh of regret. She bade him take courage, conjured him not to abandon himself to fruitless sorrow, and declared that she mourned to leave nothing in the whole world but him. While every sweet accent increased rather than lightened Lorenzo's grief, she continued to converse with him till the moment of dissolution. Her voice grew faint, and scarcely audible; a thick cloud spread itself over her eyes; her heart beat slow and irregular, and every instant seemed to announce that her fate was near at hand.

She lay, her head reclining upon Lorenzo's bosom, and her lips still murmuring to him words of comfort. She was interrupted by the convent-bell, as, tolling at a distance, it struck the hour. Suddenly Antonia's eyes sparkled with celestial brightness; her frame seemed to have received new strength and animation. She started from her lover's arms.

"Three o'clock!" she cried. "Mother, I come!"

She clasped her hands, and sank lifeless upon the ground.[1] Lorenzo, in agony, threw himself beside her. He tore his hair, beat his breast, and refused to be separated from the corse. At length his force being exhausted, he suffered himself to be led from the vault, and was conveyed to the palace de Medina scarcely more alive than the unfortunate Antonia.

In the mean while, though closely pursued, Ambrosio succeeded in regaining the vault. The door was already fastened when Don Ramirez arrived, and much time elapsed ere the fugitive's retreat was discovered. But nothing can resist perseverance. Though so artfully concealed, the door could not escape the vigilance of the archers. They forced it open, and entered the vault to the infinite dismay of Ambrosio and his companion. The monk's confusion, his attempt to hide himself, his rapid flight, and the blood sprinkled upon his clothes, left no room to doubt his being Antonia's murderer. But when he was recognized for the immaculate Ambrosio, "the man of holiness," the idol of Madrid; the faculties of the spectators were chained up in surprise, and scarcely could they persuade themselves that what they saw was no vision. The abbot strove not to vindicate himself, but preserved a sullen silence. He was secured and bound. The same precaution was taken with Matilda. Her cowl being removed, the delicacy of her features and profusion of her golden hair betrayed her sex; and this incident created fresh amazement. The dagger was also found in the tomb, where the monk had thrown it; and the dungeon having undergone a thorough search, the two culprits were conveyed to the prisons of the Inquisition.

Don Ramirez took care that the populace should remain ignorant both of the crimes and profession of the captives. He feared a repetition of the riots, which had followed the apprehending the prioress of St. Clare. He contented himself with stating to the Capuchins the guilt of their superior. To avoid the shame of a public accusation, and dreading the popular fury, from which they had already saved their abbey with much difficulty, the monks readily permitted the inquisitors to search their mansion without noise. No fresh discoveries were made. The effects found in the abbot's and Matilda's cells were seized, and carried to the Inquisition to be produced in evidence. Every

---

1 The rape and murder of Antonia are based on Clarissa's dream, in Richardson, *Clarissa* 342–43; letter 84 (7 April); and on Burke's account of the assault on Marie Antoinette, in *Reflections on the Revolution in France* (1790): see Appendix A.2.b and Appendix B.1.a.

thing else remained in its former position, and order and tranquillity once more prevailed through Madrid.

St. Clare's convent was completely ruined by the united ravages of the mob and conflagration. Nothing remained of it but the principal walls, whose thickness and solidity had preserved them from the flames. The nuns who had belonged to it were obliged, in consequence, to disperse themselves into other societies: but the prejudice against them ran high, and the superiors were very unwilling to admit them. However, most of them being related to families the most distinguished for their riches, birth, and power, the several convents were compelled to receive them, though they did it with a very ill grace. This prejudice was extremely false and unjustifiable. After a close investigation, it was proved that all in the convent were persuaded of the death of Agnes, except the four nuns whom St. Ursula had pointed out. These had fallen victims to the popular fury, as had also several who were perfectly innocent and unconscious of the whole affair. Blinded by resentment, the mob had sacrificed every nun who fell into their hands: they who escaped were entirely indebted to the duke de Medina's prudence and moderation. Of this they were conscious, and felt for that nobleman a proper sense of gratitude.

Virginia was not the most sparing of her thanks; she wished equally to make a proper return for his attentions, and to obtain the good graces of Lorenzo's uncle. In this she easily succeeded. The duke beheld her beauty with wonder and admiration; and while his eyes were enchanted with her form, the sweetness of her manners, and her tender concern for the suffering nun, prepossessed his heart in her favour. This Virginia had discernment enough to perceive, and she redoubled her attention to the invalid. When he parted from her at the door of her father's palace, the duke entreated permission to enquire occasionally after her health. His request was readily granted; Virginia assured him, that the marquis de Villa-Franca would be proud of an opportunity to thank him in person for the protection afforded to her. They now separated, he enchanted with her beauty and gentleness, and she much pleased with him and more with his nephew.

On entering the palace, Virginia's first care was to summon the family physician, and take care of her unknown charge. Her mother hastened to share with her the charitable office. Alarmed by the riots, and trembling for his daughter's safety, who was his only child, the marquis had flown to St. Clare's convent, and was still employed in seeking her. Messengers were now dispatched on all sides to inform him, that he would find her safe at his hotel, and desire him to hasten thither immediately. His absence gave Virginia liberty to bestow her whole attention upon her patient; and though much disordered herself by the adventures of the night, no persuasion could induce her to quit the bed-side of the sufferer. Her constitution being much enfeebled by want and sorrow, it was some time before the stranger was restored to her senses. She found great difficulty in swallowing the medicines prescribed to her; but this obstacle being removed, she easily conquered her disease, which proceeded from nothing but weakness. The attention which was paid her, the wholesome food to which she had been long a stranger, and her joy at being restored to liberty, to society, and, as she dared to hope, to love, all this combined to her speedy re-establishment. From the first moment of knowing her, her melancholy situation, her sufferings almost unparalleled, had engaged the affections of her amiable hostess. Virginia felt for her the most lively interest: but how was she delighted, when, her guest being sufficiently recovered to relate her history, she recognized in the captive nun the sister of Lorenzo!

This victim of monastic cruelty was indeed no other than the unfortunate Agnes. During her abode in the convent, she had been well known to Virginia; but her emaciated form, her features altered by affliction, her death universally credited, and her overgrown and matted hair which hung over her face and bosom in disorder, at first had prevented her being recollected. The prioress had put every artifice in practice to induce Virginia to take the veil; for the heiress of Villa-Franca would have been no despicable acquisition. Her seeming kindness and unremitted attention so far succeeded, that her young relation began to think seriously upon compliance. Better instructed in the disgust and ennui of a monastic life, Agnes had penetrated the designs of the domina. She trembled for the innocent girl, and endeavoured to make her sensible of her error. She painted in their true colours the numerous inconveniencies attached to a convent, the continued restraint, the low jealousies, the petty intrigues, the servile court and gross flattery expected by the superior. She then bade Virginia reflect on the brilliant prospect which presented itself before her. The idol of her parents, the admiration of Madrid, endowed by nature and education with every perfection of person and mind, she might look forward to an establishment the most fortunate. Her riches furnished her with the means of exercising, in their fullest extent, charity and benevolence, those virtues so dear to her; and her stay in the world would enable her discovering objects worthy her protection, which could not be done in the seclusion of a convent.

Her persuasions induced Virginia to lay aside all thoughts of the veil: but another argument, not used by Agnes, had more weight with her than all the others put together. She had seen Lorenzo when he visited his sister at the grate; his person pleased her, and her conversations with Agnes generally used to terminate in some question about her brother. She, who doted upon Lorenzo, wished for no better than an opportunity to trumpet out his praise. She spoke of him in terms of rapture; and, to convince her auditor how just were his sentiments, how cultivated his mind, and elegant his expressions, she shewed her at different times the letters which she received from him. She soon perceived that from these communications the heart of her young friend had imbibed impressions which she was far from intending to give, but was truly happy to discover. She could not have wished her brother a more desirable union: heiress of Villa-Franca, virtuous, affectionate, beautiful, and accomplished, Virginia seemed calculated to make him happy. She sounded her brother upon the subject, though without mentioning names or circumstances. He assured her in his answers, that his heart and hand were totally disengaged, and she thought that upon these grounds she might proceed without danger. She in consequence endeavoured to strengthen the dawning passion of her friend. Lorenzo was made the constant topic of her discourse; and the avidity with which her auditor listened, the sighs which frequently escaped from her bosom, and the eagerness with which upon any digression she brought back the conversation to the subject whence it had wandered, sufficed to convince Agnes that her brother's addresses would be far from disagreeable. She at length ventured to mention her wishes to the duke. Though a stranger to the lady herself, he knew enough of her situation to think her worthy his nephew's hand. It was agreed between him and his niece, that she should insinuate the idea to Lorenzo, and she only waited his return to Madrid to propose her friend to him as his bride. The unfortunate events which took place in the interim, prevented her from executing her design. Virginia wept her loss sincerely, both as a companion, and as the only person to whom she could speak of Lorenzo. Her passion continued to prey upon her heart in secret, and she had almost determined to confess her sentiments to her mother, when accident once more threw their object in her way. The sight of him so near her, his politeness, his compassion, his intrepidity, had combined to give new ardour to her affection. When she now found her friend and advocate restored to her, she looked upon her as a gift from Heaven; she ventured to cherish the hope of being united to Lorenzo, and resolved to use with him his sister's influence.

Supposing that before her death Agnes might possibly have made the proposal, the duke had placed all his nephew's hints of marriage to Virginia's account; consequently he gave them the most favourable reception. On returning to his hotel, the relation given him of Antonia's death, and Lorenzo's behaviour on the occasion, made evident his mistake. He lamented the circumstances; but the unhappy girl being effectually out of the way, he trusted that his designs would yet be executed. 'Tis true that Lorenzo's situation just then ill suited him for a bridegroom. His hopes disappointed at the moment when he expected to realize them, and the dreadful and sudden death of his mistress, had affected him very severely. The duke found him upon the bed of sickness. His attendants expressed serious apprehensions for his life; but the uncle entertained not the same fears. He was of opinion, and not unwisely, that "men have died, and worms have ate them, but not for love!"[1] He therefore flattered himself, that however deep might be the impression made upon his nephew's heart, time and Virginia would be able to efface it. He now hastened to the afflicted youth, and endeavoured to console him: he sympathised in his distress, but encouraged him to resist the encroachments of despair. He allowed, that he could not but feel shocked at an event so terrible, nor could he blame his sensibility; but he besought him not to torment himself with vain regrets, and rather to struggle with affliction, and preserve his life, if not for his own sake, at least for the sake of those who were fondly attached to him. While he laboured thus to make Lorenzo forget Antonia's loss, the duke paid his court assiduously to Virginia, and seized every opportunity to advance his nephew's interest in her heart.

It may easily be expected that Agnes was not long without enquiring after Don Raymond. She was shocked to hear the wretched situation to which grief had reduced him; yet she could not help exulting secretly, when she reflected that his illness proved the sincerity of his love. The duke undertook the office himself, of announcing to the invalid the happiness which awaited him. Though he omitted no precaution to prepare him for such an event, at this sudden change from despair to happiness, Raymond's transports were so violent, as nearly to have proved fatal to him.[2] These once passed, the tranquillity of his mind, the assurance of felicity, and above all, the presence of Agnes, (who was no sooner re-established by the care of Virginia and the

---

1 Misquoted from Shakespeare, *As You Like It* 4.1.96-98.
2 Cf. Henry Mackenzie (1745-1831), *The Man of Feeling* (1771), chap. 55.

marchioness, than she hastened to attend her lover) soon enabled him to overcome the effects of his late dreadful malady. The calm of his soul communicated itself to his body, and he recovered with such rapidity as to create universal surprise.

Not so Lorenzo. Antonia's death, accompanied with such terrible circumstances, weighed upon his mind heavily. He was worn down to a shadow; nothing could give him pleasure. He was persuaded with difficulty to swallow nourishment sufficient for the support of life, and a consumption was apprehended. The society of Agnes formed his only comfort. Though accident had never permitted their being much together, he entertained for her a sincere friendship and attachment. Perceiving how necessary she was to him, she seldom quitted his chamber. She listened to his complaints with unwearied attention, and soothed him by the gentleness of her manners, and by sympathising with his distress. She still inhabited the palace de Villa-Franca, the possessors of which treated her with marked affection. The duke had intimated to the marquis his wishes respecting Virginia. The match was unexceptionable; Lorenzo was heir to his uncle's immense property, and was distinguished in Madrid for his agreeable person, extensive knowledge, and propriety of conduct. Add to this, that the marchioness had discovered how strong was her daughter's prepossession in his favour.

In consequence, the duke's proposal was accepted without hesitation: every precaution was taken to induce Lorenzo's seeing the lady with those sentiments which she so well merited to excite. In her visits to her brother, Agnes was frequently accompanied by the marchioness; and as soon as he was able to move into his antichamber, Virginia, under her mother's protection, was sometimes permitted to express her wishes for his recovery. This she did with such delicacy, the manner in which she mentioned Antonia was so tender and soothing, and when she lamented her rival's melancholy fate, her bright eyes shone so beautiful through her tears, that Lorenzo could not behold or listen to her without emotion. His relations, as well as the lady, perceived that with every day her society seemed to give him fresh pleasure, and that he spoke of her in terms of stronger admiration. However, they prudently kept their observations to themselves. No word was dropped, which might lead him to suspect their designs. They continued their former conduct and attention, and left time to ripen into a warmer sentiment the friendship which he already felt for Virginia.

In the mean while, her visits became more frequent; and latterly there was scarce a day, of which she did not pass some part by the side of Lorenzo's couch. He gradually regained his strength, but the progress of his recovery was slow and doubtful. One evening he seemed to be in better spirits than usual: Agnes and her lover, the duke, Virginia, and her parents were sitting round him. He now for the first time entreated his sister to inform him how she had escaped the effects of the poison which St. Ursula had seen her swallow. Fearful of recalling those scenes to his mind in which Antonia had perished, she had hitherto concealed from him the history of her sufferings. As he now started the subject himself, and thinking that perhaps the narrative of her sorrows might draw him from the contemplation of those on which he dwelt too constantly, she immediately complied with his request. The rest of the company had already heard her story: but the interest which all present felt for its heroine, made them anxious to hear it repeated. The whole society seconding Lorenzo's entreaties, Agnes obeyed. She first recounted the discovery which had taken place in the abbey chapel, the domina's resentment, and the midnight scene of which St. Ursula had been a concealed witness. Though the nun had already described this latter event, Agnes now related it more circumstantially, and at large. After which she proceeded in her narrative as follows:

CONCLUSION OF
THE HISTORY OF AGNES DE MEDINA.

MY supposed death was attended with the greatest agonies. Those moments which I believed my last were embittered by the domina's assurances that I could not escape perdition; and as my eyes closed, I heard her rage exhale itself in curses on my offence. The horror of this situation, of a death-bed from which hope was banished, of a sleep from which I was only to wake to find myself the prey of flames and furies, was more dreadful than I can describe. When animation revived in me, my soul was still impressed with these terrible ideas. I looked round with fear, expecting to behold the ministers of divine vengeance. For the first hour, my senses were so bewildered, and my brain so dizzy, that I strove in vain to arrange the strange images which floated in wild confusion before me. If I endeavoured to raise myself from the ground, the wandering of my head deceived me. Every thing around me seemed to rock, and I sank once more upon the earth. My weak and dazzled eyes were unable to bear a nearer approach to a gleam of light, which I saw trembling above me. I was compelled to close them again, and remain motionless in the same posture.

A full hour elapsed, before I was sufficiently myself to examine the surrounding objects. When I did examine them, what terror filled my bosom! I found myself extended upon a sort of wicker couch. It had six handles to it, which doubtless had served the nuns to convey me to my grave. I was covered with a linen cloth: several faded flowers were strown over me. On one side lay a small wooden crucifix: on the other a rosary of large beads. Four low narrow walls confined me. The top was also covered, and in it was fitted a small grated door, through which was admitted the little air that circulated in this miserable place. A faint glimmering of light, which streamed through the bars, permitted me to distinguish the surrounding horrors. I was oppressed by a noisome suffocating smell; and perceiving that the grated door was unfastened, I thought that I might possibly effect my escape. As I raised myself with this design, my hand rested upon something soft: I grasped it, and advanced it towards the light. Almighty God! what was my disgust! my consternation! In spite of its putridity, and the worms which preyed upon it, I perceived a corrupted human head, and recognised the features of a nun who had died some months before. I threw it from me, and sank almost lifeless upon my bier.

When my strength returned, this circumstance, and the consciousness of being surrounded by the loathsome and mouldering bodies of my companions, increased my desire to escape from my fearful prison. I again moved towards the light. The grated door was within my reach. I lifted it without difficulty: probably it had been left unclosed, to facilitate my quitting the dungeon. Aiding myself by the irregularity of the walls, some of whose stones projected beyond the rest, I contrived to ascend them, and drag myself out of my prison. I now found myself in a vault tolerably spacious. Several tombs, similar in appearance to that whence I had just escaped, were ranged along the sides in order, and seemed to be considerably sunk within the earth. A sepulchral lamp was suspended from the roof by an iron chain, and shed a gloomy light through the dungeon. Emblems of death were seen on every side: skulls, shoulder-blades, thigh-bones, and other reliques of mortality, were scattered upon the dewy ground. Each tomb was ornamented with a large crucifix, and in one corner stood a wooden statue of St. Clare. To these objects I at first paid no attention: a door, the only outlet from the vault, had attracted my eyes. I hastened towards it, having wrapped my winding-sheet closely round me. I pushed against the door, and to my inexpressible terror found that it was fastened on the outside.

I guessed immediately, that the prioress, mistaking the nature of the liquor which she had compelled me to drink, instead of poison had administered a strong opiate. From this I concluded that, being to all appearance dead, I had received the rites of burial; and that, deprived of the power of making my existence known, it would be my fate to expire of hunger. This idea penetrated me with horror, not merely for my own sake, but that of the innocent creature who still lived within my bosom. I again endeavoured to open the door, but it resisted all my efforts. I stretched my voice to the extent of its compass, and shrieked for aid. I was remote from the hearing of every one. No friendly voice replied to mine. A profound and melancholy silence prevailed through the vault, and I despaired of liberty. My long abstinence from food now began to torment me. The tortures which hunger inflicted on me, were the most painful and insupportable: yet they seemed to increase with every hour which passed over my head. Sometimes I threw myself upon the ground, and rolled upon it wild and desperate: sometimes starting up, I returned to the door, again strove to force it open, and repeated my fruitless cries for succour. Often was I on the point of striking my temple against the sharp corner of some monument, dashing out my brains, and thus terminating my woes at once. But still the remembrance of my baby vanquished my resolution. I trembled at a deed, which equally endangered my child's existence and my own. Then would I vent my anguish in loud exclamations and passionate complaints; and then again my strength failing me, silent and hopeless I would sit me down upon the base of St. Clare's statue, fold my arms, and abandon myself to sullen despair. Thus passed several wretched hours. Death advanced towards me with rapid strides, and I expected that every succeeding moment would be that of my dissolution. Suddenly a neighbouring tomb caught my eye: a basket stood upon it, which till then I had not observed. I started from my seat: I made towards it as swiftly as my exhausted frame would permit. How eagerly did I seize the basket, on finding it to contain a loaf of coarse bread and a small bottle of water!

I threw myself with avidity upon these humble aliments. They had to all appearance been placed in the vault for several days. The bread was hard, and the water tainted: yet never did I taste food to me so delicious. When the cravings of appetite were satisfied, I busied myself with conjectures upon this new circumstance. I debated whether the basket had been placed there with a view to my necessity. Hope answered my doubts in the affirmative. Yet who could guess me to be in need of such assistance? If my existence was known, why was I detained in this gloomy vault? If I was kept a prisoner, what meant the ceremony of committing me to the tomb? Or if I was doomed to perish with hunger, to whose pity was I indebted for provisions placed within my reach? A friend would not have kept my dreadful punishment a secret: neither did it seem probable that an enemy would have taken pains to supply me with the means of existence. Upon the whole I was inclined to think, that the domina's designs upon my life had been discovered by some one of my partisans in the convent, who had found means to substitute an opiate for poison; that she had furnished me with food to support me, till she could effect my delivery; and that she was then employed in giving intelligence to my relations of my danger, and pointing out a way to release me from captivity. Yet why then was the quality of my provisions so coarse? How could my friend have entered the vault without the domina's knowledge? and if she had entered, why was the door fastened so carefully? These reflections staggered me: yet still this idea was the most favourable to my hopes, and I dwelt upon it in preference.

My meditations were interrupted by the sound of distant footsteps. They approached, but slowly. Rays of light now darted through the crevices of the door. Uncertain whether the persons who advanced came to relieve me, or were conducted by some other motive to the vault, I failed not to attract their notice by loud cries for help. Still the sounds drew near. The light grew stronger. At length with inexpressible pleasure I heard the key turning in the lock. Persuaded that my deliverance was at hand, I flew towards the door with a shriek of joy. It opened: but all my hopes of escape died away, when the prioress appeared followed by the same four nuns who had been witnesses of my supposed death. They bore torches in their hands, and gazed upon me in fearful silence.

I started back in terror. The domina descended into the vault, as did also her companions. She bent upon me a stern resentful eye, but expressed no surprise at finding me still living. She took the seat which I had just quitted. The door was again closed, and the nuns ranged themselves behind their superior, while the glare of their torches, dimmed by the vapours and dampness of the vault, gilded with cold beams the surrounding monuments. For some moments all preserved a dead and solemn silence. I stood at some distance from the prioress. At length she beckoned me to advance. Trembling at the severity of her aspect, my strength scarce sufficed me to obey her. I drew near, but my limbs were unable to support their burthen. I sank upon my knees, I clasped my hands, and lifted them up to her for mercy, but had no power to articulate a syllable.

She gazed upon me with angry eyes.

"Do I see a penitent, or a criminal?" she said at length: "Are those hands raised in contrition for your crimes, or in fear of meeting their punishment? Do those tears acknowledge the justice of your doom, or only solicit mitigation of your sufferings? I fear me, 'tis the latter!"

She paused, but kept her eye still fixed upon mine.

"Take courage," she continued; "I wish not for your death, but your repentance. The draught which I administered was no poison, but an opiate. My intention in deceiving you, was to make you feel the agonies of a guilty conscience, had death overtaken you sudden-ly, while your crimes were still unrepented. You have suffered those agonies; I have brought you to be familiar with the sharpness of death, and I trust that your momentary anguish will prove to you an eter-nal benefit. It is not my design to destroy your immortal soul, or bid you seek the grave, burthened with the weight of sins unexpiated. No, daughter, far from it; I will purify you with wholesome chastise-ment, and furnish you with full leisure for contrition and remorse. Hear then my sentence: The ill-judged zeal of your friends delayed its execution, but cannot now prevent it. All Madrid believes you to be no more; your relations are thoroughly persuaded of your death, and the nuns your partisans have assisted at your funeral. Your existence can never be suspected. I have taken such precautions as must render it an impenetrable mystery. Then abandon all thoughts of a world from which you are eternally separated, and employ the few hours which are allowed you in preparing for the next."

This exordium led me to expect something terrible. I trembled, and would have spoken to deprecate her wrath; but a motion of the domina commanded me to be silent. She proceeded:

"Though of late years unjustly neglected, and now opposed by many of our misguided sisters (whom Heaven convert!) it is my intention to revive the laws of our order in their full force. That against incontinence is severe, but no more than so monstrous an offence demands. Submit to it, daughter, without resistance; you will find the benefit of patience and resignation in a better life than this. Listen then to the sentence of St. Clare.—Beneath these vaults there exist prisons, intended to receive such criminals as yourself: artfully is their entrance concealed, and she who enters them must resign all hopes[1] of liberty. Thither must you now be conveyed. Food shall be supplied you, but not sufficient for the indulgence of appetite: you shall have just enough to keep together body and soul, and its quali-ty shall be the simplest and coarsest. Weep, daughter, weep, and moist-

---

1 Cf. Dante, *Inferno* 3.9.

en your bread with your tears: God knows, that you have ample cause for sorrow! Chained down in one of these secret dungeons, shut out from the world and light for ever, with no comfort but religion, no society but repentance; thus must you groan away the remainder of your days. Such are St. Clare's orders; submit to them without repining. Follow me!"

Thunder-struck at this barbarous decree, my little remaining strength abandoned me. I answered only by falling at her feet, and bathing them with tears. The domina, unmoved by my affliction, rose from her seat with a stately air: she repeated her commands in an absolute tone; but my excessive faintness made me unable to obey her. Mariana and Alix raised me from the ground, and carried me forwards in their arms. The prioress moved on, leaning on Violante, and Camilla preceded her with a torch. Thus passed our sad procession along the passages, in silence only broken by my sighs and groans. We stopped before the principal shrine of St. Clare. The statue was removed from its pedestal, though how I knew not. The nuns afterwards raised an iron grate, till then concealed by the image, and let it fall on the other side with a loud crash. The awful sound, repeated by the vaults above and caverns below me, roused me from the despondent apathy in which I had been plunged. I looked before me; an abyss presented itself to my affrighted eyes, and a steep and narrow stair-case, whither my conductors were leading me. I shrieked, and started back. I implored compassion, rent the air with my cries, and summoned both heaven and earth to my assistance. In vain! I was hurried down the stair-case, and forced into one of the cells which lined the cavern's sides.

My blood ran cold, as I gazed upon this melancholy abode. The cold vapours hovering in the air, the walls green with damp, the bed of straw so forlorn and comfortless, the chain destined to bind me for ever to my prison, and the reptiles of every description, which, as the torches advanced towards them, I descried hurrying to their retreats, struck my heart with terrors almost too exquisite for nature to bear. Driven by despair to madness, I burst suddenly from the nuns who held me; I threw myself upon my knees before the prioress, and besought her mercy in the most passionate and frantic terms.

"If not on me," said I, "look at least with pity on that innocent being, whose life is attached to mine! Great is my crime, but let not my child suffer for it! My baby has committed no fault. Oh! spare me for the sake of my unborn offspring, whom, ere it tastes life, your severity dooms to destruction!"

The prioress drew back hastily; she forced her habit from my grasp, as if my touch had been contagious.

"What!" she exclaimed with an exasperated air: "What! Dare you plead for the produce of your shame? Shall a creature be permitted to live, conceived in guilt so monstrous? Abandoned woman, speak for him no more! Better that the wretch should perish than live: begotten in perjury, incontinence, and pollution, it cannot fail to prove a prodigy of vice. Hear me, thou guilty! Expect no mercy from me, either for yourself or brat. Rather pray that death may seize you before you produce it; or, if it must see the light, that its eyes may immediately be closed again for ever! No aid shall be given you in your labour; bring your offspring into the world yourself, feed it yourself, nurse it yourself, bury it yourself: God grant that the latter may happen soon, lest you receive comfort from the fruit of your iniquity!"

This inhuman speech, the threats which it contained, the dreadful sufferings foretold to me by the domina, and her prayers for my infant's death, on whom, though unborn, I already doted, were more than my exhausted frame could support. Uttering a deep groan, I fell senseless at the feet of my unrelenting enemy. I know not how long I remained in this situation; but I imagine that some time must have elapsed before my recovery, since it sufficed the prioress and her nuns to quit the cavern. When my senses returned, I found myself in silence and solitude. I heard not even the retiring foot-steps of my persecutors. All was hushed, and all was dreadful! I had been thrown upon the bed of straw: The heavy chain which I had already eyed with terror, was wound around my waist, and fastened me to the wall. A lamp glimmering with dull melancholy rays through my dungeon, permitted my distinguishing all its horrors. It was separated from the cavern by a low and irregular wall of stone. A large chasm was left open in it, which formed the entrance, for door there was none. A leaden crucifix was in front of my straw couch. A tattered rug lay near me, as did also a chaplet of beads; and not far from me stood a pitcher of water, and a wicker-basket containing a small loaf, and a bottle of oil to supply my lamp.

With a despondent eye did I examine this scene of suffering: when I reflected that I was doomed to pass in it the remainder of my days, my heart was rent with bitter anguish. I had once been taught to look forward to a lot so different! At one time my prospects had appeared so bright, so flattering! Now all was lost to me. Friends, comfort, society, happiness, in one moment I was deprived of all! Dead to the world, dead to pleasure, I lived to nothing but the sense of misery.

How fair did that world seem to me, from which I was for ever excluded! How many loved objects did it contain, whom I never should behold again! As I threw a look of terror round my prison, as I shrunk from the cutting wind which howled through my subterraneous dwelling, the change seemed so striking, so abrupt, that I doubted its reality. That the duke de Medina's niece, that the destined bride of the marquis de las Cisternas, one bred up in affluence, related to the noblest families in Spain, and rich in a multitude of affectionate friends—that she should in one moment become a captive, separated from the world for ever, weighed down with chains, and reduced to support life with the coarsest aliments—appeared a change so sudden and incredible, that I believed myself the sport of some frightful vision. Its continuance convinced me of my mistake with but too much certainty. Every morning I looked for some relief from my sufferings: every morning my hopes were disappointed. At length I abandoned all idea of escaping, I resigned myself to my fate, and only expected liberty when she came the companion of death.

My mental anguish, and the dreadful scenes in which I had been an actress, advanced the period of my labour. In solitude and misery, abandoned by all, unassisted by art, uncomforted by friendship, with pangs which if witnessed would have touched the hardest heart, was I delivered of my wretched burthen. It came alive into the world; but I knew not how to treat it, or by what means to preserve its existence: I could only bathe it with tears, warm it in my bosom, and offer up prayers for its safety. I was soon deprived of this mournful employment: the want of proper attendance, my ignorance how to nurse it, the bitter cold of the dungeon, and the unwholesome air which inflated its lungs, terminated my sweet babe's short and painful existence. It expired in a few hours after its birth, and I witnessed its death with agonies which beggar all description.

But my grief was unavailing. My infant was no more; nor could all my sighs impart to its little tender frame the breath of a moment. I rent my winding-sheet, and wrapped in it my lovely child. I placed it on my bosom, its soft arm folded round my neck, and its pale cold cheek resting upon mine. Thus did its lifeless limbs repose, while I covered it with kisses, talked to it, wept, and moaned over it without remission day or night. Camilla entered my prison regularly once every twenty-four hours to bring me food. In spite of her flinty nature, she could not behold this spectacle unmoved. She feared that grief so excessive would at length turn my brain; and in truth I was not always in my proper senses. From a principle of compassion she urged me to permit the corse to be buried; but to this I never would consent. I vowed, not to part with it while I had life: its presence was my only comfort, and no persuasion could induce me to give it up. It soon became a mass of putridity, and to every eye was a loathsome and disgusting object, to every eye but a mother's. In vain did human feelings bid me recoil from this emblem of mortality with repugnance. I withstood, and vanquished that repugnance. I persisted in holding my infant to my bosom, in lamenting it, loving it, adoring it! Hour after hour have I passed upon my sorry couch, contemplating what had once been my child. I endeavoured to retrace its features through the livid corruption with which they were overspread. During my confinement, this sad occupation was my only delight; and at that time worlds should not have bribed me to give it up. Even when released from my prison, I brought away my child in my arms. The representations of my two kind friends—[Here she took the hands of the marchioness and Virginia, and pressed them alternately to her lips]—at length persuaded me to resign my unhappy infant to the grave. Yet I parted from it with reluctance. However, reason at length prevailed; I suffered it to be taken from me, and it now reposes in consecrated ground.

I before mentioned, that regularly once a day Camilla brought me food. She sought not to embitter my sorrows with reproach. She bade me, 'tis true, resign all hopes of liberty and worldly happiness; but she encouraged me to bear with patience my temporary distress, and advised me to draw comfort from religion. My situation evidently affected her more than she ventured to express; but she believed that to extenuate my fault would make me less anxious to repent it. Often while her lips painted the enormity of my guilt in glaring colours, her eyes betrayed how sensible she was to my sufferings. In fact, I am certain that none of my tormentors (for the three other nuns entered my prison occasionally) were so much actuated by the spirit of oppressive cruelty, as by the idea that to afflict my body was the only way to preserve my soul. Nay, even this persuasion might not have had such weight with them, and they might have thought my punishment too severe, had not their good dispositions been repressed by blind obedience to their superior. Her resentment existed in full force. My project of elopement having been discovered by the abbot of the Capuchins, she supposed herself lowered in his opinion by my disgrace, and in consequence her hate was inveterate. She told the nuns, to whose custody I was committed, that my fault was of the most heinous nature, that no sufferings could equal the offence, and that nothing could save me from eternal perdition but punishing my guilt with the utmost severity. The superior's word is an oracle to but too many of a convent's inhabitants. The nuns believed whatever the prioress chose to assert: though contradicted by reason and charity, they hesitated not to admit the truth of her arguments. They followed her injunctions to the very letter, and were fully persuaded, that to treat me with lenity, or to shew the least pity for my woes, would be a direct means to destroy my chance for salvation.

Camilla being most employed about me, was particularly charged by the prioress to treat me with harshness. In compliance with these orders, she frequently strove to convince me how just was my punishment, and how enormous was my crime. She bade me think myself too happy in saving my soul by mortifying my body, and even threatened me sometimes with eternal perdition. Yet, as I before observed, she always concluded by words of encouragement and comfort; and though uttered by Camilla's lips, I easily recognised the domina's expressions. Once, and once only, the prioress visited me in my dungeon. She then treated me with the most unrelenting cruelty. She loaded me with reproaches, taunted me with my frailty; and, when I implored her mercy, told me to ask it of Heaven, since I deserved none on earth. She even gazed upon my lifeless infant without emotion; and when she left me, I heard her charge Camilla to increase the hardships of my captivity. Unfeeling woman! But let me check my resentment. She has expiated her errors by her sad and unexpected death. Peace be with her! and may her crimes be forgiven in heaven, as I forgive her my sufferings on earth!

Thus did I drag on a miserable existence. Far from growing familiar with my prison, I beheld it every moment with new horror. The cold seemed more piercing and bitter, the air more thick and pestilential. My frame became weak, feverish, and emaciated. I was unable to rise from the bed of straw, and exercise my limbs in the narrow limits to which the length of my chain permitted me to move. Though exhausted, faint, and weary, I trembled to profit by the approach of sleep. My slumbers were constantly interrupted by some obnoxious insect crawling over me. Sometimes I felt the bloated toad, hideous and pampered with the poisonous vapours of the dungeon, dragging his loathsome length along my bosom. Sometimes the quick cold lizard roused me, leaving his slimy track upon my face, and entangling itself in the tresses of my wild and matted hair. Often have I at waking found my fingers ringed with the long worms which bred in the corrupted flesh of my infant. At such times I shrieked with terror and disgust; and, while I shook off the reptile, trembled with all a woman's weakness.

Such was my situation when Camilla was suddenly taken ill.

A dangerous fever, supposed to be infectious, confined her to her bed. Every one, except the lay sister appointed to nurse her, avoided her with caution, and feared to catch the disease. She was perfectly delirious, and by no means capable of attending to me. The domina, and the nuns admitted to the mystery, had latterly entirely given me over to Camilla's care. In consequence, they busied themselves no more about me; and, occupied by preparing for the approaching festival, it is more than probable that I never once entered into their thoughts. Of the reason of Camilla's negligence I have been informed since my release by the Mother St. Ursula. At that time I was very far from suspecting its cause. On the contrary, I waited for my gaoler's appearance at first with impatience, and afterwards with despair. One day passed away: another followed it: the third arrived. Still no Camilla! still no food! I knew the lapse of time by the wasting of my lamp, to supply which, fortunately a week's supply of oil had been left me. I supposed, either that the nuns had forgotten me, or that the domina had ordered them to let me perish. The latter idea seemed the most probable: yet so natural is the love of life, that I trembled to find it true. Though embittered by every species of misery, my existence was still dear to me, and I dreaded to lose it. Every succeeding minute proved to me that I must abandon all hopes of relief. I was become an absolute skeleton: my eyes already failed me, and my limbs were beginning to stiffen. I could only express my anguish, and the pangs of that hunger which gnawed my heart-strings, by frequent groans, whose melancholy sound the vaulted roof of the dungeon re-echoed. I resigned myself to my fate: I already expected the moment of dissolution, when my guardian angel—when my beloved brother arrived in time to save me. My sight, grown dim and feeble, at first refused to recognize him: and when I did distinguish his features, the sudden burst of rapture was too much for me to bear. I was overpowered by the swell of joy at once more beholding a friend, and that a friend so dear to me. Nature could not support my emotions, and took her refuge in insensibility.

You already know what are my obligations to the family of Villa-Franca. But what you cannot know, is the extent of my gratitude, boundless as the excellence of my benefactors. Lorenzo! Raymond! names so dear to me! teach me to bear with fortitude this sudden transition from misery to bliss. So lately a captive, oppressed with chains, perishing with hunger, suffering every inconvenience of cold and want, hidden from the light, excluded from society, hopeless, neglected, and, as I feared, forgotten: now restored to life and liberty, enjoying all the comforts of affluence and ease, surrounded by those who are most loved by me, and on the point of becoming his bride who has long been wedded to my heart, my happiness is so exquisite, so perfect, that scarcely can my brain sustain the weight. One only wish remains ungratified. It is to see my brother in his former health, and to know that Antonia's memory is buried in her grave. Granted this prayer, I have nothing more to desire. I trust that my past sufferings have purchased from Heaven the pardon of my momentary weakness. That I have offended, offended greatly and grievously, I am fully conscious. But let not my husband, because he once conquered my virtue, doubt the propriety of my future conduct. I have been frail and full of error: but I yielded not to the warmth of constitution. Raymond, affection for you betrayed me. I was too confident of my strength: but I depended no less on your honour than my own. I had vowed never to see you more. Had it not been for the consequences of that unguarded moment, my resolution had been kept. Fate willed it otherwise, and I cannot but rejoice at its decree. Still my conduct has been highly blameable; and while I attempt to justify myself, I blush at recollecting my imprudence. Let me then dismiss the ungrateful subject; first assuring you, Raymond, that you shall have no cause to repent our union, and that, the more culpable have been the errors of your mistress, the more exemplary shall be the conduct of your wife.

Here Agnes ceased; and the marquis replied to her address in terms equally sincere and affectionate. Lorenzo expressed his satisfaction at the prospect of being so closely connected with a man for whom he had ever entertained the highest esteem. The Pope's bull had fully and effectually released Agnes from her religious engagements. The marriage was therefore celebrated as soon as the needful preparations had been made: for the marquis wished to have the ceremony performed with all possible splendour and publicity. This being over, and the bride having received the compliments of Madrid, she departed with Don Raymond for his castle in Andalusia. Lorenzo accompanied them, as did also the marchioness de Villa-Franca and her lovely daughter. It is needless to say that Theodore was of the party, and would be impossible to describe his joy at his master's marriage. Previous to his departure the marquis, to atone in some measure for his past neglect, made some enquiries relative to Elvira. Finding that she, as well as her daughter, had received many services from Leonella and Jacintha, he shewed his respect to the memory of his sister-in-law by making the two women handsome presents. Lorenzo followed his example. Leonella was highly flattered by the attentions of noblemen so distinguished, and Jacintha blessed the hour on which her house was bewitched.

On her side, Agnes failed not to reward her convent friends. The worthy Mother St. Ursula, to whom she owed her liberty, was named, at her request, superintendent of "the Ladies of Charity." This was one of the best and most opulent societies throughout Spain. Bertha and Cornelia, not choosing to quit their friend, were appointed to principal charges in the same establishment. As to the nuns who had aided the domina in persecuting Agnes; Camilla, being confined by illness to her bed, had perished in the flames which consumed St. Clare's convent. Mariana, Alix, and Violante, as well as two more, had fallen victims to the popular rage. The three others who had in council supported the domina's sentence, were severely reprimanded, and banished to religious houses in obscure and distant provinces. Here they languished away a few years, ashamed of their former weakness, and shunned by their companions with aversion and contempt.

Nor was the fidelity of Flora permitted to go unrewarded. Her wishes being consulted, she declared herself impatient to revisit her native land. In consequence, a passage was procured for her to Cuba, where she arrived in safety, loaded with the presents of Raymond and Lorenzo.

The debts of gratitude discharged, Agnes was at liberty to pursue her favourite plan. Lodged in the same house, Lorenzo and Virginia were eternally together. The more he saw of her, the more was he convinced of her merit. On her part, she laid herself out to please; and not to succeed was for her impossible. Lorenzo witnessed with admiration her beautiful person, elegant manners, innumerable talents, and sweet disposition. He was also much flattered by her prejudice in his favour, which she had not sufficient art to conceal. However, his sentiments partook not of that ardent character which had marked his affection for Antonia. The image of that lovely and unfortunate girl still lived in his heart, and baffled all Virginia's efforts to displace it. Still, when the duke proposed to him the match, which he wished so earnestly to take place, his nephew did not reject the offer. The urgent supplications of his friends, and the lady's merit, conquered his repugnance to entering into new engagements. He proposed himself to the marquis de Villa-Franca, and was accepted with joy and gratitude. Virginia became his wife, nor did she ever give him cause to repent his choice. His esteem increased for her daily. Her unremitted endeavours to please him could not but succeed. His affection assumed stronger and warmer colours. Antonia's image was gradually effaced from his bosom, and Virginia became sole mistress of that heart, which she well deserved to possess without a partner.

The remaining years of Raymond and Agnes, of Lorenzo and Virginia, were happy as can be those allotted to mortals, born to be the prey of grief, and sport of disappointment. The exquisite sorrows with which they had been afflicted, made them think lightly of every succeeding woe. They had felt the sharpest darts in misfortune's quiver. Those which remained, appeared blunt in comparison. Having weathered fate's heaviest storms, they looked calmly upon its terrors: or, if ever they felt affliction's casual gales, they seemed to them gentle as zephyrs which breathe over summer-seas.

CHAP. XII.

——He was a fell despightful fiend:
Hell holds none worse in baleful bower below:
By pride, and wit, and rage, and rancor keened:
Of man, alike if good or bad, the foe.

THOMSON.[1]

ON the day following Antonia's death, all Madrid was a scene of consternation and amazement. An archer who had witnessed the adventure in the sepulchre, had indiscreetly related the circumstances of the murder: he had also named the perpetrator. The confusion was without example, which this intelligence raised among the devotees. Most of them disbelieved it, and went themselves to the abbey to ascertain the fact. Anxious to avoid the shame to which their superior's ill conduct exposed the whole brotherhood, the monks assured the visitors, that Ambrosio was prevented from receiving them as usual by nothing but illness. This attempt was unsuccessful. The same excuse being repeated day after day, the archer's story gradually obtained confidence. His partisans abandoned him: no one entertained a doubt of his guilt: and they who before had been the warmest in his praise, were now the most vociferous in his condemnation.

While his innocence or guilt was debated in Madrid with the utmost acrimony, Ambrosio was a prey to the pangs of conscious villany, and the terrors of punishment impending over him. When he

---

1   James Thomson (1700-48), *The Castle of Indolence* (1748) 2.80.1-4.

looked back to the eminence on which he had lately stood, universally honoured and respected, at peace with the world and with himself, scarcely could he believe that he was indeed the culprit, whose crimes and whose fate he trembled to consider. But a few weeks had elapsed, since he was pure and virtuous, courted by the wisest and noblest in Madrid, and regarded by the people with a reverence that approached idolatry. He now saw himself stained with the most loathed and monstrous sins, the object of universal execration, a prisoner of the Holy Office,[1] and probably doomed to perish in tortures the most severe. He could not hope to deceive his judges: the proofs of his guilt were too strong. His being in the sepulchre at so late an hour, his confusion at the discovery, the dagger which in his first alarm he owned had been concealed by him, and the blood which had spirted upon his habit from Antonia's wound, sufficiently marked him out for the assassin. He waited with agony for the day of examination. He had no resource to comfort him in his distress. Religion could not inspire him with fortitude. If he read the books of morality which were put into his hands, he saw in them nothing but the enormity of his offences. If he attempted to pray, he recollected that he deserved not Heaven's protection, and believed his crimes so monstrous as to exceed even God's infinite goodness. For every other sinner he thought there might be hope, but for him there could be none.[2] Shuddering at the past, anguished by the present, and dreading the future, thus passed he the few days preceding that which was marked for his trial.

That day arrived. At nine in the morning his prison-door was unlocked; and his gaoler entering, commanded him to follow him. He obeyed with trembling. He was conducted into a spacious hall hung with black cloth. At the table sat three grave stern-looking men, also habited in black: one was the Grand Inquisitor, whom the importance of this cause had induced to examine into it himself. At a smaller table at a little distance sat the secretary, provided with all necessary implements for writing. Ambrosio was beckoned to advance, and take his station at the lower end of the table. As his eye glanced downwards, he perceived various iron instruments lying scattered upon the floor. Their forms were unknown to him, but apprehension immediately guessed them to be engines of torture. He turned pale, and with difficulty prevented himself from sinking upon the ground.

---

1 The Inquisition.
2 Cf. Marlowe, *Doctor Faustus* 5.2.14–15.

Profound silence prevailed, except when the inquisitors whispered a few words among themselves mysteriously. Near an hour passed away, and with every second of it Ambrosio's fears grew more poignant. At length a small door, opposite to that by which he had entered the hall, grated heavily upon its hinges. An officer appeared, and was immediately followed by the beautiful Matilda. Her hair hung about her face wildly: her cheeks were pale, and her eyes sunk and hollow. She threw a melancholy look upon Ambrosio: he replied by one of aversion and reproach. She was placed opposite to him. A bell then sounded thrice. It was the signal for opening the court; and the inquisitors entered upon their office.

In these trials neither the accusation is mentioned, nor the name of the accuser. The prisoners are only asked, whether they will confess. If they reply, that, having no crime, they can make no confession, they are put to the torture without delay. This is repeated at intervals, either till the suspected avow themselves culpable, or the perseverance of the examinants is worn out and exhausted: but without a direct acknowledgment of their guilt, the Inquisition never pronounces the final doom of its prisoners. In general much time is suffered to elapse without their being questioned; but Ambrosio's trial had been hastened on account of a solemn Auto da Fé[1] which would take place in a few days, and in which the inquisitors meant this distinguished culprit to perform a part, and give a striking testimony of their vigilance.

The abbot was not merely accused of rape and murder; the crime of sorcery was laid to his charge, as well as to Matilda's. She had been seized as an accomplice in Antonia's assassination. On searching her cell, various suspicious books and instruments were found, which justified the accusation brought against her. To criminate the monk, the constellated mirror was produced, which Matilda had accidentally left in his chamber. The strange figures engraved upon it caught the attention of Don Ramirez, while searching the abbot's cell; in consequence, he carried it away with him. It was shewn to the Grand Inquisitor, who, having considered it for some time, took off a small golden cross which hung at his girdle, and laid it upon the mirror. Instantly a loud noise was heard, resembling a clap of thunder, and the steel shivered into a thousand pieces. This circumstance confirmed the suspicion of the monk's having dealt in magic. It was even

---

1   "Act of Faith" (Spanish): an elaborate public spectacle at which the Inquisition pronounced its sentences on heretics. These sentences were not, however, usually executed at the auto da fé itself.

supposed, that his former influence over the minds of the people was entirely to be ascribed to witchcraft.

Determined to make him confess not only the crimes which he had committed, but those also of which he was innocent, the inquisitors began their examination. Though dreading the tortures as he dreaded death, which would consign him to eternal torments, the abbot asserted his purity in a voice bold and resolute. Matilda followed his example, but spoke with fear and trembling. Having in vain exhorted him to confess, the inquisitors ordered the monk to be put to the question. The decree was immediately executed. Ambrosio suffered the most excruciating pangs that ever were invented by human cruelty. Yet so dreadful is death, when guilt accompanies it, that he had sufficient fortitude to persist in his disavowal. His agonies were redoubled in consequence; nor was he released till, fainting from excess of pain, insensibility rescued him from the hands of his tormentors.

Matilda was next ordered to the torture; but, terrified by the sight of the friar's sufferings, her courage totally deserted her. She sank upon her knees, acknowledged her corresponding with infernal spirits, and that she had witnessed the monk's assassination of Antonia; but as to the crime of sorcery, she declared herself the sole criminal, and Ambrosio perfectly innocent. The latter assertion met with no credit. The abbot had recovered his senses in time to hear the confession of his accomplice: but he was too much enfeebled by what he had already undergone, to be capable at that time of sustaining new torments. He was commanded back to his cell, but first informed, that as soon as he had gained strength sufficient he must prepare himself for a second examination. The inquisitors hoped that he would then be less hardened and obstinate. To Matilda it was announced, that she must expiate her crime in fire on the approaching Auto da Fé. All her tears and entreaties could procure no mitigation of her doom, and she was dragged by force from the hall of trial.

Returned to his dungeon, the sufferings of Ambrosio's body were far more supportable than those of his mind. His dislocated limbs, the nails torn from his hands and feet, and his fingers mashed and broken by the pressure of screws, were far surpassed in anguish by the agitation of his soul, and vehemence of his terrors. He saw, that guilty or innocent his judges were bent upon condemning him. The remembrance of what his denial had already cost him, terrified him at the idea of being again applied to the question, and almost engaged him to confess his crimes. Then again the consequences of his confession flashed before him, and rendered him once more irresolute. His death would be inevitable, and that a death the most dreadful. He had listened to Matilda's doom, and doubted not that a similar was reserved for him. He shuddered at the approaching Auto da Fé, at the idea of perishing in flames, and only escaping from endurable torments to pass into others more subtile and everlasting! With affright did he bend his mind's eye on the space beyond the grave; nor could hide from himself how justly he ought to dread Heaven's vengeance. In this labyrinth of terrors, fain would he have taken his refuge in the gloom of atheism; fain would he have denied the soul's immortality; have persuaded himself that, when his eyes once closed, they would never more open, and that the same moment would annihilate his soul and body. Even this resource was refused to him. To permit his being blind to the fallacy of this belief, his knowledge was too extensive, his understanding too solid and just. He could not help feeling the existence of a God. Those truths, once his comfort, now presented themselves before him in the clearest light; but they only served to drive him to distraction. They destroyed his ill-grounded hopes of escaping punishment; and, dispelled by the irresistible brightness of truth and conviction, philosophy's deceitful vapours faded away like a dream.

In anguish almost too great for mortal frame to bear, he expected the time when he was again to be examined. He busied himself in planning ineffectual schemes for escaping both present and future punishment. Of the first there was no possibility; of the second despair made him neglect the only means. While Reason forced him to acknowledge a God's existence, Conscience made him doubt the infinity of his goodness. He disbelieved that a sinner like him could find mercy. He had not been deceived into error: ignorance could furnish him with no excuse. He had seen vice in her true colours. Before he committed his crimes, he had computed every scruple of their weight, and yet he had committed them.

"Pardon?" he would cry in an access of phrensy: "Oh! there can be none for me!"

Persuaded of this, instead of humbling himself in penitence, of deploring his guilt, and employing his few remaining hours in deprecating Heaven's wrath, he abandoned himself to the transports of desperate rage; he sorrowed for the punishment of his crimes, not their commission; and exhaled his bosom's anguish in idle sighs, in vain lamentations, in blasphemy and despair. As the few beams of day which pierced through the bars of his prison-window gradually disappeared, and their place was supplied by the pale and glimmering lamp, he felt his terrors redouble, and his ideas become more gloomy, more solemn, more despondent. He dreaded the approach of sleep.

No sooner did his eyes close, wearied with tears and watching, than the dreadful visions seemed to be realised on which his mind had dwelt during the day. He found himself in sulphurous realms and burning caverns, surrounded by fiends appointed his tormentors, and who drove him through a variety of tortures, each of which was more dreadful than the former. Amidst these dismal scenes wandered the ghosts of Elvira and her daughter. They reproached him with their deaths, recounted his crimes to the dæmons, and urged them to inflict torments of cruelty yet more refined. Such were the pictures which floated before his eyes in sleep: they vanished not till his repose was disturbed by excess of agony. Then would he start from the ground on which he had stretched himself, his brows running down with cold sweat, his eyes wild and phrensied; and he only exchanged the terrible certainty for surmises scarcely more supportable. He paced his dungeon with disordered steps; he gazed with terror upon the surrounding darkness, and often did he cry,

"Oh! fearful is night to the guilty!"

The day of his second examination was at hand. He had been compelled to swallow cordials, whose virtues were calculated to restore his bodily strength, and enable him to support the question longer. On the night preceding this dreaded day, his fears for the morrow permitted him not to sleep. His terrors were so violent as nearly to annihilate his mental powers. He sat like one stupefied near the table on which his lamp was burning dimly. Despair chained up his faculties in idiotism, and he remained for some hours unable to speak or move, or indeed to think.

"Look up, Ambrosio!" said a voice in accents well known to him.

The monk started, and raised his melancholy eyes. Matilda stood before him. She had quitted her religious habit. She now wore a female dress, at once elegant and splendid; a profusion of diamonds blazed upon her robes, and her hair was confined by a coronet of roses. In her right hand she held a small book: a lively expression of pleasure beamed upon her countenance—but still it was mingled with a wild imperious majesty, which inspired the monk with awe, and repressed in some measure his transports at seeing her.

"You here, Matilda?" he at length exclaimed: "How have you gained entrance? Where are your chains? What means this magnificence, and the joy which sparkles in your eyes? Have our judges relented? Is there a chance of my escaping? Answer me for pity, and tell me what I have to hope or fear."

"Ambrosio!" she replied with an air of commanding dignity: "I have baffled the Inquisition's fury. I am free: a few moments will place kingdoms between these dungeons and me; yet I purchase my liberty at a dear, at a dreadful price! Dare you pay the same, Ambrosio? Dare you spring without fear over the bounds which separate men from angels?—You are silent—You look upon me with eyes of suspicion and alarm—I read your thoughts, and confess their justice. Yes, Ambrosio, I have sacrificed all for life and liberty. I am no longer a candidate for Heaven! I have renounced God's service, and am enlisted beneath the banners of his foes. The deed is past recall; yet, were it in my power to go back, I would not. Oh! my friend, to expire in such torments! to die amidst curses and execrations! to bear the insults of an exasperated mob! to be exposed to all the mortifications of shame and infamy! who can reflect without horror on such a doom? Let me then exult in my exchange. I have sold distant and uncertain happiness for present and secure. I have preserved a life, which otherwise I had lost in torture; and I have obtained the power of procuring every bliss which can make that life delicious! The infernal spirits obey me as their sovereign; by their aid shall my days be passed in every refinement of luxury and voluptuousness. I will enjoy unrestrained the gratification of my senses; every passion shall be indulged even to satiety; then will I bid my servants invent new pleasures, to revive and stimulate my glutted appetites![1] I go impatient to exercise my newly-gained dominion. I pant to be at liberty. Nothing should hold me one moment longer in this abhorred abode, but the hope of persuading you to follow my example. Ambrosio, I still love you: our mutual guilt and danger have rendered you dearer to me than ever, and I would fain save you from impending destruction. Summon then your resolution to your aid, and renounce for immediate and certain benefits the hopes of a salvation difficult to obtain, and perhaps altogether erroneous. Shake off the prejudice of vulgar souls; abandon a God who has abandoned you, and raise yourself to the level of superior beings!"

She paused for the monk's reply: he shuddered while he gave it.

"Matilda!" he said, after a long silence, in a low and unsteady voice: "What price gave you for liberty?"

She answered him firm and dauntless.

"Ambrosio, it was my soul!"

"Wretched woman, what have you done! Pass but a few years, and how dreadful will be your sufferings!"

---

1   According to Cicero (*Tusculan Disputations* 5.7) and Montaigne ("Of Experience"), the Persian emperor Xerxes I offered a reward to anyone who could discover a new pleasure.

"Weak man, pass but this night, and how dreadful will be your own! Do you remember what you have already endured? To-morrow you must bear torments doubly exquisite. Do you remember the horrors of a fiery punishment? In two days you must be led a victim to the stake! What then will become of you? Still dare you hope for pardon? Still are you beguiled with visions of salvation? Think upon your crimes! Think upon your lust, your perjury, inhumanity, and hypocrisy! Think upon the innocent blood which cries to the throne of God for vengeance! and then hope for mercy! Then dream of heaven, and sigh for worlds of light, and realms of peace and pleasure! Absurd! Open your eyes, Ambrosio, and be prudent. Hell is your lot; you are doomed to eternal perdition; nought lies beyond your grave, but a gulph of devouring flames. And will you then speed towards that hell? Will you clasp that perdition in your arms ere 'tis needful? Will you plunge into those flames while you still have the power to shun them? 'Tis a madman's action. No, no, Ambrosio, let us for a while fly from divine vengeance. Be advised by me, purchase by one moment's courage the bliss of years; enjoy the present, and forget that a future lags behind."

"Matilda, your counsels are dangerous; I dare not, I will not follow them. I must not give up my claim to salvation. Monstrous are my crimes; but God is merciful, and I will not despair of pardon."

"Is such your resolution? I have no more to say. I speed to joy and liberty, and abandon you to death and eternal torments!"

"Yet stay one moment, Matilda! You command the infernal dæmons; you can force open these prison doors; you can release me from these chains which weigh me down. Save me, I conjure you, and bear me from these fearful abodes!"

"You ask the only boon beyond my power to bestow. I am forbidden to assist a churchman and a partisan of God. Renounce those titles, and command me."

"I will not sell my soul to perdition."

"Persist in your obstinacy till you find yourself at the stake: then will you repent your error, and sigh for escape when the moment is gone by. I quit you.——Yet ere the hour of death arrives, should wisdom enlighten you, listen to the means of repairing your present fault. I leave with you this book. Read the four first lines of the 7th page backwards. The spirit, whom you have already once beheld, will immediately appear to you. If you are wise, we shall meet again; if not, farewell for ever!"

She let the book fall upon the ground. A cloud of blue fire wrapped itself round her. She waved her hand to Ambrosio, and disappeared. The momentary glare which the flames poured through the dungeon, on dissipating suddenly, seemed to have increased its natural gloom. The solitary lamp scarcely gave light sufficient to guide the monk to a chair. He threw himself into his seat, folded his arms, and, leaning his head upon the table, sank into reflections perplexing and unconnected.

He was still in this attitude, when the opening of the prison door roused him from his stupor. He was summoned to appear before the Grand Inquisitor. He rose, and followed his gaoler with painful steps. He was led into the same hall, placed before the same examiners, and was again interrogated whether he would confess. He replied as before, that, having no crimes, he could acknowledge none. But when the executioners prepared to put him to the question, when he saw the engines of torture, and remembered the pangs which they had already inflicted, his resolution failed him entirely. Forgetting the consequences, and only anxious to escape the terrors of the present moment, he made an ample confession. He disclosed every circumstance of his guilt, and owned not merely the crimes with which he was charged, but those of which he had never been suspected. Being interrogated as to Matilda's flight, which had created much confusion; he confessed that she had sold herself to Satan, and that she was indebted to sorcery for her escape. He still assured his judges, that for his own part he had never entered into any compact with the infernal spirits; but the threat of being tortured made him declare himself to be a sorcerer and heretic, and whatever other title the inquisitors chose to fix upon him. In consequence of this avowal, his sentence was immediately pronounced. He was ordered to prepare himself to perish in the Auto da Fé, which was to be solemnized at twelve o'clock that night. This hour was chosen, from the idea, that, the horror of the flames being heightened by the gloom of midnight, the execution would have a greater effect upon the mind of the people.

Ambrosio, rather dead than alive, was left alone in his dungeon. The moment in which this terrible decree was pronounced, had nearly proved that of his dissolution. He looked forward to the morrow with despair, and his terrors increased with the approach of midnight. Sometimes he was buried in gloomy silence; at others, he raved with delirious passion, wrung his hands, and cursed the hour when he first beheld the light. In one of these moments his eye rested upon Matilda's mysterious gift. His transports of rage were instantly suspended. He looked earnestly at the book; he took it up, but immediately threw it from him with horror. He walked rapidly up and down his dungeon—then stopped, and again fixed his eyes on the spot where the book had fallen. He reflected, that here at least was a resource from the fate which he dreaded. He stooped, and took it up a second time. He remained for some time trembling and irresolute; he longed to try the charm, yet feared its consequences. The recollection of his sentence at length fixed his indecision. He opened the volume; but his agitation was so great, that he at first sought in vain for the page mentioned by Matilda. Ashamed of himself, he called all his courage to his aid. He turned to the seventh leaf: he began to read it aloud; but his eyes frequently wandered from the book, while he anxiously cast them round in search of the spirit, whom he wished, yet dreaded to behold. Still he persisted in his design; and with a voice unassured, and frequent interruptions, he contrived to finish the four first lines of the page.

They were in a language whose import was totally unknown to him. Scarce had he pronounced the last word, when the effects of the charm were evident. A loud burst of thunder was heard, the prison shook to its very foundations, a blaze of lightning flashed through the cell, and in the next moment, borne upon sulphurous whirlwinds, Lucifer stood before him a second time. But he came not as when at Matilda's summons he borrowed the seraph's form to deceive Ambrosio. He appeared in all that ugliness which since his fall from heaven had been his portion. His blasted limbs still bore marks of the Almighty's thunder. A swarthy darkness spread itself over his gigantic form: his hands and feet were armed with long talons. Fury glared in his eyes, which might have struck the bravest heart with terror. Over his huge shoulders waved two enormous sable wings: and his hair was supplied by living snakes, which twined themselves round his brows with frightful hissings. In one hand he held a roll of parchment, and in the other an iron pen. Still the lightning flashed around him, and the thunder with repeated bursts seemed to announce the dissolution of Nature.

Terrified at an apparition so different from what he had expected, Ambrosio remained gazing upon the fiend, deprived of the power of utterance. The thunder had ceased to roll: universal silence reigned through the dungeon.

"For what am I summoned hither?" said the dæmon, in a voice which *sulphurous fogs had damped to hoarseness.*[1]

At the sound Nature seemed to tremble. A violent earthquake

---

1 Adapted from John Dryden, *King Arthur; or, The British Worthy* 2.1.84–85.

rocked the ground, accompanied by a fresh burst of thunder, louder and more appalling than the first.

Ambrosio was long unable to answer the dæmon's demand.

"I am condemned to die," he said with a faint voice, his blood running cold while he gazed upon his dreadful visitor. "Save me! bear me from hence!"

"Shall the reward of my services be paid me? Dare you embrace my cause? Will you be mine, body and soul? Are you prepared to renounce him who made you, and him who died for you? Answer but 'Yes!' and Lucifer is your slave."

"Will no less price content you? Can nothing satisfy you but my eternal ruin? Spirit, you ask too much. Yet convey me from this dungeon. Be my servant for one hour, and I will be yours for a thousand years. Will not this offer suffice?"

"It will not. I must have your soul: must have it mine, and mine for ever."

"Insatiate dæmon! I will not doom myself to endless torments. I will not give up my hopes of being one day pardoned."

"You will not? On what chimæra rest then your hopes? Short-sighted mortal! Miserable wretch! Are you not guilty? Are you not infamous in the eyes of men and angels? Can such enormous sins be forgiven? Hope you to escape my power? Your fate is already pronounced. The Eternal has abandoned you. Mine you are marked in the book of destiny, and mine you must and shall be."

"Fiend! 'tis false. Infinite is the Almighty's mercy, and the penitent shall meet his forgiveness. My crimes are monstrous, but I will not despair of pardon. Haply, when they have received due chastisement——"

"Chastisement? Was purgatory meant for guilt like yours? Hope you, that your offences shall be bought off by prayers of superstitious dotards and droning monks? Ambrosio! be wise. Mine you must be. You are doomed to flames, but may shun them for the present. Sign this parchment: I will bear you from hence, and you may pass your remaining years in bliss and liberty. Enjoy your existence. Indulge in every pleasure to which appetite may lead you. But from the moment that it quits your body, remember that your soul belongs to me, and that I will not be defrauded of my right."

The monk was silent: but his looks declared that the tempter's words were not thrown away. He reflected on the conditions proposed with horror. On the other hand, he believed himself doomed to perdition, and that, by refusing the dæmon's succour, he only hastened tortures which he never could escape. The fiend saw that his resolution was shaken. He renewed his instances, and endeavoured to fix the abbot's indecision. He described the agonies of death in the most terrific colours; and he worked so powerfully upon Ambrosio's despair and fears, that he prevailed upon him to receive the parchment. He then struck the iron pen which he held into a vein of the monk's left hand. It pierced deep, and was instantly filled with blood: yet Ambrosio felt no pain from the wound. The pen was put into his hand: it trembled. The wretch placed the parchment on the table before him, and prepared to sign it. Suddenly he held his hand: he started away hastily, and threw the pen upon the table.

"What am I doing?" he cried. Then turning to the fiend with a desperate air, "Leave me! begone! I will not sign the parchment."

"Fool!" exclaimed the disappointed dæmon, darting looks so furious as penetrated the friar's soul with horror. "Thus am I trifled with? Go then! Rave in agony, expire in tortures, and then learn the extent of the Eternal's mercy! But beware how you make me again your mock! Call me no more, till resolved to accept my offers. Summon me a second time to dismiss me thus idly, and these talons shall rend you into a thousand pieces. Speak yet again: will you sign the parchment?"

"I will not. Leave me. Away!"

Instantly the thunder was heard to roll horribly: once more the earth trembled with violence: the dungeon resounded with loud shrieks, and the dæmon fled with blasphemy and curses.

At first, the monk rejoiced at having resisted the seducer's arts, and obtained a triumph over mankind's enemy: but as the hour of punishment drew near, his former terrors revived in his heart. Their momentary repose seemed to have given them fresh vigour. The nearer that the time approached, the more did he dread appearing before the throne of God. He shuddered to think how soon he must be plunged into eternity—how soon meet the eyes of his Creator, whom he had so grievously offended. The bell announced midnight. It was the signal for being led to the stake. As he listened to the first stroke, the blood ceased to circulate in the abbot's veins. He heard death and torture murmured in each succeeding sound. He expected to see the archers entering his prison; and as the bell forbore to toll, he seized the magic volume in a fit of despair. He opened it, turned hastily to the seventh page, and, as if fearing to allow himself a moment's thought, ran over the fatal lines with rapidity. Accompanied by his former terrors, Lucifer again stood before the trembler.

"You have summoned me," said the fiend. "Are you determined to be wise? Will you accept my conditions? You know them already.

Renounce your claim to salvation, make over to me your soul, and I bear you from this dungeon instantly. Yet is it time. Resolve, or it will be too late. Will you sign the parchment?"

"I must—Fate urges me—I accept your conditions."

"Sign the parchment," replied the dæmon in an exulting tone.

The contract and the bloody pen still lay upon the table. Ambrosio drew near it. He prepared to sign his name. A moment's reflection made him hesitate.

"Hark!" cried the tempter: "they come. Be quick. Sign the parchment, and I bear you from hence this moment."

In effect, the archers were heard approaching, appointed to lead Ambrosio to the stake. The sound encouraged the monk in his resolution.

"What is the import of this writing?" said he.

"It makes your soul over to me for ever, and without reserve."

"What am I to receive in exchange?"

"My protection, and release from this dungeon. Sign it, and this instant I bear you away."

Ambrosio took up the pen. He set it to the parchment. Again his courage failed him. He felt a pang of terror at his heart, and once more threw the pen upon the table.

"Weak and puerile!" cried the exasperated fiend. "Away with this folly! Sign the writing this instant, or I sacrifice you to my rage."

At this moment the bolt of the outward door was drawn back. The prisoner heard the rattling of chains: the heavy bar fell: the archers were on the point of entering. Worked up to phrensy by the urgent danger, shrinking from the approach of death, terrified by the dæmon's threats, and seeing no other means to escape destruction, the wretched monk complied. He signed the fatal contract, and gave it hastily into the evil spirit's hands, whose eyes, as he received the gift, glared with malicious rapture.[1]

"Take it!" said the God-abandoned. "Now then save me! Snatch me from hence!"

"Hold! Do you freely and absolutely renounce your Creator and his Son?"

"I do! I do!"

"Do you make over your soul to me for ever?"

"For ever!"

---

1. Cf. the pact scenes in Marlowe, *Doctor Faustus* (1.3, 2.1).

"Without reserve or subterfuge? without future appeal to the divine mercy?"

ᐟ The last chain fell from the door of the prison. The key was heard turning in the lock. Already the iron door grated heavily upon its rusty hinges——

"I am yours for ever, and irrevocably!" cried the monk wild with terror: "I abandon all claim to salvation. I own no power but yours. Hark! hark! they come! Oh! save me! bear me away!"

"I have triumphed! You are mine past reprieve, and I fulfil my promise."

While he spoke, the door unclosed. Instantly the dæmon grasped one of Ambrosio's arms, spread his broad pinions, and sprang with him into the air. The roof opened as they soared upwards, and closed again when they had quitted the dungeon.

In the mean while, the gaoler was thrown into the utmost surprise by the disappearance of his prisoner. Though neither he nor the archers were in time to witness the monk's escape, a sulphurous smell prevailing through the prison sufficiently informed them by whose aid he had been liberated. They hastened to make their report to the Grand Inquisitor. The story, how a sorcerer had been carried away by the Devil, was soon noised about Madrid; and for some days the whole city was employed in discussing the subject. Gradually it ceased to be the topic of conversation. Other adventures arose whose novelty engaged universal attention: and Ambrosio was soon forgotten as totally as if he never had existed. While this was passing, the monk, supported by his infernal guide, traversed the air with the rapidity of an arrow; and a few moments placed him upon a precipice's brink, the steepest in Sierra Morena.[1]

Though rescued from the Inquisition, Ambrosio as yet was insensible of the blessings of liberty. The damning contract weighed heavy upon his mind; and the scenes in which he had been a principal actor, had left behind them such impressions as rendered his heart the seat of anarchy and confusion. The objects now before his eyes, and which the full moon sailing through clouds permitted him to examine, were ill calculated to inspire that calm, of which he stood so much in need. The disorder of his imagination was increased by the wildness of the surrounding scenery; by the gloomy caverns and steep rocks, rising above each other, and dividing the passing clouds; solitary clusters of trees scattered here and there, among whose thick-twined branches

---

1 A mountain range in Andalusia.

the wind of night sighed hoarsely and mournfully; the shrill cry of mountain eagles, who had built their nests among these lonely deserts; the stunning roar of torrents, as swelled by late rains they rushed violently down tremendous precipices; and the dark waters of a silent sluggish stream, which faintly reflected the moon-beams, and bathed the rock's base on which Ambrosio stood. The abbot cast round him a look of terror. His infernal conductor was still by his side, and eyed him with a look of mingled malice, exultation, and contempt.

"Whither have you brought me?" said the monk at length in an hollow trembling voice: "Why am I placed in this melancholy scene? Bear me from it quickly! Carry me to Matilda!"

The fiend replied not, but continued to gaze upon him in silence. Ambrosio could not sustain his glance; he turned away his eyes, while thus spoke the dæmon:

"I have him then in my power! This model of piety! this being without reproach! this mortal who placed his puny virtues on a level with those of angels. He is mine! irrevocably, eternally mine! Companions of my sufferings! denizens of hell! How grateful will be my present!"

He paused; then addressed himself to the monk——

"Carry you to Matilda?" he continued, repeating Ambrosio's words: "Wretch! you shall soon be with her! You well deserve a place near her, for hell boasts no miscreant more guilty than yourself. Hark, Ambrosio, while I unveil your crimes! You have shed the blood of two innocents; Antonia and Elvira perished by your hand. That Antonia whom you violated, was your sister! that Elvira whom you murdered, gave you birth! Tremble, abandoned hypocrite! inhuman parricide! incestuous ravisher! tremble at the extent of your offences! And you it was who thought yourself proof against temptation, absolved from human frailties, and free from error and vice! Is pride then a virtue? Is inhumanity no fault? Know, vain man! that I long have marked you for my prey: I watched the movements of your heart; I saw that you were virtuous from vanity, not principle, and I seized the fit moment of seduction. I observed your blind idolatry of the Madona's picture. I bade a subordinate but crafty spirit assume a similar form, and you eagerly yielded to the blandishments of Matilda. Your pride was gratified by her flattery; your lust only needed an opportunity to break forth; you ran into the snare blindly, and scrupled not to commit a crime, which you blamed in another with unfeeling severity. It was I who threw Matilda in your way; it was I who gave you entrance to Antonia's chamber; it was I who caused the dagger to be given you which pierced your sister's bosom; and it was I who warned Elvira in dreams of your designs upon her daughter, and thus, by preventing your profiting by her sleep, compelled you to add rape as well as incest to the catalogue of your crimes. Hear, hear, Ambrosio! Had you resisted me one minute longer, you had saved your body and soul. The guards whom you heard at your prison-door, came to signify your pardon. But I had already triumphed: my plots had already succeeded. Scarcely could I propose crimes so quick as you performed them. You are mine, and Heaven itself cannot rescue you from my power. Hope not that your penitence will make void our contract. Here is your bond signed with your blood; you have given up your claim to mercy, and nothing can restore to you the rights which you have foolishly resigned. Believe you, that your secret thoughts escaped me? No, no, I read them all! You trusted that you should still have time for repentance. I saw your artifice, knew its falsity, and rejoiced in deceiving the deceiver! You are mine beyond reprieve: I burn to possess my right, and alive you quit not these mountains."

During the dæmon's speech, Ambrosio had been stupefied by terror and surprise. This last declaration roused him.

"Not quit these mountains alive?" he exclaimed: "Perfidious, what mean you? Have you forgotten our contract?"

The fiend answered by a malicious laugh:

"Our contract? Have I not performed my part? What more did I promise than to save you from your prison? Have I not done so? Are you not safe from the Inquisition—safe from all but from me? Fool that you were to confide yourself to a devil! Why did you not stipulate for life, and power, and pleasure? Then all would have been granted: now, your reflections come too late. Miscreant, prepare for death; you have not many hours to live!"

On hearing this sentence, dreadful were the feelings of the devoted wretch! He sank upon his knees, and raised his hands towards heaven. The fiend read his intention, and prevented it——

"What?" he cried, darting at him a look of fury: "Dare you still implore the Eternal's mercy? Would you feign penitence, and again act an hypocrite's part? Villain, resign your hopes of pardon. Thus I secure my prey!"

As he said this, darting his talons into the monk's shaven crown, he sprang with him from the rock. The caves and mountains rang with Ambrosio's shrieks. The dæmon continued to soar aloft, till reaching a dreadful height, he released the sufferer. Headlong fell the monk through the airy waste; the sharp point of a rock received him; and he rolled from precipice to precipice, till, bruised and mangled, he rested on the river's banks. Life still existed in his miserable frame: he attempted in vain to raise himself; his broken and dislocated limbs refused to perform their office, nor was he able to quit the spot where he had first fallen. The sun now rose above the horizon; its scorching beams darted full upon the head of the expiring sinner. Myriads of insects were called forth by the warmth; they drank the blood which trickled from Ambrosio's wounds; he had no power to drive them from him, and they fastened upon his sores, darted their stings into his body, covered him with their multitudes, and inflicted on him tortures the most exquisite and insupportable. The eagles of the rock tore his flesh piecemeal, and dug out his eye-balls with their crooked beaks. A burning thirst tormented him; he heard the river's murmur as it rolled beside him, but strove in vain to drag himself towards the sound. Blind, maimed, helpless, and despairing, venting his rage in blasphemy and curses, execrating his existence, yet dreading the arrival of death destined to yield him up to greater torments, six miserable days did the villain languish. On the seventh a violent storm arose: the winds in fury rent up rocks and forests: the sky was now black with clouds, now sheeted with fire: the rain fell in torrents; it swelled the stream; the waves overflowed their banks; they reached the spot where Ambrosio lay, and, when they abated, carried with them into the river the corse of the despairing monk.[1]

FINIS.

---

1 The fate of Ambrosio is based on "Die Teufelsbeschwörung" ("The Exorcism," 1791), by Veit Weber, and possibly Dante, *Purgatorio* 5.112-29. It also recalls the punishments of both Oedipus and Prometheus.

Appendix A: Literary Sources

[Lewis based the main plot of his novel on an Oriental tale published by Sir Richard Steele in *The Guardian* (A.1). Lorenzo's prophetic dream (54.55) and its fulfillment in the rape and murder of Antonia (317-28) are based on two dreams in Samuel Richardson's *Clarissa* (A.2). The subplot is based on a folktale also published in Johann Karl August Musäus's *Volksmärchen der Deutschen* (A.3), and the most remarkable character in it is based on "Der ewige Jude," by Christian Friedrich Daniel Schubart (A.4). Theodore's poem, "Love and Age" (182-85) is based on a poem attributed to Anacreon, which Lewis had translated as a schoolboy (A.5). See Introduction 10-15.]

1. Richard Steele, *The Guardian* 148 (Monday 31 August 1713; quoted by permission of the University of Kentucky Press)

The History of Santon Barsisa.

THERE was formerly a *Santon*[1] whose Name was *Barsisa*, which for the Space of an hundred Years very fervently apply'd himself to Prayer; and scarce ever went out of the Grotto in which he made his Residence, for fear of exposing himself to the Danger of offending God. He fasted in the Day-time, and watch'd in the Night; all the Inhabitants of the Country had such a great Veneration for him, and so highly valu'd his Prayers, that they commonly apply'd to him when they had any Favour to beg of Heaven. When he made Vows for the Health of a sick Person, the Patient was immediately cur'd.

It happen'd that the Daughter of the King of that Country fell into a dangerous Distemper, the Cause of which the Physicians could not discover, yet they continu'd prescribing Remedies by guess; but instead of helping the Princess, they only augmented her Disease. In the mean time the King was inconsolable, for he passionately lov'd his Daughter; wherefore one day, finding all Human Assistance vain, he declar'd it as his Opinion, that the Princess ought to be sent to the *Santon Barsisa*.

---

1 "A European designation for a kind of monk or hermit among the Muslims" (*OED*).

All the *Beys* applauded his Sentiment, and the King's Officers conducted her to the *Santon*; who, notwithstanding his frozen Age, could not see such a Beauty without being sensibly mov'd. He gaz'd on her with Pleasure; and the Devil, taking this Opportunity, whisper'd in his Ear thus; O Santon! *don't let slip such a fortunate Minute: Tell the King's Servants that it is requisite for the Princess to pass this Night in the Grotto, to see whether it will please God to cure her; that you will put up a Prayer for her, and that they need only come to fetch her to Morrow.*

How weak is Man! The *Santon* followed the Devil's Advice, and did what he suggested to him. But the Officers, before they would yield to leave the Princess, sent one of their Number to know the King's Pleasure. That Monarch, who had an entire Confidence in *Barsisa*, never in the least scrupled the trusting of his Daughter with him. *I consent*, said he, *that she stay with that Holy Man, and that he keep her as long as he pleases: I am wholly satisfy'd on that Head.*

When the Officers had receiv'd the King's Answer they all retired, and the Princess remain'd alone with the Hermit. Night being come, the Devil presented himself to the *Santon*, saying, *Canst thou let slip so favourable an Opportunity with so charming a Creature? Fear not her telling of the Violence you offer her; if she were even so indiscreet as to reveal it, who will believe her? The Court, the City, and all the World are too much prepossessed in your Favour, to give any Credit to such a Report. You may do any thing unpunish'd, when arm'd by the great Reputation for Wisdom which you have acquir'd.* The unfortunate *Barsisa* was so weak as to hearken to the Enemy of Mankind. He approach'd the Princess, took her into his Arms, and in a Moment cancell'd a Virtue of an hundred Years Duration.

He had no sooner perpetrated his Crime, than a thousand avenging Horrors haunted him Night and Day. He thus accosts the Devil: *O Wretch!* says he, *'tis thou which hast destroy'd me! Thou hast encompass'd me for a whole Age, and endeavour'd to seduce me; and now at last thou hast gain'd thy End.* O Santon! answer'd the Devil, *don't reproach me with the Pleasure thou hast enjoy'd. Thou mayest repent: But what is unhappy for Thee is that the Princess is impregnated, and thy Sin will become publick: thou wilt become the Laughing stock of those who admire and reverence thee at present, and the King will put thee to an ignominious Death.*

Barsisa, terrify'd by this Discourse, says to the Devil, *What shall I do to prevent the Publication of my Shame? To hinder the Knowledge of your Crime you ought to commit a fresh one*, answer'd the Devil: *Kill the Princess, bury her at the Corner of the Grotto, and when the King's Messengers come to Morrow, tell them you have cur'd her, and that she went from the Grotto very early in the Morning: They will believe you, and search for her all over the City and Country; the King her Father will be in great Pain for her, but after several vain Searches it will wear off.*

The Hermit, abandon'd by God, pursuant to this Advice kill'd the Princess, bury'd her in a Corner of the Grotto, and the next Day told the Officers what the Devil bid him say. They made diligent Enquiry for the King's Daughter, but not being able to hear of her, they despair'd of finding her, when the Devil told them that all their Search for the Princess was vain; and relating what had pass'd betwixt her and the *Santon*, he told them the Place where she was interred. The Officers immediately went to the Grotto, seiz'd *Barsisa*, and found the Princess's Body in the Place to which the Devil had directed them; whereupon they took up the Corps, and carry'd that and the *Santon* to the Palace.

When the King saw his Daughter dead, and was inform'd of the whole Event, he broke out into Tears and bitter Lamentations; and assembling the Doctors, he laid the *Santon's* Crime before them, and ask'd their Advice how he should be punish'd. All the Doctors condemn'd him to Death, upon which the King order'd him to be hang'd: Accordingly a Gibbet was erected: the Hermit went up the Ladder, and when he was going to be turn'd off, the Devil whisper'd in his Ear these Words; *O Santon! if you will worship me I will extricate you out of this Difficulty, and transport you two thousand Leagues from hence, into a Country where you shall be reverenc'd by Men, as much as you were before this Adventure. I am content*, says *Barsisa; deliver me, and I will worship thee. Give me first a Sign of Adoration*, replies the Devil; whereupon the *Santon* bow'd his Head, and said, *I give my self to you.* The Devil then raising his Voice, said, *O Barsisa, I am satisfy'd; I have obtain'd what I desir'd:* And with these Words spitting in his Face, he disappeared; and the deluded *Santon* was hang'd.

2. Samuel Richardson, *Clarissa; or, The History of a Young Lady* (1747–48; quoted by permission of Penguin Books)

a. Lovelace's Dream

I MUST write on to divert myself: for I can get no rest; no refreshing rest. I awaked just now in a cursed fright. How a man may be affected by dreams!

"Methought I had an interview with my beloved. I found her all goodness, condescension, and forgiveness. She suffered herself to be overcome in my favour by the joint intercessions of Lord M., Lady Sarah, Lady Betty, and my two cousins Montague,[1] who waited upon her in deep mourning; the ladies in long trains sweeping after them; Lord M. in a long black mantle trailing after *him*. They told her they came in these robes to express their sorrow for my sins against her, and to implore her to forgive me.

"I myself, I thought, was upon my knees and with a sword in my hand, offering either to put it up in the scabbard, or to thrust it into my heart, as she should command the one or the other.

"At that moment her cousin Morden, I thought, all of a sudden flashed in through a window, with his drawn sword—Die, Lovelace, said he! this instant die, and be damned, if in earnest thou repairest not by marriage my cousin's wrongs!

"I was rising to resent this insult, I thought, when Lord M. run between us with his great black mantle, and threw it over my face: and instantly, my charmer, with that sweet voice which has so often played upon my ravished ears, wrapped her arms round me, muffled as I was in my Lord M.'s mantle: Oh spare, spare my Lovelace! And spare, Oh Lovelace, my beloved cousin Morden! Let me not have my distresses augmented by the fall of either or both of those who are so dear to me.

"At this, charmed with her sweet mediation, I thought I would have clasped her in my arms: when immediately the most angelic form I had ever beheld, vested all in transparent white, descended from a ceiling, which, opening, discovered a ceiling above that, stuck round with golden cherubs and glittering seraphs, all exulting: Welcome, welcome, welcome! and, encircling my charmer, ascended with her to the region of seraphims; and instantly, the opening ceiling closing, I lost sight of *her*, and of the *bright form* together, and found wrapped in my arms her azure robe (all stuck thick with stars of embossed silver), which I had caught hold of in hopes of detaining her; but was all that was left me of my beloved Miss Harlowe. And then (horrid to relate!) the floor sinking under *me*, as the ceiling had opened for *her*, I dropped into a hole more frightful than that of Elden[2] and tumbling over and over down it, without view of a bottom, I awaked in a panic; and was as effectually disordered for half an hour, as if my dream had been a reality."

Wilt thou forgive me troubling thee with such visionary stuff? Thou wilt see by it only that, sleeping or waking, my Clarissa is always present with me. (1218)

---

1 Lovelace's relations.

2 A pot-hole in the Peak District in Derbyshire.

b. Clarissa's Dream

I said I had unhappily overslept myself. I went to bed at about half
an hour after two. I told the quarters till five; after which I dropped
asleep and awaked not till past six, and then in great terror from a
dream which has made such an impression upon me, that, slightly
as I think of dreams, I cannot help taking this opportunity to relate
it to you.

"Methought my brother, my uncle Antony, and Mr Solmes had
formed a plot to destroy Mr Lovelace; who discovering it turned all
his rage against me, believing I had a hand in it. I thought he made
them all fly into foreign parts upon it; and afterwards seizing upon
me, carried me into a churchyard; and there, notwithstanding all my
prayers and tears, and protestations of innocence, stabbed me to the
heart, and then tumbled me into a deep grave ready dug, among
two or three half-dissolved carcases; throwing in the dirt and earth
upon me with his hands, and trampling it down with his feet."

I awoke with the terror, all in a cold sweat, trembling, and in agonies; and still the frightful images raised by it remain upon my
memory. (342-43)

3. Johann Karl August Musäus, "The Elopement" (1782–86); translated by Miss Corbett and Miss M. Corbett

ON the banks of the rivulet Lockwitz, in Hungary, and upon the
borders of Thuringia, where a convent formerly stood, which was
destroyed in the time of the Hussites,[1] is situated the Castle of
Lauenstein. This church property, in process of time, came under
the secular arm, and became the possession of the Count of Orla-
munda, who gave this deserted domain as a feu[2] to one of his vas-
sals, who, upon the ruins of the convent, built himself a castle, and
either gave his name to the property, or took his from it, for he was
called the Baron of Lauenstein.

It soon became manifest that the property of the church does
not prosper in the hands of the laity, and that such sacrilege is

---

1 Followers of Jan Hus, the Bohemian religious reformer burned at the
stake in 1415. Among their goals was the expropriation of church
properties.
2 "A feudal tenure of land in which the vassal, in place of military service,
makes a return of grain or money" (OED).

always punished in one way or another. The bones of the holy nuns, which for ages had reposed in peace in the gloomy caverns of the grave, could not, with indifference, endure this profanation of their sanctuary. These mouldy dead bones rebelled against the violation, rattled and rustled in the silence of night, and raised a fearful clattering and noise in the passage leading to the church, which had not been destroyed. The nuns, with solemn pomp, often made a procession round the Castle, wandered through the apartments, opened and dashed to the doors, by which the Baron was disturbed in his sleep, and could not get rest in his bed. They raged in the hall, or in the stables, terrified the maids, twitched and pinched them, sometimes here, sometimes there;—plagued the cattle—the cows were drained of their milk, and the horses pranced and snorted, and beat their stalls to pieces. This mischievous behaviour of the pious sisters, and their incessant tricks, which embittered the life of both man and beast, took away all spirit from every member of the household, down to the very bull-dog.

The Baron spared no expense, by means of the most renowned exorcists, to bring these tumultuary inmates to peace and silence; but the most powerful exorcisms, before which the whole kingdom of Belial trembled, and the sprinkling brush dipped in holy water, which generally chases away the evil spirits, as a fly-flap chases away the flies from the apartment, for a long time could do nothing against the obstinacy of those spectre Amazons, who so stoutly maintained their right to their former possessions, that the exorcists, with the holy implements of relics, were sometimes obliged to take to flight, and leave them masters of the field. At last, a conjuror, who was travelling about the country for the purpose of spying out witches, catching goblins, and delivering the possessed from the brood of evil spirits, succeeded in bringing the spectral night revellers to obedience, and again shut them up in their gloomy vaults, with permission there to wag their skulls, and rattle and clatter their bones, as much as they pleased.

All was now quiet in the Castle, the nuns again slept the still sleep of death; but after seven years, one unquiet sister spirit again awoke, and once more made her appearance in the night, and for some time continued her former pranks, until she tired, then rested seven years, and then paid another visit to the upper world, and re-visited the Castle. In time the family became accustomed to the apparition; only, when the period of her appearance approached, the domestics took care to avoid the passage through which she was to come, and kept close to their apartments.

After the decease of the first possessors, the inheritance fell to the next in descent, and there never had failed a male heir, until the time of the thirty years' war,[1] when the last branch of the Lauensteins flourished, in whose production nature appeared to have exhausted her power. So lavish had she been of the stuff which composed his body, that at the period when it had reached its highest perfection, so enormous was his size, that he weighed nearly as much as the far-famed Franz Finatzie of Presburg, and his corpulence was only a few inches less than that of the well fed Holstener, known by the name of Paul Butterbread, who formerly exhibited himself as a show to Parisian belles. However, Baron Siegmund was a very stately man till this period, when his body resembled a tun; he lived well, and though he did not waste the inheritance of his fathers, he spared himself none of the enjoyments of life. No sooner had his progenitors made way for him, and he found himself in possession of Lauenstein, than, after the manner of his fathers, he married, and at the end of a year he became a father; but, alas! it was of a girl, and as he had no hopes of succeeding children, with this he was forced to be content. The thrifty mother, who at her marriage took charge of the domestic concerns, now commenced the education of her daughter. The more papa's paunch gained the upper hand, the more obtuse became his mind, till at length the Baron took no notice of any thing, except what was either roasted or boiled.

From the accumulation of family affairs, Fraulein Emily was, for the most part, left to the care of mother Nature, and thereby found herself never the worse. This secret artist, who does not like to put her reputation at stake, and generally makes up by a master-stroke, for any error she commits, had better proportioned the body and talents of the daughter than those of the father—she was beautiful, clever, and witty. As the charms of the young Fraulein expanded, the views of the mother increased, and she resolved, that through her the splendour of their expiring race should again be restored. The lady possessed a secret pride which was not remarked in the common occurrences of life, except in regard to her pedigree, which she considered the most glorious ornament of their house; and so high were her pretensions, that, except the family of the Counts of Reiuss, there was no race in Hungary sufficiently ancient and noble, into which she would choose to transplant the last blossom of the Lauenstein stem. And much as the young gentlemen in the neighbourhood wished to secure the rich prize, the crafty mother always contrived to frustrate

1 A largely religious war, fought mostly in Germany, 1618-48.

their intentions. She watched the heart of the Fraulein with as much care as a customhouse officer does the harbour, lest any contraband goods should slip through; overturned every speculation of match-making aunts and cousins; and had such high expectations for her daughter, that no young man ventured to approach her. As long as the heart of a maiden listens to advice, it resembles a boat upon the calm unruffled sea, which sails wherever the rudder directs it; but when the winds and waves arise and rock the light bark, it no longer obeys the helm, but follows the current of the stream.

So it was with the tractable Emily, who willingly allowed herself to be led on the path of pride by the maternal leading-strings, for her still unsophisticated heart was susceptible of every impression. She at least expected a Prince or a Count to do homage to her charms; and any less high born paladins who paid their court to her, were repulsed with cold disdain. But before a suitable adorer could be found for the Lauenstein Grace, a circumstance occurred which disappointed all the matrimonial schemes of the mother; and such were its effects, that, had all the princes and counts of the Roman and German empire sued for the heart and hand of the fair Fraulein, they would have found themselves too late.

In the troubled times of the thirty years' war, the army of the brave Wallenstein[1] came into Hungary for winter quarters, and Baron Siegmund received many uninvited guests into the castle, who did more mischief than the former hobgoblins; for, although they had even less right to the property than the former, no sor-cerer could exorcise them away. The proprietor saw himself forced to put a good face on this wicked game, for the purpose of keep-ing these commanding gentlemen in good humour, and so induce them to keep up proper discipline in the castle. Banquets and balls succeeded each other without intermission; at the first the lady presided, at the latter the daughter. And whenever the military band began to play the accompanying favourite waltz, it was the signal for the gallant Fritz to lead the fair Emily to the dance. These splendid feasts made the rough warriors more pliant; they respect-ed the house which had so hospitably entertained them, and guests and host were satisfied with each other.

Among these warriors there were many young heroes, who

---

1 Albrecht Wallenstein (1583-1634) was general of the armies of the Holy Roman Emperor, Ferdinand II, during the Thirty Years' War (1618-48). He is the subject of a dramatic trilogy by Schiller, two thirds of which was later translated by Coleridge.

might even have tempted limping Vulcan's beautiful helpmate[1] to become unfaithful. But there was one in particular who eclipsed them all. A young officer, called the handsome Fritz, had the appearance of a helmed god of love. To an elegant figure, this young Apollo joined the most engaging manners; he was gentle, modest, agreeable, of a lively disposition, and, above all, a charming dancer. Until this moment no one had made the slightest impression on the heart of Emily, but this youth raised in her innocent bosom a new sensation, which filled her soul with inexpressible delight. But the wonder was, that this enchanting Adonis was neither called the handsome Count, nor the handsome Prince, but neither more nor less than the handsome Fritz. She interrogated his brother officers, one after another, about the young man's name and descent, but no one could enlighten her upon the subject. All praised the handsome Fritz as a brave man, and a good officer, and who possessed the most amiable character, but at the same time it appeared that all was not right in regard to his pedigree. There were as many reports of his birth as of that of the well known and enigmatical Count Cagliostro, who was sometimes said to be the descendant of the Grand Master of Malta, and by the maternal side, nephew to the Grand Seignior; sometimes the son of a Neapolitan coachman, then a full brother of Zannowichs, pretended Prince of Albania, and by profession a worker of miracles; and then it was rumoured that he was a wig-maker. All these reports arose from the handsome Fritz having raised himself from the pike to the sash,[2] and all agreed, that, should fortune again favour him, he would reach the highest situations in the army. The secret inquiries of the inquisitive Emily were not long concealed from the object of them. His companions thought to flatter him with the intelligence, and generally accompanied it with all sorts of favourable conjectures. His modesty attributed her advances to jest and mockery; nevertheless, the inquiries of the young damsel pleased him well, for the first look had inspired him with an ecstasy, which is the usual harbinger of love.

No language possesses such energy, and is likewise so well understood, as the sweet feeling of sympathy; through the operation of which, a first acquaintance sooner rises into love than one can rise from the pike to the sash.

---

1 Venus was the consort of Vulcan, the lame artificer god. She committed adultery with Mars, god of war.
2 The pike is a foot soldier's weapon; the sash is an officer's badge: Fritz has been promoted from the ranks.

Some time elapsed before the lovers came to a verbal explanation, but they were aware of each other's sentiments, their looks met half-way, and said what timid love dared not disclose. From the uproar in the house, the negligent mother had, at a very wrong season, removed the watch over the heart of her beloved daughter; and seeing this important post unoccupied, the crafty smuggler Love seized his opportunity, and secretly stole in. No sooner had he obtained possession than he taught the Fraulein quite a different lesson from mamma. The sworn enemy of all ceremony, he immediately removed the prejudices of his obedient scholar, and soon taught her to think, that birth and rank were not to be put in competition with all-conquering Love, and that lovers should not be classed like beetles and worms in a collection of insects.

The frosty pride of ancestry melted as quickly in her soul as the figures upon a frozen window dissolve when the rays of the sun begin to warm the atmosphere; till at length Emily cared not whether her lover had pedigree or not, and she even carried her political heresy so far as to maintain, that the prerogatives of high birth, in comparison with love, were the most insufferable yoke with which the freedom of mankind had ever been burdened.

The handsome Fritz, who adored the Fraulein, with joy perceived that his fortune in love was as propitious as his fortune in war. He seized the first opportunity which offered of disclosing the situation of his heart. She received his declaration with blushes, but with inward delight, and the lovers exchanged vows of inviolable fidelity. They enjoyed the present moment, but shuddered at the future. The return of spring again called the army into tents, and the sorrowful moment approached which was to separate the lovers. They now held a serious consultation on ratifying their vows of love, so as that nothing but death could part them. The Fraulein acquainted her lover with the sentiments of her mother on the subject of marriage; and that it was not to be expected that the proud lady would deviate one hair's-breadth from her darling system, to sanction a union of affection.

A hundred plans were adopted and rejected, for with each there was always some difficulty in the way which rendered its success doubtful. Meanwhile the young hero found his betrothed determined to take any course which would accomplish their wishes; upon which he proposed an elopement, as the surest way which love had yet thought of, which has succeeded innumerable times, and which will succeed in destroying the plans of parents, and in vanquishing their obstinacy. Emily considered for a little, and then consented; one thing was still to be considered, how she would escape from the walls and bulwarks of the castle, to throw herself into the arms of the welcome robber; for well she knew the moment that the Wallenstein garrison marched out of the castle, the vigilant mother would again take possession of her post, and her steps would be so watched she would never be allowed to go out of her sight. But inventive Love conquers every difficulty. It was well known to the Fraulein, that, according to tradition, on All-souls Day, in the approaching autumn, the Spectre Nun, after a lapse of seven years, would again revisit the castle. The terror of the inmates at the expectation of her appearance was also well known to her; she therefore determined upon the bold freak of playing the nun's part. Accordingly she secretly prepared a nun's dress, and under this disguise resolved to elope.

The handsome Fritz was delighted with this invention, and although the time of the thirty years' war was too early for free-thinking, yet the young officer was enough of a philosopher to doubt the existence of spirits, or at least to trouble himself very little about the matter.

Their plans being thus arranged, Fritz threw himself into his saddle, and commending himself to the protection of Love, departed at the head of his squadron. It appeared that Love had heard his prayer, for although he exposed himself to all dangers, the campaign terminated most prosperously, and he escaped unhurt. Meanwhile Emily lived between hope and fear; she trembled for the life of her faithful Amadis—she sought diligently to obtain intelligence how it went with them in the field. Every new rumour of a skirmish put her in terror and anxiety, which her mother took for the sign of a feeling heart, without its creating any suspicion. The hero let no opportunity slip of privately corresponding with his beloved, and through the channel of a trusty waiting-maid, he from time to time gave her intelligence of his fate, and through the same messenger received accounts from her. As soon as the campaign was ended, he prepared everything for his secret expedition, bought four steeds and a travelling carriage, and looked carefully in the Calendar for the day on which he was to be at the appointed place of meeting, in the little grove not far from the castle. On All-souls Day Emily, with the assistance of her attendant, prepared to carry her plan into execution. As had been agreed upon, she feigned herself a little indisposed, and retired early to her apartment, where she immediately transformed herself into the prettiest hobgoblin that had ever haunted the earth. The evening hours, by Emily's calculation, seemed to have doubled themselves, and as she thought of the work she had in hand, every moment increased her wish to accomplish her adventure. Meanwhile the pale Luna, the secret friend of lovers, with her soft glimmer, shone on the castle of

Lauenstein, in which the tumult of the busy day was by degrees lost in the solemn stillness of the night. None were awake in the castle but the housekeeper, who sat late in the night calculating the expenses of the kitchen—the capon-stuffer, who was plucking for the breakfast of the household a score of larks—the porter, who had also the office of watchman, and called out the hours, and Hector, the vigilant house-dog, which with his howls bayed the rising moon.

As the midnight hour sounded, the intrepid Emily set out upon her way. She had provided herself with a master-key which opened all the doors. Softly and secretly she descended the steps that led through the cloister, in crossing which she observed there was still a light in the kitchen. Upon this she rattled her bunch of keys with all her might, dashed to the doors with a deafening noise, and boldly opened the house-door and the wicket without accident. As soon as the four waking inmates of the castle heard this unusual noise, they looked for the appearance of the roving Nun. The capon-stuffer, ter-rified, fled into a closet; the housekeeper into bed; the watch-dog into his kennel; and the porter into the straw beside his wife. The Fraulein soon arrived in the open field, and hastened to the grove, where she thought she saw at a distance the carriage and fleet horses waiting her appearance. But on a nearer approach she discovered it was only the deceitful shadow of a tree. From this she concluded she had mistak-en the place of appointment. She crossed and recrossed the shrubbery from one end to another, but her knight, with his equipage, was nowhere to be found. Astonished at this circumstance, she knew not what to think. After an appointed rendezvous, not to appear, is con-sidered among lovers a high misdemeanour; but in the present case to fail, was little less than high-treason against Love; the thing was to her incomprehensible. After having waited, but in vain, for an hour long, and her heart trembling from anxiety and cold, she began to wail and weep. "Ah! the perfidious one," she exclaimed, "he lies in the arms of some coquet, from whom he cannot tear himself away; he mocks me, and has forgot my true love."

This thought suddenly brought the long-forgotten pedigree to her recollection, and she felt ashamed of having so far demeaned herself as to love a man without a name, or noble feeling. In this moment when the intoxication of passion had somewhat subsided, and reason had resumed her sway, this faithful counsellor advised her to redeem this false step, by immediately returning to the cas-tle, and trying to forget the false perjurer. The first she did without delay; and, to the great surprise of her faithful confidante, to whom she revealed everything, she reached her chamber safe and sound; but the second point she resolved to reflect upon at leisure.

Nevertheless, the man without a name, was not so much to blame as the enraged Emily supposed. He had not failed to be punctual at the place of meeting. With a heart full of rapture, he waited with impatience for the moment which was to put him in possession of his lovely treasure. As the midnight hour approached, he secretly hastened to the castle, and listened when the little gate would open. Sooner than he supposed possible, the beloved figure of the nun stepped out. He immediately rushed from his conceal-ment towards her, seized her in his arms, exclaiming, "I have thee—I hold thee. Never shall I leave thee. Dear love, thou art mine—I am thine with body and soul."

Joyfully he bore his lovely burden to the carriage, and soon they rattled over stock and stones, up hills and down valleys. The horses plunged and snorted, shook their manes, and became so wild and unmanageable, that they would no longer obey the reins. A wheel flew off, and the sudden shock precipitated the coachmen to the ground; and carriage and horses, and man and mouse, all rolled over a steep abyss into a gulf below. The fond lover knew not what had happened; his body was bruised, his head was crushed, and, from the severity of the fall, he lost all recollection; but when he came to himself, he missed his beloved companion. After spending the rest of the night in this helpless situation, he was found by some peas-ants in the morning, who carried him to the nearest village.

The carriage was dashed to pieces, the four horses had broken their necks. This loss, however, grieved him little; but the fate of the beau-tiful Emily plunged him in the greatest distress. He dispatched people in every direction, to try and gain some tidings of her; but they all returned as they went, nothing was to be heard of the runaway. The midnight hour was the first thing which cleared up this mystery. As the clock struck twelve, the door opened, and his lost travelling com-panion stepped into the apartment, not however in the form of the beautiful Emily, but of the Spectre Nun, a hideous skeleton. The hand-some Fritz, with horror, perceived that he himself had made this dreadful mistake. Death-cold perspirations burst over him; he began to cross and bless himself, and ejaculate every prayer he could think of.

The nun little heeded this; she stepped up to the bed, stroked his burning cheeks with her withered ice-cold hand, and said, "Fritz, Fritz, be resigned to it. I am thine—thou art mine, with body and soul." She thus continued to torture him with her presence for an hour, and then vanished. This game she acted every night, and she even followed him into the place where his regiment was quartered. He had neither peace nor repose from the love of this hobgoblin, which so grieved and fretted him, that he lost all spirit; so much so, that his companions began to remark his deep melancholy; and these gallant officers truly sympathized with his distress. They could not imagine what had happened to their former lively associate, for he carefully shunned the horrible secret, which he divulged to no one.

Among his companions, Fritz had one very intimate friend, whom rumour reported master of all magical arts, and who possessed the lost art of making himself invulnerable, could call up spirits, and had every day a free shot. This experienced warrior, with affectionate impatience, urged his friend to disclose the secret grief which so evidently oppressed him. This martyr of love, who was sick of his existence, at length, under the seal of secrecy, was prevailed on to divulge it. "Brother, is this all?" said the exorcist, with a smile; "I shall soon release you from this torment.—Follow me into my quarters." He began by making secret preparations, drew several circles and characters upon the floor; and, at the summons of the exorcist, in a dark chamber which was lighted only by a magician's lamp, the midnight guest for this time appeared at the mid-day hour. He scolded her very much, and banished her and her mischievous pranks to a hollow willow in a lonely valley, with strict commands at that very hour to set out to this Patmos.[1]

The spectre vanished, but at the same moment there arose such a storm and whirlwind, as set the whole town in commotion. It was an old pious custom when a high wind blew, that twelve deputed citizens should instantly take horse, and make a solemn pilgrimage through the streets, chanting a song of repentance to sing the wind away. As soon as the twelve booted and well-mounted apostles had rode out, the howling voice of the hurricane ceased, and the spirit never again appeared.[2] Fritz now perceived that this devilish ape's play was intended to entrap his poor soul, and was rejoiced that the tormenting spirit had left him. He again prepared to join the formidable Wallenstein in Pomerania, where he finished three campaigns without hearing anything of the lovely Emily, and behaved with such bravery, that on his return to Bohemia, he commanded a regiment of horse. He took his way through Hungary, and when he came in sight of the Castle of Lauenstein, his heart began to beat with anxiety and doubt, lest, in

1   A Greek island that under the Romans was a place of exile, most famously for John the Evangelist.
2   We may mention here, that it is still the custom in this town for this wind-laying cavalcade to perambulate the streets during a storm. [Note in the original.]

his absence, his beloved had been forgetful of him. He merely announced himself as a friend of the family, and, according to the rites of hospitality, gates and doors were soon thrown open to him.

Ah! how astonished was the lovely Emily, when her supposed faithless lover, the handsome Fritz, stepped into the apartment! Joy and anger by turns assailed her soul. She could not resolve to vouchsafe him one friendly look, and yet this league with her beautiful eyes cost her the greatest difficulty.

For three long years she had debated with herself whether she would forget, or not, her nameless, and, as she believed, faithless lover, and therefore he was never one moment from her thoughts. His image floated continually before her; and, besides, it appeared that the God of Dreams was his patron, for the innumerable dreams that the Fraulein had of him ever since his absence, either excused or defended him. The stately Colonel, whose high rank the harsh survey of the mother somewhat softened, soon found an opportunity the apparent coldness of his beloved to try. He related to her the horrible adventure of the Elopement, and she frankly acknowledged to him the pain the thoughts of his faithlessness had given her. The lovers now agreed to reveal their secret to mamma, and endeavour to prevail with her to favour their attachment.

The good lady was as much astonished at the secret attachment of the cunning Emily, as at the communication of the *species facti* of the Elopement. She thought it just that love, which had stood so severe a trial, should be rewarded. It was only the man without a name that was offensive to her; and, as the Fraulein observed, that it was incomparably more sensible to marry a man without a name, than a name without a man, against this argument she had nothing to reply.

They were married, and as the secret treaty had already prospered, and no Count lay at the bottom of her heart, the good dame gave her maternal consent to it. The handsome Fritz embraced his lovely bride, and quietly and happily accomplished his marriage, without the slightest interruption on the part of the Spectre Nun.

4. Christian Friedrich Daniel Schubart, "The Eternal Jew: A lyrical rhapsody" (1784); translated by Sandra Hoenle

> Out of the dark, cleft ravines of Carmel
> Crawled Ahasuerus. For almost two thousand years
> Restlessness drove him through every land.
> In times past when Jesus bore the burden of the cross,
> And wanted to rest in front of Ahasuerus's door:
> Alas! Ahasuerus refused him rest,

And pushed our Mediator obstinately from his door:
And Jesus wavered, and sank beneath his burden.
Yet he was silent. An Angel of Death stood
Before Ahasuerus, and spoke in rage:
"You have refused the Son of Man rest;
Now it will be refused you, for your inhumanity!
Until he comes!"

A black Demon, fled from hell,
Will torment you now, Ahasuerus,
As you go from land to land. The sweet solace of death,
The solace of the grave is refused you!

Out of the dark, cleft ravines of Carmel
Stepped Ahasuerus. He shook the dust
From his beard; from a pile of skulls
He took one, hurled it
Down from Carmel, so that it leapt and crashed
And shattered. "That was my father!" bellowed
Ahasuerus. Another skull! Ha,
Seven more skulls thumped down
From boulder to boulder! "And these—and these," raged the Jew
With glaring, protruding eyes:
"And these—and these—are my wives—ha!"
And still the skulls rolled. "These and these,"
Bellows Ahasuerus, "are my children, ha!
They were able to die!—But I, the outcast,
I can not die! Oh, the most fearful judgement
hangs over me eternally, shouting its terrible message.

Jerusalem fell. I crushed the infant,
I ran into the flames. I cursed the Romans:
But, oh, the restless curse
Held me by the hair, and I did not die.

Rome, the giant, collapsed into rubble,
I positioned myself under the collapsing giant,
Yet it fell without crushing me.
Nations arose and sank before me;
But I remained, and did not die!
From the cloud-girded cliffs I plunged
Down into the sea; but swirling waves
Rolled me to shore, and the flaming arrow
Of Being pierced me again.
Down I looked into Aetna's grey crater,
And raged down into its crater:
There I bellowed at the giant for ten moons
With a fearful wailing, and castigated the sulphur opening
With sighs. Ha! For ten moons!
Aetna boiled, and spewed me out
In a stream of lava. But I quivered in the ashes, and still I lived!

A forest burned. Raging, I ran
Into the burning forest. From the crowns of the trees
Fire fell upon me—
Yet the flames only singed my bones,
And did not devour me.

Then I joined the butchers of humanity,
Flung myself into the storm of the battle,
Bellowed disdain for the Gauls,
Disdain for the undefeated Germans:
But arrow and javelin broke when they hit me.
The Saracen's swords swung down
And shattered on my skull.
Cannonballs rained down on me,
Like peas flung against iron armour.
The lightening bolts of the battle twisted
Around my loins,
As around the hips of the jagged peak
That takes shelter among the clouds.
In vain the elephant trampled me;
In vain the unyielding hooves of the wrath-filled warhorse
Struck me.
The powder-filled mine, exploding with me inside,
Flung me high through the air,
Dazed and roasted I plunged down and came to my senses
Amidst blood and brain and marrow,
And under the mutilated limbs
Of my fighting companions.

The giant's steel mace burst when it hit me;
The hangman's fist became lame;
The tiger's teeth became dull;
A hungry lion tore me apart in the circus.
I lay with poisonous snakes;
I pinched the dragon's blood-red comb;
Yet the snake bit, and did not kill me!
The dragon tortured me, and did not kill me!

Then I derided the Tyrant,
I said to Nero: You are a bloodthirsty creature!
I said to the Christian: You are a bloodthirsty creature!
I said to Mulai Ismail: You are a bloodthirsty creature!
The tyrants devised
Ferocious tortures, and yet did not slay me.

Ha! Not to be able to die! Not to be able to die!
Not to be able to rest after the toils of the flesh!
To wear a shroud! With its deathly pallor
And its infirmity! Its scent of the grave!
To be forced to see through millennia
The yawning monster: Monotony!
And lustful, hungry time,
Forever bearing children, forever devouring children!

Ha! Not to be able to die! Not to be able to die!
Oh Fearful Angry One in heaven,
Have you
An even more fearful Judgement
In your arsenal?
Ha! Then let it thunder down upon me!
Let a storm throw me down
From the camel's back
So that may I lie stretched out
at its feet—
And gasp—and twitch and die!—"

And Ahasuerus sank down. There was ringing in his ears;
Night covered his bristly lashes.
An Angel carried him back to the dark, cleft ravines,
"Now go ahead and sleep," said the angel, "Ahasuerus,
Sleep a sweet sleep; God is not angry forever!
When you awaken, He will be there,
He whose blood you saw flowing on Golgotha;
And He—who forgives even you."

5. Matthew Gregory Lewis, "Imitation of Anacreon, Ode 3" (Baron-Wilson 2: 346-48)

I.

While rainy clouds obscured the sky,
And sleep, on every mortal eye,
Her midnight poppies shed;
A voice unknown (now known too well),
Assail'd the window of my cell,
And thus imploring said:

II.

"Ah! gentle swain, in pity hear,
Nor think an hostile robber near;
An helpless boy am I,
Who, wandering o'er the desert plain,
Have borne the beating of the rain,
No friend, no guardian, nigh.

III.

"Let no vain fears your heart alarm;
Nor will, nor power, have I to harm,
Then pitying grant my prayer;
For heavy showers still fast descend,
And stormy winds in fury rend
My wildly-flowing hair.

IV.

"May you in every wish be blest,
If in your cot this night I rest;

One night...... I ask no more!"
He ceased; his honey'd words mine ear
Entranced, and made the speaker dear;
I straight unclosed the door.

V.

A beauteous stripling meets my view,
Whose sparkling eyes of glossy blue,
Like purest sapphires shine;
A bow unstrung his fingers hold,
And two bright wings of glittering gold,
Proclaim his race divine.

VI.

I haste to light the extinguished flame,
And warm his cold exhausted frame
With tenderest zeal and care;
With wine renew each faded grace,
Then wipe the rain from off his face,
And wring his streaming hair.

VII.

But when the kindly warmth had spread
His cheek of down with blushing red,
His bow once more he strung;
Then meditating treacherous wiles,
While his fair face he drest in smiles,
Thus spoke his guileful tongue.

VIII.

"My gentle host, I wish to know,
Whether the rain has hurt my bow,
And fain its force would try;
Suppose I prove its power on you?"
And straight its cord the urchin drew,
And bade his arrow fly.

IX.

With aim too just it pierced my heart;
E'en now my bosom feels the smart;
And then with pinions spread,
With joyful shout he rose in air,
Paused to enjoy my fond despair,
And thus departing said:

X.

"Farewell, kind host! the trial o'er,
I leave your hospitable door,
And with you leave my dart:
Safe from the storm my bow is found,
And that my arrow too is sound,
You know it by your heart."

Appendix B: Historical Contexts

[*The Monk* expresses an ambivalent response to the French Revolution. The fate of Antonia recalls a famous passage in Edmund
Burke's *Reflections on the Revolution in France* (B.1.a) and a poem by
Lewis himself, lamenting the fate of Marie Antoinette (B.1.b); but
the novel also echoes (230-31) Thomas Paine's pro-revolutionary
The Age of Reason (B.1.c). Lewis, the son of a slave-owner, had
equally ambivalent feelings about the issues of slavery and abolition, which he expressed both in his most famous play, *The Castle
Spectre* (B.2.a), and in the journal he kept when he visited Jamaica
at the end of his life (B.2.b). Lewis was probably gay, and his period has been described as the most homophobic in English history; some of the violence in the novel may be a comment on mob
violence against homosexuals. We have chosen an example dating
from 1810, fourteen years after the publication of *The Monk*
(B.3.a). See Introduction 15-19.]

1. The French Revolution

a. Edmund Burke, *Reflections on the Revolution in France* (1790; quoted by permission of the Clarendon Press)

History will record, that on the morning of the 6th of October
1789, the king and queen of France, after a day of confusion, alarm,
dismay, and slaughter, lay down, under the pledged security of public faith, to indulge nature in a few hours of respite, and troubled
melancholy repose. From this sleep the queen was first startled by the
voice of the centinel at her door, who cried out to her, to save herself by flight—that this was the last proof of fidelity he could give—
that they were upon him, and he was dead. Instantly he was cut
down. A band of cruel ruffians and assassins, reeking with his blood,
rushed into the chamber of the queen, and pierced with an hundred
strokes of bayonets and poniards the bed, from whence this perse-
cuted woman had but just time to fly almost naked, and through
ways unknown to the murderers had escaped to seek refuge at the
feet of a king and husband, not secure of his own life for a moment.

    This king, to say no more of him, and this queen, and their
infant children (who once would have been the pride and hope of
a great and generous people) were then forced to abandon the
sanctuary of the most splendid palace in the world, which they left

swimming in blood, polluted by massacre, and strewed with scattered limbs and mutilated carcases. Thence they were conducted into the capital of their kingdom. Two had been selected from the unprovoked, unresisted, promiscuous slaughter, which was made of the gentlemen of birth and family who composed the king's body guard. These two gentlemen, with all the parade of an execution of justice, were cruelly and publickly dragged to the block, and beheaded in the great court of the palace. Their heads were stuck upon spears, and led the procession; whilst the royal captives who followed in the train were slowly moved along, amidst the horrid yells, and shrilling screams, and frantic dances, and infamous contumelies, and all the unutterable abominations of the furies of hell, in the abused shape of the vilest of women. After they had been made to taste, drop by drop, more than the bitterness of death, in the slow torture of a journey of twelve miles, protracted to six hours, they were, under a guard, composed of those very soldiers who had thus conducted them through this famous triumph, lodged in one of the old palaces of Paris, now converted into a Bastile for kings.[1] (8: 121-22)

b. Matthew Gregory Lewis, "France and England in 1793" (Ms. 114, pp. 385-87; reprinted by permission of the National Library of Jamaica)

>   Full in the splendour of meridian Day,
> Bright as its beams, the Angel Freedom lay.
> On roseate clouds the glorious Form reclined;
> Free flowed her spotless robes and unconfined;
> And her dark-golden locks, all stained with Light,
> Played in the solar blaze, and made its blaze more bright.
> Whilst on the various realms She casts her eyes,
> Which owned her sway, or dared her power despise,
> Indignant She beheld the Sultan's nod
> Give life or death, the office of a God;
> Indignant saw in Russia's hard-ruled clime
> Despots adored and Liberty a crime;
> And while her eye with pity viewed thy pains,
> It dropt a tear, lost Poland, on thy chains.
>   But how with anger did her bosom swell,
> When on the plains of France her glances fell!
> Here the wild People drenched the soil with blood,
> And bathed exulting in the crimson flood:
> Justice was spurned; Religion awed no more:
> The holiest Shrines were dyed with human gore;

---

1 The Tuileries.

And still while trampling Heaven's and Nature's laws,
Hoarse was the shout—"We sin in Freedom's cause!"—
No age, no sex, no worth could life secure;
The Young, the Old, the Guilty, and the Pure
Mixed in dread chorus their expiring breath,
And slaughtered Myriads thronged the Court of Death.
With wonder and disgust the Angel saw
Murder made sport, and wanton will held law
And blushed to see her blood-stained altars shine
Raised on the fragments of Religion's shrine.
     Now for awhile She bends her loathing sight,
Where rear the Temple's Walls their massy height,[1]
Whose threatening horrors, scowling oër the scene,
Hold in their drear embrace a Captive Queen.
Amidst these glooms profound, these frowning Towers,
Sad Antoinette consumes the fearful hours,
And mourns the day, She left the Austrian climes,
To hear her thoughtless errors taxed as crimes.
Scorned as a Sovereign, Slandered as a Wife,
Almost debarred the coarse support of life,
Wasted with agony, with sickness weak,
On her fair hand She rests her faded cheek,
While her stern Jailors gaze with eyes of stone,
And taunting mock the tear, or chide the groan.
'Tis thus, sad victim of inveterate Foes,
She waits, yet shudders at, her final close;
And oft when steps approaching fright her ear,
Trembling She starts, and thinks the Murderer near.
Yet still unchanged, in grief still fond and mild,
Doating She hangs oër either lovely Child,
And murmurs, while her tears their cheeks bedew,
—"Dear Babes, my bitterest fears are felt for You!"—
     Touched, yet disgusted at the mournful sight,
The Angel turned, and saw with true delight,
Dear to her heart and pleasant to her eyes,
The glittering Cliffs of sea-girt Albion rise.
With love maternal oër the Isle She hung;
The burst of fondness faltered on her tongue;
And in her eyes while 'rapture's sun-beam played,
In sounds melodious thus at length She said.
     —"Flourish, fair Island, long my favourite State,
Parent of all that's good, of all that's great,
Where Liberty's true Fire its light displays;
But not that fatal, that deluding Blaze,
Which, like the gleams by Lamps in Churches shed,
Shine but to show the reliques of the Dead:
'Tis that kind radiance, that pure holy Flame,
By Virtue kindled, and still fed by Fame,

---

1 Marie Antoinette was imprisoned in the Temple Prison until she was guillotined on 16 October 1793.

Which breaks the shadows of despotic Night
And oër great actions pours a clearer light.
Here every Subject's free; Here Kings possess
No power to hurt, and every power to bless;
And Liberty herself is forced to say,
'Tis sweet to rule, who willingly obey"—

c. Thomas Paine, *The Age of Reason* (1794–95); quoted by permission of the Kensington Publishing Corporation

Soon after I had published the pamphlet "Common Sense," in America, I saw the exceeding probability that a revolution in the system of government would be followed by a revolution in the system of religion. The adulterous connection of church and state, wherever it has taken place, whether Jewish, Christian or Turkish, has so effectually prohibited by pains and penalties every discussion upon established creeds, and upon first principles of religion, that until the system of government should be changed, those subjects could not be brought fairly and openly before the world; but that whenever this should be done, a revolution in the system of religion would follow. Human inventions and priestcraft would be detected; and man would return to the pure, unmixed and unadulterated belief of one God, and no more.... (1: 465)

Whenever we read the obscene stories, the voluptuous debaucheries, the cruel and torturous executions, the unrelenting vindictiveness, with which more than half the Bible is filled, it would be more consistent that we called it the word of a demon than the Word of God. It is a history of wickedness that has served to corrupt and brutalize mankind; and, for my part, I sincerely detest it as I detest everything that is cruel.... (1: 474)

Besides, the character of Moses, as stated in the Bible, is the most horrid that can be imagined. If those accounts be true, he was the wretch that first began and carried on wars on the score or on the pretense of religion; and under that mask, or that infatuation, committed the most unexampled atrocities that are to be found in the history of any nation, of which I will state only one instance.

When the Jewish army returned from one of their plundering and murdering excursions, the account goes on as follows: Numbers, chap. xxxi., ver. 13:

"And Moses, and Eleazar the priest, and all the princes of the congregation, went forth to meet them without the camp; and Moses was wroth with the officers of the host, with the captains over thousands, and captains over hundreds, which came from the battle; and Moses said unto them, *Have ye saved all the women alive?* behold, these caused the children of Israel, through the council of Balaam, to commit trespass against the Lord in the matter of Peor, and there was a plague among the congregation of the Lord. Now, therefore, *kill every male among the little ones, and kill every woman that hath known a man by lying with him; but all the women-children, that have not known a man by lying with him, keep alive for yourselves.*"

Among the detestable villains that in any period of the world have disgraced the name of man, it is impossible to find a greater than Moses, if this account be true. Here is an order to butcher the boys, to massacre the mothers and debauch the daughters.

Let any mother put herself in the situation of those mothers; one child murdered, another destined to violation, and herself in the hands of an executioner; let any daughter put herself in the situation of those daughters, destined as a prey to the murderers of a mother and a brother, and what will be their feelings? It is in vain that we attempt to impose upon nature, for nature will have her course, and the religion that tortures all her social ties is a false religion....

In short, the matters contained in this chapter, as well as in many other parts of the Bible, are too horrid for humanity to read or for decency to hear, for it appears, from the 35th verse of this chapter, that the number of women-children consigned to debauchery by the order of Moses was thirty-two thousand. (1: 528-29)

2. Colonialism and Slavery

a. Matthew Gregory Lewis, *The Castle Spectre* (1797)

HASS[AN].... Saib, I too have loved! I have known how painful it was to leave her on whom my heart hung; how incapable was all else to supply her loss! I have exchanged want for plenty, fatigue for rest, a wretched hut for a splendid palace. But am I happier? Oh! no! Still do I regret my native land, and the partners of my poverty. Then toil was sweet to me, for I laboured for Samba; then repose ever blest my bed of leaves, for there by my side lay Samba sleeping.

SAIB. This from you, Hassan?—Did love ever find a place in your flinty bosom?

HASS[AN]. Did it? Oh Saib! my heart once was gentle, once was good! But sorrows have broken it, insults have made it hard! I have been dragged from my native land, from a wife who was every thing to me, to whom I was every thing! Twenty years have elapsed since these Christians tore me away: they trampled upon my heart, mocked my despair, and, when in frantic terms I raved of Samba, laughed, and wondered how a negro's soul could feel! In that moment when the last point of Africa faded from my view, when as I stood on the vessel's deck I felt that all I loved was to me lost for ever, in that bitter moment did I banish humanity from my breast. I tore from my arm the bracelet of Samba's hair, I gave to the sea the precious token, and, while the high waves swift bore it from me, vowed aloud endless hatred to mankind. I have kept my oath, I *will* keep it![....] (12-13; 1.2)

SAIB. I trusted that his gratitude for my past services—

HASS[AN]. European gratitude?—Seek constancy in the winds—fire in ice—darkness in the blaze of sun-shine!—But seek not gratitude in the breast of an European!

SAIB. Then, why so attached to Osmond? For what do you value him?

HASS[AN]. Not for his virtues, but for his vices, Saib: Can there for me be a greater cause to love him? Am I not branded with scorn? Am I not marked out for dishonour? Was I not free, and am I not a slave? Was I not once beloved, and am I not now despised? What man, did I tender my service, would accept the negro's friendship? What woman, did I talk of affection, would not turn from the negro with disgust? Yet, in my own dear land, my friendship was courted, my love was returned. I had parents, children, wife!—Bitter thought—in one moment all were lost to me! Can I remember this, and not hate these white men? Can I think how cruelly they have wronged me, and not rejoice when I see them suffer?—Attached to Osmond, say you? Saib, I hate him! Yet viewing him as an avenging Fiend sent hither to torment his fellows, it glads me that he fills his office so well! Oh! 'tis a thought which I would not barter for empires, to know that in this world he makes others suffer, and will suffer himself for their tortures in the next! (64-65; 4.1)

b. Matthew Gregory Lewis, *Journal of a West India Proprietor* (1815-18)

It is only to be wished, that the negroes would content themselves with these fashionable peccadilloes;[1] but, unluckily, there are some palates among them which require higher seasoned vices; and besides their occasional amusements of poisoning, stabbing, thieving, &c., a plan has just been discovered in the adjoining parish of St. Elizabeth's, for giving themselves a grand fête by murdering all

---

1 Lewis has been discussing sexual relations among his slaves.

the whites in the island. The focus of this meditated insurrection was on Martin's Penn, the property of Lord Balcarras, where the overseer is an old man of the mildest character, and the negroes had always been treated with peculiar indulgence. Above a thousand persons were engaged in the plot, three hundred of whom had been regularly sworn to assist in it with all the usual accompanying ceremonies of drinking human blood, eating earth from graves, &c. Luckily, the plot was discovered time enough to prevent any mischief; and yesterday the ringleaders were to be tried at Black River.[....] (224-25; 16 March 1816)

The two ringleaders of the proposed rebellion have been condemned at Black River, the one to be hanged, the other to transportation. The plot was discovered by the overseer of Lyndhurst Penn (a Frenchman from St. Domingo) observing an uncommon concourse of stranger negroes to a child's funeral, on which occasion a hog was roasted by the father. He stole softly down to the feasting hut, and listened behind a hedge to the conversation of the supposed mourners; when he heard the whole conspiracy detailed. It appears that above two hundred and fifty had been sworn in regularly, all of them Africans; not a Creole was among them.[1] But there was a *black* ascertained to have stolen over into the island from St. Domingo, and a *brown* Anabaptist missionary, both of whom had been very active in promoting the plot. They had elected a King of the Eboes, who had two Captains under him; and their intention was to effect a complete massacre of all the whites on the island; for which laudable design His Majesty thought Christmas the very fittest season in the year, but his Captains were more impatient, and were for striking the blow immediately. The next morning information was given against them: one of the Captains escaped to the woods; but the other, and the King of the Eboes, were seized and brought to justice. On their trial they were perfectly cool and unconcerned, and did not even profess to deny the facts with which they were charged. Indeed, proofs were too strong to admit of denial; among others, a copy of the following song was found upon the King, which the overseer had heard him sing at the funeral feast, while the other negroes joined in the chorus:—

---

1 Lewis distinguishes between African-born slaves (whom he also calls "Eboes," after one of the West African peoples) and those born in Jamaica, whom he calls Creoles.

SONG OF THE KING OF THE EBOES.

Oh me good friend, Mr. Wilberforce,[1] make we free!
God Almighty thank ye! God Almighty thank ye!
God Almighty, make we free!
Buckra[2] in this country no make we free:
What Negro for to do? What Negro for to do?
Take force by force! Take force by force!

CHORUS.

To be sure! to be sure! to be sure!

The Eboe King said, that he certainly had made use of this song, and what harm was there in his doing so? He had sung no songs but such as his brown priest had assured him were approved of by John the Baptist. "And who, then, was John the Baptist?" He did not very well know; only he had been told by his brown priest, that John the Baptist was a friend to the negroes, and had got his head in a pan!

As to the Captain, he only said in his defence, that if the court would forgive him this once, he would not do so again, "as he found the whites did not like their plans;" which, it seems, till that moment they had never suspected! They had all along imagined, no doubt, that the whites would find as much amusement in having their throats cut, as the blacks would find in cutting them. I remember hearing a sportsman, who was defending the humanity of hunting, maintain, that it being as much the nature of a hare to run away as of a dog to run after her, consequently the hare must receive as much pleasure from being coursed, as the dog from coursing.[....] (227-29; 22 March 1816)

Every man of humanity must wish that slavery, even in its best and most mitigated form, had never found a legal sanction, and must regret that its system is now so incorporated with the welfare of Great Britain as well as of Jamaica, as to make its extirpation an absolute impossibility, without the certainty of producing worse mischiefs than the one which we annihilate. (402; 1 May 1818)

---

1 William Wilberforce (1759-1833), abolitionist.
2 Whites.

3. Georgian Homophobia

a. *The Trying and Pilloring of the Vere Street Club* **(1810; reprinted from Louis Crompton, *Byron and Greek Love* 164-66, by permission of Louis Crompton)**

At an early hour, the Old Bailey was completely blockaded, and the increase of the mob about 12 o'clock put a stop to the business of the Sessions.... Shortly after 12, the *ammunition waggons* from the neighbouring markets appeared in motion. These consisted of a number of carts which were driven by butchers' boys, who had previously taken care to fill them with the offal, dung, &c. appertaining to their several slaughter-houses. A number of hucksters were also put in requisition, who carried on their heads baskets of apples, potatoes, turnips, cabbage-stalks, and other vegetables, together with the remains of divers dogs and cats. The whole of these were sold to the public at a high price, who spared no expence to provide themselves with the necessary articles of assault.

A number of fishwomen attended with stinking flounders and the entrails of other fish, which had been in preparation several days. These articles however were not to be sold, as their proprietors, hearty in the cause, declared they wanted them for their own use....

The Sheriffs and City-Marshalls arrived about half-past 12, with more than 100 constables, mounted and armed with pistols, and more than 100 on foot. This force was ordered to rendezvous in the Old Bailey Yard, where a caravan, used occasionally for the purpose of conveying prisoners from the gaols of London to the hulks,[1] waited to receive the culprits. The caravan was drawn by two shaft-horses, led by two men, armed with a brace of pistols. The gates of the Old Bailey Yard were shut, and all strangers turned out, after which the miscreants were all brought out, and placed in the caravan. *Amos* began a laugh, which induced his vile companions to reprove him, and they all sat upright, apparently in a composed state; but, having cast their eyes upwards, the sight of the spectators on the tops of the houses operated strongly on their fears, and they soon appeared to feel terror and dismay. Directly the church-clock went half-past 12, the gates were thrown open, the mob at the same time attempting to force their way in, but they

---

1 Prison ships.

were repulsed. A grand sortie of the police was then made, and about 60 officers, armed and mounted as before described, went forward with the City-Marshalls. The caravan went next, followed by about 40 officers and the Sheriffs. The first salute received by the offenders was a volley of mud, and a serenade of hisses, hootings and execration, which compelled them to fall flat on their faces in the caravan. The mob, and particularly the women, had piled up balls of mud, to afford the objects of their indignation a warm reception: indeed, the depots in many places appeared like pyramids of shot on a gun-wharf. These were soon exhausted, and, when the caravan passed the old house which once belonged to the notorious Jonathan Wild,[1] the prisoners resembled bears dipped in a stagnant pool....

It is impossible for language to convey an adequate idea of the universal expressions of execration which accompanied these monsters on their journey. It was fortunate for them that the weather was dry; had it been otherwise they would have been smothered. From the moment the cart was in motion, the fury of the mob began to display itself in showers of mud and filth of every kind. Before the cart reached Temple-bar, the wretches were so thickly covered with filth, that a vestige of the human figure was scarcely discernable. They were chained, and placed in such a manner, that they could not lie down in the cart, and could only hide and shelter their heads from the storm by stooping, which, however, could afford but little protection.—Some of them were cut in the head with brickbats, and bled profusely; and the streets, as they passed, resounded with the universal shouts and execrations of the populace....

Before any of them reached the place of punishment, their faces were completely disfigured by blows and mud; and before they mounted, their whole persons appeared one heap of filth. Upwards of fifty women were permitted to stand in the ring, who assailed them incessantly with mud, dead cats, rotten eggs, potatoes, and buckets filled with blood, offal, and dung, which were brought by a number of butchers' men from St. James's market. These criminals were very roughly handled.

---

1   A famous thief and thief-taker (1682?–1725), the subject of a pamphlet by Defoe (1725) and a novel by Fielding (1743).

Appendix C: Critical Reception

[*The Monk* attracted critical comments from such eminent contemporaries as Mary Wollstonecraft (C.1), Samuel Taylor Coleridge (C.3), the Marquis de Sade (C.9), and Ann Radcliffe (C.10). Controversy over whether it was blasphemous and obscene (C.3–C.4) led Lewis to expurgate the fourth edition and to apologize both to his father and to the general public for having offended them (C.5–C.6). In Revolutionary France, the novel was more favourably received (C.7–C.8). See Introduction 19-23.]

1. *Analytical Review* 24 (October 1796): 403–4 (Review attributed to Mary Wollstonecraft)

IN the preface to this romance, which displays no common powers, the author points out the interesting tale[1] which he has chosen to amplify and alter.

The original has great dramatic merit; and the purport of it may be told in a few words. The devil, fearful of the effect the famed sanctity of a well-known hermit might produce, determines to discover his vulnerable part, and convince him, and the world, that he was not quite so impeccable as he thought himself. The devil then had all his wits about him—the temptation was a beautiful woman. Had father Anthony been thus attacked, instead of being assailed by winged monsters, and "chimeras dire,"[2] the saint, most probably, would not so cheaply have earned his canonization.

Making a more finished picture of this bold sketch of the downfall of spiritual pride, the author of the Monk has introduced some scenes to mark the progress of passion very happily imagined: particularly in the first volume. Still we do not entirely approve of one alteration, the calling up a spirit from Hell to borrow a female shape, though the gradual discovery of Matilda's sex and person (the evil spirit,) is very finely conceived, and truly picturesque; indeed the whole temptation is so artfully contrived, that a man, it should seem, were he made as other men are, would deserve to be d—ned who could resist even devilish spells, conducted with such address, and assuming such a heavenly form.

The author has deviated in another instance, and we think, still

---

1 Santon Barsisa. [Note in the original. See Appendix A.1.]
2 Milton, *Paradise Lost* 2.628.

more injudiciously, from the simplicity of the original, by incorporating a tale not indispensably connected with it; and the transitions from one to the other, when warmed by either, weakens the main interest. The story of the Monk is certainly the warp of the plot, and it is a pity that another should be wove across it of a different texture, to divide the attention.

Besides, two catastrophes have always a bad effect, splitting the interest; for, in spite of what is termed poetical justice, the imagination, constrained to rest on the unfortunate one, as on an unfinished tale, is employed in making various conjectures. Ambrosio, the monk, it is true dies; but fancy follows him to Hell, and wishes to see him meet the treacherous Matilda in her proper person, and hear his bitter upbraidings. The monk, in fact, inspires sympathy, because foiled by more than mortal weapons; yet nothing was done by Matilda, which could not have been achieved by female wiles—the monk's pride was the arch devil that betrayed him.

The style is formed, and unaffected, though many of the sentiments and descriptions reminded us of the youth of the author;[1] but the language and manners of the personages are not sufficiently gothic in their colouring, to agree with the superstitious scenery, borrowed from those times. They want the sombre cast of ignorance, which renders credulity probable: still the author deserves praise for not attempting to account for supernatural appearances in a natural way. After being awakened to wonder by the rumbling of a mountain, the reader has an unpleasant sensation of being tricked, similar to the discovery of a slight of hand, when he perceives only a mouse creep out.

A specimen from a story of this kind, would scarcely do it justice.

2. *European Magazine* 31 (February 1797): 111–15

THIS singular composition, which has neither *originality*, *morals*, nor *probability* to recommend it, has excited, and will still continue to excite, the curiosity of the public. Such is the irresistible energy of genius.

The Author acknowledges, that the main and principal event is only an amplification of the *Santon Barsisa* in the Guardian: he might have added, that his *ghost*, in one of the episodes, appears in circumstances too similar to be the effect of accident, to a spectre

---

1 He informs us, in the preface, that he had not reached twenty. [Note in the original.]

exhibited in all the horrors of corruption and *marrowless bones*, by the inventive authoress of "The Knights of the Swan."[1]

Neither *morals* nor *religion* will acknowledge themselves benefited by a work whose great scope and purport it is to shew, that the fairest face and semblance of virtue is commonly a cloak to the most horrible crimes; and unless all the other sources of *improbability* and *wonder* must be considered as completely exhausted, it is difficult to assign a reason for the revival of the exploded mysteries of *sorcery*, and the *spirits of darkness*. If it was our Author's intention, which we would not willingly suppose, to attack religious orders, and, of course, religion itself, by exhibiting the extreme depravity of its most eminent disciples, he will, in the opinion of all sound judges, be considered not only as having failed of his intention, but as having paid an honourable tribute, the more valuable for being *undesigned*, to *ecclesiastical establishments*. The *Monk* yields not to the first, nor to the second efforts even of *hellish assailants*; he resists blandishments which no mortals unsupported could have been able to repel; and becomes at last the unhappy victim of lust from excess of gratitude and attachment. His progress afterwards into the abyss of crimes is rapid and inexcuseable; and in this part of his work, our author has shewn considerable skill and dexterity; but even here, to inflame the atrocity of his character, the culprit sometimes is made to commit gratuitous and improbable enormities.

The poetry interspersed through this work would have given popularity to a composition much inferior to this both in matter and in stile. Where Mr. L. has attempted to imitate the manner of the ancient ballad, he is eminently successful; retaining all its simplicity and pathos, without the vulgarity or the incorrectness; and there are few modern elegies that surpass the *Exile* either in elegance or imagery. Indeed, the chief excellence of Mr. L.'s *prose* consists in this latter attribute of the *muse*; all the scenes on which any care has been bestowed exhibiting both the truth of nature and the animation of genius.

If the reader wishes to be instructed in the secret of raising up spirits from the *vasty deep*,[2] various specimens of that *recondite lore*

---

1 Stéphanie-Félicité du Crest, Mme. de Genlis (1746-1830), *Les Chevaliers du Cygne* (1795), was not published until after Lewis had finished *The Monk*. In a note to the fourth edition, Lewis concedes the similarity (see Appendix E, note to 179.26).

2 Shakespeare, *1 Henry IV* 3.1.53.

may be collected from this singular performance; and one by a veteran and experienced artist, no less a personage than the *Wandering Jew himself.* We shall, however, select an example from the second Volume, which is rather more highly finished, and is no unfavourable sample of our Author's adroitness in this science of *darkness* and *devils.*

[The reviewer quotes Matilda's conjuration of Lucifer, 242-44.]

That our readers may not be too much fascinated with this *angelic* appearance of the *Spirit of Darkness*, it is proper to inform them, that the arch-enemy appears again to the apostate Monk, towards the close of the story, in all his genuine ugliness and malignity, and according to the true *costume*, with *horns* and *talons.*

As a specimen of the poetry in this work, we shall select *The Water-King*, an imaginary potentate of the Danish Mythology, whose province it is to agitate the deep, occasion shipwrecks, and drag the drowning sailors beneath the waves. Mr. L. informs us, in a short Preface, that from the third to the twelfth stanza it is the fragment of an original Danish Ballad. We have not yet seen it extracted into any periodical publication.

[The reviewer quotes "The Water-King," 253-55.]

Though we readily acknowledge the genius and talents manifested in various parts of this unequal production, yet what good purpose is to be answered by an *oblique attack* upon *venerable establishments*, we are at a loss to conjecture. We know that the presses of the Continent teemed with compositions of this character while the Revolution was preparing in France; yet what have the *infidels* who produced it substituted in the place of the *religion* they have banished? The question agitated by the philosophic Bayle on the *comparative mischiefs* of *superstition* and *atheism*[1] must now *rest* for ever; for surely there is no page in the history of *bigotry* to parallel the enormities that have been perpetrated in the present day by *democratic enthusiasts* and *atheistical devotees.* The mighty ruin, with which they have overwhelmed nations, has fallen, and will continue to fall, upon themselves; and the few who may possibly escape in their *persons*, mankind shall punish in their *memory.* The *Temple* they have so successfully laboured to sink in ashes, shall indeed confer on them *immortality*, but it will be an immortality of *reproach* and *infamy.*
R.R.

---

1 Pierre Bayle (1647-1706), *Pensées diverses sur la comète* (1682-83), and *Dictionnaire historique et critique* (1697).

3. [Samuel Taylor Coleridge,] *Critical Review* 2nd ser. 19 (February 1797): 194-200

THE horrible and the preternatural have usually seized on the popular taste, at the rise and decline of literature. Most powerful stimulants, they can never be required except by the torpor of an unawakened, or the languor of an exhausted, appetite. The same phænomenon, therefore, which we hail as a favourable omen in the belles lettres of Germany, impresses a degree of gloom in the compositions of our countrymen. We trust, however, that satiety will banish what good sense should have prevented; and that, wearied with fiends, incomprehensible characters, with shrieks, murders, and subterraneous dungeons, the public will learn, by the multitude of the manufacturers, with how little expense of thought or imagination this species of composition is manufactured. But, cheaply as we estimate romances in general, we acknowledge, in the work before us, the offspring of no common genius. The tale is similar to that of Santon Barsisa in the Guardian. Ambrosio, a monk, surnamed the Man of Holiness, proud of his own undeviating rectitude, and severe to the faults of others, is successfully assailed by the tempter of mankind, and seduced to the perpetration of rape and murder, and finally precipitated into a contract in which he consigns his soul to everlasting perdition.

The larger part of the three volumes is occupied by the underplot, which, however, is skilfully and closely connected with the main story, and is subservient to its development. The tale of the bleeding nun is truly terrific; and we could not easily recollect a bolder or more happy conception than that of the burning cross on the forehead of the wandering Jew (a mysterious character, which, though copied as to its more prominent features from Schiller's incomprehensible Armenian,[1] does, nevertheless, display great vigour of fancy). But the character of Matilda, the chief agent in the seduction of Antonio, appears to us to be the author's master-piece. It is, indeed, exquisitely imagined, and as exquisitely supported. The whole work is distinguished by the variety and impressiveness of its incidents; and the author every-where discovers an imagination rich, powerful, and fervid. Such are the excellencies;— the errors and defects are more numerous, and (we are sorry to add) of greater importance.

All events are levelled into one common mass, and become almost equally probable, where the order of nature may be changed

---

1 The title character of *Der Geisterseher* ("The Ghost-Seer," 1788), which does seem to have influenced Lewis's portrayal of the Wandering Jew.

whenever the author's purposes demand it. No address is requisite to the accomplishment of any design; and no pleasure therefore can be received from the perception of *difficulty surmounted*.[1] The writer may make us wonder, but he cannot surprise us. For the same reasons a romance is incapable of exemplifying a moral truth. No proud man, for instance, will be made less proud by being told that Lucifer once seduced a presumptuous monk. *Incredulus odit*.[2] Or even if, believing the story, he should deem his virtue less secure, he would yet acquire no lessons of prudence, no feelings of humility. Human prudence can oppose no sufficient shield to the power and cunning of supernatural beings; and the privilege of being proud might be fairly conceded to him who could rise superior to all earthly temptations, and whom the strength of the spiritual world alone would be adequate to overwhelm. So falling, he would fall with glory, and might reasonably welcome his defeat with the haughty emotions of a conqueror. As far, therefore, as the story is concerned, the praise which a romance can claim, is simply that of having given pleasure during its perusal; and so many are the calamities of life, that he who has done this, has not written uselessly. The children of sickness and of solitude shall thank him.—To this praise, however, our author has not entitled himself. The sufferings which he describes are so frightful and intolerable, that we break with abruptness from the delusion, and indignantly suspect the man of a species of brutality, who could find a pleasure in wantonly imagining them; and the abominations which he pourtrays with no hurrying pencil, are such as the observation of character by no means demanded, such as "no observation of character can justify, because no good man would willingly suffer them to pass, however transiently, through his own mind."[3] The merit of a novelist is in proportion (not simply to the effect, but) to the *pleasurable* effect which he produces. Situations of torment, and images of naked horror, are easily conceived; and a writer in whose works they abound, deserves our gratitude almost equally with him who should drag us by way of sport through a military hospital, or force us to sit at the dissecting-table of a natural philosopher. To trace the nice boundaries, beyond which terror and sympathy are deserted by the pleasurable emotions,—to reach those limits, yet never to

---

1 This is the kind of pleasure that Edmund Burke calls sublime: see *A Philosophical Enquiry* 122; 4.6.

2 "Disbelieving, he despises it" (adapted from Horace, *De Arte Poetica* 188).

3 Samuel Johnson, citing John Clarke, *Essay upon Study* (1731), in "Milton," *The Lives of the Poets* (1779-81).

pass them,—*hic labor, hoc opus est*.[1] Figures that shock the imagination, and narratives that mangle the feelings, rarely discover *genius*, and always betray a low and vulgar *taste*. Nor has our author indicated less ignorance of the human heart in the management of the principal character. The wisdom and goodness of providence have ordered that the tendency of vicious actions to deprave the heart of the perpetrator, should diminish in proportion to the greatness of his temptations. Now, in addition to constitutional warmth and irresistible opportunity, the monk is impelled to incontinence by friendship, by compassion, by gratitude, by all that is amiable, and all that is estimable; yet in a few weeks after his first frailty, the man who had been described as possessing much general humanity, a keen and vigorous understanding, with habits of the most exalted piety, degenerates into an uglier fiend than the gloomy imagination of Danté would have ventured to picture. Again, the monk is described as feeling and acting under the influence of an appetite which could not co-exist with his other emotions. The romance-writer possesses an unlimited power over situations; but he must scrupulously make his characters act in congruity with them. Let him work *physical* wonders only, and we will be content to *dream* with him for a while; but the first *moral* miracle which he attempts, he disgusts and awakens us. Thus our judgment remains unoffended, when, announced by thunders and earthquakes, the spirit appears to Ambrosio involved in blue fires that increase the cold of the cavern; and we acquiesce in the power of the silver myrtle which made gates and doors fly open at its touch, and charmed every eye into sleep. But when a mortal, fresh from the impression of that terrible appearance, and in the act of evincing for the first time the witching force of this myrtle, is represented as being at the same moment agitated by so fleeting an appetite as that of lust, our own feelings convince us that this is not improbable, but impossible; not preternatural, but contrary to nature. The extent of the powers that may exist, we can never ascertain; and therefore we feel no great difficulty in yielding a temporary belief to any, the strangest, situation of *things*. But that situation once conceived, how beings like ourselves would feel and act in it, our own feelings sufficiently instruct us; and we instantly reject the clumsy fiction that does not harmonise with them. These are the two *principal* mistakes in *judgment*, which the author has fallen into; but we cannot wholly pass over the frequent incongruity of his style with his subjects. It is gaudy where it should have been severely simple; and too often the mind is offended by phrases the most trite and collo-

---

1 "This is the toil, this is the task" (adapted from Vergil, *Aeneid* 6.129).

quial, where it demands and had expected a sternness and solemnity of diction.

A more grievous fault remains,—a fault for which no literary excellence can atone,—a fault which all other excellence does but aggravate, as adding subtlety to a poison by the elegance of its preparation. Mildness of censure would here be criminally misplaced, and silence would make us accomplices. Not without reluctance then, but in full conviction that we are performing a duty, we declare it to be our opinion, that the Monk is a romance, which if a parent saw in the hands of a son or daughter, he might reasonably turn pale. The temptations of Ambrosio are described with a libidinous minuteness, which, we sincerely hope, will receive its best and only adequate censure from the offended conscience of the author himself. The shameless harlotry of Matilda, and the trembling innocence of Antonia, are seized with equal avidity, as vehicles of the most voluptuous images; and though the tale is indeed a tale of horror, yet the most painful impression which the work left on our minds was that of great acquirements and splendid genius employed to furnish a *mormo*[1] for children, a poison for youth, and a provocative for the debauchee. Tales of enchantments and witchcraft can never be *useful*: our author has contrived to make them *pernicious*, by blending, with an irreverent negligence, all that is most awfully true in religion with all that is most ridiculously absurd in superstition. He takes frequent occasion, indeed, to manifest his sovereign contempt for the latter, both in his own person, and (most incongruously) in that of his principal characters; and that his respect for the *former* is not excessive, we are forced to conclude from the treatment which its inspired writings receive from him. Ambrosio discovers Antonia reading—

[Coleridge quotes the passage about Antonia's Bible, 230-31.]

The impiety of this falsehood can be equalled only by its impudence. This is indeed as if a Corinthian harlot, clad from head to foot in the transparent thinness of the Cöan vest, should affect to view with prudish horror the naked knee of a Spartan matron![2] If it be possible that the author of these blasphemies is a Christian, should he not have reflected that the only passage in the scriptures,[3] which could give a *shadow* of plausibility to the *weakest* of these expressions, is represented as being spoken by the Almighty himself?

---

1 "Bogey" (Greek).

2 The lasciviousness of the Corinthians, the virtue of the Spartans, and the fine fabrics of Cos were all proverbial.

3 Ezekiel, chap. xxiii. [Coleridge's note.]

But if he be an infidel, he has acted consistently enough with that character, in his endeavours first to inflame the fleshly appetites, and then to pour contempt on the only book which would be adequate to the task of recalming them. We believe it not absolutely impossible that a mind may be so deeply depraved by the habit of reading lewd and voluptuous tales, as to use even the Bible in conjuring up the spirit of uncleanness. The most innocent expressions might become the first link in the chain of association, when a man's soul had been so poisoned; and we believe it not absolutely impossible that he might extract pollution from the word of purity, and, in a literal sense, *turn the grace of God into wantonness.*[1]

We have been induced to pay particular attention to this work, from the unusual success which it has experienced. It certainly possesses much real merit, in addition to its meretricious attractions. Nor must it be forgotten that the author is a man of rank and fortune.—Yes! the author of the Monk signs himself a LEGISLATOR!—We stare and tremble.

The poetry interspersed through the volumes is, in general, far above mediocrity. We shall present our readers with the following exquisitely tender elegy, which, we may venture to prophesy, will melt and delight the heart, when ghosts and hobgoblins shall be found only in the lumber-garret of a circulating library.

[Coleridge quotes "The Exile," 197–99.]

4. "An Apology for the Monk," *Monthly Mirror* 3 (April 1797): 210–15

MR. EDITOR,

IT is with no inconsiderable pain that I have remarked the numerous attacks which have been made by the host of critics on the ingenious author of the MONK, for the supposed vicious tendency of that excellent romance. The author is universally allowed to be endowed with nature's best gift, genius, and in the work before us is generally acknowledged to discover throughout an imagination, rich, powerful, and fervid. This able writer is, however, attacked on a point which, I am sure, must make him feel little satisfaction in the applause which his genius commands. It is asserted by almost all the critics who have sat in judgment on this admirable performance, that its *tendency* is to deprave the heart, to vitiate the understanding, and to enlist the passions in the cause of vice. Dif-

1 Jude 4.

fering as I do with these censors, as to this and other objections, I wish, through the medium of your impartial publication, to rescue his production from this undeserved obloquy. I have not the pleasure of Mr. Lewis's acquaintance, and I know not how this apology may be received on his part, but the defence of genius is the common cause of all men of the least pretensions to literature; and every person who can enjoy works of taste, has the right of rescuing them from unmerited attacks. I should, as little as the critics, wish to be the apologist of vice, or the defender of lasciviousness; but justice requires that error, and error of such magnitude, as it regards Mr. Lewis's character, should be detected and exposed.

The error of the principal objection to this romance, viz. that of its vicious *tendency*, appears to me entirely to arise from inaccuracy of observation of the author's work, of the human heart, and of the meaning of the word tendency. It is not a temporary effect, produced upon the imagination or the passions, by particular passages, which can fairly be cited as the tendency of the work; we must examine what are the probable general results from the whole, and not judge from these partial and fleeting effects.

In this view, I maintain, this beautiful romance is well calculated to support the cause of virtue, and to teach her lessons to man. I am not old enough to have my heart steeled against the effects of the strongest of the human passions, nor young enough to riot in lascivious descriptions, or wanton in the regions of obscene imagery. I can feel as disgusted as the critics with such defects; but I entreat these *grey bearded* gentlemen to consider again whether there are any such images in the work before us. The lessons of virtue which I see in the Monk, are striking and impressive. In the character of Ambrosio we see a man delineated of strong passions, which have been for a long period subdued by as strong resolution; of a natural disposition to virtue, but, like all other men, with some portion of vice, which has been fostered by the situation into which his fate had thrown him; he is haughty, vindictive, and austere. The greatest error of which he is guilty, is too great a confidence in his own virtue, too great a reliance on his own hatred of vice. We are taught by his conduct that this unbounded confidence, by blinding the mind as to the real consequences which result, lays the foundation for vice, and opens an easy road to great excesses. We have again a very forcible illustration in Ambrosio, a man of the strongest understanding and the highest powers of reason, of the danger of receding even in the least from the path of virtue, or giving way in the slightest degree to the insidious approaches of vice. *C'est le premier pas qui coûte*,[1] is a truth long established, and is well illustrated in the present instance. We see and feel strongly this danger, and the lesson is the more forcible, in proportion to the strength of understanding which is shown in the Monk. We learn that when once a man ventures into the pool of vice, that he plunges deeper and deeper till he is completely overwhelmed. These are striking and impressive lessons.

There are many other moral lessons which are inculcated by the work in the strongest manner; the tendency, therefore, i.e. the general effect likely to result, is favourable to the cause of virtue and morality. We are however told, that "the temptations of Ambrosio are described with a libidinous minuteness, which leaves the painful impression of great acquirements and splendid genius, employed to furnish poison for youth, and a provocative for the debauchee."[2] If this were the case, I must give up my author in part, though still the tendency of the whole would be good. But I deny the fact. I request that the character and circumstances of Ambrosio may be seriously considered. To a man of strong understanding, austerity of manners, and great self command, strong temptations must be offered. If the author had made the Monk sink under a slight temptation, he would have offended against the laws of probability, and shocked the reason of his readers. I ask if it be possible to describe such temptations as were calculated to seduce such a man, with greater delicacy and decorum than our author has done: and I will take for example the strongest instances—the conclusion of chapter 2. vol. 1. p. 253 of vol. 2. and his attack on Antonia in p. 36 and 37 of vol. 3.[3] The answer, I am persuaded, must be—No! Highly coloured as these passages are, I maintain that no heart but one already depraved, could rise from them, if the preceding part of the work had been perused, with the least impurity. The mind that could draw food for vicious appetites from this work, must have made no little progress in the paths of profligacy and debauchery; so strong are the entrenchments erected before the heart, by the *general tendency* of the work.

The previous part is calculated to prevent all the evil which may arise from warmth of description, by the interest we take in observing the gradual progress of vice in Ambrosio's bosom, and the hatred we of course must feel for this insidious adversary. The work can be

---

1 "It is [only] the first step that is difficult": the comment of Mme du Deffand (1697-1780) on being told that, after his decapitation, St. Denis had walked for two leagues, carrying his head.

2 Critical Review, for February, 1797. [Note in the original.]

3 See pp. 103-04, 233, and 262.

read only by three descriptions of persons; either those whose minds, by habitual vice, are prepared to turn every the least hint to the purposes of food for their depraved appetites, or as incitements to their dormant desires, which require stimulants; or those who are wavering between vice and virtue, whose minds may be led to either, by interesting their passions strongly for one or the other; or else, young, innocent, and undepraved persons. The first deserve not notice: purity itself would be poison to their hearts, and the modestest allusion would excite depraved ideas. The passions of the second will be, I contend, excited more strongly to virtue than to vice by the Monk, because the horrors consequent on his vicious conduct are so strongly pourtrayed, as to destroy the momentary effect, if any were produced, of the passages which are rather warm in description. The last, from the very supposition of their being yet innocent and unpolluted, and in consequence ignorant, can not have improper ideas excited, or their passions roused to vice; as, in the first place, they will not be able to understand as much as our *knowing* critics, nor can the confused notions of felicity which may be excited destroy the purity of their minds, or the effect of the moral lessons inculcated. The writer of this paper felt not a single loose idea excited by the warmest passages, so perfectly had he imbibed the moral lessons which the author has so forcibly brought forward.

The critics themselves seem aware of this tendency of the work, and therefore endeavour to deprive the author of the defence, by roundly asserting that "a romance is incapable of exemplifying moral truth; and that he who could rise superior to all earthly temptation, and whom the strength of the spiritual world alone would be adequate to overwhelm, might reasonably be proud, and would fall with glory." As applied to the Monk, there are two errors in this assertion. The reader of this romance has no reason to imagine, till the greater part of the mischief has been done, that any but earthly temptations are used against the hero. The fall of Ambrosio is precisely that which would happen to any man of a similar character, assailed as he was by the fascinating arts of a woman, skilled in exciting the strongest passions, and endowed with the most attractive charms. We see the gradual progress she makes in undermining his virtue by merely human means. His feelings, his gratitude, and finally the strong desires of human nature are all combined to ensure his fall. But still the temptations appear to be no more than human. We see where a man of truly virtuous principles would have commenced resistance; we observe and lament his first deviation from the path of virtue; and cannot withhold our wishes that he may remain firm when the first disposition to yield manifests itself. Matilda appears to be merely a woman, though a woman of the greatest charms, and of an extraordinary character; but still there is nothing improbable or unnatural in the means of temptation, nothing that a man of a strong mind and pure virtue would not have resisted. The lesson therefore is taught and deeply imbibed before the discovery of supernatural agency is made, and that discovery does not and cannot eradicate the morality before inculcated.

Nor is it true in general that moral truth cannot be conveyed in romance. The general sense of mankind is against the critics in this assertion. From the earliest ages fiction, and incredible fiction, has been thought a proper vehicle for moral instruction, from the fables of Æsop, to the tales, allegories, and visions of modern days. The religion itself which these gentlemen profess inculcates the notion that Lucifer is the author of all our vicious propensities, and that he is the continual seducer of man. An allegorical representation of this being visibly interfering is no more therefore than adopting popular belief, and turning it to the purposes of instruction. It is no more improbable, on the notion of this great tempter, that a man should yield to his agency, when he himself assumes the human figure, than when he is supposed, as he is, to inhabit the bodies of all the vicious, and supply the crafty and artful with the means of operating on inferior minds. We do not the less blame Eve, because we are told that she yielded to the temptation of the serpent.

As to the minor objections made to the conduct of parts of the story, and defects of style and description, I feel not myself called on to defend, my object not being to establish the literary but moral excellence of the work. The only remaining objection which I shall attempt to answer is that "our author has contrived to make his romance pernicious, by blending, with an irreverent negligence, all that is most awfully true in religion, with all that is most ridiculously absurd in superstition. He takes frequent occasion, indeed, to manifest his sovereign contempt for the latter, both in his own person and in that of his principal characters; and that his respect for the former is not excessive we are forced to conclude from the treatment which its inspired writers receive from him."

In support of this observation we have a garbled passage quoted by the critics, in which the author has noticed with too much warmth, we must confess, some of the passages of the bible, which are undoubtedly improper for the eye of a young female. It is not fair to quote this passage without adding the eulogiums which the author has passed on the morality of the sacred writings, both in that passage and others in the work. Whether the author be or be not a Christian, is not the inquiry, but whether there be any foundation for the observation made on the indecency of some parts of our religious code; this the critics are obliged to allow is the case in one instance, viz. Ezekiel chap. 23. There are also other examples which must be in the eye of every man who has read these writings with attention. The indiscriminate perusal of such passages as occur, in which every thing is called by its vulgar name, in which the most luxuriant images are described, as in Solomon's Song, must certainly be improper for young females. So fully aware were the Jews of this truth, that they prohibited the reading of Solomon's Song, till a certain age, when the passions are in subjection. The warmth of expression is too great, but we may pardon this, since we see a desire of preventing the mischievous effects of even the most generally excellent productions.—The author, so far from deserving to be stigmatized as an enemy to Christianity, appears to me to be acting as one of its best friends, when he endeavours to prevent the mischief which may ensue from mixing what may be improper for young minds, with the rest of a work so generally excellent in its morality, so pure in its doctrines. The mischief which might be produced would be the greater, because of the reverence with which young persons are generally taught to regard the sacred writings. The impressions of such images as are blamed, would be the more deeply engraven on the mind, as they believe that nothing can be learned there but purity and innocence. I should have thought that these critics might have overlooked an error into which they themselves have fallen to a still greater excess: for they cannot allow the moral tendency of the romance to plead the pardon of two or three passages, which appear to them to be too luxuriant, and too replete with wanton imagery.

I have thus, Sir, endeavoured to shew that the attacks made on Mr. Lewis are unfounded, and that when the critic stares and trembles to find the author of the Monk a legislator, his horror is not reasonable; and that with propriety we may apply to those men who can drink vice at the fountain of the Monk, the expression of this very critic: "The most innocent expressions may become the first link in the chain of association, when a man's soul has been poisoned and depraved by the habit of reading lewd and voluptuous tales; and we believe it not absolutely impossible that he might extract pollution from the word of purity, and turn the grace of God into wantonness."

I hope I have succeeded in showing, that "the author has not endeavoured to inflame the fleshy appetites, and then to pour contempt on the only book which would be adequate to the task of reclaiming them." If I have not failed in this object, I shall feel a satisfaction in having employed a leisure hour in a task so delightful as rescuing from disgrace, in my opinion unmerited, a man of such talents, taste, and brilliancy of imagination, as the author of the Monk. I hope this attempt will not be displeasing to him who is the most concerned, nor fail of its effect on the public mind. My motives are, however, pure; I know I am as great an enemy to licentiousness as the critics themselves, and I trust I have shewn myself

A FRIEND TO GENIUS.

5. Matthew Gregory Lewis, letter to his father (Baron-Wilson 1: 154–58)

February 23, 1798

MY DEAR FATHER,

Though certain that the clamours against "The Monk" cannot have given you the smallest doubt of the rectitude of my intentions, or the purity of my principles, yet I am conscious that it must have grieved you to find any doubts on the subject existing in the minds of other people. To express my sorrow for having given you pain, is my motive for now addressing you; and also to assure you that you shall not feel that pain a second time on my account. Having made you feel it at all, would be a sufficient reason, had I not others, to make me regret having published the first edition of "The Monk;" but I have others, weaker indeed than the one mentioned, but still sufficiently strong. I perceive that I have put too much confidence in the accuracy of my own judgment; that, convinced of my object being unexceptionable, I did not sufficiently examine whether the means by which I attained that object were generally so; and that, upon many accounts, I have to accuse myself of high imprudence. Let me, however, observe that TWENTY is not the age at which prudence is most to be expected. Inexperience prevented my distinguishing what would give offence; but as soon as I found that offence was given, I made the only reparation in my power: I carefully revised the work, and expunged every syllable on which could be grounded the slightest construction of immorality. This, indeed, was no difficult task; for the objections rested entirely on expressions too strong, and words carelessly chosen; not on the sentiments, characters, or general tendency of the work.

That the latter is undeserving censure, Addison will vouch for me:

the moral and outline of my story are taken from an allegory inserted by him in "The Guardian," and which he commends highly, for
ability of invention and propriety of object. Unluckily, in working it
up, I thought that the stronger my colours, the more effect would
my picture produce; and it never struck me, that the exhibition of
vice, in her temporary triumph, might possibly do as much harm as
her final exposure and punishment would do good. To do much
good, in deed, was more than I expected of my book; having always
believed that our conduct depends on our own hearts and characters, not upon the books we read or the sentiments we hear. But
though I did not expect much benefit to arise from the perusal of a
trifling romance, written by a youth of twenty, I was in my own
mind quite certain that no harm could be produced by a work
whose subject was furnished by one of our best moralists, and in the
composition of which I did not introduce a single incident, or a single character, without meaning to inculcate some maxim universally allowed. It was, then, with infinite surprise that I heard the outcry
raised against the book, and found that a few ill-judged and
unguarded passages totally obscured its general tendency.

To support the charge of irreligion, a single one only has been,
or can be, produced. I am heartily sorry that this passage was ever
published; but I must say, that I have been very unfairly treated
respecting it. Those who have made it the subject of public censure,
have uniformly omitted such parts as would have palliated those
offensive expressions. Those expressions, certainly, are much too
strong, and I now see that their style is irreverent; but it was not
intended to be such, nor was the passage meant to counsel any
more than that the bible should not be read before a certain age,
when its perusers would be capable of benefiting by its precepts and
admiring its beauties. It also suggested the propriety of not putting
certain passages before the eyes of very young persons. This advice
I was induced to give from experience; for I know that schoolboys
do not (neither, if my informers may be credited, do schoolgirls)
always read particular chapters of the bible for the purpose of edi-
fication. In stating this, I thought, by representing the advice as having been given to the heroine by her mother—a woman pious and
sensible—I had guarded against the idea of attacking the bible.

My precaution was ineffectual: I have given offence; I am sorry for
having given it. I have omitted the passage; and can now do no more
than say, that neither in this, nor any other part of "The Monk," had
I the slightest idea that what I was then writing could injure the principles, moral or religious, of any human being. Since this work, I have
published others; and, taught by experience, I have avoided the inser-

tion of any word that could possibly admit of misrepresentation. As their propriety has not been questioned, I trust that I have succeeded in the attempt; and I do not despair of some time or other convincing my censurers that they have totally mistaken both me and my principles. Those principles I need not justify to you, my dear father: I need only again request your pardon for the uneasiness which this business has given you, and beg you to believe me,

Your most affectionate son,

M.G. LEWIS

6. Matthew Gregory Lewis, Preface to *Adelmorn, the Outlaw* (1801)

A fault, were it one ever so serious, committed at twenty, and followed during a course of years by no error of a similar nature, might, I should think, be forgiven without exercising any dangerous lenity, or requiring any very great exertion of candour. That I have not found such candour, however, I do not very poignantly regret: what pains but little, is not worthy a complaint, and censure is only terrible to me, when I feel it to have been merited. I have nearly served a seven years apprenticeship to patience, under the attacks of the most uncandid criticism, unmitigated censure, and exaggerating misrepresentation; nor have I ever written a line to right myself, or blame those who magnified a single act of imprudence into charges equally discordant with my principles, and insulting to my understanding. Hitherto I have only listened with contempt to censure inflicted without justice; for once, and for once only I will alter my conduct, and address a few words on this head to those who may feel any interest respecting me.

Without entering into the discussion, whether the principles inculcated in "The Monk" are right or wrong, or whether the *means* by which the story is conducted is likely to do more mischief than the *tendency* is likely to produce good, I solemnly declare, that when I published the work I had no idea that its publication *could* be prejudicial; if I was wrong, the error proceeded from my judgment, not from my intention.

Without entering into the merits of the advice which it proposes to convey, or attempting to defend (what I now condemn myself) the *language and manner* in which that advice was delivered, I solemnly declare, that in writing the passage which regards the Bible (consisting of a single page, and the only passage which I ever wrote on the subject) I had not the most distant intention to bring the sacred Writings into contempt, and that, had I suspected it of producing such an effect, I should not have written the paragraph.

To those who know me well I am certain these assertions are superfluous: it is to those who know me not that I address them, and whom, if they do not convince, I must be contented to leave in error. (v–vi)

7. *Le Décade philosophique, littéraire et politique* 23 (20 Floréal, Year 5 [9 May 1797]): 290–97, translated by D.L. Macdonald and Nikki Sheppy

[The reviewer begins by quoting the epigraph from Horace, in Latin and French.]

It's a very strange and extravagant work, this novel of the *Monk*. Stories of robbers, of sorcerers, of ghosts, of the *wandering Jew*, of the devils, everything that can be imagined of the incredible and the ridiculous is to be found there, and it is all interesting, one reads it and eats it up without stopping.

> The world is old, they say; I believe it; nonetheless
> One still needs to amuse it like a child.[1]

One is sometimes astonished at how the ancient poets displayed such noble genius, such rare talents, in dealing with absurd and inept fables; but it is precisely because they trained themselves with fables that they were so sublime, so pathetic, so animated; what would you have the reason compose? An epic poem or a tragedy? Reasoning is difficult; it has a hold on only a few minds, and on trained minds: the imagination, the passions warm, move, transport all men. That, among other causes, is why in our reasoning, dissertating, analyzing century, one should not expect great orators and great poets. When Boileau said: *Nothing is beautiful but the truth*, he meant to speak only of the truth of execution; that's why he took care to add: *It should hold sway everywhere, even in fable.*[2]

It is true that the religious fables of the ancients were more pleasant, more cheerful, more inspiring than ours: even though we were to be accused of *philosophy* again, we would say that the Christian religion and its mysteries are sad, degrading, and contemptible in comparison to the pagan mythology. Attributing to the Gods the passions of men, one almost raised men to the rank

---

1 Jean de La Fontaine (1621–95), *Fables* 8.4, "Le Pouvoir des fables" (1678).
2 Nicolas Boileau-Despréaux (1636–1711), *Épîtres* 9.43–44.

of Gods. Mythology peopled the world, raised the soul; Theology has nothing but scholastic arguments and frightful dogmas.

The character of the Monk is drawn with power and truth. Two things surprise me; that this work should be English: one would have believed it written in Spain or Italy, so well is the monastic race depicted in it! and that it should be by a young man of twenty; it displays a great deal of experience and a profound knowledge of the human heart.

[The reviewer summarizes the main plot of the novel and quotes the ending, from Ambrosio's escape to his death.]

This catastrophe is enough to give an idea of this singular novel. Ambrosio dies the victim of his desires, against which, from the beginning, he has not kept himself sufficiently on guard.

The seductions are managed with the greatest art; and that is not surprising, since they are hatched and carried out by a Devil metamorphosed into a woman.

There are many passages in the book which one cannot read without an involuntary shudder; such as a story of robbers in a forest of Alsace; such as that of *the bleeding nun of Lindemberg*, which has apparently provided madame de Genlis with the ridiculous story of *the Little heels*, on which she based her novel of *The Knights of the Swan*; in short, the author seems to have had the aim of terrifying, like Shakespeare, by supernatural means, by dreams, spells, communications between the living and the dead, between men and fantastic beings; all that is very impossible, very absurd; and all that nonetheless produces an effect; so great is the power of the imagination over us at every age! In vain one tells oneself that these are stories; these stories make one tremble and affect one powerfully. Then one shrugs one's shoulders in pity; but only when one has finished the book.

8. "Novels of Mrs. Radcliffe," *Spectateur du nord* 6 (April–June 1798): 324–38, translated by D.L. Macdonald and Nikki Sheppy

Another novel, of the same genre and published at almost the same time as those of Mrs. Radcliffe, *The Monk* has obtained and deserved the same success. This novel is full of interesting situations, almost all of them well rendered. The fall of the Monk Ambrosio is well enough paced, although his first scene of sensual pleasure with Matilda, whom he must believe to be on her deathbed, appears a bit precipitate. Two of the victims of the Monk, Agnes and Antonia, excite a lively interest and compassion. What could be more fit to inspire terror and pity than the description of the terrible punishment to which Agnes is condemned; that black, damp, and foul vault; that chain which binds her there; that half-rotten straw which serves her as a bed, those reptiles which besiege her there! and her childbirth in that tomb! and the neglect to which she is abandoned with her child, amidst the horrors of that dreadful entombment!..... To make a counterpart to this picture, the Author could not have imagined anything more dreadful than Antonia waking from her lethargy amidst cadavers to pass into the arms of the villain who has buried her alive, and who gluts his infamous desires on her, surrounded by bones and skeletons.

This novel has the merit of offering a great and fearful lesson, the danger of a first offence, and of vices, apparently excusable, which lead to the greatest crimes. It seems that the Author wanted to develop and put into action the maxim that la Fontaine has expressed in the following verses:

> Just as the virtues are sisters
> Likewise the vices are brothers;
> And when one of them gets a hold of our hearts,
> They all come in a file, hardly any are missing.[1]

There is a very remarkable difference between this novel and those of Mrs. Radcliffe: it is that the Author of *The Monk*, in order to inspire terror, has not restricted himself to natural means: he has made use of ghosts and magic. With such means, great effects are easier to obtain; but since no-one believes either in ghosts or in magic, when the machinery is laid bare, must not the illusion vanish? In that case, at least, a great talent is needed to keep it up: the Author of *The Monk* does not lack one. Besides, this reef is perhaps not so dangerous as it appears at first glance. The hunger for the marvellous accompanies us from the cradle to the grave: men, *for the most part*, are children in this regard at fifty as at ten; and one can point out at least three reasons for it: the constant awareness of our weakness, which makes us esteem and admire whatever is above our reach; the pleasure of surprise, which belongs to all ages; and the belief in invisible powers, which is bound up with the religious principles of our education.

Moreover, when an able painter shows you a *bleeding Nun* with her dagger, her funereal veil, her sepulchral lamp, her habit stained with blood, her wound still bleeding, leaving a cavern in the middle of the night, lifting her veil, and revealing the face of a spectre to a lover who was waiting for his mistress there;—or when the

---

1 La Fontaine, *Fables* 8.25, "Les Deux Chiens et l'âne mort" (1678).

same painter shows us the phantom of Elvira appearing to her daughter and pointing out to her, with a finger on a clock, the hour when she must die;—if the picture is well painted, of what use will be our disbelief in ghosts? Our senses will be stronger than our reason, and our mind will immediately share in their shock.

The writer has in his style more resources to make a good picture than the painter with his brush and his colours. Speaking only to your mind, the style paints to all your senses; and the brush speaks only to your eyes. In regarding the writer's picture, the eye, the ear, the touch, the smell, everything is affected: you see the spectre and her rags, you hear the noise of her chains, you feel her icy hand seize your own, you smell the odour of death that accompanies her [...] And, if the writer leads you for a long time from underground passages to underground passages, from caverns to ruins, from ruins to dungeons, from dungeons to sepulchres, always accompanied by owls, spectres, chains, daggers, skeletons, assassins; the senses remaining always violently affected, and the reason never being able to find a moment of calm to make itself heard, if, after several hours of reading, your eyes leave the book which has presented you with this succession of lugubrious pictures, you can hardly recognize anything around you, you are drunk with horror and fright[.......] And, if you were doing your reading, on a long winter's evening, in the vast hall of an ancient castle, by the flickering gleam of a single light, amidst the concert formed by the whistling of the winds, the murmur of the waves, the cries of the screech-owls and the harsh sound of the weather-cocks;—busy reading about phantoms and ghosts, how many times would you not perhaps glance with a kind of anxiety at the obscure depths of the hall, at its old and sombre pictures, at its tattered tapestries, at its doors and windows shaken by the hurricane! [...] No doubt your imagination, however exalted it might be, would be easily overcome by your reason; but if it cost the latter a single effort, a single instant of labour, that would be enough to justify to a certain extent the means employed by these writers, who, with their phantoms and their ghosts, aim only at your imagination. If their own, at least, in giving itself up to its caprices and disorders, knew how to brighten instead of blackening itself, and to make us laugh instead of frightening us, far from incurring our reproaches, they would earn the right to our gratitude, and perhaps, like Ariosto, to our admiration. (330-34)

9. Marquis de Sade, "Reflections on the Novel" (1800; quoted by permission of Penguin Books); translated by Mario Praz

This genre [the Gothic novel] was the inevitable product of the revolutionary shocks with which the whole of Europe resounded. For those who were acquainted with all the ills that are brought upon men by the wicked, the romantic novel was becoming somewhat difficult to write, and merely monotonous to read: there was nobody left who had not experienced more misfortunes in four or five years than could be depicted in a century by literature's most famous novelists: it was necessary to call upon hell for aid in order to arouse interest, and to find in the land of fantasies what was common knowledge from historical observation of man in this iron age. But this way of writing presented so many inconveniencies! The author of [*The Monk*] failed to avoid them no less than did Mrs Radcliffe; either of these two alternatives was unavoidable; either to explain away all the magic elements, and from then on to be interesting no longer, or never raise the curtain, and there you are in the most horrible unreality. (14)

10. Ann Radcliffe, "On the Supernatural in Poetry," *New Monthly Magazine* ns 16 (1826): 145-52

["]In the scene where Horatio breaks his secret to Hamlet, Shakspeare, still true to the touch of circumstances, makes the time evening, and marks it by the very words of Hamlet, 'Good even, sir,'[1] which Hanmer and Warburton[2] changed, without any reason, to 'good morning,' thus making Horatio relate his most interesting and solemn story by the clear light of the cheerfullest part of the day; when busy sounds are stirring, and the sun itself seems to contradict every doubtful tale, and lessen every feeling of terror. The discord of this must immediately be understood by those who have bowed the willing soul to the poet."

"How happens it then," said Mr. S——, "that objects of terror sometimes strike us very forcibly, when introduced into scenes of gaiety and splendour, as, for instance, in the Banquet scene in Macbeth?"[3]

---

1 Shakespeare, *Hamlet* 1.2.167.
2 Sir Thomas Hanmer (1677-1746) and William Warburton (1698-1779) both produced worthless editions of Shakespeare.
3 Shakespeare, *Macbeth* 3.4. The epigraph to Lewis's Chapter IV (p. 133) is from this scene.

"They strike, then, chiefly by the force of contrast," replied W——; "but the effect, though sudden and strong, is also transient; it is the thrill of horror and surprise, which they then communicate, rather than the deep and solemn feelings excited under more accordant circumstances, and left long upon the mind. Who ever suffered for the ghost of Banquo, the gloomy and sublime kind of terror, which that of Hamlet calls forth? though the appearance of Banquo, at the high festival of Macbeth, not only tells us that he is murdered, but recalls to our minds the fate of the gracious Duncan, laid in silence and death by those who, in this very scene, are revelling in his spoils. There, though deep pity mingles with our surprise and horror, we experience a far less degree of interest, and that interest too of an inferior kind. The union of grandeur and obscurity, which Mr. Burke describes as a sort of tranquillity tinged with terror, and which causes the sublime, is to be found only in Hamlet; or in scenes where circumstances of the same kind prevail."

"That may be," said Mr. S——, "and I perceive you are not one of those who contend that obscurity does not make any part of the sublime." "They must be men of very cold imaginations," said W——, "with whom certainty is more terrible than surmise. Terror and horror are so far opposite, that the first expands the soul, and awakens the faculties to a high degree of life; the other contracts, freezes, and nearly annihilates them. I apprehend, that neither Shakspeare nor Milton by their fictions, nor Mr. Burke by his reasoning, anywhere looked to positive horror as a source of the sublime, though they all agree that terror is a very high one; and where lies the great difference between horror and terror, but in the uncertainty and obscurity, that accompany the first,[1] respecting the dreaded evil?"

"But what say you to Milton's image—

"On his brow sat horror plumed."[2]

"As an image, it certainly is sublime; it fills the mind with an idea of power, but it does not follow that Milton intended to declare the feeling of horror to be sublime; and after all, his image imparts more of terror than of horror; for it is not distinctly pictured forth, but is seen in glimpses through obscuring shades, the great outlines only appearing, which excite the imagination to complete the rest; he only says, 'sat horror plumed;' you will observe, that the look of horror and the other characteristics are

---

1 Evidently a mistake for "the second." Uncertainty and obscurity are attributes of terror, not horror.
2 Misquoted from Milton, *Paradise Lost* 4.988-89.

left to the imagination of the reader; and according to the strength of that, he will feel Milton's image to be either sublime or otherwise. Milton, when he sketched it, probably felt, that not even his art could fill up the outline, and present to other eyes the countenance which his 'mind's eye'[1] gave to him. Now, if obscurity has so much effect on fiction, what must it have in real life, when to ascertain the object of our terror, is frequently to acquire the means of escaping it."] (149-50)

---

1 Shakespeare, *Hamlet* 1.2.185.

Appendix D: Cultural Responses

[*The Monk* was so popular that it inspired a number of spin-offs and rip-offs. We have chosen three, all from popular culture: one play (D.1), one poem (D.2), and one fiction "chapbook" (D.3). See Introduction 23-26.]

1. Charles Farley, *Raymond and Agnes; or, The Castle of Lindenbergh* (1797)

IN order to shape the Episode of *Raymond* and *Agnes*, from the romance of the MONK, for dramatic effect, the situation in which the Countess (step-mother of Agnes)[1] is placed in the cottage, according to the romance, is now occupied by AGNES. Another variation occurs in making the NUN, whose SPECTRE appears, the *mother* of *Agnes*, and former Countess of Lindenbergh.

The progress of the story will occur in the following scenes.

BALLET,
RAYMOND and AGNES;
OR THE
CASTLE OF LINDENBERGH.

SCENE I. *A Gothic library in the castle of Don Felix.*—Raymond discovered at his studies, is interrupted by the entrance of Don Felix (his father) who informs him it is his wish he should go upon his travels.—Theodore, his favourite domestic, intreats to accompany him.—After which the scene changes to

The outside of a castle.—Theodore takes an affectionate leave of his favorite (Annette).—Several servants enter, preceding Don Felix, Raymond, and a holy father of the Church—Raymond receives their benedictions, and departs on his journey, accompanied by Theodore.

Scene. *Madrid; with a view of an hotel and a convent.*—PROCESSION of NUNS and FRIARS—

---

1 In the novel, the Baroness is Agnes's aunt.

CHORUS.[1]

SOME yield their breath to hoary time
And others perish in their prime
But he whom death the longest spares,
Is but the witness of most cares.

Agnes, the daughter of Count Lindenbergh's departure from the convent—Raymond and Theodore enter, order refreshments from the hotel, and proceed on their journey, under the guidance of Claude, one of a banditti infesting the neighbouring forest.

Scene, *A forest—midnight, with a distant hovel.*—Enter Baptiste (one of the banditti) disguised as a woodman—The carriage with Raymond and Theodore breaks down—Claude, pointing to the hovel, informs them they may there find shelter for the night.

Scene, *A nearer view of the hovel.*—Baptiste is seen to enter it.—Raymond and Theodore are conducted in by Claude and Baptiste.

Scene, *Inside of the hovel.*—Maugerette and her child are discovered. Raymond and Theodore are introduced by Baptiste—Theodore is shewn to his room by Maugerette—Robert and Jacques (sons to Baptiste) enter armed, making a servile obedience to Raymond, who is conducted to his chamber by Robert.

Scene, *The bed room prepared for Raymond*—Maugerette wishing to preserve the life of Raymond from the assassins, conveys a pillow stained with blood upon his bed, thereby to inform him of his danger—she conceals herself—Raymond retires to rest, but is prevented by finding the bloody pillow and struck with horror, falls into a swoon—Robert enters—Attempts to murder him—Is prevented by Maugerette—and Raymond, at her request, retires.

Scene, *The Lower Apartments of the Hovel.*—Robert informs his father and brother of the ineffectual attempt on the life of Raymond; who is brought in by Maugerette—A knocking is heard without—Agnes (who has been also benighted in the forest) is led in by Claude, attended by servants—Supper is prepared—Opiates are mixed with the wine—Agnes drinks, and falls into a slumber—Maugerette begs Raymond not to drink, but to put on the semblance of sleep—Baptiste sends Robert and Jacques to secure the servants, who have retired; and supposing Raymond at rest, prepares to murder him—Raymond seizes him, and Baptiste falls by

---

1 In the published version, the songs are printed separately, at the end of the text, and cross-references (sometimes) indicate where they should appear. We have deleted the cross-references and inserted the songs at the appropriate points in the action.

the hand of Maugerette—who points out a secret avenue; through which she, taking her child, Raymond and Agnes escape, followed by Theodore.

Scene, *Inside of Lindenbergh Castle.*—The mother of Agnes, the late Countess, pourtrayed in the habit of a Nun.——The Count discovered viewing the picture with agitation—kneels to implore forgiveness for the murder.—Agnes brought in by Raymond, is introduced to the present Countess—she becomes enamoured of him, offers him her picture, which he rejects with scorn.

Scene, *The Chamber of Agnes*—Portrait of a Nun, with a wound upon her breast, a lamp, dagger, and a rosary on her arm.—— Agnes enamoured of Raymond, enters, and prepares to draw his Portrait—Raymond entering unperceived, throws himself at her feet, and obtains a promise of her hand—He requests an explanation of the picture of the bleeding Nun.—She informs him (in a Song), 'tis the resemblance of a Spectre which haunts the Castle every fifth year.—

AIR—AGNES.

FULL fifteen Years have past away
        Since first within these walls,
Appeared the ghost, whose gliding form
        The stoutest heart appals.
Long time here nightly stalk'd this bleeding NUN,
Her entrance at the awful hour of one!

II.
Her face she'd veil, and on her arm
        A chaplet still appear'd,
One hand a burning lamp sustain'd,
        A dagger t'other rear'd;
O what amazement to behold the NUN,
When ent'ring as the midnight clock struck one!

III.
At chamber doors she'd sometimes stop,
        And heave a piteous wail:
Now curses deep wou'd shake the roof,
        Now anthems soft prevail.
At length the spectre for a time seem'd gone
And ceas'd her visits as the clock struck one!

IV.
Now each fifth year, on May's fifth morn,
        Still constant to the hour;
That door she passes and descends,
        The steps of yonder tower:
And then that Gothic hall she'll cross anon,
Just as the warning midnight bell strikes one!

The Count and Countess approach; and in anger order Raymond to quit the castle.

AIR—AGNES.

When warn'd this Castle to depart,
On me fond glances Raymond threw;
Love seiz'd for once a Parthean dart,
And gave him victory as he flew.

Scene, *The Outside of the Castle*—Raymond, about to depart, is diverted by the sound of Mandoline—a paper is lowered by Agnes from the Castle, containing a drawing of the Nun, with the following scrolls.

"When the castle-bell tolls one,
Expect me like this bleeding Nun."

Scene, *The outside of the castle as before*—Raymond waiting for the appointed time—the clock strikes one—the gates fly open—the apparition of the nun comes from the castle—Raymond (supposing it Agnes) follows in extacy—Theodore approaching, is met by Agnes in the habit of the nun—agitated by the apparent neglect of Raymond, they retire.

Scene, *A dreary wood*—Raymond following the spectre (still supposing it Agnes) attempts to embrace it when suddenly vanishing,[1] a cloud rises from the earth bearing the following inscription:—

"*PROTECT the CHILD of the MURDER'D AGNES.*"

Scene, *The Mountains*—

GLEE—MULETEERS.

BRING, bring the generous flask to cheer,
The weary, drooping Muleteer!
Those Alps, whose tops in clouds are lost,
Since break of morn with toil we crost,
O full of danger is the way!
The Wolf twice mark'd us for his prey;
With sudden swell the torrent broke;
The winds with loudest fury spoke!

O bring the generous flask to cheer
The spirits of the Muleteer!
Bring too the Flagelot and Tabor,
To soothe the heart, and sweeten labor,

---

1 In 1801, Lewis recalled this stage effect: "at Covent-Garden the bleeding Nun in 'Raymond and Agnes' has been for many years in the habit of ascending to heaven with great applause in a sort of postchaise made of paste-board" (*Adelmorn* v).

The dance, the dullest mind will brighten,
The foot most weary it will lighten!
                        lara, lara, lol,
                        lara, lara, lol!

Such joy the ev'ning yet can give:
        The day till twelve at night will last,
        And when in merriment 'tis past,
We've only one day less to live!
Your smiles, ye Damsels, too shall cheer
The spirits of the Muleteer!
                        lara, lara, lol,
                        lara, lara, lol.

Robert, Jacques, and Claude (the Robbers) discovered at the grave of Baptiste—Theodore and Agnes enter—Agnes is seized and borne into the Cavern.

Scene, *A wood*—Theodore and Maugerette meet Raymond and inform him of Agnes being seized by the Robbers—They hasten to her rescue.

Scene, *Inside of the Cavern*—The three Robbers cast lots for the possession of Agnes—she becomes the prize of Robert—He attempts to seize her—She resisting, he aims a stiletto at her breast.—At this instant Raymond, Theodore, and Maugerette rush in—Robert falls by the Dagger of Raymond, Jacques by the sword of Theodore—and Claude by a pistol from the hand of Maugerette.

Scene, *The castle of Don Felix.*—Raymond presents Agnes to his Father, who joins their hands; and the piece concludes with

A FINALE SPANISH FANDANGO.

STRIKE the lute's enchanting wires!
Every chord the dance inspires!
In the brisk *Fandango* meeting,
And with smiles each other greeting;
The *Castinet* shall time our measure,
And the night dissolve in pleasure!

2. Anon., "The Bleeding Nun" (1801)

I am not at liberty to publish the name of the author of this Ballad: it is founded on the fourth chapter of the Romance of "Ambrosio, or the Monk."[1]

---

1 Lewis's note; the poem was included in his anthology *Tales of Wonder* (1801). In 1798, *The Monk* had been re-titled *Ambrosio*.

WHERE yon proud turrets crown the rock,
    Seest thou a warrior stand?
He sighs to hear the castle clock
    Say midnight is at hand.

It strikes, and now his lady fair
    Comes tripping from her hall,
Her heart is rent by deep despair,
    And tears in torrents fall.

—"Ah! woe is me, my love," she cried,
    "What anguish wrings my heart:
Ah! woe is me," she said, and sigh'd,
    "We must for ever part.

"Know, ere three days are past and flown,
    (Tears choak the piteous tale!)
A parent's vow, till now unknown,
    Devotes me to the veil."—

—"Not so, my Agnes!" Raymond cried,
    "For leave thee will I never;
Thou art mine, and I am thine,
    Body and soul for ever!

"Then quit thy cruel father's bower,
    And fly, my love, with me."—
—"Ah! how can I escape his power,
    Or who can set me free?

"I cannot leap yon wall so high,
    Nor swim the fosse with thee;
I can but wring my hands, and sigh
    That none can set me free."—

—"Now list, my lady, list, my love,
    I pray thee list to me,
For I can all your fears remove,
    And I can set you free.

"Oft have you heard old Ellinore,
    Your nurse, with horror tell,
How, robed in white, and stain'd with gore,
    Appears a spectre fell;

"And each fifth year, at dead of night,
    Stalks through the castle gate,
Which, by an ancient solemn rite,
    For her must open wait.

"Soon as to some far distant land,
    Retires to-morrow's sun,
With torch and dagger in her hand,
    Appears the Bleeding Nun.

"Now you shall play the bleeding Nun,
    Array'd in robes so white,
And at the solemn hour of one,
    Stalk forth to meet your knight.

"Our steeds shall bear us far away,
    Beyond your father's power,
And Agnes, long ere break of day,
    Shall rest in Raymond's bower."—

—"My heart consents, it must be done,
    —Father, 'tis your decree,—
And I will play the Bleeding Nun,
    And fly, my love, with thee.

"For I am thine," fair Agnes cried,
    "And leave thee will I never;
I am thine, and thou art mine,
    Body and soul for ever!"

Fair Agnes sat within her bower,
    Array'd in robes so white,
And waited the long wish'd-for hour,
    When she should meet her knight.

And Raymond, as the clock struck one,
    Before the castle stood;
And soon came forth his lovely Nun,
    Her white robes stain'd in blood.

He bore her in his arms away,
    And placed her on her steed;
And to the maid he thus did say,
    As on they rode with speed:

—"Oh Agnes! Agnes! thou art mine,
    And leave thee will I never;
Thou art mine, and I am thine,
    Body and soul for ever!"—

—"Oh Raymond! Raymond! I am thine,
    And leave thee will I never;
I am thine, and thou art mine,
    Body and soul for ever!"—

At length,—"We're safe!"—the warrior cried;
    "Sweet love abate thy speed;"—
But madly still she onwards hied,
    Nor seem'd his call to heed.

Through wood and wild, they speed their way,
    Then sweep along the plain,
And almost at the break of day,
    The Danube's banks they gain.

—"Now stop ye, Raymond, stop ye here,
    And view the farther side;
Dismount, and say Sir Knight, do'st fear,
    With me to stem the tide."—

Now on the utmost brink they stand,
    And gaze upon the flood,
She seiz'd Don Raymond by the hand,
    Her grasp it froze his blood.

A whirling blast from off the stream
    · Threw back the maiden's veil;
Don Raymond gave a hideous scream,
    And felt his spirits fail.

Then down his limbs, in strange affright,
    Cold dews to pour begun;
No Agnes met his shudd'ring sight,
    —"God! 'Tis the Bleeding Nun!"—

A form of more than mortal size,
    All ghastly, pale, and dead,
Fix'd on the Knight her livid eyes,
    And thus the Spectre said:

—"Oh Raymond! Raymond! I am thine,
    And leave thee will I never;
I am thine, and thou art mine,
    Body and soul for ever!"—

Don Raymond shrieks, he faints; the blood
    Ran cold in every vein,
He sank into the roaring flood,
    And never rose again!

3. Anon., *Almagro & Claude; or Monastic Murder; Exemplified in the Dreadful Doom of an Unfortunate Nun* (1810)

——————————————"Ah! how dark
These long extended realms and rueful wastes,
Where nought but silence reigns and night.—
——————————————The sickly taper,
By glimm'ring through thy low brow'd misty vaults,
Furr'd round with mouldy damps and ropy slime,
Lets fall a supernumerary horror,
And only serves to make thy night more irksome."
                                BEATTIE.[1]

---

1 Actually (mis)quoted from Blair, *The Grave* 11-20, the epigraph to Lewis's Chapter VII (p. 228).

ALMAGRO & CLAUDE,
OR THE MONASTIC MURDER.

THE Marquis d'Axala, after leaving the University of Salamanca, set out immediately on his travels. He was liberally supplied with money and letters of introduction by his father, who insisted on his concealing his rank, and travelling as a private gentleman. Before he entered upon his tour, the prudent parent addressed his son in a long speech upon the principles which ought to direct his conduct, and the reasons why he had enjoined him for a time to drop his title; which were, that he might appreciate the estimation in which he himself would be held by the world when their judgment was not biassed by his rank, and that he might examine the customs and manners of the multitude, without derogating from his exalted birth. The Marquis saw the propriety of this advice, and quitted Spain, calling himself by the plain title of Don Almagro di Cordova. Paris was the first station he made, attended by a faithful servant. Here he found the manners of the people trifling, unstable, and insincere; and, dissatisfied, bent his way towards the German Courts, intending to make some stay at Strasbourg. The Marquis arrived safely at Luneville, and on stepping out of his chaise to alight at the inn, observed a rich equipage at the door, and soon after saw an elegant female, followed by two attendants, enter the carriage, which drove off immediately. He directly enquired of the host who the lady was, and learned that she was a German Baroness of great rank and fortune, who had been on a visit to the Duchess of Bellecour, and was returning to Strasbourg, to her husband, previously to their return home. Almagro set off, and intended to reach Strasbourg that night. In this, however, he was prevented by the breaking down of the chaise in the middle of a dark forest. There seemed no alternative but for Almagro to take the servant's horse, and ride on; but the old postilion, after stating the intricacy of the way in such a gloomy night, said it was only five minutes walk from the cottage of Dubois, a very honest friend of his, and a wood cutter. The proffered help was immediately accepted, and the shattered vehicle was, with much labour, drawn to the cottage, through the window of which they beheld the blaze of a comfortable fire. They soon made the cottager awake, who apologized for not opening the door till he heard the voice of his friend Jacques, as there were a sad number of rogues about. He then introduced Almagro into an inner room, where sat a female whom he supposed to be the wife of his host, who received him with a slight reverence, but did not rise to assist in providing for his accommodation till reproved by her husband and Jacques.—A churlish gloom overspread her countenance, and, though she might be called handsome, her very look and action expressed discontent. The woodman seemed to be about sixty years of age, and appeared to have absorbed all the fatness and fresh colour of his wife, who was haggard, though not yet thirty.

The postilion would have proceeded to Strasbourg that night for workmen to return and mend the chaise, but Almagro over-ruled this, as the night was bitterly cold, and his arrival there at a particular hour was of no consequence.—Not long after Dubois put his head out of the cottage door, and said, "I wonder what detains my boys so long. O Monsieur, they are such fine young men, that you will say, when you see them, their equals are not to be found any where."

"Such sons, indeed!" exclaimed Antoinette, in a growling accent. "Come, come, Antoinette," said the host, "chear up a little; if your two sons are not quite as old, I hope you will yet live to see them just such lads as Martin and Philip." "Heaven forbid!" cried Antoinette, clasping her hands together: "I would rather see them perish first!" She then quitted the room, and the Marquis could not help remarking to his host how ill-fated he was in being united to such a woman. The man briefly informed him, that her affection for two sons she had had by a former husband made her play the step-mother with his two sons; but, cross as she was, she managed his family excellently. This discourse was interrupted by a loud halloo, followed by a carriage, attended by several cavaliers, who were proceeding to Strasbourg, but through the ignorance of the drivers had lost their way. A lady inside appeared to be principally distressed, and whom Almagro recognised to be the lady he had seen at Luneville, the Baroness Wildenheim. The woodman shewed evident chagrin at the arrival of these strangers, but his countenance afterwards cleared up, upon learning the quality of his guest, and he soon arranged matters for the Baroness to have one chamber, and Almagro the other. The servants were to be well accommodated in a large barn, a few yards distant from the house. This arrangement being gratefully accepted, Dubois was just going to conduct the male domestics to their outhouse, when Martin and Philip appeared, who started at coming in, but, being assured by Dubois that the good company would find a corner for them, they staid, and were presented to the Baroness and Almagro, after which the two waiting women were conducted by Antoinette to their lady's apartment.

The two young men were tall and stout, and acknowledged Jacques as an old acquaintance. They then drew a cutlass and a brace of pistols from under their clothes, and laid them on the shelf, remarking at the same time they had just come from Strasbourg, and it was necessary to be well armed, as the forest was much infested with robbers. The Baroness earnestly wished to convey a letter to her husband, but the account of the forest rendered it too hazardous to send any servant. When Jacques understood this, he informed her he was under the necessity of reaching Strasbourg that night, and would convey a letter safely, as he was too insignificant an object to be interrupted by banditti. The Baroness accepted his offer, and at the same time she gave her letter, the Marquis sent a few lines to his banker. The lady, finding herself much fatigued, was conducted to her chamber; and on Antoinette's return, the Marquis, perceiving he was in her way, said he would go to his room till supper was ready.—Philip asked what chamber it was, and Antoinette replied, the one with the green hangings; and having put clean sheets on the bed, if the gentleman chooses to lounge on it, she should not make it over again. Philip, having remarked that it was no novelty to see his mother out of humour, opened the door, and began to ascend the staircase. "You fool, to go without a light!" exclaimed Antoinette, and passed the Marquis to put the candle into Philip's hand; in returning she met the Marquis just going to ascend: no one was near at the moment, and she instantly took the Marquis's hand, pressed it, and whispered, "Look at the sheets!" Don Almagro was startled, but Philip's voice calling him, he ascended to his room, where an excellent fire was lighted. No sooner was his conductor departed, then he turned down the coverture of the bed, and stood petrified at seeing the sheets crimsoned with blood. The circumstances which had taken place convinced the Marquis of the horror of his situation, which was further confirmed by hearing some one pacing hastily backwards and forwards under his window, whom he discovered to be Dubois, looking round with anxiety as if he expected some one. Having extinguished his candle, and repaired to the window, he saw Dubois joined by the postilion, Jacques, whom he had supposed on his way to Strasbourg.—They entered into a deep conversation, the result of which was, that, as the Marquis had above 2000 pistoles in his chaise, and the Baroness had also a casket of jewels of immense value, Jacques should immediately set out for the cavern, where some confederate banditti would be waiting till eleven o'clock; he was then to conduct them by twelve to the cottage of Dubois, and if any resistance was made by the cavaliers, the latter were all to be poniarded. The feelings of the Marquis at the prospect before him may be easily imagined; unarmed as he was, courage could do but little against so many; however, to avoid suspicion, he re-lighted his candle, and, on descending, found the table spread for six persons. The Baroness sat opposite the Marquis, who by a single glance informed Antoinette that he had taken her hint. He could not escape his confusion being seen by the young men, who enquired the cause, which he attributed to fatigue. The Marquis then talked upon his visit to Germany, and received an invitation from the Baroness to pass some time at her castle; at which the brothers cast a malignant smile, that seem to say they might never reach there. During all the supper time the Marquis talked incoherently, his attention being fixed on escaping from the cottage, and getting to the barn, to alarm the domestics; but the circumspection of Philip and Martin prevented this, and his only hope lay in Jacques not finding the banditti, in which case the guests might escape unhurt.

The host lamented the poorness of his fare, and he insultingly remarked, that, if his guests should be detained longer than they at present intended, he hoped to provide them with better entertainment. Dubois, then observing, that it very rarely happened he had such noble company, said he would celebrate the accidents of the night, by uncorking a bottle of most excellent wine made by his father, who was now in a better world! He gave his wife the key of the closet, which she received with a look of fear and distress. When she returned, the Marquis's eye caught her's, and she looked frowningly at the wine, and then expressively at him. In the mean while the host had drawn the cork, and filled two goblets, one of which the lady, at the instance of Dubois, drank. The Marquis, by its look and smell, took it for champaign, but seeing some grains of white powder floating on the top, he raised it to his lips, and seemed to have swallowed two or three mouthfuls of it, when, suddenly starting up, and declaring that this sort of wine always made him ill, he feigned to spit it out, and unperceived emptied the liquor into a vase of water behind him. Martin and Dubois looked distrustful; and Philip, in a side whisper, said, he had drank *sufficient*. The Marquis anxiously watched the effect of the wine upon the Baroness, who sunk into a profound sleep, which he did not dare to notice, but continued the conversation. The banditti now no longer seemed to preserve appearances, but whispered among themselves, and his danger seemed proceeding fast to extremity. In this situation he was relieved by Antoinette, who, placing herself behind the seats of her step sons, closed her eyes, and reclined her head upon her shoulder, pointing to the Marquis. He understood the hint, and in a few minutes seemed overcome with slumber. Dubois now congratulated his sons, that the Spaniard was gone to sleep, as he began to suspect him, and regretted they had not come a few minutes before the arrival of the Baroness, in which case the Don and his servant might have been dispatched out of the way, and their property secured. It was agreed, if the gang did not arrive that night, the travellers should be waylaid in the forest on the morrow. Dubois had just asked his wife, if she had given the sleeping draught to the female attendants, and been answered in the affirmative, when the trampling of horses announced the arrival of the troop, and Antoinette horrified the Marquis by an exclamation of, "Gracious heaven, then they must die!" "Let us in," was vociferated outside the cottage. "Yes, yes!" cried Dubois, joyfully; "they are our friends; you lead them to the barn, and do the business there; I will manage my gentleman here, and the women!" Martin would have shot the Marquis upon the spot, but Dubois bid him follow his brother, and assist the new comers, who had dismounted, and were silently moving towards the barn. Dubois then went to a small cupboard, and unlocked it. At this moment Antoinette whispered in the Marquis's ear, "Now!" and on opening his eyes, he saw Dubois standing with his back towards him, feeling the point of a dagger. Not a moment was to be lost. The Marquis, unarmed, sprang from his seat, and being possessed of a powerful arm, he grasped the villain by the throat with such violence, that he threw him on the floor breathless, while Antoinette, taking advantage of his unrecovered state, wrested the dagger from his hand, and plunged it repeatedly into his heart.

"Our only safety now lies in flight!" exclaimed Antoinette; "follow me! quick as lightning!" The Marquis seized the Baroness in his arms, and hastened after Antoinette, who mounted one of the banditti's horses, while the Marquis did the same with his charge. As they galloped by the barn, they could distinguish the shrieks of the dying, and the Marquis, unable to relieve them, felt a pang too great for utterance. Their flight was perceived by Martin, who with a torch recognized the fugitives in passing, and ordered a pursuit. The Marquis and his guide were in view of the steeple of Strasbourg, when the banditti were found to be gaining fast on them. The horses were spurred to the utmost, and at the moment when Antoinette had exclaimed, "We are lost!" a numerous band of cavaliers approached, of the foremost of whom she most piteously implored protection from robbers. "It is she herself!" exclaimed the man, jumping on the ground; "It is my mother! Stop, my Lord, they are safe."

Antoinette now descended, and clasped the cavalier in her arms. "Where is the Baroness Wildenheim?" inquired another stranger, (her husband) and on beholding her in the arms of the Marquis, he ejaculated, "God be thanked, she has escaped uninjured!" The Marquis, having pointed out to the company the approach of the brigands, they hastened to meet them; but the latter perceiving their danger, fled towards the wood. Immediately, upon their arrival at Strasbourg, the Baroness, on whom the effects of the opiate had not ceased to operate, was put to bed, and a physician administered medicine to counteract its effects. The Marquis was pleased that his banker had provided apartments for him before his arrival, whither he had the lady conveyed.

While the Marquis was relating the adventure to the Baron, the pursuing party returned, with the complete subjugation of the banditti, who had submitted, to the number of sixty, without resistance. Their first visit was to the barn, where they found two of the Baron's servants alive, though much wounded; but the Marquis's faithful servant, Lopo, had perished. The waiting women, being overlooked by the brigands, in their hurry, were found still sleeping, and, with an infant about four years old, which proved to be the child of Antoinette, were removed to the Marquis's residence. When the first burst of Antoinette's maternal affection was over, the Marquis requested to know the cause of her being united to such a man as Dubois. She blushed, and proceeded thus:

"I was born of respectable parents in Strasbourg, where my father still lives. Betrayed by a villain, I quitted my father's house: I dearly loved my seducer; and this baby and the youth who warned you of your lady's danger, were the offspring of our love. Having squandered away his paternal inheritance, his noble relations discarded him; he sunk into distress, and at length joined the banditti who infest the forest, many of whom were respectable young men, reduced like himself. I followed, and shared in his losses and gains, and at eight years end found his love for me remained undiminished. He cautiously concealed from me that he ever imbrued his hands in innocent blood, and it was not till after he had been killed in attacking an English traveller, that I learned this horrid feature. When my grief had subsided, I resolved to return to Strasbourg, with my two babes, and implore my father's forgiveness; but, think of the bitter disappointment I felt when the banditti informed me, that they suffered none of their body ever to depart, who were acquainted with their retreat, and that I must make choice of a husband. They decided this by lot, in spite of my remonstrances, and I became the property of the infamous Dubois. A robber, who had been a priest formerly, said a burlesque ceremony, and I and my children were delivered into the custody of my new husband, who proved the reverse of my first lover, and strove to bend my nature to an approbation of scenes of blood and slaughter. I should certainly have put an end to my existence, but I trembled for the virtue of my children. The youngest was not capable of receiving my instructions, but the eldest shewed how little he was calculated for the society of villains, by his detestation of their proceedings. This was my situation, when the perfidy of Don Almagro's postilion conducted him to the cottage, and I resolved to risk every thing to save one so young and innocent. Dubois watched me so closely, that my only hope lay in procuring succour from Strasbourg. My son, Louis, was then ill in bed, but I seized an opportunity to steal to his room; he directly entered into my plan, let himself down from the window, took Jacques's horse, and rode to Strasbourg, where he applied to a magistrate, and the news reaching the Baron, who knew his wife was travelling that road, they set off with an armed party, conducted by Louis; the fortunate issue of which you are all acquainted with."

They afterwards learned from Antoinette, that she had put the sheets on the bed, in which a traveller had been murdered a few nights before, that Don Almagro might be aware of his situation, and feel the force of her hint. The sleeping potion, she also said, was administered, that, if the victim were armed, they might the more easily search him, and prevent a desperate resistance. The Baron, having asked Antoinette what were her future plans of life, she replied, that it was her wish to enter a convent, hoping that her father, through the intercessions of the gentlemen before her, would accept her repentance, and provide for his two grandsons. The Baron and Almagro assured Antoinette, that, if her father proved inflexible, they would provide for the children; and the poor woman's heart was read in her eyes.

On the recovery of the Baroness, Almagro was persuaded to accompany the Baron to his castle in Bavaria, prior to which the interests of Antoinette were not forgotten at Strasbourg. The good old man received his repentant and only daughter, after an absence of fourteen years, with open arms, and persuaded her to remain with him; but no inducement could influence Louis to leave the Marquis, who requested to be taken into his service, and with all the innocent eloquence of a youth of thirteen, set forth the little services he might render him. The Marquis then dubbed him his page, and, before leaving Strasbourg, faithfully promised to restore him to his mother within the year.

The journey to Wildenheim Castle proved very pleasant, and Almagro found in the Baron an uninformed man, remarkably fond of hunting; and the Marquis being a tolerable good sportsman, his dexterity soon fixed him in the Baron's friendship. At the castle of Wildenheim it was that Almagro first saw the lovely Claude, then scarcely sixteen, and blooming in every beauty and accomplishment. From the Baroness Almagro learned that Claude was her niece, and sister of his friend Olphos; that she herself was his country-woman, and sister to the Duke of Calvados; that Claude was the daughter of Don Farojez, her second brother, and that she had been devoted to the convent from her cradle, and would soon make her profession at Madrid, in consequence of a vow made by her mother in child-birth, who, being then taken dangerously ill, vowed to dedicate the child, if a girl, and she survived, to St. Clare. She did survive, and Don Farojez readily chimed in with his wife's wishes; but, knowing the aversion the Duke, his brother, had to a monastic life, Claude accompanied her newly married aunt, Donna Lemnosa, to the castle of Wildenheim. The Baroness then placed her in a neighbouring convent, where her education was liberally attended to, and the acquirements she made estranged her heart from a life of seclusion. She did not conceal her repugnance, and Don Farojez, fearful it might come to his brother's ears, fixed the time for her taking the veil when he was on his travels. Olphos was never made acquainted with his mother's fatal vow, and all his letters to Claude were always opened and inspected, which was the case with her answers.

Almagro, master of these cruel particulars, determined to attempt the rescue of this lovely girl from such a fate. He spoke to her of his friendship with her brother, of his willingness to serve her, and soon received a confession of esteem and love. The Marquis proposed her quitting the castle of Wildenheim, but this she indignantly rejected, and advised, in its place, that Almagro should endeavour to gain the consent of her austere aunt to the union; and next those of the Baron and her guardian, and then her hand should be his.—The Marquis set about this plan directly, and applied the chief battery of his attentions to the Baroness, who was now about forty years of age, and yet retained several traits of former beauty. Her passions were amorous and violent, and her hatred was as inveterate. Don Almagro laboured incessantly to please her, and succeeded but too well. He read to her every day, for several hours, from old Spanish romances, till he was tired to death. Every day the Baroness seemed more pleased with him, and her partiality at length became so marked, that Claude advised the Marquis to seize the first opportunity of declaring their mutual passion to her aunt.—This occurred one evening, after he had finished a romance. "Do you think it possible," said the Baroness, "for any man to feel a love so sincere as the hero of this tale?"—Almagro replied, that his bosom could answer in the affirmative, were he permitted to name the object of his affection. "She has long been known to me," said Donna Lemnosa, "and laments most sincerely the cruel bonds which separate her from you." "Then you have discovered my secret," exclaimed Almagro, taking her hand; "and now what may I hope?"—"For my consent!" replied the Baroness. "Ah! Don Almagro, I no longer can stifle the violence of my passion; I own I adore you! Respect for myself, and regard for the Baron's honour, are all vanquished; they all bend to my love for you!" Almagro was silent—he stood astonished, contemplating the dreadful mistake to which his assiduities had led. Notwithstanding the knowledge of her revengeful disposition, he resolved to clear up the mistake at the moment, concealing only the name of his mistress. This he did in the handsomest terms his eloquence could supply; but it abated nothing of the exclamatory fury which followed. She demanded who the happy rival was. "Let me," exclaimed she, "but find her who dares to rob me of your heart, and I will inflict upon her all the tortures of jealousy and disappointment.—Spies shall watch your steps and your eyes, till she is discovered, and then tremble, Almagro, for her and your own safety."——

Her rage here ending in a fainting fit, Almagro called her attendants to assist, and took the opportunity to escape. Not knowing where he strayed to, he entered the garden, and saw Claude sitting at the window of a room that looked into it; some drawing instruments, & several large sketches lay before her. He entered the room, and before he had determined whether she dare be trusted with her aunt's vengeful determination, he was struck with the subject of one of the pictures. It represented the great hall of the Castle Wildenheim. A door stood half open, which conducted to a narrow staircase. In the front were several characters in caricature positions, arising from terror at seeing a gigantic female figure, clothed in the habit of some religious order. Her face was veiled, and her dress was in several places stained with blood, which trickled from a gash in her neck. One hand held a lamp, and the other a large dagger, and she was advancing towards the iron portal of the hall. Almagro asked Claude, if the picture was an invention of her own; but she replied, by asking him if he had lived three months in the castle of Wildenheim without having heard of the bleeding Nun?—Almagro rejoined, that he had never heard about the lady, and asked who she was. Claude replied, that she had been handed down in a traditional story from father to son; and that her aunt, as well as the Baron, firmly believed she haunted the castle. "But sit down," said Claude, "and I will tell you the whole of this alarming story.

"The Nun did not begin to be known till after she was dead; but not choosing to remain for ever quiet, she fixed on the castle of Wildenheim for her theatre of action, and, being a person of taste, took the best room to perform her ghostly pranks in. Sometimes she visited the other chambers and galleries, to the universal terror of the inhabitants, who described her as here traced on the paper. The Nun, full at times of execrations and blasphemies, and at others, of the most religious exercises, soon made the castle scarcely habitable, and its lord was so frightened by these midnight revels, that one morning he was found dead in his bed.

"The next lord exorcised her by a pious and tough priest, and for some time after no news was heard of her; but this lord died in five years, and then she appeared again, somewhat more tractable than before. She then walked about in silence, and never made her appearance but once in five years—a custom which the Baron firmly believes is continued. He is fully persuaded that, on the fourteenth of February of every fifth year, at midnight, the door of the haunted chamber opens, which has been continued for a century. On this night she marches with a lamp and dagger, as in the picture, when the porter out of respect leaves the castle gate open for her ghostship, who, after an hour's absence, retires to her chamber, and is quiet for another five years. The sketch I have here taken is from the description of Dame Barjona, my governess, who tells that fifteen years ago she saw the spectre *with her own eyes*."—The caricature which the playful imagination of Claude had correctly drawn for the Dame Barjona was so correct, that it excited both the laughter and admiration of the Marquis. "If that please you," said Claude, "I will present you with a likeness much more ridiculous than Dame Barjona. Do with it as you think proper." She then unlocked a small cabinet, and drew forth a miniature portrait of herself. Transported with gratitude, the Marquis threw himself at her feet, and was declaring to her well-pleased ears the ardour of his passion, when she suddenly uttered a loud shriek, disengaged her hand, and escaped from the room by a door that opened into the garden. On turning round, the Marquis beheld the Baroness standing near him, choking with rage. She had seen the portrait given, and heard their mutual declarations of everlasting attachment; the embarrassment of the Marquis and Donna Lemnosa was equal; but the lady first recovered the use of speech, and told him he should know what it was to love without hope, since Claude should be sent to Spain on the arrival of an order from her parents, and there take the veil. She then added that her niece should be confined till he took his departure, which she expected would be the earliest possible.

The Baroness then darted from the room with a look of contempt on the Marquis, who, after seeking the timid Baron, and vainly endeavouring to interest him in his cause, quitted the castle without a sight of Claude. The Marquis was attended only by a French servant, and Louis, whose ability and disposition had endeared him to his master. He had learned Spanish sufficient to be understood, by going to school for that purpose, from the time the Marquis adopted him. "Courage, Signor," said he in Spanish; "I have watched the moment when Dame Barjona was absent, to mount to the chamber over that of Donna Claude, and sung so loud that she heard me, and opened her window. I then let down a string, and drew it up in a few minutes, with this scrap of paper fastened to it." "When my aunt believes you have quitted Wildenheim, I shall be restored to liberty. Conceal yourself in some neighbouring village, till the night of the thirtieth, when I will be in the West Pavilion at twelve, and we will concert our future plans. Adieu. Claude." The Marquis obeyed the instructions of Claude, and proceeded to Munich, leaving the care of the chaise to Fouet, his French servant; who was ordered to remain there till his master and Louis returned.—The latter, having disguised themselves, repaired to an inn at a village about four miles from Wildenheim, where a fortnight passed away, and Almagro had the pleasure of seeing Claude with her Duenna pass through the village in good health and spirits, whither she came every Friday to the convent there. Almagro attended the following Friday, and had the pleasure to see himself recognized by Claude in his disguise. At length the long-expected thirtieth night arrived, and the Marquis, with Louis, who had provided a ladder of ropes, scaled the garden wall, and posted themselves in the west pavilion. As the castle bell tolled twelve, the light footstep of Claude announced her approach. The Marquis flew to receive her, and conducted her to a seat. "We have no time to lose," said Claude impatiently, "for Dame Barjona watches me every moment. In a week I am to depart for Madrid, to be sacrificed. I have no hope left but in your honour, and this is the plan of escape I have formed. On the fifth day from this time, the visionary nun is expected to appear, and by means of a friend I have provided a dress proper for the character. You must be ready with a carriage, at a little distance from the great gates of the castle; then, as soon as the clock strikes one, I shall quit my chamber habited as the ghost, and easily reach the door; thus far success is certain; but, if you reward my confidence with perfidy, the world will not hold a more wretched being than your Claude." Had the Marquis's carriage been ready, he would have carried her away at the moment, but Munich was the nearest place to obtain one, and that lay at a distance of two day's journey; the plan of Claude was therefore acceded to, and the lovers sat making mutual vows of love and honour. Suddenly the door of the pavilion was opened, and Barjona entered; she had watched her mistress out, and overheard the whole conversation.—"But I shall mar all your projects," said the Duenna; "and as for you Don Almagro, you ought to be ashamed of yourself, to seduce an innocent young creature away from her family. Good by, Signor.—Come, Claude, your ghostship will please to return with me." The Marquis interceded with the cruel Barjona; but, finding all remonstrance vain, after having premised her obstinacy would be her punishment, he took the veil of Claude, and enveloped Barjona's head in it, threatening her with instant death upon making the least noise; he then bound her hand and foot with handkerchiefs, and bid Claude regain her apartment, and carry her plan into effect on the day appointed. Claude then departed, and the antiquated intruder was hoisted over the wall, and carried to the inn at the village, where Louis managed by knocking out the light to get her conveyed by Almagro, without being perceived, into his room. The Marquis, when all the bustle was over, strove to reconcile Barjona to her temporary confinement, but such was the fury of the virago, that he was compelled to gag and lock her up, except at meal times, when he stood over her with a drawn sword. The greatest alarm was excited at the castle on account of the lost Duenna; thus in various conjectures the five days passed away, and in making preparations on the part of the Marquis, who had written to Fouet to be ready with a coach and four, at ten o'clock in the morning of the 14th of Feb. at the village of Hauser. He was punctual, and before twelve o'clock on that day, he and Louis repaired to the important scene of action. The coach was hidden in a large cavern, called Wildenheim vault, close to the castle.—The night was still; the moon faintly shone, and the castle clock struck twelve, the usual signal for the family to retire to bed. Not long after the porter opened wide the portal gates, the lights disappeared, and the whole fabric was eclipsed in darkness. The Marquis then ventured to draw near to the castle, and observed a few rays of light glimmering in the chamber of Claude. While he was going, a figure drew near the window and the curtain was carefully closed to conceal the lamp burning there. Almagro, convinced that Claude was there, returned to wait for the appointed hour. At length, the solemn hour of one tolled, and in five minutes after a light again appeared. The light soon faded away, and all was dark and gloomy. Not many minutes however elapsed, when he saw Claude pass through the folding gates, habited exactly like the spectre, with a lamp and dagger. She advanced to where Almagro stood; he flew to meet her, and clasped her in his arms. The terrified maid, overcome by joy, sunk upon his bosom, and in this state he conveyed her to the carriage. Louis remained behind to release Barjona, and take a letter to the Baroness, explaining Almagro's rank and intentions to her niece. Being seated in the carriage, the postilions drove away with great fury; the horses became restive, and a dreadful storm of thunder and lightning coming on, they were no longer manageable, but dragged the carriage at their pleasure, till all farther progress was stopped, by its striking against a tree, and being shattered to pieces. The shock threw the Marquis out, and wounded him so desperately on the temple, that his senses forsook him, and he lay without animation till broad daylight, when he saw himself surrounded by several peasants, of whom he immediately demanded if they had seen Claude. They replied no person answering her description had been seen by them, and they had been attracted to the spot by hearing the groans of the only surviving horse.— Almagro immediately dispatched some of the peasants in search of her, while four that remained made a litter of boughs, and conveyed him on it to Ratisbon; a surgeon being sent for, it was found that Almagro had dislocated his arm, broken a rib, and his left leg was dreadfully bruised. The arm however was set with success, and the surgeon announced no other consequence from his hurts than a tedious and painful cure. It was conceived both by the surgeon, the hostess, and the peasants, that he was delirious, when he talked about the lady he had brought with him since one o'clock that morning from the village of Hausen, which lay at a considerable distance from Ratisbon. All efforts to trace the lost Claude proved fruitless, and the furious agitation the Marquis had at first displayed sunk into a mild despondency.—On the third night, as he lay tossing from side to side, and vainly endeavouring to invite sleep, he heard slow and heavy steps ascending the staircase. A rush light glimmered on the hearth, and by an involuntary sensation, the Marquis raised himself up in his bed, and drew back the curtain. At that moment the clock of a neighbouring church tolled one, the door was thrown open with violence, and the figure of the bleeding Nun entered, but without the lamp and dagger. His astonishment was changed into horror, when she lifted up her veil in a solemn manner, and instead of presenting the face of the beautiful Claude, he saw before him nothing but an animated corpse. The glaring eyeballs of the visionary female now fixed upon the Marquis, and in a sepulchral voice she repeated the first effusions of affection which he had uttered on her escape from the castle. The apparition then seated itself opposite to him, with her eyes fixed on his, till the clock struck two, when it rose and approached the bed: then taking hold of his hand with her bony fingers, and pressing her icy lips to his, she repeated her former words, and quitted the chamber. The Marquis fainted with a loud groan immediately that she had disappeared; the sound was heard by the host and his wife, who entered his chamber, and found some difficulty in restoring him to his senses. The following night the Marquis had a servant to sit up with him, and by the assistance of opiates had slept several hours till the neighbouring clock struck one, when he awoke, and felt all the terror of the preceding night renewed. His servant was fast asleep, beyond his strength to wake him, and the bleeding Nun entered the room with the same appearance as the preceding evening, saying, "Signor, Signor, thou art mine! Signor, Signor, I am thine!" in a hollow voice, and after again pressing his lips, and staying till the clock struck two, disappeared.—This was repeated every night, and so little did his terror abate by familiarity to his nocturnal visitor, that several months elapsed before he was able to cross the room without assistance. The ghost was invisible to every eye but his, and whenever any attendants sat up with him, they were seized with an irresistible slumber from the entrance of the spectre till its departure.

Louis, who had, during this interval, been confined at Wildenheim, had some difficulty to find his master at Ratisbon, and from him and the subsequent relation of Claude, he learned the following particulars. On the fatal night when her elopement was to have taken place, accident had prevented her from quitting her chamber at the exact time; nevertheless, she found no obstruction in getting through the castle gate, in her ghostly attire. Finding that Almagro was not there, she staid till past two o'clock, in traversing the avenues of the castle. When she returned, the door was shut; but, on knocking, the porter admitted the supposed spirit, and Claude passed quietly to her chamber. In the mean time, Louis, seeing the carriage drive off with the false Claude, returned to the village, released Barjona, and accompanied her to the castle. He found the Baron and Baroness disputing upon the porter's relation; but the mystery was soon developed, on his being interrogated, and the ghost that appeared at past two o'clock was resolved into the person of Claude. The Baroness now artfully suppressed the letter, and the real rank of the Marquis, who from a vanity of being beloved only for his own sake, had not even revealed to his mistress that he was any other than plain Don Almagro di Cordova. This artful lady instructed Barjona to tell Claude, that the scheme had failed entirely through the perfidy of her fortune-hunting lover; and Louis, lest he should contradict it, was kept confined in the castle. Incensed at Almagro's perfidy, Claude passed another month before she consented to receive the veil, and then set off for Spain with Don Farojez. Louis was set at liberty, and, after finding his master had not been at Munich, succeeded in joining him at Ratisbon. One day, while Louis was looking through the window, and Almagro was lying on the sopha, he exclaimed, "There goes the great Bashaw, who is the most singular man in the world! Some suppose him an astrologer, from Arabia, others, Doctor Faustus, and others, the devil. He told me, when I was seeking you out, that he had a message for you, Signor, and that he alone could dissipate the bloody phantom!" Almagro bid him fly after the Bashaw, and request his attendance. In a few minutes he returned with this stranger, who was tall and majestic in his appearance. A band of black velvet encircled his forehead, and his wild black locks gave force to the secret awe his countenance inspired. Having motioned to Louis to retire, he said, "Marquis, I have the power to release you from the nocturnal visitor. After Saturday, you shall see her no more! She is perpetually by your side, though visible to you only one hour in the day, nor will she ever leave you till her request is granted, which she will explain on Saturday night next!—Ask no more till then!"

The Marquis then entered into conversation with him, and found that he had visited all countries; which he accounted for by saying, that an irresistible fate compelled him to stay no longer than a fortnight in one place; and that, although he had courted death in a thousand shapes, heaven had ordered that neither animals nor elements should injure him.

The stranger, then bidding Almagro expect him at twelve on Saturday, retired. This was the last day of his fortnight at Ratisbon; and, true to his appointed time, he entered the Marquis's room at midnight, with a small chest in his hand. After saluting him, he opened the chest, and took out a wooden crucifix, which he kneeled to, and kissed three times. He then produced a goblet, and sprinkled the floor with a liquor which appeared to be blood. The end of the crucifix was next dipped in the fluid, and he described a circle in the middle of the floor, round about which were laid relics, sculls, and other human bones, in the form of crosses. Having taken out a large bible, he beckoned the Marquis to move into the circle, and be silent. He had scarcely commenced reading, when the spectre entered at the hour of one, and advanced to the circle. After some unintelligible words on his part, he extended the crucifix towards the ghost, and in a solemn voice pronounced thrice the name "Malvoglia!"——"Speak!" faltered out the spectre. "Say why," rejoined the sorcerer, "you haunt this youth? How can thy spirit be laid at rest?" ——"It is forbidden me to tell," replied the Nun; "fain would I repose in the grave, but my punishment is prolonged!"—"Look at this blood!" rejoined the stranger. "Knowest thou not in whose veins it flowed! By his manes I charge thee to answer me!"—The spectre shook her head in dissent.——"Now shalt thou obey me!" exclaimed the Bashaw, and he drew from his forehead the velvet band, and a burning cross was visible on his brow. The horror the Marquis felt was equally imparted to the spectre, whose limbs trembled, while her quivering lips spoke thus. "At that mark I obey: learn then, that in Wildenheim vault my bones rot in obscurity, and this youth only can consign them to the grave; his own lips have made over his soul and body to me, and never shall he rest till my mouldering remains are at rest in his Andalusian castle. There let 30 masses be said for my repose, and then I disquiet the earth no more. Oh! that burning crucifix scorches me!"—The Bashaw now let drop the crucifix, which till that moment he had pointed towards her, and the apparition bowed her head as she vanished into air.

The exorciser then led Almagro from the circle, replaced his bible, &c. in the chest, and addressed him thus: "Don Almagro, fail not to fulfil those conditions punctually. Malvoglia is your relation, and, when living, bore the name of D'Axala. She was great aunt to your grandfather: She took the veil at an early age, but when her ungovernable passions began to expand, she contrived to elope from the convent, and fled to Germany with the Baron Wildenheim. Here she lived several months as his avowed concubine, professed herself an atheist, and disgusted the whole country by her grossness. Soon after her arrival, the Baron's younger brother attracted her affection, and she found in him her equal in turpitude. He made the return of his love the price of his brother's murder, and the night was fixed on for the deed. Rolan said that he would wait for her in Wildenheim vault, on the night of the murder, then with some friends proceed to make himself master of the castle, and conclude by marrying her, which the Baron had ever refused to do.

"On the fatal night, Malvoglia plunged her dagger into the heart of her lord, as the castle clock tolled one, and then quitting her bed hastily, took the lamp in one hand, with the bloody dagger in the other, and repaired towards the cavern. She reached Wildenheim vault unopposed, where she saw Rolan waiting for her. He listened to the narrative of the atrocious deed with transport, and before she could half enquire why he had brought no attendants with him, or defend herself, he wrested the dagger from her, and plunged it, still reeking with his brother's blood, into her bosom, and terminated her life by repeated blows. Rolan now succeeded to the barony, and the murder was solely attributed to the fugitive nun. But his crime did not remain unpunished; her bones lying still unburied in the cave, the spirit of Malvoglia continued to inhabit the castle, dressed in her nun's habit, and holding the lamp and dagger. Every night she stood thus before the bed of Rolan, uttering alternate prayers and blasphemies. At length Rolan's life became insupportable, and he was one morning found dead in his bed.

"The castle next fell to a distant relation, who, terrified by the accounts of the bleeding nun, called in a holy man, who forced the spectre to silence during his life-time.—At his death, which happened five years after, she again appeared, but only once within every fifth year, at the same hour she murdered her sleeping lover; she then visited the cavern holding her mouldering skeleton, and returned at two o'clock, when she disappeared for five years.—She was doomed to suffer during the space of a century, which being past, nothing now remains but to obey the injunctions of the spectre—I now feel some consolation in having released you from her visits, and wish you farewell." The Marquis entreated the Bashaw to stay, and reveal some of the mystery attending himself, which the latter promised to do, if he would let him defer his explanation to the next day; but on the following morning the Marquis learned that he had quitted Ratisbon, and who this singular person was, unless he were the celebrated character known by the name of the *Wandering Jew*, he was never able to discover. Relieved of his terrors, Almagro rapidly grew well, and soon set out for Wildenheim, where he was welcomed by the Baron and his lady, whose passion the Marquis was sorry to see was not diminished by his absence. Wishing to avoid the latter's revenge, and perform the obsequies of the murdered nun, he collected her remains, and bent his course, with Fouet and Louis, towards Spain.

He arrived at his father's castle in Andalusia without any accident, deposited the bones of Malvoglia in the family vault, and performed the masses. He now set about tracing Claude, but found that her mother was dead, that her brother Olphos was from home, and her father on a visit to the Duke of Calvados. Neither the ingenuity of himself, nor Louis, could develope the mystery, till the following adventure effected it.

Returning home one night from the playhouse, he was attacked by three men in an unfrequented street. One he laid at his feet, but he would have vainly opposed the others, had not a cavalier with his servants heard the clashing of swords, and rushed to his assistance. The bravoes then fled, and the Marquis, finding he was severely wounded, requested to be carried to the Hotel D'Axala.

On mentioning the name, the Cavalier said he knew the father of the Marquis very well, and insisted on his being taken to his brother's, (the Duke of Calvados,) hard by.—When they had entered, the family surgeon was sent for, and declared, that the wounds were of no consequence, and only required rest. "I esteem myself happy," said Don Farojez di Calvados, "to render you any service; and am infinitely obliged to my daughter for detaining me so late at the convent of St. Clare. I am certain my brother will lament his absence, but in the mean time every thing in the hotel di Calvados is at your disposal." This was a double discovery for the Marquis, nor did he feel uneasy when he afterwards learned that Claude had taken the vows in St. Claire, as he flattered himself that his uncle's credit at the court of Rome could easily procure a bull to remove that obstacle. There was little doubt that the Marquis's intended assassination had been attempted by the means of Donna Lemnosa, yet he carefully guarded this knowledge from her brother Don Farojez, who had no suspicion that the Marquis was the person who had been attached to his daughter under the name of Don Almagro di Cordova at Wildenheim.—The Marquis now closely attacked the gardener of St. Clare with bribes and promises, and succeeded in persuading the old man to introduce him as his assistant. The Prioress suspected no deception, and for three days he worked in the garden, without meeting with the object of his disguise. On the fourth morning the Prioress and Claude advanced, and seated themselves on a bench; she was lecturing the fair recluse on her obstinacy in giving way to an ill-requited love, when a young pensioner came, and called the old lady out. Claude then shewed the charming girl several letters, which the latter read with pleasure, and begging leave to copy them, retired to her cell.—The Marquis now came forward, and the eye of Claude recognised him in his disguise. She accused him of falsehood, and would have retired; but he detained her with an assurance that she had been deceived by the artifices of her relations. She listened, and the next night at eleven o'clock they agreed to meet again on the same spot.—The weather was cold, but it secured them from interruption, and the Marquis had a full opportunity of declaring the cause of his absence on the fatal night of the spectre deceiving him, and assured her, that, even the dreadful barrier to their happiness in having taken the veil, might be overcome by the Cardinal Duke of Parma's influence at Rome. Claude listened, but combated his arguments, stating, her father's superstition would never pardon her leaving the convent in any manner, and she concluded with saying, that she felt her voluntary vows to heaven were binding, and that her father's curse would follow her if she broke them. The Marquis continued to refute her scruples till the convent bell rang, when he persuaded her to meet him at the same hour next evening.

These meetings continued for several weeks uninterrupted, and in one unguarded moment the honour of Claude was sacrificed to their mutual passions.—When the burst of delirium was over, Claude started from the bank on which she was seated, and after venting the reproaches of conscience on the Marquis, she hurried to the convent, in spite of his efforts to detain her. The next morning and night the Marquis attended at the garden, but Claude came not. Several nights passed away without seeing her, and at length the old gardener informed him, that the lady whom he used to meet had threatened, if he continued any longer in the convent, to unfold the whole business to the lady prioress, and that regard for his own safety required he should withdraw himself. Finding all efforts to see Claude were ineffectual, he submitted not to visit the convent. In a fortnight after, he was summoned to attend his father, who was taken dangerously ill. He lay several months before he died, and a week more passed after his decease, before the Marquis could arrange his affairs so as to return to Madrid. On his arrival, he found a letter from Claude, announcing that she was with child, and both the innocent babe and herself would be lost if he could not extricate her from the tyranny of the vengeful prioress; that the gardener having been dismissed, and one of inflexible integrity in his place, the only chance of her receiving an answer from him was by concealing it under the statue of St. Francis, in the Capuchin cathedral, whither she went to confess every Thursday morning. Her father's death, she added, had removed one obstacle to their union, and she now intreated him to procure with all speed the dispensation from her vows, as the only means of saving her life!—The Marquis felt pleasure at this epistle, because he thought he had power to execute the prayer of it. From the first he had interested the Cardinal-Duke of Parma to procure the necessary bull, which he had just received a letter from him he expected to arrive in a few days; but he also said it was necessary to get Claude out of the convent privately, lest the fury of the prioress should counteract his Holiness's mandate.

The Marquis saw the necessity of this, and immediately had the new gardener seized, and conveyed to his hotel.—Master of the key, he entered, and deposited at the shrine of St. Francis a letter for Claude, to prepare her for elopement at twelve the next night. The Marquis, in doing this, became accidentally known to the vigilant Olphos, his friend, the brother of Claude, who promised to assist, and informed him that he had now nothing to fear from Donna Lemnosa, who, in a fit of passion, had died by bursting a blood vessel. At twelve the following night the friends attended at the garden wall of the convent, with a coach and four. Don Almagro drew out his key, and they entered the garden, where they waited a long time, but Claude came not. The fact was, the prioress had learned the situation of Claude, and the plan; she knew that to arrest the lover would only have provoked inquiry about the government of her convent, and therefore she left them to wait as long as they thought proper, and then retire unmolested. The next morning Olphos repaired to the convent, and requested to see his sister. He was informed by the Prioress that she had been taken ill, and confined to her bed the last three days, owing to something which secretly preyed on her mind, and which she would not reveal. Olphos requested to be admitted to her cell, but the Prioress was shocked at such a horrid proposition, as admitting a man into the convent. Finding his sister was not to be seen that day, he repaired early the next morning to the convent, and received an account that the physician had ordered no one to see her. Regularly did he attend the convent every day, and received always a more unfavourable account. Convinced that her indisposition was feigned, these accounts did not alarm him; but how to extricate her from the fangs of the Prioress was a very serious consideration, as she was cruel, superstitious, and never suffered a nun of rank to depart.

Fortunately at this time arrived the Pope's expected bull for the release of Claude. This essential paper decided at once the proceedings of the Marquis and his friends. On the following day Olphos was commissioned to present the instrument, and repaired to the convent early in the morning. When the matin service was over, he demanded to see the Prioress, who replied, as usual, that the only chance of her dear child's recovery, was in keeping her from being agitated. To end the business, Olphos placed the Pope's bull in her hand; she received it with humility, but, on perusing the contents, her hypocrisy forsook her, and, in a rage, she exclaimed,—"The Pope's mandate cannot be obeyed; it has arrived too late! I cannot deliver up Claude either with or without delay, for she expired on Friday last!"—Olphos started with horror, but recollecting that the Prioress had said the moment before that she was alive, he taxed her falsehood, and insisted on her being produced.—"If I concealed her death," replied the Prioress, "it was only to soften the sad event to you.—What interest have I in detaining one who long has wished to quit our holy society? But her crimes are great, and it is not to be regretted such a wretch no longer exists. On Thursday last, in returning from the Capuchin chapel, she was taken ill, and, thanks to the Virgin, we were *too ignorant* to suspect her malady. Judge then of our horror, when she was delivered the next day of a dead child, and followed it herself immediately! Claude is therefore no more, and, if you have any doubt, I swear by this sacred crucifix she has been buried three days!"—She then, with a scornful smile, left the room, first observing, that he might now obtain a second bull from the Pope for her resurrection. Olphos also retired, and communicated the result to the Marquis, who was firmly convinced that the walls of St. Clare still confined her, and tried every means, without success, to procure intelligence of her. Olphos thought she was taken off by unfair means, and two months elapsed without any thing arising to create a contrary supposition. All the researches of the Marquis d'Axala proved in vain, and the despair he felt brought on a long and severe illness. Olphos attended him constantly with the most fraternal affection; but no one was more sensibly afflicted than the amiable lad Louis, who left no means unemployed to gain an entrance into the convent.

Among other schemes, he one day took it in his head to disguise himself as a beggar; he put a patch over his left eye, took his guittar in his hand, and posted himself at the gate of the convent, imagining that if Claude were at liberty, and heard his voice, she would recollect him, and find means to let him know it. His sweet songs soon attracted the notice of the nuns, and when the rest of the beggars were dispersed from the gate, he was desired to come in, and partake of their charitable donation of soup. The nuns all admired his youth and beauty, and agreed that he would be a worthy pillar of the Catholic church. This was represented by the porteress to the Domina, who ordered him to be introduced. After having asked him several questions, to which he replied artlessly, the Prioress was so pleased with him, that she ordered him to attend the next day, to speak further upon his entrance into the church.—The Domina then retired, and the nuns crowded round him, to whom he related his strange adventures, and amused them so highly, that each of them gave him some little relic, waxen image, or consecrated cross. He had just remarked, that he should want a basket to put his presents into, when the Mother St. Urbana presented him with one, lined with satin, saying, significantly, that, though it seemed of little value, it had many hidden virtues. Louis, in receiving the present, came as close to the grate as possible, and she whispered in a low voice, "Claude!" He immediately after withdrew, and hastened to the Marquis, who started from his pillow on hearing what Louis had to say. With eager haste he ripped up the satin lining, and found the following note on a scrap of paper:—"I have recognised your page, and venture to send these few lines. Procure an order from the Cardinal Duke to seize my person and the Domina, and let it be executed at midnight on Friday, during the festival of St. Clair. Be secret, or I may perish before I can unfold the dreadful tale. St. Urbana."

This note, instead of giving comfort to the Marquis, deprived him of sense and motion. From the tenor of these lines he was convinced that Claude was no more; but when he recovered, both he and Olphos broke out into execrations against the assassin of Claude, and vowed to take a signal vengeance. The Marquis raved till he relapsed into insensibility, and his friend flew to the palace of the Cardinal Duke, who was out of town. Olphos however set off immediately, as it wanted five days to the festival of St. Clare, and succeeded in obtaining the order for arrest, with which he arrived on the evening of the festival. Having shewn it to the Marquis, who remained very ill, he took it to Don Gomez, an uncle of Claude's, and an officer of the Inquisition, who was petrified with horror at the recital of his niece's unhappy fate, and promised to accompany him at night, with a band of trusty archers, to prevent every opposition on the part of the populace. They repaired full an hour before the time to the convent gates, where a great crowd was assembled to witness the procession. The archers mixed among the populace, and Olphos being recognized as a person of rank, was permitted with his party, to place himself opposite the great portal, through which the pilgrims were to pass. The convent service lasted till midnight, the finish of which was announced by a bell.

The procession then began by the Capuchin monks chaunting hymns in honour of St. Clare, and marching two and two; next came the novices, without tapers, and the professed with. To these succeeded a beautiful young girl, representing St. Lucia, her eyes covered with a velvet band, and led by another nun. St. Catharine followed, and then St. Genevieve, surrounded by grotesque imps, who endeavoured to abstract her attention from a devout book, on which her eyes were fixed; at this the spectators laughed heartily. After a band of choristers, came the reliques of St. Clare; the nun who bore the heart was the mother St. Urbana, and Olphos recognised her by Louis's description. Next appeared the damsel representing St. Clare, selected from the most lovely of all the nuns. Her dress was inestimably rich, and she was seated on a moving throne. Her beauty attracted every eye, and was contrasted with the sour visage of the prioress, who followed at the head of the remaining nuns, with her eyes raised to heaven. The populace blessed her as she passed, but what alarm and confusion followed, when Don Gomez arrested her in the name of his Holiness! When she had recovered her first surprise, she called upon the people to protect her from sacrilege and impiety; they were eagerly preparing to obey her, when Don Gomez rushed forward with his band of archers, and threatened the populace with the vengeance of the Inquisition. All was again quiet, and Don Gomez declared he must next arrest the Mother St. Urbana. At this moment Olphos stepped forward, and the prioress exclaimed, "Holy Virgin, I am betrayed!"—"Yes," retorted St. Urbana, "betrayed by your villainies! I am your accuser.—I charge you with murder, and stake my life for the issue of the accusation."—A murmur ran through the multitude, and an explanation was vociferously demanded. The procession in the mean time dispersed, and the mob ordered St. Urbana to harangue them from the vacant throne, which she ascended, and addressed them as follows. "I am now at liberty to relate a tale, which had I been in the power of the prioress would have cost me my life, and numbered me with the once lovely and gentle Claude di Calvados. I was entrusted with her secrets, and she shared the love of every one—even of the proud and forbidding prioress. Alas! Claude had her faults, and who is free from error?

She violated the rules of our order, and the sentence adjudged by the unforgiving Domina was cruel and inhuman, though conformable to the rigour of a law, altogether obsolete till she revived it. This law decreed that the offender shou'd be plunged into a private dungeon, be there condemned to perpetual solitude, and her friends be induced to believe she was dead. Here for the remnant of her life her food was to be bread and water, and the straw-covered earth her bed.

"A council of twelve elders was called to try the unfortunate Claude, and I was of the number. Except the Mothers Anna and Ladrona, and myself, the rest were for her sacrifice: but this we over-ruled by our remonstrance, and the Prioress demanded time to reflect on a system of punishment that might be agreeable to the sisterhood. On the evening of the third day it was announced that Claude should be examined, and her punishment be regulated by her behaviour. In the night preceding this examination, I flew to the cell of Claude, while the other nuns were asleep; I cautioned her not to be ensnared into a confession prejudicial to her interests; I exhorted her to fortitude, and, after mingling my tears with her's, was about to retire, when the sound of steps approaching the cell, compelled me to place myself behind a curtain which veiled a large crucifix. The Prioress in a moment after entered, followed by four other nuns. The Superior reproached her in the bitterest terms, and commanded her to drink the contents of a goblet which she held in her hand, as an expiation of her crimes! The unhappy girl, aware that the liquor was poison, sued for life in the most piteous accents and affecting prayers,—for a month, a week, a day longer!—The Prioress bid her recommend herself to heaven's mercy, which had been insulted, and whose avenging instrument she was. Perceiving it was vain to implore this religious monster, Claude sprang from her bed, and was about to call for assistance, when the Prioress seized her by the arm, pushed her back on the bed, and, drawing a dagger, vowed by heaven if she uttered a cry, or hesitated to drink the poison, she would stab her that instant! The fatal goblet was presented by a nun. Claude drank it off, and the deed was soon accomplished. They embittered her pangs in dying by their reproaches, and such were her agonies, that they must amply have gratified the inhumanity of her enemies. When the victim ceased to breathe, and the Domina, with the assistant nuns, retired, I ventured out, and scarcely had strength sufficient to regain my own cell. As I took the last farewell of the lovely lifeless body, I vowed to bring her assassins to shame and death. No marks of violence appearing on the corpse, it was given out she had expired suddenly.

"At her funeral, I unguardedly dropped some hints, and have ever since been so closely watched, that it was at the utmost hazard of my life I conveyed my secret to the unhappy lady's relations. I again repeat, and will answer it with my life, that the Prioress is a murderer, a barbarian, and a hypocrite, and I also accuse the nuns Melina, Porcella, Dolla, and Teresa, as accomplices!"

Such was the address of St. Urbana, which raised the indignation of the mob to so high a pitch, that they demanded the immediate surrender of the Prioress to their fury. To this Don Gomez positively objected, and surrounded her with the archers, but the ungovernable assailants soon forced a passage through the guards, and dragged their destined victim from their shelter. The wretched woman shrieked out for mercy, but she spoke to those who were now as deaf to that quality as she had been. They stifled her cries with howlings and curses, dragged her through the streets, trampled on her, and spurned her with savage fury. At length, a well-directed stone struck her on the temple; she staggered, and fell to rise no more!—Their next object, after the Prioress, was her convent; thither they repaired, set fire to it, and swore not a nun of the order of St. Clare should be left alive. Olphos entered with the rabble, and vainly endeavoured to repress their indiscriminating fury, till the progress of the flames compelled him to seek for his own safety. The mob now hastened out with more eagerness than they had entered; the door-ways were suddenly closed up, and the flames rapidly advancing, many perished from this cause as well as pressure. Olphos, more fortunate, made his escape at a small door in a further aisle of the chapel, which led him to the foot of St. Clare's sepulchre. Here he stopped to breathe, and found he was followed by Gomez and some of his people. A wicket door in the wall opened into the garden of the Capuchins, and they all passed through except Olphos, who, being the last, observed the door of the sepulchre to be softly opened. Some one looked out, but, on seeing a stranger, uttered a shriek, flew back, and descended the marble steps. Olphos immediately pursued, and followed through dark and subterranean vaults, till he could only trace the object he was in quest of by the sound of the feet. He at length became quite bewildered, and with his sword drawn, groped his way till he caught the glimmer of a lamp, which, as he drew near, he perceived was placed before the statue of Saint Clare.

Several females stood round it, and, from their conversation, Olphos learned they had flown there for security from the mob. They were thrown into the most dreadful alarm when he presented himself, but he soon dissipated their fears. While he was assuring them of protection, a loud groan seemed to issue from the middle of the vault in which he and the nuns were. A second groan followed, and the noise plainly came from the statue. The nuns accounted for the noise as a miraculous intimation from the saint that she was offended at the proceedings of the people, and shewed Olphos a human hand, grasping her arm, which had once belonged to a man who had sacrilegiously mounted the statue of St. Clare to steal a valuable ring from her finger. The robber could be released only by amputation, since which he had turned hermit, and no one had dared to touch the statue under the fear of certain destruction.

This extraordinary legend led Olphos to examine the arm of St. Clare with particular attention; and jumping over the iron railing which inclosed her, he ascended the pedestal, and discovered a small iron knob between the shoulder and the supposed man's hand; on pressing it, it seemed to loosen a chain that attached the wooden image to the base. Lifting this off, he perceived a heavy iron grate in the hollow of the pedestal, which, with some difficulty, he raised, inviting the nuns to follow; this they declined, and he descended a flight of rude mishapen steps to a cavern, and thought he perceived a spark of light:—as he wandered on, he lost sight of it, but a plaintive moan stole upon his ear, and he directed his steps towards it. It became more audible as he advanced, and at length conducted him to a narrow gloomy dungeon in one side of the cavern. Through the vapoury and pestilential fog that clouded this cell, by the glimmering beams of a lamp, he saw a pale emaciated human being lying on a bed of straw. She was partly naked, her disordered hair concealed her face, and a tattered rag enveloped her limbs. With one hand she pressed a small bundle to her bosom; the other hung inactively down. Her sunken eyes were directed to a crucifix, and beside her straw was a basket and an earthen pitcher. Olphos stopped a moment to contemplate this horrid object: she cast her eyes towards the staircase, and then in a feeble voice uttered, "No one comes to me!—Two long days have passed, and no food!—Oh, cruel, to lengthen out my miseries by a death of hunger!" She then shivered, drew the rug closer over her shoulders, and addressed the bundle which lay on her breast. "Dear babe, once so lovely, so like him, how have a few days changed thee!—Yet still art thou dear to me, and I will weep over thy putrid form!" She then shed some tears, which she wiped away with her tresses, and stretched out her hand to the pitcher, but put it back again, exclaiming, "Not a drop! Oh! I would give worlds for a drop of water to allay my burning thirst! Saviour, Saviour, have pity on me, and turn the hearts of my persecutors!"

Olphos, no longer able to contain his feelings, entered the dungeon, and in a soft voice said, he was come to relieve her woes. The captive started, and eagerly demanded if the Prioress had sent him to destroy her. Olphos briefly related that he was come to give her liberty and comfort, and that she had nothing to fear from the Prioress, who had been sacrificed to the popular indignation. As Olphos stooped to raise her, the beams of the lamp struck full upon his face, and the captive exclaimed, "Gracious heaven! is it possible!—Those features!—Ah! it is——" She said no more, but sunk upon the straw in a fainting fit. Olphos lost no time in removing an iron chain, which encircled the body of the unknown victim, and taking her in his arms, by the iron lamp, he gained the iron grate, where he met the nuns, who were waiting his return with the greatest anxiety. They busily employed themselves in restoring the inanimate female, till they were alarmed by the sound of Don Gomez's cries, calling on Olphos to know if he were safe.

When Gomez joined them, he brought the pleasing intelligence, that the riot had all subsided, and that the nuns, with their helpless charge, were consigned to his care, while Olphos penetrated into other parts of this subterranean abode, and succeeded in rescuing two more victims of the Domina's fury. Don Gomez conducted all the nuns to their respective friends. The beautiful Almira, who had personated St. Clare, requested not to be separated from the rescued prisoner, and Don Gomez conducted them both to her house. Here the unfortunate was immediately put to bed, and medical assistance procured. As her illness had principally arisen from weakness and want of wholesome food, she very soon assumed an altered appearance; and when her history was related, she proved to be the supposed deceased and sacrificed Claude!—The account which Claude gave of her sufferings and imprisonment ran thus:

"My imagined death was attended with the greatest agonies, and when I awoke from my trance, an hour elapsed before I was sufficiently collected to examine the surrounding objects. I found myself extended upon a sort of wicker couch, with four handles, which doubtless served the nuns to convey me to my grave. A lamp was over my head, and four narrow walls encompassed me. Perceiving my grated door was unfastened, I rose to endeavour to explore my way out; but the first thing I put my hand on was the corrupted head of a nun, who had died some months before. This dreadful discovery prompted me the more eagerly to remove, and I ascended through the grated door, and got into a vault, which was strewed with sepulchral fragments and mouldering bones. I advanced eagerly to the door which formed the outlet, and to my horror found it fastened on the other side.

"I now abandoned myself to the prospect of perishing with hunger, and projected destroying myself, but the sake of the infant I bore prevented me. Suddenly a neighbouring tomb caught my eye, on which was a basket containing some coarse bread, and a small bottle of water. I blessed the friendly hand which had placed these viands there, and devoured them with eagerness. I then sat down, debating on the cause of finding this relief, and was inexpressibly delighted with hearing the sound of footsteps approach, and seeing a light advance; but all my hopes were dashed to pieces when I heard the door unbolted, and saw the Prioress enter, with the four nuns, who had been witnesses of my supposed death. She gazed upon me with angry eyes, and exclaimed, "Do I see a repentant or a criminal?—I fear those tears are shed less for your fault, than to excite my compassion.—But I do not wish for your death, but your repentance. I administered an opiate, not a poison, that you might feel the agonies of a guilty conscience, without dying. I shall now purify you with wholesome correction, and revive the long neglected laws of our convent, for such incontinent crimes as your's. All Madrid thinks you dead; I have taken sufficient caution to continue the mystery, therefore abandon all thoughts of this world, and prepare for that which is soon to come. Now listen to the sentence of St. Clare. Beneath these vaults are dungeons allotted to such criminals as yourself. Thither are you to be conveyed. Food and raiment, just sufficient to support nature in the coarsest manner, will be supplied you. There, chained down, and illuminated only by a feeble lamp, you will have leisure to repent. Follow me!" Thunder struck at this sentence, I fainted, and was conveyed by two of the nuns to the principal shrine of St. Clare. The nuns then raised an iron gate, hitherto concealed by the image, which was taken from the pedestal, and we descended. I was conducted down a frightful abyss, and forced into one of the cells that lined the walls of the cavern. I now interceded for mercy, for the sake of my unborn babe, but the Prioress cursed my innocent offspring, and vowed that I should bring it into the world, feed, and bury it, unbefriended! Her gross inhumanity threw me into a second fit, and when I recovered, my tyrant had departed. I then awoke to the horrors of my situation, but scantily supplied with clothing, food, and oil for my lamp. To add to my misery, the pains of child birth came on, and I was delivered of my forlorn burthen. It came alive into the world, but soon perished from my ignorance, and a want of proper attendance. The bitter wind that whistled through the vaults, the misty damps that arose from the ground, in a few hours finished its existence, and I witnessed its death with agonies that even wound me severely now.

"Sister Theresa visited me every twenty-four hours, and would fain have buried the infant, but the contemplation of its features was my only comfort, and I would not have it separated from me; nor, when I quitted my prison, could I scarcely be persuaded to entomb the precious remains. The reason of Theresa's not visiting me as usual with my stipulated allowance, I have been since informed by the Mother Urbana; she was suddenly taken ill, and a dangerous infectious fever confined her to her bed, from which cause no one would attend her, but the lay sister who was appointed to nurse her. The Prioress, and the nuns in the mystery had given me over entirely to her care. One day passed away without food; another, and a third arrived, but no Theresa, no sustenance! The lapse of time was discernible by the wasting of my lamp, to feed which, fortunately, oil enough for four days had been left me. In this dreadful dilemma, I thought the Domina had ordered the nuns to let me perish. I was become an absolute skeleton; I had the pangs of hunger gnawing at my vitals, and groans were all I had strength to utter. I was looking for the moment of my dissolution, when my beloved brother arrived in time to save me. My dim sight at first could not recognise him, but when I did, the burst of rapture overpowered me, and my emotions found refuge in insensibility. O Olphos, Axala, how shall I repay the debt of gratitude I owe to your exertions, how compensate ye for the affluence and ease I now feel, surrounded by those I esteem, and about to become the wife of him who has long before been wedded to my heart! Axala, think not, because you once found me frail, that you will witness such another error in my future conduct. No!—I am fully sensible of the great and grievous error I have committed, but I trust heaven has accepted the sufferings I have endured, as an expiation of that crime. Had it not been for the consequences of that unguarded moment, I had never seen you again: but, Fate has ordained it otherwise, and I rejoice in the wise dispensation of Providence! Here then shall the subject rest, and my future life convince Axala that the error of his mistress shall operate to render her more exemplary as a wife." Here Claude ceased, and her friends replied to her address, in terms equally affectionate and encouraging. It may easily be expected that Claude had before commencing her narrative made enquiries concerning Don Almagro. The wretched situation in which he lay, gave her a great shock, but as there did not appear any danger of not surviving his malady, she secretly exulted in the cause of his illness, since it proved the strength of his affection. Olphos undertook the pleasing duty of communicating to his friend the happiness that awaited him, in the liberation of Claude, and her rapid convalescence. Notwithstanding the caution Olphos used in relating the intelligence, Almagro's transports were so violent, as to threaten his life from an excess of joy. These once past, assured of the completion of his wishes, and above all blest with the presence of Claude, who, immediately that she had recovered under the care of Almira, hastened to attend her lover, and soon enabled him to overcome the effects of his late malady. The ease of his mind communicated itself to his body, and he recovered his health with astonishing rapidity. The next time the happy party met, Olphos expressed his satisfaction at the prospect of being so intimately connected with a man, for whom he had so much esteem. No obstruction could now present itself, (the Pope's bull having liberated Claude from all monastic engagements) except the illness of Don Olphos—which now threatened to place him in the same situation his friend had just escaped from.

His uncle, the Duke di Calvados, had before solicited his affections in favour of Almira, the young nun who, with several others, had taken refuge, during the riots, in the sepulchre of St. Clare. He could have no objection to this beautiful girl, who, from person, accomplishments, and rank, was a fit match for the first nobleman in Spain. He begged only delay till he had overgotten the shock he had experienced in the sepulchre, which, added to the affection he had long felt for a beloved and sacrificed object, whom he had discovered in the vaults, had terminated in a fit of despondency. The story involves some interest, and may not be unacceptable to the reader.

Father Clement was the Abbot of the Capuchins, and bore the surname of the Man of Holiness, from his austerity and sanctity. His stature was tall, and his features uncommonly handsome;—the glance of his eye was penetrating, and his manner inspired universal awe. This reverend father was about thirty years of age, and had been brought up by the late superior of the Capuchins, who had found him an infant left at the Abbey door. He was educated in the monastery, and had remained there ever since, even without quitting it, till a short period back, when he had been induced, on Thursdays, to deliver a lecture in the cathedral, which all Madrid constantly attended to hear. The common people esteemed him as a saint, and he was looked upon as a miracle of chastity and purity. Such was the man whom Donna Gardana, and her beautiful niece, Nerina, had come to hear. The press of the crowd was so great, that seats were invaluable, and the old lady and her charge would have retired, if Don Olphos and his friend Lopez had not politely offered to accommodate them with the seats they had procured. The beauty and elegance of Nerina, when she had, by her aunt's persuasion, unveiled, sunk deep into the heart of Olphos. They learned, in conversation with Donna Gardana, that Donna Camilla, Nerina's mother, had come from Mercia to Madrid, to solicit the continuance of a small income from the son of her father-in-law, which by the death of the latter was discontinued. Olphos, having learned the name of the gentleman, informed Nerina that he was well acquainted with him, and made an offer of his services in her mother's favour, as he was well acquainted with the generosity of his friend. Nerina raised her blue eyes, and thanked him by a look of inexpressible sweetness. This conversation preceded the sermon, which had the effect to interest every one of the auditors most profoundly, but none more than Nerina, who listened with admiration to the clear, nervous, and sublime language in which he inveighed against the vices of humanity, and described the punishments reserved for them in a future state. When he descended from the pulpit, he was loaded with blessings, and Nerina's eyes followed him with anxiety as he quitted the church. The absence of this pious father seemed to deprive her of something essential to her happiness. Olphos observed the interest she seemed to take in him, and spoke with delight of his powers and eloquence. Nerina felt an assurance that he was superior to temptation, and here the conversation ended. The ladies soon after retired, and Olphos told his friend how much he was pleased with Nerina, and that he thought her sufficiently interesting and charming to make her his wife. When they parted, Olphos repaired to the Convent, to call on his sister Claude. When he entered the church, the cool and refreshing air invited him to sit down, and as he sat contemplating the perfections of Nerina, he went fast asleep, and did not awake till the sound of the monks performing Vespers disturbed him. He was about to retire, when he observed a man, who seemed suspicious of being observed, advance towards the colossal statue of St. Francis, and, placing a letter beneath it, he retired. Not long after the sisterhood entered, with the Prioress at their head, who made a profound reverence as she passed the statue of St. Francis, the patron of the cathedral. She was followed by the rest, unveiled; but guess the astonishment of Olphos, when he saw his sister Claude, in bending to the shrine, *accidentally* drop her rosary, and extract the letter from the Saint's foot. Upon this the unknown quitted his concealment, & was hastily retiring from church, when Olphos insisted on knowing the contents of the letter, and who he was. This produced an éclaircissement, to the great joy of Olphos, who found in the stranger his much valued friend, the Marquis d'Axala, who had just then come from Wildenheim, and whose history has been previously detailed. The Monk, after the above service had been performed, retired to his cell, where he looked round in conscious exultation, considering himself as a being in many respects superior to his fellow creature.

Suspended opposite to him was the picture of a Madona, on the fine face and bosom of which he constantly gazed with delight.—He was one day indulging in a train of free ideas on the beauty of the Madona before him, when Giovanni, a young novice, opened the door, with a small basket of flowers in his hand.—He intended to make his profession in three months, and had a considerable degree of mystery about him. A stranger, whose rich habit and magnificent equipage had declared him to be of high rank, had engaged the monks to receive the novice, and with him had left the necessary sums. The youth had carefully avoided all society, except that of Father Clement. His face was so muffled up in his cowl, that no one ever had seen it, not even the Monk, who was charmed with the sweetness of his manners, and his particular attention to him.—Giovanni had come to applaud his decided conduct in not listening a few nights before to the prayers and intreaties of Claude.—The latter, in stooping to make her confession before the Abbot in his official chair, let fall the letter which she had a little before obtained from the statue of St. Francis, containing the plan of her escape from the convent, and signed by the Marquis d'Axala. The Monk shewed her what he had picked up, and deaf to her intreaties, sent it to the Prioress, who thereby became acquainted with the whole plot, and prevented, as before-mentioned, the escape of Claude.

When Giovanni had done speaking, the father said he felt pity for her. "If you pity her father," said Giovanni, "Oh! then pity me! for I have no friend, and my secret bows me down with its weight!"—The Monk took Giovanni's hand, and vowed that his happiness was as dear to him as his own. "Swear then!" said Giovanni, "that I shall not quit the monastery before my noviciate expires!" The Monk swore, and then intreated an explanation of the mystery. "I obey you, father!—Reverend Clement, pity my weakness, my love; pity the passions of one who is a woman!" The father started, and would have flown, but Malina prevented him, and the Monk seated himself beside her. She then informed him that her father died when she was an infant, and left her rich; that she was brought up under an uncle, who instructed her in erudition and magic; having refused many offers, her heart had remained uninfluenced by love, till she saw him in the pulpit of the cathedral. The father disapproved of her conduct, at the same time he felt the pleasure with which he had contemplated the Madona transferred to this living representative of her. It will be sufficient to say, that, after various interviews between them, in which the seductive charms of Malina had been displayed partially to his view, he repaired one night to her cell, having received a message that she was unwell. The syren, raising herself half out of bed, threw her arms round him; the impression was irresistible; the rays of the lamp darted upon her half-undressed figure, and the vows of the Monk yielded to passion! The barrier of holiness was broken down, and the gulf of desire was ready to cancel in a short time every other remaining virtue.—Intoxicated with pleasure, the Monk rose from the fair one's couch; habit made her necessary to his pleasures for a time; but, as in the course of his confessional duty, new faces and other charms succeeded, he grew cloyed with the easy conquest he had obtained over the person of Malina, and panted only for new enjoyments, regardless of his sacred character, and satisfied with avoiding the danger of detection from the unimpeachable purity of his character.

One morning the confluence of penitents was greater than usual; he was detained till it was late, and was about to retire, when the beautiful Nerina and another female solicited him to pray for her mother, and send some pious Monk to comfort her in her dying moments. He was charmed with the supplicant, and took the card with the address of the sick Donna Camilla on it. When the Monk retired to his cell, he felt a thousand new emotions spring up in his bosom: he felt a mingled sentiment of tenderness, admiration, and respect: he felt now the purer influence of love, and in a fit of indignation dashed the picture of the Madona from the wall. He resolved to be the confessor himself, and the gratitude of Nerina shone through her eyes when the holy father entered her mother's chamber. Camilla was highly gratified by this visit; the pious Monk laid all her fears at rest, and in case of her death, promised to provide for the future comforts of her daughter.

In the anti-room he met Nerina, gave her hopes of her mother, and received with delight the artless expressions of her gratitude. When Clement returned to the abbey, his mind was filled with the most pleasing images, and he failed not to profit of Camilla's indisposition, to visit her daughter every day, whose innocent familiarity encouraged his desires; and as her mother was getting better, he thought the attempt to try his influence over the innocent Nerina must not be delayed. One day he entered her room, which adjoined that of her mother, and found her sleeping on the sopha, in consequence of an opiate he had given her.

He gazed for some minutes in rapture on the sleeping beauty, and he was bending his head to salute her, when Camilla entered from a private closet that opened into her room, and detected the guilty monk. The Abbot made an effort to get to the door, conscious, if he could but once reach his convent, his reputed sanctity would protect him from imputation. The enraged mother, however, opposed his progress, and called loudly to the servant to witness his guilt. Not a moment was to be lost. Suddenly with one hand he grasped Camilla by the throat, threw her on the floor, and placing a pillow over her face and bosom, knelt upon it till she was suffocated. The horrible act once perpetrated, he beheld the enormity of his crime. The shock of Camilla's unexpected death produced its natural effect on the daughter; it brought on a despondency, and in this dilemma the Abbot again visited her; as she mended, his flame revived, and Malina recommended to him the administration of a second draught. This plan the Monk executed, successfully, and Nerina was conveyed to St. Clare's, supposed really dead. During Nerina's lethargy, the Monk effected his lustful purpose, and she awoke to the horrors of her situation. Scarcely had the terrors of conscience visited the Monk, when Malina informed him the convent was beset. She then drew a dagger, and recommended that Nerina should be poniarded. He hesitated to do the deed, resolving to lock her up in the secret dungeon; but the noise of archers, and Olphos, impelled Nerina to call for help, when the Abbot twice plunged the dagger into her bosom, and fled. Nerina died in the arms of Olphos, and the Monk and Melina were afterwards convicted of witchcraft and murder, and executed.

These circumstances for a time clouded the mind of Olphos, but at length they gave way to the remonstrances of his friend, and the beauty of Almira, and he eventually entered the regions of Hymen, with his friend Almagro and Claude.

FINIS.

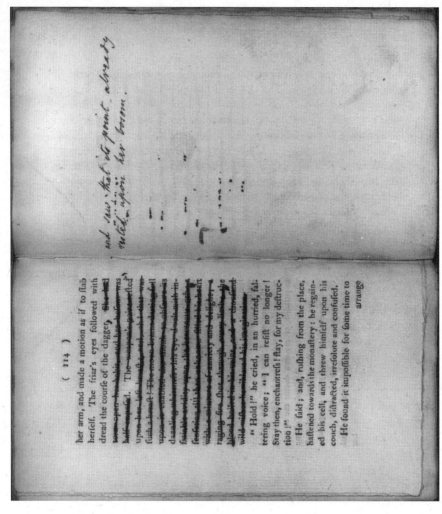

(114)

her arm, and made a motion as if to ſtab herſelf. The friar's eyes followed with dread the courſe of the dagger; ſhe was ~~...~~

~~...~~

"Hold!" he cried, in an hurried, faltering voice; "I can reſiſt no longer! Stay then, enchantreſs! ſtay, for my deſtruction!"

He ſaid; and, ruſhing from the place, haſtened towards the monaſtery: he regained his cell, and threw himſelf upon his couch, diſtracted, irreſolute and confuſed.

He found it impoſſible for ſome time to arrange

A page from the third edition (C.28.b.4-6, British Library) with Lewis's handwritten revisions for the expurgated fourth edition (see p. 84-85). Reproduced with the permission of the British Library.

Appendix E: Variants

[Almost as soon as he had published *The Monk*, Lewis began to have second thoughts about its sensationalism. He made at least one major change to the second edition (the first to which he signed his name), and he made many more to the fourth edition, in response to critical controversy (and perhaps the threat of legal action). See Introduction 20-22, and Appendix C.

The following collation was prepared by Chris Olbey, Darren Matthies, and Renée Laaja. We have also drawn on the previous textual work of William B. Todd, Louis F. Peck, and Howard Anderson. The collation lists all the substantive variants between this edition of the first edition of *The Monk* and the four later lifetime editions. (For emendations in this edition, see the Note on the Text.) The format is as follows: first we give the page and line numbers, and the reading, of this edition; then, after a right square bracket, the number(s) of the edition(s) in which the variant is to be found, then the wording of the variant. Passages more than six words long in the first edition have usually been abbreviated. Additions and omissions are indicated by the words *add* and *omit* in italics. Accidental variants are not listed.]

VOLUME I

35.17 criticised] 4-5 *add a footnote*: Neglected it has not been, but criticised enough of all conscience.

37.10 4-5 *add to* Vol. III The Erl-King, The Erl-King's Daughter, *and* Giles Jollup the Grave and Brown Sally Green.

39.12 influenced by] 4-5 influenced with

40.35 both started] 2-5 but started

45.21 cavalier was] 4-5 cavalier were

45.36 in her company] 4-5 in company

45.42 not you speak] 2-5 you not speak

47.15-17 he is reported ... common people therefore] 4-5 the common people

47.19-29 "Does that make ... through the church] 4-5 Here Don Christoval was interrupted by an universal murmur, which ran through the church; it

48.26 conscience] 3 confidence

49.7 amidst the spectators] 3-5 amongst the spectators

49.10   greater vivacity] 3 great vivacity
50.37   failings] 2-3 feelings
51.37   make] 3-5 made
52.7   amours still further] 2 amour still further] 3-5 amour still
        farther
54.36   Sudden] 2-5 Suddenly
55.5-6 unutterable] 4-5 evident
55.12   4-5 *omit* Lust!
55.25   embrace] 2-5 embraces
55.28   above] 4-5 *add a footnote:* Lovelace dreams, that Clarissa left
        her robe in his grasp.
55.33   sunk] 4-5 sank
60.15   was their lodging.] 4-5 they lodged.
61.22   What I in fortune's mirror view;] 4-5 In fortune's mirror
        what I view;
62.31   lust] 4-5 whims
63.24   Lustful] 4-5 Vicious
65.25   you—Madona] 2-5 yon Madona
65.36-37   with my lips ... that snowy bosom!] 4-5 to my lips
        that hand of snow!
66.2   a common virtue] 4-5 common virtue
66.5   become woman] 4-5 becoming a woman
66.10   your virtue] 4-5 thy virtue
66.26   observation] 2-5 observance
67.39   dispersed] 3-5 disposed
69.8   4-5 *omit* at last
69.13   picked] 4-5 took
70.14   lust;] 4-5 pleasure;
71.19   the opinion] 4-5 an opinion
72.10   sunk] 4-5 sank
72.39   jessamine] 4-5 jessamines
73.28   O God!] 4-5 Oh!
73.32   his place] 4-5 the mossy couch
73.33   seated] 4-5 placed
73.34   place himself] 4-5 be seated
74.26   *After* Consume the day. 2-5 *insert this stanza:*

        This rock my shield when storms are blowing;
        The limpid streamlet yonder flowing
        Supplying drink; the earth bestowing
                        My simple food;
        But few enjoy the calm I know in
                        This desert rude.

75.29   Time] 5 time
76.33   of fair] 4-5 of the fair
76.42   God] 4-5 heaven
77.1   God] 4-5 heaven
77.24   sunk] 4-5 sank
80.1-2 they had been touched] 4-5 had they been touched
80.21   4-5 *omit* lust for the enjoyment
81.12-13 4-5 *omit* Oh! surely on ... of his charge!
84.36-85.2 dagger. She had torn ... bewildered his imagination.]
        4-5 dagger, and saw that its point already rested upon her
        bosom.
85.40-41 to judge by her—by what] 4-5 to judge by what
86.6-24 unrefreshed. During his sleep ... was he less ashamed] 4-5
        unrefreshed; and started from his couch, heartily ashamed
89.15   sunk] 4-5 sank
89.36   lancet] 2-5 instrument
90.1   lancet] 2-5 instrument
90.21   lancet] 2-5 instrument
94.29   backwarder] 4-5 more back
96.12   to you] 4-5 to thee
96.12   on you] 4-5 on thee
96.13   you would] 4-5 thou wouldst
96.14   you have] 4-5 but thou hast
96.14   you have] 4-5 thou hast
98.37-38 4-5 *omit* aided by the natural warmth of his temperament
99.2   seductions to lust,] 4-5 seductions,
99.3-4 the devil,] 4-5 Satan,
99.21-29 4-5 *omit* but the dreams ... shame and disappointment
99.30-31 dawned. Fatigued, harassed ... provoking dreams, he] 4-5
        dawned, but he
100.13 hearts] 2-5 heart
102.18-19 forgotten the day already] 4-5 forgotten the day
103.5-6 4-5 *omit* either I must die ... of unsatisfied desire.
103.9-10 4-5 *omit* I lust for the enjoyment of your person.
103.16-20 I shall no longer ... enjoy you or die."] 4-5 No, no,
        Ambrosio, I feel that I must not live!"
103.33-35 4-5 *omit* She took his hand. ... Feel this heart, father!
103.38-104.2 4.5 *omit* Thus will I expire ... that kiss is my
        assurance."
104.5-19 No prying eye ... upon her bosom.] 4-5 Nothing was
        heard but her melodious accents. Ambrosio saw before
        him a young and beautiful woman, the preserver of his
        life, the adorer of his person; and whom affection for him

had reduced to the brink of the grave: her life or death rested upon his decision: which should he sacrifice, his vows or her existence? A thousand noble feelings, blended with a thousand base ones, impell him to prefer the former. He obeys; his vow is violated! Tremble, Ambrosio! the first step is taken; and he who breaks his faith with heaven, will soon break it with man.—Hark! 'twas the shriek of your better angel: he flies, and leaves you for ever!

111.39   forgotten] 4-5 forgot

120.18-19   a better treatment] 4-5 better treatment

123.15   that my sleep] 3-5 my sleep

128.23   I had had too many] 5 I had too many

130.10-11   met with nothing] 4-5 met nothing

VOLUME II

133.21   as it had been a battle] 2-5 as if it had been a battle

137.2   her aunt] 2-3 our aunt

137.28   they made] 2-5 they had made

138.36   into her cheeks] 3-5 in her cheeks

139.26   raised] 4-5 had raised

141.26   paternoster] 4-5 *Paternoster*

141.27   De profundis] 4-5 *De profundis*

144.4   talk nonsense] 4-5 make love

146.34   long wished-for night] 2,5 long-wished-for night] 3 long-wished fortnight] 4 long-wished for night

152.34-41   her, and clasped ... thine my soul!"] 4-5 her; and, clasping her in my arms, I exclaimed,

> "Agnes! Agnes! Thou art mine!
> Agnes! Agnes! I am thine!
> Fairest! Dearest! Thou art mine!
> Fairest! Dearest! I am thine!
> Leave thee will I never!
> Thou art mine!
> I am thine!
> Body and soul for ever!"

156.9-12   "In thy veins ... Mine thy soul!"—] 4-5

> "Leave thee will I never!
> I am thine!
> Thou art mine,
> Body and soul for ever!"

157.28   sunk] 4-5 dropped

160.26   some] 2-5 no mean

160.27 sometimes] 2-5 occasionally
160.28 occasionally] 2-5 frequently
162.4 was unpowdered] 2-5 hung wildly upon his brow
162.23 nor night] 2 or night
164.7 sunk upon his knees,] 4-5 knelt down and
164.17 bible] 4-5 Bible
164.21 bible] 4-5 Bible
165.24 bible] 4-5 Bible
166.5 avowed concubine.] 4-5 acknowledged mistress.
166.16 inclinations] 2, 4-5 inclination
168.15 persons] 2-5 people
168.27 already quitted] 2-5 quitted
169.6 riddle] 4-5 *add a footnote*: I imagined the tradition of the Wandering Jew is to be known universally. But, as many people have expressed to me their ignorance on the subject, it may be as well to state, that the Wandering Jew is said to have insulted our Saviour, while leading to the Cross, saying "Go, go, Thou King of the Jews!" on which Christ, looking at him, answered "Yea, I will go; but thou shalt tarry till I come again!"
169.34 hoped] 2 hope
171.2 brought me to] 4 brought to] 5 brought us to
172.6 doubting] 4-5 suspecting
173.23 4-5 *omit* in spite of my disguise,
178.2 you to write] 2 you write
179.9-10 till the arrival ... the cardinal-duke's estate.] 3-5 in the cardinal-duke's estate till the arrival of the expected bull.
179.26 heart] 4-5 *add a footnote*: There is certainly a very strong resemblance between some parts of the story of "the Bleeding Nun," and that of the Apparition in "Les Chevaliers du Cygne." I can only account for it by supposing that Madame de Genlis had heard, while in Germany, the same tradition which I have made use of. It is at least certain, that "The Monk" was already in the press, when I read for the first time "Les Chevaliers du Cygne."[1]—The story which was related to me, was merely, that the castle of Lauenstein was haunted by a spectre habited as a nun (but not as a bleeding one); that a young officer by mis-

---

1 This is Lewis's response to the charge of plagiarism in the *European Magazine*: see Appendix C.2. In fact, Stéphanie-Félicité du Crest, comtesse de Genlis (1746-1830), *Les Chevaliers du cygne* ("The Knights of the Swan," 1795) was not published until after Lewis had finished *The Monk*.

take ran away with her, instead of the heiress of Lauenstein; that she used to appear to him every night; that, on
going to a foreign country, neither he nor the phantom
was ever after heard of; and that the words which she used
to repeat to him were in the original,

> "Frizchen! Frizchen! Du bist mein
> Frizchen! Frizchen! Ich bin dein!
> Ich dein!
> Du mein,
> Mit lieb' und seel."

180.22 excess] 2-5 access
181.21 of the morning] 4-5 in the morning
181.31 little] 4-5 youthful
182.4 cheerful] 4-5 kindly
183.25 led thee] 2-5 led you
185.18 lyre] 4-5 *add a footnote*: The last stanza is taken from the
first Ode of Anacreon.
186.27-28 only seem introduced] 2-5 seem introduced only
188.7 woke] 4-5 awoke
192.15 else] 4-5 *add a footnote*:

> Pour chasser de sa souvenance
> L'objet qui plait,
> On se donne bien de souffrance
> Pour peu d'effet.
> Le souvenir durant la vie
> Toujours revient;
> En pensant qu'il faut qu'on l'oublie
> On s'en souvient.[1]

195.34 approve of the] 3-5 approve the
203.33-35 While in each ... coming day. LEE.] 4-5

> "What is't ye do?
> —A deed without a name!"   MACBETH.[2]

204.1-205.21 The burst of transport ... in her possession.] 4-5

> We now must revisit the monastery of the
Capuchins. There we shall find bosoms agitated by very
different emotions from those which were felt by the
innocent inhabitants of Elvira's dwelling.

---

1 "To chase from our memory / The object that pleases, / We suffer greatly
/ To little effect. / Memory during life / Always returns; / In believing
that we must forget something / We remember it" (adapted from "Les
Constantes Amours d'Alix et d'Alexis" [73-80]; trans. Nikki Sheppy).
2 Shakespeare, *Macbeth* 4.1.49.

With every step that Ambrosio made in the path of vice, he at first looked back with regret to the station which he had quitted: but, alas! with every step that regret became weaker. Matilda's eloquence and beauty, the power of habit, and the frailty of human nature, gradually diminished the sensation, and at length it scarce could be said to be felt by the monk's bosom at all. He no longer reflected with shame upon his conduct, or dreaded the vengeance of offended Heaven. One fear alone possessed him. He trembled to lose Matilda, who still laboured under the influence of poison. He therefore pressed her with earnestness to use the means of preservation which she had before declared to be in her possession.

205.36 are you possessed of] 4-5 do you possess
206.19 secret charms] 4-5 charms
206.24 incontinence] 4-5 weakness
206.28-30 The pleasures which ... brain was bewildered,] 4-5 His brain was still bewildered,
206.31 4-5 *omit* voluptuousness,
206.33-34 indulged in excesses whose very idea] 4-5 committed an error, from whose very idea
206.34 four-and-twenty] 4-5 a few
206.34 had recoiled at] 4-5 would have recoiled
206.42-207.1 beauty, and those ... never be forgotten.] 4-5 charms and tenderness.
207.2-3 he considered ... night] 4-5 and he considered her possession
207.16 incontinence,] 4-5 that which is
207.19-21 4-5 *omit* he threw himself ... repetition of his pleasures.
209.26 of obtaining] 4-5 to obtain
210.37 into a low murmur] 2-5 in a low murmur
210.39 into the cavern] 2-5 in the cavern
212.8 makes] 2-5 make
212.13 4-5 *omit* wanton
212.15-18 The friar returned ... were frequently repeated.] 4-5 This the friar hesitated not to promise, or Matilda to believe.
212.28 desires] 4-5 emotions
212.31-32 4-5 *omit* The monk was ... fullness of pleasure.
212.33-35 paramour: his warm ... quitted her with disgust,] 4-5 conquest,
212.39 he had obtained her favours,] 4-5 she was become his,
212.39-40 become dearer] 4-5 dearer
212.40-41 4-5 *omit* and she felt ... equally been sharers.

212.41 Unfortunately] 4-5 but unfortunately,

213.12-16 4-5 *omit* Still, however, their illicit ... indulge his passions safely.

215.8-9 4-5 *omit* he was ignorant ... power to bestow;

215.37 The eyes of the luxurious friar] 4-5 The friar's eyes

215.38 those interpreters] 2-5 these interpreters

215.39-216.3 4-5 *omit* For his misfortune ... entered their imaginations.

216.21 it] 4-5 her

216.22 himself to Matilda's person.] 4-5 his addresses to Matilda.

218.2-3 He felt not the provocation of lust; no] 4-5 No

218.4-5 bosom; nor did ... his eyes. On] 4-5 bosom. On

218.19 first] 4-5 one

218.19 lustful] 4-5 glutting

218.20 second] 4-5 other

218.20-21 4-5 *omit* gluts me with enjoyment even to loathing,

218.22 her prostitution.] 4-5 what should be her shame!

218.22 4-5 *omit* Disgusting!

218.26-27 refuse to sacrifice] 4-5 not sacrifice

221.13 said] 5 says

223.5 Such alone] 4-5 Such a one alone *and the sentence is
italicized.*

223.7 and distrust] 2-3 and disgust] 4-5 *omitted*

223.10 that some] 2-5 that on some

226.1 HYMN] 4-5 *add a footnote:*
Probably these stanzas were suggested by Imogen's prayer
in Cymbeline—
    "From fairies and from tempters of the night
    Guard me, good angels!"[1]

227.27 has 'scap'd] 2-5 escapes

228.25 encouraged his desires.] 4-5 gave him encouragement.

228.28 4-5 *omit* quality

228.29 Warmth of passion, ... of which latter,] 4-5 His natural
penetration, of which,

229.22-23 While he waited ... his unwarrantable lust,] 4-5 In
the mean while

230.26 secure of his principles and her own] 4-5 secure

230.27 prattle to] 4-5 discourse with

230.29-231.16 4-5 *omit* He examined the book ... upon the table.

232.10 passion] 4-5 love

232.30 these sentiments] 4-5 those sentiments

---

1 Shakespeare, *Cymbeline* 2.2.9-10.

233.3-4 4.5 *omit* wild with desire,

233.5 sucked] 4-5 and sucked

233.6-7 breath, violated with ... and yielding limbs.] 4-5 breath.

233.12 4-5 *omit* licentious].

233.12-13 prayers: he persisted ... still greater liberties.] 4-5 prayers.

233.18-19 quitted his prey, ... the couch. Antonia] 4-5 released
Antonia, who

233.29-30 his being in ... heat of manhood] 4-5 his youth

233.36-37 the disorder of her daughter's dress] 4.5 her daughter's
alarm

233.39 but too well founded] 4-5 well founded

235.35 which I complain] 4-5 that I complain

235.35-36 not of your indifference to my person.] 4-5 for though

235.37 but nothing] 4-5 nothing

235.40 and a confident: in] 4-5 of a confident, and in

235.40-41 4-5 *omit* needful

236.10 4-5 *omit* your attempt to enjoy Antonia's person,

237.13 lust,] 4-5 desire,

237.14 enjoyment] 4-5 possession

239.28-240.3 The scene was ... worked up to phrensy.] 4-5
Ambrosio gazed upon it for a few minutes; those few were
sufficient to fix his irresolution.

243.28 sunk] 4-5 sank

245.7 your voluntary servants] 5 our voluntary servants

245.9 enjoying] 4-5 possessing

245.14-15 4-5 *omit* deprive her of ... attempts. Sleep will

245.35 adventure, and,] 4-5 adventure:

245.36 looked] 4-5 he looked

245.37-38 4-5 *omit* Imagination retraced to ... the enchanted mirror,

245.38 4-5 *omit* he

VOLUME III

252.3 name but] 2-5 name than

253.10 are worth] 4-5 is worth

253.18 sung] 4-5 sang

253.19 WATER-KING] [4-5 *add a footnote*:
Since writing these Stanzas, I have met with two old
Scotch ballads which have some resemblance with "*The
Water-King*:" one is called "*May Colvin*," and relates the
story of a king's daughter, who was beguiled from her
father's house by *a false Sir John*: the other, entitled "*Clerk
Colvil*," treats of a young man, who fell into the snares of
a false Mermaid: the latter, indeed, bears a still stronger

resemblance to the Danish tradition of "*The Erl-King's Daughter.*"—The fragment of "*The Water-King*" may be found in "Herder's Volk-lieder."[1]

254.30 partner] 2-5 bride-groom

255.34 Water-Spright] 4-5 *add a footnote:*

Many enquiries having been made respecting the elementary monarchs mentioned a few pages back, I must inform my readers, that all I know respecting the Water-King (called in the German translation "Der Wasser-Mann"), and the Erl-King (called in German "Erl-König"),[2] is gathered from the foregoing ballad, and two others which I shall here insert. With respect to the Fire-King and the Cloud-King, they are entirely of my own creation; but if my readers choose to ascribe their birth to the "Comte de Gabalis," they are very welcome.

THE ERL-KING.
[The Original is by Goëthe, Author of Werter.]

WHO is it that rides through the forest so fast,
While night frowns around him, while chill roars the blast?
The father, who holds his young son in his arm,
And close in his mantle has wrapped him up warm.

—"Why trembles my darling? why shrinks he with fear?"
"Oh! father! my father! the Erl-King is near!
The Erl-King, with his crown and his beard long and white!"
—"Oh! thine eyes are deceived by the vapours of night."

—"If you will, dear baby, with me go away,
I will give you fine clothes; we will play a fine play;
Fine flowers are growing, white, scarlet, and blue,
On the banks of yon river, and all are for you."—

—"Oh! father! my father! and dost thou not hear
What words the Erl-King whispers low in mine ear?"—
—"Now hush thee, my darling, thy terrors appease:
Thou hear'st 'midst the branches when murmurs the breeze."

—"If you will, dear baby, with me go away,
My daughter shall tend you so fair and so gay;
My daughter, in purple and gold who is drest,
Shall nurse you, and kiss you, and sing you to rest."

—"Oh! father! my father! and dost thou not see?
The Erl-King and his daughter are waiting for me?"—

---

1 Johann Gottfried Herder (1744-1803), *Volkslieder* ("Folksongs," 1778-79).
2 Johann Wolfgang von Goethe (1749-1832), "Der Erlkönig" (1782).

—"Now shame thee, my dearest! 'tis fear makes thee blind:
Thou see'st the dark willows, which wave in the wind."—

—"I love you! I dote on that face so divine!
I must, and will have you, and force makes you mine!"—
—"My father! my father! Oh! hold me now fast!
He pulls me! he hurts, and will have me at last!"

The father, he trembled; he doubled his speed;
O'er hills and through forests he spurr'd his black steed:
But when he arrived at his own castle-door,
Life throbbed in the sweet baby's bosom no more.

THE ERL-KING'S DAUGHTER.
[The Original is Danish; but I read it in a German Translation.]

O'ER hills and through forests Sir Oluf he wends
To bid to his wedding relations and friends:
'Tis late, and arriving where sports the elf band,
The Erl-King's proud Daughter presents him her hand.

—"Now welcome, Sir Oluf! Oh! welcome to me!
Come, enter our circle my partner to be."—
"Fair lady, nor can I dance with you, nor may:
To-morrow I marry, to-night must away."—

—"Now listen, Sir Oluf! Oh! listen to me!
Two spurs of fine steel will I give unto thee;
A shirt too of satin receive as thy boon,
Which my Queen-mother bleached in the beams of the moon.

Then yield thee, Sir Oluf! O! yield thee to me,
And enter our circle my partner to be."—
—"Fair lady, nor can I dance with you, nor may:
To-morrow I marry, to-night must away."—

—"Now listen, Sir Oluf! Oh! listen to me!
An helmet of gold will I give unto thee"—
—"An helmet of gold would I willingly take,
But I will not dance with you for Urgela's sake."—

—"And deigns not Sir Oluf my partner to be?
Then curses and sickness I give unto thee;
Then curses and sickness thy steps shall pursue:
Now hence to thy lady, thou lover so true!"—

Thus said she, and laid her charmed hand on his heart,
Oh! never Sir Oluf had felt such a smart!
Swift spurred he his steed till he reached his own door,
And there stood his mother the castle before.

—"Now riddle me, Oluf, and riddle me right:
Why look'st thou, my dearest, so wan and so white?"—

—"How should I not, mother, look wan and look white?
I have seen the Erl-King's cruel Daughter to-night!

She cursed me; her hand to my bosom she prest:
Death followed the touch, and now tortures my breast.
She cursed me, and said—'To thy lady now ride!'—
But ne'er shall my lips kiss the lips of my bride!"—

—"Now riddle me, Oluf, and what shall I say
When here comes the lady so fair and so gay?"—
"Oh! say, I am gone for a while to the wood,
To prove if my hounds and my courser be good."—

Scarce dead was Sir Oluf, and scarce shone the day,
When in came the lady so fair and so gay,
And in came her father, and in came each guest
Whom the hapless Sir Oluf had bade to the feast.

They drank the red wine, and they ate the good cheer.
"Oh! where is Sir Oluf? Oh! where is my dear?"—
—"Sir Oluf is gone for awhile to the wood,
To prove if his hounds and his courser be good."—

Then trembled the lady so fair and so gay:
She eyed the black curtain; she drew it away:
But soon from her bosom for ever life fled,
For there lay Sir Oluf, pale, breathless, and dead.

257.10 the basket] 3 a basket
257.25 nor sealed] 2-4 or sealed
259.12 encourage] 2-5 give way to
261.6   4-5 *omit* lustful
261.12 her daughter's ravisher.] 4-5 the culprit.
261.14-16 4-5 *omit* that it would seem ... or by whom;
261.36 ravisher] 4-5 intruder
262.4-5 mistress. No] 4-5 mistress; and no
262.6-7 4-5 *omit* and his eyes flashed with lust and impatience.
262.10-12 4-5 *omit* The heat of the weather ... hastened to remove.
262.20-21 pervaded her whole form;] 4-5 was spread over every
         feature.
262.21-31 and there was a sort ... of his lust] 4-5 But the mod-
         esty visible in her whole appearance, instead of persuad-
         ing him to renounce them, served only to confirm the
         monk in his designs.
             He remained for some moments lost in motionless
         admiration! Her mouth half opened seemed to solicit a
         kiss: he bent over her: he joined his lips to hers, and drew
         in the fragrance of her breath with rapture.
262.32 exclaimed] at that moment exclaimed 4-5.
262.35 it.] 4-5 the voice.

263.4   just in time] 4-5 in time

263.4-5 grasp of the ravisher] 4-5 betrayer's grasp

263.14 incontinence] 4-5 infamy

263.41-42 perfidy, your hypocrisy, and incontinence] 4-5 perfidy and hypocrisy

264.12-13 4-5 *omit* gathered up such ... thrown off, and

265.14 4-5 *omit* gathered up his garments,

266.28-29 longed more eagerly than ever to enjoy Antonia.] 4-5 was now bent more earnestly than ever on procuring its gratification.

267.14 the mistress] 4-5 mistress

270.28-29 caught her eye ... been her mother's.] 4-5 conducting to that which had been her mother's caught her eye.

271.31-32 "If e'er I, by lust or by wealth led aside, / Forget my] 4-5 "And if e'er for another my heart should decide, / Forgetting

272.15 told—] 5 tolled—

272.33 God!] 4-5 then

273.33 Imagine] 4-5 *add a footnote*:

> After this raw-head and bloody-bones history, perhaps it may be agreeable to some readers to peruse the following parody. I must observe, that the lines in Italics, and the original idea of making a Brewer of the Baron, and a Physician of the Knight, are borrowed from another parody which appeared in the newspapers under the title of "Pil-Garlic the Brave and Brown Celestine."

GILES JOLLUP THE GRAVE
AND
BROWN SALLY GREEN:
A PARODY.

A DOCTOR so prim and a sempstress so tight
    Hob-a-nobbed in some right marasquin;
They sucked up the cordial with truest delight:
Giles Jollup the Grave *was just five feet in height,*
    And four feet the brown Sally Green.

"And as," said Giles Jollup, "to-morrow I go
    To physic a feverish land,
At some sixpenny hop, or perhaps the Mayor's show,
You'll tumble in love with some smart city-beau,
    And with him share your shop in the Strand."

"Lord! how can you think so?" brown Sally Green said;
    "You must know mighty little of me;
For if you be living, or if you be dead,
I swear, 'pon my honour, that none in your stead
    Shall husband of Sally Green be.

"And if e'er for another my heart should decide,
    False to you and the faith which I gave,
God grant, that, at dinner too amply supplied,
Over-eating may give me a pain in my side;
    May your ghost then bring rhubarb to physic the bride,
        And send her well-dosed to the grave!"

Away went poor Giles, to what place is not told.
    Sally wept, till she blew her nose sore!
But scarce had a twelvemonth elapsed, when behold!
A Brewer, quite stylish, his gig that way rolled,
    And stopp'd it at Sally Green's door.

His wealth, his pot-belly, and whisky of cane,
    Soon made her untrue to her vows:
The steam of strong beer now bewildering her brain,
He caught her while tipsy! Denials were vain,
    So he carried her home as his spouse.

And now the roast beef had been blest by the priest,
    To cram now the guests had begun:
Tooth and nail like a wolf fell the bride on the feast;
Nor yet had the clash of her knife and fork ceased,
    When a bell—('twas a dustman's)—tolled—"one!"

Then first with amazement brown Sally Green found
    That a stranger was stuck by her side:
His cravat and his ruffles with snuff were embrowned;
He ate not, he drank not, but, turning him round,
    Sent some pudding away to be fried!!!

His wig was *turned forwards, and short was his height;*
    His apron was dirty to view:
The women (oh! wondrous!) were hushed at his sight:
The cats, as they eyed him, drew back (well they might),
    For his body was pea-green and blue!

Now as all wished to speak, but none knew what to say,
    They looked mighty foolish and queer.
At length spoke the bride, while she trembled—"I pray,
Dear sir, your peruke that aside you would lay,
    And partake of some strong or small beer!"

The sempstress is silent; the stranger complies,
    And his wig from his phiz deigns to pull.
Adzooks! what a squall Sally gave through surprise!
Like a pig that is stuck how she opened her eyes,
    When she recognized Jollup's bare skull!

Each miss then exclaimed, while she turned up her snout,
    "Sir, your head isn't fit to be seen!"—
The pot-boys ran in, and the pot-boys ran out,

And couldn't conceive what the noise was about,
　　While the Doctor addressed Sally Green:

"Behold me, thou jill-flirt! behold me!" he cried;
　　"You've broken the faith which you gave!
God grants, that, to punish your falsehood and pride,
Over-eating should give you a pain in your side:
Come, swallow this rhubarb! I'll physic the bride,
　　And send her well-dosed to the grave!"

Thus saying, the physic her throat he forced down,
　　In spite of whate'er she could say;
Then bore to his chariot the damsel so brown;
Nor ever again was she seen in that town,
　　Or the Doctor who whisked her away.

Not long lived the Brewer: and none since that time
　　To make use of the brew-house presume;
For 'tis firmly believed, that, by order sublime,
There Sally Green suffers the pain of her crime,
　　And bawls to get out of the room.

At midnight four times in each year does her spright
　　With shrieks make the chamber resound:
—"I won't take the rhubarb!" she squalls in affright,
While, a cup in his left hand, a draught in his right,
　　Giles Jollup pursues her around!

With wigs so well powdered, their fees while they crave,
　　Dancing round them twelve Doctors are seen:
They drink chicken-broth, while this horrible stave
Is twange'd through each nose—"To Giles Jollup the Grave,
　　"And his patient, the sick Sally Green!"

274.34 was whispering] 3 were whispering
276.34-35 upon Antonia's ruin, ... of whose person] 4-5 to pur-
　　sue his designs upon Antonia, for whom
280.32 this resolution] 4-5 his resolution
283.11-12 not for a single night, but] 4-5 and yours
283.13-14 her. You shall riot ... your mistress. This] 4-5 her; but this
283.25-26 and heart] 5 and her heart
283.38 Matilda's gift] 4-5 your gift
283.38-284.5 4-5 *omit* I shall clasp ... wild tumultuous wish?
284.20 hesitated] scrupled 4.5.
284.20 desires] 4-5 passion
284.22-30 Antonia. As he sat ... vigilant duenna. Inflamed] 4-5
　　Antonia; and, inflamed
284.22 discovered] 2-3 again betrayed
284.23-25 which till then ... had pictured them.] 2-3 on which

his eyes had dwelt with such delight on the night of Elvira's murder.

284.30 these beauties] 4-5 her beauties

287.15-16 no better than a procuress.] 4-5 being no better than she should be.

288.21 to his own] 4-5 for his own

294.22 sweeter] 4-5 *add a footnote*:

> "In notes by distance made more sweet."
>
> COLLINS.[1]

294.27-28 at their hypocrisy] 4-5 of their hypocrisy

298.17 none] 2-5 known

299.32 day] 4-5 morning

302.33 mob was] 2-5 mob were

306.40 These terrors] 3-5 These dangers

307.6-7 4-5 *omit* Not we, indeed;

307.22-23 dare ask] 3-5 dare to ask

313.3 slow] 3-5 1ow

314.31 him] 4-5 them

316.22 2-5 *omit* Don

317.12 his monks] 2-5 the monks

317.15 comply with his desires] 4-5 fall an easy victim to his villainy

317.17-18 prevent him from enjoying her] 4-5 be permitted to counteract his plans

317.21-22 affection, and wishing ... no one but herself.] 4-5 affection.

318.18 their rotting bones] 3-5 the rotting bones

318.26-321.25 He lifted her ... dishonour of Antonia.] 4-5 Antonia! wretched Antonia! Too soon were the villain's words verified. Heaven, for purposes no doubt wise in themselves, but whose aim the sight of mortals is too weak to discern, interposed not in the unhappy girl's behalf. Animation was only restored to make her sensible that the monk was a villain, and herself undone!

318.29 passions] 2-3 passion

320.30 loves] 2-3 commerce

321.26 than he shuddered] 4-5 when he shuddered

321.28 eagerness to possess] 4-5 passion for

321.31 her arms] 4-5 her

321.34-36 4-5 *omit* The unfortunate had ... of her misfortune.

321.36 She] 4-5 The unfortunate

---

1 William Collins (1721-59), "The Passions: An Ode for Music" (1749) 60.

322.14 4-5 *omit* a ravisher,
322.14 lust,] 4-5 luxury
322.22 be in the horrors] 2-5 feel the horrors
322.26 into infamy?] 2-5 in shame?
322.26-27 4-5 *omit* Have you not made ... ravisher, an assassin?
322.29 damn me!] 4-5 *add a footnote*:
    "When we shall meet at compt,
    That look of thine will hurl my soul from heaven,
    And fiends will snatch at it!"   OTHELLO.[1]
323.12 lust] 4-5 passions
323.13-15 bosom. The wealth ... person. His nature] 4-5 bosom:
    his nature
323.15 the very idea] 4-5 their very idea
324.20 ravisher,] 4-5 betrayer,
324.30-32 as her person ... first intended; that] 4-5 in keeping
    her concealed as he had at first intended, 4-5
325.10 done, Ambrosio?] 4-5 done?
329.13-14 of the death of Agnes] 4-5 that Agnes had died in child-bed
329.42 and desire] 5 and to desire
330.10 been long a stranger] 5 long been a stranger
330.31 inconveniencies] 3-5 inconveniences
339.11 but my excessive] 4-5 but excessive
341.4 shrunk] 4-5 shrank
343.7 most employed] 3-5 thus employed
344.15 to supply] 2-5 to feed
347.30 His partisans] 2-5 The abbot's partisans
348.4 whose fate] 4-5 whose probable fate
348.11 being] 4-5 presence
350.5-6 tortures as he dreaded] 2-5 tortures, as he yet more
    dreaded
351.26 a sinner like him] 2-5 a sinner like himself
354.7 4-5 *omit* your lust,
354.36 God.] 4-5 Heaven.
361.21 "Carry] 4-5 "Bear
361.37 lust] 4-5 passions
361.41 chamber; it] 4-5 chamber; and it
361.42-362.3 bosom; and it ... of your crimes.] 4-5 bosom!
362.3-6 4-5 *italicize* Had you resisted ... signify your pardon.
362.11 restore to you] 3-5 restore you to
362.42-363.16 2-5 *omit* Life still ... languish.
363.16 On the seventh] 2-5 Instantly

---

1 Shakespeare, *Othello* 5.2.274-76.

363.21 2-5 *add:*

Haughty Lady, why shrank you back when yon poor frail-one drew near? Was the air infected by her errors? Was your purity soiled by her passing breath? Ah! Lady, smooth that insulting brow: stifle the reproach just bursting from your scornful lip: wound not a soul that bleeds already! She has suffered, suffers still. Her air is gay, but her heart is broken; her dress sparkles, but her bosom groans.

Lady, to look with mercy on the conduct of others, is a virtue no less than to look with severity on your own.

Works Cited and Recommended Reading

Manuscripts

The Monk. Holograph manuscript: printer's copy for the first edition. Townshend MS ix. Wisbech and Fenland Museum, Wisbech, Cambridgeshire.

The Monk. Sheets of the third edition interleaved and with holograph additions
and alterations: printer's copy for the fourth edition. C.28.b.4-6. British
Library.

Lifetime Editions

The Monk: A Romance. London: J. Bell, 1796.

The Monk: A Romance, by M.G. Lewis, Esq. M.P. 2nd ed. London: J. Bell, 1796.

The Monk: A Romance, by M.G. Lewis, Esq. M.P. 3rd ed. London: J. Bell, 1797.

Ambrosio, or The Monk: A Romance, by M.G. Lewis, Esq. M.P. 4th ed., "With
considerable Additions and Alterations." London: J. Bell, 1798.

Ambrosio, or The Monk: A Romance, by M.G. Lewis, Esq. M.P. 5th ed., "With
considerable Additions and Alterations." London: J. Davis for J. Bell, 1800.

Contemporary Reviews of *The Monk*

Analytical Review 24 (1796): 403-4. Review attributed to Mary Wollstonecraft.

British Critic 7 (1796): 677.

Critical Review 2nd ser. 19 (1797): 194-200. Review by Samuel Taylor
Coleridge.

Décade philosophique, littéraire et politique an V, 3e trimestre [9 May 1797]: 290-97.

European Magazine 31 (1797): 111-15.

Flapper 1.55 (17 September 1796): 4.

Journal de Paris 28 février 1797: 641-42.

Mercure de France 8 (5 prairial, an X [25 May 1802]): 344-52. Article entitled
"Spectacles"; ref. on 346.

Monthly Magazine 4 (1797): 120-21.

Monthly Mirror 2 (1796): 98, 323-28; 3 (1797): 210-15; 5 (1798): 157-58.

Monthly Review ns 23 (1797): 451. Review attributed to Richard Brinsley
Sheridan (Parreaux 76 n. 1).

Morning Chronicle 26 July 1796: 3.

Scots Magazine 64 (1802): 470-74, 545-48. Article entitled "On Novels and
Romances," by "W.W."; ref. on 546-48.

Spectateur du Nord 6 (avril-juin 1798): 324-38. Article entitled "Romans de
Mistress Radcliffe"; ref. on 330-34.

Modern Editions

Anderson, Howard, ed. and introd. *The Monk: A Romance,* by Matthew Lewis.
London: Oxford UP, 1973.

MacLachlan, Christopher, ed. and introd. *The Monk: A Romance*, by Matthew Lewis. London: Penguin, 1998.

Peck, Louis F., ed. *The Monk*, by Matthew G. Lewis. Introd. John Berryman. New York: Grove, 1952.

Other Works of Matthew Gregory Lewis

Adelmorn, the Outlaw; a Romantic Drama, in Three Acts. London: J. Bell, 1801.

The Castle Spectre: A Drama. In Five Acts. London: J. Bell, 1798. Rpt. in Cox 149-224.

"France and England in 1793." Ms. 114. National Library of Jamaica. Pp. 385-87.

Journal of a West India Proprietor, Kept during a Residence in the Island of Jamaica. London: John Murray, 1834. Ed. and introd. Judith Terry. Oxford: Oxford UP, 1999.

Tales of Wonder. 2 vols. London: J. Bell, 1801.

Venoni; or, The Novice of St. Mark's: A Drama, in Three Acts. London: Longman, Hurst, Rees, and Orme, 1809.

Other Primary Texts

Anonymous. *Almagro & Claude; or Monastic Murder; Exemplified in the Dreadful Doom of an Unfortunate Nun*. London: Tegg and Castleman [1803].

Baron-Wilson, Margaret. *The Life and Correspondence of M.G. Lewis....* 2 vols. London: Henry Colburn, 1839.

Burke, Edmund. *A Philosophical Enquiry into the Origin of our Ideas of the Sublime and Beautiful*. 1757. Ed. and introd. Adam Phillips. Oxford: Oxford UP, 1990.

—. *The Writings and Speeches of Edmund Burke*. Gen. ed. Paul Langford. 9 vols. Oxford: Clarendon, 1981—.

Cazotte, Jacques. *Le Diable amoureux et autres écrits fantastiques*. Introd. Henri Parisot. Paris: Flammarion, 1974.

Farley, Charles. *Airs, Glees, and Chorusses in a New Grand Ballet Pantomime of Action, Called Raymond and Agnes; or, The Castle of Lindenbergh*. London: Printed by T. Woodfall for T.N. Longman, 1797.

Flammenberg, Lorenz. *The Necromancer*. 1792. Trans. Peter Teuthold. London: Skoob, 1989.

Godwin, William. *Caleb Williams*. 1794. Ed. Gary Handwerk and A.A. Markley. Peterborough: Broadview, 2000.

Goethe, Johann Wolfgang von. *Goethe's Faust*. Trans. Barker Fairley. Toronto: U of Toronto P, 1972.

The Guardian. Ed., introd. and notes by John Calhoun Stephens. Lexington: UP of Kentucky, 1982.

Musäus, Johann Carl August. "The Elopement." Trans. Miss Corbett and Miss M. Corbett. *The Odd Volume*. 2nd ed. Edinburgh: Daniel Lizars, 1826. 105-24.

Paine, Thomas. *The Complete Writings of Thomas Paine*. Ed. Philip S. Foner. 2 vols. New York: Citadel, 1945.

Radcliffe, Ann. *The Italian; or, The Confessional of the Black Penitents*. 1797. Ed. Frederick Garber. Oxford: Oxford UP, 1981.

—. *The Mysteries of Udolpho*. 1794. Ed. Bonamy Dobrée. Introd. and notes by Terry Castle. Oxford: Oxford UP, 1998.

—. "On the Supernatural in Poetry." *New Monthly Magazine* ns 16 (1826): 145-52.

Richardson, Samuel. *Clarissa; or, The History of a Young Lady*. 1747-48. Ed. Angus Ross. London: Penguin, 1985.

Schiller, Friedrich. *The Ghost-Seer*. Trans. Henry G. Bohn. Introd. Jeffrey L. Sammons. Columbia, SC: Camden House, 1992.

Schubart, Christian Friedrich Daniel. *Gesammelte Schriften und Schicksale*. 8 vols. 1839. Hildesheim: Georg Olms Verlag, 1972.

Walpole, Horace. *The Castle of Otranto and The Mysterious Mother*. 1764, 1768. Ed. Frederick S. Frank. Peterborough: Broadview, 2002.

Secondary Texts

Anderson, Howard. "The Manuscript of M.G. Lewis's 'The Monk': Some Preliminary Notes." *Papers of the Bibliographical Society of America* 62 (1968): 427-34.

Ashton, John. *Chap-Books of the Eighteenth Century*. London: Chatto and Windus, 1882.

Berryman, John. Introduction. *The Monk*, by Matthew G. Lewis. Ed. Louis F. Peck. 11-28.

Brooks, Peter. "Virtue and Terror: *The Monk*." *ELH* 40 (1973): 249-63.

Clery, E.J. *The Rise of Supernatural Fiction, 1762-1800*. Cambridge: Cambridge UP, 1995.

Conger, Syndy M. *Matthew G. Lewis, Charles Robert Maturin and the Germans: An Interpretive Study of the Influence of German Literature on Two Gothic Novels*. Salzburg: Institut für Englische Sprache und Literatur, 1977.

—. "Sensibility Restored: Radcliffe's Answer to Lewis's *The Monk*." *Gothic Fiction: Prohibition / Transgression*. Ed. Kenneth W. Graham. New York: AMS, 1989. 113-49.

Cox, Jeffrey N., ed. and introd. *Seven Gothic Dramas, 1789-1825*. Athens: Ohio UP, 1992.

Crompton, Louis. *Byron and Greek Love: Homophobia in 19th-Century England*. Berkeley: U of California P, 1985.

Day, William Patrick. *In the Circles of Fear and Desire: A Study of Gothic Fantasy*. Chicago: U of Chicago P, 1985.

Dias Marques, José Joaquim. "Une Ballade gothique anglais dans la tradition orale de Trás-os-Montes." *Littérature orale traditionnelle populaire: Actes du colloque, Paris, 20-22 novembre 1986*. Paris: Fondation Calouste Gulbenkian/Centre Culturel Portugais, 1987. 257-99.

Ellis, Kate Ferguson. *The Contested Castle: Gothic Novels and the Subversion of Domestic Ideology*. Urbana: U of Illinois P, 1989.

Eribon, Didier. *Michel Foucault*. Trans. Betsy Wing. Cambridge: Harvard UP, 1991.

Frank, Frederick S. "M.G. Lewis's *The Monk* after Two Hundred Years, 1796-1996: A Bicentenary Bibliography." *Bulletin of Bibliography* 52 (1995): 241-60.

Friedman, Albert B. *The Ballad Revival: Studies in the Influence of Popular on Sophisticated Poetry*. Chicago: U of Chicago P, 1961.

Genette, Gérard. *Narrative Discourse: An Essay in Method.* Trans. Jane E. Lewin. Foreword by Jonathan Culler. Ithaca: Cornell UP, 1980.

—. *Palimpsests: Literature in the Second Degree.* Trans. Channa Newman and Claude Doubinsky. Foreword by Gerald Prince. Lincoln: U of Nebraska P, 1997.

Grudin, Peter. "*The Monk*: Matilda and the Rhetoric of Deceit." *Journal of Narrative Technique* 5 (1975): 136-46.

Guthke, Karl S. "Some Unpublished Letters of M.G. Lewis." *Notes and Queries* 202 (1957): 217-19.

Howard, Jacqueline. *Reading Gothic Fiction: A Bakhtinian Approach.* Oxford: Clarendon, 1994.

Howells, Coral Ann. *Love, Mystery, and Misery: Feeling in Gothic Fiction.* London: Athlone, 1978.

Jones, Wendy. "Stories of Desire in *The Monk*." *ELH* 57 (1990): 129-50.

King, Stephen. *Stephen King's Danse Macabre.* 1981. New York: Berkley, 1983.

Laws, G. Malcolm. *The British Literary Ballad: A Study in Poetic Imitation.* Carbondale: Southern Illinois UP, 1972.

Macdonald, D.L. *Monk Lewis: A Critical Biography.* Toronto: U of Toronto P, 2000.

Malchow, H.L. *Gothic Images of Race in Nineteenth-Century Britain.* Stanford: Stanford UP, 1996.

McAllister, Harold Stanwood. "Apology for Bad Dreams: A Study of Characterization and the Use of Fantasy in *Clarissa, Justine*, and *The Monk*." Diss. U of New Mexico, 1971.

McWhir, Anne. "The Gothic Transgression of Disbelief: Walpole, Radcliffe and Lewis." *Gothic Fiction: Prohibition / Transgression.* Ed. Kenneth W. Graham. New York: AMS, 1989. 29-47.

Miles, Robert. "Ann Radcliffe and Matthew Lewis." *A Companion to the Gothic.* Ed. David Punter. Oxford: Blackwell, 2000. 41-57.

Miller, Alice. *For Your Own Good: Hidden Cruelty in Child-Rearing and the Roots of Violence.* Trans. Hildegarde Hannum and Hunter Hannum. New York: Farrar, 1984.

Parreaux, André. *The Publication of* The Monk: *A Literary Event, 1796-1798.* Paris: Marcel Didier, 1960.

Paulson, Ronald. *Representations of Revolution (1789-1820).* New Haven: Yale UP, 1983.

Peck, Louis F. *A Life of Matthew G. Lewis.* Cambridge: Harvard UP, 1961.

Pound, Louise. "'Monk' Lewis in Nebraska." *Southern Folklore Quarterly* 9 (1945): 107-10.

Praz, Mario. Introductory Essay. *Three Gothic Novels.* Ed. Peter Fairclough. Harmondsworth: Penguin, 1968. 7-34.

Rosenmeyer, Patricia A. *The Poetics of Imitation: Anacreon and the Anacreontic Tradition.* Cambridge: Cambridge UP, 1992.

Todd, William B. "The Early Editions and Issues of *The Monk*, with a Bibliography." *Studies in Bibliography* 2 (1949): 3-24.

Todorov, Tzvetan. *The Fantastic: A Structural Approach to a Literary Genre*. Trans. Richard Howard. Cleveland: Case Western Reserve UP, 1973.

Trumbach, Randolph. *Sex and the Gender Revolution, Volume One: Heterosexuality and the Third Gender in Enlightenment London*. Chicago: U of Chicago P, 1998.

Watkins, Daniel P. "Social Hierarchy in Matthew Lewis's *The Monk*." *Studies in the Novel* 18 (1986): 113-24.

Weiss, Harry B. *A Book about Chapbooks: The People's Literature of Bygone Times*. 1942. Hatboro PA: Folklore Associates, 1969.

Williams, Anne. *Art of Darkness: A Poetics of Gothic*. Chicago: U of Chicago P, 1995.

Winter, Kari J. *Subjects of Slavery, Agents of Change: Women and Power in Gothic Novels and Slave Narratives, 1790-1865*. Athens: U of Georgia P, 1992.